Knocking on the
Moonlit Door

Knocking on the Moonlit Door

Gillian Coleby

To order additional copies of this book, contact:
Xlibris Corporation
0-800-644-6988
www.xlibrispublishing.co.uk
Orders@xlibrispublishing.co.uk
301332

For all my team,
who have been there;
and for Mandy,
who knows.

The Listeners

"Is there anybody there?" said the Traveller,
Knocking on the moonlit door.
And his horse in the silence champed on the grasses
Of the forest's ferny floor:
And a bird flew up out of the turret,
Above the Traveller's head:
And he smote upon the door a second time;
"Is there anybody there?" he said.
But no one descended to the Traveller;
No head from the leaf-fringed sill
Leaned over and looked into his grey eyes,
Where he stood perplexed and still.
But only a host of phantom listeners
That dwelt in the lone house then
Stood listening in the quiet of the moonlight
To that voice from the world of men:
Stood thronging the faint moonbeams on the dark stair,
That goes down to the empty hall,
Hearkening in an air stirred and shaken
By the lonely Traveller's call.
And he felt in his heart their strangeness,
Their stillness answering his cry,
Whilst his horse moved, cropping the dark turf,
'Neath the starred and leafy sky;
For suddenly he smote the door, even
Louder, and lifted his head:-
"Tell them I came and no one answered,
That I kept my word," he said.
Never the least stir made the listeners,
Though every word he spake
Fell echoing through the shadowiness of the still house
From the one man left awake:
Ay, they heard his foot upon the stirrup,
And the sound of iron on stone,
And how the silence surged softly backward,
When the plunging hoofs were gone.

Walter de la Mare

Chapter One

Sometimes Joe Mortimer really disliked his role as Britain's most celebrated astronaut in the new era of space exploration, even though it was years since he had flown missions. Combined with everyone wanting a piece of him as the current UK head of *BUSSTOP—British and United States Scheme for Travel to Other Planets*—it all became a little wearing sometimes. But today he could play his part to perfection. He smiled disarmingly at the image of the caller on the screen. Rob Masters was part of the *BUSSTOP* family, a highly respected engineer. He could be given the polite brush-off, followed by being redirected to someone who had time to listen.

"I'll let you into a secret.," he said confidingly to Mr Masters. "I gave up speaking foreign languages for Lent a while ago and then discovered that I could kick the habit completely. So I can be confident I'm not using Outer Mongolian. On that basis, which part of *This isn't something I can deal* with do you not understand?"

"Mr Mortimer, please! Something made me look again at Ichiro Matsushita's original wiring schematics on the Lander of *Ariadne One*. It's very late in the day but I think that I have found a fundamental—"

"Rob, I'm a very busy man. *BUSSTOP* doesn't run itself. Vicky will help you."

Joe touched a console button, cutting off Rob Masters in mid-sentence, and gave some instructions to his PA about finding someone who might like to spend half an hour talking technicalities with someone who was so bouncing and keen early on a Friday afternoon. Then he sat back in his chair, reflecting that it was a good thing *BUSSTOP* didn't run itself. He would be out of a job, as would a large collection of talented people.

After a suitable pause, he hit the same button again, summoning the face of his personal assistant, Vicky Tennant. With the newly developed

S-Creen monitor technology, it was as if she was in the room with him, and not thirty miles away in *BUSSTOP*'s north London headquarters.

"Vicky, you're slipping," he said in mock severity. "How did Rob Masters get past you? You don't usually fall for the *It's really important* sob story."

"I'm so sorry!" she said, not realising her boss was joking. "He said that this was top priority and I thought-"

Joe looked out of the window of his home office. It was a beautiful sunny afternoon. He wanted to be part of it. Enough was enough for one week.

"Mother ship calling Space Explorer One!" he said gently. "Vicky, do I look like I'm angry?" Vicky shook her head. "Obviously it's not a good day for teasing you. Remind me. Is there anything important in the diary for the rest of the day?"

"Bruce Dougall will be contacting you. I'm sure you hadn't forgotten that. He said after three o'clock, which will be his three o'clock."

"Ah, Bruce! How could I forget? He'll contact me here. So conscientious!"

Joe was sure that Bruce Dougall enjoyed flying his desk as much as he did a Zeus space ship. He did become so . . . wrapped up in what he was doing. And he clung to this old-fashioned notion that he needed to be in *BUSSTOP*'s Washington D.C. building quite a lot; so with the five hour time difference on the East coast of America, it could be the middle of the night by the time the United States chief came through.

It had been a long week. Joe wasn't sure why. One of the few perks of being in charge of an organisation was that he didn't have to give reasons for disappearing. This was the day for an early finish.

"That's fine," Vicky replied briskly when he told her that he was shutting down his work system for the weekend. "Does anyone need to know, Mr Mortimer?"

"Bruce will call after our office hours on my personal line. If the Prime Minister needs a word, that's okay, of course. Send him my way. But he would probably contact me on my personal line. If he's got any sense, he'll be having the weekend off. I want to relax for a bit. Your inventiveness knows no bounds for these occasions. Where will I be for everyone else for the rest of the day?"

Vicky's head dipped for a moment in thought. Her long brown hair dropped forward, momentarily obscuring her eager, shining face.

"Hmm." She looked up. "How about a not-to-be-interrupted session with Kurt Somers, head of Space Tech? It's a closely guarded secret that he's drying out in a rural retreat. So no one will know you're not really with him."

Joe raised his eyebrows. He didn't even know that Somers had an alcohol problem. Vicky had been in post for a mere six months and already Joe had stopped wondering about her sources of information. He was just thankful.

"Vicky, what would I do without you? I'll see you for real on Monday. I'm walking some government bods round the factory floor."

In her office, Vicky held Joe's image on her screen for a while. She took him in, feature by feature. The guarded grey eyes, the artfully tousled thick brown hair, the youthful but strong face with the hint of dimples in the cheeks; a face that was saved from being almost pretty by that nose. She stared for a while. She flushed and her blue eyes sparkled behind the lenses of her glasses. When Mr Mortimer was around, even via the screen, her office in the London *BUSSTOP* building seemed less impersonal. She could get as far as appreciating the computer console and the bank of screens that kept her in touch with the world, the light-reactive glass in the windows and the intelligent materials used on the floor, walls and ceiling to maximise heating and air-conditioning efficiency.

Vicky knew what they called her in PA-land: *Miss Cool.* Most women disliked her because she was ultra-organised, always well groomed and unthreateningly attractive, which therefore made her threatening. Men had a weakness for her healthy peaches and cream appearance. These days bosses, male and female, schemed like mad to employ her when it was known that she was out in the job-market. There were a lot of disappointed executives when the thirty year-old had signed up to *BUSSTOP* last year.

Vicky sighed and cancelled the picture, before Miss Cool lost her cool. She turned back to her work. There was more and more to do as a possible launch date drew near and Mr Mortimer would have to spend more time in the London base.

Every cloud had a silver lining.

*   *   *

Bonny the dog greeted Joe when he emerged from the office at the back of his house as if he had been away for months. Her barks became hysterical squeaks when she realised he was changing into his running gear. Although she liked nothing better than to lie around, it seemed that she was born to run as well. She was a gloriously unidentifiable mix of breeds, although her deep chest proclaimed a bit of greyhound in there somewhere. To an outsider she was a massive black and white fur ball with a leg at each corner, an inquisitive nose at one end and a wagging tail at the other. To Joe she was the placeholder of unconditional love, who put up with his tastes in twentieth century music, didn't mind his books all over the place and who listened for as long as it took to tell the story of the day.

Man and dog came out into the lane and began a steady jog. It was a beautiful spring afternoon. Drifts of daffodils waved in the breeze, which brought promising damp smells of new life. The grass was yellowed by the most recent of the heavy snowfalls that had punctuated the winter of 2108-09. This one would go down in the record books, for sure. But today all plant life seemed to be doing its best to soak up the sunshine and turn green again.

At the top of the road Joe stopped to wait for Bonny. She was distracted by scents under the hedge. It gave him a chance to appreciate all over again just how lucky he was to live in this village. His family had owned the house for a very long time. Documentation tracked Mortimers living at Stable End as far back as the 1960s.

With a yelp, Bonny realised she was a long way from her master and galloped after him. They ran past the ancient church, dedicated to Saint Margaret of Antioch. They skirted across the top of Pond Lane, dominated by the village school where Joe had spent his formative years. Then they struck out across the headlands of the fields belonging to Marsh Farm before angling back to the centre of the village and home.

Stable End was a house that caught the eye. The core of it was sixteenth century and it had grown in a random fashion over the centuries. Joe opened the door and a panting Bonny charged in. He glanced up at the windows looking out from the second floor. As children, he and his brother Philip loved it when visitors came to stay. They were moved up into those special rooms under the roof to make way for the guests. They spent hours talking, with no one to hear them and tell them to be quiet and go to sleep.

Joe was in the shower when he heard the messaging signal. This was no ordinary signal. It was the Prime Minister's personal pattern.

"Oh, bugger you!" he said out loud. "I'm sure you haven't declared war in the last hour or so. You can wait a few minutes."

Damp and wearing a bathrobe, he was put through to Kevin Crane.

"Prime Minister! You do pick your moments! I was in the shower."

"So I see. Your wonderful Miss Tennant said you would be at leisure." The fanciful would have said that Mr Crane smiled. "I have the feeling that she has a different story for everyone else as to your whereabouts."

"She has."

Kevin Crane had been given the run-around in the past by Vicky, which he appreciated sincerely—afterwards. The Prime Minister's face didn't change when he heard Vicky's latest effort. He wasn't called "A well-kept statue" for nothing, a label that had become a gift for the cartoonists. He was usually portrayed on a plinth in Nelson-like pose, staring out across the House of Commons chamber, his glasses slipping down his nose.

"I see. To business. Bruce Dougall will be calling you later, I understand. You deserve to have some warning about what he will be saying to you." The burr of Hampshire was evident in his speech. "Surprises can be hard work, be they good or bad."

Joe did not possess Crane's studied impassivity. He looked dumbfounded by the time the Prime Minister had finished. He ran a hand through his wet hair.

"Right. It means that everything can go ahead now. I just didn't think it would be on these terms!"

"It is a massive honour, much of it down to you, I'm sure. Once you have spoken with Dougall, we have a timetable of publicity to follow. You don't need me to tell you that things can really start moving now. Sarah—*my treasure*—will send it through to you. Amongst other things, Buckingham Palace will be informed officially and *BUSSTOP* will be sent a note of congratulation. You will have a personal letter from the King."

"So get this wrong and I'll be sent to the Tower."

"Get this right and you'll receive a knighthood."

"Are you being indiscreet, Prime Minister?"

One corner of Kevin Crane's mouth definitely curled upwards.

"No," he said after a pause. "Merely applying a little honesty. You know more of the detailed history of space exploration than I do, as does His Majesty, but I doubt that either of you would say the word honesty crops up a great deal in its pages. I won't take up any more of your time. My wife and I are going home to Winchester for the weekend."

Joe was tempted to say "Give my love to Janet" but, even though he had known Kevin Crane for many years, long before either of them came to national prominence, there were still bits of this man that he hadn't worked out, so he left it at hoping they had a pleasant stay.

Talking with the Prime Minister about the King was a combination that sent Joe wandering down Memory Lane. He called up a batch of photographs onto the screen. He looked at the crowd of eager young RAF recruits. There they were. Joe and Prince Richard, as he was then. And close by them was Jack Crane, the Prime Minister's younger brother. He was talented, popular and the best of the lot of them. When Jack was killed in a flying accident, Joe was so angry about the botched safety procedures leading to the crash that he could easily have walked away from the RAF. He didn't take that drastic course of action because his eyes were on a higher prize.

Joe knew that he and his royal friend had both done all right for themselves. He was the British chief of *BUSSTOP* after his career as an astronaut and a stint training the next generation of space explorers. Richard was His Majesty.

It was a pity. Richard had been one hell of a pilot and had the right temperament to be out in major space missions. When *BUSSTOP* was headhunting in the Air Force, they made the first informal enquiries together. After a couple of days, Richard came to Joe, crestfallen.

"I won't be able to join you on this one, Joe. My family has hit the roof."

Joe resisted the urge to ask if any tiaras had been damaged and sympathised instead. Some of his own family were none too keen but they were not crowned heads of state. He got his dream of going into space on the experimental long haul flights and Richard got Buckingham Palace. No comparison really.

The heir to the British throne in space exploration would have been a belter. Some Americans still tended to be a bit patronising about Britain as a voyaging partner. They reckoned that history gave them the right to look on the stars as their personal back yard. They had never quite recovered from the fact that Britain came first in the organisation title—*British and United States Scheme for Travel to Other Planets.* Unable to come up with a better acronym, they had to live with it. *HRH Prince Richard, astronaut* would have seen them faint clean away.

Bonny's wet nose brushed against Joe's foot and he jumped. He had been sitting there far too long. He was cold and his muscles were stiffening. The dog placed a large paw on his knee.

"Yes, Bonny, you can have your dinner. I'd better have dinner myself. Bruce on an empty stomach is not to be recommended." He glanced fleetingly at the drinks table. "And I need a clear head for this one too."

It wasn't too late when Bruce Dougall made contact. He looked disapprovingly at Joe, sprawled on a sofa with Bonny. Joe had been listening to The Beach Boys and Meatloaf. *Bat Out of Hell* seemed to be one of Bonny's favourites.

"I see you still have that flea-ridden mutt, Joe."

"And a very good evening to you, Bruce." Joe wanted to keep this pleasant and he could be affable tonight. He was the victor after all, wasn't he? "How is your day going?"

"It's going," he replied heavily.

Joe was concerned as they traded the usual insults and observations. The two men had come to dislike each intensely but, when working as part of a team in space, all personal opinions were irrelevant. In the ultimate hostile environment, each person's life depended on the other members of the group. With Bruce, he had been pushing up against the boundaries of the science and technology of the day. One error and a bunch of people would be dead. They had come to know each other well, in spite of themselves.

Tonight he could see that the fires of Bruce's personality were burning low.

"I'm sure that a satellite in low orbit is picking up your grin," Bruce observed. Joe straightened his face hastily but it was too late. "You know what I'm going to say, don't you? Who has been opening his big mouth this time?"

"The Prime Minister contacted me earlier on," Joe admitted. "I'm sure that the President, or someone in your government, would have done the same for you if the circumstances were reversed. Why, Bruce? I thought that Britain and America might have to come to blows over who got the final oversight of the Mars project. Basically, that agreement is all we've been waiting for. This is not like America, handing over jurisdiction of the new flights to *BUSSTOP* to us here. It's a daft thing to say, I know, but I presume that the President is happy with this."

"Yes," was the curt reply. "We'll still have our say and up to half of the crew. You won't be doing it all on your own."

"I know. It will be a joint effort. That's a given."

"We will want our share of the glory. Not that I think there will be much."

"What?"

"I've come to the conclusion that this project is flawed," Bruce told him, revealing his part in the astonishing turn-around. "Deeply flawed. I think we're rushing it. We shouldn't be sending people to Mars yet. No one listens to me. You haven't listened to me."

Joe blinked. In moments of painful honesty he knew he could be impatient with Bruce, but when had his colleague said *anything* along these lines over the past months? Why had no one from America spoken to him about such reservations? Bruce was still droning on.

"Your Prime Minister has been listening to your King too much. Filled his head full of nonsense. Damned armchair astronaut! We're putting some distance between Ariadne and us. The approach to it has become careless."

Bruce stopped. He knew he was being totally unfair. Joe Mortimer had set the gold standard in space safety. He drove the Zeus flight crews and ground engineering teams mad with his insistence on rigorous procedures. But everyone had to admit that there had never been the slightest hint of a problem, never mind an emergency, on Joe's watch. Apart from—. No. Never mind that for now.

Joe laid aside the multiple reasons behind his antipathy towards his space project partner and was saddened as he saw Bruce's hazel eyes dancing with anger. He had only seen Bruce in such an irrational state once before. He was unwell, fortunately on the homeward bound leg of a mission.

He looked okay now, didn't he? His sharp features were not as angular as he approached fifty but otherwise he wasn't all that different from when he was in the space flight spotlight. His light brown hair was brushed back from his forehead as usual and wearing glasses most of the time these days minimised the appearance of a slightly crooked nose. Joe had a fleeting sense of a heaviness of spirit about his colleague, and it was not anything to do with what he was saying.

This extraordinary decision didn't rest with Bruce alone and could not have been reached quickly. What was eating at this man? He had obviously swayed important people to his way of thinking. The exploration of Mars was almost an article of faith with the current President of the United States of America.

"Okay Bruce, we'll leave it there," he said quietly, slipping back naturally into his former role of commander speaking to his right hand man. "Thanks for letting me know how you feel, even if you have left it a bit late! Will you write me a report on your reservations about Operation Ariadne? For my eyes only, of course."

"With the greatest of pleasure."

Joe broke the connection and his personal monitor went back to the peaceful vista of a country park screensaver. He sat watching the flames licking round the logs in the massive grate for some time. Bonny leaned against him and went to sleep.

*   *   *

"Professor Hanson, do you realise what the time is?"

Irene Hanson looked up from the bank of computer monitors. She found herself meeting the gaze of a concerned University security guard.

"Oh my goodness, Sid!" she exclaimed apologetically, catching sight of a clock.

"It's no bother to me, Prof. I'm on duty all night. I don't like the thought of you working this long, especially on a Friday night. You should be at home, or out on the town."

Irene was touched by the concern of this white-haired, stocky little man, who was everyone's surrogate father or grandfather. He was a security guard in name only. It was doubtful he could have knocked the skin off a rice pudding!

"I think I might be a little long in the tooth for being 'out on the town', Sid, but you're right, it is late. I hadn't realised how late. I'll call it a day. I'm leaving this batch of computers on automatic. Everything else I use has been shut down as per procedure. The staff on weekend duty will be here as usual. I'll say goodnight then."

"Good night, Professor."

Sid Brotherton watched her gather her bags together and walk off down the corridor, a tall, perfectly proportioned figure, an expensive coat slung over one arm. He shook his head. He couldn't understand why such a fine woman was on her own nine times out of ten. What was wrong with these younger fellers today? He had to conclude that the men in her circle of acquaintance thought it was only used for stirring their tea.

Sid was indignant on her behalf. He had known her since she was a student. She was a lovely lass then. They had grown older together in the service of Cambridge University.

Irene reached the staff car park. Her vehicle standing forlornly on its own told her just how late she had stayed. Night staff left their vehicles in a more secure location. It's a good job I haven't got a houseful of children and a mutinous partner, she thought as she headed towards home.

A parcel was waiting for her when she got there, safe in the electronically secured delivery box. She knew it was from her publisher, ready for the big launch the following day, but Irene ripped off the packaging with all the excitement of a child opening a much-anticipated gift. She turned the book over. *Signals From Other Places by Irene Hanson.*

She read the blurb on the back, although every word had been chosen with care, hammered out as usual over lots of coffee with Tanya.

> *Irene Hanson, Professor of Space Communications at the University of Cambridge, has done it again—explaining the nature of signals from space, how they are tracked and what they might mean. This is achieved in the accessible yet rigorously scientific style that has become so popular in her previous books.*

She looked at her photograph critically. Yes, it was the best one after all. She wasn't too keen on pictures of herself but this would do nicely. Her trademark necklace showed up well. Her blond hair looked good. She had spent a fortune at the hairdresser. Her heart-shaped face hadn't sagged—yet. She could thank her father for her blue eyes. They always gave a photograph a touch of the dramatic.

She smiled as she placed the new book on the shelf that held her three previous volumes. In the excited frenzy that gripped the popular imagination, following the real take-off of computing in the mid 1990s, the death of the physical book was predicted confidently. Everyone would be reading electronic copies. Well, many people would purchase this work in electronic form but just as many would buy the actual book. Gutenberg and Caxton had really started something in the late fifteenth century and it wasn't going away any time soon.

It was time for a cup of tea. Irene headed towards the kitchen and then returned to the bookshelf. She picked up her new book again and reread some of the words on the back dust jacket. *Rigorously scientific* . . . In her line of work it was the only way to be. Yet she knew the idea that had kept her at the college late, checking and rechecking data, was little more than a fancy.

She looked out of the window at the sparkling night sky, focusing in the direction that was bothering her. What was the point in growing older if you couldn't be a little crazier from time to time? And was it so crazy anyway? Surely no computer could be making such a mistake. Or was she making mistakes at the end of an endless week?

Irene decided to forget all about it until Monday morning.

*   *   *

Joe found his eyes closing. He realised that he had dropped his book on Bonny, who looked at him reproachfully. He made a huge effort to get up and walk through to the back door to let the dog out for a final run around the garden. The draught of cold air jerked him into real wakefulness and then he heard the messaging signal. Doubting that it was Bruce coming back for round two, he trailed back to the living room.

It was his nephew, Sam.

"Greetings, Uncle!" He was way too lively for this time of night. "How are you?"

"Tired," he replied pointedly.

"Ah, the burdens of office! I won't keep you long, Nunc, but we just had to share some good news with you." Joe was aware of Sam's wife, Natasha, waving and jumping up and down in the background. "We're having a baby! We've kept it quiet until Natasha was past that first tricky stage. So how's that, Great Uncle to be?"

Joe enthused appropriately and at great length with Sam and Natasha. He had a great deal of time for these young people and he loved his brother Philip dearly. But at this time on a Friday night he felt suddenly old, far beyond his fifty years.

"Where are your Mum and Dad?" he asked at a suitable pause in the flow of family nonsense; he had lost track of where Philip and Daphne were meant to be. "They'll be the doting grandparents. And how about Neil and Stella?"

He was imagining the reaction of his own parents. Neil and Stella Mortimer usually met the world head-on and at full speed.

"I've been in touch with Gran and Granddad," Sam assured him. "They were speechless with delight for a moment or two."

"I'm sure they were. It's not every day you're told you will be great grandparents."

"We left them about to open a bottle of champagne!" laughed Natasha. "I'm not sure whether it was to celebrate or to face up to the shock!"

Joe knew his parents very well. Prospective great-grandparenthood would be another glowing tick on the checklist of life as far as they were concerned. He had visions of them rounding up immediate neighbours to party for days. He made a mental note to contact them at a *considerate* time in the morning, to allow the champagne haze to disperse.

"Mum and Dad are trekking through the Andes—I think," Sam said vaguely. Was he on a two-minute time delay? "You know what they're like. I've left a message for them to pick up."

Joe had no time for false modesty. He knew what he had achieved, but his brother usually managed to make him feel inadequate, without even trying. Philip and Daphne Mortimer were doing their best to live up to the centuries-old tag of *Growing older disgracefully*. Or perhaps, in their case, very actively. All of two years his senior, sometimes Philip looked at his little brother in jesting disappointment.

"You don't get about much these days, do you?"

It was all part of the family routine and Joe had stopped retaliating a long time ago. He knew that Philip, like everyone else, was immensely proud of him and would bore anyone rigid with stories of what his brother had done, given half a chance. Joe had been part of enough "getting about" to last several lifetimes.

The conversation over, he called Bonny, who bounded back into the house.

"Bed!" he ordered.

With a final wag of her tail and a sneaky lick of her master's hand, Bonny trotted through to the kitchen to settle down for the night. Joe wished that some people were as biddable as his dog. The business of Bruce was gnawing at him.

He turned out the lights and sat down on the floor facing the window, which gave him a good view of the night sky. He was glad he had developed the habit of meditation, which helped him to empty his mind. Otherwise Bruce would have been coming between him and his sleep tonight.

Most people who had been in space were changed. Some followed a destructive path of addiction. Early on, Joe was fortunate enough to meet a veteran astronaut who gave him good advice on how to cope with his altered life.

"Think about where you've been, boy, then leave the stars where they belong. There's no sense in dragging them around with you. Most folks don't have the first notion of what you are talking about. Oh, when the time comes, do your interviews and write your articles. Get into the after-dinner speaking racket if that's your style. But last thing at night, let it go. Let everything go."

Joe turned his gaze to the clear sky, full of twinkling points of light, and offered his silent thanks and thoughts.

*   *   *

His glasses magnified the shine in Neil Mortimer's grey eyes.

"Good morning, Great Uncle to be!" he bellowed from the screen at Joe.

"Morning, Dad!" replied Joe. "You beat me to it. I wasn't thinking of calling you for a while yet."

"Why's that?"

"Last night Natasha said that you and Mum were about to hit the champagne."

"We did that, I promise you. Very seriously." Neil was obviously puzzled as to why that meant a morning contact should be delayed. "Didn't you have a small celebration before you turned in?"

"I'd been talking to Bruce Dougall earlier in the evening. That sort of took the shine off the rest of the day."

"Oh, him!" His father grunted an acknowledgement of Joe's discomfort. "You and I need a little chat, I can see. Your mother's organising a bit of a family get-together for tomorrow. Sunday lunch and all that. We must congratulate Sam and Natasha properly. Can you make it?"

"Of course. But what about Philip and Daphne? It's their first grandchild we're celebrating!"

"If they decide to be half-way up a Peruvian mountain at the wrong moment, that's their look-out! No, seriously. It'll be a good excuse to have another do when they come back, won't it?"

Stella appeared behind her husband, beaming

"See you about midday tomorrow, Joe?"

"You're on, Mum!"

"Bring the dog," said Neil conspiratorially when Stella had gone. "Everyone loves her to bits and you and I can take her for a walk later on—and have a talk."

Joe could only feel gratitude when he thought of his parents. Later, as he ran through the lanes and fields with Bonny, he decided that they had the right attitude. Life was one big celebration. But that was not to say that they were frivolous people. Far from it. They were a rock to both of their sons and were there for them during various bumps in the road. Oh, they had thrown their hands up in horror when they realised Joe was serious about his application to *BUSSTOP* to train as an astronaut. But that was only natural and he and his father had come to a light-hearted agreement.

"What's more dangerous than flying wing-tip to wing-tip doing aerobatics in a miniscule metal can?" Joe asked Neil.

His father had been the flight leader of an RAF display team. He had hoped that Joe would make a long career in the air force, following in his footsteps.

"At least I could have got out of my metal can in most emergencies!" he replied, conceding defeat.

Of course, Mum and Dad had been wonderful when—.

Even now Joe's mind swerved away. He had to stop and distract himself by throwing a few sticks for Bonny to fetch and deposit at his feet with panting eagerness.

After twenty minutes of this surprisingly energetic pastime, he rubbed her head. Playing with sticks was over. It was time for a good attacking run back to the house.

"Come on, girl! Race you home!"

They ran a dead-heat and Bonny waited impatiently for Joe to open the door. She tore down the hallway, heading for the kitchen. Her master followed at a more sedate pace.

Joe realised, not for the first time, that a dog was what had been missing from Stable End when it was the family home. Both he and Philip had badgered their parents for a pet but gave up in the face of point-blank refusals. He never had worked out why Mum and Dad kept saying no. These days, they adored Bonny and they had been nervous wrecks when the dog required minor surgery.

Bonny had moved on to the living room and was arranging herself in front of the fire. Her feathered tail waved languidly when Joe heaved some more wood into the grate. This room was part of the original house. The fireplace took up most of the wall and there was an uninterrupted view up the chimney to the sky in the summer when there was no fire. Joe remembered standing inside the fireplace with Philip one night, looking up at the stars.

"I'll visit them some day," he vowed with nine year-old earnestness.

Philip said nothing but looked suitably impressed before they set off playing hide-and-seek.

The house was made for such a game, with creaky-floorboard corridors, unexpected rooms and cupboard doors in the most unlikely places. That was why the children moved up on to the top floor when people came to stay. Those bedrooms would have made excellent guest rooms, full of olde-worlde charm, wonky roof struts and worn floors. But strangers to the house would never have been seen again, lost somewhere between the top and the bottom of the Mortimer home.

Joe wondered now why he and his brother hadn't been given permanent residence on the top floor. It would have been so much simpler. They hadn't been *that* untrustworthy, surely! Still, at the time it was all a big adventure, not something to be weighed up with prosaic adult eyes.

He was glad that he shared the house with Bonny. Having a large pet made it seem marginally less ridiculous that one person was rattling around in such a big place. Still, it was handy for the entertaining that he did in his official capacity as head of *BUSSTOP*. The caterers bounced about in spasms of delight on such occasions.

*   *   *

Bonny jumped into the car the next morning. She didn't have the chance to do much car riding. Although a general switch to hydrogen-cell powered vehicles was helping to deal with the global pollution problems, Joe didn't use the car any more than was strictly necessary.

Man and dog were met by a cheering mob at the front door of his parents' house. Joe's first impression, that half the road was there, was incorrect. The crowd consisted only of the people who were meant to be present—Neil, Stella, Sam and Natasha. The problem was that they all wanted to say hello at once. Bonny would guard Joe to the death and was anyone's for a kind word, but this time she sat down out of the way in safety until everyone was disentangled. Then she moved forward for her share of attention.

This was the kind of occasion that Stella loved. Sunday lunch was her speciality and it was a joy to have most of her family round a table. Considering what hectic lives everyone lived, five out of seven wasn't a bad score.

She bustled about, scorning all offers of help—especially from Natasha.

"You need to be taking life a bit easier, young lady. Yes, I know that you're pregnant, not ill, but take a breather when it's offered."

"That's me put in my place," Natasha whispered to Joe.

"It's done in total love," he whispered back.

It was difficult for Joe to remember that both Mum and Dad would soon be eighty. These days it was no longer clear what eighty was supposed to look like but Stella was nowhere near it. Her white hair was neatly coiffed and her make up was lightly but effectively applied. She had one of those timeless, soft and twinkling faces, which came into its own when the children first managed "Mummy" and reinvented itself when Sam declared "Granny." A few wrinkles later and she was limbering up to be a great grandmother.

Pregnancy didn't appear to be hindering Natasha's appetite and Stella was happy as her meal disappeared like the last snow of winter. She hated people who pushed food around a plate and didn't really eat. That didn't apply to anyone today although she thought Joe looked thinner. She could see he was tired too, so she began to scold Neil when he announced that he and Joe would take the dog for a walk.

"It's okay, Mum." Joe put a hand on her arm. "I could do with a breath of air. You've flatted the youngsters with your wonderful lunch." They looked over at Sam and Natasha, dozing on the sofa. With his face relaxed in sleep, Sam looked so like his father, and thus very like Joe. "And you'll be cross if I offer to help you clear up. We won't be long. Have some coffee ready for when we return."

Father, son and dog walked along the road in silence.

"So what's Bruce Dougall been up to now?" Neil asked after a couple of minutes.

Joe trusted his father. Discretion was as natural as breathing to him. As a former Wing Commander in the RAF, Neil knew a bit about being part of a system and how the system can be wearing, even when you have a handle on a chunk of it.

"Well now," he said when Joe had finished recounting Friday's conversations with the Prime Minister and Bruce Dougall. "Congratulations, Joe. And the PM is right. It's about time old Ricky boy down at the big house got round to awarding you something a bit more serious." Joe had received his MBE from Richard's mother, Queen Matilda. "An MBE is a special honour, certainly." He was the proud owner of one as well, also from the hands of the late Queen. "But for what you've done? And for what you are yet to achieve? That gong is just for starters. As for Dougall . . . Let's begin with the obvious. Are any of his observations justified?"

"Dad!"

"Just checking." His son was as thorough and meticulous as he had been and heaven help anyone in his outfit who didn't work to the same standards. "So what has put him in such a spin?" Joe gestured futilely. "It's a recognised phenomenon that space does odd things to people. You admit it yourself. Let's apply the principle of Ockham's Razor to this."

Joe looked blank for a moment. Then they spoke in chorus.

"The simplest working explanation is taken to be the correct one."

"Exactly," Neil continued. "I think he's going off his rocker." Joe stared at him. "Dear me! You're not exactly firing on all cells today, are you lad? Going mad! Losing his mind!"

"I know what you mean. But Bruce?"

"Why not Bruce Dougall? Don't imagine he has superhuman powers just because you two didn't see eye to eye. He'll have no special immunity to the ills of body and mind which can result from prolonged space travel."

Neil bent to take the stick that Bonny was desperate to give him.

Joe reckoned that he was a fairly matter-of-fact person, by inclination and training. But when he was in his father's company, he remembered that he wanted to bottle Neil's personality, administer a dose of the elixir to himself regularly and share it with friends and colleagues. He watched him playing tug-of-war with Bonny. Dad had become a corpulent figure ("I don't think anyone will be expecting me to squeeze into a cockpit tomorrow!" he observed ruefully) and he had grown through the top of his white hair. There was serenity in his smile as he finally won his battle with the dog.

"We'd better get back, Dad. Mum will be waking up Sam and sending him out to find us. Oh, and—"

"Not a word to Mum. I think I know the drill by now."

It was good to sit and talk about everything and nothing as a family. At one point, Stella picked up a book.

"Do you know this lady, Joe?"

Joe squinted across the room.

"Irene Hanson? The glamorous prof! By reputation, mainly. Is that her new book?"

"Launched yesterday in the city," put in Neil. "We went along. She was doing a big book signing. Your mother waited very patiently in the queue."

"I wasn't very patient in the end!" She frowned. "There was this silly woman prattling on about why couldn't the launch have been down in London."

"I'm probably being a very silly woman," said Natasha. "Aren't most book launches in London?"

"Generally." Joe offered an explanation. "But Professor Hanson was a student at the University, has done all her work here and lives in the area. It would be rather churlish to turn her back on Cambridge when it comes to the books."

"Yes. I suppose it would." Although he was family, Natasha was still in awe of Joe. "Have you ever met her? She sounds quite an amazing person."

"Once. She gave a lecture at *BUSSTOP* headquarters a couple of years ago. There was no sense or meaningful work to be got out of any of the men for the rest of the week. And I include myself in that," he admitted cheerfully. "A very attractive, sexy woman in her late forties, talking scientific . . . a devastating package."

That's it! Natasha was thinking to herself. He's not gay. I *knew* he wasn't.

It wasn't something that she felt she could blurt out to Sam . . . "By the way, is your uncle gay? There never seems to be any hint of a woman in his life."

Definitely not. And she had a developing instinct that there were stories about Uncle Joe that Sam didn't tell—probably because he was none to clear himself on some of the details.

When it was time for him to leave, Joe had a pang of guilt as he discovered Sam and Natasha were staying with Neil and Stella for the night. It would have been much easier if Mum and Dad still had the family house. But they had gifted it to him legally five years previously when he became head of *BUSSTOP.*

"A man in your important position needs the abode to go with it," his mother had told him. "And we've seen this lovely smaller place just outside Cambridge. You can sell your property and buy this one for us. Effortless upgrading and downsizing in one fell swoop."

A complex documentation and money shuffle had seen this happen. Joe had one reservation about the location of their new property. There was a nuclear fusion plant in the area. It blended into with the landscape and was of no danger in itself. The only problem might come with occasional practising for security or safety alerts. The whole area would shut down. Neil and Stella decided they could live with that. The house was part of a modern development and Joe appreciated the practicalities of a maintenance-free place with all the mod cons for his parents, who were not getting any younger. *He* was finding that some aspects of living in an old house like Stable End were an ongoing nightmare. Three bedrooms, a large living room with a dining area, a kitchen that would have been fine for a small restaurant and a compact garden equalled a perfect home for them.

"You look after this girl, Sam," Joe ordered his nephew as he gave Natasha a hug and a kiss on the forehead. "She's doubly precious now."

Sam saluted in acknowledgement.

Yes. Doubly precious.

Neil caught his son by the elbow.

"You know where I am, lad. Any time. Your mother can enjoy the news as it's given out via the media."

In the car, Joe turned and waved. The impact of unexpected emotion caught at his breath. Natasha was standing framed by the doorway. This young woman's black hair was cut stylishly short but she had the pale complexion that often accompanies such colouring. She was tall and well made, a good match for Sam, who managed to tower over most people. It was a different house, obviously, but the echo of another scene and another person was there.

Natasha's appearance had never struck him until now.

"Let's go home, Bonny," he murmured. "I haven't had sight of the Prime Minister's publicity timetable yet but it's bound to run everyone ragged."

Chapter Two

"Prime Minister!" Joe began enthusiastically as the familiar figure came on screen. "What can I do for you on this fine morning?"

Kevin Crane looked slightly puzzled.

"I know that you are stuck out at Whetstone, Joe, but I wouldn't have thought your weather was *that* different to the centre of London."

The world beyond the *BUSSTOP* buildings would be cloaked in the same gloom and rain that Crane was looking out on from his Downing Street window.

"No, it's not. Vicky has just made me laugh until I hurt." The Prime Minister looked as interested as he ever could. "She informed me that she was thinking of calling in first thing and saying she wouldn't be able to come to work today because Einstein, her dog, had eaten her make-up."

"I would have paid serious money to listen in on that conversation if it had happened! So your wonderful Miss Tennant is squaring up to the world barefaced today?" He reflected for a moment. "Not that that would be a bad thing. She is a very appealing woman."

"Yes she is, I suppose," replied Joe, who had never thought about it before. "She found emergency supplies of war paint in a drawer, I believe."

He gave himself a mental shake. He was talking like this with the Prime Minister? It was a pity that they had to move on to more mundane matters.

"Are you happy, then, with the details that were sent to you for the publicity launch of Operation Ariadne?" the Prime Minister asked.

"*Happy* isn't the word I'd use. But it has to be done."

"If you can foresee any difficulties, Joe, now is the time to tell me. I can get something done about them. I can't do much about today's press conference, though. That has to go ahead. We have to get this show on the road."

"No difficulties, Prime Minister. I just have this urge to be somewhere else doing something different. You know me and the publicity thing."

"I do indeed. But *BUSSTOP* has never had such an eloquent chief—or astronaut for that matter. Promise me that you won't become too scientific today or in subsequent media interviews. Journalists are very simple people and they are easily confused. I swear that Reece Thompson's eyes were crossing when you were on his programme a few months ago. As you were giving everyone a history lesson about the old-style theories about conventional minimum-energy launch windows for Mars and opposition-class trajectories, I thought he was about to lie down on the studio floor."

"I'll do my best, Prime Minister."

"Have your best suit ready, by the way. It's not on the timetable but, in a day or so, after the congratulations from the Palace and your personal note, His Majesty will be inviting you to one of his private luncheons for movers and shakers."

Joe was not at all bothered by the invitation to the Palace. Whilst etiquette meant he couldn't walk up to the King and say "Wotcha, Richard! How's it going?" he would be talking to the person he knew and had worked with, not the figurehead that many looked up to. It was the Prime Minister who was fascinating him right now. He had never known him to be so animated. A newspaper columnist had bestowed upon him that "well-kept statue" tag after a particularly rumbustious session in the House of Commons early in his premiership. Everyone began to notice his amazing physical stillness, as well as his grave face; a short, edging-towards-the-rotund figure—an island of calm in the midst of a front bench full of fidgeting, squirming and gesticulating people.

Today, here was this totem pole fancying Joe's personal assistant and quoting space jargon accurately and sounding as though he understood it.

Bruce Dougall accused the King of being an armchair astronaut. It looked like the Prime Minister was just as bad. It had put a twinkle in his eye and no mistake. The media pack might see a whole new PM this afternoon. The next few months were shaping up to be very interesting.

Joe raised a hand to the intercom buttons to put him in contact with Vicky and then stopped. She's just through that door! he told himself. You'll lose the use of your legs if you're not careful.

Vicky looked up and smiled brightly when Joe came in. Thanks to Einstein the Jack Russell terrier, she was at her most alluring, she decided. After he had inexplicably chewed her make-up bag, she was forced to dip into her expensive reserves, which were there for special occasions. She took off her glasses. Thank goodness Einstein hadn't got hold of them. The frames alone cost a king's ransom.

This venture with Einstein had better be worth it. She had deliberately adopted her great aunt's dog three months previously, when Marcia Graham died, so that she would have a point of contact and a topic of conversation with Joe Mortimer.

Vicky swept back her hair with a careless hand and smiled again.

Joe wanted to check various things with her in the diary and then warn her about the impending invitation from the Palace. He had already given the visiting dignitaries their guided tour of *BUSSTOP*. Then he would be disappearing into a meeting to confirm details of what could be let out at the afternoon's press call.

"There shouldn't be any hitches there, Mr Mortimer," she said, scanning the screen. "I'll get Sarah—the PM's assistant—to put her ear to the ground so that we can have as much notice as possible regarding the date for lunch with the King."

On past form, Vicky would have the information within five minutes of the decision being made.

Joe kissed his fingertips and pressed them to her cheek.

"Vicky, you are a star!"

Vicky's eyes followed him hungrily as he left the office.

"I hate men who are in love with their jobs!" she muttered under her breath.

*   *   *

Nine a.m. local time and Bruce Dougall was to be found where he always went when he wanted to think. He was in Arlington Cemetery, where the honoured dead of the United States were buried. He was standing in front of the memorial to the seven astronauts who died when the *Challenger* space shuttle exploded before the disbelieving eyes of families, friends, *NASA* and a world television audience. This was a comparatively new monument, dedicated on 28th January 2086, exactly one hundred years on from the day when a brutal reminder was dished out that no nation could ride its luck forever. He had been part of the dedication ceremony, as had Joe Mortimer and the rest of the Zeus missions team. They had to be there. They were the young guns of *BUSSTOP*, who travelled to the Moon and the international Space Station as a matter of course; who were nearly ready for the most daring flights yet in the new Zeus spaceship, which would further the effort to put people on Mars.

No one was there to watch the lone figure who laid a cluster of spring flowers at the foot of the stone. Bruce looked around him without seeing, as he had done for the previous few days. He felt really ill for the first time, which had prodded him to come here instead of arriving promptly at *BUSSTOP* or settling down to work at home.

Washington D.C. was special during this season, when Nature ransacked her closets to look her very best. The swathes of daffodils across the city centre flowerbeds were still going strong and the tulips were in position to bloom soon. More sunshine like this and the flowering cherry trees and the dogwoods would create a blaze of pink and white. Generally he loved this time of year.

But not today.

Bruce trudged down to the grave of President John F. Kennedy. It might be said that he started this whole space business, declaring that America would have men on the moon by the end of the 1960s. His murder gave those words urgency and a sanctity that they might otherwise have never had. It became a holy mission.

A few early arrivals gave Bruce curious, sidelong glances. They knew that they should know who he was, but just couldn't put name and face together first thing in the morning. Bruce liked it that way right now. He wasn't sure he could be polite to adults or interested in young people who told him that he had inspired them and they wanted to be astronauts too.

He had to get back to *BUSSTOP* or go home. If he didn't—

What if he didn't?

The place would not grind to a halt if he were not sitting in his office or working from home. He had no meetings scheduled today. Yes, there was the media launch at London *BUSSTOP* but he had made it clear that this was a British show. Today there was nothing for America to say.

Most of the time, only his assistant knew where he was.

Genevieve Stanforth looked anxiously at her boss from the small screen of his palm-sized communicator.

"This is most unusual, Mr Dougall."

Bruce was tempted to tell her that she wasn't paid to comment on his actions but he bit back the instant retort. He was oddly detached from all this on one level. It was as though he was watching it happen to someone else. It was no good getting snippy with Genevieve. Her reaction was natural. In her eyes, this was a day when he should be available. But he needed to be away from everything.

"I'm feeling unusual today. Anyone can get in touch with me. I'm not about to throw this communicator into the Potomac or do something crazy like that. Anything that I should be reminded about?"

"You won't need reminding about this." She appeared to be looking up at a point somewhere above his head. "Joe Mortimer and the British Prime Minister will be starting the press conference at London *BUSSTOP* within the next half hour, to announce the Ariadne project properly." Bruce grimaced and felt a real sympathy, at least for Joe. Politicians deserved everything they got, although Prime Minister Crane seemed a decent enough guy. "Your statement is ready to be released and we also have something from the White House, so that's under control."

"Thanks, Genevieve! I won't be in the office or at home today"

The thought of her boss haunted Genevieve as she turned back to her work. The same age as Bruce Dougall, she remembered everyone joking about the newly assembled Zeus mission crew who would be aboard the groundbreaking flights. These were necessary before people could go to Mars. Ironically, it was said that each astronaut must have been picked by Central Casting. They were a fine-looking collection of men and women, for sure, with Bruce Dougall and Joe Mortimer leading the field. It became one of the longest-running gags of all time because, as the years went by, none of these people appeared to be aging anywhere near as quickly as their contemporaries. Was the fountain of youth located out there in space or was this a random collection of genetically blessed individuals?

Genevieve envied Dougall his apparent continued defiance of the years. Up to now, she would have said that the only real change in his appearance was the wearing of spectacles. ("If you think I'm putting up with having my eyes lasered, think again!" was the reaction from one of the pioneers who had sailed through the heavens not missing a beat). She didn't realise that many people envied *her*, remarking on her glossy, short fair hair, the smooth cheeks that owed nothing to facelifts and little to cosmetics, and the voluptuous figure that made any healthy man stop for a second look.

Yes, Bruce Dougall was a good boss. He lightened the day with clever jokes and smart comments about some of the more pompous members of the space community who appeared on screen or who made it as far as his office. The asides to her were not really wounding, always delivered with his ready smile.

Except that something had switched off that smile and suddenly he wasn't the Peter Pan of space any more. He looked drawn and weary and, although he was slim and athletic in build, he appeared to have lost weight. Genevieve didn't know what was going on there. Two divorces hadn't dented him noticeably. So what was having such an effect on him? Generally she could pick up some kind of a hint. Thus far she had drawn a blank.

*   *   *

Tom Garner heard the unmistakable click of heels along the corridor, heading for this computer lab after the owner of them had been in a meeting. He wondered if he should clear the screen of the television pictures and at least look as though he was doing something useful. When Irene Hanson came in, he could see that she didn't look as grimly cross as she sometimes did when she had been talking to the Master of the college, so he took his chance.

"The press conference is just about to begin, Professor."

"Which conference is that, Tom?"

"It's being held at *BUSSTOP* London. The Prime Minister and the boss of *BUSSTOP* are speaking, I believe, so it must be big."

Irene almost fell over a chair in her haste to get a better view of the screen. She watched Kevin Crane and Joe Mortimer enter the *BUSSTOP* media centre and take their seats. A Downing Street publicity flunky stood up along with an opposite number from *BUSSTOP* and they began an interminable double act of opening comments.

"Have you ever met Joe Mortimer, Professor?" Tom wanted to know. "He's some guy!"

"What?" Irene eyes were glued to the screen. "Oh yes, once. I gave a lecture a couple of years ago at *BUSSTOP.* He certainly is—er—some guy."

"When I was a child, my friends and I used to play Zeus missions. I insisted on being Joe Mortimer every time."

"Goodness!" Irene smiled. "Didn't your friends have something to say about that? As a matter of interest, did you have any friends left?"

"They didn't have much choice in the matter. I had the tree house in the back garden, which became the Zeus craft. Dad put up some extra ropes on the big outer branches so that we could do the space walks. I became pretty good at space walks. Then Bruce Dougall did that incredible inspection out round *Zeus Three*, so I was him for a while."

My bat, my ball, my wicket, Irene observed silently. You'll go far, young man.

He was well on the way there already, putting together a formidable doctoral thesis under her supervision.

Preliminaries were over and the Prime Minister had the floor. Looking very pleased with himself, he delivered a statement that the British division of *BUSSTOP* would have control of the Ariadne project to send people to Mars.

"Preparations are at a very advanced stage because both parts of *BUSSTOP* have been working together, as usual. This co-operation will continue. Half of the crew will be chosen by the United States and half will be chosen by Britain. We anticipate a launch within months, not years."

There was the sound of one hundred jaws dropping open and not going back. This was the stuff of science fiction being announced calmly as science fact.

Of course, Joe Mortimer and his impossibly glamorous crew had made everyone's eyes stand out on stalks. They had taken the Mars mission as far as orbiting the planet. They went out and proved the hard way that the new space ship, capable of generating a velocity that couldn't have been contemplated even a few years previously, wouldn't come apart at the seams in real space conditions with a full payload of people and equipment. The high orbits had also given *BUSSTOP* priceless data on surface conditions and what humans landing there could expect to find.

Following these dramatic advances, it was presumed that there would be one of those prolonged and inevitable periods of nothing, the likes of which had dogged the development of space travel from its beginning. Well yes, it was a long time since the last flight to Mars, but the pause had been one full of great activity, as the concept of Zeus had been stripped down to the wires and reborn as Ariadne. The crew of Zeus was suddenly about to see the fruit of its labours as *Ariadne One* headed for Mars.

The Prime Minister finished his prepared speech.

"I'll hand you over to someone who needs no introduction. But I don't want to take his achievements away from him, so here goes. He is British head of *BUSSTOP*. And without his team's work in the Zeus missions towards Mars, we would not be in this happy position today." He gestured. "Joe Mortimer."

Irene edged her stool a little closer to the screen as the camera focus moved to Joe Mortimer.

"Thank you for those kind words, Prime Minister. I can't add any more factual substance to what Mr Crane has just said. I could blind you with science all afternoon." Looking down at his papers, the Prime Minister gave the slightest of nods. Good man! "But that might not answer your queries. So let's take some questions. Mina, you start us off," he concluded as at least fifty journalists leapt to their feet and the inevitable cacophony of voices began.

Joe was something else, the Prime Minister concluded, even though he knew the little signs that gave away this person's unease at being in such a forum. He gripped the pen he wrote with very tightly, and when he spoke sitting down, his fingers were clenched behind his folded arms. But for all that, this was a man of action who knew how to deal with a baying press corps. He charmed, he laughed, he drew quick diagrams on a flip chart and he was able to address most of the people in the room by name because he had been mixing with them for five years and the faces didn't change much.

His father, Wing Commander Neil Mortimer, had been a bit of a smooth operator in his time. In his capacity as leader of one of the aerobatic display teams, he became a public face and voice of the RAF. Because of him, for a while everyone wanted to throw planes about the sky at silly speeds. Whatever magic the father had, the son possessed in spades. Joe Mortimer made everyone want to be an astronaut.

Crane knew that he must put a word in the royal ear during his next audience with the King. The Honours Committee wasn't a problem. If Joe didn't get some substantial award after this—along with the Britons in the team who went to Mars—as a seasoned politician the Prime Minister could write the future tabloid newspaper headlines quite accurately: *GIVE HIM A SIRHOOD, SIR! (And don't be mean with the gongs for our other brave boys and girls!)*

Back in the college monitoring lab, Tom Garner was impressed.

"That was interesting, wasn't it, Professor?"

Irene only responded when her student said her name for a third time and asked if she was all right.

"Sorry, Tom." She left her trance regretfully. "Yes, that was very good. What an amazing man," she said dreamily.

"You never know. Joe Mortimer and *BUSSTOP* might come calling," Tom suggested in all seriousness. "The discussion about the speed of communication between Earth and Mars is ongoing. Anyone with the smallest suggestion will be grabbed. When I was over at Goonhilly, the people there had some interesting ideas. But they weren't saying anything that I haven't heard you say. Mr Mortimer may seek out your expertise."

"Yes please," said Irene, in a voice low enough for Tom not to hear.

*　　*　　*

Bruce Dougall was footsore but pleasantly tired after wandering for hours around his beloved city and taking the occasional ride on the Metro. He felt a lot better. He had stopped a couple of times to buy coffee and something to eat. If startled food stand staff recognised him, they were too polite to say anything. His walking had brought him to the Washington Monument.

The vertical construction was behind him, piercing the late afternoon sky. He stood looking along the length of the reflecting pool. Across the river, the lights of Northern Virginia were coming on one by one to banish the encroaching darkness.

Bruce was seeing very different lights, a very different darkness. He was back on board *Zeus Three*.

"Bruce, I'm sure it's something and nothing," Joe Mortimer had said when he heard his report. "I'd rather we upset *BUSSTOP* and came back in late, in one piece. Will you take a stroll outside around this old lady and have a look?"

It had been a standard space walk, if much longer than usual, and Bruce had enjoyed himself outside. As a rule, Joe helped himself to this kind of job. The external inspection established that nothing was wrong. A computer must be giving a false reading. Still, it was a good enough reason to get kitted up and enjoy the unique freedom of floating in space, albeit on the end of a safety line.

But this time something was different. Bruce became ill after completing the walk. There seemed to be no explanation for the sudden onset of his malaise.

Joe spent time sitting with him every day for the duration of the voyage back to Earth, as well as carrying out his routine work, cursing *Zeus Three* because she wouldn't fly any faster and annoying Mission Control as he did his best to override computer protocols to coax more speed out of her. A space ship hurtling through the stars was hardly the ideal place for a dizzy and nauseous passenger, who could do nothing to help himself or the rest of the team. Over the long days Joe talked cheerful banalities to his invaluable assistant. When Bruce was really in a bad way, he held the delirious man's hand in reassurance, unsure as to what else he could do.

Back on Earth, in his capacity as Commander of the flight, Joe harried the doctors day and night to get an answer from them as to what had ailed Bruce, to the point where medical staff were seen to flinch at the mention of his name. Bruce recovered and appeared none the worse for the ordeal but the doctors could find nothing wrong with him or put forward any meaningful explanation for what had happened.

The whole mystery was kept under wraps. Only a small group knew what had happened. Bruce had been seen leaving *Zeus Three*, walking unsteadily. The explanation for his uneasy gait and his non-appearance at the post-flight media calls was that he had developed a minor back problem. This required immediate treatment to prevent it becoming a major problem that could jeopardise his place on subsequent missions.

Everyone swallowed the story. By the time *Zeus Three* was involved in the longest round trip ever, the world had got used to seeing at least *some* of what the astronauts got up to, on television. Everyone waited with bated breath for the daily dose of edited film. So Bruce's total absence from the flight deck or the leisure areas of Zeus had to be dealt with too. He had been seen to good effect during his unexpected space walk. Working on the basis that most viewers are remarkably unobservant, *BUSSTOP* authorised the insertion of film from *Zeus Two* into the daily broadcasts. Bruce was only seen in long shot, undertaking non-specific tasks that could not be attributed to any particular flight.

"After all," said the archivist who selected the appropriate sequences and supervised their inclusion, "the moving image has been fooling the human eye for over two hundred years. We can do a pretty convincing job here."

Bruce risked the wrath of his superiors by telling girlfriend Shannon Pierce what had really happened. She was more concerned about his well being and kept the secret.

All was fine until six months ago.

"I wish I could offer you a better prognosis, Mr Dougall," the doctor said when Bruce had regained a measure of composure. "I'm so sorry. As far and as fast as medical science has progressed, sometimes we're just plain stumped. I can give you medication, which will help you considerably for a good long time. We are a lot further forward in that respect. In your great grandfather's time, patients were put through the hell of chemotherapy and radical surgery, almost to justify the doctors' existence, and then they were stoned out of their minds with industrial strength painkillers, which must have hastened the end anyway. But even if I could, there would be no point in setting up an aggressive and invasive programme like that for you. I can't cure you.

"We've done some work on the cell structure of your cancer. That leads me to think that at some time in the past you have been exposed to dangerous levels of radiation. The obvious culprit is when you were in space on mission. I know that you were tested extensively after your famous space walk and nothing unusual was found. There would have been a major panic if anything had been found! Exposing astronauts safely to the massive radiation out in space depends on the integrity of the intelligent materials used in the manufacture of space suits and in the building of your spaceships. Joe Mortimer noted that no alarms were set off when you re entered the *Zeus Three* airlock. The sensors detected nothing. There's no point in telling the *BUSSTOP* medical people because there is nothing to tell. But *something* must have happened to you. You get used to surprises in this line of work."

You bastard, Joe! Bruce decided viciously. You and your safety-first attitude. If you were that bothered, you should have done the space walk yourself. Why did you decide to sit that one out, when you were usually so keen to go on space walks? I'll bet you knew you were sending me into danger.

The lights across the Potomac were coming on in their tens, hundreds and thousands. The scene became blurred with his tears.

Damn you, Joe! he thought. I'll even the score yet.

* * *

Kevin Crane and Joe Mortimer made an interesting new pairing as spokesmen of the impending space challenge. In the feeding frenzy that followed the announcement of the next stage of the exploration of Mars, the reaction was universally good. One newspaper was lost for words the next day—almost. Its front page was filled with a press-conference picture of the Prime Minister seated beside the astronaut-turned-administrator and a one—word headline: *WOW!*

Like any good politician, Crane had occasional waking nightmares about what some of the tabloids might make of certain events and this was music to his ears.

The general public was a lot more sophisticated these days about space exploration and the inherent risks involved. People could look back in amazement at what appeared to be a cavalier attitude to safety in the early days. They could be certain that the launch of *Ariadne One* would not have been bounced forward just so that the Prime Minister could milk the inevitable feel-good factor. This man's caution was legendary. His detractors said that he must have held a debate with himself before deciding to emerge from the womb but even the most grudging of them acknowledged him as the safest pair of hands in Downing Street for a long while.

Joe was known for his ultra-steady approach to matters when flying the Zeus missions and it was as inevitable as night following day that he ended up in the big chair at *BUSSTOP*, where his attitudes could count for even more. He was something of a media enigma. Chunks of his life were a frustrating blank for those who liked the human-interest angle. But everyone felt they knew him well enough to be sure that, if he discovered politicians had decided to score cheap points at the expense of thorough preparation, he would have locked the entire Cabinet in a secure room and then told the world why he did it.

The Prime Minister and His Majesty King Richard the Fourth were less of an odd-couple set-up simply because everyone was more used to it. Very occasionally, the weekly audience between PM and King was turned into a photo call and the Thursday following the *BUSSTOP* press conference was an obvious candidate for this treatment. The two men were seen strolling in the sunshine through the gardens of Buckingham Palace, deep in conversation. The King was a photogenic subject. He was a strapping six feet two and solidly built, with fair hair and an expansive smile. The Spencer inheritance was still alive and well in the royal family and the cameras loved him.

Kevin Crane was less concerned about what he looked like, although he did not want to appear as a total fool. Smaller and dark-haired, he was the perfect foil for the pin-up King.

Although this was an exciting time, it would be a very challenging one. All sections of the media were feeling less winded upon reaching the morning after the morning after. A nation could begin to consider the enormity of what lay ahead.

The King was laughing and Kevin Crane was half-smiling.

"It has to be a compliment, Prime Minister."

"I'm taking it like that, Sir."

They were referring to that day's newspapers and the editorial column of an influential tabloid, which couldn't be relied upon to be the Prime Minister's biggest supporter. This time the message was unequivocal.

> *Kevin Crane is undoubtedly the man to be leading the country at this time. He has shown us during some times of difficulty that he does not shirk the job. He is an unlikely commander of the new Space Age. He wears steel-rimmed spectacles but—more importantly—he has balls of steel.*

*   *   *

Joe was glad to let them get on with it. It was part of their very different job descriptions. For a few days a press and television group did trail him when he was away from the safety of his home or *BUSSTOP* but they had to give up in the end. No one could continue forever with spinning new slants on the fact that the Ariadne project had the green light, with Britain in the driving seat. There was some lively speculation amongst the specialist correspondents as to exactly why Britain had ended up with overall control but there wasn't an excess of analysis. It was as though nobody wanted to question it too much in case a spell might be broken. It could all be part of a feverish dream.

It wasn't. The publicity juggernaut rolled on. *BUSSTOP* was sent its note of congratulation by the Palace and Joe received his personal letter from the King. Hard on heels of that came his expected invitation to lunch with His Majesty.

In the middle of this Philip and Daphne Mortimer arrived back home from Peru and, for the first forty-eight hours after their return, they were joyfully bemused as they caught up with family and national news. Natasha's pregnancy was top of the list but the confirmation of the Ariadne project, with all that it meant for Joe, came close behind.

Three days after returning home, Philip was paying a solo evening visit to his brother.

"Will I have to curtsy or anything to you now?" Philip wanted to know as Joe closed the front door. "You'll get your knighthood, for sure!"

He slapped Joe on the back, high on multiple delights.

"It's good to see you!" Joe exclaimed, crushing Philip in a bear hug. "But let's wait until we get the team safely to Mars and back home again before we start talking about stuff like that."

"You're nervous about this, aren't you?" Philip asked wonderingly as he accepted the whisky glass and sat down.

Joe took a deep breath.

"I'm something. I don't know if nervous fits the bill."

He sat down then stood once more, restless. He opened the patio doors and looked out over the darkening garden. Philip joined him.

"What is it, bro?" he asked quietly. "This is not like you."

There was a long pause, and then Joe turned and faced his brother. Apart from the greying hair, Philip could have been his twin. The vigilant concern for his little brother was always there, even in the banter, and it was very evident in his face.

"When I—" Joe stopped. "During the—"

He stopped again. Philip waited. This was not the time to interrupt.

"Tell me," he had to say eventually, as the seconds dragged by.

"Phil, what if it all goes wrong?"

The words came out in a rush. It was as though holding them in had held him upright. Now he physically drooped and stepped back into the room to drop into an armchair. Philip was stunned. This was not the lad who had joined the RAF at seventeen or the man who was enrolled in the space programme by the time he was twenty-two.

As a Human Resources consultant, he knew a bit about what makes people tick.

"God, this is going to be a long night." He stuck his empty glass under Joe's nose. "Do the honours, big fella."

This term of endearment, all the way from childhood, showed his deep concern. The young Joe flourished like a weed, overtaking his older brother in the growth stakes for a while. In the uneven march towards maturity, the two ended up at much the same height of six feet, with a similar muscular build. But the tag was there forever, as were the height marks still on the kitchen doorframe, drawn by doting parents.

Philip took a sip from his replenished drink and sat down on the floor next to his brother's chair.

"You've been mixing with the bad people, haven't you?"

That raised a smile from Joe. *"Watch out for the bad people, boys!"* had been their grandfather's mantra back through to their earliest memories. When they were young and were learning one of the first harsh lessons of life—that not everyone is as loving and caring as family—they accepted it at face value. As the years passed, Gerry Mortimer expanded the advice, to include those with negative attitudes.

"They will suck you in and drag you down. You can reach the point where you begin to doubt whether you know your own name. Keep out of their reach as much as possible."

"I think I have," Joe replied faintly to Philip now.

"Who?"

Joe found himself telling Philip about the bizarre conversation with Bruce Dougall.

"He knows something that I don't, Phil. I was ready for it to be data presentations at dawn to sort out the jurisdiction of Operation Ariadne. I didn't expect him to roll over so tamely. And then he kept banging on about the project's flaws . . ."

"Hmm. I take it that you have this conversation saved? Let's have a look."

Joe put all communications on automatic storage. Personal material went in one file, official business in another, where even the security codes had security codes. It was a precaution that many public figures took these days. Joe routed the exchanges with Bruce to his personal console in the living room where he and his brother were seated.

As usual, Philip couldn't help noting the contrast between the hi-tech equipment and the room it was in. All the furniture was at least a hundred years old. He and Joe had been merciless with it as small children. Chairs had been moved and roped together to make American Western stagecoaches. But everything retained an air of battered elegance, especially the overstuffed armchairs, which their parents had no room for when they moved out.

Afterwards Philip looked thoughtful.

"You're right, little bro. You are as good at people watching as I am. Give yourself some credit. Dougall gets to you every time, even across the stretch of the Atlantic, without even trying. What is it with you two?" he wondered, even though he knew the story. "Anyway, he does know something that you don't know."

"Oh."

Joe looked and sounded devastated.

"Only I don't think it's anything to do with spaceships. In fact, I'd stake everything I hold dear on it. That was nothing to do with flying to Mars and everything to with Bruce Dougall as a person. And I think we'll be hearing about it before too long."

"He gave up formalising his life after two marriages," mused Joe. "There's no one to divorce again. It can't be that."

"I don't know what it is, Joe. There's no point in going round in circles wondering what his problem might be. But it's not the integrity of this mission. There's nothing wrong with your expedition. Just as you know, the Prime Minister knows and your precious King knows."

*   *   *

Joe attended his luncheon date at Buckingham Palace with refurbished confidence. According to royal etiquette, he bowed formally to the King upon meeting him and murmured "Your Majesty." Both men were smiling inwardly at the games tradition made them play.

It was a select gathering. Joe found himself rubbing shoulders with two captains of industry and three merchant bankers. The table was enlivened by the presence of Her Royal Highness Princess Charlotte, the heir to the throne. Her mother, Queen Alice, had memorably declared herself—privately, of course—to be "luncheoned out." So mother and daughter split the duties of being hostess with the King. As the next monarch, it was a sensible move for Charlotte to become accustomed to the grind of such occasions. But she didn't appear to be finding it a grind. She was witty and gracious and as well briefed as her father, asking each guest informed questions. Although Joe knew that he was watching a stellar performance, he couldn't help being beguiled.

Imbued with a love of history by grandfather Gerry, he also couldn't help doing a double take on the quiet. As a child, he spent hours with granddad watching film from the twentieth century. Devouring grainy footage from the 1960s race to the Moon first fired his enthusiasm for space exploration. He was equally fascinated by the 1980s and 1990s and, because of this, he knew that he was sitting opposite an echo from the past at the luncheon table. This tall, blonde and attractive young woman with the winning smile bore more than a passing resemblance to another royal back down along the line—Diana, Princess of Wales.

The process of the gathering frustrated Joe. Yes, he was part of a far-reaching and lively conversation but he was speaking in press release snippets, expanding on what everyone already knew about upcoming events. He wanted to really *talk* with Richard and that wasn't possible on this sort of occasion.

Everyone scrambled gallantly to their feet when Princess Charlotte withdrew from the gathering. The King thanked everyone for coming, wished them a safe journey home and then he too left the room.

A grey-suited official caught Joe's eye.

"Mr Mortimer," he said quietly. "His Majesty has taken the liberty of sending instructions to your driver to be prepared to wait for a while. His Majesty additionally wonders if you would care to join him for a walk in the gardens."

Joe wondered what the penalty might be for kissing a senior member of the Royal Household. Instant beheading, probably. There were so many arcane and ancient rules, grown like an unruly thicket around royalty and all matters pertaining to the Crown. He had discovered, to his amazement and amusement, that MPs were forbidden to die within the House of Commons, poor sods, because Westminster was a royal Palace and commoners were not allowed to do anything as ordinary as shuffle off the mortal coil there.

When a member of Kevin Crane's Cabinet collapsed and expired within the precincts, his death had to be recorded officially as having occurred in St Thomas' Hospital.

Joe, trampling on all his instincts to jump up and down on the spot with glee, looked very solemn, and followed another official through a maze of rooms and corridors out into the afternoon air. His Majesty was inspecting a rose bed.

"Joe!" he exclaimed when he spied his old RAF colleague.

"Your Majesty."

"Oh, stuff that, Joe! How are you? You looked tired at that *BUSSTOP* do the other week. You look much better now. Come on, there's nobody to get in the way here. Let's have a good chinwag!"

Both men loosened their ties. The King threw down his jacket on a low wall and took a couple of exaggerated breaths of fresh air.

"You never were one for being indoors too long, were you?" Joe remembered.

"Sometimes this lot pisses me off." Richard waved a hand at the palace buildings. "I'll bet *BUSSTOP* does the same to you." Joe agreed. "But that's the way it is. I'm a guardian of this country's heritage and you're making sure that we don't make a cock-up of the greatest exploration opportunity *ever*. How do we manage it?"

"I guess we've both learned a little tact and diplomacy along the way, Richard."

"True." Richard was silent for a moment, also remembering. "I'm glad you hadn't picked up any tact when you gave evidence at the inquiry into Jack Crane's death. You rattled the top brass good and proper!" He halted. "Does Kevin ever talk about Jack to you? No, he doesn't to me, either. Odd."

"Perhaps not," Joe said. "By my reckoning, the fact that we know is enough for him. I suppose it's a link, a bond, that doesn't have to be spoken about."

The years dropped away and they were young men again, with life opening up before them. Joe had visited a world that most could only imagine and, following the death of his formidable mother Queen Matilda, the King had worked tirelessly within his own sphere. It was great to go back to where it all began.

They walked and talked for a good half an hour, remembering their RAF days and Joe's space exploits, before the appearance of a servant at a door indicated that the King had stretched the afternoon timetable as far as it would go. His Majesty groaned and looked around for his jacket.

"You know, Joe, I think there must be a secret annexe in this dump that I don't know anything about, where they teach the staff to *hover*. If there's one thing that gets me down, it's people hovering discreetly. One thing before you leave. Not a word to anyone about what I'm going to tell you. I will personally hang you from the flagpole if I thought it got out via you."

"Richard! You know me better than that!"

"Yes, I do. Charlotte is getting married. Squadron Leader Michael Timpson, of course. We've decided that he ought to have some sort of title, hence the delay in announcing the engagement. The genealogists and the College of Heraldry are having a dig around in his family tree. He could well be an unofficial twig of some house or other."

"If they dig too far, he could well have a better claim to this lot than you. There was an interesting television programme made a hundred years or so ago. I remember watching it with my grandfather. The presenter reckoned that the real monarch and descendants were living in Australia."

"That must have been fun! Anyway, the wedding will be at St Paul's. We're looking to the end of November. The full works. You'll be receiving an invitation. The invitation will be for you and a companion. I don't like to see you wandering about alone, Joe. I wish you would do something about it. Settle down with a good woman. Mind you, she'd need stamina to share your music. Still listening to everything from Sinatra to The Sex Pistols, I suppose? I know that you will turn up with a lady appropriate to the occasion." He winked as the courtier drew closer. "Good to see you again, Mr Mortimer," he continued, for the benefit of their audience.

"Your Majesty," replied Joe, bowing once more.

Chapter Three

It can be difficult to ignore a fact. Once the decision to turn away has been made, the shunned information crops up all over the place, like an orphan tapping on the windows of the house, beseeching to be brought in out of the storm.

The data that Professor Irene Hanson was trying to sideline was contained within Heinrich One Hundred, one of the University space computer programs. But that didn't stop her thinking about it as she went on with her daily life. It was in her mind as she drifted into sleep at night and it was awake and bouncing when she opened her eyes each morning. It was reaching the point where she didn't want to check out this monitoring again. It was becoming ridiculous.

Everything was quiet that day. No students wanted to bend her ear, she had no lectures or seminars and Tom Garner was visiting Jodrell Bank, mixing with the specialist experts there to further his thesis. Squaring her shoulders, she opened up the listening and tracking system that was taking over her life.

At first Irene was relieved. Only the expected signals of space were there. Earlier generations thought that the planets made heavenly music, as they swung around in their orbits. She loved the notion. It was almost a pity it wasn't true. But that didn't stop the solar system being a very noisy place when computers and radio telescopes listened in, especially with the racket from a cacophony of stars in the background.

Irene noticed that the computer settings meant she was tracking across a very narrow band of frequency. Perhaps Tom had altered it and failed to reset. She was helping him to watch on Heinrich, as part of his studies. She widened the band.

And there it was.

The signal was rhythmic, steady. Just as before. Groups of sounds were repeated to make a pattern. Irene had never heard anything like it. On that basis alone, she had to keep working at it. She had built her career and her reputation on doing this type of analysis. Not for the first time she set the program to provide a possible origin and location for the signal. She knew already that the results would be exactly the same as before and she had no idea how to explain them.

That wasn't quite true. There was *one* explanation. It was a pity that the old organisation of *SETI* no longer existed. The *Search for Extra Terrestrial Intelligence* had been set up to monitor precisely this sort of signal. It had been disbanded after a century with no results. Irene could have done with its expertise.

"Time for lunch!" she said under her breath and scuttled out of the room before Heinrich could start going over old ground. She wanted to be able to go through the results step by step, at her own pace.

No one took much notice of her walking down the corridors, apparently lost in thought. It meant that she was about to produce another stunning paper or was planning her latest book. The woman was a powerhouse and no one could ever be sure what was coming next.

For the first time in a long while Irene was feeling lonely. Oh yes, she was used to being alone. That was quite different and mostly she revelled in it because the memory of being with another person was still a horror, after all these years. But as she sat at table with three colleagues and ideas were shared, she was suffering from professional isolation. Dan and Parvinder and Donna were trotting out their latest fancies. Whilst some of the theories might be a bit skewed, they were based in solid scientific fact and such on-the-hoof conversation might put them back on track.

But what about her own observations?

If there was a rational way of saying "I'm picking up signals from Mars," she hadn't worked it out yet.

*   *   *

Whilst he knew that he could never come near to achieving the poker face of the Prime Minister, Joe Mortimer had a calm and serious professional exterior, especially when doing something as important as rounding up a flight crew to make history.

"Gianfranco, that's superb!" he concluded. "We'll do all our bits and pieces at this end. How's Rome efficiency-wise these days?"

Gianfranco Rosso definitely stopped to consider his words—not something that happened very often. Were they still in formal mode, at the end of what amounted to an on-screen interview?

"A little slow," was what he settled for.

"Tell me something new! We'll stir them up from this end. Don't worry about a thing. Get ready for Cape Canaveral. Bring Paola, of course, for some or all of the time. The training will mean a long stretch away from home. Welcome to *Ariadne One!*"

"I'm honoured, Mr Mortimer."

The small, neat black-haired Italian beamed at him. He looked like a cherubic choirboy—suspiciously so; he would be the one messing about when he thought no one was looking, but would be the one to perform like an angel when the moment came.

Joe shut down the screen and punched the air in delight. Not only was Gianfranco a prodigious young space engineering talent; his *joie de vivre* would be the secret weapon against the low times that plague every crew during preparation and in flight.

"Yes!" he exclaimed. He activated the screen again. "Vicky, that's it. List complete. We have Gianfranco Rosso on board as rear gunner."

"Mr Mortimer, I thought you were talking to Mr Rosso as—"

"Sorry, Vicky. I come from a flippant RAF family. Gianfranco will be our engineer. Send the whole list over to Washington D.C for Bruce Dougall to check. Our half of the proposed crew plus our reserves, with their relative positions on the list"

"Yes, Mr Mortimer. Will you want to talk to Mr Dougall about it?"

"Oh. I'm sure we'll have a talk about it. I understand that Bruce is in *BUSSTOP* today. He should be nicely settled down at his desk by now."

Joe made a wager with himself. When Vicky confirmed that the list of London-selected *BUSSTOP* flight crew for *Ariadne One* had been dispatched, he started counting the seconds. With the two-minute mark approaching, he heard the words he was expecting from his assistant.

"Mr Mortimer, I have Mr Dougall to speak to you on your secure line. And he doesn't look or sound very pleased."

Oh, Bruce! mused Joe. You are so predictable.

"Good afternoon, Bruce," he said out loud. "Or in your case, good morning."

Joe was so busy thinking about what he could say to soothe Bruce's ruffled feathers, and score a few points at the same time, that he nearly missed the most important thing of all.

Bruce looked shocking.

"Hello," he said flatly to Joe, not wanting to become involved in word games about the time difference. "I've received your crew list for *Ariadne One.*"

"And you don't like it."

"Does it make any difference what I think?"

"Tell me about the selections I've made. I would like you to be on board with this."

Suddenly, all the smart comments that Joe could have made were unimportant, childish almost. Bruce's eyes were enormous in his shrunken cheeks.

"Okay." Even the word sounded tired as Bruce said it. "What the hell are you playing at?" he demanded, coming to life. "Especially putting Masahide Shimamoto in the crew! And are you trying to found the Space Chapter of the United Nations?"

That was more like the Bruce Joe knew, with a ready wit. It was part of what attracted S—.

Don't go there! he ordered himself sharply.

"Bruce, I have picked the people who are best for the job, in computing, space engineering and so on. Does it matter which country they come from? And why don't you want Masahide on board?"

Joe's tone challenged Bruce to be truthful. The American didn't have the stomach for a fight today about Masahide's lifestyle choices.

"He's a very quiet guy," he offered lamely.

Joe couldn't disagree with that. It was partly Masahide's nature and partly an attempt to keep his head down and avoid prejudiced and hostile attitudes. His friends and loved ones said that he should speak up more. He let his abilities do the talking. But there was more than reticence going on there. His broad, untroubled face and understanding black eyes showed him to be one of the world's listeners. To those who didn't know him, Masahide gave a first impression of being formidable. He was quite short but obviously ultra physically fit. But when he bowed in greeting, or offered an hand to shake, the person who was being acknowledged felt as though he or she was the only person in the world. Every team needed a Masahide.

"I think that Gianfranco has enough personality for everyone!" Joe noted.

"*BUSSTOP* is primarily an American and British initiative." Bruce was not to be denied. "Our predecessors way back nearly came to blows founding it."

"And the only reason we can smile at their stupidity is because *BUSSTOP* went ahead, in spite of them. We can't have things happening in spite of us, when it comes to landing on Mars for real this time. We must have the very best from the start. I had final oversight in the training of each person I have named. I guess you'll be able to say the same about your people. I can't see your problem. I'm the one who could be accused of something—short-changing his own country! In case it has escaped your notice, there's only one British person on board. The next Brit—Fay Shaw—is down the back-up list, behind Arty Rowe and Jackson Metz. I could have done with her on board but no, I won't juggle with the rankings. Mind you, I'm guessing that you'll select Emily Alexander. She counts as half a Brit." Emily's parents had left England to live in the United States when Emily was about three years old. "That reminds me. I presume Simeon Turner will be on your list? Unless you're being a racist too. And yes, I know you have your reservations about a couple on board."

"I'm thinking about it."

"Good." Joe paused then continued in a more conciliatory manner. "Bruce, are you all right? You look as though you should be taking a break from work."

The fierce duty of care that Joe had felt for the people on the Zeus flights was stirring again. He would have gone outside *Zeus Three* and pushed the spaceship home if he had thought that it could get Bruce back quicker to medical attention.

"Don't you start! You're as bad as my doctor."

"Doctor?"

Joe was on the word in a flash.

"Yeah. No big deal. He reckons I've picked up some virus or other. We're putting the finishing touches to our crew roster at this end. You'll receive it tomorrow."

Bruce closed down the communication abruptly.

Making his point had been exhausting, as well as useless. He removed his glasses and buried his face in his hands for a minute or so. Then he straightened himself up and spoke to his assistant.

"Genevieve, please may I have the details of Simeon Turner, Systems team, on screen."

Bruce looked out of the window at the lowering skies. After all the debates, he was still in a quandary as far as Simeon Turner was concerned. He barely glanced at the information as it appeared. He knew exactly what all the evaluations said. He had written the initial training stuff himself!

He stared at the picture of Simeon on screen and had a moment of sudden clarity. It was as if a hitherto unused part of his brain had been switched on, by some force beyond his control. It was a bizarre feeling. He shuddered as he realised how unfair he had been at times during the young man's training. Simeon didn't always snap into action in a split-second but he was much improved by all accounts and his computer skills would be a huge asset. He *had* to go to Mars.

This was the beginning of a long apology to the whole Turner family, framed in the only way Bruce thought might make some sense.

* * *

At the end of a burdened day, there was a bright spot for Irene.

"You have a personal call waiting, Professor," her secretary announced. "Professor Marmaduke Dawson. Did I get that right? Is anyone called Marmaduke?"

"He is." Irene smiled. "You haven't been here long enough to meet him, have you?"

As a result, Irene found herself stepping out of a taxi some hours later, ready to walk into one of Cambridge's smartest hotels. Professor Dawson moved forward to greet her as she came through the door.

"Irene!" he exclaimed, hugging her and kissing her cheek. "How are you, my dear?"

"All the better for seeing you, Marmaduke. Don't tell me you've been prowling up and down the foyer waiting for me to arrive."

"Oh no! I had advance warning. All the birds were dropping out of the sky, dazzled as you made a triumphal entrance in your chariot."

Irene had heard Cambridge taxis called some things in her time, but she didn't recall the word "chariot" being one of them. Marmaduke was on top form, as usual. She wondered what they were making of him in New Zealand, this huge bear of a man with long wavy hair and a neatly trimmed beard. His blue eyes were much paler than Irene's, but right now they were on fire with equal intensity. He was in the midst of a three-year exchange project between Cambridge and the University of Wellington and was home for a week or two, taking a break. His opposite number was going down a storm here in Cambridge, teaching Antipodean Studies. Marmaduke, in his own words, was "putting the Kiwis right about early mediaeval English history."

"Irene, I thought we'd eat here in one of the hotel restaurants, if that's up to scratch with you. *Parker's Piece* would be my choice."

Parker's Piece was the holder of just about every culinary award going. Irene accepted graciously, as if dining in such a place was an everyday occurrence for her.

Half way through the main course, Marmaduke put down his knife and fork.

"Good God, it's great to see you, Irene Hanson." He poured more wine into both glasses. "You look more lovely every time I do clap eyes on you. Blue really is your colour, isn't it?"

"Flattery will get you everywhere, Marmaduke."

"Will it?" he wondered hopefully. "Still living on your own, I gather. It's not right, a splendid woman like you."

"You of all people know my reasons for not making any kind of long-term commitment again."

"Of course I do. It was a bad business, but how many years can anyone go on being angry and frightened?"

"I don't sit on my own *all* the time."

"Delighted to hear it!" Marmaduke said cheerfully, attacking his beef once more. "Glad to know that you are not withering away in your ivory tower."

The conversation flowed effortlessly, as if both parties were picking up from where they left off yesterday, instead of filling in a gap of many months. Their fathers had been good friends. Over the years Irene had come to look upon Marmaduke as the brother she never had. Well, she had thought other things at one time, but bitter experience had made her realise the benefits of a deep and lasting friendship with no complications.

Marmaduke ordered large brandies to go with the coffee.

"We can't come to much harm. We don't have far to go, do we? It's only a short ride in the lift to bed."

"That's where *your* bed may be, Marmaduke. Mine is a taxi ride away."

Marmaduke grinned, unabashed.

"God loves a trier, as my dear old father used to say. A man can't be blamed for trying. I was duty bound, you might say."

Irene laughed off the suggestion, which they both knew would never come to anything.

"Thank you. You were paying me a compliment."

"Every time, Irene. Every time. But listen to me, Irene Hanson." He paused whilst the coffees and brandies were served. "If I can't be your lover tonight, let me be your father confessor. What's wrong?"

"Pardon?"

"You are as charming and enchanting as ever, but it's as if there's a great big question mark hovering over you. What has put it there? Tell me. I can listen, even if I can't help."

"It's work!" she replied. "Something I can't seem to categorise."

It was probably the unexpectedly large quantity of alcohol hitting her system that finally broke down Irene's reticence. Marmaduke did listen until finally she rambled to a halt.

"That's it," she said. "In a rather large nutshell."

"Absolutely fascinating! Some sort of structured message coming from Mars. Perhaps I'm being a little dim here, Irene, but what's your problem? You organise your data and you go public with it. It will blow everyone's socks off!"

"How long have you been away from Britain? I'd be on the front pages and at the top of every news programme one day and standing in the unemployment queue the next."

"I think you are judging your fellow countrymen a little harshly. Remember that the King was a wannabe astronaut in his youth and from what I see and read in the news reports, the Prime Minister has caught the space bug badly. The King and Joe Mortimer were in the RAF together. Imagine the three of them working together! It's like putting kiddies in charge of the sweetie shop. And space fervour is spreading. You could stand up and say that the Moon was made of Gruyere cheese and you would be believed right now." Marmaduke drank the last of his brandy and waved to a waiter. "If you won't go public, our all-time hero Joe Mortimer is someone you should talk to."

"Why?" asked Irene, going pink and feeling hot and flustered like some silly teenager gazing at a picture of her latest fancy.

"If you can control yourself for a moment, think! He and *BUSSTOP* will be sending a spaceship full of people to Mars in the next few months. Generally, when one travels anywhere on this planet, one needs to know if the natives are friendly. I think Mr Mortimer and his gang will be more interested in the fact that it appears there are natives on Mars, friendly or otherwise."

*　　*　　*

Later in the evening, Joe was still smarting from the rebuff. Usually he shrugged off such a rare event. For some reason, tonight it hit home.

"Dinner?" Marilyn Bailey had repeated. "That's very sweet of you, Joe, but no thank you."

"No?"

He couldn't believe it.

"That's what I said. No. Ah, you can't understand why I'm turning down dinner with Joe Mortimer. Hang on, let's get this right. I'm turning down dinner and sex with Joe Mortimer. Both guaranteed to be incredible. If word of the offer got out, women would be queuing round the block. But not this particular woman and not tonight."

"Why?"

Joe felt very foolish and didn't know what to say to move this conversation on.

"Do you really want an answer?"

An alarm bell should have been ringing. When someone says such a thing, it's time to retreat because that answer is bound to be painful. But he was like an animal dazzled in the headlights of an oncoming vehicle, unable to run out of the way.

"Yes please."

"In case you hadn't noticed, Joe, I'm a human being. I am not a toy that you can pick up and put down as the mood takes you. I don't hear from you for weeks and then it's all supposed to be lovely again when you decide to contact me."

"I've been busy," he said lamely.

"I know. Your "busy" is all over the news." She looked at him from out of the screen with an expression of faint disapproval. "I really hoped for a more original excuse from you!"

"I'm not making excuses."

"And neither am I. Good night, Joe."

Marilyn, with the mane of auburn hair and those astonishing green eyes, disappeared from the screen.

Bonny had been stretched out fast asleep for most of the evening at her master's feet. Suddenly she woke up, shook herself so that her collar tags clanked and rested her chin on Joe's knee, sighing heavily.

"Is life getting you down as well?" Joe wondered, stroking her head. "It happens. The sun will rise tomorrow morning and we can get on with everything again. It'll be all right. Promise."

Bonny followed Joe round the house like a clinging toddler. She sat behind him in the kitchen whilst he made coffee. She was at his side as, in a mood of introspection, he rummaged for a small box in a bedroom cupboard. She flopped down on the sofa next to him when he returned to his original seat.

"What's this, dog? You don't need to show your paces for the *Faithful Hound of the Year* competition. You're the permanent winner of that."

Joe opened the box. Bonny's nose was close to his hand as he picked up different items. His *BUSSTOP* medals glinted in the lamplight, along with the recognitions from the RAF. He opened up the small velvet-covered case that contained his MBE.

"The whole country salutes you and your achievements, Mr Mortimer." He remembered the words of the Queen so clearly. "How long do you think it will be before people actually walk on the surface of Mars?"

Her Majesty Queen Matilda the Second had given him a warm smile along with his award. He allowed himself to wallow in the old glow of pride and satisfaction once more. He recalled every detail of the opulent Ballroom in Buckingham Palace, where the investiture had taken place. That was strange, because at the time he was concentrating on not tripping over.

Joe closed the case and tried to put it back in the box. It would not sit evenly in its place because something small had slid down into the space it usually occupied. Joe's fingers felt the shape of the object and he froze. He closed his eyes. If the contents had not been so special, he would have hurled the box across the room. Instead, he pulled out the little thing. For a moment he couldn't look. But he had to.

"No, Bonny."

Joe pushed away her questing nose. Offended, she retreated to the other end of the sofa as he held the tiny teddy bear.

He hadn't looked at it or touched it in a long time. He had forgotten how small it was. He judged it to be about three and a half inches long. Teddy wore an old-style blue duffel coat and a lopsided embroidered grin. Again, the memories came flooding back.

"Look, you can put his coat hood up when he's cold." Sally laughed. "It's cold in space, isn't it? His name is Barry. He belonged to my great-grandmother. Goodness knows how I've ended up with him. Take him, Joe. He can be the first teddy bear to visit the stars. And a bit of me can be with you all the time."

Laika the dog may have gone into orbit before him but surely Barry was the original bear space traveller, flying out on *Zeus Four*. It was as that spacecraft was returning to Earth that Sally had been involved in a senseless hit-and-run accident. A medical team at Addenbrooke's Hospital kept her alive as long as they could.

When the spaceship landed. Bruce gave Joe the terrible information. It transpired later that Philip Mortimer had been allowed to speak to Bruce on a secure link. No one at *BUSSTOP* knew what Philip was saying, beyond that fact that there was a family problem that needed Joe's attention. Sally had never been to America and she was not for public consumption at home. She had met Bruce when he was in Britain preparing for *Zeus Two*.

Joe rushed back to England. Although in a coma, Sally had seemed stronger when he was at her side. He was holding her hand when she died two days later.

He had never known such heartbreak but, as he looked at Barry the bear now, something occurred to Joe for the first time. How must Bruce have felt when Philip spoke to him and he was given the task of passing on the news? He hid it very well.

Joe pulled the hood up onto the bear's head and pulled it back again. Tears ran down his face.

"Sally, why did you have to leave me?" he wept.

Bonny, sensing she was needed, abandoned her sulk and dropped down beside Joe. He didn't stop her when she sniffed the miniature figure. She wagged her tail hopefully but soon realised that it was not a toy for her amusement.

Joe looked up at the night sky through the window.

"Sally, I didn't mean to end up living like this," he said desperately. "Behaving the way I do sometimes. A bit of a shit with women. You knew what the real me was like."

"I know," a quiet voice seemed to say inside his head. "And I love you."

*   *   *

Joe opened his eyes very slowly. The sun shone brightly through the curtains and the wind mumbled round the eaves of the house. His head ached abominably and his mouth was sour and dry. The whisky bottle and a glass standing on the bedside table came into gradual focus. He groaned loudly.

"What was I doing?" he demanded of the empty room.

He didn't even particularly *like* whisky. He only drank it as a rule when Phil was around, to keep him company.

The clock entered his line of vision and then his mind slid into gear.

Uttering words that should never pass the lips of a twenty-four carat national icon, he leapt out of bed and immediately regretted the speed of his movement. He had to wait until his reeling senses steadied and he could formulate a plan of action. He caught a glimpse of himself in a mirror and wished he hadn't.

Yes. That was it. Try and appear to be a bit respectable. He didn't fancy contacting *BUSSTOP* looking like this. Vicky was loyalty itself but even her particular brand of discretion must have a breaking point and this would surely be it.

For once Joe understood the true meaning of a family saying that had come down from the Mortimer East Anglian agricultural roots.

"You'll feel better when you have your collar and 'ames on."

As a child, he heard the phrase used when someone was grumbling about going through the processes of getting ready for the day. Later on he found out that the "collar and hames" referred to parts of a working horse's harness.

Joe was dressed and this side of respectable in his collar and hames when he called *BUSSTOP*.

"Vicky, I overslept badly," he said, without a word of a lie. "I'll be in as soon as I can. Various people are expecting me to be in London today."

Vicky's heart went out to him in a fluttering rush. As usual, Joe could have stepped from the pages of a men's clothing catalogue but this morning there was something slightly *rumpled* about him.

"That's fine, Mr Mortimer. There's nothing important going on." No, she thought, nothing much. Nothing, apart from the continuous clatter of events towing everyone towards the launch of *Ariadne One*. "If you're not feeling one hundred per cent," she continue to the woebegone face on the screen, "we can manage without you for the day. Everyone knows what's to be done. There are others who could do your meetings."

That was true. And part of the art of leadership was delegation.

It was tempting. Bonny nuzzled against him. The idea of throwing off his work clothes and slobbing out in a tracksuit for the day, taking the dog for a long walk to clear his head—it all beckoned like a mini paradise. He made his decision.

"I'm on my way," he said firmly.

He was telling Vicky, and himself, before he could change his mind.

When Joe arrived at *BUSSTOP,* he learned that he had missed an important caller.

"Professor Irene Hanson from Cambridge University came through about ten minutes ago. She wonders if she could talk to you about certain aspects of the Ariadne launch," Vicky said.

Joe decided that he must make an extra effort to be civil today, so he asked her about her dog.

"Einstein's still chewing things," she said sadly.

"You need to be firm with him," Joe told her. "Set some boundaries. He's not a puppy. Shut him in a small space with only his bone and his toys to gnaw on. He'll get the message. He's trying—very successfully—to be top dog. Unless you become top dog, you'll always have problems."

"Here endeth today's lesson," Vicky said quietly as she gazed adoringly at the door through which Joe had just gone.

She guessed that he was hung over and tired. That was most unusual! Professor Hanson had looked as though she was in the same predicament. She didn't know the professor's habits, so she couldn't pass judgement on her. For a few moments Vicky indulged herself in a fantasy of being a ministering angel to Joe, and a lot more when he felt better. She blushed at her thoughts and tapped industriously on her console keyboard to file information that kept the Joe Mortimer show on the road.

Joe dealt with a few minor matters and then turned his attention to the business of Professor Hanson. What did this expert in Space Communications want to say to him? His sluggish pulse was quickening. There was only one way to find out.

He was disappointed to be speaking to a secretary.

"Thank you for contacting us so promptly, Mr Mortimer. Unfortunately, Professor Hanson is tied up in lectures for the rest of the morning. She apologises for doing this via an intermediary. She has asked me to invite you to lunch in the college Buttery at about one o'clock. Do you know where to find us?"

"Not exactly but I'm sure my navigation system will show me the way. Tell the Professor I'd be delighted to join her for lunch," Joe lied.

His stomach heaved mutinously at the very thought of food, but at least this was a valid reason to be out of the office. To make this possible, he spent a few minutes rounding up colleagues who could meet the people he should have been seeing in the afternoon. He would have time to be pleasant to those in the diary for the morning.

Joe marvelled that he was prepared to do this and to drive from north London to Cambridge to talk with a total stranger. He had to qualify that straight away. Irene Hanson wasn't a stranger. He had met her once before. She was respected across the world and if she had something to say—however trivial—about Ariadne, then he had to listen. Fresh air, brains and beauty—just the combination to put a man back on his feet again. He wasn't so sure about the eating bit but then no one ever claimed that life was entirely fair.

Joe arrived with a few minutes to spare. He checked in with the secretary, who confirmed that Irene was waiting for him. A passing student was commandeered to show him the way.

"John, could you take Mr Mortimer here to the Buttery?"

Joe followed John, who looked about fourteen years old.

Half way across the quadrangle the guide stopped suddenly as he put two and two together.

"Mr Mortimer!" he uttered in strangled tones. "Mr Joe Mortimer?"

"That's me!" smiled Joe, praying that this boy wouldn't tell him he wanted to be an astronaut.

"Wow! I hope the Ariadne mission goes well, sir."

"Thank you," Joe replied, charmed by such courtesy

He could see Irene standing outside, enjoying the sunshine. The light glinted on her fair hair. She was dressed for summer, wearing an emerald green top and a green print skirt. Cerise shoes and matching chunky necklace provided a splash of colour.

"Thank you again, John," he said. "That looks like my date." John began to smirk. "Space stuff, you know. I think Professor Hanson is worried that our ship might bump into a star en route to Mars."

He moved away from a mystified undergraduate.

"Hello, Mr Mortimer."

Irene was surprised to see that Joe Mortimer looked a bit rough round the edges today but he was still too attractive for his own good—or hers. She put out her hand, expecting him to shake it. Instead, he took the hand and kissed it.

"Professor Hanson! It's a pleasure to see you again."

"I've reserved us a table out on the patio. It's such a lovely day. I don't think there will be many people out there. They all prefer to be crowded indoors in the gloom, watching the screens."

"Are students really troglodytes in disguise?" Joe wondered. "Hey, that could be a good title for a doctoral thesis."

Irene's shoulders shook as she suppressed a giggle. Oh yes, do that some more, Joe thought.

"I take it you don't have a very high opinion of students, Mr Mortimer?"

"I don't have any opinion at all, professor. I wasn't a university student so I simply observe. And please call me Joe."

"Joe it is. So you'd better drop my title as well. I'm Irene. Let's eat."

That wasn't as difficult as Joe anticipated. His outraged stomach was growling with hunger and he ordered a mackerel salad with some confidence.

"I'm intrigued," he said after a few minutes of general politeness and comparing notes on their meals. "I must be a poor lunch companion because most people just say what they have to say on screen and push off to eat with someone else. What have you got that could affect Ariadne?"

"I'll come straight to the point, Joe. I am overseeing a very talented young man for his doctoral thesis, although he's not writing about students or troglodytes, alas." Joe grinned in acknowledgement. "So I've been doing a lot of general scanning and listening across our solar system, along with him, to help him out. The usual bread and butter stuff."

"Narrow band out to broad band and all the way back in again," Joe said automatically.

"Yes." Irene was impressed and lost the thread of what she was saying. "Where was I?"

"You were coming straight to the point a few sentences ago," he reminded her and they both laughed.

"Thank you. I heard what I thought was a signal. Repeated definite patterns. At first I thought I'd made a mistake. It took some isolating! I've done that on my own. My student doesn't need unnecessary complications. I can't find a computer program to decipher it."

"This is very interesting, but is it relevant to the Ariadne project?"

"It most certainly is, Joe. The signal appears to be coming from the surface of Mars."

Joe dropped his knife and fork onto the plate with a clatter. A few people looked round briefly then turned back to their own tables.

"Let me get this straight," he said slowly. "Repeated definite patterns. You mean messages, don't you?"

"Possibly."

"And there's no doubt these patterns or messages are coming from Mars?"

"No doubt at all. I've checked everything out so many times that I can run the damned Heinrich One Hundred computer program with my eyes shut."

From the strain in her voice, Joe guessed that she must have been doing just that.

"So you've known about this for some time?" he wanted to know.

"A little while," she said defensively.

"Irene." Whether by accident or design, he rested his hand on hers. "I'm not getting at you. If I had found something like that, I don't know whether I'd like to stick my head over the parapet, especially standing alone. Is it possible to listen to some of this tracking?"

"I rather hoped that's what you would want to do. Let's finish lunch first."

When they had finished the meal, Irene led Joe back through the Buttery and hailed the manager.

"Thanks, Melanie. In the book, please."

"Of course, Professor."

"The occasion goes down as entertaining an official guest, on college expenses," Irene explained. "I hope you don't mind being classified as a freebie."

"I always knew I was a cheap date!"

Joe laughed good-naturedly.

In the computer lab, Irene patted one particular machine.

"The star of the show."

"Heinrich?" Joe asked, eager to keep up.

"Heinrich One Hundred is the program. This is Attila. Some students named it that a while back. Don't ask me why."

"Can Attila-running-Heinrich perform for us?"

"It certainly can," said Irene, working with the speed that only comes from total familiarity with a piece of equipment. "This is a saved scan."

The pulsing rhythms echoed in the silence of the room. Joe listened intently. There was something scratching away at the back of his mind and it wouldn't make a move forward.

"That's that, then." She bent over the computer. "I'll see if we can get a live feed."

Irene worked her way through the bandwidths on which the signal had been arriving. There was nothing of interest to be found; only the usual racket of space, with which they were both familiar.

"I guess the Martians must be bye-byes," Joe said.

Irene spun round to face him. Her eyes were blue flints.

"Don't mock me, Mr Mortimer!" she snapped.

Me and my big mouth! Joe said to himself. He held up his hands in a gesture of surrender.

"I'm not mocking, Irene. I promise you that." He watched some of the tension ease from her posture. "That's better. There are all kinds of reasons as to why the transmissions are not continuous. A finite, poor power source might be one. It takes huge amounts of energy to whack out a message across the distances that we are talking about. The relative distance between Earth and Mars varies from a mere thirty six million miles to over two hundred and fifty million miles. Those were the approximate measurements the last time I looked. Surface dust storms are another communications hazard." He saw Irene's smile. "Sorry. You know all this."

"And I'm forgetting that you know it, Joe. That's one of the problems of being a teacher. You presume that everyone needs teaching."

"I'm always up for learning," Joe reassured her. "Everyone should be."

"Yes. But I just know the theory. I look at space, the planets and the stars and try to understand what they are telling us. You've been there. I'm the one who should be apologising." She had watched the lights come on in Joe's eyes and colour return to his pallid face. "You really think there is something in this, don't you?"

"I do. And there's another possibility for why there is silence. Who knows how long this transmission has been broadcasting? You've only picked it up recently because of the work you are doing with your student. Perhaps those who are sending it are running out of hope for a reply."

"You know what you are saying, don't you? That there is intelligent life on Mars."

"I am saying it. Why shouldn't there be? It's only the supreme arrogance of human beings that makes us think that we are all there is. Only a few hundred years ago people believed that the planetary system revolved around Earth."

"A bit of a historian, then, as well as a scientist!" she said admiringly.

"Anyone who came within arm's reach of my granddad was a historian by the time he'd finished with them."

"He was a history teacher?"

Irene knew there were more pressing things to do than talk family backgrounds but she let the conversation run. Somehow this was important.

"No. He was an engineer in the RAF. He said to his dying day that we forget our history at our peril." Joe was perched on a stool. He jumped up suddenly. "Yes! That's it! Irene, run the saved scan again. Have you got some paper and a pen?"

Joe listened once more. Irene noticed his grey eyes darken to the intensity of thunderclouds as he concentrated and scribbled. She stood closer to see what he was writing down and was disconcerted by the sheer physical energy flowing from his body.

At the end of the message cycle she looked at the piece of paper, covered in dots and dashes.

"You've got me there," she admitted.

"And you the Professor of Space Communications!" Joe said, wagging a finger. "See? Granddad was right. We forget our history at our peril. Mind you, I wouldn't expect Martians to be attempting to transmit in Morse Code, either."

"The signal I've been tracking is Morse Code?"

"I said that someone is *attempting* to use Morse. And they've made a right mess of it. As it stands, it's gibberish. Can Morse Code be gibberish? Anyway, it's full of mistakes."

"Oh," said Irene disconsolately. "Computers can only do what they are programmed to do and no one uses Morse any more"

"Got any plans for this evening?" She shook her head. Joe fished out his communicator. "Afternoon, Mum. Can I invite myself and a colleague to dinner? And we'll need Dad ready to advise us on twentieth century Morse Code."

Chapter Four

The dust storm that was blocking the outbound communications system of Mars howled across the Amazonian Plain.

The temporary fatigue and distress that followed the initial complex transformation from Martian to corporeal Earth form had eased. The difficulty and the fear were put on one side for the moment. Everyone inspected each other's appearance and attire with frank interest.

"Comments?" the obvious leader invited when the murmur of conversation had died away.

He looked around. All was as it had been anticipated. He and three others were starting to establish themselves within the forms of named human beings. He liked this Tony person whom he had acquired, even if he had a regrettable tendency to denim, just like the rest of his sub-group.

The remaining three stood a little apart. They had different roles to play. The ones now known as Adam and Sophia were designing their own appearances, to be as welcoming as possible when the visitors arrived. Tony could use his newly acquired feeling of pity for his sister Raii. She had taken human form but as yet had no identity. That too was part of the plan, as yet not understood, and bound to be difficult.

A terrible bond and a huge responsibility linked the seven.

Tony's eye was taken by one of the human forms, probably about thirty Earth years in age. He must have been a handful in his last Earth life. Tony hoped that his brother could assimilate such a character without too much pain.

"This is an historic day!" said that handful Justin, rather unnecessarily.

"We have a unique opportunity here," Tony continued when no one else spoke. "No species has ever had our chance. The chance to move so far back in time and see where we came from. We must embrace it fully."

"And embrace the finer points of language too!" said another voice.

All eyes turned to the human manifestation known as Sally as she moved forward. She was stunning woman, no more than twenty five at the most, a tall, curvy figure with long and wavy dark hair and even darker eyes.

"Behave yourself, Justin!" she admonished as she walked by, not even turning her head in his direction. "And close your mouth. Humans don't look good gaping. And in your present form you're gay—sexually drawn to other men, in case you haven't found your point of reference yet."

Justin's head drooped in disappointment for a moment. The wind tangled his black curls. His face was as finely boned and attractive as Sally's. He raised a hesitant hand to touch the one diamond earring he wore. The Martian within was finding human emotions and he was confused. Yes, he had such an important job to do, but how high was the price?

"And that is not fair!" he protested. "Earth people are not telepaths."

"A few are. And right now we're still on Mars, with a huge amount of detail to master."

Having listened to the general murmur of talk and the way each person was using the language, Sally treated the group to a brisk lecture on the contraction of certain common words, using her exchange with Justin as the prime example.

"He should have said *that's* instead of *that is*," she told everyone. "*Aren't* instead of *are not*."

"Go quietly with us, Va—I mean, Sally," Tony said to her later as they sat alone. "And with yourself. We are on the brink of the next stage of our own future—becoming pure energy and thought—and we have to step backwards into human bodies. It is a huge shock to the form, mind and psyche, lowering our vibrations so far. You did not need to be a telepath to sense the distress everyone has already been through. And there is more to come as we grow into our individuality. We need time to adjust. I know you queried why we had to transform so far in advance of human visitation to this planet. Your behaviour has answered your own question. You are still settling in, as we all are. Physically you are Sally but that is all. Inside you remain Vara, our linguistics guide. If we are to be heard and allowed to help, we must be those we represent. Tony Johnson, Sally Tillman, Justin Connor, Ichiro Matsushita." He recited the names in a slow, thoughtful manner. "It seems strange, having two names. But that's how things have been done for a very long time on Earth. Historically the second name showed where or to whom an individual belonged."

"You've always been so wise. Was Tony that wise? I must be developing as a human already. I can't get a proper sense of him."

"I think he was. That's why I was drawn to him."

"Listen to you!" she cried. "You've got it! You said *that's*—not *that is*."

"I told you he was wise. A fast learner too. He was much loved, and mourned greatly when he moved on from his Earth life."

Sally stood up and walked around him in critical appraisal.

"Let's see. About forty-five Earth years in age. Dark hair, cropped close to minimise the appearance of balding. A bit on the short side for a human male but never mind. Your eyes crinkle at the corners in a beautiful smile. You have a sensuous mouth."

"And you have a one-track mind, obviously."

"Sally was young—and so in love. And she was so loved. And that love caused such division." A visible wave of unease washed over Sally. It was her turn to shy away from her task. "Tony, I don't know if I can do this."

"You can. We have already been undertaking one of our tasks for some time, supporting our brother on Earth. This is simply the next step in the process."

"Now that I'm becoming Sally, with her emotions, that supporting will be more challenging for me," she admitted. "I suppose that's part of my burden, my learning."

"Ah! Human emotions!" Tony marvelled. "We've worked so long and so hard to tame and refine them as we grew. And what do we do when we are called to this mission? We have to grab back all the passions, fears and grief of humanity, with both hands."

He studied his hands, the hands of Tony Johnson, for a moment. They were strong and he knew they were skilled, marked with the inevitable scars collected working as a carpenter.

"I know." Sally experienced human tears. "We can't move on until the wrong has been righted."

"Sally, it will be all right. Don't fret."

Tony put his arm round Sally. He didn't know where the gesture or the phrase came from but he liked the sensation of both. Memories of intimacy with a woman, physically and emotionally, began to form in his mind. He moved away.

"So what now?" Sally wondered.

"Representatives will soon arrive from Earth. Then we can begin the real healing process."

*   *   *

Stella Mortimer had the front door open as Joe parked the car. The rain fell in stair rods and there was an ominous rumble in the distance from inky clouds.

"Are you ready?" Joe asked Irene. "Go!"

They jumped from the car, slamming the doors and running into the house in record time.

After a less than conventional arrival, Joe made some introductions.

"It's lovely to see you, Professor!" said Stella fervently.

"Irene, please. I can see that Joe favours you but it's more than that. I feel that I've met you before. Is that possible?"

"Yes. I was at the launch of your book *Signals from Other Places* in the city centre a while back. You signed my copy and we had a little chat."

"That's right!" Irene exclaimed. "I remember. You said that your younger son was involved in the space industry. I wondered at the time exactly what he did." She cast a glance at Joe, who was enjoying this hugely. "I never imagined . . ."

"Well, I was telling the truth, wasn't I?"

"Greetings and things!" said Neil Mortimer, clanking into the hallway with some bottles of wine. "I'm sorry that we couldn't arrange you better weather, Professor." He put down the bottles, took hold of her hand and kissed it. "Welcome to Mortimer Towers."

What a lovely family, Irene mused. She understood that Joe had a brother. Such a pity he wasn't around. She was sure that she could have achieved the hat trick of kissed hands. Twice in one day ought to qualify her for some kind of record achievement anyway.

"Have you got a copy of the transmission you want me to listen to?" Neil asked Irene when everyone was comfortable. "I presume you're doing this the old-fashioned way. I can't say I blame you. I wouldn't want to send something like this directly from one computer to another." Irene handed him a memory stick. "The prehistoric technology still has its uses!" he commented. "Now let's not think about it until after dinner."

Joe followed his father out of the room.

"Where did you find her?" Neil chuckled.

"In her college. She invited me over. These transmissions are coming from the surface of Mars, Dad. Irene's very nervous about putting this into the public arena. She decided to start with me."

"A wise choice," he said heavily. "I can think of a few characters who will tear her limb from limb."

Irene proved herself to be great company round the dinner table. There was much hilarity and laughter as everyone enjoyed one of Stella's winning impromptu menus—lamb casserole followed by home made ice cream. Neil loved having a new audience for his stories of display flying in the RAF. His family had heard them all before and in some cases had lived through them. Stella had been part of them and had a rather annoying tendency to correct him if he got carried away.

"So you were awarded the MBE for your work, Neil?" Irene asked.

"Yes. And Joe has kept the family thing going," he said, glowing with pride.

"That is truly amazing. I wonder if there is any other instance of a father and son receiving the same accolade?"

Joe was happy to listen and let the chatter flow. Because he was driving, he was also very happy to spend the evening drinking water. He made a mental note to bury every bottle of alcohol in his house at the bottom of the garden when he got home. But then he thought about Phil. He would be heartbroken if he couldn't put the world to rights with his brother over a glass of whisky.

"Are you all right, dear?" Stella wondered when Joe carried some dishes out to the kitchen for her.

Joe braced himself to be totally honest with his mother.

"I—er—had a drop too much to drink last night."

"That's not like you." Her eyes searched his face. "If you drank to excess, it was because you were upset. Am I right? You weren't celebrating or socialising."

"I was going through some things at home. I found Barry bear." Stella nodded. He clutched at his hair and walked round the kitchen. "Mum, this is stupid! After all these years . . ."

"It's not stupid and time has nothing to do with it. In the twentieth century, Queen Elizabeth the Queen Mother was supposed to have commented on her long widowhood by saying '*It doesn't get better. One gets better at it.*' And here's the wisdom according to Stella Mortimer. No one is too big or too grown-up or too important for a hug. Even the British head of *BUSSTOP* is allowed to have had enough of everything from time to time." She held out her arms. "Come here, you big dollop!"

"Joe, I take it you were sober when you wrote this lot down," Neil said later as he looked at the transcription of the signals from Mars. He didn't understand why Stella was glaring at him so he ignored her. "It's twaddle." He turned to Irene. "We'll presume that whoever is sending it doesn't know what he's doing. Joe generally knows his arse from his elbow. Sorry," he added with a smile.

Totally charmed, Irene could only smile back.

"Will you listen to it for me?" she asked.

Neil moved over to the desk and played the saved message, following Joe's written version. On arriving, Irene said that Joe looked like his mother. He did. But as Neil concentrated, she could see that father hadn't lost out totally in the appearance department. That set of the jaw and the angle at which the head was held were in evidence in her computer lab earlier in the day.

"A perfect transcription, lad," Neil pronounced at last. "I don't know how you did it. The mistakes in the letters and numbers are too many to count."

"I wasn't trying to form words, or even letters," Joe admitted. "I was trying to take down the dots and dashes in the right order and then make some sense of it all later. I only fully appreciated the errors—."

Father and son looked at each other across the room.

"Random Error Code!" said Neil in quiet satisfaction. "It was an early twenty first century development in communications secrecy," he explained to Stella and Irene. "Keeping messages secret and breaking them wide open had reached such a pitch that you could check on someone changing their mind. Morse Code hadn't yet gone away. Commercial airline pilots were still required to have a rudimentary working knowledge of it, if only to be able to recognise certain emergency signals that might be transmitted. A chap called Kirk Fitzpatrick developed a variation on the Morse Code—the Random Error Code—which was a bugger to crack because random mistakes were put into the individual symbols—the letters and numbers—which were then blocked together in groups, not words. He was laughed at to begin with and everyone told him he'd been watching too many films about Bletchley Park and the breaking of the Nazi Enigma Code. Morse Code had had its heyday in the Second World War. Anyway, he won over the top brass in the armed forces of this country and America. It was used for a while before the development of Infinity Loop Hyper-encryption."

"Which reigns supreme in encryption-land to this day," concluded Joe.

"Thank you for the history lesson, dears," said Stella, leaning back in her chair. "I feel quite worn out by all that!"

"But it leaves the good professor—and Joe and the whole Ariadne project—with an interesting situation," Neil reminded her. "Who is sitting out there on Mars using Random Error Code?"

"I've started something here, haven't I?" Irene sounded worried. Stella reached over and squeezed her hand. "I'm so sorry if this will cause trouble."

"It's not trouble!" said Joe cheerfully. "It's just one more thing to be aware of. I don't think that beings utilising one hundred year-old encryption to send messages to Earth are waiting to zap Earth's representatives when they arrive on Mars."

"Many people have thought for a long time that there is a civilisation on Mars," mused Neil. "Not monsters in machines in the *War of the Worlds* sense, but a considered and rational life form. I remember my grandfather telling me about *Beagle Two*, Britain's unmanned Mars probe. It reached Mars on Christmas Day 2003 and promptly went off line. Ground control struggled for weeks to re-establish contact. He always said that they were wasting their time. Someone had taken *Beagle Two* home to amuse the kids or some bright young thing was walking around wearing parts of the probe on its heads." Everyone laughed. "But granddad wasn't really joking, not deep down."

Irene admired the photographs on display whilst Stella and Neil disappeared to the kitchen to make some more tea and coffee. There was a beautiful shot of them with their two sons. Irene was surprised at how alike the brothers were. She picked up the photograph to take a closer look.

"That's Phil, my big brother," said Joe, behind her.

Irene whirled round, badly off-balance. He caught her by the elbows. "Whoa! It's only me."

"Joe! I was miles away, looking at these lovely pictures. You startled me. Tell me about these photographs. Who is this?"

"That's Phil, as you may have gathered. Here he is with his wife Daphne. Oh, you've noticed my nutter nephew Sam and his wife Natasha. They're both in television. We don't like to talk about them too much. A bit of a family embarrassment."

Joe couldn't keep a straight face long enough to sustain the joke any further.

"I was believing you there for a minute!" Irene said.

"I hope you were. I'm always being told I'm a very plausible man. I've not been found out yet. They do work for a television production company, by the way."

As Joe continued the guided tour of the photographs, he was occupied with something else. In that split second when she turned, there was raw terror in Irene's face. Her arms were going up in a classic defensive posture, right in front of left, which enabled him to steady her as he did. He sensed that if he had had to take hold of her body to stop her falling, she would have struck out at him.

"This is you at Buckingham Palace with the family, isn't it?" Irene asked. Joe confirmed it. "And when was this taken?"

He looked closely. There he was, a very young man, in the middle of a cheery, waving group.

"A few hours after returning from the Moon. It was my first trip into space." He shook his head wonderingly. "They were all old hands. Flying to Base One on the Moon and out to the Space Station was routine for them. They looked upon me as the flight mascot, the baby of the bunch, which I was. I couldn't have set off with a better crowd of people. I learnt more from them in one trip than I did in months of training. I suppose that's why *BUSSTOP* put me with them. I owe them a lot."

"Were you nervous?"

"Nah!" he said in apparent nonchalance. A pause. "Of course I was. I was shitting bricks before we left. Pardon me, Irene. There's nothing like that first flight, though. It makes you keep going back for more, just to check that your memory isn't playing tricks."

"Mr Mortimer, I think you're wishing you were flying out on *Ariadne One*. You are, aren't you?"

"Yes. And even more so now we've established that we have a real message. I'd love to come face to face with the ones who are sending it."

"You know what they say. Be careful what you wish for. You might just get it!"

"A nice thought, Irene. I'm fitter than most of the whippersnappers we'll be sending to Mars but I'm on the scrap heap at fifty! I ask you. My colleague Bruce Dougall thinks the same, but I suppose the youngsters must have their chance."

*   *   *

Doctor Michael Doherty looked far too kind to ever be annoyed with anyone. His face was round and solemn but he possessed a winning smile, which he didn't use nearly enough. The pale brown eyes had seen it all professionally. He was good at his job and he charged appropriately for his expertise. The plush surroundings of his Georgetown office, in which he met with his patients, underlined that. Even the styling of his prematurely greying hair and the cut of his suit hinted at it. Usually he was very detached. In his line of work he had to be. But occasionally someone got to him. The patient, the case details, the number on a computer file, became a person, along with all that person's baggage. It had happened here. He was both concerned and irritated as he looked at the man sitting across the desk from him.

"Bruce, didn't they give you enough medals from *BUSSTOP* and the USAF?"

Bruce Dougall shrugged his shoulders.

"I don't follow you, doc."

"I'm wondering if you're looking for that extra medal as Jackass of the Year. When I said we couldn't cure you, that doesn't mean we can't help you. It's just that if you are struggling between the visits to see me, you have to holler. It's easy enough to change your medication. There's a new drug I've been waiting to try on someone—ZFF. But when you don't say anything, everyone presumes you're okay. Would you like to give it a go? You have the perfect medical profile." He looked again at his screen, checking Bruce's latest test results. "Heaven only knows how, but most of you is still working reasonably well, so you can tolerate the drug. You can start taking it and I'll sort out the red tape of a clinical trial. It should help you a lot. A physician can't usually bounce someone in like this but I don't think many potential subjects have such a detailed medical history that I can hand over on the spot. Of course, you must give your permission for that. People I know in the pharmaceutical manufacturing company owe me a favour. What do you say?"

"I've nothing to lose," Bruce replied bleakly.

"Don't hold back, will you? Nothing like looking on the bright side, is there?"

"Any particular regime I need to follow to go with the new drug?" Bruce asked.

He was quite the expert now when it came to various medications.

"Rest. Take a break from work. Two weeks. You need it anyway. You've been a fool to keep on working. And don't quote to me how little time you've spent in the *BUSSTOP* building. I know how much you do at home. Switch off that damned screen. Or use it just for chatting with friends. I'm serious."

"Two weeks?" Bruce echoed in horror.

"Listen here, Bruce." Doctor Doherty shifted in his chair. He was plagued by a bad back. "I see patients on a daily basis, sitting where you are sitting, who beg, demand and even threaten, in order to be given time away from work. I don't think two weeks out will slow the Ariadne project down any and it will speed you up no end. Is it so impossible to have some time out?"

"No. A few people have been concerned about my health."

"You don't say!" interrupted the doctor but it was said with that smile.

"I told them I had a virus. So no one will be that bothered if I do take some sick leave."

"Good. You can nurse your "virus" for two weeks. And more importantly, simmer down until the ZFF has got a hold of your system."

"What if I don't rest?" Bruce wondered, still not quite at ease with the idea of putting *BUSSTOP* on the back burner for a while.

"You'll continue feeling lousy for longer. The ZFF will work more slowly and may not be quite as effective. Give me a break here, Bruce. I'm trying to improve the quality of your life."

"And it is much appreciated. Thank you."

"I still don't like the notion of you battling on with all this alone. Let me talk to some people for you. After all, a trained professional—"

"That's the way I like it," Bruce said firmly.

"Okay. But we're getting a bit ahead of ourselves here. I'll tell you a bit more about ZFF and its therapeutic actions. The medical breakthrough behind it is probably a hundred years old. The drug acts as a genetic brake on the cancer cells and—"

"It's okay, doc. Knowing what cutting edge research has cooked it up isn't going to alter the way it works on me. I trust you. As long as you tell me what the doses are and any contraindications, that will do."

"Hmm." Usually Doctor Doherty was annoyed when someone interrupted his sales pitch, but today he turned back to the keyboard meekly and rattled some keys. "I'm ordering it up for you."

Half an hour later Bruce was walking down the street, enjoying the bustle of his native Georgetown. He would have that rest. Two weeks sounded good. Whether he liked it or not, *BUSSTOP* was working well on both sides of the Atlantic and, thus far with the Ariadne project, Joe Mortimer appeared to be moving mountains unaided.

He knew that, realistically, there was little more he could do to speed the process along. The crew list, plus a long roll call of replacement astronauts, had been agreed. Everyone was playing a waiting game, whilst the *Ariadne One* team hopefuls who were already in Florida were training for all they were worth. Gianfranco Rosso and Illya Abelev were joining them today.

Bruce stopped for coffee at *Billy's*. Taking the doctor's advice seriously, he ordered a sub and a cake as well. He sat at a sidewalk table, wanting to be in the bright midday light. A few people paused momentarily as they clocked him and then they moved on, not sure that they had seen who they thought they had seen. He was pleased. As ever, the simplest tricks were the best. He often went out and about without his glasses now. As long as he didn't have to look at anything in too much detail, everything was fine, and it confused those who would have thought nothing of invading his private space.

He was hearing whispers that there was some conflict between the potential Ariadne team and Steven Bradbury, the Training Director. Bradbury always drove people hard and the astronauts would thank him when they got themselves out of a tight spot without even thinking about it. Gianfranco and Bradbury could make an interesting mix. He hoped—

Leave it! Bruce told himself sternly. There was a whole organisation down at Cape Canaveral to deal with stuff like this. Barging in to micro-manage the training, when he had just been put on the sick list, was rather dumb.

Enjoying the sunshine and the warm breeze, he knew how extravagant, how wasteful folks could be with time. In the past, he had complained about time dragging. Everyone did. From where he was sitting, time was rocket-propelled.

Bruce put his hand in his pocket. The small container with the ZFF was there. *BUSSTOP* would pick up the tabs for anything like this. So be it. His goal was to still be around when *Ariadne One* touched down on Mars. In the meantime, he might as well enjoy the ride and that began with trying to forget work.

Based on what Doctor Doherty had said, he could look forward to being in better shape quite soon. He paid for the coffee and the food, leaving a generous tip, as he had been brought up to do. He had had quite a chat with the man who served him.

Bruce could hear his father's voice.

> *"When you've got a good pile of dough like we have, make sure you spread it about. I wouldn't want to earn my living waiting on tables. And never forget that it's a person standing next to you and running about after you."*

Bruce set off down the street quickly, as if hurrying towards the things he could enjoy during this unexpected leisure time.

*   *   *

Professor Irene Hanson had thrown a huge problem his way, however gallantly Joe tried to laugh it off at his parents' house. Where was the best place to begin defusing the situation?

Joe had enjoyed spending time with Irene and she obviously liked being around him. She had fallen hook, line and sinker for his parents. Quite right too!

"I want to be adopted by them," she said on the way home in the car.

Joe took her home at the end of the evening because, after all the mad gallivanting around and partly solving the mystery of the message from Mars, her car was still sitting in the college staff car park in Cambridge. It would be perfectly safe there but it meant that she had no transport. It turned out that although they were in different counties, she and Joe lived only a few miles away from each other. She would be able to take a taxi in to work the following morning.

"Thank you for the most amazing day," she said when Joe halted his car outside her home. "I think I've had all the fun and left you with all the difficulties. I had to tell someone. A dear friend persuaded me that I should tell you. The friend will not say anything about this, by the way. You have my solemn promise on that."

"I'm glad you were persuaded. Don't worry, Irene. The Ariadne project will go ahead. I'll contact you as soon as possible and tell you what we all need to do. I'll—er—contact you anyway, even if I haven't decided what to do. I'm afraid you are stuck with me in this for a while."

"I like the idea of that."

Joe's mind was already in overdrive when he woke the next morning. He was thankful for feeling so much better than he had done the previous day. Never a big drinker, he and alcohol were beginning to disagree seriously.

Joe set off for London, even though he hadn't planned to be in the office that day. By the time he arrived at *BUSSTOP*, a plan was clear in his mind.

"Morning Vicky!" he said, bouncing into her office. "Any messages?"

"Good morning Mr Mortimer," she replied, delighted with the change from the miserable figure he had cut the previous day. "Nothing yet. Most people don't reach their desks as early as this. Anything I can get you?"

"A large black coffee and Downing Street on screen would be nice. I need to speak to the Prime Minister in—let's say—ten minutes."

"It's a bit early."

"If the Prime Minister is still cleaning his teeth like a good little boy, he can call me back when he's done."

Vicky brought Joe his coffee and some unwelcome news.

"The PM is unavailable."

"Who told you that?"

"A very nice man called Toby."

Whilst Joe could be confident that the Prime Minister wasn't climbing out of the window even as they spoke, this wasn't good enough.

"Please talk to his PA. Sarah, isn't it?"

"I shouldn't really by-pass the system, Mr Mortimer."

"For me. Please?"

Vicky nodded and headed back to her office.

"Prime Minister!" Joe was saying a few minutes later. "I need to talk to you."

"You are talking to me, Joe. Even if it is a bit early."

"I mean talk as in sit and talk face-to-face. I've got some exciting news for you about Mars."

"I see. I have a Venezuelan trade delegation arriving this afternoon so it would be better if you came here. Is that possible?"

"I'll be with you in an hour."

"I await your arrival with interest, Joe. I'll tell the Press Office that you are visiting to give me a personal update on the Ariadne project. It looks better if we're saying the same thing. There will probably be a few press and television people around outside."

As ever, the Prime Minister was the master of understatement. Joe was taken aback when his car was allowed through the security gates and eased its way into Downing Street. He knew that the press conference at *BUSSTOP* had sharpened media interest in space exploration but this was beyond belief.

"Bloody hell, Mr Mortimer!" said his driver. "I didn't think they allowed demos in here any more."

The throng of people more like a medieval army sitting outside a beleaguered town. In the hour since Joe had talked to Kevin Crane, the press release had been picked up and this was the result.

"It's not a demonstration, Roland. It's the media circus waiting for us. Smile. Somewhere you and I are going out on live TV."

The car whispered to a halt right outside Number Ten. Roland shot out of his seat, rushed round the front of the vehicle, opened the door for Joe and almost bowed him out.

"Don't overdo your part, Roland," Joe murmured as he stepped into the mob.

"Mr Mortimer!"

"Joe!"

His name was shouted from all directions and countless lenses fixed on him.

"Why are you here, Joe?"

"I presume you must have read the Downing Street release," Joe said very patiently, "or *you* wouldn't be here. I've come to give the Prime Minister an update on Ariadne."

He beamed at the bank of cameras, half looking over his shoulder. That would be the money shot filling the next day's papers, sending every female in Britain with a pulse into a spasm.

"Mr Mortimer, is there a problem with the Ariadne project?"

Joe was known for thinking fast on his feet and this was a moment for it. If he didn't give this lot something, they would broadcast and print exactly that—that there were difficulties with the Mars landing before it even happened.

"The crew list for *Ariadne One* is finalised. I've come to talk to the Prime Minister about it. I believe in the personal touch. I shall be going to Buckingham Palace later on to consult with His Majesty."

Joe couldn't be certain that Richard was at home. He'd better be. Early in his career as head of *BUSSTOP*, Joe had developed a simple technique for the media. If a lie needs to be told, make it a whopper and say it with a great big smile.

The black door of Number Ten opened and he was swallowed up into the safety of the building.

"That was an powerful show you put on at my doorstep," observed Kevin Crane as they sat down. "I was watching you on the television news." He fixed Joe with an unnerving stare. "What has gone wrong?"

"You're as bad as the people out there," Joe began.

"I'm far worse. They don't know you as well as I do. What's wrong?"

Joe handed him a memory stick.

"Irene Hanson, Professor of Space Communications at Cambridge University, has picked up this transmission. We're pretty certain it's beaming out directly from the surface of Mars."

Even Crane's façade came close to cracking. He began to formulate a sentence several times.

"Ah," was what he came up with eventually. "What does this transmission say? Or is that a silly question?"

Joe had to admire him for cloaking an avalanche of natural feelings so well.

"Not a clue. I've identified it as Random Error Code, which was used about a century ago." He was keeping his family out of this. "REC was the hyper-encryption of its day. What it says isn't top of my list, Prime Minister. The fact that it is there at all is crucial."

"Professor Hanson came to you directly with this?"

"Yes."

It was best to leave the unnamed friend out of it too.

"Why did she come to you?"

"As a member of the public, who else would she know about to approach? I'm sure that she could have dug up other names by asking colleagues within the Space faculty in Cambridge but they might have become curious. The chain of command is not very clear around British space exploration, is it Kevin? I had to sit down myself and try to work out who is my boss. You are about the closest thing I have to a superior. You and the King, I suppose, in his capacity as head of state. The military has been kept out of *BUSSTOP* all the way along, so no one can pull rank on me in the RAF."

"I see."

"I wish I did!"

"I presume Professor Hanson's calculations are correct for the origin of the transmission?"

"You can take it from me that they are," Joe assured him. "I may not have a university degree or a professorial chair but I think I still know a correct tracking when I see one. I've been over her mapping."

"I do apologise, Joe. I didn't mean to cast aspersions on your abilities, or those of the professor. Why has no one else picked up this signal?"

"They may well have done and not realised it. Have you ever listened in on space? It's the Tower of Babel out there! Everything from echoes of the Big Bang downwards. Someone really needs to know what they're doing to isolate and track down one strand in that lot. Professor Hanson was only working that section of space to help a student and she is one talented lady. Mars is old hat for the professional listeners, especially now we're going there. Everyone in astronomy and astrophysics is involved in academic fisticuffs about wormholes or having stand-up fits about fractures in the fabric of space. And the business of folding space to travel mega-distances is still up for debate. They are all looking and listening and thinking way beyond the solar system."

"So what shall we do?"

"I'd better find out if I can call on His Majesty first and then think. Saying I was seeing the King was the first thing that came into my head. The press all know that he and I go way back. It could work in our favour. Richard is always good value as a distraction."

"You've got a nerve, Joe."

"It shut that lot up outside when I said I was going to Buckingham Palace, didn't it?"

"I'll get someone to contact the Palace straightaway. I happen to know that Richard is having a day with his red boxes. So you picked the right time to invite yourself to the Palace! There's a lot going on government-wise at the moment and he likes to be properly in the loop. I'm sure he'll welcome a distraction, especially when it's you. The journalists are probably already harassing the Press Office there to find out when you're arriving. Ben Meyer is good but he won't be able to bluff the media for long if he hasn't got any information. No one can. Sit tight and I'll see what I can do."

Courtesy of the watching cameras, the nation had a grandstand view of Joe leaving Downing Street and heading off for Buckingham Palace.

"This is getting quite boring, isn't it Mr Mortimer?" Roland asked as he steered the car through the gates of Buckingham Palace. "Here twice in how many weeks?"

"Make the most of it, Roland. It'll be something to put in the family memoirs, won't it?"

*   *   *

"I haven't done a stroke of work today," Irene told Joe that night.

He looked at her on the screen.

"Irene, you mustn't worry about this."

"No one has done any work in college today. It's because you were with us yesterday and then you've been all over the television today. The Prime Minister *and* the King! I'm impressed. You have stood the place on its ear and that's for sure."

"You don't think anyone is making a link?"

"With what? It's a happy coincidence, that's all. You were in Cambridge yesterday and you have been on television today shuttling between Downing Street and Buckingham Palace. John Berry, the young man who acted as your guide to the Buttery—well, I think he'll be drunk from now until Christmas. Everyone wants to hear all about meeting you and most of them are prepared to pour pints of beer down him in payment. What exactly did you say to him?"

Joe went over the brief words he had with the student as Irene recounted what John was saying.

"He actually believed me?" he marvelled. "He thinks a spaceship could bump into a star?"

"Let's put it this way. I've been told several times today, by individuals who should know better, that surely Ariadne's automatic guidance systems will keep it out of the way of a star."

Joe leaned back on the sofa and laughed until the tears came to his eyes. Bonny trotted in and sat down by him. Following her usual routine, she copied her master and stared at the screen.

"Oh, what a beautiful dog!" Irene said.

"This is Bonny. I'm glad you like her." He thought of Bruce. "A colleague of mine calls her a flea-ridden mutt."

"Shame on him. It's got to be a man, saying something like that."

"Back to more serious matters, Irene. I can tell you now that you will be able to ride the gusts of hot air that will whistle up and down the corridors of *BUSSTOP* and Whitehall when we tell the world about your discovery. But I can deal with that. It's partly what I'm paid for. I've been out there, as far as Mars. I don't judge the risks to Ariadne to be any higher now than when I assessed them long before you spoke to me. All of *NASA's* accidents happened within sight of home, so to speak. It's incredible to think that, in the 1960s, one group of astronauts was actually killed on the launch pad whilst testing the instrumentation, in an oxygen-fuelled fire." Irene winced at the thought of it. "What I'm trying to say is that take off and re-entry remain the crunch points for any space vehicle and its crew to this day, not beings sending out messages. I beg your pardon, Irene. I do tend to go on a bit."

"You know what you're talking about, Joe, and your enthusiasm is catching. I want to learn. You said something about when we tell the world. Was that a rhetorical *we*?"

"Not entirely. Have you ever done a press conference?"

"Good heavens, no! I do interviews for the print and screen media but they're one-to-one and edited before transmission, so there's nothing too challenging about them. A couple of my book launches have become a bit top-heavy with the press. The last do, where I was meeting your mother and didn't know it, was lovely and quiet in that respect. Just lots of potential readers who wanted to talk and buy the book and I signed the copies."

"You'll be fine then. Kevin Crane is the real pro. I'm still picking up tips from him. We'll guide you through it."

Irene looked as though she had been hit by a thunderbolt. Her mouth dropped open.

"You want me to do a press conference with the Prime Minister?"

"And with me. Look on the boys and girls of the media corps as a bunch of undergraduate students." He thought of the hapless John Berry and began to laugh again. "And they are not much brighter."

Joe's confidence was as contagious as his enthusiasm. She could cope if he was there.

"You're on! When? Where?"

"Where will be *BUSSTOP*. There's not much point in having a perfectly good media centre if we don't use it. I'm still sorting out the when. In the meantime, we say nothing. But I'd like to talk to you some more about this. How about we meet up at the weekend for lunch? I know a lovely little country pub. It must be a natural halfway point between us. I'll know by then when we can hold the conference. We can confirm tactics."

"Lunch and a council of war. What more could a girl ask for?"

Chapter Five

It was warm and muggy in the early evening. The Braddock Road Full Gospel Evangelical Church in Alexandria, Virginia was packed and an ever-growing tide of worshippers stood outside, the sights and sounds taking place inside relayed to them via a large screen. The modern building was large, built to accommodate an influx of worshippers in the wake of a local revival of faith, but the number of people trying to get in tonight was staggering. Three police patrol cars were parked along the road, on watch simply because of the number of people involved. The officers might be needed at the end of the meeting to make sure that everyone got on their way safely, although this crowd was hardly likely to exhibit rowdy or drunken behaviour. The man behind the wheel of one car yawned hugely.

"The singing sounds good."

The congregation was reaching some kind of frenzy point, culminating in the twentieth century song by the English writer Graham Kendrick; *Lord, the light of your love is shining*. There were a few shouts of "A—men!" and "Hallelujah!" after it had been sung through twice.

"They don't write 'em like that any more!" observed one woman to her neighbour. "I don't hold with all this modern music, do you?"

An expectant hush settled over the crowd.

"And now!" An amplified voice boomed across the church and out into the street with a roar, like a missile taking off. "Let's give a huge and holy welcome to our very own Pastor Philemon Brown!"

As the band reprised the Kendrick melody, Philemon Brown walked out onto the temporary staging and into the spotlight and deafening cheers, waving both of his hands to the adoring upturned faces.

"Greetings in the name of the Lord!" he declared. "Do you know Jesus?"

"Yes!" the crowd yelled.

"I can't hear you, brothers and sisters! Do you know the saving love of Jesus?"

"Yes!" they screamed even louder.

"Are you washed in the blood of the Lamb?"

"Oh yes!" they moaned, well into the script by now.

Philemon Brown was a compact, thickset figure, black haired and black suited. His tie supplied the relief from this monochrome. Members of his congregation ran a book on the colour he would wear on any particular day. Tonight's offering was pink. His lantern-jawed appearance and dental broadside were made for television evangelism. His eyes had an oddly unfocused appearance, making it tricky to say what colour they were, and there was an uncompromising I-have-visions-before-I-get-out-of-bed-in-the-morning air about him.

"Brothers and sisters, my text tonight is Genesis One verse thirty seven. *God looked at everything he had made and he saw that it was good.*"

"A-men!" shouted a woman at the very front.

"And a-men to you, sister! God made the world, Genesis tells us. Everything in it was good. Everything in it is good, because God made it!"

As the evening wore on, the calls of approval drifted over to the watching police officers.

"Hey Todd," said one cop uneasily. "Do you think we need some reinforcements here?"

"No, that's just Pastor Brown stoking them up, sarge." The sergeant looked worried. "Stoking them up to be the holy people of God. That's his way."

Todd would not have been as understanding if he had heard clearly where Brown's spontaneous tirade was going.

"Now take this *BUSSTOP* business!" he cried.

"You take it, brother!" a man called out. "I've got enough with a wife and six kids."

"God bless you, brother," Philemon continued smoothly, with a note of approval in his voice as befitted the father of five, "and praise the Lord for the fertility of your family. *Blessed is the man who has his quiver full.* God made the world. He made us. We are unique. We are the pinnacles of his creation. Say it with me. *We are the pinnacles of his creation!*"

"We are the pinnacles of his creation!" everyone declared and some wept.

"Brothers and sisters, I am here to say to you tonight that the money that has been wasted on the exploration of space is obscene! Jesus commands us to feed the poor and heal the sick, not pay former astronaut Bruce Dougall to sit in a plush office here in D.C. and oversee sending *more* people in to space." He waved a hand in the general direction of *BUSSTOP* headquarters across the Potomac. "And brothers and sisters, we must pray for our friends in Jesus in London, England. Another astronaut is hiding there in another building. That is Joseph Mortimer, who led those wicked journeys closer and closer to Mars. God save him!"

"Hallelujah!" a group of women chimed in, undoubtedly torn between God and the flesh.

"A-men. He is organising the most wicked journey of all—landing people on the surface of Mars. I tell you, my blessed people, that this is not being done for scientific research! They are looking for signs of life on another planet, just as they did on the Moon so long ago. They failed to find life there and God punished them for their transgressions. A—men!" If anyone had reservations about seeing the hand of God in the terrible events that befell assorted *NASA* projects, this was hardly the place in which to voice them. "This exploration is being done to undermine the holy word of God. The Bible says that God made the world and he made us and he did it all in six days and on the seventh day he rested. We know that there are those who doubt this. We must bring them to the light, brothers and sisters! We must bring them to the light! A—men!"

Bruce Dougall's ears were not burning. He was calmer and more relaxed and settled than he had been at any point since he was given the crushing news of his diagnosis. He wasn't sure that the new medication could be having an effect so quickly, but not working and making a huge effort not to think about work was certainly helping. Genevieve was ready to contact him if anything of real importance cropped up. As far as everyone was concerned, he was recovering from a virus.

He felt like a student let out of classes. He was reading books he hadn't picked up in a long time and he was able to appreciate his music collection. As he carried coffee back into the main room of his discreetly luxurious apartment, the piercing beauty of Allegri's *Miserere* stopped him in his tracks as he was caught up in its rapture. It was no hardship spending some time here. There was a sprawling sense of airiness in his home. This very large room with its dining area saw to that. If that meant that the kitchen was a little smaller than would be anticipated in a property of this calibre, he wasn't worried. He was no kind of cook and appreciated the food that *BUSSTOP* rustled up when he was in the office.

Bruce sat on the balcony awhile, enjoying the evening urban view. The house where he lived as a child had been demolished, along with most of the surrounding buildings, about ten years previously. He had been annoyed by the fact that the family to whom he sold it after his mother died had not taken care of the property. It had fallen into a state of ramshackle disrepair, as had most of the neighbourhood. Homes of that age took some looking after. This apartment complex was slap bang in the middle of where the old properties once stood. It was difficult to explain to strangers how it used to be. The road and the sidewalks had been rerouted and the whole area redesigned. Friends looked in disbelief when he put photographs on screen.

Bruce remembered being told that Joe Mortimer now lived in what had been *his* family home. It was ironic. Two people who traipsed across the solar system both ended up back at the beginning in one way or another. Some lines written by John Donne, the seventeenth century poet, came to mind:

> *So wilt thou be to mee, who must*
> *Like th'other foot, obliquely runne.*
> *Thy firmness makes my circle just*
> *And makes mee end, where I begunne.*

Five hours further on into the night across the Atlantic Ocean, there was silence and darkness and sleeping in Joe's house. Downstairs, in the kitchen, Bonny whiffled happily and her paws twitched as she raced through dreamland, chasing a never-ending supply of sticks and half-chewed bones. Upstairs, Joe was motionless but anyone listening would have heard him utter one word in his sleep.

"Sally."

*　　*　　*

"What do you think of the place?" Joe wanted to know.

"The pub or the village?" asked Irene.

"Both."

"The village looks like something out of a film set and this place is wonderful."

May was living up to its reputation for being a treacherous month. An overcast sky and an icy wind put paid to plans to eat outside in the beer garden. Moving into the lounge had its compensations. A log fire was burning brightly in the grate and the pub cat was curled up fast asleep on the chair closest to the warmth.

"It looks like Tiddles is settled in for the duration," said Joe, who had encountered the cat on a previous occasion when they both wanted to sit in the same place. "Let's work round him."

"The voice of experience?" Irene wondered.

"You could say that. I've still got the scars to prove it."

After the food had been served Joe began to unfold the plan of action.

"We're looking at Tuesday for the press call. The Prime Minister will attend. Is that all right for you?"

"Yes," she said, sounding more confident than she felt. "I put all meetings and other bookings for this coming week on hold until you gave me a day. I have warned Sir Arthur Downey, the Master of the college, about what I will be doing. He huffed and puffed a bit, but he came round in the end"

"Kevin Crane pulled a couple of faces. He would have preferred Monday, simply because he has this old-fashioned notion that Monday is a quiet news day and we'll be able to hog the headlines."

"I should think that we will blast our way into the headlines, whatever day of the week it is," said Irene, allowing the first touch of apprehension beginning to appear, as it was all getting a bit too close and a bit too real.

"True. Anyway, I'm busy on Monday away from work. It's a family thing. So let's talk rough stuff, Professor. How will you blow everyone away with your facts?"

Irene found her nerves were steadied by Joe's approach. He listened, he encouraged, he made suggestions but at no point did he scorn anything that she put forward. You're a natural teacher, she thought. And you are a dear, dear man.

Joe watched Irene closely as they talked. He noticed the movement of her fair jaw-length hair, the light catching on her ear rings, the way she smiled and used her hands to emphasise a point. Her voice receded into the middle distance as he imagined moving very close to her and—

"Do you think that will be enough, Joe?" Irene was asking.

He pulled himself back to reality and told her that it would be perfect.

"I'm trying to imagine what kind of fuss there will be," Irene said after a companionable eating silence. "When we break the news."

The cat stood up and stretched in one continuous, fluid movement, eyed the people in his space and made a beeline for Irene, assessing her to be the soft touch when it came to wheedling food from the plate.

"You must appreciate that all the people who need to know have already been briefed." Joe ran his hand along the cat's back to show that there were no hard feelings. "Otherwise, they won't be ready with their polished "reactions" when the media come calling."

"I haven't told anyone in the University!" Irene declared hotly.

"And I'm glad you haven't. Academic circles are a bit different from government circles. The knack to a public secret is picking your people to tell."

"Who have you told?"

"That's easy," Joe smiled. "Personally, I've told two people since my meeting with the PM. The King and Bruce Dougall."

"Then how do all these other people know?"

"That's the Prime Minister's department, Irene. Politicians are a wonderful breed. They're quick enough to jump on the glory bandwagon when things go right and they have armies of people who organise all their publicity. Kevin Crane's popularity rating will soar when we land on Mars. So they are well prepared." He looked very solemn for a moment. "In just the same way, we will have contingency plans for if the Ariadne project went tits up. Pardon me."

"Oh."

Irene looked thoughtful.

"Welcome to the real world, Professor."

"I was getting the idea that you liked Kevin Crane," she said.

"I do! I have the greatest respect for him. I think it's mutual. I couldn't do his job under any circumstances and he admits that even thinking about being out in space makes him sweat, although he's fascinated by the whole business. But don't be fooled. If he thought it would solve a problem, he would hang me out to dry. And I'm sure that President Harper would do the same to Bruce Dougall in America."

"Bruce Dougall. He's Washington *BUSSTOP*, isn't he? And he was second in command on the Zeus flights?"

"Oh yes and yes."

"How did he react to the news?"

"He's excited by it. Like me, he would love to be on the Ariadne flight. That's even more unlikely than me going. He's poorly at the moment, with some virus. He's a lot better than the last time we spoke. He looked as if he was at death's door then. I don't think that being in space has done him any favours in the long run."

*   *   *

Daphne Mortimer was beginning to get a little anxious. Phil was very late. But she resisted all urges to contact him. She hoped nothing drastic had happened. She knew that he was with Joe and the last thing either man needed was her calling and asking what time Phil would be home for dinner.

She had scarcely finished thinking this when she heard the messaging signal. It was Phil.

"Hello, poppet. I'm staying to have something to eat with Joe. I hope you don't mind."

"Of course not. Take all the time you need. I'll see you when I see you"

Daphne was not surprised by the last-minute decision or particularly bothered. She could have dinner with her husband any time. Joe—well, Joe needed his brother today. That was why she had given very little thought to an evening meal for two.

She opened and shut cupboards in a desultory fashion, gave up and made herself a cup of tea instead. Then she went to sit down in the living room.

Daphne found that she couldn't settle to read or even to watch television. Oddly enough, it was the call from Phil that had unsettled her. Why was he staying longer with Joe? She hoped that it was because Joe was all right at the end of this tricky day and the brothers could talk into the night. Or was it because he was still in pieces? She would find out soon enough.

A few weeks previously Daphne had watched several episodes of an early twenty first century science fiction television series, shown on *Archive Three*. Amnesia pills figured from time to time in the story lines, given to people to make them forget what they had discovered or experienced. A hundred years on and Daphne was not entirely sure if such a drug had made it from a writer's imagination into actual use. She wished that it was around and could be given to Joe to work selectively on parts of his mind. Then the painful memories of Sally could be sponged away.

Daphne had never seen two people who were more meant to be together than Joe and Sally. They shone in each other's company. She understood that there had been some problems with one of Joe's *BUSSTOP* colleagues, who fancied a bit of the action. And if the truth were told, Sally had been tempted. But they rode out that storm and lived in peaceful rural seclusion when Joe wasn't flying through the heavens.

"We'll get married one of these days," Joe had said. "When we don't have the world's news media turning up for the ceremony."

That time appeared to be some way off. He was the glamour boy of British space exploration, in the national and international eye, back in the headlines every time another space ship thundered up into the sky. The pace was relentless. Everything was new, new, new and needed to be tested to the nth degree. Once Brent Dyer and the Jarnsen Corporation of New Jersey had made the breakthrough with the engines which would revolutionise flight times to Mars, each time Zeus took off it was fitted with the next incarnation of the CPT-300 series.

"I've lost track of which Mark we're on," Joe admitted memorably at a post-mission press conference when he gave the wrong designation to the engines on a particular flight and was corrected, rather unkindly, by a member of the news pack.

That pressman was probably taken outside and lynched quietly.

Zeus Four was on what Joe called a "shake down" mission.

"We'll be playing with the old lady this time," he explained to the family. "Opening everything up to full throttle and seeing what happens!"

Sally had total confidence in Joe and what he was doing because he was confident. Daphne could still remember Stella going white as Joe said those words. She knew that his mother had nightmares about spaceships coming apart.

Joe and his crew were bringing *Zeus Four* back to Earth when Sally's accident happened. She was found unconscious at the roadside, apparently struck by a car when she was walking home from the village shop.

Thanks to a subscription to the full range of *Archive* television channels, Daphne had developed a taste for the overblown "soaps", which really came into their own at the end of the twentieth century and kept on rolling for a long time. What happened next was worse than the worst script ever concocted for one of those shows. It wasn't enough that Sally was in a coma and dying. The doctors revealed that she was pregnant. Joe didn't know, that was for sure. He wouldn't have kept that from anyone. He and Sally were looking forward to children.

"Four would be a good number," Sally had said on more than one occasion.

It was thought that she was keeping the news to be a surprise for when Joe returned from his latest mission.

The family took the decision to give Joe this information themselves. They couldn't fault the care given to Sally by the medical team at the hospital but, when push came to shove, they were professional strangers, paid to do a job.

Daphne thought that all of them—Phil, herself, Neil and Stella—were candidates for those amnesia pills. The details of the small room where friends and family could retreat, where they sat with Joe, were burned into her memory and she knew that it was much the same for the others. There were multicoloured carnations in a vase on the table. Blue curtains moved in the breeze, which filtered through the partly open window. Outside birds were singing. The smell of coffee pervaded everything. Joe was living on the stuff.

To the taking of her final breath, she would never be able to forget Joe's face when Neil told him. It went totally blank. He was beyond pain, beyond grief, beyond anything. He just stopped.

How many years was it since Sally had died? Daphne gave up counting a long time ago. All she knew was that today was the anniversary of her death and Phil had taken Joe to Sally's grave, as he did every year.

The people of the village where Joe and Sally lived were the unsung heroes throughout this terrible time. They were proudly protective of the celebrity in their midst. As a result, very few in the wider public arena had the slightest idea where Joe lived and even fewer were aware of Sally's existence. Now they wrapped the cloak of anonymity even tighter round heartbreak. No one outside the family and the community knew and no one, least of all Joe, was saying anything.

"Daphne?"

Her reverie was broken. She looked up and smiled a watery smile. How long had she been sitting thinking?

"Hello, Phil."

Philip pulled her to her feet and put his arms around her.

"You've been crying. What's the matter?"

"I was thinking about Sally and Joe—and everything. But never mind me. What about Joe?"

"He's doing okay." He stopped an escaping tear half way down her cheek with his finger. "But are you?"

Her compassion was one of the things that had attracted Philip to the new personal assistant of his immediate boss, when he had seen her in action with a distressed employee. And a petite body that still managed to be shapely helped, as well. The freckles remained splodged on her nose and her thick chestnut hair, a little shorter these days, was maintained in a vibrant colour.

"I'm fine, Phil."

"You can't imagine what's happening now with Joe."

"A woman? One who actually means something to him?"

"You never know. You are an incurable romantic, Daphne. Joe always plays his cards very close to his chest and that won't change. But this is even more interesting."

Daphne sat down, ready to hear about what could possibly be so wonderful in Joe's world.

By the time Philip had finished, she was spellbound.

* * *

The stress was showing in Professor Irene Hanson. Her delivery was measured, controlled, steady. She looked cool and crisp in a blue dress. The inevitable necklace was black, made with tiny pieces of lava from Mount Etna. The giveaway for the tension was the timbre of her voice, the natural cadences flattened out with apprehension. She was making very little eye contact with her audience. But it was unlikely that this audience would have noticed if she had broken into grand opera. The press and television people gathered in the media centre at *BUSSTOP* turned up with no real idea of what was on the agenda. All they knew was that Kevin Crane and Joe Mortimer always made for good copy and news slots and the merest mention of the space programme sent circulation and viewing figures soaring.

As a result, once Irene made it clear what she was saying about messages from Mars, she had one of the most tractable groups ever to sit in that room. An occasional involuntary "Ooh" was heard and that was it. Joe realised that he was gripping the table edge tightly behind his folded arms, willing her on to the end of her statement.

"Thank you, Professor Hanson!" Albert Wright, head of *BUSSTOP* press office, seized the initiative. "The professor has given us a great deal to think about here." He was a media man to his fingertips, the perfect poacher turned gamekeeper. "I'm sure that you all have many questions to ask our distinguished panel." He sensed that the journalists were on Irene's side and he wanted it to stay that way. "So, ladies and gents, can we have a bit of decorum here instead of your usual impression of yobbos come up to London for the Cup Final? I believe that this is Professor Hanson's first press conference. Let's not frighten her away and make it her last."

Albert Wright always looked as though he had rolled out of a press room after a late night. Even new clothes were a mess on him. His tie was askew and his shirt collar dog-eared. One shoelace dangled from beneath slightly-too-long trousers. Yet for all the untidiness that was crammed into a short and tubby body, his grey hair and moustache gave him a distinguished air. And anyone who had been on the *BUSSTOP* beat for more than a week knew not to mess with Albert.

The barbs in his humorous asides struck home. Kevin Crane had never seen such a well-behaved press corps. Whilst no one was let off the hook if they gave a sloppy or unhelpful answer, he would not have believed it if he hadn't witnessed it. Barney St John, the ugliest and most aggressive newspaperman it had ever been his misfortune to meet, was saying *Please* and *Thank you*.

"Yeah, well," Barney said afterwards. "She's a real lady, isn't she? You don't cut up rough with a quality bird like that."

The real lady dealt with the questions about the accuracy of tracking the signal and just how she had come across it. Joe took over with the identification of the type of signal and what this all meant for the Ariadne programme. The Prime Minister was a kind of benign umpire. Most of his sentences began with likes of *The government thinks* or *I have advised His Majesty*. It all came together in a truly spectacular team effort.

The conference was being shown live on the television news programmes. After an hour there was an orderly stampede from the room as the TV journalists left to do their pieces to camera and print journalists disappeared to write and file their stories.

Four people were left.

"That went very well!" declared Mr Wright.

Three figures, motionless in their chairs, managed brief nods.

"If anybody had told me, a week ago, that I would talking about Martians with press and television and that I would come out alive and credible . . ."

Kevin Crane's voice petered out.

"You can move yourselves now," suggested Albert Wright. "You're making the place look untidy. Not you, of course, Professor. You are lighting up the room."

His fleshy, timeworn face was also lit up.

The Prime Minister had no choice in what he did next. Two of his entourage were standing outside the door, looking very obvious.

"I have to go. Professor Hanson, it has been a pleasure working with you. May I borrow you sometimes when I have a lively press briefing on the horizon? You have a very positive effect on our friends from the press and television. I'll speak to you tomorrow, Joe."

"You tease! Is that a promise?"

Moving past the initial stages of relief and recovery, Joe's natural sense of humour was reasserting itself.

"I think I could do with something to eat," he said to Irene.

"I'm starving now," she confessed. "I couldn't eat anything this morning. I think I would have been sick."

"Let's go up to my office," Joe suggested. "We will only provoke curiosity if we go out anywhere. Vicky can organise something to be sent in."

Neither said anything as they hiked along corridors and rode in the lift. They smiled and murmured incoherently when people stopped them to say how well they had done.

"That was brilliant, Mr Mortimer!" Vicky declared when they entered her office. "Good afternoon, Professor Hanson" she said to Irene. "I'm honoured to me you."

Joe introduced Vicky Tennant, his personal assistant.

And his willing slave, Irene thought. There was dogged devotion in the young woman's eyes, devotion that would keep her slogging on until one day she was noticed. There was a hint of hostility in Vicky's demeanour as she looked at Joe's guest but today's media stars were too weary to notice.

"Vicky, could you be an angel and track us down something to eat?" Joe asked. "It doesn't need to be anything special. We're both suffering from post-stress hunger."

"Is that what it's called?" Irene marvelled, flopping into a comfortable chair in Joe's office.

"It will do, as a label." Joe collapsed in similar fashion. "Irene, you were a sensation. Well done!"

Irene took a few moments to look around her. There was no mistaking that this office was used by a man; a man who didn't like spending too much time in it, either. Vicky had softened the edges of her workspace with pictures, plants and trinkets. When the time came for Joe to leave this job, he would literally be able to walk out of the door. Irene could not identify anything that was not *BUSSTOP* property, and functional property at that.

"Are all press calls as draining as this?" she wondered.

"Not really. It's more like choreographed war most of the time, following strict rules. We come in from one side, the press come in from the other. We say what we need to say and they don't listen. They ask questions and we give prepared answers, whether or not those answers fit the questions. We are all suitably rude to one another and Albert calls full time." He sat up straight. "Today was *fun*. Thank you for being part of it with me, Irene."

"I can't wait to see the television news and tomorrow's newspapers. We've just told the world that there is life on Mars."

"I know." He indicated the screen. "We can check on the news now. Compare performances."

"I'm not quite the seasoned campaigner that you are, Joe. I shall watch, in the privacy of my own home tonight, through my fingers."

"Irene!" he chided. "Give yourself some credit. You hit them straight between the eyes with all the facts and—" He took a breath "—you looked wonderful whilst you were delivering it, if you will excuse me being so personal."

"You are excused," said Irene, feeling quite overcome.

It would have been too bad if anything else of importance decided to happen that day. The story was round the world within minutes and news channels were running and rerunning the recording of the actual press conference. No one was safe if they knew the slightest thing about the history of space exploration, the original race to the Moon, the collapse of *NASA* and the founding of *BUSSTOP*, the planet Mars, the monitoring of space signals, the programme which developed the rocketry, hardware and software necessary to travel to Mars or the three principals who sat in that media room. Someone, somewhere wanted every expert in a television studio or on a live feed into a programme right now.

The communications systems of London and Washington D.C. *BUSSTOP* were both jammed. There was a lively crowd outside Washington's headquarters but the main problem was in London, as Joe and Irene were soon to find out.

The chief of *BUSSTOP* security asked to see the boss. Walter Bland looked harassed as he came through the door but that wasn't of immediate significance to Joe. He was convinced the man was born looking like that.

"Good afternoon Mr Mortimer, Professor Hanson. We could have a bit of a job getting you two out of the building. The place is surrounded. Not just press and television. Members of the public too. There are a couple of demonstrations growling at each other."

"Demonstrations? Come on, Walt!" Joe laughed. "What the hell can anybody be demonstrating about?"

Walter cleared his throat.

"Well, sir, there's a fundamentalist Christian group claiming that you are the incarnation of the Devil, squaring up against a group from the Church of England who are saying that this is proof of the omnipotence of the creator God. There being life on Mars and all that."

"Oh bugger!" Joe put his head in his hands. "Are the police coping?"

"They're doing a great job, sir."

"The Prime Minister!" said Irene suddenly. "Is he all right?"

"Yes, Madam," Walter assured her. "He left quite quickly to attend another engagement and he was away before the crowds started forming. This has taken a while to build up. Then in five minutes it was massive. How did you both arrive this morning?"

"My car is in the underground car park. I sent Roland to fetch Professor Hanson," Joe told him.

"Thank you, sir. I would advise that you stay put for a while and we'll get this sorted out."

Joe and Irene remained very still for a few moments after Walter Bland had left. It wasn't fun any more.

"Why, Irene?" Joe wanted to know.

"Let's have a look at the television pictures," she suggested. "I'm sure one of the news channels will be showing what's going on outside the front door."

"I can do better than that." He went over to his desk. "Vicky, please hook my office in to the external security cameras. Front and rear doors and the car park entrance and exit on a four-way split screen."

In each case there was a wall of humanity. There was a lot of movement at the front of the building with the demonstrations, but no apparent violence.

"What does one group of Christians do when it faces another group of Christians in a demo?" Joe wondered. "Do they sing hymns at one another? Or throw each other to the lions?"

Irene stood next to him, looking at the screen.

"They're frightened, Joe."

"What?"

"All these people. They're frightened. These are just ordinary people and they're scared."

Joe stared at Irene, studied the pictures and then looked back at her.
"But why?" he asked helplessly.

"We forgot one thing. We know and they don't. You know all about being
in space and getting to Mars. I know a lot of information about the planets
and the stars. So when we realised that there is life on another planet, we
slotted it in alongside what we already know. All they have got is a faulty
recollection of a map of the solar system that they learned at school, *War
of the Worlds* and *Doctor Who* on the *Archive* channels. Bug-eyed monsters
are coming to harm their families and their way of life."

"Surely at the beginning of the twenty second century—" Joe started
to say.

He stopped and looked again. In the fundamentalist Christian group an
elderly woman was waving a placard. She was grim-faced and dishevelled.
In the crowd by the car park entrance he spotted a woman with two toddlers.
She held each child's hand really tightly—a tigress guarding her cubs.

Fortunately the weather came to their rescue. Black clouds had been
building for some time. Rain began to fall, increasing in intensity. A flash
of lightning stilled the urban landscape and a crack of thunder crashed
directly overhead. The rain turned to hail stones, bouncing off the pavements
and roads, bouncing off heads and backs and hands, stinging and hurting.
This was the point at which many people gave up. By the time the storm
was passing over, the crowd standing firm round the *BUSSTOP* building
was significantly smaller. Panic buttons had been pressed and no less than
ten police officers from the Mounted Branch had arrived with their horses.
They moved in amongst the milling people, encouraging them to move along.
Adults held children up to stroke soft horse noses and the riders passed the
time of day with the individuals and groups, whom they were nudging so
gently along the street. The situation was defused. It was an example of a
law and order strategy that hadn't changed in more than a hundred years.

"I don't like thunderstorms," said Irene unexpectedly. "But I like this
one. Joe?" she said, when there was no response.

Joe's hands were on the desk and he was leaning against his braced
arms. He head was down. Eventually he looked up.

"I'm sorry," he said. "I'm so, so sorry. I just never imagined that such a
thing would happen. And this won't be the end of it." He stood up. "Vicky,
I need words with the Hertfordshire and Cambridgeshire police forces. Do
we have an encampment of press outside my house or Professor Hanson's
place yet? They'll know where the professor lives. And since I moved back
to Graffenby, everybody knows where I live."

The police confirmed that there was a growing and restive public
presence in both villages. Senior officers hid their fears behind cautious
phrases. Joe knew what they meant. It wasn't safe to go home. Mobs like

this could get ugly, especially if restraining orders were issued and arrests were made.

It was all rather scary but Irene was fascinated to see a man of action and decision in action and making decisions.

"Irene, do you think you can tough it out for forty eight hours?"

"I don't know. It will be a bit tricky if I can't get through my front door. I could stay in college, I suppose."

"Too obvious. And the college authorities won't be best pleased if the place is invaded." He walked up down the room for a minute or two. "Got it! How do you fancy camping out with Mum and Dad? They'd love it, I know."

Joe was a whirlwind now, leaving Irene breathless.

When she tried to recall the events of the afternoon at a later date, she found that the fine detail was blurred. Joe made call after call. He confirmed with the police that neither of them would be home that night and he said where they would be staying. Neil Mortimer agreed with Joe's plans. He had been watching the television coverage of the crowds and he was worried. The most startling conversation came last of all.

"Afternoon, Richard!" Joe said.

Irene's eyes widened when she realised that he was talking to the King.

"Hello, Joe. I'm aware of what's going on. Are you and Professor Hanson all right?"

Joe beckoned Irene over to the screen.

"As you see," he said.

"Good afternoon, Professor Hanson," the King said with a smile. "I hope that rascal Joe is looking after you properly."

"Good afternoon, Your Majesty. He is, thank you."

Irene was on automatic pilot.

"Now Joe," His Majesty continued. "You were right, although I don't think you anticipated the reaction to the news about Mars being as agitated as this." Joe nodded his agreement. "So we could do with that little distraction we talked about. Everything is ready. It can be tomorrow if you would like that."

"I think some people would smell a rat there. Thursday morning?"

"Thursday morning it is then. Eleven o'clock. Are you sure? The media can be very persistent. I should know."

"We'll stay with my parents and the police can deal with any problems. The house and the village are easy enough to watch over."

Everything now became totally unreal for Irene. She was ushered into the official car by a solicitous Roland at the back entrance of *BUSSTOP*. Both ignored questions and shouts from the crowds, who were held back by police. They were soon heading out towards Cambridgeshire.

"You said that you wanted to be adopted by Mum and Dad," Joe reminded her, breaking off from making an almost continuous stream of calls. "Now's your chance to have a trial run."

"That sounds nice. But why are you so sure that we will only have to sit this out for forty eight hours?"

"That would be telling." He could see that Irene needed more reassurance. "I promise you that everything will work out."

*   *   *

Irene opened her eyes and didn't know where she was. Then she remembered. The events of Tuesday were not a dream. They had happened and she was waking up in a spare room in Neil and Stella Mortimer's house. Those two lovely people had done all they could to make her feel welcome and comfortable. Stella had stood out of view on the previous evening, giving thumbs up signals of encouragement, whilst Irene had a brisk exchange of views with the Master of the college. She battered him down in the end with the very valid point that if she had stayed in college, the press pack would have descended there.

Going downstairs slowly, she wondered if she would still have a job after Joe's mysterious forty-eight hours. She was also concerned about the newshounds ending up here.

Joe looked very pleased with himself when he joined everyone at the breakfast table.

"I haven't got my running gear so I've been for a long walk. I went and had a chat with the police."

"Police?" queried his father, looking towards the window.

"Dad, hasn't it struck you as odd that not a single journalist has made it here? The police have cordoned off the whole area. There's a combined security and safety alert going on up the road at the nuclear fusion place. Only there isn't," he added quickly, to calm Stella. "It was about time they had a dummy run of their procedures and it's happening now."

"Let me guess. The police won't be stood down until some time tomorrow," said Irene.

"That's right. There are some very big boys and girls up the road with some very big guns. The Army is around as well. As far as the outside world, and the rest of the village, is concerned, this is a routine drill. Nothing to do with us being here. It makes the place journalist proof."

Irene didn't feel strong enough to ask how he had managed all of that. One small detail was bothering her.

"What about your lovely dog? Bonny, isn't it?"

"My neighbours went into the house with a police escort and Bonny is staying with them. Freda and Ron have my key for emergencies."

Irene was losing the will to live. Even Superman can become irksome after a while.

The day passed pleasantly enough. Joe and Neil were fiddling about endlessly on the computer and Irene had a long talk with Stella. It isn't very often that an author is stuck in the middle of a practice lock-down with one of her readers. Irene took advantage of this and wanted Stella's opinion on her latest book—and on the others. Joe discovered them deep in discussion, with Stella's copies of the books spread around them.

Thursday morning dawned bright and warm.

"So what's your trick today?" Irene wanted to know of Joe.

"Wait and see," he said mysteriously.

"Joe, I'm tired of waiting and seeing! I just want to go home and get back to normal." She was instantly contrite. "That didn't come out at all how it sounded in my head. I do apologise. I am being less than gracious here. I could have spent this time barricaded in my house on my own, hiding from the press and the public. That's presuming that I could have got in there in the first place. Thank you, for everything."

Joe took her hand and bowed over it to kiss it.

"That's what friends are for, Irene."

As the morning wore on, Joe was becoming edgy. Irene thought back to the call he had made to the King on Tuesday afternoon. That must have something to do with it, only she couldn't think at all how His Majesty King Richard the Fourth could do anything to help here.

"Nearly eleven o'clock," said Joe, rubbing his hands together. "We need to look at the television news."

"Why, Joe?" his mother asked.

They had steadfastly ignored the news. Newspapers, like all other commodities, couldn't get through to the village. There was a temporary Category Five filter on all incoming calls to the Mortimer household.

As the screen came to life, the newsreader was wearing the broadest smile imaginable.

"These are the headlines at eleven o'clock. We have learned from Buckingham Palace that, at this moment, the following announcement is being made:

> "*It is with the greatest pleasure that the King and Queen announce the betrothal of their beloved daughter, Her Royal Highness the Princess Charlotte, to Squadron Leader Michael Timpson, oldest son of the late Mr Matthew Timpson and Mrs*

Mary Timpson. It is anticipated that the wedding will take place at St Paul's Cathedral in the late autumn."

Joe had been standing behind his armchair. Now he jumped over it and sat down.

"Yes!" he exclaimed. "You beauty, Richard!"

Chapter Six

There is one big drawback to being part of a mob. Eventually, the minds that came together to create it have to separate and then the reality starts to kick in.

The reality that was kicking in now included the joyous announcement of a royal wedding and many people who had jumped up and down in protest—protesting about what?—following the *BUSSTOP* press conference began to feel very foolish indeed.

One of the newspapers summed it up best with a *montage* of pictures. First there were the happy, laughing photos of Joe Mortimer and Irene Hanson, taken as they joked with those gathered in the media centre on the Tuesday morning and everyone saw the funny side of a comment. Underneath was a picture of the two of them being driven away from the *BUSSTOP* building in the afternoon. Irene was obviously frightened and Joe looked less than comfortable.

SORRY JOE! SORRY PROF! was the sheepish headline, as a nation hung its head in shame.

Kevin Crane had an enviable fingertip feel for a situation. On the Friday evening he made a special live broadcast to the nation. This was the Prime Minister at his best. The headmaster was berating the naughty children in his study—more in sorrow than in anger.

Joe came in part way through the broadcast. Bonny sat and watched with rapt attention, none the worse for her little adventure with the neighbours.

"Sometimes our nation comes out onto the streets to make a point for very good reasons. We celebrate those occasions in our history as stepping-stones on the road to democracy. Sometimes our nation comes out onto the streets in a way that is uniquely British. I am thinking of the events that followed the death of Diana, Princess of Wales, in 1997. Or the month-long silent protests in 2020 following the arrest of the television reporter Peter Sanders, who exposed such corruption in the City of London. And we should never forget the devotion of Beatrice Cooper, who with her friends and growing public support, lobbied her local police force for a year until it was agreed to review the circumstances surrounding her grandson's death. We can watch all this and more on archive film. But *never* should our nation come out onto the streets to follow the unthinking reactions of a minority with a point to prove.

"The events of Tuesday afternoon and Wednesday morning are a disgrace, a blot on our national character, which will take some removing. I count Joe Mortimer as a friend, as well as a person with whom I work. As the elected leader of this country, I shall find it very difficult to look him in the eye when I think how he—an applauded, decorated national hero—felt so threatened that he couldn't go home. And I cannot begin to say how I feel about Professor Irene Hanson—a world-respected academic—being hounded in this way.

"What did these two people do? They shared with us exciting knowledge, which makes the upcoming Ariadne flight to Mars even more important. What did a minority do? Attack." Kevin Crane looked at a nation sternly via the camera lens. "I count myself as having a Christian faith but I despaired when I found out from police chiefs that so-called Christian fundamentalists were leading these demonstrations. Those who tried to counter them were, alas, playing into their hands, whatever their good intentions.

"We live in exciting, rapidly changing and modern times. We should look forward with eager anticipation to the take-off of *Ariadne One* and be ready for whatever encounters there may be on the surface of Mars." He paused, for dramatic effect. "And yet, thank goodness, there are some things that never change, as we celebrate the engagement of Her Royal Highness Princess Charlotte and Squadron Leader Michael Timpson. We send our congratulations to the King and Queen and to the happy couple. Let us unite in the very new and in the constant."

"That was a Prime Ministerial broadcast by the Right Honourable Kevin Crane," intoned the station announcer. "Normal programme scheduling will now be resumed."

"Say what you mean, won't you?" murmured Joe, surprised but pleased that the Prime Minister had been so direct.

When he emerged from the news-free bunker of his parents' home along with Irene, he had been taken aback by the amount of civil unrest their press conference had caused. Irene was right. A slice of the nation panicked. During his impromptu visit to Buckingham Palace, he had arranged with Richard that the announcement of Charlotte's engagement should be made in the days after the press conference, just to take the attention from everyone involved. He had no idea what a lifeline it would become in the calming-down process.

Joe smiled contentedly. It had all worked out in the end and Irene was revealing herself as a perceptive woman. A perceptive and fascinating woman. He had to talk to her.

He was surprised that he got through to her at the first time of trying.

"I thought your communications system would have been filled with callers," he said. "Did you see Kevin Crane's broadcast?"

"I did indeed. He believes in saying what he thinks, doesn't he?"

"When the occasion demands it. He can be the most opaque of men when he decides on it. Irene, are you sure that you're all right?"

"Perfectly, Joe. You are so sweet to be concerned. I don't appear to have lost my job, by the way."

"None of what happened after the press call was your fault and if someone had been misguided enough to write your dismissal notice, they'd be deleting it after that statement from the Prime Minister."

"An old school friend has invited me to go and see her tomorrow and stay over into Sunday," Irene said, cutting off Joe's next line of conversation. "She lives in Hunstanton. We can have some bracing coastal walks if the weather holds."

"Have a great time," he said.

"I'll call you next week, if that's not being too presumptuous. I will need your help to write a proper report about this. I think I can keep Sir Arthur quiet if I do that for him."

"Consider it done!" Joe replied, very happy at the prospect.

He found himself unexpectedly wishing he could be the one walking a beach with Irene, not an old school friend. Looking forward to their next meeting, he almost stopped wishing that it would rain on Hunstanton for the whole weekend.

Almost.

*　　*　　*

The police presence was serious this time. No fiddling about with a few patrol cars to keep an avuncular eye on proceedings.

Pastor Philemon Brown was using much bigger premises tonight within Alexandria—a sports stadium—but an overspill was being catered for. The preacher never said in advance what he would be speaking about—"I let the Holy Spirit dictate to me"—but many of his followers hoped for one particular topic.

They were not disappointed.

"Pastor! What about the Martians?" someone called out from the crowd.

"I'm coming to that right now, brother!" he replied. "We know that God created the world and made us in his own image to populate this world and this world only. Hallelujah!"

"Hallelujah!" the congregation responded.

"And yet, in these last days we have seen that iniquitous man Joseph Mortimer and that painted whore Professor Irene Hanson telling the good folks of England and the world that they will find people living on Mars. This is an abomination! We must fight the good fight against this, brothers and sisters!"

"Fight the good fight!" the congregation shouted.

The singing of *He is Lord* started in one section of the stadium and the refrain was passed around for a few minutes.

Those filming for the news reports couldn't believe their luck as Brown went on attacking Joe and Irene in the most lurid terms. When Bruce Dougall saw this on television he was horrified. He was aware that he and Joe had been mentioned in one of Philemon Brown's earlier sermons. But this was outrageous.

He sat waiting for the footage to go on and show the police moving in to arrest Philemon Brown. It didn't happen. He was baffled.

The next morning he unfolded the newspaper, anticipating reports and reactions. There was a brief summary of the fact that Pastor Philemon Brown had conducted another packed service and voiced his opposition to the Mars landing. The story appeared to have dropped out of the news shows.

Bruce sat on the balcony for a long time. He knew that sometimes the best way to deal with a contentious person like Brown was to ignore him. Publicity was what this man was looking for. Deny him a wider audience and he and his message were confined and eventually went out like a candle burnt down.

Bruce knew that this was nothing to do with him. He wasn't mentioned or slandered in this outpouring. It *was* nothing to do with him. It was part of the rough and tumble of public life.

No it wasn't. This was character assassination.

Why was he bothering about this? Bruce could answer his own question immediately. Like many before him who had been told that their days were numbered, he was doing a pile of thinking. It was only natural that a fair bit of that thought involved Joe Mortimer.

They started to clash over various matters not long into the Zeus programme. Why? The simplest explanation that he could come up with was they were both breathing. Although they came from very different backgrounds and had very different interests, in some ways they were too alike. That was why he was so attracted to—.

Anyway. They were a great team in space but were a disaster otherwise. Those teamwork occasions had to count as really good times in his life. But even so, why should he be bothered with the rantings of a small-time holy roller, even if the jerk was painting Joe and this Professor Hanson in terms of an adult-rated movie? Why should he care?

The answer to that was in the Earth-bound journey on *Zeus Three*.

Bruce wasn't frightened by the prospect of dying. It was the cutting short of opportunity that really rankled with him. But he had to admit that he swerved round frightened and went straight to terrified out of his mind when he became sick after that space walk. It was the suddenness of the thing that had unhinged him. Nothing could come close to that experience surely, not even death. On the space ship he didn't know it was possible to feel so ill and so scared. But then there was Joe, who sat with him for hour after hour. There was the pressure of a hand on his and a voice saying "I promise I will get you home, Bruce. I will make this box of electronics and computer chips fly like no other spaceship has ever flown. Mission Control wanted to see what this crate could do. We all want to see what she can do. We will show them and no one can complain about a mercy dash. I promise you we will reach home in record time and you will be helped and you will get better. And you will be on the next mission with the rest of us."

* * *

President Phoebe Harper was not the stereotypical formidable harridan that one would expect to find succeeding in a man's world. A woman being elected to the office of President of the United States of America had been a lot longer in the happening than the even the most pessimistic of observers would have dared to predict. But now that she had made history, Mrs Harper was doing a great job. She was a softly spoken, no-nonsense little Southern lady. Her hair was a flattering shade of grey these days but those greeny-hazel eyes reminded everyone that she had been a flaming redhead. She retained a fiery streak and a youthful air; a lot of people thought that she was a lot younger than the figures on her birth certificate showed her to be. Invariably making public appearances wearing muted shades of soft colours, always with black accessories, she escaped any accusations of mutton dressed as lamb. This President had initially divided the nation into those who applauded her go-getting attitude and those who thought she should be sitting on a porch somewhere, being the grandmother that she was. Mrs Harper had won over the majority of her opponents.

Many said that she won in spite of her Vice President, Ted Rodriguez. But the hint of him as her running mate had been key in ensuring that some of the influential Eastern states swung behind her in the primaries. In the Presidential election itself, he couldn't have worked harder if he had been up for the White House himself. Between them they had all the corners covered, in Congress and in the country.

President Harper was pleased to be speaking on screen to Bruce Dougall. They got on well. And she always had time for a good-looking man who also had a brain in his head. Ted Rodriguez ticked those boxes but there was *something* about the former astronaut. His insistence that the United States should not take the lead in the Ariadne project had been puzzling but his written report put the case very succinctly.

"Mr Dougall!" she said brightly. "It's good to talk to you again. I understand you have been under doctor's orders for a while. I hope that you are feeling better?"

"I am, thank you, Madam President."

"So what can I do for the boss man of *BUSSTOP* today? I can't tap into any more money, if you were hoping to lobby personally for a budget increase. The pennies are a bit tight right now."

"No, nothing like that."

"So what is it then, boy? Tell me what's on your mind."

So he did.

Phoebe Harper listened politely to begin with but her annoyance began to show after a while.

"What's this all about, Mr Dougall?" she asked sharply. "You're bending my ear because you don't like something a preacher man has been saying? May I remind you that this is a country which prides itself on the freedom of speech!"

"This isn't free speech, Madam President. This is muck-raking and rabble rousing."

"So you decided to speak to me."

"After I had spoken to a lot of other people, whom I hoped would do something. But they didn't."

Bruce listed the individuals and authorities he had tackled on the uphill advance to the White House.

"Very commendable, Mr Dougall. Now what exactly do you expect me to do about this Pastor Philemon Brown?"

"Stop him. Before I do."

"And if I don't do whatever it is you want me to do, how do you propose to "stop" him?"

"I own a hand gun and a rifle with a telescopic sight. I go hunting sometimes. I'm a good shot. I don't often miss."

"Mr Dougall!" she thundered. "That is not very funny!"

"I wasn't being funny. I'm deadly serious, Madam President."

"Are you aware of the grave consequences of even contemplating such an action?"

"I am," he said.

He was almost sorry for her as she tried to rattle him. He was one man who had little left to lose.

*　　*　　*

Tony was finding some confusion amongst the group who had set themselves apart to transform, ready for the visitors from Earth. He was uncertain as well and was not sure what he could say.

"Can we sort out one or two things?"

Justin, again! He was obviously settling into his character. Tony was glad that his Earth *persona* had been a patient man. Justin was calming down a bit now but he must have been a challenging and persistent person as a human.

"We have been given these human appearances, characteristics and personalities for a reason. Correct?" Justin began.

"Yes."

"These transformations will help us to communicate in a rational way with humans when they arrive on this world."

"Yes."

"There will be individual humans who will recognise these forms when we meet them."

"Yes."

Tony knew where this was leading.

"No!" said Justin. "That's the problem. None of us can identify with the people who will be physically walking in our world. Sally has the best links. She has ties to two key people on Earth. The one, as we know, will not be coming, for sure." There was a moment's silence. "The other will not be here, either. My link is to a public figure in the United States of America, who will not be coming. And your link is?" he concluded, knowing the answer full well.

"My link is to a woman who has the esteem of the world but who has not yet realised her full potential. She, too, will not be on the spaceship," Tony answered honestly.

"Then what are we doing in these forms? In these personalities? No one will be on the ship for Ichiro, either. Sophia and Adam are here to represent the learning of Earth and no one knows the identity of our seventh member. So it is up to you, me, Sally and Ichiro. But what's our point of contact?

Yes, we want to greet our visitors with appearance and language that they will understand. But what about the greater mission? How can we right the wrong, if the one we wronged isn't with us? How can we face up to our karma if the one harmed doesn't travel from Earth?"

"I don't know," said Tony. "When I called out to the Universe, the people that we are becoming came gladly and willingly, because they recognised the cry. It is not just us here who have unfinished business with the one. Each of our human links needs an answer, or a closure; maybe a move on to the next level of understanding. I know that they won't tread this world. But we will see the answer when the explorers arrive from Earth. Trust me."

It is unusual for brown eyes to really shine. Tony's eyes shone. His human frame seemed taller, stronger as he spoke. From what he sensed already about this human, Justin knew it was not like Tony to make a mistake. Yes, clarity would come later.

Tony realised Sally was not around. Being cramped down into human form was rapidly becoming tiresome. Harnessing his curtailed senses, he found her, sitting on a rocky outcrop staring into nothingness.

"Hello, Tony," she said before she looked round.

"To quote Justin—that's cheating."

When she did look round, her face was streaked with tears.

"I'm finding human emotions very difficult to cope with," she admitted. "And I have an extra burden to deal with, which I have only just come to recognise."

Tony held her hands and bowed his head to clear his mind and identify her problem.

"Sally, that's difficult," he said at length. "But that is the way the laws say it must be. We must all be as our characters were when they left Earth life. No exceptions. The child must be—No, we'll leave that for another time."

"But what's the point? Neither of my links will be here! Your link, whoever she is, won't be here. I can't sense her. My senses are becoming scrambled. I don't like it. I feel so . . . limited."

"Welcome to the life of a human being. We were like this once, long ago. We will keep out telepathic links with each other. We will have to read humans as other humans read each other—the hard way—until the levels of vibration are raised. We will also retain a degree of psychic ability beyond most human reach. But we can't bring out a whole array of powers. Humans are so far behind us in their evolution. They would be frightened, and frightened humans are potentially dangerous humans."

As he spoke, Tony knew that he was developing an unwelcome human trait—that of secrecy. He did not share with Sally the identity of his Earth link in words and he closed off that knowledge in his mind so that she could not check it out. There was no need for this. The group of Martians were linked by a shocking mistake, so there was nothing that they did not share. But the human Tony was winning the battle. This information was his, to enjoy, to anticipate, to delight in—on his own.

*   *   *

As Irene waited for Debbie to arrive, she knew what a blessing it was to have good friends. Without saying a word, those friends were rallying round her in an unobtrusive way. Heavy rain thwarted the planned walks but she had spent an enjoyable weekend with Sandra in Hunstanton. She hadn't been home long on Sunday evening when Debbie contacted her. She and Debbie became bosom pals in their undergraduate student days and they had kept in touch through the ups and downs that life had to share out to them.

"I shall want to hear about *everything*," said Debbie when they had sorted out that she would come to dinner on Tuesday evening. "You can't trust the TV or the newspapers to give you the complete story." She raised and lowered her eyebrows several times. "And everything includes all about you and your spaceman. Spare me none of the delicious details. I could do with a vicarious thrill—middle-aged rapture, lust and love and all that business. I had you booked down to find yourself a toy boy some day. But you've always had an eye for top quality and it hasn't failed you. Good girl!"

Irene was confused for a moment.

"I don't know what . . ." She checked. "Are you rambling on about Joe Mortimer by any chance? Debbie! He's not my spaceman! He's not *my* anything."

"Have it your way. I've got to go. Be ready to reveal all on Tuesday."

Checking on the progress of the food, Irene went hot and cold in turn as she recalled what had been said. Could she cope with an evening of innuendo? Actually, with Debbie it would be the straightforward approach, as it had been in their university days. When Irene had been seeing her boyfriend of the time for a while, Debbie collared her one lunchtime.

"It's time to tell all about Nathan," she had said. "The world needs to know about him, as do I. Can we have some marks out of ten for sex?"

These days Debbie was Director of Clinical Psychology in a London hospital, where her husband was lead consultant in Emergency medicine. "Look at me, all grown up," as she once put it, but underneath the respected healer and teacher, the sparky undergraduate was still going strong.

The door buzzer sounded and there was Debbie.

"Bye!" she was shouting out towards the road. "Alisdair brought me," she said to Irene. Irene waved to Debbie's husband. "He'll come and collect me at the end of the evening. So how is the latest star of screen and print?"

"Don't!"

"Then I won't, for the moment. Hello, you!"

Debbie hadn't changed much over the years. She retained the same elegant and correct posture that was so noticeable in Irene. Both had attended ballet classes for several years as girls and it was through fencing, another activity where body stance is so important, that they first met at university. Two children and domestic contentment had filled out Debbie a little so that now she was a fashionable and styled mother earth figure. Her face was a little less sculpted these days but that only added to her striking features. Her brown hair was pinned up casually for the occasion.

The two women were soon caught up in a tide of reminiscing, which stretched out over their meal and continued on into the evening. Debbie accessed some of her home computer files to show Irene the latest pictures of Mhairie and Rhona. Irene felt guilty. She was their godmother and she had been a little negligent recently.

"You've been steamrollered by events," said Debbie understandingly. "And with a positively edible man to amuse as well—."

She saw the look on Irene's face and subsided. Along with husband Alisdair, Irene had a rare claim to being an effective wrangler of Debbie MacIver.

"You'll be able to make it to Rhona's twentieth birthday, won't you?" she continued, as if there had been no break in her speech.

They laughed and remembered and even shed the odd tear, especially when they looked at Debbie's wedding pictures. They hadn't glanced at these in years.

"Don't we all look so young!" Irene exclaimed. "And what a sensation Alisdair was."

Keen to keep up the family Scottish Highland traditions, Alisdair cut a dashing figure as the groom, dressed in the full tartan regalia

"Trust me to marry a man wearing a skirt," Debbie observed, not for the first time. "Have you got any pictures of the old gang to hand, Irene?"

There was nothing for it but that Irene went delving into her picture collection, calling on so many memories via the screen.

"Oh!" she said suddenly. "An escapee in the wrong file."

Debbie looked at the picture. This was one she had never seen before.

"What a lovely man!" she breathed, hardly aware that she was saying it.

It was crazy to say that an image hummed and brimmed with life, but it did. Debbie could almost feel his energy reaching out and touching her.

"Who is that, Irene?" she asked, shaken.

"Have you never seen this picture? I know I've mentioned him, many times. That's my mother's father. He was only forty-five when he died. I never knew him, of course. And yet, sometimes I think that I know Tony Johnson very well. Odd, isn't it?"

Debbie took another look at the picture before Irene moved it to the file where it belonged. His dark hair was cropped close to minimise the appearance of balding. He looked a bit on the short side but never mind. His presence dominated the picture. His smile could only be described as beautiful and crinkled the corners of his eyes.

"I'm pleased to have met you, Tony," she said to the picture in a way that Irene couldn't hear.

When Alisdair called to say that he was on his way to collect her at the end of the evening, Debbie could contain herself no longer.

"It's no good, Irene. I've got to know. What about you and Joe Mortimer?"

"Debbie! Last week I told the world that there is life on Mars, there was rioting in the streets and all you want to know about is Joe Mortimer!"

"You know me, Irene. I always have been the one for gossip. Like all your friends, I saw what happened. I love you dearly and I'm so proud to be able to say I know you. But the thing is, the world simply cannot continue spinning round on its axis if I don't have the full starting price on the spaceman."

"There isn't anything to say, Debs." Debbie looked stricken. "Joe and I have been thrown together by circumstance. He fronts *BUSSTOP*, which is sending people to Mars. I tracked a message from Mars. That's all."

"Really? You only had to look at his body language in that press conference to see what he's all about. I'm not very often wrong."

"I was too busy trying not to make a fool of myself in front of the representatives of the media to notice anything else."

Debbie spotted the telltale downward glance to the left.

"You're smitten by him, aren't you?" she said. It was noticeable that Irene did not deny it. "But you are telling me there has not been a kiss, a gesture, a word?" Debbie was properly vexed. "Dearie me! Do I need to draw both of you some diagrams? Or perhaps the rumours about him are true."

Irene could see that she would have to give *something* to her friend. Debbie's knowing comments were making her return to being a boy-obsessed teenager again. What did she really think about Joe? She would have to be really honest with herself later, after Debbie had gone.

"He says some very flattering things. He's kissed my hand a few times but I think that's a charming family habit. His father is a bit of an old smoothie. Oh, and he held me up one night and prevented me from tripping over my own feet."

"I'll bet he's got gorgeous hands."

"My elbows didn't register that information," Irene told her dryly.

"I shall await developments," Debbie said firmly, not to be defeated.

As Debbie prepared to leave, Irene hugged her.

"What about the poor world, not able to continue spinning on its axis?" she asked quietly.

"Don't tell the world," was the whispered reply.

* * *

Philemon Brown was shaken to his core. He watched the car pull away from the house. He went through to the kitchen, stood at the sink and dashed water against his face to wash away the cold sweat. He was so glad that the family was out. This humiliation was for sharing with no one.

His eyes were smouldering pits as he went over what the unexpected arrivals said. How dare they speak to him in that way? He, who had been hailed as *the new buckle of the Bible Belt.*

He was still gathering his wits when the doorbell sounded again. Surely they hadn't returned to make more veiled threats? Should he pretend he wasn't in? He could hide. This was a large house, one of Alexandria's finest, which the church had bought for him and his wife and five children. Brown's insides tightened as he checked the door monitor. He nearly dropped to the floor. Two of the biggest men he had ever seen were standing on his front porch. They looked like personal security for someone, except that it wasn't clear who was being watched over. With a slipping grip on reality, he opened the front door.

"Am I addressing Pastor Philemon Brown?" one of the men asked. After a moment's hesitation, Brown agreed that he was the man. "My colleague and I are part of the staff of Mr Ted Rodriguez, Vice President of the United States of America." The preacher held on to the door to keep himself stable. "Mr Rodriguez wonders if he might take up a few minutes of your time?"

Philemon Brown's brain told him that he said yes. An affirmative whimper was what actually came out of his mouth.

"We have a green," said the other man cryptically into a personal communicator.

Whilst the preacher was still trying to work out what this was all about, a car with tinted windows slid to a halt outside the house. The driver got out and Brown's jaw sagged. This one had to be seven feet tall if he was an inch because when Vice President Rodriguez stepped out of the car, his six feet of height was dwarfed.

For a hysterical moment, Philemon Brown wondered if this was some sort of elaborate prank. But no. Ted Rodriguez was a very distinctive figure.

Here was this powerfully built man striding up the path, taking the porch steps two at a time, hand outstretched, eager to say hello.

"Pastor Philemon Brown!" he said, with the kind of satisfaction that most people reserve for arriving at journey's end. "I am so pleased to meet you, sir. I am a great admirer of your preaching and your message."

Brown was sagging mentally. He couldn't keep up with this. His previous visitors—three men, who never *quite* made it clear which federal agency they came from—had suggested that he might like to keep some of his thoughts to himself. They gave him some guidance on which thoughts in particular they were concerned about. He was glad that he lived in a twenty second century benign democracy. In another time and place he would have just disappeared, never to be seen again. And now the Vice President was happening along, saying the exact opposite to those people.

Within ten minutes, he was serving coffee and cookies to Ted Rodriguez in the family room. They were talking as if they had known each other for years.

Rodriguez gave Philemon Brown one of his vote-winning smiles. It was like having a publicity poster come to life sitting opposite to him—the greying hair, the strong face not quite as firm as the man reached into his fifties, the dark eyes that never really showed what he was thinking. He leaned forward eagerly.

"I particularly applaud your opposition to the Mars exploration programme, Pastor Brown."

Brown blinked. As an electioneering presidential candidate, Phoebe Harper struck a chord with the nation when she pledged to make the continuous funding of space projects one of her top priorities. With echoes of President Kennedy, she made it clear that, if she reached the White House, people would walk on Mars during her watch, thanks to the transatlantic cooperation of *BUSSTOP*. Could her Vice President be so at odds with her on this topic? Come to think of it, the pastor couldn't recall Rodriguez ever speaking on the subject. He had presumed that was because it was considered a personal topic for Mrs Harper. Now he was beginning to wonder.

"More coffee, Mr Vice President?" he offered. "And thank you so much for your words of support, sir."

*   *   *

Irene Hanson electronically mailed her draft report to Joe Mortimer at his office. He could have read it, suggested any amendments and sent it all back within the hour. Instead they met at the country pub again. This time the weather was kind and they enjoyed sitting out in the garden on a summer evening.

The birds were twittering and chirruping and they didn't stop as the cat came strolling nonchalantly towards them. It was as if they knew he was too indolent and well fed to worry about such mere details as chasing birds. He was concentrating on winding himself round Irene's chair and her ankles.

"You've got a friend for life there," said Joe. "That's what comes of giving animals titbits."

"I'll bet you spoil Bonny!" she challenged. "You can't say that you never do."

"Occasionally she has a treat," he admitted. "The cat is called Tigger, by the way. I checked with Don behind the bar."

Tigger lay down under the table to wait patiently. All manner of voluptuous smells were working their way out from the kitchen on the warm, still air. He had learned that it was better to besiege tables than the kitchen. Some of those smells would end up out here as food.

"I've got a few suggestions for your report," Joe said, as if it was an afterthought. "I've written them up for you. Nothing drastic. Just expanding a few of your comments, that's all."

"Thank you."

"I'm off to America on Monday. Washington D.C. and then down to Cape Canaveral to look over *Ariadne One* and check on how the crew is coming together. We've got ourselves a good group of people there. They are all seasoned astronauts, who have flown around with the propulsion systems that are used on *Ariadne One*. It's down to hours of practice in the simulator, putting the Lander part of Ariadne down on the surface of Mars and docking with Orbiter again afterwards."

"I've never been to the States," Irene said enviously.

"You've never—." Joe looked faintly incredulous. "No lecture tours? No book promotions over there?"

"The good people of America don't have the same appetite for my writing as Britain and the rest of Europe. My publisher has never thought it worthwhile sending me. I'm quite a home bird, really."

"So am I. Even more so when faced with being in Washington at this time of year. It's like a sauna. Cape Canaveral won't be much better. Come with me, Irene!" he offered impulsively. "The Americans are always going on about my "people." They can't work out that I don't travel with an entourage, even though I'm given the budget for one. I'm quite capable of making my own notes and writing them up. And I can manage to follow an itinerary that has already been arranged—all on my own. I'm sure the University term is over by now. Come and be my people!"

"It's very tempting," she said, weakening, swept along by the madness of the moment.

"So be tempted."

"I have a lot of end-of-academic-year business to attend to," she said, with genuine regret. "Otherwise I really would love to come with you."

"I'll be back at Cape Canaveral for the launch." Joe told her when that would be, at the end of the year. "That is a big secret, by the way."

"Is that a public secret or a secret secret?" she wondered.

"You're a quick learner! That is strictly a top of the command heap *BUSSTOP* piece of information. Even the Ariadne crew don't know for sure, though if they sat down and did the maths, they could probably work out the summer season in the northern hemisphere on Mars. So you really will come with me for the launch?"

"Joe, I wouldn't miss it for the world."

"I look forward to holding your hand all the way to America, then," Joe said with some satisfaction. Irene glanced at him, puzzled. "I hate flying," he admitted.

Another look at his face was enough to stop Irene's bout of hysterics before it started. This was a major confession and had to be treated as such.

"Let me get this straight," she said slowly. "You started off in the RAF. You got your wings, or whatever they call it. And you flew all those missions in space. And you hate flying on a commercial plane?"

"Yes. It would be okay if I were in the cockpit. Drivers hate being driven."

The conversation drifted elsewhere, before Irene's self-control came under too severe a test. She was beginning to appreciate the fact that the surprises this man could spring might be never-ending. There was far more to him than his action hero label.

"I'll bring you a tacky souvenir from Cape Canaveral," Joe promised as they stood to go their separate ways. "Oh, I nearly forgot. Here's your report, with my suggested alterations." He leaned in and kissed her cheek. "See you soon, Irene."

Irene watched him walk along the path to the car park. Suddenly she was wishing the time away so that Joe Mortimer would be back with her under the same sky.

* * *

Ted Rodriguez altered the screen quickly so that it showed a document when his wife came into the room.

"Still working?" Maureen wanted to know.

"Yeah, still working."

He didn't raise his head as he spoke to her.

"Ted, I'm going on up to bed. Are you coming?"

"Later. I've got some things to finish off here."

Maureen knew when she was defeated. Each footstep up the stairs was like a mountain—an all-consuming effort to climb. She kept trying to find other reasons, other excuses but it was no use. She had to face up to it. Ted must be messing about again. He had hardly looked at her at all for a week. Not because he was busy, her instincts told her, but because he didn't want to look. When was the last time he touched her?

She sat on the edge of the bed and wept. What more could she do? Everyone told her that she was an attractive woman. She was a dainty New Englander of Irish descent, well-dressed as opposed to madly fashionable, but commented upon favourably in her role as the wife of the Vice President. She made sure that there was no grey in her dark hair and she was toying with the idea of wearing tinted contact lenses, to ensure that her eyes remained a sparkling blue.

But why was she bothering? She had known for most of her married life that she was fighting a losing battle.

Downstairs, Ted glanced at the document he had put on screen instead of the picture. In his haste, he had lunged at the filing system. He couldn't believe what was there. He knew what it was as soon as he saw the *BUSSTOP* logo: five stars arranged in a crescent that cradled a planet. Every time he came across this he knew he should delete it. It was a reminder of painful rejection. But the pain had informed his life and he couldn't let go of the words on the screen.

Ted switched back to the picture he had hidden so guiltily. This person belonged to that dark time and had helped pull him out of his despair. He had other friends now, whom he needed so much. But the memory of this man was special.

It was a foolish thing to do, keeping this picture on the system. The protection level was high and Maureen couldn't access this file but there might be some bright spark from MIT or some such place, who might think it was clever to hack into the Vice President's computer. Back at the beginning of the last century there appeared to be regular incidents involving high school kids working their way into the Pentagon's computers.

Rodriguez came to his senses. Come on, now! This wasn't a treasonable document he was worrying about. It was a picture of a person who had been known in his day as a model on both sides of the Atlantic. What was wrong with that?

By the look of it, the young man in the picture was finding something funny. As his head went back in laughter, the sun flashed and sparkled on his diamond earring and the wind ruffled his hair.

Ted could remember the day, remember the conversation, and remember the actions with laser-etched clarity. He couldn't keep up running and took this picture as an excuse to stand still.

"Get a move on, Ted! Are you twenty-five or two hundred and fifty? Do I have to come and resuscitate you?"

The distinctive English accent was in the room with him. He could almost feel lips brushing softly against his.

"Justin!"

He said the name out loud, a cross between a sigh and a prayer.

Chapter Seven

Joe managed the flight to Washington D.C. without a hand to hold. He coped by looking forward to what the trip held in store for him. The highlight would be seeing *Ariadne One* for real. He had watched extensive film footage of her construction and, more recently, had looked in via screen link on the crew becoming familiar with her layout and physical possibilities and limitations. He knew that, as head of British *BUSSTOP*, he had the right to be there in person for any, or all, of this. He preferred to stay out of the way. He was a great believer in the Expert Theory. Different groups and individuals were responsible for the design and building of the space ship. He couldn't do their work, any more than they could do his, so he didn't interfere. A handpicked crew would fly her to Mars. His job was to—.

What *was* his job, exactly?

In his cynical moments, Joe might say that he and Bruce Dougall were there as the smiling, recognisable faces. When *BUSSTOP* began to wind itself up for landing people on the surface of Mars, it needed public opinion on its side more than ever—if only to cushion the blow of the eye-watering amounts of money that continued to be poured into the project.

He thought back to when he had been appointed to his present position in *BUSSTOP*. On both sides of the Atlantic, the top jobs in the organisation became vacant within a month of each other. He and Bruce were taken from the relative obscurity of astronaut training and put in post. It was a universally popular move.

Joe smiled as he settled back in his seat on the plane. *BUSSTOP* and the two governments only had themselves to blame if they hadn't realised what they were taking on. Having done everything by the book when in space, he had allowed himself to be more of an individual when working in Britain's Space Training School. Bruce had been similarly refreshed in America. Keen young recruits came into practical sessions like tornadoes, firing theoretical regulations from the hip. Two men who had been there, seen it and done it said, very simply, "Now let's see what you really need to do, as opposed to what the manual says should be done."

Or words to that effect. As a result, trainees worshipped them.

They continued with their unintentional brand of sedition after promotion. Joe and Bruce developed a taste for administration. It was a soothing antidote to the loneliness of command. On the Ariadne flights, millions of miles away in space and out of reach as far as instantaneous communication was concerned, decisions and actions began and ended with the commander and his right hand man. Suddenly they both had whole organisations to talk to and an endless supply of staff, who did what needed doing. And they had met and worked with a lot of people in their time as members of their national Air Forces and as active astronauts. Neither man was afraid to call in favours and remind people of past loyalties when this could be useful. If the governments of Great Britain and the United States of America were expecting lionized figureheads to keep the media happy, they were in for a bit of a shock. The former astronauts didn't go looking for trouble, but both were ready to tell anyone what was what, be they a Prime Minister, a President or a King.

Whilst Joe held out stubbornly against the whole entourage circus, he was more than happy to take advantage of some of the benefits that being a member of a prestigious international concern brought. Roland drove him from home to the airport, where his credentials saw him whisked through the departure formalities. The same thing happened on arrival in America. Few people within that airport knew he was passing through and he was in a car and being driven into Washington and on to his hotel before most of them could gather their wits.

Joe couldn't help but think about Irene, not that she was ever completely out of his mind at the moment. She would love all this attention and he was confident that the grade of hotel *BUSSTOP* went in for would be the knock-out blow when she travelled with him.

His opinion of the academic world was sinking by the day, based on what he had observed as he became acquainted with her. It seemed to treat its leading players with scant regard.

Would she join him for the launch? He was banking on it.

Joe presented himself obediently at the front door of *BUSSTOP* in Washington the next morning. A respectful young man on the Reception desk told him to go right on up, as Mr Dougall was expecting him.

"Thank you, Laurence," said Joe, reading the name badge on his lapel.

As he trundled up to the top of the building in the lift, Joe didn't know what to expect from his meeting with Bruce. It was a while since they had been in the same room and, taken as a whole, the last few on-screen conversations with him had made for a bizarre mix of behaviour and attitude. He couldn't forget the evening when Bruce handed over Ariadne to Britain. It just didn't add up. Perhaps his father was right and Bruce was losing it.

This morning Bruce Dougall was bright-eyed and bushy tailed. He welcomed Joe cordially and offered the ultimate in early morning hospitality for his colleague—a pot of Kenyan tea. He didn't make any of his usual disparaging comments about the brew and accorded Joe the politeness of also having a cup of tea, instead of his usual coffee.

They were soon talking about *Ariadne One*, checking over the latest images sent through from Cape Canaveral. At one point, Bruce took something out of a drawer rather self-consciously.

"This arrived by express delivery late yesterday afternoon." He handed Joe a perfect scale model of the spaceship. "I've got one too. The boys and girls down at the Cape thought we needed these to put on our desks."

"So we do. Over these next weeks there will be such a ballyhoo going on that it will be easy to forget what everyone is trying to do."

Bruce put his model on the desk.

"I am now reminded," he said with a grin.

Somehow a whole morning went by, sharing the anticipation of the flight.

"I meant to ask earlier," Bruce said in a lull. "How are the messages from Mars going? It seems you and Professor Hanson created quite a stir in Britain."

"I think we did initially but it has now gone quiet, both on Mars and on Earth." Joe leaned back in his chair. "Everyone here on Earth is quiet because they're plain flummoxed. Send messages by all means! *SETI* listened in interminably for the likes of some such thing. But Random Error Code?"

"No chance of breaking the code, then?"

"A couple of specialists with nothing better to do are working on it, but without any context or starting point . . ." Joe's voice trailed away. "Perhaps," he continued, "the meaning is unimportant and the aim was just to catch our attention."

"It did that all right!" Bruce exclaimed. "Martians with a sense of humour! Now there's a thought! Anyway, the flight crew are up to speed on it all and are ready for any Take Me To Your Leader scenario when they reach Mars."

"How is Steven Bradbury doing with the crew and their training?" Joe wanted to know. "He can be a little . . . unforgiving."

"That's a neat way of putting it!" said Bruce appreciatively. "I don't think Gianfranco Rosso would use *quite* those words. I don't know what he does say," he sighed in response to Joe's querying look. "But it isn't complimentary. As you know, Gianfranco speaks perfect English. I've discovered that he lapses into Italian when he's swearing. He swears a lot about Bradbury and I don't know any Italian. But going back to the Martian messages, the public reaction has been quite positive here. Of course, there are always one or two lunatics." Bruce looked thoughtful for a moment. "I did offer to shoot one of them."

Joe turned very deliberately in his chair to make sure that he wasn't missing one bit of Bruce Dougall.

"You did *what*?"

Bruce told him about the meeting led by Pastor Philemon Brown. Joe didn't know which information was more astonishing—the personal attack on himself and Irene or what Bruce said that he would do in the aftermath.

"You threatened a Christian preacher?" he said slowly.

"Credit me with a little sense. I've had no contact with this Brown guy."

"You said you—So who did you speak to?"

"Oh, the President," he answered airily.

Joe gripped the arm of the chair, just to make sure that he was still in touch with reality. Bruce was not joking. And Joe knew how good a shot he was. Or what an unerring aim he used to have, and probably still did. On the Zeus flights they laughed about it, saying it was a pity that their spacecraft was not armed to the teeth in the style of *Star Trek* and *Star Wars*. If they had met any hostile aliens, Bruce would have been able to take out the threat single-handed.

"And what did President Harper have to say about it?" he wanted to know.

"She was a bit surprised," Bruce replied, in the understatement of the century. "But like the Martians, Philemon Brown has gone very quiet. It's standing room only out on the sidewalk at his meetings if you arrive less than thirty minutes before the start time, but I understand that he won't be drawn on the subject of Mars."

Joe said no more. He couldn't. Obviously someone had leaned on this character. But what if they hadn't? He had always known Bruce as a man of his word. He didn't make idle threats and no one said something like that to a head of state on a whim or in a fit of pique. That was laying life and limb on the line big time and it might yet cost Bruce his job. Governments were in the business of playing a long game. He might be eased out of *BUSSTOP* after the Mars landing.

Why would Bruce do such a thing? Well, he always did fancy himself as a bit of a knight in shining armour. Sally saw him as that, for sure, at a low point in her life. He must have considered Irene to be the latest damsel in distress—even though she knew nothing about what had been said, thank goodness, and he hadn't yet met her. This was Bruce deciding to saddle up and ride to the rescue in a honourable cause—the disgraceful treatment of a lady. There was no other explanation. He wouldn't have gone to this trouble for his former space comrade.

Joe was glad when Bruce suggested a lunch break. It was a welcome distraction. They walked down the street, oblivious to occasional stares and whispered comments. They were ushered to Bruce's favourite table in *Barty's*. The hum of dining room small talk and the scrape of silverware on plates were suspended as they took their seats. After a few seconds, normal activity was resumed.

One patron of the restaurant, bolder than the rest, asked if they minded having their picture taken. They didn't mind and they both signed a menu for him.

These were the smiling, recognisable faces of *BUSSTOP*. Two men who had been there, seen it and done it.

Joe was unable to rid himself of a feeling of unreality when they travelled down to Cape Canaveral the following day. He was shaken by Bruce's casual account of telling the President he was prepared to shoot someone. And there was stillness—an inner calm—about his colleague that was almost eerie. It was as though he didn't know Bruce at all. But then, had he ever known him, really?

There was no more time for such thoughts when they reached Mission Control. This was partly a media jamboree and partly a genuine fact finding journey by the *BUSSTOP* chiefs.

There were reunions within Mission Control. Men and women who had been reassuring voices at the other end of the communications system and the hawk-eyed monitors of data for the Zeus flights had grown older too. But whereas there was no room for fifty year-olds on a space ship, the youngsters from the ground team of the Zeus glory days were now the seasoned campaigners, and ready to write the next chapter with *Ariadne One*, working alongside a new generation of specialists. There was plenty of reminiscing on both sides, incomprehensible to these younger people, but where a word or a phrase was full of meaning for those who knew, who had experienced everything first hand in those awesome pioneering days.

It was more stilted to begin with when Joe Mortimer and Bruce Dougall entered the huge hangar and appeared on the flight deck of *Ariadne One* to see what the crew was doing, trailed by a large media contingent. They were not strangers. Between them, Joe and Bruce had had oversight of the initial training of all the Ariadne personnel, whatever their country of origin. Now that these new astronauts were about to follow in their footsteps and push their work to a logical conclusion, the seven felt as though two historical monuments had stepped down from their plinths and were offering the benefit of their wisdom and knowledge.

"How have the initial firings of the reactor been?" Joe wanted to know from Brian Hammond, the English commander of the flight. "The first one was a total nightmare in *Zeus One.*"

"They have been better than you experienced," Brian replied, painfully ill at ease because of the media presence.

Joe leaned forward, apparently looking at new equipment.

"Don't take any notice of the press, Brian," he murmured. "If you think that being an astronaut it a strange way of earning a living, look at them!"

The comment worked. Joe was pleased. He had a lot of time for this man. He had spotted Brian's potential from Day One in Training School. He had been quieter, more reserved, than his fellow trainees, physically smaller than the rest, and so therefore easily missed. But Joe had noted him. He had an eye for . . . Now what was the phrase that Bruce used? That was it. He picked up on the second banana, not going straight away for the obvious.

Of course, the girls all thought Brian was wonderful. That was inevitable, with the black hair and the blue eyes. His smile usually ran on meg-wattage, transforming his narrow, high cheek boned face.

"I understand you had problems back then with *Zeus One,*" Brian continued now. "One of the senior engineers was telling me that you came close to blowing up the whole place."

"With that guy saving the day, of course," put in Bruce, appearing unexpectedly from behind a computer bank. "Let me guess. It had to be Boris Tyler telling you such a story! There was a major imbalance. The nuclear boys blamed it on the americium-242m. They could get away with that simply because most people hadn't caught up with what it was at the time. The ground engineers worked round the clock for days to sort it out. That won't ever happen again. We all learned the hard way."

The ice was broken as all three men nodded in homage in the general direction of the nuclear reactor that powered *Ariadne One.* Brian Hammond was able to talk comfortably, one professional to another, as he outlined the numerous tests and results that he had overseen.

The concept of powering a spaceship with americium-242m, an isotope of an artificially produced element, in a nuclear reactor was hardly new technology even when Joe and Bruce were pioneering its application. Yigal Ronen, a professor of nuclear engineering at Ben-Gurion University of the Negev, in Israel, first suggested using this material at the very beginning of the twenty first century. Am-242m was produced by irradiating another isotope, Am-241, with neutrons. It was a process that was ruinously expensive to begin with, which is why the idea took a while to catch on.

Once its full potential was appreciated—reducing the length of a journey to Mars from months to weeks—the fledgling *BUSSTOP* organisation took up the idea, which Brent Dyer dangled before them, with all the zeal of a convert. Along with the creation of artificial gravity within a spaceship not requiring the centrifugal forces that threatened to make a crew ill, the planet named for the Roman god of war was suddenly tantalisingly within reach as the first Zeus craft took off.

The media had a field day, making an almost historical documentary type record of the people at the forefront of the latest scientific adventure. The participants managed to ignore the reporters and the camera operators for two quite different reasons. Joe and Bruce both guarded their privacy ferociously but, when they were out on show for public consumption, they had learned a long time ago to carry on as if no one was looking. Brian Hammond had been given a new perspective by Joe, and he and his team were so determined to soak up every drop of information from these two legends that they too were able to pretend that the prying lenses weren't there.

Some remarkable television film and stills for newspapers were recorded that day. Donning glasses for the first time in public, Joe gave the AD249 computer the once—over in the company of Brian and Simeon Turner. The computer brought together data from all over the spacecraft in a coherent form. A possible problem anywhere inside or outside the ship registered first on this array. It was an earlier version of this system, giving a false alarm, which led to Bruce undertaking that precautionary space walk inspection of *Zeus Three*.

The photograph that was published on just about every newspaper front page in the world was equally good. Most of the media frenzy had calmed down and the press pack was losing interest by the time this frame was taken. The innards of *Ariadne One* had been captured from every possible angle, as had the crew and distinguished visitors. One photographer, with more stamina than most, tracked the astronauts and veterans down to one of the payload bays. Everyone was sat on the floor. The Ariadne crew was listening with rapt attention as Joe and Bruce shared some of their experiences.

It could have been a kindergarten class, spell-bound by adults telling the most enthralling story ever.

Newspaper editors rarely had human-interest angle stories on Joe Mortimer and Bruce Dougall. The business with Philemon Brown had been left alone because of the slander potential of what he said. This time they were handed two gems on a plate. Joe putting on a pair of glasses would keep the women's pages (*Are spectacles the new fashion accessory?*) and medical commentators (*Why so many are turning against laser eye treatment?*) going for weeks. Bruce's appearance was the cause of some lively comment. Never as solidly built as Joe, he seemed almost frail beside his colleague. But the consensus of opinion was that he looked good. They both looked good. *FIFTY IS THE NEW . . . WHAT?* as one paper put it so memorably.

Joe marvelled again at the human capacity for nonsense and trivia and accepted that public interest, however it was generated, helped to shake the money tree funding all this. He had heard unsubstantiated rumours that Vice President Ted Rodriguez did not see eye to eye with President Harper on the seemingly limitless budget being nodded through Congress for the exploration of Mars.

Bruce continued to be glad that he had dumped overall responsibility for Ariadne on Britain, even if he had done it for all the wrong reasons. He was becoming very fragile, both mentally and physically, at the time. His anger back then puzzled him because he felt so different now. It was as though he was seeing things through new eyes. The news of the discovery of signals from Mars thrilled him but he harboured an unspecified doubt. His instincts, honed by years of thinking out beyond what computers and Mission Control told him, were prodding him to understand that something was not right. No. That was the wrong word. Something unexpected was over the horizon.

What he had said and done was beyond recall. However, there was something to be concerned about. Talking about all their yesterdays with the *BUSSTOP* old timers was fine but it stirred up some memories that were best left alone. And the medication that was giving him his life back for a while by putting a genetic brake on the cancer probably wasn't helping. Anecdotal evidence was showing some minor side effects in patients taking the drug, including disrupted sleep patterns and vivid, terrifying dreams.

Bruce's recurring dream was vivid all right but there was nothing nightmarish about it. As a result, back at home he was using the computer at half past one in the morning, going through old pictures. He decided that his dreams were nothing to do with a doctor's prescription and everything to do with yarning about times past.

After such a disturbance, Bruce went back to sleep remarkably quickly. The moon shone in through the bedroom window.

"Hello, Sally," he said out loud, back in his dream.

*   *   *

". . . and you have just stuffed the Lander into the surface of Mars," said a voice in Brian Hammond's earpiece. "You most likely made a new crater, which we could name after you. Broken bones for sure among the crew, broken hardware *and* the propulsion systems for leaving the planet damaged." Brian muttered at length under his breath. "And that is plain rude, Commander!"

"I'm so sorry. That wasn't meant for you, Jacintha." As ever, Jacintha melted as she listened to his quiet English tone. "We're tired and it's making us careless. We'll take a break, if you don't mind."

Brian and his landing team climbed out of the simulator and back into reality. Steven Bradbury, the Training Director, was about to say something and thought better of it. He was getting really irritated with the crew and he didn't know why. A calmer, more rational part of his mind was behaving like another person, tapping him on the shoulder and telling him that these folks were working their asses off. But he couldn't stop himself. He knew he was being a bad-tempered bully and he was biting back angry comments all the time. Yes, he was proud of his reputation as a hard taskmaster, but he wasn't proud of this.

Bradbury watched the Ariadne astronauts stomp away. The white-hot fury bubbling away just beneath the surface made him want to scream out loud, especially when he looked at Brian Hammond. The Brit was a cheerful man as a rule. Right now he reminded the Training Director of Eeyore, the morose donkey from *Winnie the Pooh*. This Eeyore was resigned to a bad day in the computer representation of space and the planet Mars. The whole team was rebellious. Simeon Turner was the only person wearing an expression that wasn't potentially murderous.

Ten minutes later Brian reappeared, clutching a cup of coffee as if his life depended on it. The Commander of *Ariadne One* was thankful that this was not a slot when the Orbiter astronauts were around as well. Emily Alexander was a sweetheart and kept Simeon in line. But Gianfranco . . . Unlike Bruce Dougall, Brian understood Italian. His mother was a modern languages teacher and, as a child, his school holidays had been spent in Italy, France and Spain. The anger that he had just fielded from the Lander group was more than enough. Gianfranco in flowing vituperative Italian would have been too much. He grimaced at the thought of what the engineer might have said.

Bradbury saw Brian's expression darken. Feeling a bit like a matador, he walked over to the astronaut.

"Are you okay?" he asked, more in hope than confidence.

"No, but that won't stop you sending us back in again and again until we get it right. And yes, I know that we will only have one chance to get it right on the way down to Mars but we've about had enough for one day. Don't be fooled by Simeon. He will soon begin to do dreadful things to you; he'll write a letter of resignation and he'll go to the media. I'm just not sure in which order."

"Where are the rest of your team?" the Director asked, suddenly aware that he had an audience of one instead of five.

"I've stood them down for the rest of the day," Brian told him with deceptive calmness. "And I'm going home myself." Not for the first time he was glad that his wife and children had decided to come out to America with him. "We will be in good and early tomorrow morning. And then, we'll get it right so many times that you will be sick of perfection."

Steven Bradbury watched, stupefied, as Brian Hammond walked away. The sweat glistened on his face and bald head, despite the air conditioning. He looked around him and then hurried to his office, shutting and securing the door. He was shocked to find himself struggling for breath. He was a bull of a man, the epitome of physical fitness. When he pushed a team in training, he was proud of the fact that he never asked anyone to do anything he wouldn't do himself.

He drank some chilled water and then coughed until he thought he would vomit. As long moments passed and he began to feel better, he didn't fancy telling anyone that the landing team had just walked off site.

*   *   *

Joe knew that this was where he was really earning his money. He'd been hard at work in the London office since early morning. It was now nearly seven o'clock and he could actually start thinking about going home. Vicky was beavering away next door. Of course, she was clocking up plenty of overtime pay but he couldn't think of many young women who would give up summer evenings so willingly.

He yawned and stretched. Definitely home time.

His hand was half way to starting the procedure for shutting down and locking the communications system when Vicky appeared on screen.

"Mr Mortimer, I've got Steven Bradbury, Training Director of Ariadne, wanting to talk to you. I haven't said whether you are here or not. I told him I'd have to check. He looks like he's in a bit of a state. So much so that I think he's forgotten the time difference."

"I'd better talk to him," Joe said uneasily.

He was concerned as to what was happening that warranted the Director himself coming on line.

"Steven!" he said with a forced cheerfulness. "You timed it perfectly. I'm just about to go home. It's seven o'clock in the evening here," he reminded him when Steven looked confused.

"Yes," he said, not really taking in the information. "We've got a bit of a problem at this end."

"I've worked that out. I can tell from the look of you that this isn't a social call. Do tell, or have I got to try and guess?"

The Director's plump face registered real pain as he recounted the events leading up to the landing team doing a disappearing act. His whole body seemed suddenly thinner, corseted by terrible tension.

"I see." Joe knew that he must stop saying that. He was beginning to sound like Kevin Crane. He didn't know of any other way to cover his confusion. "But they'll all be back tomorrow?"

"Yes."

"Send me through the film of the training session and I'll talk to the team if I can get hold of them. Incidentally, why didn't you contact Bruce Dougall? He's more on the spot that I am."

"You're in charge," Steven reminded him bleakly.

"So I am." Joe wondered if this was turning into a poisoned chalice. "Bruce needs to know. I'll tell him. You go home and—well, tomorrow is another day."

Joe went through into Vicky's office.

"Go home, Vicky. This is way beyond the call of duty. Set up Redirect for anything that comes through. I'm going home too."

"Anything, Mr Mortimer? There could be a lot of routine stuff from America."

"I can't risk not hearing from someone. We have some unhappy people down at the Cape and I'd rather listen to them at home tonight than try and pick up the pieces tomorrow morning."

Vicky could see that her boss was exhausted. His smile didn't reach his tired eyes. He had returned from America and plunged straight back into the thick of things. And were those the first flecks of grey that she could see in his brown hair? This job wasn't the cushy number that some ignorant people made it out to be.

*   *   *

Man and dog sighed in unison.

"I make that three down, two to go, Bonny."

Sat beside Joe, Bonny's tail whisked across the floor in a hyper-wag that seemed to involve the whole of her body.

"I'm glad that one of us is keen. Now for Simeon Turner and Brian Hammond."

Joe didn't mind trying to sort out the situation. He wasn't one to shirk responsibility and this came with the territory of being the lead for the Ariadne project. All credit to Bruce; he had offered to deal with some of the stray lambs himself.

"It's better that the shit comes from one person," Joe said to his colleague. "And you did hand over the bit about being the overall boss to me, if you remember."

"Oh yeah, I did," said Bruce in wonderment, as if someone else had taken that drastic step.

As Bonny pressed herself against him, hearing the thunderstorm rolling in the distance, Joe did a weary recall of some of the problems that *BUSSTOP* and its predecessor *NASA* had dealt with over the years as probes and manned spacecraft were launched. They were all difficulties to do with machinery and computer software. In the early days of 2003, the *Columbia* space shuttle flew with computing capability that hadn't altered much since the days of the Apollo missions. Hence the craft re-entered Earth's atmosphere with no one knowing that the left wing was disintegrating. The crew was lost as the spaceship broke up. Bruce had reminded him of the magnitude of the near miss they had with the reactor on *Zeus One*. The americium-242m based propulsion system was newly out of Research and Design and freshly into manufacture. They dodged a bullet there. But *never* had the stumbling block been a crew walking out.

He watched the film of the training session and realised where the problem lay. That didn't make it any easier.

Joe tried to look affable when Simeon Turner called.

"Please don't tell me I can't tear Bradbury into little pieces and spread him all over space as we fly to Mars," Simeon launched in with no preamble. "I may well cry."

Joe was saddened to see Simeon angry like this. He was a truly placid soul, despite what Bruce might say. Simeon knew his family history and was quietly proud of his African slave origins.

"Tobacco plantation to the stars isn't bad, is it?" he had said to Joe during the visit.

Tonight his eyes flashed warning signals. He was of average build and height but he filled the screen like a thunderous exclamation mark. His flared nostrils reminded Joe of illustrations of mediaeval warhorses, who were trained to fight just as viciously as the knights they carried into battle. If Simeon did something about this incident, it would be calculated and devastating.

Joe counted to ten very slowly and said all that he had rehearsed.

"Hmm. You will speak to that . . ." Simeon stopped himself. "You will speak to the Training Director," he continued correctly.

"I will. I didn't find a magic wand when I was out in space, but I promise you that I will do my very best. Forget about Ariadne for the rest of today. Take that lovely girl friend of yours out to dinner. How did Emily react?"

"Emily is just fine, Mr Mortimer. She was mad at first when she found out why I was home so early. The support crew weren't in today, so she didn't know what had happened." Emily Alexander was one half of the chorus line of *Ariadne One*, who would keep the main ship orbiting Mars whilst the Lander went down to the planet's surface. "She understands. Bradbury has yelled at her a good few times." His frown deepened. "It's not how you should treat a lady."

Joe knew that Steven Bradbury's attitude was uncompromising. If women wanted true equality, they had to take the rough with the smooth.

"I'll talk to you really soon, Simeon."

Keen on making it to bed the right side of midnight, Joe contacted Brian Hammond and was speaking with another uncharacteristically cross astronaut.

"Kiss your wife, hug your children and enjoy the evening," he suggested when Brian finally ran out of steam. "Everybody gets things wrong and putting the Lander down on Mars is the ultimate game of patting your head and rubbing your tummy. Oh, and probably spinning plates with your feet at the same time. I understand what a challenge you are up against but you will only get one shot at this. You won't be able to fly yourself out of trouble like Apollo Eleven did prior to touching down on the Moon. The Moon has no atmosphere or weather. We don't have that luxury on Mars. Both are big problems when it comes to touching down in one piece."

"You're sounding just like Steven Bradbury," Brian said suspiciously.

"No. I'm reminding you of the basics, that's all. I will sort this. Enjoy your evening."

Joe took the dog for a quick walk and then it was back to soothing the choppy waters again.

"Steven, you're pushing," he told the Training Director when he finally tracked him down. He was concerned at the image he saw on screen. Bradbury gave the impression of a pot slowly coming to the boil. "You're pushing too hard. There is plenty of time for the landing team to get sorted. The crew as a whole can fly the likes of *Ariadne One* in their sleep. They will get the landing craft right. I've watched and listened to today's session. Give them a bit of encouragement."

"Encouragement!" Bradbury spat back. "They need threats, not encouragement! Their actions today put them in the realms of incompetence and gross negligence!"

Joe was taken aback by this display of vitriol.

"Hey, Steve! Take it easy! I'm not criticising you, just offering some suggestions."

He was trying in vain to calm the outraged figure on the screen.

"It's all right for you!" said Bradbury, cornered and aggressive. "Your flying days are over and you didn't make mistakes."

He sounded bitter and was still taut with unexpressed anger.

"Don't put me on a pedestal, Steven. I'll only collect cobwebs and need dusting." He watched as his attempt at humour appeared to help Bradbury relax a little. "I've made as many mistakes as the next person. Not at crucial moments I admit, or I wouldn't be sitting here talking to you tonight. I'll be honest with you. I'm glad that the Zeus remit didn't go as far as landing on Mars. I would have done it but I'm happy that it is Brian Hammond and his team rather than me and my team. I'll check in with you tomorrow. If necessary, I'll come back out to the Cape. But get that group of men and women feeling as though they are achieving something in double quick time or we will have problems forever. Understood? If this goes wrong, it's not only Ariadne that is wasted. Bruce, myself and the others might as well have stayed at home and not bothered with Zeus."

He bade Steven a curt goodnight and turned off the screen with an air of finality. That was it for the evening.

Joe couldn't help wondering at the perceptions of others. *You didn't make mistakes.* Flattering but wildly inaccurate, of course. It was a matter of public record that the Training Director of the day wanted to sack Bruce Dougall and himself part way through the preparatory work for *Zeus One*, claiming they were totally unsuited to working in space. And Bruce was in the legends of the USAF for most of the usual—and not so usual—reasons. The first time he flew a training flight as a youngster, the instructor accompanying him was seen afterwards tottering across the tarmac. Fortified by several measures of bourbon, he wrote a blistering memo to his Commanding Officer, stating that Dougall would be useless as a pilot.

"We live and we learn, Wing Commander," one of Joe's schoolteachers said to his father when Joe himself had brought home a series of poor report cards. "We all get there in the end."

"I hope he bloody well gets there soon!" was Neil Mortimer's response.

Everybody made mistakes. Joe knew that Brian Hammond and his crew would get there. He was less certain about Steven Bradbury getting it right.

*   *   *

Bruce had spoken to Joe again and insisted that he took some part in dealing with this unprecedented behaviour in the ranks. He looked at each one of them in turn. They were hardly the stuff of which rebellions are made. Brian Hammond. Masahide Shimamoto. Illya Abelev. Jethro

Norman. Simeon Turner. And yet, each one of them looked right back at him, quite happy to stare him down if necessary via the screen. They were convinced of the justness of their cause. Jethro was particularly belligerent. He was almost a physical caricature of the all-American hero, a chunky and chiselled blonde, with a smile to make a dentist weep with pleasure. Usually his eyes were liquid chocolate. Today they held the slow but deadly burn of lava.

Whatever else they might be, these men were not ashamed of what they had done.

Bruce had thought long and hard about whether he should go back down to Cape Canaveral or deal with this on screen. After all, he and Joe had only recently visited the Ariadne teams before the eyes of the world. He knew enough about the way the media worked to understand that, after a prolonged love-in between the space programme and press and television, someone might think that it was the right time to have a little judiciously applied negativity—just to make sure that the viewing and reading public didn't nod off and lose interest.

And no one with the remotest connection to the Mars adventures could ever lift a finger without being aware of the popular perception of "The curse of Mars." If the doctors were right and his *Zeus Three* space walk was the ultimate culprit behind his cancer . . .

The five were beginning to fidget as the seconds ticked by. No one was sure what game Bruce Dougall was playing but it was making them nervous. Little did they know that he was racking his brains to find the right thing to say. He decided on total honesty.

"Steven Bradbury has gone on sick leave," he informed them.

"What a surprise!" exclaimed Jethro.

Bruce turned towards his protégé, about to really lose his temper, then realised that his anger was probably being fuelled by thoughts of Philemon Brown. One Biblically named character was quite enough to handle. He doubted that Norman or his parents even knew what the Bible was. He once asked Jethro where his family had acquired such an exotic handle for him.

"I think Ma was watching some Archive television series the summer she was waiting for me to be born," was his laconic answer. "She liked the sound of the name of one of the characters."

Now *that* was much more like it.

"Steven is sick, for real," Bruce continued and the gang of five had the grace to look abashed. "He went to see his doctor with chest pains and he is in hospital awaiting major heart surgery as soon as he is judged to be strong enough. He is in a bad way. It's a wonder he didn't collapse when he was working with you."

"I suppose that explains the way he has been rampaging about," put in Brian. "It was becoming a nightmare, Mr Dougall. I wish he'd said something."

"Don't we all," went on Bruce. "He's been struggling like this for some time and doing nothing about it. Which leaves us with a problem. Who will take over as Training Director? Can I trust you lot not to drive someone else into the ground? Will you stamp your feet again and have temper tantrums? What do I need to do for you guys? Would you like Joe Mortimer and me to train you through the landing simulations up to launch day perhaps?"

Bruce was making a sarcastic comment but he was shocked to see five faces spark up like a row of lights going green on a control panel. They thought he was being serious. And more to the point, they thought it was a good idea. He was trying to be funny. What was that saying about true words spoken in jest?

Bradbury had undermined them more than he realised.

"And they responded to that?" Joe asked later. He puffed out his cheeks. "They thought you meant it?"

"You should have seen them," Bruce confirmed. "The five of them looked like drowning men who have been thrown a life raft. But it does bring into focus something that we must do anyway—or make sure that it is done for our respected leaders. We must do a Nixon. There is every possibility they could make a hole in the surface of Mars for real."

"In every mission there is always the possibility of problems and accidents. We know that, but . . . no!"

Bruce could feel Joe's anguish as if he was in the same room.

"Joe, this is accepted, standard practice in media and politics already," he said quietly. "You can't tell me that the Presidents and Prime Ministers of our day didn't have statements at the ready for if we had been killed out in space. You have a British citizen in charge of the Lander. You have more citizens in the reserve crew if we get that far down the line. And we have citizens of Italy, Russia and Japan on board too. Your Prime Minister and your King must be prepared. I don't know the niceties of who would do what."

"The statement would come from the Prime Minister and the King would offer public and private condolences," said Joe dully. "Bruce, you are sitting there casually talking about what will happen if five people die putting the Lander down on Mars and leave two more stranded in the Orbiter."

"It's an ever-present possibility." Bruce's gaze was unwavering. "The trouble the team are having with the Lander set-up has just made me think about it sooner. That's all. Shall I copy you the text of President Nixon's speech? Historically, this was the benchmark that has been adapted over the years. I've sent it to appropriate people in the White House, even though the original will be in the archives there. It will give your officials something to work from."

"I suppose you must. What's happening with the training?"

"Deanna Sorbin has taken over. Sex appeal will give her about ten days of grace, by which time she will have asserted her authority. She knows what she's talking about."

We must do a Nixon.

After his first nerve-filled flight to the Moon, Joe never gave another thought to the inherent dangers of his work in space. The day an astronaut started thinking like that was the day to quit. But sitting safe and sound on Earth and sending others into space was quite another matter. Bruce was right. It was their job to worry about all possibilities—even the unpalatable ones.

When *Apollo 11* took off in July 1969, with the mission to put men on the Moon for the first time, there was a fifty-fifty chance that *NASA* might not be able to get them back to Earth. Presidential speechwriter William Safire wrote a memo to the White House Chief of Staff with a suggestion as to what President Nixon should do and say in the event of astronauts Neil Armstrong and Buzz Aldrin being stranded on the Moon.

Joe put on his glasses and from the screen read the text that was never needed by a President who was able to reap the glory of the astronauts when they returned.

> *Fate has ordained that the men who went to the Moon to explore in peace will stay on the Moon to rest in peace.*
>
> *These brave men, Neil Armstrong and Edwin Aldrin, know that there is no hope for their recovery. But they also know that there is hope for mankind in their sacrifice.*
>
> *These two men are laying down their lives in mankind's most noble goal: the search for truth and understanding.*
>
> *They will be mourned by their families and friends; they will be mourned by the nation; the people of the world will mourn them; they will be mourned by a Mother Earth that dared to send two of her sons into the unknown.*

Joe saved the document without reading any more. He couldn't.

In such an event, Prime Minister Kevin Crane and His Majesty King Richard the Fourth could be relied upon to play their parts to perfection.

Joseph Joshua Mortimer! he berated himself. This will *not* happen on your watch.

Chapter Eight

The calm acceptance and understanding were worse than any reproach or anger.

"It's all right, Joe," said his mother. "It sounds as though you have some problems to deal with. I'm so sorry for you and the team. I wish we could do something to help. Still, you'll have Bruce Dougall to assist you. I know you two aren't the greatest of buddies but he's a very able man. You've said so yourself. You'll sort this out, I know."

Joe put his head in his hands. With a glance at Neil, Stella moved over to where their son was sitting. She perched on the arm of the chair.

"Have I said something wrong?"

Joe looked up.

"No, Mum. Here I am screwing up the family plans and you're offering *me* sympathy."

"Why not?" she wondered. "These difficulties aren't of your making. You're not doing this to annoy us. You can celebrate our birthdays with us at any time."

"I know. But your eightieth birthdays are a bit special."

"We're not on a timetable," put in Neil. "*Ariadne One* is. I think what your mother is hinting at is that the two of you will be able to knock everyone and everything into shape quickly and then you can join us for part of the holiday."

The plans had been made for some time. Neil and Stella Mortimer's birthdays fell within five days of each other during the summer. As Neil once said, holding joint parties had saved them a fortune over the years in celebrating landmark ages. This time they were opting for a quiet family get together, staying in a large holiday house in the coastal resort of Minehead, on the Somerset-Devon border. This was the town that Stella called home as a child. A distant cousin was letting the sea front dwelling to them at a very favourable rate. The idea was that she and Neil, Philip and Daphne, Sam and Natasha and Joe plus dog would gather there for a few weeks.

Joe's father had painted the idyll for Joe in simple terms.

"You know what the air is like down there. All everyone wants to do is eat and sleep." Joe agreed. Being by the sea there was the most powerful relaxant he knew. "Natasha could do with some of that and so could you. I've checked the tides for the time we're there. You'll be able to take Bonny along the beach at sparrow-fart each morning *and* get some rest! I don't lecture like your mother does but you look knackered. No one will give you a medal for making yourself ill."

Now this prospect had been taken from his grasp.

Well, no it hadn't, not really.

Joe reminded himself that he had not been forced into this. He had taken the decision to go back to Cape Canaveral himself, as had Bruce. Both men blamed themselves for not taking more notice of the signs of difficulties between the Ariadne crew and Steven Bradbury. They had not foreseen in their wildest imaginings that the situation would explode as it did. So they felt that they must do something about it all. It wasn't just a case of making sure that the Lander crew was technically perfect. Those astronauts needed some urgent morale building.

Neil made the most pertinent observation after Joe had gone home.

"You have to hand it to Joe," he said to Stella. "And to Bruce Dougall," he added grudgingly. "They will deal with whatever is going on with the astronauts. If they can't help, nobody can! But the point is that they think *they* should do it.

"You mean that there are lots of other folks who could sort out the problems."

"Exactly!" Neil drained his mug of tea emphatically. "Joe and Mr Dougall have only to say the word and there would be an army of experts lining up to get the Ariadne team through their present difficulties."

"Joe believes in the personal touch in the most hierarchical of settings." Stella looked at her husband fondly. "And he gets that belief from you."

"Is that a good or a bad thing?" he wondered anxiously. "The RAF is not the same as *BUSSTOP*."

"It's always good, Neil, even if it means some hard work in the short term. And I'm sure that what Joe has done in the past encourages people to go to him when they might turn elsewhere." Stella poured them both some more tea. "If you think for a moment, he has said to us on several occasions that individuals or groups approach him with variations on the same opening line. *You've been out there. You know what it's like and you know what we mean.* I imagine that Bruce Dougall hears the same kind of song in America. Both men do know what's what when it comes to spaceships and flying in them."

"True." Neil's sigh disturbed the surface of his tea. "Being hands-on is good. But handling stuff that could be done by others . . . Joe's on a slippery slope here. He doesn't need to make things worse by putting a set of wheels under his arse. The Zeus crews were hailed as Supermen and Superwomen at the time. I hope that our lad hasn't taken to believing that in his middle age."

Joe had never fallen into the trap of believing his own publicity. But perhaps, if he and Bruce really could be miracle workers just for once, he would be able to get to Minehead a few days late. Just thinking about the place, he could feel the stones and patches of sand on the beach under his feet, taste the tangy salt air, hear the lazy slap of halyards against masts as small boats rode at anchor in the harbour, whilst seagulls bobbed up and down on the waves or hung, motionless, in the sky.

That was his goal.

He was also annoyed because his decision meant that he couldn't catch up with Irene. He spoke to her on screen and apologised for the fact that he had to return to America on *BUSSTOP* business. He didn't specify why.

"Goodness! You are leading a busy life at the moment," she said. "Actually, I'm to be whisked off soon for a while, for enjoyment, not duty like you. Some dear friends, Debbie and Alisdair, have insisted that I join them and their grown-up daughters for a long holiday in Scotland. The girls are my godchildren and I have been neglecting them. They're going to Ballater, which is near Balmoral. Alisdair is a saint, willing to put up with yet another woman in his leisure time."

"If you see Richard around, give him my best wishes."

"What? Oh, of course!"

Irene could hardly forget the conversation Joe had with the King on the day they both provoked a riot, a conversation in which she had a small part.

"I will be in touch with you when I get back from everywhere, Irene. I've already got one far-from-tacky souvenir for you." He had wheedled another model of *Ariadne One* out of the person who made them. "I'll have to find you a second one, won't I?"

"I'll buy you a haggis!" she laughed. "And I won't tell Alisdair about the face you just pulled."

Spending some time with Irene and sharing traveller's tales was another very important goal.

*　　*　　*

"We'll have to stop meeting like this. I've got better things to be doing," Joe said honestly when he and Bruce joined forces at Cape Canaveral.

"So have I."

Bruce's tone was wistful. This was the year he had decided to take up the open invitation to join his disgracefully wealthy friend, Bob Broomfield. The prospect of total indolence in a beautiful house at Martha's Vineyard was a powerful one.

Two people could feel precious time slipping through their fingers and they wanted to be in a place of their choosing very badly. Their dealings with the whole Ariadne crew would be brisk and to the point.

Deanna Sorbin was doing a great job with the flight team but she sensed that there was still a way to go. A veteran of many journeys to the Moon, she knew all about putting a landing vehicle down on that surface with no atmosphere and no weather to contend with. Like everyone else, she was entering new territory when it came to landing on Mars.

She was learning with the astronauts as they worked on the computer simulations. Joe had gone over the facts and the new technology until he could recite it all like verses from a poetry book. He suspected that Bruce was in much the same position. The atmosphere of Mars is only one per cent as dense as Earth's. Any object returning to Earth is slowed down naturally by flying through the planet's thick atmosphere. Without an array of systems to steady it, a heavy landing vehicle would drop to Mars like a stone.

For those final few seconds before touch down on Mars, a Hypercone had been developed for the Lander craft. It was effectively a giant doughnut-shaped airbag, which girdled the vehicle, inflating almost instantaneously with gas rockets. This would act as an aerodynamic anchor to slow the vehicle. Ordinary parachutes, such as had been used since the *Apollo* days, could then be deployed. There would only be a few seconds of use for these. The parachutes then had to be jettisoned and thrusters used to bring the Lander to a controlled halt on the surface of Mars.

Even with computer aid, it was a matter of split-second human reaction, from both the landing crew and the team remaining in orbit aboard the mother ship.

That split-second human reaction was not there yet, as Joe and Bruce saw on the first simulation run that they observed. Naturally jittery at having such informed eyes watching them, the orbiting and landing crews managed to smash the Lander into the surface of the planet.

"Ouch! That would have to hurt in reality!" Bruce shuddered. "I don't think there would even be any pieces left for the Martians to pick up."

"We're not helping, sitting here taking notes," said Joe. "We'll have to fly Lander ourselves in the simulator. Apart from anything else, we can't make any helpful comments until we know what it feels like to land that bird. Are you ready to make a fool of yourself?"

"The things I do for the cause!" marvelled Bruce.

Before an open-mouthed set of astronauts and a clutch of technical staff, the two heroes of yesteryear took over from Brian Hammond and Jethro Norman in the simulator to bring the Lander down. Pride dictated that they would not try to make the team feel better by putting in any deliberate errors.

The voices of Emily Alexander and Gianfranco Rosso echoed in the exact reconstruction of the flight deck, mingling with the statements of two people who were once more feeling the exhilaration of being there. The concentration in the silences between messages was ferocious.

"You are free of the mother ship."

BUSSTOP jungle drums brought more spectators to stand and watch.

"Hypercone deployed."

"Inflated."

Deanna had to remind herself to breathe.

"You are now in subsonic speed."

"Ready with the parachutes."

"Confirmed."

"Hit those chutes!"

"Deployed."

"Jesus! They're going to do it!" someone whispered.

"Chutes away."

"Thrusters on."

No one dared move a muscle.

"Oh, bugger!" exclaimed Joe, spoiling a perfect science fiction script as the Lander crunched to a halt a little too firmly in a cloud of computer-generated dust and the screens displayed the possible damage that could have been caused.

Everyone cheered and clapped. Deanna was already deciding to use the footage of this for training future astronauts, as long as the stars of the show didn't mind.

Despite some natural annoyance with his own shortcomings, Joe was secretly pleased to discover from an initial look at the computer read outs that he and Bruce had made the best landing yet. They still made a good team.

"It's the business of getting those chutes out just right," he decided, looking at the fractions of seconds that divided the almost successful from success. "It made us just short of time on the thrusters. We'll crack it."

Brian and Jethro went into a huddle over the data, along with Deanna. She may have had the model-girl figure and the blonde looks, but right now all that anyone was concerned with was getting this right. The rest of the crew took a golden opportunity to raise a whole host of minor queries with their heroes.

Joe could feel the prevailing atmosphere changing from leaden-footed worry to get-up-and-go enthusiasm. He was glad that he had made the trip.

"Let's see." Bruce considered options, seated at the main computer with Masahide Shimamoto. "We could try . . . No. Let's go for this," he said, amending some details on the program.

"Thank you, Mr Dougall!" Masahide grasped his hand. Bruce had never known him to be so animated. "You and Mr Mortimer are our saviours."

"Let's wait until you can all put this puppy dog down quietly instead of whacking Mars, but you're welcome."

Bruce was glad that he had made the trip.

The rest of the day was spent in mind-numbing analysis and rehearsing sections of the manoeuvre, which would make all the difference in the next full practice and, most importantly, in the real landing.

BUSSTOP had booked its two chiefs into the same hotel. It would have been unnecessary bad manners to ignore each other so Joe and Bruce continued to be in each other's company over dinner.

"So where would you rather be?" Joe wanted to know.

"Martha's Vineyard. Bob Broomfield and his wife have been inviting me for years. I'm supposed to be there now."

"Ah yes. The mighty Mr B! Multi-millionaire at thirty! You do have some interesting friends." He knew that Bruce had gone through school days with Bob. "The crew seems to be getting their act together so perhaps we can go home soon. You can have a shortened break in paradise and promise yourself a longer stay there next year."

"Perhaps," Bruce said carefully and turned the question back to Joe so that he didn't have to talk about the future. "Where are you supposed to be?"

"A family celebration."

They were united in mutual frustration, which was eased considerably the next day. Confidence gives wings of inspiration and new, shiny competence and the Lander and orbiting crew worked as one to make a safe landing in computer simulation. Just to prove that the age of wonders was not over yet, the Lander crew executed a perfect take-off away from the surface of Mars for good measure and joined the main ship without a hiccup.

There was instant bedlam, with people running in all directions. Gianfranco Rosso grabbed Bruce before he could duck and kissed him soundly on both cheeks. Illya Abelev waltzed Deanna across the room and she then kissed Joe. Some people had all the luck. Emily Alexander almost jumped into Simeon's arms. Brian and Jethro were immobile, staring at their instrument panels as if they couldn't believe what they had just done.

When some measure of order was restored, Joe could be the firm but fair teacher.

"Well done! That was spot-on. You need to mark those readings and measurements and know them better than you know your own names. We want this landing routine to be as instinctive as breathing. Then we will leave you alone until launch day, in the capable hands of Deanna."

"And launch day can't come soon enough," Bruce said that evening. "This may sound heretical, but I'm getting tired of *Ariadne One*."

"That's because we're not flying her," was the judicious reply from Joe. "We'll all be keen enough when the moment arrives. But one thing is bothering me. It's great that the crew have got the landing and take off sorted. All credit to them. I knew they could do it. It's the bit in between that's sort of up for grabs."

"Everyone has a pile of equipment to set up on Mars and there are tests and observations to . . . Ah, you mean the possible company they'll be keeping."

"Something like that."

"There's nothing we can do about that, Joe. The landing crew are going to Mars knowing as much as anyone else about who or what is waiting for them. I want another medal for this."

"Don't bother yourself about it. It would only need polishing."

"How much longer do you think we need to stay? Bob and Belle keep sending me messages, informing me of what a great time they're having. I don't think that they are natural sadists but I am beginning to wonder."

"Tell me about it," Joe said ruefully. "I'm getting similar stuff from my family. I want to make sure that Brian can land that machine in his sleep and the orbiting crew could do with some sharpening up on a few bits and pieces. If they make a mess of any of their tasks, we might as well all go home. Can we sort them out between us? Let's set ourselves the target of three days."

"Three days of Masahide and Gianfranco?" Bruce wondered. "Gianfranco needs tying to his seat and Masahide needs a kick up the ass. He's way too laid back for my liking. But let's see if we can get these people feeling proud of themselves. Bradbury did a real demolition job on them. I know he was sick, but he tore the group apart and then put them through a meat grinder for a big finish."

Joe was a fair prophet. Four days later he and Bruce were heading home and on to some well-deserved, if interrupted, holiday.

*   *   *

"Why didn't you tell me sooner?"

Joe realised that he was speaking out loud as he surfaced from a dream. He could see clearly the room in which he was sleeping. It was a page from one of those country living magazines come to life, all muted earthy colours and artless design. The pearl light of dawn was flooding through the small window but he didn't know where he was. Still in the States? At home? Where?

The haunting, manic call of seagulls and the distant rush of waves gave him his answer. The wind must be strong this morning. The yacht halyards were drumming out a staccato beat on both wooden and metal masts.

It was strange how shifting time zones in a commercial airliner always had the power to disorientate him, whereas flying through space, with no obvious points of reference, had caused little or no trouble.

Joe rolled out of bed and went to the window. His dream was evaporating as quickly as sea fret. The only thing he could be sure of was that he had put the question to Bruce, when he was astounded by some information his colleague gave him. What that information was and why Bruce Dougall was even in his dreams were mysteries that he wasn't going to worry about too much.

Joe dressed quickly and tiptoed downstairs. Joining the conspiracy of silence, Bonny didn't bark a greeting. She wagged her tail with minimal effort and said good morning to her master by planting her front paws on his chest.

The wind was powerful. It tugged at hair, fur and clothing. It was exhilarating as man and dog came out of the lee of the harbour side hotel and met the full force of the breezes. Far out to sea, white horses danced across the tips of the waves. If seagulls could be said to be disconcerted, five of them were that for sure, as they found themselves being driven backwards. This was no time to be riding the air currents.

Joe looked out across the Bristol Channel automatically. Reassuringly, the coast of South Wales was shrouded in mist. From visiting this part of England since he was a child, he knew that was the promise of a fine day ahead.

Bonny streaked up and down the water's edge, her barks carried away out to sea. Locals greeted Joe as a fellow dog-walker. The anonymity was as refreshing as the unruly wind.

*   *   *

Irene sighed in contentment. Her head was full of images of the holiday so far. There was Ballater itself, with all the *By Royal Appointment* signs over the shops and businesses. The brooding hills and mountains framed an achingly blue sky, which made a fabulous backdrop to it all. And the air was as intoxicating as the local whisky. Today they had ambled along the banks of the River Dee. Cambey O'May was desperately beautiful.

She lay back in her chair and wriggled her toes, enjoying the warmth of the log fire. The days were glorious but summer evenings in the Highlands can be chilly.

"One happy person," observed Alisdair MacIver from the depths of a similar armchair. "The toes always give it away."

"What?" said Irene, looking at her feet with some alarm.

"Just a doctor's observation. Most of my patients are distressed and frightened when I first see them. After all, they've usually just been brought in to hospital after an accident or a sudden collapse. However stout and brave they might be, I can always tell if what we're doing is hurting them more. A person may be able to control everything else, but the curling of the toes when in pain or under stress is a reflex action. Your bonny feet are well relaxed."

"What are Irene's feet doing?" asked Debbie, bringing in after dinner coffee.

"Telling Alisdair of my good state of mind, apparently," Irene informed her.

"Quite right, too. The girls have gone down into Ballater to see Francine and Moira. So we can be as boring and middle-aged as we like."

"Speak for yourself!" Alisdair retorted. "But I will be very boring if you don't mind and catch up with some television news. It's wonderful being isolated up here in God's own country but it is good to check from time to time to see if the world is still going round."

Irene was out of the room when Debbie called her.

"Irene! Your hunk is on!"

Irene hurried back in, despite herself.

"The date of the flight to Mars has been announced," Alisdair said, "so we are being given a potted history of the Ariadne project."

Film of the recent public visit to *Ariadne One* by Joe Mortimer and Bruce Dougall was on screen.

"Oh dear!" exclaimed Debbie, who hadn't seen the film when it was originally shown

"The poor wee man!" Alisdair said quietly, who hadn't taken much notice first time round.

Irene stared harder at the screen, flummoxed. All she saw was the film footage, which she had viewed previously, showing the *BUSSTOP* bosses giving the hardware, the software and the crew the once-over.

"What was wrong with that?" she wanted to know when the next story came on.

"Yon American man—the American *BUSSTOP* big noise," Alisdair began.

"Bruce Dougall," Irene reminded him.

"That's him. He is one truly poorly person, that's for sure."

"Are you sure?" asked Irene. "Joe hasn't said anything about him being unwell."

"Ah!" Debbie leapt in, triumphant. "You talk this about this kind of stuff with the great man. I told you," she said knowingly to her husband.

Ever a kindly person, Alisdair could see Irene turning pink with embarrassment. He suggested that they watched that section of the article again. This time Irene tore her eyes away from Joe and watched Bruce Dougall. Certainly he appeared to be thinner than she remembered him from photographs and his appearances on the news. But that was nothing. Lots of men at fifty panicked suddenly about growing old and fat and became health and diet fanatics overnight—not that she imagined Bruce had let his physical fitness go when his space days were over, any more than Joe had done.

"Look! There!" said Alisdair, sitting forward in his chair. "He thinks no one is looking and he doesn't know the camera is still on him. That is one tired and drained man. He's fighting something and he has nearly had enough. And it's not a bad cold."

"What do you think is wrong?" Irene wondered.

"It could be anything." Alisdair's tone was vague but he had a good idea. "Irene, I'm surprised that your boy wasn't announcing the date of *Ariadne One* personally."

"He's not my boy and he's on holiday," Irene told them.

"Ah!" Debbie repeated. "Privy to personal arrangements, eh?"

"Give it a rest, Debs," Alisdair suggested, seeing Irene's red face. "Although I do bring Mark Twain's adage to mind. *Man is the only animal that blushes—or needs to.*"

Irene loved the bones of Alisdair and she had a proprietorial air when it came to the MacIvers as a couple. She was responsible for their first meeting. Any woman with sense would fall for him at first sight. Debbie did, for sure. Irene would have done so herself when she first met him if her heart hadn't been elsewhere at the time, and he was still an attractive package. His lilting Scottish accent was beguiling and was probably as good as a light sedative for some of his patients. His large brown and expressive eyes danced with fun as he grinned hugely. The firelight caught the coppery tones in his dark hair—so common amongst natives of Highland Scotland. The passing of the years had failed to put much flesh on his bones. Most women would want to mother him first before moving on to more important things.

But right now Irene could have killed him.

"I'm sorry, Irene," Alisdair apologised later when he and Irene sat by the embers of the fire. "I don't mean to tease, but I think you're a bit sweet on the space hero, aren't you?"

"Isn't it ridiculous? At my age?"

"No. Not at all. You were put into his company with the business of the signals from Mars and you obviously like what you have seen. Debbie knows for sure that Mr Mortimer likes what he has seen. Take no notice of Debbie, although I don't think that's advice I need to give you. She is a total romantic and I can be too. After all, in my family we've only just stopped drinking toasts to *The gentleman in velvet* and *The King across the water.*"

Fortunately Irene's seventeenth and eighteenth century English and Scottish history was sufficiently up to scratch to understand those comments. Supporters of the exiled King James the Second on both sides of the border were delighted when the usurper William of Orange died as a result of complications following a fall from his horse. The animal had stumbled over a molehill, throwing its royal rider, hence the acknowledging of *The gentleman in velvet*—the mole that created the obstacle. The death of William did not bring the return of James Stuart and his family to the throne and many were left with nothing more than forlorn remembrances of *The King across the water*—whichever current member of the Stuart clan was claiming the Crown and being helped by the King of France in order to annoy the government in London.

"But the Jacobite cause was a futile one," Irene mused.

"Only because individuals made it that way," Alisdair said firmly. "James Edward and Charlie both wanted to be King, but they wanted to be King without putting in any of the prolonged effort necessary to get back the Crown. They couldn't be bothered. What I'm saying is this, Irene. Debbie and I so want to see you really happy. This world is not meant to be a vale of tears for anyone, but you especially deserve to be content and really belonging somewhere, after what you endured in earlier days. I'm sure Joe Mortimer is a good man. You must go for it, lassie—if that's what you want. Don't do a Charlie and turn away when the prize is there for the taking. It looks to me as though Joe Mortimer won't need much encouraging. I reckon that the only thing that might come between you two is your appointment books."

*   *   *

The continuous background whisper of the sea was joined by something else on this particular morning. At first Joe thought that someone was throwing stones against the window. As his senses began to march as one, he realised that gusts of wind were dashing handful after handful of rain onto the front of the house. Hmm. Bonny would get a *very* quick walk this morning.

Weather didn't normally bother him. But he knew of old what conditions would be like down at the water's edge. The gales came barrelling up the Bristol Channel, did a neat pivoting turn round North Hill and the protective arm of the harbour and roared onto the beach and up into the town.

Another five minutes and it would be time to get up.

Joe was astonished that he was thinking such a thing. He was even more taken aback when he heard voices downstairs. He had the selective ear of one trained through long experience to make sense of every internal sound generated by a space ship in flight. Although no one was speaking loudly, he identified all six voices swiftly—his parents, Phil and Daphne and Sam and Natasha. What were they all doing up and about so early?

He looked at the clock and realised.

It was quarter past nine.

There was no point in rushing about and, oddly enough, he couldn't be bothered. He readied himself for the day at a leisurely pace and finally appeared in the kitchen at about twenty to ten. Everyone was seated round the large table at different stages of breakfasting. Lying in her basket, Bonny gave Joe an out-from-under-the-eyebrows glare, which condemned him as a traitor to the cause. She tucked her tail round her nose and slept.

"Afternoon, Joe," said Neil.

That earned him a kick under the table from Stella before she rose to put the kettle on.

"I'm glad that you decided against taking the dog out in this weather, Joe," she said.

"I didn't even know it was raining," he admitted. "I only woke up about half an hour ago."

There were mutterings of approval from all round the table and no one was more pleased than Stella. It had only taken a few days for the particular magic of the air here to have an effect on Joe. He had always been an early riser. The only time she had ever known him to be late down the stairs for a while was after Sally's death, when the rituals of mourning were over and some semblance of normality had to be striven for. The iron mixture of grief, stubbornness and adrenaline finally gave out and he was running on physical, mental and emotional empty. For a week he slept the clock round.

There was another source of noise, below the wind and rain, as thunder rumbled across the bay. Joe sat down in time to see Natasha take hold of Sam's hand.

"I'm frightened of thunderstorms," she said sheepishly, reminding him of what he already knew.

What he was less familiar with was the look of weary impatience on Sam's face. Joe wanted to give his nephew a good thump. Irene had said she didn't like thunderstorms but hell, if she admitted to a fear such as Natasha had . . .

"You can hold my hand if Sam can't be bothered," he said pointedly. "Everyone is frightened of something. Everyone."

So far, the weather had smiled on this celebration-cum-holiday. Now it was as if the saved-up meteorological wrath was being poured out on the morning. Stella looked out of the window and predicted that it would all be gone by midday.

"Mother Leakey has spoken," said Philip fondly.

"Wasn't Mother Leakey the supposed ghost around here who called up storms?" Daphne queried. "Not someone who sent them away."

"She was," Stella confirmed. "But whoever and whatever, this lot will be gone by midday."

Her confidence in the changeability of the weather of West Somerset seemed misplaced. The thunder was still crashing around when everyone began to drift away from the table. Daphne cleared up silently and efficiently around Joe and Natasha, before disappearing.

Joe noticed how Natasha jumped at every flash of lightning and crash of thunder.

"It's okay, Natasha," he said, holding both of her hands. "You'll frighten that babba of yours."

The Froglet, as Sam and Natasha named her ever-growing bump of pregnancy, didn't appear all that bothered.

"I'm silly," she said. "Sam says I'm silly."

Joe could have done a nice line in undermining his nephew in the eyes of his adoring wife. He had clear memories of Sam's childhood fears and foibles. But that was unworthy—a bit like showing the naked-on-the-rug baby pictures. Instead, he started telling her about his trip to America and the preparations for the *Ariadne One* flight at the end of the year. He knew that the date of the flight would have been announced by now. Natasha asked some very pertinent questions.

"Why is it so important that the rocket goes then?" she wondered. "I've heard you talking on the television about the power system that these ships use. How close or how far away Mars is doesn't matter too much. Not like it did when everyone was thinking about going to Mars years ago."

"But the weather does matter," explained Joe. "Mars is a planet with an atmosphere, weather and seasons. We want the astronauts there at the height of the summer in the northern hemisphere of the planet. That way our explorers and the Lander have a fighting chance of not freezing solid. *Ariadne One* has to go after Christmas."

The loudest peal of thunder yet cracked over the house.

"Everyone is afraid of something."

Natasha repeated it like a guiding mantra, hanging on to Joe's hands.

After that eruption of sound, the weather began to calm down rapidly. The storm dissipated and the rain began to slacken. By quarter to twelve the sun was out and Stella's reputation as the local weather sage was secure.

The warmth of the sun made wet pavements and roofs steam when Joe took the dog out. The tide was right in and slopping messily against the sea wall, so he walked along the sea front. Bonny was happy to trot along beside him and she was enjoying the attention from holidaymakers' children. One little boy came up to them when she was stopped, sniffing interesting smells. Joe had watched the child in earnest conversation with his parents.

"Can I pat your dog, mister?"

"Of course you can. Bonny loves being fussed over. She never gets tired of it."

The boy stroked Bonny's back, tentatively at first, then with growing confidence. The dog lifted her face to the child and he rubbed one finger on her forehead.

"Thanks!" he shouted over his shoulder, running back to the family. "Dad! I want a dog!"

Joe smiled and walked on.

The strong cross currents were evident as they ran over one another on the bay, creating patches of frothing turbulence in the sea. The rasping sound of the shingle being sucked this way and that indicated the power of the undertow. As his mother often said, this was a stretch of water that you called "Sir." Every year visitors got into difficulties here and there was occasional tragedy.

Bonny was happy enough when Joe turned round and headed back towards home. They were nearing the house when Joe spotted a familiar figure sitting on a bench looking out to sea.

"Natasha! What are you doing out here? Had a row with Sam?"

"No. Nothing like that. I wanted a bit of sea air. The others are playing poker. I don't really enjoy the game."

"I hope they're not playing for money," said Joe uneasily. "Dad goes into killer mode when he plays cards, especially any form of poker. He'll bankrupt everyone."

"They're only playing for pennies. Philip is really unhappy. Your father is doing rather well."

"He will. Continuously. I've only met one person who I think could really take him on at the game and that's Bruce Dougall, my Zeus flights colleague. Those two playing would be a true clash of the heavyweights. It's a pity it will never happen because I really wouldn't be able to predict who would come out of it ahead."

"What are you frightened of?" Natasha wondered casually, her mind still running on the earlier talk with Sam's uncle. "You said that everyone is frightened of something. What will you admit to?"

It took Joe a moment or two to catch up with her thought processes. He was still mesmerised by the never-to-be prospect of his father and Bruce squaring up to each other over a hand of cards.

"Flying in commercial airliners," he confessed. "I hate it."

Unlike Irene, Natasha didn't find that at all strange.

"I can understand that. You must have a pretty good idea of what could go wrong with a plane. You just mentioned Bruce Dougall. You must have got to know him as well as anyone. What's he frightened of?"

"That would be trampling on his life and his story," said Joe gravely, thinking of the hours of terror that Bruce endured journeying home on *Zeus Three*. "It's his to tell, not mine. Ask him yourself sometime. When *Ariadne One* is safely back on earth, I'm sure that Bruce will be over here in Britain at some point. I'll organise it that you meet him, if you would like to."

"Oh, I don't know about that."

Her usually pale face was flushing.

"Don't be star struck, Natasha. He's a human being, like anyone else. He's a native of Georgetown, Washington D.C., from an old monied family. He's a natural charmer. You'll love him. Most women do," he concluded with a grimness of tone that she didn't understand.

As he talked with Natasha, Joe was recalling fragments of his dream from a few days previously. He had an uncomfortable feeling that the news Bruce gave him was not good.

"What has Mum planned for everyone this afternoon?" Joe continued after they had sat for a minute or two watching the sea. "I can't imagine that they'll want to be in the house forever playing cards, especially when Dad will beat them hollow and the sun is shining."

"She said something about going along to Porlock Weir. And everyone feels the need for a cream tea. I could eat several cream teas. What is it about this place, Uncle Joe? I'm permanently hungry. I know that the idea of "eating for two" when a woman is pregnant was discredited a long time ago but at the moment I'm a big believer!"

"It's part of the peculiar charm of the area. The air here is a real tonic." Joe couldn't help wondering if Martha's Vineyard was having the same effect on Bruce. He hoped it was. "If we're headed out Porlock way, Bossington is the cream tea port of call. Shall we go and break up the poker school? I don't want anyone coming to blows over a card game, especially on holiday."

Chapter Nine

The flat, stony and dull brown ground of Mars was swirling with dust. The sky was choked with dust. It was difficult to tell where one ended and the other began. The wind built up to a crescendo and died down again repeatedly.

"What have you been doing?"

Tony looked very concerned as he asked the question.

Sally was developing the human skill of lying. She managed to look puzzled but she hadn't quite mastered the air of innocence to go with the expression.

"I don't know what you mean!" she protested.

"You do. Earth Sally wasn't very good at telling untruths," said Tony, "so perhaps you're just practising the character. You have been influencing dreams on Earth."

"I've appeared to my two links—yes. I don't know why I bothered. Neither of them responded when Sally came to them after her death, although they were shocked at the time. So I'm not sure why I expended such effort in the hope that they might react this time."

"It's not just that, though it's bad enough." Tony looked perplexed. "How did you manage your next trick? To have the one appearing in the dreams of the other, to tell him what he must not yet know. That calls for skill of a very high order."

"You have always underestimated me!"

That was pure Vara.

"Perhaps. But it's not time for anyone to know about Bruce Dougall. We cannot force his hand and make him tell other people. We certainly cannot involve his space comrade prematurely."

"Why not?" Sally flashed back. "Joe Mortimer was in charge of the space ship. He could easily have been the one to check the exterior of the

144

craft and he would now be the one stricken. He showed great care for Bruce Dougall when the others weren't quite sure what to do. He is linked closely to what we . . . to what happened. But no harm has been done. Many people on Earth are rediscovering that their dreams are important and should be heeded. Very few have reached the point where they think about them and try to find the importance. Joe Mortimer has lost the crucial parts of his that dream and gives it no thought."

"A lucky escape, then. I wouldn't trespass into the dreams of my link."

"She wouldn't know who you were, anyway," Sally said. "Don't worry. I have worked out who she is. It took effort because our senses are dulled. So you came to see me to be cross about what I failed to do?"

"Not only that. The time for the spaceship travelling here has been set. It is not long now."

*   *   *

"NOT LONG NOW!"

After trumpeting the launch date of *Ariadne One* on its front page in this inevitable style, one British newspaper set itself up as the official calendar and count-down to the event, noting on each front page how many days, hours and minutes there were until lift-off. Joe was beginning to agree with Bruce. He was tiring of Ariadne and it was all becoming a bit too much. He and everyone within *BUSSTOP* had enough real things to do without someone having to field the continuous queries from press and public alike, based on a speculative timetable of events in the paper. Just about the only thing that was correct was the launch date and it became someone's full-time job correcting the misconceptions that arose from the errors appearing in print.

A lesson for next time, thought Joe. A launch date is not enough. If other information wasn't given out at the same time, someone would be enterprising enough to make it up and be creative enough for it to sound spot-on.

Irene Hanson didn't have a government organisation behind which she could shelter. The furore over her revelations about the signals from Mars had died down quickly, especially when public appetite was tossed the well-timed bone of a royal wedding to gnaw. A definite launch refocused everyone's thoughts and, on her return from Scotland, there was increasing pressure on her to explain why the messages had stopped, what that meant for the expedition and what she thought the landing party would find when they reached Mars. Irene was unable to answer these questions. No one could. But she bluffed her way through a couple of interviews with as much aplomb as she could muster.

BUSSTOP drew the fire of the curious media by releasing the latest pictures of the surface of Mars, highlighting the area where it was anticipated that *Ariadne One*'s Lander crew would end up. The pictures of the Martian landscape hadn't changed much since the days when the *NASA Spirit* and *Opportunity* vehicles trundled across the surface of the planet, in a journey worthy of Homer's *Odyssey*. The images were starkly beautiful and continued to point towards previous volcanic activity and the once-upon-a-time presence of water—oceans of it, in fact.

The images were also starkly empty.

This led to another baying campaign in the media, which could have landed everybody back at Irene's front door. If there were beings who could transmit messages in Random Error Code, where were they? Where were their buildings? Where was their hardware?

The Who-What-Where-and-Why chorus was deafening and to begin with no one was sure how to quieten it.

Joe consulted with Bruce. The American media were becoming equally fidgety about the apparent emptiness of Mars and how this did not tally with the business of the mysterious signals from the planet. Each man rounded up two astro-biologists from within their *BUSSTOP* ranks and suggested that it was about time that they earned their retainer fees properly. They had free rein to educate and speculate with television and press about who and what might be found on Mars. The Sherlock Holmes process of deduction was to be employed. Once the impossible has been ruled out, go with whatever is left—however improbable. That would keep the newspapers in copy and the television people in story slots until final countdown.

"But don't get too nutty," was Bruce's parting shot of warning. "This country has never recovered from Orson Welles' dramatisation of *War of the Worlds* in the 1930s. So no *Doctor Xargle* look-alikes, please, when you start doing possible constructs of Martian beings."

He wasn't sure that either person understood that last reference. The *Doctor Xargle* books were precious family heirlooms, originally belonging to a family member in the twentieth century. He kept the volumes on a shelf at home and hadn't looked at them recently. He made a mental note to get them out and read them again. He wondered if Joe had ever read them.

Joe hadn't.

But he was delighted to have the routine of the day broken by a call from Irene.

"You look great!" he exclaimed. "Scotland suited you, that's for sure."

Continuous sunshine had given Irene a good tan, drawing attention to her fair hair and blue eyes.

"I can see that you benefited from being on the coast." Joe was tanned too and looked more rested. "I was calling to say a big thank you."

"I'm always up for being thanked, Irene, but I'm not sure what I have done for you."

"Your two astro-biologist people. They have taken the press away from me and from the college."

"I'm glad about that. We must meet up really soon."

"Yes please."

"And you're coming to the launch with me?"

"The date is in a ring of fire in my diary. It has been since you told me. I told no one before the announcement. I looked very interested when the date was given. I was on holiday with the MacIvers when I heard the news." She hesitated, unsure if she should say what ought to come next. "That reminds me. Alisdair MacIver is a doctor—a very good one—and when he saw your colleague Bruce Dougall on the television, he was concerned about him. He thought he looked ill. He didn't say anything about what he thought was wrong with Mr Dougall, but I know Alisdair. He was worried."

"Bruce was in need of a holiday, like all of us. He spent some time with his seriously rich friend and that man's family. From what I know of the Broomfields and their set-up, he will have been waited on hand, foot and finger. So we've all had a boost to get us ready for the fray."

*   *   *

Maureen Rodriguez smiled at her husband.

"It's been a long day and I'm tired."

Ted had been far more attentive recently, allaying her fears that he was back with his young men again.

"I'll be down here a while yet, Mo. You go on up. I've got some visitors coming in a little while. I'll make sure you're not disturbed."

"Visitors at after ten o'clock in the evening?" she queried.

"I agreed it was a tad late for a meeting. But these are busy people and it was the only time we could get together. Here was the most convenient place to gather. It's just boring politics but it has to be done. I'm sorry. You don't need to try and stay awake."

You want a bet? she murmured to herself.

In all fairness, if Ted hadn't said anything, she would scarcely have been aware of the late night callers. There was a vague hum of conversation downstairs after they arrived and an hour later they left, with no clue as to who they were and why they were there.

Ted was surprised when he came upstairs to find his wife still very much awake and reading a book.

"I hope we didn't make too much noise," he said.

"I hardly knew anyone was here. And I couldn't make out a word anyone said."

"That's good. I mean, I'm glad we didn't disturb you."

"Ted, you could have dropped ten ton bombs and I wouldn't have heard you. This is one amazing read."

Ted glanced at the cover. *Signals from Other Places by Irene Hanson.*

"That's the British professor who picked up the signals from Mars, isn't it?" he said casually.

"Too right! She's some lady. You ought to read this. It'll put you in the mood for the take-off of *Ariadne One.*"

"I think it would take more than a well-written book by an attractive woman to make me think kindly of an escapade that eats money."

* * *

Brian Hammond was sick and tired of his bickering children. He watched as his wife separated and consoled their son and daughter, who had started hitting one another as they argued about a toy cat. Five year-old Fred glowered as his little sister Susie sobbed and sucked her thumb at the same time.

"I hate you!" he declared with all the venom and angst that only a small child can summon. "And I—I don't care if . . . you are only three!"

As he marched off in high dudgeon, echoing what his mother reminded him of continuously, Brian had to stop himself agreeing with the first part of what his son had said.

Sat on her mother's knee, an over-tired and fractious Susie slept.

"You were a great help there," Georgina said bitterly. "I'll get these two to bed. You've got such important things to do."

Brian was glad to see her go upstairs. What she said wasn't entirely accurate. He could hardly practice here, in the family room, the thousand and one manoeuvres that were needed to ensure that *Ariadne One* went safely to Mars and came back again. But at the end of each long day, he was desperate for some peace and quiet when he reached home. Instead, most times he arrived to find the children knocking lumps out of each other and Georgie at the end of her tether. It had been particularly tough when everyone was under the cosh with Steven Bradbury. Deanna Sorbin was a much more amenable taskmaster but Brian still looked forward to some domestic harmony.

He was beginning to wonder if it had been the right thing bringing his wife and children out here. He had not wanted to be separated from them for so long and they had been devastated by the mere thought of such an absence. But Georgie was close to her family too. They were thousands of miles away and she was feeling isolated, even though she could talk to them on screen every day if she wanted to. He did appreciate that on-screen parents could not give her a break from the youngsters, who were obviously feeling unsettled.

Brian had sold it to his family as a big adventure. There was not much point in trying to hook them into the history of the area, with "Canaveral"—a canebrake or area of cane vegetation—already on the maps of Spanish explorers in the first half of the sixteenth century. Georgie was interested in the original space race reasoning behind Cape Canaveral as the location for rocket launching, to take advantage of planet Earth's movement and velocity. The southerly location of the Cape allowed space ships to launch eastward, in the same direction as Earth's rotation, relatively close to the Equator. It was also a good idea to have the downrange area sparsely populated, in case of accidents. An ocean is a good place for debris to fall. This was proved horribly correct when *Challenger* exploded. Brian didn't dwell on that too much with his wife.

So the adventure ticket it was and, at first, being in the City of Cape Canaveral, Brevard County, Florida was like exploring a new playground for all of them. They loved the spacious modern house that was provided for them by *BUSSTOP*. Many of the original houses, built during the Apollo days of the1960s and 1970s, were modernised or knocked down as the twenty first century progressed and the city was now a gleaming, bright advert for the twenty second century. A turgid history of high divorce rates and drug addiction problems in the area had been swept away with the demolition rubble.

The proximity of the beach was a lure and there were many interesting places to visit, such as Mosquito Lagoon, The Indian River, Merritt Island itself—which saw the launch of all *NASA* and *BUSSTOP* manned space flights, the National Wildlife Refuge and Canaveral National Seashore. Orlando was not so far away.

Brian had convinced himself that it would be a continuous holiday for the children. Certainly it was the thrill of Fred's short life to look round Daddy's spaceship. He might have been a touch hazy on exactly *where* Daddy was going in the spaceship but he knew it was somewhere important. But interspersed with these high points was a question that the boy repeated frequently.

"Daddy, when are we going home?"

Susie watched everything through the eyes of a bewildered three year-old. The chatterbox had slowly fallen silent and now she vented her feelings on her brother, regularly.

There were inevitable comparisons being made between the Zeus team and the group of new pioneers that Brian headed. In Brian's mind, there was no comparison at all. To start with, neither Joe Mortimer nor Bruce Dougall had any family responsibilities when they flew their missions. Dougall married for the first time between *Zeus Four* and *Zeus Five*. Shannon was his school sweetheart, so presumably they knew each other very well. That lady was unimpressed, it seemed, by running second to *BUSSTOP* and soon divorced him. Mr Mortimer's life outside of space exploration was a fascinating unknown, but even the most outlandish snippets of gossip about him didn't include any children.

No. They were footloose and fancy-free when they roamed the heavens, as anyone should be when trying to make *Star Trek* fiction a reality.

Brian had to remind himself sternly that he loved his wife and his children.

There was an incoming call. His parents were checking how he was and how the preparations for the flight were coming along. As ever, they hid their feelings under a bushel of jollity and comments along the lines of "Is Georgina thinking about what outfit she will wear when you are summoned to Buckingham Palace?" There were plenty of rational questions, especially from his mother. But he never had a moment's doubt as to what they really thought. As a teacher, his mother was a good actor and Dad was doing his best. He laughed with Brian about great aunt Marjorie. She was renowned within the family for getting her words wrong from time to time. The latest was priceless. She was telling her friends proud stories about *"My great nephew the astronut."*

Brian was sure that his parents agreed heartily with her slip of the tongue.

He was the astronut. They thought he was mad.

Brian couldn't imagine that Joe Mortimer's family, steeped in RAF tradition and ideals of service, entertained such thoughts for a moment. Bruce Dougall had no one to fret over him when he was in space, apart from Shannon. His father had died as the result of a sudden brain haemorrhage when Bruce had been in the USAF about a year. His mother never recovered from the shock and within six months she was dead. A healthy and fun-loving woman, it seemed as though she had just given up.

"Mum and Dad just called," Brian told his wife when she finally came back downstairs. "They send hugs and kisses to you and the children."

Georgina looked at her husband and remembered how much she loved him. From the word go, she was very taken with the new recruit in Space Training School, where she worked in administration. The women in his training group had been all over him but he was unimpressed.

"They were so bloody obvious," he would tell Georgina when he knew her a lot better. "It might be some men's idea of heaven, but not mine. I obviously wasn't cut out to be the stud of the solar system! Anyway, when I spoke to you on that very first day, it was as though the life I had lived up to then had ended and a new one started. I was fulfilling my dream of becoming as an astronaut and I had just met the most beautiful girl in the world."

Even now, the memory of those words made Georgina's heart beat faster.

"I'm sorry, Brian," she said, sitting down beside him and putting her arms around him. "I suppose I'm getting a bit nervous about *Ariadne One*. The launch is getting closer. My nerves are affecting the children."

"Don't be nervous," he said, tweaking her nose. "Joe Mortimer and Bruce Dougall and co did all the grunt work and went in for the danger stuff, didn't they? No one knew for sure what would happen when they let that new reactor cut loose for the first time in space. They did all the checking—at the sharp end of proceedings."

"Don't belittle what you're doing. You'll hardly be turning up on the day on a casual off chance and flying that space ship. You're all working so hard."

"True. Joe Mortimer did say that he wanted Jethro and I to be able to put that Lander down on Mars in our sleep."

"I can't pass any comment on Jethro but I could reassure Mr Mortimer right now that you can put that damned thing down in your sleep. You do it most nights—and I've got the bruises to prove it."

Brian was contrite.

"Georgie! I thought I'd stopped that. You should wake me up."

"You need your beauty sleep. I'm becoming quite the expert. You do have problems with those chutes and thrusters some nights! You need to be in with those thrusters a good half second quicker."

Her droll sense of humour was one of Georgie's many admirable qualities. Of course, Brian thought, being a full-figured fair-haired, dark-eyed goddess, with boobs that any man would want to get his hands on, *and* the mother of his children, were pretty important considerations too.

* * *

After a brief hunt along the bookshelves at home, Bruce Dougall located *Doctor Xargle's Book of Earthlets*. He sat down and began to read out loud, transported back to another time. Dinner could wait. He wasn't that hungry anyway.

> *"Today we are going to learn about Earthlets. They come in*
> *four colours. Pink, brown, black or yellow . . . but not green.*
> *"They have one head and only two eyes, two short tentacles*
> *with pheelers on the end and two long tentacles called leggies.*

*They have square claws which they use to frighten off wild beasts
known as Tibbles and Marmaduke. Earthlets grow fur on their
heads but not enough to keep them warm."*

He smiled at the illustrations, especially the ones of Doctor Xargle and
class. The newspapers would love these as images of Martians.

He was still smiling when he took a call.

"Shannon!" he exclaimed.

"You look happy," she said. "Am I disturbing something?"

His first wife contacted him from time to time. Over the years, such
occasions had gradually morphed from the wary to the almost cordial.

Bruce held up his book for her to see.

"Going back over a few childhood memories."

"Doctor Xargle! Are they the original books that you had way back
when?"

"Yes. What can I do for you, Shannon?"

"It's more a case of what I can do for you. May I take my ex-husband
out to dinner some time soon?"

"How about tonight?" he asked, always eager to gain the upper hand in
such encounters. "I don't have a sensible thought in my head about what
to cook and eat. I can call *La Casa*, if you're up for Italian. Mario owes me
a favour. He'll fit us in, however busy the restaurant is."

"You're on!" said Shannon gamely, not expecting such a positive and
prompt reply.

Shannon Dougall managed to reach *La Casa* before her former husband.
Mario himself led her to the best table in the house. She studied a menu
as he watched her from a distance. Such a lovely lady. Her thick long hair
had gone grey very early and she made it a feature of her look, wearing it
pinned up in a variety of ways. Tonight the candlelight gave her a silver
halo, which seemed to extend around her tall, rangy frame. She frowned a
little as she read the list of dishes available tonight, highlighting some fine
lines on her sculpted face and round her blue eyes.

"Don't do that, lovely lady," Mario muttered. "You are a very attractive
person still."

As a rule, Mario preferred a little more meat on a woman, but he knew
that if Shannon was to crook her little finger in his direction, he would be
able to do no other than to go running. Bruce was a fool.

Shannon glanced in Mario's direction and smiled. Mario knew he was
putty in her hands. It was a smile that would have lit the darkest corner of
a room, or the furthest recess of someone's soul. He began to wonder if he
understood people any more. He had known the Dougalls for more years
than he cared to remember and he was genuinely distressed when Shannon

and Bruce split up. It should have taken more than space ships to come between those two. Still, that was human nature for you.

Shannon looked across the restaurant at the exact moment Bruce walked in. She hadn't met with him in a while. A lifelong follower of astrology, she could see that, as ever, he was the Leo. It was very underplayed, but there was an unspoken statement that hung around him. *"Make a hole. The King of the Jungle is coming through. I'll park my throne right here."*

She knew that Joe Mortimer was born on the cusp of Leo and Virgo, which made him a *very* interesting brew to begin with. Although it was not inevitable, the potential was there for those two to piss each other off big time. And they did.

Once the back-and-to of ordering was done, Bruce looked at Shannon very directly.

"To what do I owe this honour, then?"

"The glasses," she said, totally inconsequentially. "They've become part of your public image. I can hardly imagine you without them now." Bruce removed them for a moment, to remind her. "Thank you, honey. Anyway, they make you look very wise. They suit you."

"I'm glad that you approve!" He put the glasses in his pocket. "Still as good as ever at avoiding a question, Shannon."

"Of course. I saw you on television when you and Joe Mortimer visited Cape Canaveral. Just for a moment, when you thought no one was paying attention, you had me worried. You looked tired, sick. I decided I must check you out in person when I had a minute."

"Do I look tired or sick now?"

"No."

"It has been a long year for everyone involved with Ariadne. I made it to Martha's Vineyard to spend some time with Bob and Belle. They worked their magic and here I am. I wonder. Should I be doing this? Does this mean I'm being bought dinner under fraudulent circumstances?"

"Bruce!"

Shannon remained unconvinced. Bruce was the consummate actor. He always had been. Although she knew that he cringed about such things, getting a write-up in the gossip columns after the Cape visit as *Fine at fifty* could be his biggest triumph yet.

They managed to spend a whole evening talking about everything and nothing. Shannon wanted a blow-by-blow account of the progress of *Ariadne One* and, like many others, she was puzzled by one thing.

"All the pictures from Mars show this awful dull emptiness. I liked it better when the film made it look as thought the planet was red, because of the illusion of the colour from Earth. Where are the Martians who have been sending these messages?"

"I don't know. Perhaps they're camera shy. I don't know, honestly," Bruce said, when she raised her eyebrows. "I'm putting my money on there being some sort of underground civilisation. The planet's surface is not the most welcoming."

"You envy the Ariadne crew, don't you?"

"Part of me does. But middle age does strange things. I've gotten quite cautious these days. I'm glad I don't have to put the Lander down on Mars."

"Bruce the stay-home!" she smiled. "That's a new one!"

"I suppose you're out and about every night. You're not in the gossip columns, but that doesn't mean anything."

The Dougalls had been viewed as a golden couple, of great interest to the purveyors of tittle-tattle. Bruce had placed himself squarely in the firing line again for a while through a second marriage and divorce but Shannon had effectively dropped off the radar.

Bruce knew that look. His ex wife was bursting to tell him something. He waited expectantly, but nothing could have prepared him for what she said.

"As a matter of fact, Bruce, I've seen a lot of my home recently as well. I've been writing a book. No gossip writer would be interested in that, even if he or she knew, and my publisher hasn't cranked up the publicity machine yet. Oh yes, it's accepted and in production but we haven't decided yet when to dish it up to an unsuspecting world."

Bruce grounded his coffee cup very deliberately. He had clear memories of Mrs Wheatley, their grade school teacher, reading out Shannon's stories to slack-jawed classmates who couldn't push their writing beyond the first line. The written word and the student had always gone together. But . . .

"And what is it about?"

"Don't worry, Bruce. It's no kind of lurid autobiography. It's fiction. Historical, I suppose you'd call it, about a family seeing in the Millennium and all that springs from the celebration."

"I'm . . . I'm impressed."

"I could tell you more. But then I'd have to kill you."

By the end of the evening, Shannon Dougall was at screaming point. She knew Bruce and she was convinced that there was something that he was not saying to her, but she couldn't get at it.

She was still hoping, even when she had paid the bill.

"Bruce, is there something you want to share with me?"

He opened his mouth to speak. It was good and *comfortable* to be spending an evening with Shannon. She had the right to know.

Then he stopped and thought for a moment.

"I could tell you more. But then I'd have to kill you."

*   *   *

Ted Rodriguez took in his surroundings with a certain satisfaction, as he did most days. The novelty would never wear off. He liked being Vice President of the United States. He and his wife enjoyed a lot of the trappings of high office in Washington D.C., without the onerous responsibilities that might otherwise be attached to such privileges. He had his suite of rooms here, on the second floor of the Old Executive Office Building, as Vice Presidents had done since the early 1960s. Mo loved the official residence, the former Admiral's House at the Naval Observatory on Massachusetts Avenue. She had taken to using her staff and aides like a duck to water, as had he.

Most importantly, the Vice President had few formal duties. The job may have been an afterthought for the Constitutional Convention, but it had its advantages. The President could not issue orders to him, nor could she remove him from office. He was one of her inner circle of senior political advisers simply because she couldn't ignore him. It was up to the incumbent to make the post his, all the while remembering that, as the cliché went, he was just a heartbeat away from the Presidency.

That suited Ted Rodriguez just fine. Especially today, as a stream of individuals and small groups with appointments trooped through to his inner office to talk with him. He was seen as a man of the people and so no one was a bit surprised to see two traffic cops go in, followed by a truck driver, then the truck driver's boss, with an Emergency Room doctor and nurse close on his heels.

This was quite usual. Those with a taste for history likened him to a Senator of ancient Rome, receiving petitions and pleas from plebs in the street.

The last person to see him that morning was more exotic. Bob Broomfield was a multi-millionaire—maybe a billionaire, who could be sure?—who had made several blameless fortunes in the importing of foodstuffs. He and Rodriguez nodded at each other. Broomfield sat down, looking wary and uncomfortable.

"I was disappointed that you couldn't make it to my late-nighter," Rodriguez opened carefully. "Now, you know what I would like to do—and what I will do if you don't help me. I need to know that you will help with your bit."

"I'm with you, Ted. I don't have much choice, do I?"

"There's always a choice," the Vice President observed smoothly. "I understand that you and Belle go pretty much your separate ways these days. I thought I might have to find another method of persuasion."

"I can't have you saying that stuff to the children about their mother. I owe her and them that protection. You know you've got me, you bastard."

It was one of the shortest meetings on record but Ted Rodriguez had won what he wanted. Bob's influence and reputation would count for a lot in this undertaking and his cash would oil some wheels as well. His nickname of *The Blonde Bomber* was justified. He took a very direct and robust route when solving problems. Whether he was a willing or an unwilling recruit was unimportant.

It had been a good morning's work, decided the Vice President. He had thought the unthinkable and decided he could do it. The ease with which plans were made was a sign that this was the right way to go. Even so, the random way in which the information about Belle Broomfield came to him was astonishing. It was a chance remark from Jared, pillow talk of the hottest kind from one of his most trusted friends, telling him what Mrs Broomfield had been up to with two men in a gay night club.

Rodriguez kept that picture locked up tighter than Fort Knox on his computer. He didn't need to look at the image again. It was burned into his mind. He thought he was pretty inventive when it came to sex, with both men and women, but this was amazing. Even now, he wondered at what Broomfield had said. It was obvious that the businessman knew all about his wife's . . . proclivities.

Would Mo ever be so understanding? He wasn't sure.

*   *   *

"Natasha, she is a prize-winner. Just like her mother."

Joe gazed in awe at his great-niece. Natasha beamed back at Sam's uncle. He had the knack of making people feel good, and she needed that. She didn't look much like a prize-winner at the moment. She decided she was a wreck. She was still very tired after a long but routine labour. Fortunately, Abigail was establishing herself already as a placid baby, intent on showing the ropes to her nervous new parents. Thoughtfully, Joe stayed away from the mob that besieged her in hospital, waiting until she and the latest addition to the Mortimer tribe were safely back home.

Abigail stirred in her mother's arms and stared up at Joe with big blue eyes

"Say hello to your great-uncle Joe," Natasha told her. "He is a famous and important man. He will soon be even more famous and important."

"Hello, little one," said Joe, offering a finger to her star-fishing hand. "Take no notice of your mother. I'm just Uncle Joe."

"Well, just Uncle Joe. Would you like to hold your great-niece?" Natasha asked.

Carefully, and rather awkwardly, Joe took the baby in his arms. Within seconds, that awkwardness was gone. Nestled against his chest, Abigail continued to look at this new man in her life. He looked back and they understood one another completely.

Still on an emotional roller coaster, Natasha found herself wiping away the tears. If ever a man was meant to nurture and love children, it was this one. The words were in her mind:

"You would have made a great father."

But somehow she was unable to say them, as if something was preventing her. Instead, she shared an intense silence with the child and the man that seemed to last forever.

The door opened and in poured the family. The moment was gone, but what a moment it had been—for reasons that Natasha could not fathom or begin to explain.

Joe watched the dynamics of the group with some amusement. His mother and his sister-in-law were under strict instructions not to fuss unnecessarily.

"I've given your mother her marching orders," Neil had told him. "She'll help that poor girl to death, given half a chance."

Brother Philip had said things along a similar line to Daphne. So every time Abigail whimpered or moved, both women made to get up and then remembered and were still again. Natasha put them out of their misery.

"I think this young lady has had enough adoration for a while. I'll take her upstairs and put her down in her cot to sleep properly."

She left the room with the baby, followed by Sam. He had been wearing the same dazed smile since the moment Abigail drew her first breath and he realised that there was a very real point to the pains his wife was enduring. He had been on Cloud Nine ever since.

Neil Mortimer was as proud as anyone and adored his great-grand daughter already but enough was enough when it came to baby chatter. He wandered out to the kitchen and Joe joined him.

"Another Mortimer safely gathered in, Joe," his father observed with great satisfaction. "But how's this Mortimer doing?"

"Okay, Dad. Some mornings I find myself wishing I was back down in Minehead. *BUSSTOP* is manic, as you can imagine, but everything is going smoothly towards launch day—at the moment. I'm beginning to think it would be easier if there were one *BUSSTOP* headquarters. I know we've got the lead on this but most everything ends up being referred to the appropriate department in Washington as a matter of courtesy."

"Perhaps that's the next stage in the organisation's development. The headquarters was only split between London and D.C. to get everyone to agree to *BUSSTOP* as the successor to *NASA*. Perhaps that will be another of your lasting legacies, Joe. The man who brought about the unification of *BUSSTOP*! How are our beloved leaders holding up?"

"Kevin Crane is just Kevin Crane. You know that he doesn't give much away to the outside observer. But he would be odd if he weren't enjoying the attention of the world homing in on Britain. It's a good job that space ships don't launch from here. I think that Richard would be totally overcome. He's away with the fairies as it is."

"And he's got the wedding to do before the launch."

"True. But unlike most parents of the bride, he and the Queen don't have to worry too much about the organising of it. They say yes or no to suggestions and then they pay up and turn up."

Neil took off his glasses and polished the lenses carefully.

"Talking of turning up, I've heard from a very good source that you have been invited to the wedding." Joe's expression was too studied. His father leapt on it. "You have! Bloody hell, Joe! Who are you taking?"

"I—er—haven't asked her yet."

"Then you'd better get your skates on, lad! Have you ever taken a woman to a wedding? I thought not." A look of real pain crossed his face. "Any woman who has ever outfitted herself to be a guest at a wedding could run a medium-sized war with no effort. The logistics of bringing together the dress or the suit, the shoes, the bag, the hat—."

"The hat?" Joe echoed.

"At a formal do, yes. And I think that Princess Charlotte's wedding will count as a very formal do. Tiaras might not be worn but hats certainly will. And are you sure that the aforementioned lady will be free on that day? I know the wedding is on a Saturday but even so. Shape up, Joe!"

Not for the first time, Neil Mortimer realised that his action man son could be a very impractical person. He had an idea who the mystery lady might be, thanks to a few flying leaps of the imagination that Stella had made. She would be there at a moment's notice. But it was no bad thing to shake Joe out of his complacency from time to time, a complacency born of having so many things done for him throughout his working life.

Joe had sat in spaceships and sat in *BUSSTOP* headquarters. His Majesty King Richard the Fourth sat in Buckingham Palace. They had moved on from the RAF but as products of their individual worlds, there wasn't much between them.

Chapter Ten

"No man is worthy of you until he can walk backwards up Mount Everest, playing the banjo and singing *God Save the King* in Italian, also backwards, with punctuation and speech marks. You know that, Charlotte. So Michael had better turn out to be first rate as your husband and your future consort or I will want to know why!"

His Majesty King Richard the Fourth and Her Royal Highness Princess Charlotte were enjoying the autumnal sunshine in the palace gardens. They stopped to take in the view and Richard linked arms with his daughter in a protective gesture.

"He will, Papa," Charlotte replied very seriously. "He was just very apprehensive this morning. I hope that you can understand that. We all do silly things when we are a little uncertain. I think Mama went a bit over the top. She's becoming all mother-of-the-bride."

"She *is* the mother of the bride, chicken."

Earlier in the day, Charlotte and her parents had visited St Paul's Cathedral, along with Squadron Leader Michael Timpson. The Royal Family were totally familiar with the cathedral but they decided that it would be helpful to undertake a quick private recce in the context of the forthcoming wedding. All concerned were feeling slightly overwhelmed by well-meaning advice from the hundred and one individuals and groups that royal protocol demanded should have a hand in making the day happen. They needed reminding of the great space in which it would all take place, so that they could say Yes and No to each proposition with total confidence.

Michael's nerves got the better of him whilst they were there and he ended up telling some rather dubious jokes. The Queen was not amused.

Charlotte turned to face her father. Even though she had grown to be on a level with him a long time ago, Richard still found it odd to conduct eye-to-eye conversations with his little girl.

"Thank you for being so concerned about us," she said. "It will be a wonderful occasion. A wonderful occasion that will be the beginning of something very special for Michael and myself and for the whole family. You'll see."

"Hmm." Richard cleared his throat noisily. "You know that your mother and I only want you to be happy. We wouldn't dream of making any trouble. You were legally an adult when you decided to marry him and he's not a Roman Catholic, so we couldn't stand in your way."

He gave a wry smile at the reference to an old, outdated but still-enacted tradition concerning royal marriages.

Charlotte was backlit by the afternoon sunshine. She shone like some blonde beacon. She had his height and her mother's lovely figure. Seeing her in a few moments of silence and reflection, she reminded Richard of his own mother. That was no bad thing. Matilda had been a tough woman when she needed to take a stand and he knew that Charlotte had inherited some of her qualities. She would need them. Like her father, she could play her part to perfection but was wearied by some of the ridiculous conventions surrounding British Kings and Queens. He was chiselling away at restrictions. Charlotte would use a sledgehammer. But she would charm everyone whilst she was smashing things down.

"But most importantly, Michael and I love one another," she said, picking up the theme of the conversation again.

"Yes, I think you do."

They strolled on.

"Papa, I was studying the guest list, now that it is beginning to come together. Don't look like that, please. I'm not about to complain. It's fantastic that so many interesting people will be there. I could see your hand in one particular name."

"And who might that be, young lady?" asked Richard, having a good idea who she meant.

"Mr Joseph Mortimer. Your RAF friend and, of course, the man of the moment. I noticed that there has been no reply from him, one way or the other. I hope he will be at the wedding. He was the most fascinating company at the luncheon he attended earlier in the year."

"I would imagine that his mind is on other things—like *Ariadne One* taking off after Christmas. That's why he won't have replied. I'll contact him personally to boot him up the arse. Joe is a bit of a one for the quiet life but he'll be with us on the day. It'll be fun to see who is the lucky lady that he brings."

"It will be a woman then? Someone told me he's gay. Some of my friends have been making bets amongst themselves as to which outed public figure he would turn up with."

"Don't be so bloody ridiculous, girl! Where on earth did you get that idea? He has his funny ways. We all do." A glazed look of reminiscence came over his face. "But I can tell you that wearing the green carnation isn't one of them." He saw her questioning face and explained further. "That's a reference from a very old musical drama of the twentieth century. All the gay boys belonged to *The Green Carnation Club* and they wore one as a badge of office!"

* * *

Joe was apology itself when he discovered that he was putting a spanner in the works by having failed to reply to the wedding invitation.

"It's all right, Joe." Richard beamed at him from the screen in an evening call. "It was Charlotte who picked up on it. We know you're coming. But someone in the palace food chain will soon start having palpitations. You should have received a reminder by now. I'll make sure that the appropriate person looks into it, because the Household department that's doing all this will need to put a tick or whatever it is next to your name. Tell me whom you are bringing and I'll get dear old Angus to ensure that you are on all the lists. You can then reply formally at your leisure. I know that you have a lot to think about at the moment. I'd rather be worrying about Charlotte's wedding than dealing with your stuff."

"But I still shouldn't have been so rude, Richard. It sounds rather pathetic, blaming pressure of work, but you have an idea of how it is. Professor Irene Hanson has said that she will be delighted to accompany me."

Richard nodded in approval.

"Now there's a pairing made up in the heavens!" he laughed, in an almost a passable joke. "Can you find some time in your overflowing diary to come down to the palace and give me an update on Ariadne? The Prime Minister keeps me informed. It's difficult to get him to talk about anything else sometimes when we have the weekly get-togethers, but it would be good to have some details directly from you."

* * *

Irene didn't bother about the rain sluicing down as she drove to college. When her car was stationary in traffic, she noticed that the raindrops bounced like silver coins as they hit the road and pavements. Headlights glowed soft and golden in the morning murk that was created by this prolonged cloudburst. She could have floated into work through the downpour, minus the car, quite happily. She sang along to the music playing on the sound system.

As a result of a call from Joe the previous evening, today everything around her seemed beautiful. They arranged to meet up at the weekend at their pub. Then Joe dropped his glorious bombshell. He was invited to the wedding of Princess Charlotte and he wondered if she would do him the honour of being his companion for the occasion.

The tingle of warm excitement still suffused Irene's body. Nothing could squash her spirits, not even the prospect of a long and tedious tutorial with some of her least favourite students.

She parked the car, pulled up the hood of her coat and stepped out into the rain, clutching books and files to her body. There was no point in running to the building. It was an occasion to accept being soaking wet and, on this of all days, she could accept it gladly

As she approached the entrance, Irene saw her favourite security man, Sid, holding the door open for her, so that she didn't have to stop and fiddle about with the number system. She quickened her pace.

Sid had a perfect view of Professor Hanson slipping on wet leaves and falling to the ground. He hadn't moved so fast in years as he rushed to her aid.

*   *   *

Debbie MacIver squeezed Irene's hand.

"How are you feeling now?" she wanted to know.

"Rather foolish," said Irene. "First I was helped by Sid, who was very worried and having the time of his life simultaneously. Then I had the paramedics moving me around, which doesn't do a lot for the professorial image, especially when some of your students are watching and being alternately concerned and hysterical. And of course, I fell into the biggest muddy puddle in the car park."

"That's the law of sod," replied Debbie. "But being manhandled by two sexy paramedics? I'd risk the down side. And Sid helping you couldn't have been that bad. It must have been like your Dad or favourite uncle rushing over."

Irene's face crumpled as she began to cry. Debbie thought nothing of this beyond the fact that her friend was badly shocked and in pain.

"Debs, this isn't fair!" she sniffed. "I arranged to meet Joe Mortimer tomorrow for lunch."

"Oh dear! That won't be happening, for sure. Well, not this weekend, anyway. You've done some damage to yourself there, my girl."

Irene was trying not to look at her left leg, which was supported and packed with ice around the knee and thigh. She was scarcely aware of the hubbub of the hospital Emergency Department going on around them.

"I hope you didn't mind my getting the hospital to call you. I couldn't think of anyone else to contact, off the top of my head."

"I would have been cross if you hadn't," Debbie said firmly. "You know that I'm generally at home on a Friday and luck would have it that Alisdair wasn't working today either."

"Where is Alisdair?"

"Talking to the medical staff about you."

"I hope he isn't giving them a bad time."

"I doubt it, Irene. Wendy Ransome is a bit of a legend in her own lunchtime in Emergency medicine. I'm sure that she and Alisdair will be sharing ideas as fellow professionals."

Doctor Ransome was feeling rather intimidated by her fellow professional Alisdair MacIver. He had a justifiable national reputation and she wanted to be seen doing the right things for a friend of the great man.

"The initial scan examination is inconclusive, as I suspected, Doctor MacIver. Take a look yourself." Alisdair studied the images and had to agree. "It's impossible to have a clear view yet of what's going on. There are vast amounts of localised swelling and trauma. Professor Hanson must have hit the ground with her knee twisted. It's a classic footballer's injury—falling one way with the lower leg going in the opposite direction. But seeing as she isn't a professional player, we don't need to jump in with all guns blazing immediately. We can afford to wait over the weekend and then examine again when some of the swelling is reduced. I'll make sure that Professor Hanson is booked in to the out patients clinic for Monday morning. I'm certain that nothing is broken. In the meantime, I hardly need tell you that our patient needs total rest. We'll do the usual support strapping and hope like hell that there isn't too much soft tissue damage. This could be a long job."

"She'll rest," said Alisdair firmly. "We'll be looking after her. I'll do the checks over the weekend. What are you prescribing for the pain?"

Irene gave way completely and sobbed when she discovered that the MacIvers had already made the decision to take her home with them and care for her. Debbie held her close and stroked her hair.

"It's okay, Irene. It's what friends are for."

"You manage to see me at my worst, Alisdair," Irene hiccupped eventually.

"Aye. Sometimes. That's what medical friends are for," he said cheerfully. "You were bonny enough on holiday. At least this was an accident, which can befall anyone." His mouth straightened into a hard line as he remembered an earlier time. "The other stuff was not."

Annoyingly, the rain clouds had rolled away and the sun was shining by the time Irene and the MacIvers left the hospital. Alisdair pushed her in a wheelchair to their car and Debbie carried the crutches that Irene would need for when moving about from one place to another was unavoidable.

"We'll do all the talking and telling people," Alisdair assured her as he threaded the car out of the hospital complex and onto the road. "The college will need to know where we're up to. Anyone else on the immediate horizon who needs to know that you're out of circulation?"

"We need to contact Joe Mortimer," said Debbie. "Irene was meeting him tomorrow."

"He'll be one disappointed man, then," observed Alisdair.

Joe's disappointment was tempered by anxiety and sympathy for Irene when Debbie spoke to him. He was thankful that she was with the MacIvers.

"I would like to come and see Irene at some point, if that's at all possible, Mrs MacIver."

"Not so formal! Debbie, please. I would leave it for today and tomorrow. How about Sunday?"

Debbie went back to a woebegone Irene, who was sitting with her leg elevated.

"Joe Mortimer sends his love. Those were his exact words, Irene. At the moment, as long as your leg doesn't fall off, he will call to see you on Sunday. A visit from your lover boy should help lift your spirits." Irene made to speak. "Yes, okay, he's not your lover boy. I concede the point. He jolly well should be, though"

*   *   *

The curtain of rain and menacing clouds were turning day into night. So much for all the Saturday plans, thought Bruce, in which the word *outdoors* had figured prominently. Glorious fall weather had changed overnight into this black shroud that hung over Georgetown and the whole D.C. area as he looked out of the window. He poured more coffee and realised that he had not yet taken his medication. That was a vital moment of every day.

Doctor Doherty was delighted with the way he was responding to the drug.

"You and ZFF were made for one another, Bruce. I'll have to write this up for one of the medical journals. And the bosses of the pharmaceutical company behind the drug haven't stopped dancing yet each time I send in an update on your condition."

"You'll write for the journal when I'm dead?"

"I don't want to have to wait that long. ZFF is going to give you a good run yet. You should know that by now. You will be my anonymous patient, of course, as you are anonymous to the drug company."

"Damn! And there I was, hoping for some fame at last."

The storm moved up a notch, with a crash of thunder. The echoes of the thunder were still reverberating when Bruce heard the unmistakable call signal from Cape Canaveral. It was going to be one of those days.

It was. Deanna Sorbin didn't beat about the bush.

"Illya Abelev has been taken ill. I've just been talking to his sister. He's in our Medical Centre and in surgery right now. It was easier to bring extra personnel to him than to take him anywhere else."

"Surgery? What's happened?"

"Peritonitis."

"Pardon me? You don't just develop a condition like that."

"It seems that Illya has been suffering with intermittent abdominal pain for some time but decided to ignore it. It turned out he had a grumbling appendix. Everything blew up big time overnight."

"And so did his appendix," Bruce concluded with grim humour "Oh shit!" He squared his shoulders. "I'd better come down and see him. Illya deserves a visit and some sympathy, even if I beat him senseless afterwards. And you and I can have a quick word about who replaces him in the Lander."

"Shouldn't Joe Mortimer be in on this?"

"It's not really necessary. We're here. He's not. And we've got an agreed line of who should come next. If you can have the list ready and all the training assessments, we can move the astronauts around and put the new person in. I'll let Joe know what's happening. This isn't what I had planned for today, but never mind. I'm on first name terms with most of the ground staff at Washington National airport. I might as well keep a good thing going. We'll have to start swapping contact details soon at this rate. I wonder if Marge's daughter has had her baby yet. Some good news on that front may well ensure that I don't kill Illya."

The baby hadn't been born but Bruce could only feel sorry for a sick man when he finally reached the Russian's bedside. Illya cut a woebegone figure, lying very still. Monitors beeped and chattered around him. All the paraphernalia used to help the human body fight a tough fight was in place. It was hard to summon any real anger.

"You concentrate on recovering your health," Bruce said, when the astronaut ran out of ways of saying he was sorry. "But tell me this, Illya. Say you'd managed to get as far as flying to Mars. Say your performance was not being impaired and no one noticed that anything was wrong. Carrying the most minor condition is not a good idea. Apart from anything else, it's a long way back home from the next planet if someone suddenly becomes really sick, even with our present propulsion systems. I know that our spaceships have moved on in terms of design and comfort since the first moon landing days, with a few little bitty extras like gravity as well, but we're not yet up to *Starship Enterprise* standards. You know—complete with a fully equipped and staffed Sickbay. *Ariadne One* would not have been a good place for you to develop peritonitis, any more than *Zeus Three* was . . ." He stopped, not sure how much of the story Illya knew or was supposed to know. "Had you thought about that?"

Illya's eyes were closed and a single tear escaped and rolled down his cheek. At the moment he was a fair-haired limp rag doll.

"I suppose not. I so wanted to be on that ship."

"We need you. You won't be going to Mars this time, but you work on getting better and you'll be in *Ariadne Two*. I'm not letting your expertise go to waste. We'll shift the crew around and call in one of the back—up crew to fill your slot. That's why we go to all the bother and expense of training extra personnel."

Illya Abelev opened his eyes. He looked more cheerful now that he realised his chances were not totally blown.

"The curse of Mars, eh, Mr Dougall?"

"Don't even go there."

It was a day to keep moving. Bruce left the Medical Centre and prowled along the endless corridors of Mission Control to meet briefly with Deanna. Arty Rowe headed the list of replacements and Deanna rated him very highly. So he would be in the Orbiter and Gianfranco Rosso was promoted to the Lander. This would mean a disruption to the routines and camaraderie that the crew members were developing but, long term, it might be a good thing. Bruce had been thinking for a while that Gianfranco's talents would be wasted baby-sitting the Orbiter. This swap certainly wasn't the disaster that it would have been if Brian Hammond or Jethro Norman were suddenly taken out of the reckoning. He didn't like to even think about how *that* scenario could be sorted out. Was it possible to put those two under twenty-four-hour surveillance until the final countdown, to make sure that they reached the launch pad in one piece?

"Hello, Bruce," said a voice behind him. "Long time and no see."

Bruce turned to see Hagar Turner.

"Hagar! It's good to see you. How are you keeping?"

"Very well, thanks. I didn't expect to see you wandering the corridors of this joint, especially on a Saturday. You can't be tired of Georgetown, and I could think of plenty other places to swap it for before I reached Cape Canaveral."

"Something cropped up here that needed my personal attention."

"And I'd do well to mind my own business, I suppose."

"Perhaps. Can I buy you a coffee?"

It was a sight that had not been seen for a while—the *BUSSTOP* chief and Mission Control's leading computer expert heading to the restaurant together, talking like the great friends that they were. The lighting in the corridor gave Hagar's fabulously smooth black skin an extra polish. Bruce knew that she was about his age but she looked at least fifteen years younger. The glass beading she wore in her mass of braided locks of hair glinted and twinkled. Her smile started with her generous mouth but worked its way through the bunching of her wide cheeks, the lighting of her eyes and her expressive eyebrows. Even her hair beads seemed to get involved in a smile, clinking together like tiny bells. She could almost look down on Bruce as they walked along. She was an imposing figure and the contrast between the two could not have been greater. Next to her, Bruce looked as though he was about to break in two.

Bruce Dougall had the greatest respect for Hagar Turner and he was delighted to be sharing some time and some coffee with her. He had some serious talking to do with her regarding Simeon, when he dared broach the subject.

Later, his thoughts ran on again during a natural pause in the conversation. Hagar had been put in a difficult position during Simeon's initial astronaut training, being his aunt and an employee of *BUSSTOP* at the same time. The rest of Simeon's family were furious with Bruce. They thought that he judged the young man with undue harshness. It was a tricky time and she handled everyone and everything with diplomacy and tact. She emerged from the situation still on speaking terms with everyone and became the matriarchal figure for a cantankerous bunch of people.

Bruce was hearing glowing reports about Simeon's work on *Ariadne One* and he was glad. Back when Hagar's nephew was undertaking his initial training, he had to acknowledge all over again that neither instructor or trainee were at their shining best. Simeon was the only child of hopelessly indulgent parents and his aunt's tough love had not prepared him fully for the realities of the world. The *BUSSTOP* chief could see now that he was in a bad place then, with his second divorce looming on the horizon. But he was supposed to be an experienced and seasoned man, who didn't lash out at a bit of a kid because he happened to be there. It had been teaching and learning train-wreck style.

Fortunately, although Bruce was the chief instructor in Space Training School, other people's opinions counted as well. Thank God they did. He didn't know what Simeon thought of the experience, and he didn't want to know either. He recalled it with horror.

Bruce felt once more the shame that had swamped him when he selected Simeon to be on the Ariadne team. Was that only months ago? It felt like years and it was as though another person had been processing those thoughts.

How could he put all this to Hagar?

"A penny for them?"

Hagar was looking at him quizzically.

"Sorry, Hagar. I was miles away."

"You certainly were. But we all need those moments. Were you out in space, perhaps?"

"Something like that."

The poor weather had pursued Bruce right down the coast. Outside the rain clouds rolled in.

"I'm sure it was simpler flying a spaceship," she suggested. "Now you have to stay down here, making the decisions and giving the orders."

"I think so. As astronauts, we had our instructions and we followed them. End of statement."

"Now Simeon will be part of the team following the instructions. It's amazing. I've not had the chance. Thank you for picking him for the Ariadne crew. It takes a big man to realise that his long-held thoughts were wrong and then to go on to do something about it."

Bruce wanted to crawl into a hole. Here was this genuinely strong woman praising him for a strength of character which he most definitely did not possess. Hagar gave him a long, shrewd look. She patted his hand as she stood up.

"We're all going to be rushing here and there until that spaceship takes off. When all the dancing in the streets is over, you and I must have a heart-to-heart. And Bruce!" He looked up at her, expectantly. "It's okay. No apology is needed. If I'd had to work with Simeon as he was then, I would have been pleading provocation on a murder charge in a court of law. And you were . . . troubled. But don't be troubled now. Till next time" she concluded softly and was gone.

Bruce could only stare stupidly at her retreating back

*　　*　　*

"Irene."

The voice was low and quiet but Irene looked up. She had fallen asleep with the bedside light on. She expected to see Debbie, tiptoeing in to turn off the lamp.

"Oh," was all she said.

She had always wondered what she would do in such a situation. A woman was supposed to scream, probably. Or faint. At the moment she could hardly leap up and run away. But she wasn't at all scared. She was intrigued, and oddly calm.

"I'm glad you're not frightened," said the man. "If you did start yelling and someone came in, I wouldn't be here and it would be a bad dream, brought on by your pain relief. But I want this to be a good memory, a special dream for you."

"Who are you?" she asked, immensely curious.

"I have watched over you from the day you were born. I am so proud of you, Irene Hanson. I know you feel that, in your life, every time you have got hold of something good, it has unravelled before your eyes. You are thinking it right now, in your present situation. I can't see yet exactly what road you will tread. I'm sure that there will still be some difficult places in it but I know that you will end up where you truly want to be. That is my promise, given to you with my love."

"Who are you?" she repeated.

"You came across me a while back and you will come across me again. Don't fret. Sleep tight, my angel"

Irene did just that and she felt a lot better the next morning after her odd experience. Alisdair gave her a doctor's glance as she hopped into the kitchen to share some breakfast. She was already quite nifty on those crutches. And, most importantly, the instant face-lift that shock gives a person was beginning to disappear. She was still very pale but nowhere near as tense.

"Is it okay if I use your computer in a while?" Irene asked. "I want to access some files back home. Yes, I know that could be done via my communicator but I'm an old-fashioned girl at heart. I prefer to have a decent-sized console in front of me as opposed to working on something I could crush under my heel. And I need a decent-sized screen anyway."

"I hope this is nothing to do with work!" said Alisdair sternly.

"Goodness, no! I had the most curious dream in the night. I just want to check something."

"Dreams can be funny things at the best of times, Irene. Even more so when you're taking the happy pills you've been prescribed. But you play away on the computer—as long as it is play. Doctor's orders."

"I hope that Joe Mortimer's visit today is part of doctor's orders," she said.

"Oh aye. That's fine."

Irene found that her mind was rather fuzzy and she had to stop and think how to remotely access her home system. She made a couple of false starts. She had to force herself to really concentrate. Another wrong entry and she would be locked out of her own computer. She was beginning to realise how much the pain and the drugs were affecting her.

This time she managed it and went to her picture files. She was almost hoping that the photograph didn't exist, but she knew it did. She had looked at it with Debbie. She found it with no trouble.

His dark hair was cropped close to minimise the appearance of balding. He was a bit on the short side. His smile could only be described as beautiful and crinkled the corners of his eyes.

"Well, well, well," she whispered. "Tony Johnson. Hello again, granddad. I don't know how that all happened. I wonder what you would have made of Joe Mortimer." She smiled at the image. "I think you would have liked him. You're two generations apart, but it would have been lovely if you could have met him. Come to think of it, I wouldn't have minded meeting you myself." She stopped, realising the contradiction in what she had just said. "Did I meet you, in the night? I'm sorry. I'm talking nonsense here, aren't I? Blame it on the painkillers I'm taking."

She looked round, to make sure that no one was listening to her talking to a picture. Today she would have a real, live Joe to talk to and she couldn't wait. Judging by the reactions of Debbie and Alisdair, neither could they.

When Joe did arrive, Debbie served up tea and then she and Alisdair made themselves scarce, leaving Irene seated in splendour with her propped-up leg and Joe Mortimer in attendance. Their conversation flowed as easily as it would have done if they were enjoying lunch in *The Three Tuns*.

"You haven't mentioned Ariadne as much as I thought you might," Irene said during a lull. "Is that good or bad?"

"We've been talking about you and your accident, which is what we should be doing. If you want some breaking news, Bruce Dougall has been in contact with me a couple of times. A member of the flight crew is ill. He won't be flying with them this time. But we've shuffled everyone around. It will be all over the papers and television tomorrow."

"I shall wait patiently."

"That's more than Bruce and I are doing. The sooner this bird takes off the better. That reminds me." Joe reached over for the box that he had put on a table when he arrived. "A less-than-tacky souvenir from Cape Canaveral, as promised. Bruce and I both have one on our office desks, in case we forget what we are trying to do. I managed to wangle one for you."

He stood by Irene's chair whilst she fumbled with the box. At last the graceful lines of *Ariadne One* were revealed in model form.

"I didn't know she was quite that beautiful, Joe," said Irene, quite overcome. "Thank you for such a wonderful present."

"The gift of a beautiful lady for a beautiful lady. That's only right and proper." It was the most natural thing in the world to sit down on the arm of her chair and kiss her. "You can't get up and run away. Am I taking unfair advantage here?" he wondered. "You could have slapped me, I suppose."

"Now why should I do that, even though I'm drugged to the eyebrows. I could make a small fortune selling the pills I'm taking to some of my students."

"I hope you remember this tomorrow, then," Joe said, after he had kissed her again. "I'd hate you to deny all knowledge of something that I won't be able to forget. Do you think you will be able to remember?"

"I will. But you'd better try that just once more for luck. And it will keep my memory sharp."

"She is positively *glowing*, I tell you." Debbie reported back to Alisdair in the kitchen after Joe had left.

She held the canvas bag of potatoes to her heart.

"Are you peeling those tatties by the power of thought?" Alisdair remarked.

"No. Just commenting on what a difference the visit of a fine man can make."

"Well, they can't have got up to much. In Irene's present condition, I can hardly see Joe Mortimer throwing her onto the carpet and—"

Debbie put a hand over her husband's mouth.

"Has anyone ever told you that you can be a bad man, Alisdair MacIver?"

He wriggled free.

"Yes, and you love me for it. Now, not a word to Irene on the subject. She's a dear friend and I want things to stay that way."

* * *

The popular media decided to make a hero out of Illya Abelev, on the basis that he was ready for the call of duty, even though he was unwell. There was endless film footage of him in hospital, with his family at his side. Most newspapers carried a picture or four along those lines. No one in *BUSSTOP* could do anything about this unwelcome publicity because Illya's family had invited the world in to share the astronaut's bad luck, or so it seemed. The short and dignified press release that Bruce had sanctioned was trampled underfoot.

"What an idiot!" said Joe in controlled fury when he had a longer on-screen conversation with Bruce about the subject. "If he'd gone into space, it could have jeopardised the whole mission."

"I did point out to him that it's a long way back from Mars, even with our current reactor and engines."

"You *pointed that out*? I hope that you told him what was what, Bruce."

He knew that Bruce could flay someone with words when necessary.

"I promised him a place on *Ariadne Two*."

"You promised him . . ." He looked at Bruce narrowly. "You are joking. Aren't you?"

"We're on a secure link so I can say this. Only you and I know that we were both probably unfit to be out in *Zeus Five*. Emotionally unfit, that is. I was, seeing as I had married for all the wrong reasons. And I'm guessing that you were too."

Even after all these years, with the safety of a secure line, Bruce could not bring himself to talk about Sally's death. Joe knew what he was hinting at.

Joe's head was spinning. The previous day with Irene had taken on an air of delightful unreality. This afternoon was becoming painfully unreal. The small but significant shifts that he had detected in Bruce Dougall when they were at Cape Canaveral were now becoming seismic. What was going on with the man?

"There was ultimately no harm done, I suppose," he conceded grudgingly and ambiguously. "It's given the media something different to chunter about and Gianfranco Rosso has been handed the chance of a lifetime. He will do well in the Lander."

"When they meet with the Martians, I hope he doesn't start kissing them!" Bruce chuckled. "He could start the first inter-planetary war."

That was more like Bruce.

*   *   *

"What have you been doing?"

It gave Sally great pleasure to throw the comment back at Tony, although she regretted it immediately. Vindictiveness was such an unattractive trait of the human female and she wasn't at all sure that Earth Sally was much like that. Was it coming from deep down inside her?

"I had to give Irene some hope," he said. "I couldn't bear to see her so distressed. She is Tony's grand daughter."

"When everything else had escaped from Pandora's Box, hope was left," Justin put in unexpectedly.

He was so quiet that they had forgotten he was there. His head hung low.

Sally put a hand on his shoulder.

"What's wrong?"

"My link—Ted. He was a good man, to begin with. I thought he was a kind man. That was why I was drawn to him. He was so kind to me at a difficult time. It was a difficult time for both of us. But now—I'm horrified at what he is contemplating."

Tony took his hands and shared his thoughts.

"This is hard for you, Justin. You can't do anything about it. Sally and I can appear in dreams to give comfort and to warn but what we did doesn't alter the course of events. You would have to be able to change what might be. That would not be allowed, even if you had the ability to make it happen, which you don't possess."

"And I still don't understand what use we will be here, with our links out on Earth," Justin continued. "Yes, the explorers need to see human forms that they can cope with, when they arrive. But any human forms would have done."

Tony said nothing. He was beginning to see where this might be leading, although he was not sure of the circumstances that would bring them to that point. He shielded that part of his mind from them.

Tony, Sally, Justin and Ichiro sat in silence, sharing their thought images. Joe Mortimer. Bruce Dougall. Irene Hanson. Ted Rodriguez. Brent Dyer. It was a mingling of joy and sorrow. Ichiro was the only one who could remember with a smile on his face as he recalled his co-designer Brent Dyer. Although Tony had never known his granddaughter, that lack of knowing hurt his human half.

"No wonder we moved down another path of development," Sally sighed.

"And there are beings in this galaxy that yearn to be like humans," Justin marvelled. "They want this. I wonder if they understand the confusion, the limited abilities, the isolation and the pain."

"Welcome to the human condition," Tony said soberly. "But it's not all doom and gloom for humans. Please don't forget the joy, the creativity, the reaching out, the learning and the sharing that is uniquely human."

The Earth part of Tony was recalling his wife and his children and the delight he took in his carpentry, especially the doll's house that he made for his daughter Judith. Oh, and the special desk and chair for son Mark's teddy bear, so that he could do his school work as well.

Daughter and father were very close. As Judy grew through her late teenage years to be as beautiful as her mother, Tony made her a promise.

"When your first child is born, I shall craft a cradle for her. Family members gave us cots and cradles for you and for Mark, so I didn't have the chance when you were babies. And I think my woodworking has improved a bit over the years!"

"I could have a boy first, Dad! That's presuming anyone will want me in the first place."

"We'll see, won't we?"

The path that Tony Johnson took meant that the cradle was never made.

In spirit, Tony had stood close to his daughter as she gave birth to a daughter of her own, fairer than herself, in a wild and windy early morning. He blessed Irene Elizabeth as her parents marvelled at the new arrival.

"This one has been here before," the midwife remarked as the newborn girl gazed at the person whom no one else could see.

Tony felt the warmth of tears in his eyes. Sally rushed to his side.

"I'm all right! In fact, I'm so happy." He laughed at their bewildered faces. "Oh yes. We have travelled so far and gained so much. We have had to wrap ourselves in cold clay to undertake this mission and we see that as a backward step. There are lessons for the people of Earth to learn, which somehow we will have to teach. I wonder if we have lessons to learn as well—about some of the special things we lost along the way."

Chapter Eleven

Irene made the return trip to hospital on the Monday morning, filled with apprehension. Her knee still hurt horribly, despite the medication she had been given, and her thigh muscles were joining in the protest too. Alisdair tried to put her mind at rest on Sunday night, explaining what was going on inside her knee. He went on to say that time was the only healer, combined with physiotherapy as she recovered. It all sounded very reassuring but Debbie knew that her friend was very nervous as they arrived at the out patient clinic.

Irene continued to feel gratitude towards the MacIvers that words could never express adequately. Alisdair went off to his hospital work as usual but Debbie made an executive decision to be based at home for the next few days.

"Most of my diary this week is taken up with meetings," she said. "That's one of the penalties of having the word *Director* in your title. I'm sure I won't be the only one joining in these discussions via the screen. The days when everybody had to be physically in the same room are long gone but old habits can be hard to shake off. Thank goodness I can do this. Alisdair can't help his patients remotely. He has found himself being dragged into a few meetings when he's at the hospital and he really resents that. When he's in the building, he's there to help the sick and injured. He has become very cunning. When he can't avoid a meeting, he organises one of the Emergency staff to call him back to cases that need his expertise. He's had *me* page him before now. It's amazing how many desperately ill people come through the front door of that hospital when he has been sat in a conference room for about ten minutes! Anyway, as long as one of us is around at home to keep an eye on you, for this week at least."

Doctor Fowler smiled brightly at Irene after he had studied the latest scan of her knee.

"You caused a bit of a stir on Friday, Professor," he said. "It's not every day we have a celebrity wheeled in to Emergency. But I promise I won't say a word about Martians! Now let me guess. You're still in a lot of pain and that worries you." Irene nodded. "This is usual. You're still in the first acute phase of ligament injury. It lasts about one hundred hours and you're still inside that time frame, when all hell breaks out as your body's defence systems react to the damage."

It was very naughty, but Irene listened only intermittently after that. Doctor Fowler was using the same phrases as Alisdair, so he could fill her in on anything important. She had learned the knack of looking fully alert—and yet mentally elsewhere—at school, to deal with the purgatory of lessons like Art and Design and Technology. So as the good doctor droned on, she was thinking about Joe and the time they had spent together the previous afternoon.

Alisdair was pleased to see a much happier Irene that evening.

"The clinic doctor said all the things that you said," Irene marvelled.

"Let me see." Alisdair winked at his wife. "*Acute stage, granulation phase* and *injury contraction and remodelling.*"

"That's it."

"We studied the same textbooks at medical school, Irene. And all the textbooks give the same information anyway. So what does yon Doctor Fowler say you've done?" He put a hand to his forehead in mock drama. "Let me prophesy! You have sprained all four ligaments in your knee—medial collateral, anterior cruciate, posterior cruciate and lateral collateral. The most damage is to the anterior and posterior cruciates because they have only half the strength of the medial collateral. In other words, you've wrenched those knee ligaments about as far as they will go without the need for surgical repair. This will all take a few months to heal totally and you'll never play centre forward for Cambridge United. How am I doing so far?"

"Very well indeed!" exclaimed Irene. "I'm impressed."

"You don't need to be. Wrists, knees and ankles are the basic fodder of front line Emergency medicine. They are the bits of the body that take the brunt of an impact when a person goes over unexpectedly and the knees suffer a lot in car crashes too. Despite all the safety technology built into vehicles these days, it's amazing what a knee will find to crunch up against, especially with very rapid deceleration. Anyone who has ever spent any amount of time working in an Emergency department could write the book on such injuries, their immediate treatment and their care."

"Apparently the doctor on Friday commented on my good general muscle tone and how that might have saved me from worse injury."

"You never knew, did you Irene, when you were hauled off to ballet class as a wee bairn, that one day it would stand you in good stead."

"And the fencing, which you still do," said Debbie. "That must help."

"I think that Doctor Fowler was trying to say that I was in good shape for my age," Irene observed grumpily. "What is it about doctors and age?"

"The medical profession has tended to set its milestones a bit early," Alisdair admitted, "because for the majority of medical history, most people died before their time. And then those milestones became cemented into the ground. Patients do take their revenge. I once saw a pregnant woman hit a colleague because he called her an elderly *prima gravida*—an older first time mother-to-be. He was a pompous ass and he deserved it. Professional terminology has its uses but that was the wrong occasion."

"How old was the woman?"

"Thirty two, if memory serves me right."

"Goodness! So I would—. Oh."

All three knew that they had come to a subject that was rarely mentioned. It was time to move on.

"How about contacting Joe Mortimer? He'll be busting a gut to know how you are," suggested Debbie. "He spoke to me before he left yesterday. He was very concerned about you."

Irene gathered up her crutches and hopped out of the kitchen, a woman on a mission.

Suddenly the world was a brighter place when she was talking to Joe.

"So the knee will heal up as and when," Irene concluded. "But I shall be throwing these crutches away at record speed."

"And you can have one of my medals for such bravery," said Joe. "I've got a few. I don't like to be greedy. I'll bet your doctor at the hospital wishes that all his patients were so attentive. You sound like a medical text book, Irene."

"That's Alisdair, filling in the gaps," Irene admitted. "I wasn't listening very much to Doctor Fowler. I was thinking about your visit yesterday."

"I'm glad you remember. Wasted effort is always frustrating! I've been thinking about it too. All day." He stopped, looked at a point beyond Irene, and grinned. "Tell Debbie that I'd be delighted. Thank you."

By the time Irene managed to turn round, she saw the corner of a piece of paper disappearing back behind the partly open door.

"What was that?" she asked, looking back at the screen.

"That was Debbie inviting me to dinner on Wednesday."

Later, Debbie showed her the sheet of paper that she had held up for Joe to see, with its message in capital letters: *JOE, WOULD YOU LIKE TO COME TO DINNER ON WEDNESDAY? SEVEN O'CLOCK?*

"Debbie!" she said.

"Well, Joe has accepted, hasn't he? Was he annoyed?"

"No, he thought it was funny and said that he wished he had friends like you."

"There you are then. Someone has to organise you two. It might as well be me. You were responsible for Alisdair and me getting together. I'm simply returning the favour. I wrote the message good and big because I know that Joe wears glasses now sometimes. There's not much wrong with his distance vision, though."

Irene went to bed feeling very contented. She had so much to be thankful for. She looked around the small downstairs study that had been transformed at lightning speed into a room for her. With a bathroom just along the passageway, the problem of stairs had been eliminated whilst she was here. Old rambling houses came into their own at a time like this.

Rhona and Mhairie had called her, full of sympathy and best wishes.

"You should be receiving some flowers tomorrow," said Rhona.

"And we will both be coming down from Liverpool at the weekend to check that Mum and Dad are looking after you properly," put in Mhairie. "Sorry we can't get to you before then. There are some cruel people at this university. We both have impossible timetables at the moment."

"My students tell me that all the time. Bless you, girls. I look forward to the flowers and, more importantly, your company."

After the slow and painful process of readying herself for the night and actually getting into bed, Irene picked up the book she was trying to read then put it down again. She hadn't made much progress with it thus far because her knee was the uppermost thought in her head. Tonight, lots of good things were jostling around in her mind and she needed to mull them over. In those first distressing hours, her fall had seemed to be a disaster. Of course, in some ways it was. But it was a disaster that came complete with all kinds of fringe benefits.

*   *   *

"So Rhona decided to find out if cats do always land on their feet," Alisdair continued. "She got hold of the wee beastie and threw it out of an upstairs window."

"Tabitha did land on her feet," said Debbie. "She tore off up the garden and was never seen again. Rhona was made to feel totally wretched by everyone."

The evening was a great success. Debbie thought Joe was wonderful anyway and Alisdair found that he had a kindred spirit. Like him, Joe was a successful public figure and he had a similar self-deprecating take on his achievements. And there was another unspoken item on Alisdair's agenda. Anyone who was interested in Irene was of interest to him.

Alisdair could see that Irene was really enjoying herself. As predicted, that first stage of pain, which no safe dose of drugs would properly quell, was past. She had lost the preoccupied look that people routinely wear when in extreme discomfort. Her eyes were only for Joe. The best of luck to them both. Joe was a good man.

At the end of the evening, Joe thanked his hosts in charming manner and Irene hobbled to the front door with him.

"I'm sure you know that you have the most amazing friends," he said. "I do know."

"Debbie and Alisdair have invited me for lunch on Sunday. They are gluttons for punishment. I understand their daughters will be here for the weekend."

"I can't wait for Sunday."

Debbie and Alisdair were clearing up in the kitchen. Alisdair inclined his head in the direction of the hallway.

"I'd forgotten how long it can take to say goodnight."

*   *   *

Joe had been in the house five minutes when he heard the messaging signal. He looked at the clock. It had to be America. Who had forgotten about the time difference? He decided it would have to be Bruce. Now what?

Bonny drew closer, as if knowing her master might need a little moral support.

"Okay, Bruce. I'm ready for anything. What is it?"

"Arty Rowe was playing soccer with his nephews and nieces in the back yard this afternoon and fell over the ball. He has broken his leg. A really nasty fracture."

Joe blinked. The circumstances surrounding this mission were becoming surreal.

"I know it's odd, Bruce, having to replace a replacement in the Orbiter crew but we have plenty more back-up people. I trust you and Deanna to pick the right one. Unless he's made a total hash of training, if memory serves me right it's Jackson Metz next, isn't it? At this time of night, I can't see your problem."

"The media are the problem—specifically the television companies. Someone has picked up on this and every East Coast six o'clock news show has gone out with *The Curse of Mars* as the lead story."

Joe closed his eyes. That phrase again! Anyone who had worked on the Zeus project was haunted by it. It was first coined in an early twenty first century piece of writing called *Beating the curse of Mars*, a response to the phenomenal financial cost of the exploration of the planet. At that time, two thirds of all unmanned spacecraft heading for Mars failed before they completed their tasks. Some failed before they even began.

These days the tag was used by anyone who opposed the Mars programme, and all opposition had to be treated with the utmost seriousness. *The Curse of Mars* was a handy stick with which to beat everyone, and it made a slick rallying flag. It hinted darkly at money being thrown away on an endeavour that was bound to end in tears because travelling to Mars was something that humans were not supposed to do.

Joe was aware of another writer from that era, who talked about *The Great Galactic Ghoul*, which seemed to live on a diet of Mars probes. Thank God no one had liked the sound of that one—so far.

"Who is your media person now?" he asked Bruce.

"They went straight past Morgan and jumped on me."

Albert Wright kept a stern but fatherly eye on the media people in Britain. As a rule he had them under control but Joe wondered if even he could rein them in with a story like this.

"So what do they want?"

"If I go on one of the breakfast shows tomorrow morning, I should be able to dampen this down."

"Fine." Joe was doing sums in his head. "I could just about make it. Do you want me to fly over? Present a united *BUSSTOP* front?"

Bruce looked taken aback. He didn't expect such a generous offer.

"Let's save that for if this thing goes totally wrong. A live link with you into the programme would do the trick. Could you manage that?"

"No problem. I'm sure that the television people here will want their interviews. I'll set up shop in the *BUSSTOP* media centre and do it all from there. Couldn't you do the same in Washington? Those breakfast shows of yours are bear pits, not places where you find out what's going on in the world!"

"Only me sitting for real in the studio will do, apparently."

"Hold on!" Joe said suddenly. "How did this get out so quickly? You say that Arty broke his leg this afternoon, your time. Who knows?"

"His father informed me. He made it very clear he wouldn't be talking to anyone. No one from the family wanted it. They didn't fancy the media all over them as happened with Illya Abelev. The hospital had been instructed to keep quiet, and they did. Arty's parents took some convincing that I didn't have anything to do with the leak. Oh, and the President and Vice President were told, as a matter of courtesy. That's it."

"Right. I'll get messages to the duty officers at Downing Street and Buckingham Palace. They may already have had enquiries from your side of the water. I'll just make sure that the PM and the King don't wake up to a nasty surprise tomorrow morning." The brevity of the list of people who knew about Arty now dawned on Joe. He pushed Bonny from his feet. "Are you thinking what I'm thinking, Bruce?"

*   *   *

Bruce Dougall was not a stranger to television studios, but right now he wished he were at home. Perhaps he was. He was still fast asleep and this was a nightmare.

But if it was, it was going on for a long time. Monty Silverton, the anchorman, was affability itself as they ran through some of the questions that might come up but silence fell as everything and everyone was counted in.

Stand by, studio floor. Sixty seconds.

This was worse than waiting to blast off into space for the first time, Bruce decided.

Desk ready. Thirty seconds.

Bruce took a few deep breaths.

Ten seconds. Run opening visuals and sound . . . five, four, three, two, one, on air.

Instead of the firing of rocket engines, Monty Silverton lasered the East Coast with his smile and they were away.

"A very good morning from *WMA*, Washington D.C. This is Monty Silverton, bringing you all the latest news. This morning, as the Ariadne space project to land people on Mars hits yet another problem, we ask if we should be taking more notice of the notion of *The Curse of Mars*. With me in the studio is my special guest Bruce Dougall, second in command for all the Zeus space flights, which paved the way for the Ariadne project. He was sometime chief instructor of our next generation of astronauts and is currently head of *BUSSTOP* here in D.C. We will be joined via screen link from Britain by Joe Mortimer . . ."

In amongst other news items, Bruce undertook a few opening rounds of verbal sparring with Mr Silverton. About half an hour in, Joe joined the show from London *BUSSTOP*. Like a defence lawyer questioning the legality of the court putting his client on trial, Joe and Bruce undermined the whole idea of *The Curse of Mars*. Joe was in fine form, with the historical facts and figures at his fingertips. He had already had a warm-up canter with his own domestic breakfast news programmes, so he was good to go. Bruce weighed in with the science and computing facts and figures. He landed what might be considered the knockout blow.

"I've enjoyed sitting here with you this morning, Mr Silverton, although I could have done with a bit more sleep. I hope that Joe and I haven't been wasting your time and the time of the viewers. After all, there isn't really a problem here, is there? If we didn't have a fully trained back up crew and the *Ariadne One* take-off had to be postponed, or even cancelled for lack of personnel, that would be something else. But I don't think that it would be *The Curse of Mars*, somehow. It would be total *BUSSTOP* inefficiency. Whatever Joe and I may be, we are not inefficient. I think our space flight record speaks for itself."

The unspoken *I rest my case* hung over a mesmerised studio. The director was signalling frantically to Monty Silverton to wind this up as quick as was decently possible. The interview had not gone his way.

There was a sense that the people of the Eastern seaboard of America were standing shoulder-to-shoulder, ready if necessary to physically lift *Ariadne One* off the launch slope at the end of December. If Bruce had appealed on the spot for volunteers to train as space crew, the line would have stretched from the studio building down to the Navy Yard.

On a quiet news day, journalists are happy to gloat over each other's problems. Monty Silverton was seen as a bit of a jerk in some circles and already one newspaper was planning tomorrow's front page headline: *DON'T MESS WITH OUR HEROES*.

Bruce was ever so slightly sorry for Silverton. He still had an hour to go.

"Having dragged me in here," he said to Joe afterwards, "the least this outfit can do is give me a half-decent breakfast. Will you be at *BUSSTOP* for the rest of your day? I'll catch you there later, then."

They still made a good team.

*   *   *

Ted Rodriguez had gambled and he lost. He was hearing that as he spoke to people in his office and received messages from his network of contacts across Washington D.C. That was the way things went oftentimes. If you were not prepared to take a risk, you shouldn't play the game. Some days you get the bear. Some days the bear gets you. But it was an unexpected bear that stood up on its hind legs, in the shape of Bruce Dougall. Ably backed by Joe Mortimer, he gave Monty Silverton the interview equivalent of a resounding slap. Although he had been as good a spokesman as Joe Mortimer for the Zeus programme in his flying days and had developed into the accomplished public face of *BUSSTOP* in America, no one expected him to pull out a performance like that. When the Vice President leaked the news about Rowe and got WMA the interview, he demanded that Silverton must demolish Dougall. With this television man's track record and Bruce Dougall's public persona as the quiet guy who just got on with things, it should have been a case of taking candy from a baby. But it wasn't.

The WMA studios informed Rodriguez that the calls had been pouring in. Almost every person was angry about the obviously hostile stance that Silverton took on the subject of exploring Mars and women ranging in age from twelve to one hundred were full of praise for "our boy, and that lovely British Mr Mortimer."

When those two went on the offensive, generating their grit and that indefinable *something*, which had taken a generation by the throat and the heart, all bets were off. The Vice President knew that he should have known better.

Maureen Rodriguez would have been shocked if she could have watched an expression settling on her husband's face. It was a blend of sneering contempt and a hardness that hinted at unplumbed depths of indifferent cruelty—something that she would never have seen before, or could have dreamt was part of her husband's character.

He asked his personal assistant to put him through to Dessie Shaffer. Even though they spoke on a secure line, the conversation was elliptical.

"Dessie, we need to go for the third option."

"Whatever you say. When?"

"We don't want to be too obvious. Give it five days."

"Understood."

"Okay," Rodriguez said under his breath, speaking to himself "Now you can find out what happens when you fail to deliver to Ted Rodriguez."

*   *   *

Tony knew that each assimilation of human form, complete with the memories and experiences of a particular person, was almost accomplished within the group. He had been almost overwhelmed by his developing awareness of his Earth life. He had heard the pain when Justin talked of his link, and identification with the original human was nearly in place.

> "*My link—Ted. He was a good man, to begin with. I thought he was a kind man. That was why I was drawn to him. He was so kind to me at a difficult time.*"

Tony knew he had been chosen as their leader because he would be the strongest at holding himself and his human entity apart in his mind. His was the weakest link. Although Tony Johnson had watched over his grand daughter all her life, he had never met her in corporeal form and, alas, she did not remember the first minutes of her life when he stood so close to her. And yet he was finding it all so difficult! Sally and Justin had complex relationships to deal with. He was glad that Ichiro had a straightforward history. In his present weakened human form, Tony couldn't have coped with anyone else going through so many crises as they came to terms with the back-stories of their characters. Sophia and Adam had no links and the seventh human entity was still undecided. And of course, the whole Martian group had been picked to meet the explorers from Earth because each one carried some of the blame for the shocking mishap that occurred out in space with *Zeus Three*, when an experiment went wrong. There were some interesting conversations to be had when *Ariadne One* finally arrived.

Thinking of the events surrounding the Zeus flight, he spoke to Sally, as he would speak to them all.

"Thank you for your help with Bruce Dougall. He continues to be physically stronger and mentally calm. And his better state is affecting those around him."

"Yes. That doctor thinks he's helping Bruce. He'll be very disappointed if he ever has to know that we have been supporting his patient."

"No. Doctor Doherty will win many honours in the medical world on Earth, ultimately being awarded the Nobel Prize for Medicine for his pioneering work in the new treatments of cancer. ZFF is a true breakthrough in managing the many manifestations of the disease. The drug really works. Bruce went back to him too late but because the medication is so new and its therapeutic nature so different, no one was really aware of that, or even sure what are the parameters of the medication. With something so untried, everyone is making it up as they go along. This apparent success will give Doctor Doherty the final lift to his professional confidence that he needs. As a result, his insights and knowledge will help countless people until such times as Earth catches up with our expertise and technology. It will happen, eventually," Tony said, when he saw the disbelief on Sally's face. "They may look like the poor country cousins and there are occasions when I wonder that we all spring from the same stock. They are on the slow path, that's all. So it doesn't matter that we bolster Bruce and give him strength. The important thing is that he has to live until we have come to a reckoning over our harm to him. To coin an Earth phrase, you have been working overtime on Bruce. Thank you again."

"Yes. Sally is doing what she can. Tony, how will this all work? Us here and our links out on Earth."

"I don't know," he lied. "When *Ariadne One* arrives everything will be a lot clearer. I promise."

*   *   *

The East Coast of America woke to the news that one of its favourite sons, breakfast television anchorman Monty Silverton, had died in a car crash on the Washington D.C. Beltway. A truck swerved after a tyre blow out and it careered on to smash into Silverton's car. He died in the ambulance taking him to hospital.

Ted Rodriguez paid public tribute to the man and asked for all the reports of the terrible accident to be on his desk within twenty-four hours. He had made road safety in general, and the racetrack nature of The Beltway in particular, one of his special concerns. This had gained him a nod of approval from the President. The odds attached to being killed or seriously injured on the roads of the United States of America had not improved much in one hundred and twenty years. The switch to hydrogen fuel cell-powered cars during the second half of the twenty first century might be saving the planet's atmosphere, but it wasn't doing much for preventing people driving recklessly. President Harper was glad that her Vice President was attached to such a popular and vote-winning campaign.

Rodriguez skimmed through the reports in his office on screen, asked for a hard copy and took the papers home to read that night. It wasn't fair on Mo to be always stuck in front of the screen in his study. Yes, it had been a very good practice for what he had planned at a later date.

Maureen didn't think it got much better than this. She and Ted sat either side of the log fire, snug and warm. Outside the wind was swirling the first snow of the season through the air. Music played softly in the background. The only other sounds were the rustle of documents and the crackle of the fire.

"Those papers are sure taking your attention," she commented.

Ted looked up at her. Mo was always there for him. He was a lucky man.

"These are the reports that I asked for about the Monty Silverton smash."

"Oh yes. That was dreadful! I saw Mr Silverton's wife and kids on the television earlier on."

"Dreadful," Ted agreed.

"Do the reports tell you what you need to know?"

"They tell me exactly what I need to know. Just what I was hoping for." Maureen gave him a funny look. "I mean, they are very comprehensive."

"You'll be able to use them in your road safety campaign?"

"Yes. That's it. I will."

"That's good. Perhaps there will be some good that comes out of Mr Silverton's death then."

"There will be, Mo. I can promise you that."

*   *   *

Joe fell into a comfortable and easy routine of visiting Irene whilst she was away from work and convalescing with the MacIvers. His time alone with Irene and being with Alisdair and Debbie were islands of sanity in an increasingly busy timetable as launch day drew ever closer.

"I often wonder what I was put on this Earth for," Debbie remarked one night to her husband. "If it is just to keep Joe Mortimer fed and watered and therefore make sure that the space thing is on track, I'm happy. And we're giving Irene and Joe a neutral space in which they can get to know each other a lot more. That's the bonus."

They both laughed but Debbie was not speaking entirely in jest. And for all her previous girlie patter with Irene about wanting her to plunge into a frantic affair with Joe, she was glad that circumstances had given them this breathing space, where they could engage first simply as two lonely people.

It was a shock to Debbie when she had that last part of the thought, but she knew that it was true. Despite all their friends, despite the busy worlds they inhabited and the regard in which those worlds held them, they were two lonely people.

Irene was making progress, albeit slowly. Her hospital doctors were concerned, as was Alisdair, but soon everyone began to make more hopeful noises. There were a few terrible days when she began to wonder if she could make it to Princess Charlotte's wedding. It was difficult to summon any enthusiasm for finding an outfit. Debbie sat down with her at the computer and they went through the on-line catalogues. Within half an hour Irene had made her choices and ordered them. Then it was a case of waiting for the clothes to turn up.

Joe called in on the Saturday before the wedding, when Irene and Debbie were purring over the newly arrived purchases, spread out over the kitchen table. Debbie snatched up the skirt and jacket, put them back in their bags and held them behind her back conspiratorially.

"Ready for a fashion parade, Joe?" she wondered. "Get this kit on, Irene, and wow us all."

Irene disappeared with several bags and boxes.

"I don't know how I can ever thank you," Joe said when Debbie automatically put a mug of black coffee in front of him on the table. "The way you're helping Irene. And I appreciate what you are doing for me."

"Irene is a dear friend. You fall into that category too, now. The girls look upon you as an honorary uncle. We don't need thanking. Irene is very precious cargo. I know that you treat her as such."

"She's still very fragile cargo," Joe mused, finally voicing his worry. It seemed to be the morning for honesty. "She really did herself a mischief, didn't she?"

"She's beginning to recover. I don't think she'll go back to work until after Christmas. She'll be back on form by then."

"I hope so. I've invited Irene to come to Cape Canaveral with me for the launch of *Ariadne One*."

"Have you now? You are one for coming out with surprises." Debbie looked at him over the rim of her mug for a moment and then busied herself pouring more coffee "Take good care of her, Joe."

"I intend to," he replied as they heard Irene's dot-and-carry-one footsteps returning. "I know I'll have you to answer to if I don't."

Joe sprang to his feet in admiration when Irene came into the kitchen.

"You look amazing!" he exclaimed.

"Oh, yes!" confirmed Debbie. "Everyone else at that wedding might as well give up now—apart from the bride."

After days of miserable weather, the day of the wedding dawned clear and bright. The die-hard witnesses, who turned up for all state and Royal occasions, had been camping out on the pavements for several days, to ensure that they had the best vantage places. Some of the old-timers were part of a long-standing camaraderie, swapping reminiscences about past events, such as the funeral of Queen Matilda. They were the heirs of a doughty tradition that reached back as far as the Coronation of 1953. One or two were defeated when the odd snowflake began to fall before dawn on Friday morning but, on the whole, they were made of stern stuff and were rewarded with a sunny end-of-November day.

They were joined on the Saturday morning by the less hardy bulk of the crowd, who took up their positions behind the barriers along The Mall, in Trafalgar Square, the Strand, Fleet Street and up Ludgate Hill to St Paul's Cathedral. They looked pityingly on the invited guests, who came from warm houses and hotels, well breakfasted and impeccably dressed.

Most of the congregation were requested to be in their seats by ten o'clock, an hour before the ceremony began. So it was an early start for Joe and Irene.

"We're doing this properly," said Joe as their plans were finalised. "Richard may have given me a personal invitation, but I'm going in my official capacity. Enjoy the ride, Irene. It will take us right up to the front steps of St Paul's Cathedral."

He arrived at the MacIver's house to pick up Irene in the *BUSSTOP* car, driven as ever by Roland. Debbie had already taken several photographs of

Irene in her outfit. Now she took some more pictures of her friend about to depart. She made sure that she didn't photograph the moments when Irene was easing her damaged leg into the car.

"You look fabulous," Joe whispered as he sat down beside her.

As soon as Debbie had waved them off, she was in position in front of the television, watching the Wedding Special programme, which had begun broadcasting at seven o'clock.

"Give me a shout when anything interesting comes on," Alisdair instructed her. "Especially when our bonny couple arrive. I'm not particularly interested in looking at the guests—apart from Irene and Joe."

"Wimp! Apparently the whole of America is taking the ceremony live. That should be an endurance test for those who want to watch it as it happens."

Alisdair happened to be in the room when the cameras fixed on Joe and Irene, stepping out of the official *BUSSTOP* car.

"And here we have a well-known face," said the commentator Luke Prentice. "Joe Mortimer, MBE, Britain's former lead astronaut and head of *BUSSTOP,* very much in the public eye at the moment, in the weeks leading up to the launch of *Ariadne One* to Mars. Accompanying him is Professor Irene Hanson of Cambridge University, who sprang to renewed international prominence some months ago when she announced that she had been tracking messages from the planet."

"Professor Hanson looks stunning," was the verdict of fashion guru Marcia Hollander. "She is wearing a flowing mid-calf light blue skirt and a close-fitting navy blue jacket with matching light blue trim. Her hat, shoes and bag are a clever shade of slate grey-blue—from the same colour palette, and yet so different. You can see with us the professor taking the steps up to the Cathedral very steadily, leaning on Mr Mortimer's arm. It is believed that she damaged her left knee badly some weeks ago. Undoubtedly the length of her skirt will have been selected to hide the support strapping on her leg.

"Joe Mortimer is ultra-smart as ever in a conventional three-piece suit. Look there at the *BUSSTOP* logo lapel badge, which he wears on all public occasions."

"I don't think we can quibble with that," said Alisdair. "They were well and truly noticed and given due praise."

In the Cathedral, Joe and Irene were settling into their seats.

"Are you okay?" Joe wanted to know, looking at Irene's pale and tense face.

"I will be in a moment," replied Irene. "I'm realising now why I've been with the MacIvers all this time. Those steps were murder."

There was organ music to listen to and then heads of state and foreign royalty began to show up. It was fun playing spot the public figures as further contingents entered the building. Joe picked out Kevin Crane, looking very solemn as he took his place with his wife.

The Queen and various dignitaries paced along the nave.

The playing of Handel's Water Music marked the bridegroom's procession. Michael Timpson was dressed in the full uniform of his rank—Squadron Leader. That very morning the title of Duke of Cambridge had been bestowed upon him. Charlotte would not become HRH Mrs Timpson upon her marriage.

The opening bars of Jeremiah Clarke's *Trumpet Voluntary* brought everyone to their feet. His Majesty King Richard the Fourth and Her Royal Highness Princess Charlotte were beginning the long walk up the nave. The music was chosen for personal and practical reasons. It was Charlotte's nod to her ancestor Diana, Princess of Wales, who walked into her own wedding accompanied by this piece of music. And with the journey up through Wren's masterpiece of a building being such a long one, the music had to be of sufficient length to get them to their destination without any repeats.

Joe noted that Richard was wearing the uniform of an honorary Air Chief Marshall. He was a former serving officer. More importantly, he was head of state and titular head of the Air Force, so he could do that. A little bit of effortless outranking was going on here. The bridegroom might have been lifted up through the pecking order as the new Duke of Cambridge, but he was still a mere Squadron Leader in the RAF. Richard was reminding everyone who was the boss.

All eyes were on Charlotte. Her ivory silk dress was a creation of total simplicity, with a minimum of ruffles and embroidery. It emphasised her trim, tall figure. Her veil was held in place by one of the Royal tiaras and two bridesmaids attended to her train. This was a ready-for-anything, no-frills princess of the twenty second century, who still retained that air of dignity, who promised so much for the time ahead when she would become monarch and head of state. She made her vows in a clear, firm voice that rang out through the building. If she had any nerves, they weren't for the congregation or the television audience to see or hear.

Many had looked at their history books and had watched the archive film. They saw more than an echo of a previous blonde princess. But as HRH Duchess of Cambridge walked back down through St Paul's Cathedral with her new husband, this was one princess with whom no one would fool.

Joe held Irene's hand as they stood for the bride and groom.

"You've done really well, Irene," he murmured. "Just the reception to go and then we'll be able to head for home."

"Don't, Joe. You make it sound like some kind of test that I have to pass. My leg might be hurting, but this is a *royal wedding* that we're attending and now we're off to Buckingham Palace. I wouldn't have missed this if I'd had to crawl on my hands and knees!"

Irene was strengthened by excitement and Joe was sure that she would make it through the rest of the celebrations.

Roland was ecstatic that he was driving the boss to Buckingham Palace for a *third* time. Irene said little, soaking it all in. For all her brave words, this was turning into a test. She found that she was registering snapshots of action, with most of the peripheral detail disappearing.

When Princess Charlotte and her husband appeared in the room where the reception guests were gathered, Irene managed a curtsy of sorts when she was introduced. The discipline of ballet came to her aid at that point.

"Professor Hanson!" exclaimed Charlotte. "It is so good to meet you. How is your injured leg? And Mr Mortimer! The King speaks often of you, with great affection. We will all be watching the launch of *Ariadne One* with the utmost interest."

The Duke asked Joe what he had flown during his time in the RAF and wondered with Irene if she had any plans for another book.

This was the timeless ceremony of royalty, for which the British nation has a matchless touch. Irene wondered if she was back in a dream world with her grandfather when she sat down with Joe in the Ball Supper Room for a three-course luncheon prepared by the Palace kitchens. Putting aside the obligatory French on the printed menu, along with Joe she enjoyed poached salmon, Beef Wellington and a deceptively simple lemon mousse, which was given added vroom by Italian lemon liqueur. A fine wine accompanied each course. The cake was cut with all due ceremony. Eloquent toasts were proposed and even more eloquent replies offered.

The events tumbled over one another. Irene was trying to keep a grip on each of them as best she could, because she was sure that she would never be part of anything like this again. Every time she looked at Joe he smiled encouragingly and once he winked.

"It would never do to upstage the bride," he whispered. "But after Charlotte, all eyes are on you."

"Flattery will get you everywhere," she whispered back and remembered the last time she said that, to Marmaduke, in another lifetime, before she met Joe.

When it was all over and the guests had cheered the happy couple on their way, tossing a cloud of rose petals and confetti, it was with a genuine sense of regret that Irene found herself settling in the *BUSSTOP* car and heard Joe speak to Roland.

"Back to the MacIver household, Roland, and don't spare the camels."

Chapter Twelve

As the calendar marched on towards the launch date of *Ariadne One*, no one remotely connected with this chain of events had any doubt that time moved at different speeds. This depended on where each person stood and what had to be done. For the present design teams, this was the last crawl along an interminable home straight. Their baby was long gone from their care and they couldn't wait to see how the modifications to the Zeus model improved her performance. They were fidgeting impatiently already, anticipating the telemetry readings from *Ariadne One* to see if any tweaking was needed before she took to the skies again as *Ariadne Two*.

Like some crazy jigsaw puzzle, *Ariadne One* had come together over a long stretch of time, but those who built her had been out of the equation for months. Their finished craft was waiting proudly for the great event, protected from the elements by an enormous moveable hangar, as were all spaceships these days. Never again would a space craft stand with foot long icicles hanging from her superstructure, as had happened prior to the launch of the doomed *Challenger* space shuttle at the end of January 1986.

Decisions based on weather predictions on Earth and conditions on the surface of Mars, which help govern when the spaceship would fly, had been made a while ago. Meteorologists of Earth and Mars could only stand by their advice and the likes of Joe Mortimer and Bruce Dougall trusted their experts implicitly. And everyone could be certain where Mars would be in its leisurely orbit of the Sun, in its relative position to the Earth.

For the *BUSSTOP* chiefs, time skittered away one moment and dragged the next, the latter usually happening when they were trapped in some interminable meeting or screen conference. Bruce's complaining was at a minimum. He knew that he was living on borrowed time, however generous Doctor Doherty might claim his extra portion to be, and it was all beyond price.

The people who had the most secure grasp on the passing of the days were the Ariadne crew themselves. They took the disappearance of Arty Rowe and the advent of Jackson Metz in their stride. They worked as a group and they were trained to be interchangeable in the tasks that they carried out within the main ship. The Lander crew all had to be able to put the vehicle down safely on the surface of Mars. Once Brian Hammond and Jethro Norman landed the simulator smoothly as a matter of routine, they worked with the rest of their team as conscientiously as Joe and Bruce had done in those training sessions that the outside world would never know about. The whole group spent time getting the feel of the artificial gravity system used in Ariadne, which was slightly different from what was current on other spaceships. The landing team practised walking and undertaking tasks in the simulated conditions of Mars. On that planet, with thirty eight per cent of the gravity of Earth, the human body would give the impression of being one third of its actual weight.

Like the Zeus crew before them, they had the confidence that comes from being part of a first-rate team that has worked together and has anticipated most eventualities. If the launch date had been brought forward suddenly, they would have settled into position on Ariadne and got on with the job.

The newspapers and television programme makers knew that all their birthdays and Christmases had come at once. There was apparently no end to the people prepared to add their two cents' worth to the torrent of information that was being pumped out to a bewildered public in the run-up to the launch. Everyone who wanted a say about the upcoming adventure had a guaranteed platform and the reluctant were encouraged to speak by the sheer weight of data being put out there, complete with the inevitable mistakes and misunderstandings that crept in and needed correction. It was chain reaction fusion, human-style.

Brent Dyer, whose design vision with the reactor engines made the Zeus flights—and thus Ariadne—possible, was lured into the media arena. He lived quietly these days with his family in rural Vermont. He was not about to make the process easy for those who wanted his thoughts.

"I'm an engineer, not a performing monkey," he said testily on more than one occasion.

So a top television journalist and film technicians had to travel to see him. It was worth it. He had picked up the label "reclusive" but the now white-haired man who smiled like a benign shark and looked like everyone's much-loved and eccentric uncle, was the unexpected hit of the weeks leading up to the departure of *Ariadne One*. No one commented on how he had altered with the passing of the years. Television viewers and newspaper readers had grown beyond holding the childish idea that those in the public gaze, however briefly, should be unchanged and unchanging and hey, everyone gets older. Yes, Brent Dyer might have a few lines on his face now. His neck was chunkier and his jowls heavier. But his lively and restless mind, mirrored in his dancing grey eyes, was as sharp as ever. The interview was pure gold and broadcasters were able to edit it into three programmes, as he shared his insights into the ongoing development of his original idea. He remembered his colleague Ichiro Matsushita, who died tragically young. He was generous in his praise of Joe Mortimer and Bruce Dougall and the people they led into space.

"Sure, I could design things all day long and the geniuses who worked alongside me could build them, but we would have gotten nowhere without those brave men and women who flew *Zeus One*. They didn't know, and we didn't know for certain, whether she was the next great thing in travelling to the stars or a hi-tech, big-bucks bomb."

Such comments made everyone stop and remember. Because history recorded the triumphant and happy ending to the story, time had been allowed to blur the edges of the very real potential jeopardy that surrounded the first Zeus missions. It was a bit like not quite appreciating Cinderella's grief when she is forced to stay at home and not go to the ball. The audience knows that she will end up with the Prince and can't see what all the fuss is about.

Joe and Bruce were suitably flattered by the kind words from Brent Dyer. They had met him a few times early on in the Zeus project, when he was hanging around anxiously, swinging between doubt over the propulsion system he had created and pride in the fact that he and his team had taken something from the *Too difficult* list and had made it happen.

"Look after this old lady," he had said to them, prior to the take-off of *Zeus One*. "We've tried to make sure that she'll look after you."

Joe, in particular, fell into the habit of calling Zeus "the old lady" as a result of that talk.

BUSSTOP on both sides of the Atlantic had any number of publicity people, with a whole raft of information to hand. It was their job to keep the newspapers and television people happy. But Joe and Bruce felt that they had to become involved. As well as *The Curse of Mars* brigade, there was the school of thought that maintained that the Zeus missions had never flown as far as it was claimed they flew and that *Ariadne One* would not really be landing on Mars. This was a natural extension of the late twentieth and early twenty-first century fantasy that *Apollo Eleven* didn't land on the Moon at all; it had all been a big con trick, filmed in a studio. The not-going-to-Mars idea was fuelled by ignorance and poor memory. It was clear from the much-trumpeted television schedules that coverage of the flight and the landing on Mars would consist of a programme of highlights each day. Therefore, some believed, there must be something to hide. Everyone had forgotten that the Zeus flights were covered in exactly the same way.

Joe, Bruce and their ranks of media representatives explained it time and again. The time lag for a message travelling back and forth to the Moon is just over a second, hence the characteristic "beep" that has punctuated all Earth-Moon communications traffic since the 1960s. So broadcasts can be virtually in real time.

That couldn't be so with signals to and from Mars, as Bruce showed on several occasions in interviews. He had no Kevin Crane figure at his elbow to remind him to go easy on the techy bits. The Prime Minister knew the country he represented and was well aware that, deep down, the British can't abide a smart-arse. The romantic notion of the bumbling amateur, dreaming dreams sitting in the garden shed, had never quite gone away.

Bruce Dougall was speaking to a national audience with very different tastes and temperament. Those watching him saw him as a tried and trusted expert, sharing the benefit of accumulated knowledge, in time honoured fashion.

"Even at their closest approach when Earth and Mars are on the same side of the Sun, they are roughly thirty six million miles apart and a radio wave travelling at the speed of light will take over three minutes to cover this distance," he told journalists and interviewers. "The two planets can be at a maximum of two hundred and fifty million miles apart and that means that messages will take over twenty two minutes to arrive." He demonstrated the working of the standard formula that was used to calculate the time it would take for a message and pictures to travel between Earth and Mars at any given moment in the mission and then added a flash of humour, which viewers were coming to expect. "And Mr Stewart, my Math teacher, I hope that you can see that I was listening in your classes."

Mr Stewart, well into his eighties, was listening to one of these patient explanations and mailed a message to his former pupil.

"I've boasted shamelessly for a long time that you were in my Math classes. You have made an old man very happy now that you have demonstrated publicly your grasp of arithmetic."

Bruce found, as did Joe in Britain, that while most understood what he was saying, there were those who didn't want to understand, who had shut their minds deliberately. They formed part of the anti-Mars movement, which needed a watchful eye kept on it just in case things got really silly. Bruce had been troubled by the way in which the news of Arty Rowe's accident had been leaked to the media. There was only one person who could have done such a thing. It didn't bear thinking about. The sooner *Ariadne One* landed on Mars, the better.

Joe was cheerful about there being contact with Martians—whoever and whatever they were. Once Irene had put the idea in his mind a seeming age ago, it had become a natural extension of the mission. Bruce tried to paint similar scenarios for himself but there was something wrong with every picture he created. That nagging doubt, which had been with him ever since he came to his senses, and which was undoubtedly there when those senses were scrambled, would not let him go. When he was raging at his illness, he managed to convince a national government that the whole enterprise was fraught with danger. Mission oversight was tossed ungraciously to Britain as if it was a grenade with the pin out. At that time, he was thinking of the problems of sustaining an orbit round Mars for any length of time, which was a pathetic excuse, and the no-second-chance accuracy that was needed to land on the surface, which had proved itself to be a real difficulty. Now, he was pursued by poorly formed feelings, impressions and thoughts that were just out of reach. It was like a shadowy figure that whisked away out of view when he turned to face it fully. He went over the anticipated sequence of events repeatedly and it all looked good every time, so he was at a loss to understand his own reservations. He mentally itemised every step:

The launch. A routine flight. Establishing an orbit round Mars. The Lander touching down with barely a whisper. Human beings stepping out on to Mars for the very first time—was Brian Hammond's script finalised, by the way? Being met by . . . .

That was the point at which Bruce began to bother. Would the Martians be hostile? Impossible to communicate with?

Something was not right.

He didn't know what and he had to leave it on the back burner of his mind. There were far too many real matters taking up every waking moment and, if he was not careful, they followed him into his dreams.

*   *   *

Irene was recovering well. Her knee was still stiff and occasionally painful. She was attending physiotherapy sessions to aid the healing process. The MacIvers let her go back home full time with some reluctance.

"If I don't get back into some routine soon, I will never do it," she said quite reasonably. "I don't think you want a permanent lodger."

Also, she was hoping that Joe would call round.

That wasn't happening any time soon. Joe Mortimer's days were crammed full. The main ingredients of any twenty four hours were administrative slog and media calls—both related to Ariadne—plus some perfunctory time put aside for eating, sleeping and remembering that he was responsible for a dog who never asked to be owned by someone who played with spaceships for a living.

He managed to keep in contact with Irene.

"I'm sorry that things are so mad," he said sorrowfully on more than one occasion from the screen. "There just don't seem to be enough hours in the day. I wouldn't blame you if you turned round and said that you won't accompany me to the launch."

"Of course I will!" Irene exclaimed. "I mean—you do still want me to, don't you?"

"Irene! We both know what we feel about the trip. Vicky is sorting out all the practicalities for our visit. How does this grab you for a timetable?"

*   *   *

This was a hard task for Vicky Tennant. Not that she faced any difficulties in how to go about it. She knew the people she needed to speak to and they knew her. Booking anything to do with Cape Canaveral at this time required the personal touch and she gave it. She laughed and joked with the airline company representative when sorting out the flights. The man she spoke to dealt with her personal account when she visited Washington D.C. to see her brother Jamie, who was working there as a doctor. She had a long talk with the hotel manager, who could offer her rooms, despite the fact that his hotel had been full, with a waiting list, since the launch date was announced.

"You'd better make it two rooms, Vicky," Joe had said. "The press will have a field day otherwise."

"Of course, Mr Mortimer."

It broke her heart. She had met Professor Irene Hanson just that once, after her joint press conference with the head of *BUSSTOP*. She was a nice enough woman, very polite and composed in the circumstances of the fraught day in which she became embroiled. But what was *she* doing going to Cape Canaveral with the boss?

It was propinquity, she guessed. Two people, thrown into each other's company . . .

Vicky felt tears prickling her eyes as she messaged confirmations of the arrangements she had made. She spent a lot of time with Joe Mortimer in her capacity as his personal assistant. She knew as much about him as any wife or partner, she was sure. She knew his moods, the weaknesses that he displayed inadvertently through what happened in the work arena, and the people he liked and disliked—although she was becoming confused about where he stood with Bruce Dougall. But to her boss, she ranked alongside the computer and communications system.

"I hope you have a wonderful time, Professor Hanson," she said quietly, with a kindness that she did not feel. "The launch will be pretty amazing too."

For more and more people, the launch couldn't come soon enough. Mars fever was gripping everyone and, like any fever, it was debilitating. Chic dinner gatherings and the in-crowd restaurants managed to put *Mars* or *Martians* somewhere in the menu every time. Children's parties in the run up to Christmas had one theme only: *Fancy dress! Come as a Martian!* Demented parents and grandparents were roped into making the most original costumes yet. And as no one knew what a Martian looked like, the inventive went to town.

Joe and Irene reported to each other with considerable amusement that the schools in both of their villages were stretching the Nativity play narrative to include some Martians arriving in time for the birth of the baby Jesus. Teachers of older children were getting their heads round the topography of Mars, finding out as much as possible about *Amazonis Planitia*, the proposed touchdown site for the Lander vehicle of *Ariadne One*.

Much against his better judgement, Joe found himself facing one of his toughest audiences yet in the events prior to the take-off. He was invited to talk to the eleven year-old children in his local school. This was nothing new. As Pond Lane Primary School's most famous ex-pupil, it was something that had to be done occasionally. It didn't mean that he had to enjoy it, though. Generally he didn't like going back, because of some of the memories that were conjured when he walked through the front door of the school. In the foyer were the original keystone and plaques, which denoted the original construction of the school and subsequent major rebuilding projects: 1875; 1957; 2040. Looking at the last date, Joe was amazed that the school he knew had gone so long without a major rebuild. How long it would be before someone decided that *this* building had outlived its useful life?

It was always an embarrassing trip back in time. He and school had not got on, initially. Philip had watched over him from a distance on his first day and was delighted by the way his little brother coped.

"Did you enjoy today, Joe?" their mother asked anxiously at home time.

"Oh yes," said Joe. "But I don't have to go any more, do I?"

When it dawned on the five year-old that he had to turn up every day for the foreseeable future, like his brother, he wasn't so happy about it. Philip died a thousand deaths of humiliation and Stella Mortimer got used to handing over a screaming child to his teacher. Well, as used to it as any mother could be, when her last view each morning of her little one was a small figure, rigid with anger and apprehension and yelling at the top of his voice, being carried through the classroom door.

Joe was glad that, in later years, he had a chance to thank his teacher from those days. Miss Watson, who had been near retiring age when he turned up in her class, was delighted to welcome him into her home on several occasions. On what turned out to be his last visit before her death, Joe gave her the most amazing news of all.

"I've been selected to train at *BUSSTOP*, Miss Watson." He could never bring himself to call her Mary, even though she encouraged him to do so. It was disrespectful in his eyes. "I will be going into space. I'd really like to go in for the new long-haul missions towards Mars."

"That's very exciting, Joe. I knew you would do very well."

"Did you really? Even when I was sitting in the corner crying and disturbing the whole group?"

"Even then. It may have seemed harsh at the time, but I let you get on with it until you were ready to do something. The last thing you needed was an audience, or any sympathy. And then you came out of that corner and jumped into that classroom. That showed real character, young man, which will stand you in good stead for your chosen career."

"I don't know what I was making a fuss about back then. Not really."

"Does anybody truly know what is going on in the mind of a small child?"

"I did enjoy being in your class, Miss Watson. It might not have seemed like it at the time."

"And you were fun to have around. Good luck in your new venture, Joe."

On this occasion, the Head teacher of Pond Lane had asked Joe to talk about the landing site on Mars, why it had been chosen, and how it contrasted with rest of the planet's terrain. He had to do a bit of research—or rather, he got the information from the appropriate department within *BUSSTOP*. There was a presumption that, as a former lead astronaut and now the British boss of the space agency, his knowledge was all encompassing.

He walked down corridors that were engraved upon his soul. As ever, he expected to see old familiar faces through the classroom windows and doors and, as ever, they weren't there. Some of his old teachers had been honoured by their names being given to classes. There was a Watson class for the five year-olds.

The purposeful buzz of activity, which Joe had always sensed, was much in evidence. There was that unmistakable school smell, a mixture of polish, cleaning fluids and an indefinable something else. And he never ceased to wonder about how *small* everything looked, when he delved into his recollections of the six years he spent in the building.

Joe found that he had an interested and responsive group of young people on his hands. They listened, they laughed at most of his jokes, and asked pertinent questions. He had prepared a computer display of photographs and diagrams to show the contrast between the flat northern plains, smoothed out by ancient lava flows and the pockmarked and cratered southern highlands. This rugged appearance was caused by multiple meteorite strikes.

"There was no contest as to where we would land. It had to be Amazonis Planitia, the Amazonian plain. It is *the* flat place, ideal for putting down any kind of vehicle and hopefully not smashing it into pieces," he told the children. "If you look at a map of the northern hemisphere of Mars, it is found centred on 24.8° N 196.0° E. It is between the Tharsis and Elysium volcanic area to the west of Olympus Mons, or Mount Olympus. That is the highest known mountain in the solar system, nearly three times bigger than Mount Everest."

Some of what Joe was saying was over the children's heads but they gave him their full attention, wearing their name badges prominently so that Mr Mortimer could address them personally. They felt as though they were being initiated into some great and grown-up secret. It was incredible enough that Joe Mortimer had sat in the classrooms where they sat. They may have been apparently sophisticated eleven year olds but they found it hard to imagine him as a child, although his class photographs, along with those of his brother Philip, were there for everyone to see.

The mind-blowing element came as the talk became a relaxed conversation, which broadened out into the whole space exploration project, which preceded Ariadne. Joe's replies were littered with casual references to *Bruce Dougall* and *Brent Dyer*—people who were up there with him in the Hall of Fame.

Neville Class kept Joe long beyond the time he was meant to be there but this was one occasion when no one minded the timetable being sabotaged. One child summed it all up.

"Mr Mortimer, you know that all the class groups are named after people who have contributed to the life of the school. I'm the School Council representative for this class and I shall be asking the Head teacher at the next meeting that we should name a class after you. You have done so much for space exploration."

"Thank you, Dawn. I hope that I can live up to such high expectations. I'm sure that you'll all be watching the launch on television."

The projected television viewing figures for the launch of *Ariadne One* were so big as to be incomprehensible. Every country was taking the broadcast live. It felt as though the whole world would be tuned in.

By Christmas Eve something unexpected was happening.

The possible audience in Great Britain was shrinking by the minute.

Influenza stalked the land. The healthy and the strong were taking to their beds in droves. They were weak, feverish, aching, coughing and knowing—if they were capable of thought—that if someone lit a fire under them, they would have to burn, because they were incapable of moving. The numbers involved made this an official pandemic, on a par with the outbreak of 2045.

Irene was staying with the MacIver family for a few days before she flew out with Joe on the twenty seventh of December. She stumbled down to breakfast on Christmas morning, heavy-eyed and pale. By early afternoon she was poorly and in bed.

Debbie did her best to make Irene comfortable and Alisdair left a message for Joe, asking him to make contact urgently. He guessed that Joe wouldn't be too far away, seeing as he appeared not to have his personal communicator with him. Probably he was spending Christmas Day with his family. Alisdair did wonder if he ought to gamble on Joe being there and speak to him straight away. He decided to let the poor man enjoy his day before he had to tell him what was happening.

Alisdair had guessed correctly. Joe was with his family and he was wishing that he wasn't.

Stella Mortimer had to resist the urge to fuss too much over Joe. It was obvious that he was going through the motions and rituals of the day and not enjoying it. He was tired and distracted and had little to say to anyone. It dawned on her, belatedly, that he had really meant what he said when she issued the invitation. Left to his own devices, he would have preferred to be alone with Bonny, perhaps calling in at the MacIvers in the afternoon to check that Irene was all ready for their journey. She would hear none of it and insisted on gathering everyone up, mother-hen style, for a get-together.

In the afternoon, she had to admit to her younger son that she had misjudged the situations.

"Oh, Joe! You really should have stuck out for the day on your own," she said candidly when she found him in the back garden, counting the tips of daffodils that had already broken through the surface of the flower beds in anticipation of Spring. "I forced you into this. And after all the hard work of preparation for the launch, this really has been the last thing you needed. Forgive me. It seemed such a good idea—celebrating Ariadne's launch, little Abby's first Christmas, all that kind of thing. You know."

"I know, Mum. And you're forgiven," he said, enveloping her in a hug. "I shall be fine. Once we get to Cape Canaveral, the adrenaline will take over."

"Hmm. I think you've been running on adrenaline for some time. And *we*?"

"Irene is coming with me. Didn't I tell you?"

"You know full well you didn't. I'm not surprised. I—." Stella stoppered the urge to make any more motherly comments. "Come back and join the others, please. Abby has stopped crying and is asleep. I don't know why she is so fretful today. She has been such a placid child thus far. I could see that she was beginning to annoy you."

Yes, it had been a day that Joe would not look back on with any pleasure, and he wasn't proud of the way he had behaved. Abby was only a few months old. He had no excuse. The bright spot on the horizon that kept him going was the thought that in less than forty-eight hours he would be on his way to America with Irene. *Ariadne One* would lift off and Irene would be there to share it with him.

She would be there to share so much with him.

Arriving home and talking with Alisdair MacIver was like a punch in the face.

"This is desperate bad news, I know," said the doctor. "I understand how much Irene and yourself have been looking forward to making this trip together."

"Can I speak to Irene?"

"She's fast asleep right now. She is really unwell. If she was awake, she wouldn't be making much sense. And I wouldn't recommend calling round tomorrow, Joe. Irene is in a bad way and flu is very easily caught. We are discouraging anyone coming to call. We're a bit like a stricken house in the Great Plague of London. We should have a red cross scrawled on the door, along with *God have mercy on us*. You're the history man. Have I remembered it right? There is every chance that Debbie and I might develop the infection. We'll have to care for each other as best we can if that happens. You don't want to be poorly for the launch, or be the one who spreads this across the Atlantic." He leaned forward earnestly. "Irene cares a great deal for you, Joe. She'll still care about you when you return." He grinned. "Debbie is making me as bad as her. You enjoy the launch and haste ye back."

Joe didn't have much choice in the matter. He crashed around the house and realised he was being ridiculous when he found Bonny cowering fearfully behind a chair. He managed to coax her out and reassured her that everything was all right. Mum and Dad would be looking after the dog whilst he was away. He could have taken her over to their house today but he was glad that he hadn't done so. She was a creature of habit and would have found the freewheeling excitement of the day too much. Philip was calling round to collect her early on the twenty-seventh, before Joe left for the airport.

"That showed real character, young man."

Miss Watson's words came into Joe's mind yet again. He just wished that he didn't have to wheel out his strength of character on quite so many occasions.

* * *

It was all building up to be the biggest block party in recorded history. Anyone who was anyone was due to be there, but the people converging on

Cape Canaveral fell into two distinct groups. There were those who wanted to be seen, to have their column inches and pictures in the gossip pages and a report on the more lightweight television programmes. They were of great annoyance to the other group—those who could be loosely classified as the Ariadne family. They were the swathes of individuals without whom the spaceship literally would not take off and fly safely, the many who had devoted months and years to make this possible, and the actual families of the astronauts, there to support their loved ones as they stepped into history.

On the subject of loved ones, Brian Hammond was feeling like the old man of the crew. He was the only one with a wife and children who would be watching the take-off. Everyone else had parents, brothers and sisters, girl friends and boy friends who would be willing *Ariadne One* up into the sky.

Joe found Bruce to be unusually sympathetic when he explained why he was here on his own, as he had said previously that Professor Hanson would be accompanying him.

"That's real tough. I hope the professor recovers soon. Your influenza outbreak has been reported over here. The World Health Organisation is hoping that it doesn't become a global thing."

"I don't think I've brought it with me." Joe looked down on the heaving hotel foyer from their perch in the mezzanine bar. "I don't know why half of these characters are here."

"All publicity is good publicity," Bruce reminded him. "Although I'm not sure whether I'll be saying that tomorrow. Jonathan Farmer clocked me earlier with Shannon. I don't know if he was totally sure it was her."

Jonathan Farmer was one of the most predatory gossip writers.

"Your ex-wife is here?" Joe marvelled.

"My first ex-wife," he corrected. "I have no idea what Belinda is doing these days. Shannon insisted that I needed some moral support. She made her arrangements quite independently of me. She has a bit of leverage in her own right these days, as an about-to-be-published author. She's around somewhere," he concluded vaguely, as if she was a book that he had put down carelessly and couldn't remember where he had last seen it.

"Brent Dyer is supposed to be here for the launch," Joe mused. "If he has any sense, he'll take one look at this lot and head straight back to Vermont. I wish I was back in Hertfordshire."

Joe was keeping in contact with the MacIvers. Irene remained very ill. He wanted to be with her, that's all. Comfort her, hold her, and encourage her. Seeing as the MacIvers would not let anyone near the house, public duties had to be fulfilled.

Public duty day, the thirtieth of December 2109 dawned bright and cold. *Ariadne One* looked breathtaking. The sun glanced off her sweeping white body and dazzled those looking her way. The traditional vertical take-off was a curiosity of the past. Ariadne, like her Zeus predecessor, used an elevated ramp for launch. But some things hadn't changed that much. Added extras, in the form of boosters, spoiled her fine lines. Liquid fuel was still the best way to create enough power and thrust to ascend rapidly and break free of Earth's atmosphere. The empty tanks would be dumped when their job was done. Then Ariadne became a proper spaceship, a plane in space, powered by the phenomenal reactor in her tail.

There was some surprise that figures such as Joe Mortimer, Bruce Dougall and Brent Dyer would be outside watching the launch. The "experts" surmised that they would be inside Mission Control. Joe disabused some journalists of that idea.

"Talk-back at a launch is not a place for visitors. We would have nothing to do and we would probably be in the way. Remember that Bruce and I have never seen these machines take off for real."

"We were in the damned things," Bruce reminded the newshounds when they looked confused. "I must be getting old," he said to Joe when they had gone. "I think that all journalists are growing stupider by the day."

"They probably are. At home, it used to be that thinking police officers were getting younger was a sign of age."

"Yeah." Bruce shook his head. "The kid playing dress-up in cop's uniform, who quite rightly asked for my ID last night, must have been about twelve. I wanted to ask her if her mother knew she was out so late."

"Good morning, gentlemen!" A chirpy Brent Dyer appeared beside them, well muffled against the cold. "It'll make a change for you two, seeing a launch. It's the first one for me, in the flesh, so to speak."

They found out after the flight that he had hidden in a small room within the Cape Canaveral complex when *Zeus One* took off. Following that, a degree of superstition took over and Dyer stayed at home for all the Zeus launches, with the television and computer shut down, watching the take-off later, safe in the knowledge that all was well.

All eyes were turning to a disturbance in another knot of people within the crowd. A child was crying and the noise was growing.

"That's my Daddy there!" a quivery, quavery voice hiccupped. "Daddy! Daddy!"

"Fred Hammond—Brian's little boy," Joe murmured in Brent Dyer's ear.

Georgina Hammond was becoming flustered as Fred got louder and louder. She could see the tears welling in Susie's eyes. She would kick off in a moment, simply because her brother was in a state. Those standing close by were becoming more perturbed by the moment. There was nothing that anyone could do.

Brent Dyer strode over to the Hammond group, indicating that Joe and Bruce should follow. Neither was sure what help they could be. Joe was slightly better versed in small children than Bruce because of Sam, but Sam never had a screaming fit before the eyes of the world. They were relying on the engineer, a family man with children and grandchildren.

"Hey, little soldier!" Brent said. "What's the problem?"

Fred looked up at him. Curiosity won out over his distress.

"Who are you?"

"I'm Brent. I helped in the building of the spaceship your pa is in and these amazing guys—" He indicated Joe and Bruce "—flew a whole heap of times in another of my rockets. D'you think I'd build spaceships that don't fly properly?"

"No," Fred conceded.

"I'm sure you can't see much down there. How about a better look sitting on my shoulders? Is that okay, Mrs Hammond?" he enquired.

Georgina nodded, speechless that the great man should even be bothered about her son. Brent swung Fred up in his arms and Joe asked if he could do the same for Susie. The Hammond children had the best view in the house.

The countdown had raced on during that interlude. Everyone went quiet. Apart from the occasional sniff from Fred, there was silence. Bruce could see that Brent had his eyes closed. Whether he was praying or pretending he wasn't there, the former astronaut could not be sure.

Joe caught sight of a man who was obviously wishing that someone could pick him up, take him away from the cares of the moment and soothe him—Emily Alexander's father. Doug Alexander's eyes never left *Ariadne One*. The *BUSSTOP* chief guessed that Mr Alexander was torn between pride the size of a planet and the overwhelming urge to somehow board the spaceship and snatch his daughter to safety. Emily was all he had. His wife had become bored with their new life in America some years ago and went back to England and then filed for divorce.

Bruce was watching him too, with concern. Here was an overweight, middle-aged Brit, who fascinated everyone he worked with in the New York world of finance by never losing his bizarre English accent. Those in the know said it showed he came from Birmingham, in the West Midlands area of England. He made a huge contrast with his daughter, who was so obviously raised on Long Island every time she opened her mouth.

Yes, it had been so easy to climb into the next space ship and zoom around without a care, trailing the good wishes and prayers of the world. It was far harder sending others out there, with all the responsibilities and possibilities that went with such an action.

Joe and Bruce were mentally going through the checklist that the astronauts were following in the last five minutes. Joe could hear the ground team inside his head, following the script but livening things up with the unexpected comments.

"Joe, Bruce, bring me back a stick of rock," Martin Baker said on a few occasions, just before the clock swept into the last minute.

Martin hailed from Blackpool, in northwest England. Every seaside town sold its own confection, with its name written through the middle and, naturally, he insisted that Blackpool rock was the best! Joe had never had a particularly sweet tooth, even as a child, and Bruce had been appalled when the general idea of seaside rock was explained to him.

It was a private joke that eased the tension.

Ariadne One was obviously powering up. She was a sleek, white missile, long and slender, pointed at the stars. But like Zeus, this missile packed a crew of seven rather than an explosive warhead.

The final countdown began.

Ten, nine . . .

The words were lost as a ground-shaking roar reached the spectators. Hot gases thundered against the curved protecting shield that stood behind Ariadne's tail. The sound reached new decibel levels as the spaceship slid free of the forty-five degree angled ramp and climbed slowly into the air, leaving behind an acrid vapour plume.

Brent was holding Fred's ankles tighter than necessary but the boy didn't mind.

"Bye bye Daddy!" Fred called, waving frantically and bouncing up and down on his point of vantage.

Bruce realised that he hadn't breathed for a while. He had watched film of the Zeus launches many times, of course, but nothing could have prepared him for the raw power of *Ariadne One*, which he felt within his body. Her crew would have no idea either. All busy with their appointed tasks, they would have little time to note the noise or the slight increase in vibration as their craft kicked herself free of the sloping surface.

There wasn't a dry eye in the place.

Susie looked down at her mother from Joe's commanding height.

"Dat's the fugest rocket I ever be seed!"

Somehow, there wasn't much else to say.

Joe was following every yard of the ship's progress. *Ariadne One* was well down range and she was going like a winner. He had thought that nothing could ever compare with the pride he felt as the Zeus flights took to the skies with the crew under his command. This was a different kind of pride, equally satisfying. The crew of Ariadne were still his crew for sure, but in a different way. He glanced across at Bruce, who relaxed as the spaceship disappeared from sight. Make that *their* crew.

"Haste ye back," Joe whispered, borrowing Alisdair's words.

Chapter Thirteen

Humans have always been infinitely adaptable. Never has that been more obvious than in their methods of travelling. Once the first journey had been made that was more than a day's walk away from home, people were hooked on seeing what was round the next corner and wanted to make the process as safe, swift and satisfying as possible. The horse moved off the daily menu and turned into a prized symbol of transport. Wooden boats took to the seas and one day wooden aeroplanes took to the skies. It was only a matter of time before the craft of another age headed towards the stars.

The crew of *Ariadne One* was not about to have a great deal of time to ponder on its place in the great scheme of history. Each member of the team would busy doing the thousand and one thing that *BUSSTOP* had made sure were put their way. There was the obligatory payload bay of experiments to think about, for starters. The whole scientific world wanted something of theirs to travel to Mars—or that's how it seemed. And from a human psychology point of view, it was a good idea to keep individuals moving. Two weeks in the enforced company of others can be a long time. There would be natural friction. But busy people don't have as much time to take offence or to brood. Despite this, each person did manage to marvel in his or her own way. They were all veterans of space flight but this mission was completely different. There was no comparison between *Ariadne One* and the bog-standard craft that flew between Earth and the Moon and undertook astronomical observations and mapping. Or if there was a comparison, it was an unkind one—the difference between a highly trained racehorse and a plodding dobbin.

Now it was all happening for real, Brian Hammond could appreciate how well he and his crew had been trained. Although Deanna Sorbin would take all the credit, he had the beginnings of a grudging regard for Steven Bradbury. And the brief time Joe Mortimer and Bruce Dougall had spent with the team was beyond compare. He had to remind himself that this was not yet another session in one of the simulators. He and the crew were actually flying to Mars.

They were ready for anything and computerised control meant that, once some course corrections were made as she left Earth's atmosphere, *Ariadne One* was almost flying herself. Brian was still glad that he had *two* systems people on board. Gianfranco Rosso was an engineer, strictly speaking, but so much of the ship was controlled by microchips that he was almost as good as Simeon Turner when it came to computers.

Almost. Brian was not impressed when he gave the command to bring the reactor fully on line and Gianfranco was offering a *Hail Mary* as he entered the relevant codes.

> *"Ave Maria, piena di grazia, il Signore e con te.*
> *Tu sei benedetta fra le donne e benedetto e il frutto del tuo seno, Gesu.*
> *Santa Maria, Madre de Dios, prega per noi peccatori, adesso e nell'ora della nostra morte Amen."*

All this in the time it took to enter three blocks of numbers.

Brian did not object to anyone having religious beliefs. But there was a time and a place for such matters.

But for all that, Gianfranco was a good second string to the computer bow. Computers had come a very long way from the cumbersome machinery that took up whole rooms and needed filtered air. Folks from a hundred years back, who screamed at their desktop PCs, could not have dreamed of the power and speed of the present day machines. But as the Commander of the flight, it was Brian's job to anticipate possible problems. The mechanical engineering was impeccable, the offspring of sometimes-bitter experience, and the reactor power was a stroke of pure inspiration. For him, computing systems were the weak spot of any spacecraft, simply because everything depended on them. Brian was more than competent in the use of the on-board systems but he was glad that he had crew members who could talk right back at a computer having a strop. He was still amazed that Simeon Turner had been selected, given his history with Bruce Dougall. Anyway, he was truly thankful, because Simeon was pretty nifty round a computer. And he left it at that.

Knowing that the journey to Mars would take two weeks, everyone settled into natural routines and made themselves at home. Once Ariadne was truly on her way and everyone could think about the little things, photographs appeared at workstations and in sleeping quarters, as did familiar objects. Emily Alexander brought along her teddy bear, which Brian "borrowed" to perch above his command position. Nothing escaped the glassy stare of Bruno, who sat there solemnly—arms outstretched and patchy golden fur a testament to much childhood loving—and was every inch the ship's mascot. A vase of silk flowers appeared next to a computer console. A scrawled notice fixed to a bulkhead proclaimed *Mars or bust!* Someone had been watching too many old time movies.

Having heard Gianfranco's lightning rendition of the *Hail Mary*, Brian noticed that his engineer wore a small crucifix. His rosary beads were hung by the reactor computer when he was working. The Commander knew that Simeon Turner was skirting round the edges of Islam. He wasn't too sure about what the others believed—or didn't believe. He knew that he should know. It was in a briefing file on his computer and he held the access code to it. He had never looked at it. Joe Mortimer would have had a rare explosion of anger if he had been aware of this omission.

"It's not prying," he said to Brian when he transferred the file to his care. "You hope like hell that you will never need the information, but if someone died or became very ill, you might be outraging a family and their sensibilities if you took the wrong course of action."

Joe Mortimer obviously didn't have a problem with this sort of thing but Brian retained a very English discomfort with knowing too much about matters as personal as someone's belief system. He knew that his own information would not be that helpful. When pressed on the topic of any kind of religious faith, he shrugged his shoulders and murmured, "C. of E., I suppose."

Ariadne One rapidly took on a littered and comfy air. The likes of Brent Dyer might have had palpitations but Joe Mortimer and Bruce Dougall looked at the images being beamed back from the interior of the spaceship and understood completely. Joe carried Barry bear in his pocket on the *Zeus Four* flight. As the distance between a rocket and Earth widened and the radio traffic time grew longer, there had to be immediate and tangible reminders of home. When "This is Mission Control; comm check" came through, it was all very reassuring. But as the hours and days went by, the words would be heard many minutes after they were spoken.

Any crew was effectively out there on its own and anyone with power of command knew that split-second decisions had to be made with no practical reference possible to Earth.

"You'll be monarch of all you survey, Brian," Joe Mortimer had said to him.

Brian was beginning to appreciate fully what the boss man meant, as he walked around the ship. Flying this old lady was like being the mayor of a small self-sufficient community. Hydrogen cells provided huge the amounts of electricity that were needed and the by-product of this process was pretty useful as well—pure water. The power output, combined with the artificial gravity, meant that the crew of *Ariadne One* could live in comparative luxury, as had the Zeus crews, with comfortable beds and freezers full of decent food just waiting to be cooked in small ovens. Showers and flushing toilets were a final flourish of civilisation.

The records noted that Alan Shepard was the first American to make a space flight in May 1962. Thanks to Joe Mortimer's penchant for the oddities of history, for Brian he would always be the man who had to pee in his spacesuit because he was sat atop his rocket on the launch pad for so long waiting for lift-off and there was no provision for the call of nature. As Joe observed to horrified trainees, "There's being a pioneer, there's roughing it for the cause and then there's bloody stupidity."

And the showers and the toilets were part of an endless recycling system. All waste water was purified and pumped back into the system and solids and rubbish were dealt with in an anaerobic digester.

Brent Dyer was rightly hailed as a genius. But the unsung heroes who worked out the day-to-day living conditions of Zeus and Ariadne were right up there with him. Brian couldn't help stopping and patting a bulkhead.

"Good girl," he said.

* * *

Georgina Hammond waited until the next morning to give the children the presents that Brian had left for them. She spent the intervening day swinging between embarrassment, anger and distress about the show that Fred had put on. The media were bound to love it, especially when the trinity of the Zeus project—Brent Dyer, Joe Mortimer and Bruce Dougall—became involved. Mostly she was upset, because it had never crossed her mind that Fred might be frightened by the whole business. She had on-screen chats with the two Americans, who were concerned that Fred was all right. Bruce Dougall promised her that the media would not be banging on the door. She wasn't sure how he would achieve that but, so far, the pledge seemed to be holding.

Joe went one better and called round at the house to see that everybody was okay.

"I've got an idea how your lad was feeling," he said as Georgina made him some tea. "The first few times I saw my father flying in the RAF display team, I don't think my brother and mother had any hands left. I was hanging on to them so tightly. Where are your rascals, anyway? I have pressies for both of them."

Fred and Susie were called in. Joe gave the children a gift-wrapped box each. Fred tore off the paper—a one-boy demolition squad. Georgina helped Susie with her package. Soon, both children were admiring scale models of *Ariadne One*.

"Daddy's rocket!" Fred shouted.

He ran around in ever-widening circles, flying the spaceship in his hand. *Ariadne One* was about to zoom off into outer space via the family room door when Fred remembered his manners.

"Thank you!" he said shyly and was gone.

"Fank you," Susie said, copying her brother.

She stayed put and sat on the floor, pushing the spaceship along the carpet.

"We're doing regular comm checks with the real Ariadne," Joe told Georgina quietly. "The messages are coming back well. Ship telemetry is registering perfectly. Ariadne is looking very good. I know that you probably don't want to sit and watch television broadcasts. You're welcome to go into Mission Control any time. Just call first and then you can see anything that's coming through—if you want to. By the way, when Fred was a bit tearful about his Dad, no one was seeing television pictures from the crowd outside. At that time, the broadcasters were all taking a feed of scenes from inside Mission Control. But it was a tempting story for anyone who was aware of what went on and you don't need journalists on the doorstep. Bruce Dougall and I have had words in various ears. You won't be bothered by any media people on the subject. If you are, let me know. Or Bruce."

"I don't know what to say," Georgina said, genuinely touched by this concern.

"It's all part of the service. And Bruce deserves most of the credit. He has developed a good line in menacing threats over these past few months," he observed to a puzzled astronaut's wife.

Georgina Hammond was close to tears when she gave the children Brian's gifts. The children were beside themselves with joy. Susie hugged the teddy bear as if she would never be parted from it.

"What will you call teddy?" Georgina asked her daughter.

"Tudder," Susie replied promptly, if a little mysteriously.

Fred was thrilled with the child-sized space helmet and gloves that made up his present.

Half an hour later, Georgina was concerned that everything had gone *too* quiet. She tiptoed to the door of the family room. Her eyes widened in horror as she took in the scene that greeted her.

Tudder had arrived complete with a red ribbon tied round his neck. That was long gone. But it was the state of the bear that shocked her. His long white fur was scattered in small piles across the floor. Fred was finishing some close trimming round Tudder's ears with a pair of scissors.

Georgina pounced so suddenly and silently that the children were genuinely shocked.

"What have you been doing?" she roared at them, grabbing the scissors in one hand and the scalped bear in the other.

"Susie did it too!" Fred told her, eager to shop his sister and absolve himself of guilt in one fell swoop.

"Where did you get the scissors?"

Fred scuffed the carpet in an agony of realisation that the game was up.

"From the big table in your bedroom," he said, truthfully.

"But why?" Georgina asked, looking at the few threads of fur that remained on Tudder after the shortest short-back-and-sides in history. "Why cut off all teddy's beautiful fur?"

"We have our hair cut," said Fred doggedly. His lip trembled as he saw his mother's tears. "Tudder's fur grow will grow again. It will, won't it? My hair grows. Susie's hair grows."

"My hair grows," Susie confirmed.

Georgina sat on the floor and sobbed. It wasn't just the vandalising of a father's gift that upset her. It was the culmination of weeks, months of tension and Tudder's haircut was the conduit for everything that had to come pouring out.

"Don't cry, Mummy!" Fred begged, tugging at her sleeve.

*　　*　　*

Irene Hanson was sure that she could never cry again. She knew that she had used up a lifetime of tears since that fateful day when she slipped and fell. There had been tears of pain, tears of joy, tears of gratitude and, above all, tears of frustration. It was as though some malevolent hand of fate was keeping her away from Joe when it really mattered. The morning she sat up and took notice, when she had come through the worst of the flu, she was told that the trip to Cape Canaveral, the launch and everything associated with it had passed her by. She nodded limply at Debbie and, for her friend, this was the worst thing of all. Those who knew Irene said that, above all, she was a fighter. There was real tenacity about her. It was a quality which had seen her make her mark in a world that was still male-dominated, survive a brief, disastrous and abusive marriage, rebuild her life and forge on with her career and come to the place where she was now, enjoying the warm regard of her peers. The pretty girl had matured, like fine wine, into the sophisticated and attractive woman. Joe Mortimer was there on the front row with his tongue hanging out and, this time, Irene was taking some real notice of a man who was noticing her.

Debbie knew and understood the suspicious and watchful look that crept into Irene's eyes sometimes. As a rule, no admiring man was allowed to get too close for too long but the spaceman was about to be the exception—if the gods would ever allow it to happen in the first place.

"Happy New Year!" Debbie said as Irene wobbled to a kitchen chair on her first foray downstairs.

"Yes, of course, the New Year." she marvelled. "That's the first time I haven't seen in the New Year for ages."

"It's the second of January 2110," Debbie confirmed. "Alisdair and I celebrated Hogmanay quietly. The girls went back up to Liverpool to be with their university friends for all the turn-of-year nonsense. They've both written you notes. Joe will be calling tonight from America, as usual," she added cunningly.

"As usual?"

"That's right," smiled Debbie, making herself busy with the teapot. "Our man has been calling every evening. He may be thousands of miles away, chewing his fingernails ragged as Ariadne travels to Mars, but he's still thinking about you and worrying about you. I told him last night that you'd be properly back in the land of the living today, so tonight he'll be expecting to talk to you in person, my girl. Now, that medicine has hit the spot, hasn't it?" she asked as Irene smiled back.

*   *   *

"I think we're making everyone jumpy," Bruce said when he and Joe had paced round the Mission Control nerve centre. "Let's face it. We want and are anticipating a straightforward flight to Mars and if anything needs sorting, it's up to the Ariadne crew and the people in here to deal with it. We're not looking for the kind of problems that need us."

They exited as gracefully as they could and Bruce could almost hear the collective sigh of relief when everyone realised they were gone. Joe stood in the corridor, strangely indecisive.

"It was easier flying the spaceships, wasn't it?" he said after a pause.

"It was." Bruce bowed in mock obeisance. "Would the mighty overall project leader deign to allow his humble sidekick to buy him coffee—or tea if he insists?"

"That sounds like a good idea."

They sat by the panoramic window in the restaurant. They had a distant but clear view of the ramp from which Ariadne had begun her journey. The place was still and quiet now. It was incredible to think that only three days previously this spot had been the focus of the world's attention.

Joe stirred his coffee idly. Bruce watched his colleague for a few seconds. Joe didn't take sugar.

"Go home, Joe," he suggested, taking the spoon away from him. "Back to England. I'm thinking of returning to Georgetown. Prime Minister Crane disappeared quickly enough. So did the President. There's nothing more for us to do here. We know when *Ariadne One* will be establishing orbit and we know when the Lander should touch down on Mars. We can both be back here for that. Two weeks is a long time away from home when you've got little to do and no real purpose. And I know you've plenty waiting for you at the other end."

"Have I? I imagine that London *BUSSTOP* is very quiet at the minute," Joe replied, innocently enough. "Britain tends to come to a halt for a couple of weeks over Christmas and the New Year. And with Ariadne safely on her way, no one will be doing much for a few days yet."

"You always were a poor actor. Professor Hanson! I've haven't seen that look on your face since . . . Not for a long time. You've lit up now like a Christmas tree, at the very mention of her name."

Later, back in his hotel room, Joe pondered for a long time. Daily he was becoming more confused by Bruce. How did he get to be so wise, or so concerned, when no one was looking?

* * *

Brian Hammond gazed around him with satisfaction. This was a good team and they were already working well. And, borrowing a phrase that originally pertained to family life, *The team that plays together stays together.* It was almost inevitable that the cards had come out. A poker teach-in was in full swing. The ferocious games on the Zeus flights, with Bruce Dougall in charge, were already the stuff of space legend, as everyone in those crews ended up playing frighteningly well.

This time there was a poker novice and a total beginner. Emily was helping Jackson. Brian was glad that he was settling in so easily. Being a replacement was bad enough but being the replacement for the replacement was a tough one. Simeon was giving Masahide the benefit of his advice. Jethro appeared to be the organiser. Everyone urged Brian to join in. He declined, saying that someone ought to keep a general eye on everything. He would sit in later. He hoped by then that the competition would be over for the day. He was not a good card player. It was silly but he didn't want to parade this weakness before his crew.

Also, with everyone's attention elsewhere, Brian was able to look at his family pictures in peace. Sitting at his command station was a good cover for this. Fred was turning into a small version of his father. The dark hair was already there and the sharp chin. The fine facial features would emerge as he grew. Susie had his dark colouring but she was so like her mother. The picture was an action shot of her skipping from foot to foot down the front path. Georgie had caught her with both feet off the ground. Her head was to one side, her hair was flying and she was laughing. Brian could hear her bubbly little-girl giggle.

He looked at the photo of Georgie for a long time. When he returned home, they would pin a medal on him, no doubt. Georgie was the one who deserved all the accolades, for putting up with all this, for doing the hard bit and waiting whilst he went off on the jaunt of a lifetime.

"Let's get the chief into this game!" said Jethro as he concluded a resounding defeat of the company. "Brian!" he called in the general direction of their commander.

Emily had noticed what Brian was doing and shook her head.

"No," she murmured. "I think he's got other things on his mind."

When card school was out, she saw Simeon wander away down towards the crew quarters. Curious, she followed him. She found him sitting on his bed, turning something over and over in his hands.

"Am I interrupting?" she wondered, standing by the open door.

"Never! Come in and close the door. I have something to show you."

Emily did as asked and sat on the bed beside him. On closer inspection, she could see that Simeon was holding a bracelet.

"You know a bit about jewellery," he said. "What do you reckon?"

"It's beautiful!" she exclaimed. "May I?"

Simeon watched her looking at the bracelet, stone by stone and link by link. Her long bob of dark hair fell forward. Her blue eyes were gleaming with interest, as was her open and honest face—the face that he loved so much.

"What do you make of it?" he asked.

"You've got Red Tiger's Eye here, pure jet, gold beads and other precious metal beads," she said at last. "It's so unusual! Where did you get it from and why did you bring it on the flight?"

"Auntie gave it to me."

"Hagar?"

"Yes. It was her parting gift to me. She was insistent that I brought it with me and she said the strangest thing '*Use this wisely. Keep it with you at all times. You'll know what to do with it when the time comes.*' How weird is that?"

"Did she buy it specially for you?" Emily wondered.

"I don't think so. You know that I went round to see her the night before launch, and you went to see your Dad. She rummaged around in one of those carved wooden boxes of hers and dredged this up from the bottom.

It looked like it had been there for years." He smiled in an embarrassed, puzzled way. "And as if that wasn't bad enough, she insisted I also bring a stone with me. I have to leave it on the surface of Mars."

"A stone?"

"A stone, a pebble, whatever. From her back yard." He handed Emily the smooth, freckled stone. "I know you think she's wonderful and reckon she is a phenomenally wise lady. Mostly I think it too. But this time I say she's lost it, very seriously."

"Why? Just because you don't understand yet what she said? You may be looking at Islam, Simeon, but I've told you before. That lady is plugged into wisdom that is far, far older. She's asked you to do some simple things—keep the bracelet with you at all times and leave the stone on Mars. Not a big problem, is it?"

"You are amazing, Emily," said Simeon, kissing her. "You always want to see the very best in everyone. Just like Hagar. I'm trying to as well."

*   *   *

Debbie had told Joe that Irene should be up and about that night but he still couldn't believe it when he found himself looking at her. Joe could see that she had been ill and she was still far from well. Her face was thinner and strained and her eyes were ringed with dark circles.

"Don't look at me too closely, Joe," she said. "I'm still a wreck."

"Proper influenza is no joke and you look fine to me. I wanted to see you before I came out here, but the MacIvers suggested that I shouldn't. If I had been able to see you and spend time with you whilst you were so ill, I would have stayed in England."

"What, and miss the launch?"

Irene was breathless at his might-have-been audacity and now appreciated the strength of the pull she was exerting over him. It was almost scary.

"Why not? Bruce was there to fly the *BUSSTOP* flag and everyone was so delighted when Brent Dyer—the designer of the reactor—turned up. No one would have missed me. Kevin Crane was there too, doing all the handshaking. Bruce and I are definitely superfluous to requirements now. Bruce reckons we're making them nervous in Mission Control when we go in and see what they are doing."

"It must be a bit like having a school Head teacher and Deputy wandering around," Irene mused. "Rather off-putting."

"Have you watched the launch yet?"

"I have, with Debbie this afternoon. *Ariadne One* looked splendid. Everyone should be really proud. Who was the fetching young lady perched on your shoulders?"

"That's Susie Hammond, Brian's little girl. Brent was giving the Hammond boy, Fred, a good view."

"The television commentator was rather vague about the identity of the tiny tots."

"Irene, I'm hoping to come home in the next day or so. Bruce and I are just sitting around. He's going back to Washington. I can't wait to see you."

"Likewise, Joe."

* * *

Tony was uneasy. Whilst human emotions could be a nuisance, they were useful right now. He was seeing images of the immediate future and he felt very human fear. The group would never lose their mind links whilst they were in human guise and they came together instinctively as they sensed his anxiety.

"Yes. *Ariadne One* is about to hit trouble," said Sally. "What can we do? The powers that we need to help the spaceship are shut down."

"Then we must ask the others," Tony decided.

They joined minds with full force to summon the rest of the planet. They could do this as well as continuing to pour out the power needed to help Bruce Dougall. Making use of the fact that they had bodies, they joined hands too, still marvelling at the comfort of human touch. In response to the call, their brother and sisters appeared, shifting continuously in appearance. One moment they took definite humanoid form and shape, the next they blurred into amorphous clouds, with points of light twinkling and shining brightly. If any of the seven needed a reminder of the point of their mission, this was it. All were caught in a limbo of evolution until the wrong was put right.

"We know," said a voice. Everyone was surprised. "We are communicating with you in human mode because it is easier for you at the moment. Continuous telepathy might become a strain for you in your present state. We have identified the problem. It is a computing error. The AD249 is giving erroneous readings. We do not think the humans flying *Ariadne One* have realised yet."

"The AD249?" Sally shook her head. "That was the problem on *Zeus Three*. So Bruce Dougall went out to do an exterior inspection of the ship and—."

"Exactly. We want no more tragedies. We believe that human ingenuity will overcome this. But we are standing by. Listen! We believe the crew is finding the difficulty."

"Brian!"

Simeon Turner's tone of voice brought the Commander to his feet. He walked over to where Simeon was standing, by the AD249.

"A problem?"

"It could be." Simeon sighed. "I thought everything was too quiet! I've just been doing a check of our systems. The AD249 is not saying what the other computers are saying and that's wrong. Its job is to gather together all the data from the other systems."

"AD249 gave one of the Zeus flights some problems. Bruce Dougall had to go on that walkabout outside, chasing a false reading as it turned out."

"I'll settle for a false reading on this bad boy." Simeon's dark eyes were troubled. "Because otherwise we could have major problems anywhere in the computing system—problems that could cascade."

They both knew how vulnerable *Ariadne One* could be to a systems failure. However many redundancies were built into her schematics, in the end everything came down to sub processors.

"Suggestions?"

For a moment Simeon's old indecision, which Bruce Dougall had jumped on in initial training, threatened to spark into life. He dug one hand deep in a pocket as he thought. His fingers felt the lumpy contours of Hagar's bracelet.

Of course! It was childishly simple. He outlined his plan to Brian.

"I'll need Gianfranco. And Masahide is pretty sharp with our systems."

"I'll contact Mission Control. They'll have kittens when things start dropping off their screens. Our radio messages are taking forever to reach home. They'll be registering what they think are computer failures before anyone knows what we are doing"

Gianfranco and Masahide appeared in double quick time.

"We have to take several computers off line, one at a time, check them out, and bring them back on line," said Brian briskly. "A certain amount of rerouting of computer functions will have to be done if we don't want to end up drifting, freezing to death or running out of air. Take your orders from Simeon. And Gianfranco." His engineer looked at him expectantly. "No Our Fathers and *definitely* no Hail Marys. I shall knock your bloody head off before you can get as far as *il Signore e con te.*"

"I shall be saying an Our Father for all of us silently, Brian," Gianfranco replied in all seriousness. "And I'll say a Hail Mary for everyone at Mission Control." He glanced at a chronometer. "Apart from anything else, we might be giving the teams on Earth an early morning surprise."

Joe had woken at the usual silly o'clock. Knowing that his flight home was not until the afternoon, he drifted back to sleep and was having a very pleasant dream about Irene. The reality of the messaging signal broke in just when things were becoming interesting.

Bruce looked as dazed as he felt.

"Mission Control is having a meltdown," he informed Joe. "Some of Ariadne's computers have gone off line. All life signs are still registering, although if there is a major computer problem, we don't know how accurate that information is. Hagar Turner is on her way in to run an eye over things. Perhaps between us we can bring a little sense to proceedings."

The three dead-heated at the outer door of Mission Control's main room. Hagar was the coolest. She was her usual calm and serene self. Either that or she was a very good performer, who was hiding fears about her nephew being in some kind of danger.

"Good morning gentlemen," she said. "Shall we?"

There was a general easing of tension as they entered the room. It was as if all the superheroes of the two preceding centuries had walked in, ready to do battle. People leapt away from computers to give Hagar a free run, eager to explain what had happened.

"Any word through from Ariadne?" Joe wanted to know.

"Nothing," was the wretched reply.

"I wouldn't worry too much about that," said Bruce with a confidence he didn't feel. "Radio traffic is so slow at the moment that you could walk back quicker from *Ariadne One* with a message. There seem to be some distortions out there in space, which we don't understand. Telemetry readings are being received at the anticipated speed. You've sent them a comm check, of course."

Bruce couldn't help but admire the rapidity with which Hagar worked. He knew he was good on a systems console but this woman was the best. Like him, she was blessed with supple "concert pianist" fingers and there was another similarity between them. She was left-handed.

The corners of her mouth turned down as she concentrated. At last, she looked up at a circle of expectant faces, which now included project Director Dieter Goldberg, who looked as though he had just rolled out of bed.

"I think that computers have been taken off line deliberately by the crew. I'm pretty sure this is not uncontrolled failure," she suggested.

"They're checking the computers for something, then," said Joe, his spirits lifting considerably.

"That's my guess. Come on, team! Give me something to work with! Put one machine back on line and I can get some idea of what's going on with you guys upstairs. Oh yes!" she exclaimed quietly and stroked the screen.

Hagar was off again, rattling through reams of information, oblivious to her audience, which carried on growing.

The minutes were ticking by but no one noticed, or cared. Making sense of this was all that mattered.

"I've got it!" she declared. "The AD249 is not functioning properly. The crew must be checking that the problem is isolated within that system. Their best bet will be to shut it down for the rest of the trip. They'll just have to be extra vigilant on all the separate readouts."

Bruce found that his hands were balling into fists. That damned AD249 computer! He would personally take a sledgehammer to the thing when *Ariadne One* returned.

The radio came to life and everyone could hear Brian Hammond confirming what Hagar had told them—that a ship-wide check of the computer systems was in progress. It was nothing to worry about.

"So Simeon and the others think that it is AD249 playing silly buggers," he concluded. "In which case, we'll take it out of the loop. Toodle pip! *Ariadne One* over and out."

There was uproar as everyone in the cavernous room leapt to their feet in an orgy of hugging and kissing.

Joe and Bruce managed to extricate themselves from the melee and step back.

"What will they do when the Lander arrives on Mars?" Joe wondered.

"I don't know," Bruce replied. "But I aim to be here to find out. I haven't been so thoroughly handled in a while."

"After this, I'm having second thoughts about going home," Joe said as the hubbub died down.

"Me too. Let's go and find some breakfast."

"I need to disappoint a lady first of all."

Bruce looked at him wonderingly.

"You two must really have something going there. Shannon divorced me for less."

Bruce became aware that Hagar was impaling him on a Don't Go Anywhere glance. He waited patiently until she too detached herself from the mob.

"I think it's time we had that heart-to-heart we promised ourselves a while back, Bruce. Anyone with any sense is still in bed but do you fancy breakfast?"

"Why not? My treat, Hagar. You put everyone's minds at rest before Brian Hammond came through. Dieter Goldberg having hysterics is not a pretty sight."

"I thought only women had hysterics," Hagar said with a grin as they wandered along corridors.

"You haven't seen Dieter in full flight, obviously."

Hunger can be very sharp when the body and mind have been forced into unscheduled early action. As a result, conversation took a little while to get going.

"We've got the joint to ourselves for a little while." Hagar looked around the restaurant. "Everyone will soon be pouring in, Bruce. So tell me. What aren't you telling everyone?"

Bruce was disconcerted by her direct approach.

"Don't be all wide-eyed with me, Bruce Dougall. I've known you too long. When I gave you a hug back along in the Mission Control room, I was shocked. I've told you before about how I used to stay with my grandma when I was a child. One of Grandma's scrawny old chickens would have had more meat on it than you. I saw you taking some pills with your coffee. So what is it? You know that whatever you tell me stays with me."

Bruce had had the presence of mind to grab his medication as he left his hotel room. The pretence had to be halted at some point and he could think of no better person with whom he could practise being honest. Without a word, he handed Hagar a small container.

She read the label.

"The name sounds familiar, as if it's been in the news. Is this some kind of quiz where I have to work out various puzzles to reach an answer?"

"Of course not. You are the first person I'm telling about this. I don't know what to say."

"Just say it," she suggested.

"I have cancer. Inoperable and terminal. This ZFF is a radical new treatment, which acts as a genetic brake on key cancerous cells. What's already there won't go away but the medication brings it to a virtual halt. My doctor says that ZFF and I were made for one another."

Hagar looked at him steadily.

"I'm not surprised. And no one knows? How long have you been going around with this knowledge, Bruce?"

"Long enough. ZFF is a more recent addition to the armoury, when the standard medications began to fail."

"Don't you think there are a few more people who need to know?"

"I can't think of anyone who would really be that bothered."

"Bruce John Dougall!" Hagar growled at him, upset because he really meant it. It hadn't been said for effect. "Don't ever say such a thing again. I'm bothered! Plenty of people will be devastated when they know. Joe Mortimer for one. Shannon still loves you, deep down. Anyone who had worked with you in *BUSSTOP* on either side of the Atlantic will be shattered. That's before we start on your friends. Don't you realise? America and Britain will sit down in sackcloth and ashes," she said, sounding positively Biblical. "But never mind everyone else. What about you?"

"I was really angry at first." She nodded. "I blamed Joe for sending me out on that space walk on the *Zeus Three* mission. At one point I would have killed him if I could have gotten hold of him. My doctor thinks that going outside Zeus on that walk is the most likely cause of the cancer, although no one can work out exactly what I was exposed to. Then I was scared." She nodded some more. "And now . . ."

"And now?" she prompted.

"I feel like a different person. I'm keeping a journal for my doctor. He has never seen anything like it and I've never felt anything like it. It's a kind of mild euphoria, although I'm not walking around in a cloud—or on one! Events earlier on this morning worried me, like they worried everyone. I'm not beyond the cut and thrust of life." He studied her face. "You don't seem a bit shocked by any of this."

Of course! Hagar had a moment of revelation, which she hid by reading the dosage instructions of Bruce's medication and then handing the container back to him.

"Individuals process information in different ways, Bruce. I don't think you'd want me to break down and cry right now, would you? I thought not." Her eyes were bright as she returned his hesitant smile. "You're not done yet, by any stretch of the imagination. There's a lot to do yet. Not just in your life, but in the lives of those linked to you in different ways. You will see what you need to see and do what you need to do before your time here is over."

Bruce made to speak. Hagar put a hand on his arm.

"Hush for now. When we've spoken about stuff before, have I been wrong?"

"No." He grinned sheepishly, acknowledging the relief he felt at sharing his burden fully. "Never!"

Chapter Fourteen

Joe Mortimer and Bruce Dougall might have been able to keep Georgina Hammond and her family out of the media via a little informal cajoling, but nothing and no one could have squashed the news that began seeping out of Mission Control. *Ariadne One* was experiencing computer problems.

The fact that the two heads of *BUSSTOP* and the agency's leading computer expert, closely followed by the Flight Director, had been roused from their beds to help deal with this situation only added to a heady brew of story and rumour that was soon swirling around.

Nothing like this had happened in the history of *BUSSTOP*. Or so it was thought. The general public was unaware of what lay behind Bruce Dougall's impromptu space walk on *Zeus Three*—a computer malfunction. Everyone enjoyed watching his journey round the exterior of the spaceship on television at the time. The inexplicable symptoms that struck him down soon afterwards and the rigorous medical testing he underwent following the flight were closely guarded secrets, not known outside the confines of *BUSSTOP*.

The age of general public innocence was sputtering to an end for the Mars programme thanks to an intermittent fault on a computer which filtered data on *Ariadne One*, just as it had ended abruptly for *NASA* when the first lives were lost.

In an echo of the weeks leading up to the launch of *Ariadne One*, everyone had something to say and there were the usual limitless platforms from which to say it. But it was a twisted echo. In December the contributors to television programmes and newspaper columns were dewy-eyed with optimism and visions of the steady forward march of humanity. In January the voices of criticism were being raised. Should a crew be risked when no one could guarantee the reliability of the computer systems?

It was a ridiculous argument, which was quickly demolished by those who came out to defend *BUSSTOP* and the Ariadne project. No machine can ever be completely proofed against problems. Joe Mortimer and Bruce Dougall thought it unnecessary to point out that, when they flew the first Zeus mission, even the designers were not totally convinced that the space ship would hold up. There were question marks over the new power system too. But there were plenty of individuals who were ready to put about those reminders on their behalf.

The criticisms became more insidious and the searching questions were tabled. When it was announced that *Ariadne One* would finally be taking to the skies, in the jubilation of the moment no one stopped to wonder why Britain had been given mission oversight. Kevin Crane announced proudly that his country had finally come of age in space exploration and America was pleased that Cape Canaveral would again be the hub of the world.

Now the wondering began.

With the faintest whiff of difficulty hanging around proceedings, the anti-Mars lobby was on the warpath once more and everyone was fair game.

*   *   *

Philemon Brown muttered under his breath when he heard the doorbell. He was organising his thoughts for his latest sermon. Although he said that the Holy Spirit guided him when he preached, a few topic headings were a big help to both of them to get the ball rolling.

Approaching the front door and glancing at the security screen, he saw that the crowd on the porch was, in reality, two large men. He recognised them. As he opened the door, he could see the limousine with the tinted windows pulled up at the kerb.

Vice President Ted Rodriguez was paying another visit.

"I hope I'm not disturbing you, Philemon," Rodriguez said very humbly.

"Of course not, sir," he replied. "My wife and children are all out."

He would marvel afterwards that this was two out of two for the Vice President, arriving when he was alone in the house. That was a *very* rare event. With Darlene and five children, generally someone else was around. He valued his few occasions of solitude.

Brown was flattered that Rodriguez had come back but he was not so pleased once the pleasantries and the serving of coffee and cookies had been dispensed with.

"You want me to do what?" he asked bluntly.

All outward forms of deference were gone.

"Don't tell me you've changed your mind on the subject, Philemon," marvelled Rodriguez, totally unruffled.

"Of course I haven't. But I don't want the prize apes from . . . whichever agency it was, appearing at the door again."

"I can promise you that such a thing won't happen any more."

"Have you started controlling these people then?"

"No. But the days of some of the people behind that visit are numbered."

"You will pitch folks out of office?" Philemon wondered.

"That's a little extreme. Changes will be made."

The briefest of smiles accompanied Ted Rodriguez's reply. Philemon was a big people-watcher. He spent a lot of time watching faces. It was his biggest clue to how sincere the individual might be about what he or she was professing. Rodriguez might have gained a few pounds over the years but he was still a fine looking man. But it was a miracle that he charmed as many as he did. Or was it that he had changed through time and no one had taken that much notice? Had the expression turned into a mask? His lips became thin and mean when he smiled and there was no warmth in his eyes. In fact, Philemon felt a chill of apprehension ride his spine. He almost felt like asking the Vice President to leave but that might have been a little tricky. The two men accompanying Rodriguez were not for show and they were very intimidating. One stood just inside the front door. The other was out in the back yard. Philemon remembered from the previous visit that the driver looked pretty useful as well.

Additionally, the lure of being able to ride out on his favourite hobbyhorse was too great.

He contented himself with a silent arrow prayer aimed at Heaven.

"God help me."

*　　*　　*

Irene was growing weary of being understanding and tolerant when Joe contacted her yet again to say that he was stuck in America. But she was left with little choice. The ripples of *Ariadne One* experiencing computer problems, however briefly, came storming across the Atlantic to Britain like a *tsunami* gathering energy. She knew that Joe could do nothing but stay within arm's reach of Mission Control, in case there were any more difficulties, which might lead to decisions having to be made. He was at the top of the heap and he had to be there.

Britain being Britain, the focus was on the small, insignificant details of the story, particularly Brian Hammond's laid-back demeanour when his message about the computers finally came through to Mission Control. That cheery "Toodle pip!" at the end enchanted everyone.

"It's was like listening to an old World War Two RAF film!" editorialised one newspaper.

Irene had got over her illness and had moved back home. As much as she had been longing to be in her own house again, she had taken a few days to settle. Since her tumble in the college car park, she had spent very little time on her own. The nights were worst. In the care of the MacIvers once more, she had slept well, safe in the knowledge that there were other people around. Now she noticed and worried about every unexpected sound and creak of her cottage in the silence of the night. Finally, to her great relief, she was allowed back to work.

The first day in college was a bizarre experience.

Irene had never been out of the workplace for so long. Returning was a real shock to the system. The world had moved on without her. Everyone was delighted to see her and welcomed her wholeheartedly but within minutes friends and colleagues were referring to matters of which she had no knowledge. They laughed at comments where she didn't understand the joke. The refrain became tedious.

"This happened whilst you were away, Irene. You see, Parvinder . . ."

She felt like last year's dead leaves.

She was glad to be able to share her feelings with Joe, who contacted her most evenings, wanting to be in her company, if only on a screen. He was truly sympathetic.

"I know what you're going through," he said. "As a child I hated going back to school after every holiday break and I did have one longish spell away from things when I was about thirteen. I picked up some weird form of gastro-enteritis, which took quite a time to clear up. Of course, I was past crying every day by that age but it took me a long while to get back into the routine of school. Also, you begin to develop a kind of invalid mentality. I had Mum's undivided attention whilst I was at home ill and you feel all at sea when that level of attention is no longer there. You've had the MacIvers on care duty for a bit. You're bound to miss it. Still enjoying being back home in your own place?"

"Yes," she lied.

A huge smile was creeping across Irene's face.

"What's so funny?" Joe wanted to know.

"You cried when you went to school?"

"As a little one, yes. Mum handed me over to the teacher every day, literally, kicking and screaming."

"The secrets of Joe Mortimer!"

"We all have them, Irene. I'm looking forward to you confessing to a few of yours. What dark secrets do you harbour?"

"Wouldn't you like to know," she said, a little uncomfortably. "I'm glad to know that everything seems to be okay with Ariadne now. Remind me, when is she due to reach Mars?"

* * *

In America, the idea of attacking Bruce Dougall was on a par with questioning whether Saint Peter was worthy to hold the keys of the Kingdom. But in the atmosphere that pervaded everything after Ariadne's technical glitches, everyone was fair game. The report written and submitted to the President by Bruce Dougall, recommending that Britain take overall control of the first Mars landing, was out in the public domain for anyone who cared to look. Plenty did and the star astronaut found himself being stalked by the document. He was skewered by it in a television interview.

"So you had reservations about the project, Bruce," Gordon Scott insisted.

"At the time, I did," Bruce agreed.

"You keep using that phrase *at the time*. What was so special and different about when you made your recommendations to the President?"

In a hyper-rush of memory that took a split second to chase through his mind, Bruce remembered an occasion in school when a situation had gotten completely out of control, because various children were not honest about some simple matter. By the time the teacher reached the bottom of the complexities of it all, it was worthy of the attention of the United Nations. He delivered a dictum that none of his charges ever forgot.

"You will never regret telling the truth."

Fair enough. Did he tell all on live, early evening, prime time television? Did he win the sympathy vote and make Gordon Scott look like a heartless fool by admitting that, when he railroaded everyone into seeing things his way, he was struggling daily with having been handed a death sentence and this coloured all his judgements? It was tempting.

But in that fraction of a moment, he also knew that the fall-out from such a statement would continue raining down on him and many others for weeks and months to come. He couldn't do it. The topic of discussion was Ariadne, not his health.

"I had various reservations, yes. A report crystallises someone's thoughts at a moment in time. My reservations proved to be groundless and I'm happy to admit it."

"But your report lost this country overall jurisdiction of the Mars Ariadne project."

"*Lost?*" Bruce picked up on the word sorrowfully. "I was always under the impression that *BUSSTOP* is an act of co-operation between America and Britain, not a forum for some private competition."

"Maybe. But did you talk to anyone about this, before the report was handed over formally to the White House?"

"I did." Bruce's skin crawled at the recollection of that conversation he had had with Joe. "But who said what and when is irrelevant. Joe Mortimer and London *BUSSTOP* did a fine job getting us to launch day, with the established space expertise of this country. We're all doing our bit now to ensure the success of this mission. Like I said, it's based on co-operation. When Brian Hammond steps onto the Martian surface for the first time, no one will be remembering who did what within the agency to make that possible. That it happened at all and the date on which it happened will be enough for most people, along with recalling the *BUSSTOP* logo on *Ariadne One* and on the astronauts' spacesuits and equipment."

The interview was judged a draw—an honourable result when being questioned by Gordon Scott. For Bruce, it was as though he had gone several rounds with a prizefighter. For the first time in a while he felt drained and unwell. He headed back to the hotel, ignoring all offers of studio hospitality and went to bed, tumbling straight into sleep.

When he awoke, he noted the time and grunted. There were words ringing in his head.

> "*It is not time to give up yet. You have so much to do and a great deal depends on you, although you may not realise it at the moment. Gather your energy for a while and keep going! You are being given the strength.*"

He knew he had been dreaming—yet another of those vivid dreams that the doctors said could be a side effect of his medication. So many people from his past shoehorned themselves into this one and it was so real—the conversation, the laughter, the praise and appreciation of all that he had achieved. His parents were there, as were other relatives and older friends long gone. Above all, Sally appeared.

Bruce turned on the light. He could see the soulless surroundings of the room—comfortable enough and paid for out of someone else's pocket. But he desperately wanted to be back at home in Georgetown. Apart from anything else, he could engineer accidentally on purpose bumping into Shannon. He had enjoyed her company, however briefly, when she travelled down for the launch. He couldn't think of any good reason why he should contact her from here in Cape Canaveral.

It was one o'clock in the morning but he felt better already.

*   *   *

Philemon Brown ran onto the platform. The auditorium was packed, despite the bitterly cold D.C. night.

"Greetings in the name of the Lord!" he declared. "Brothers and sisters, I welcome you all here tonight."

"Hallelujah!" the crowd yelled back. "A-men, brother!"

"My text tonight is James Four verses seven and eight. *So then, submit to God. Resist the Devil, and he will run away from you. Come near to God and he will come near to you. Wash your hands, you sinners! Purify your hearts, you hypocrites!*"

"Praise the Lord!" one group cried. "Resist the Devil!"

"A-men, brothers and sisters! I am resisting! All those of you who have been washed in the blood of the Lamb are resisting! But we have the perfect example before us of those who are *not* submitting to God, who are *not* resisting the Devil! I speak of that limb of Satan—the organisation known as *BUSSTOP*—and its sinful representatives, who even now are flying in the face of the Almighty by sending a spaceship full of people to Mars! I prophesy to you tonight, brothers and sisters, that this computer failure that we have heard about on *Ariadne One* is only the beginning of things! God will exact his revenge! This will end in tears, fire and destruction! The iniquity of putting men and women on the same vessel is beyond belief. It, too, flies in the face of God! The wrath of the Lord is being readied to pour down on all sinners and hypocrites!"

Many remembered that there was only one woman aboard Ariadne and she was with her boyfriend but this was hardly the time to raise such a detail.

Brown continued with his mesmerising tirade, which had the crowd on its feet and howling approval.

In something of a lull, there was a call from the audience.

"What about these *BUSSTOP* leaders, Pastor?"

He threw in another firecracker.

"Now how about these so-called leaders of *BUSSTOP*! At least Joseph Mortimer has not polluted our shores by bringing with him his whore and concubine Irene Hanson! The Lord got the message through to him that she would not be welcome in this God-fearing country. But what do we see instead? Bruce Dougall consorting and fornicating with the woman who was once his wife! Brothers and sisters—he is twice married and twice divorced! Oh, the iniquity of it all!"

"The iniquity of it all!" repeated the crowd, raising their hands to Heaven to bear witness to the wickedness they had to endure.

"How do we explain this to our children and grandchildren, that such a sinner should apparently be reaping a harvest of success? God will punish, my brothers and sisters! God will punish!"

This was too good to pass by. The press and television had a field day.

So did the combined forces of *BUSSTOP* and local law enforcement when they reacted. A security barrier was put round the hotel where Joe and Bruce were staying. Men and women in body armour nursed powerful weaponry and dared representatives of the media to come any closer. Fortunately, no one was prepared to die for the sake of a better story. Inside, two wounded and puzzled men wondered what would happen next.

Legal advisors from *BUSSTOP* went in under armed escort to talk to Joe and Bruce, who were furious and shaken. They listened patiently to the professional-speak, which underlined the processes already underway. The space agency would be filing actions on their behalf against Philemon Brown, the newspapers who printed his words and the television companies who broadcast them.

When the lawyers had gone, the atmosphere was sombre in the small lounge that had been set aside for the meeting. The anger they both felt, and had to bottle up in public, burst out.

"I can't threaten to shoot Brown a second time!" Bruce said at last through gritted teeth. "Maybe I'll just go do it. Not bother the President or anyone at all. Then I'll win a medal for services rendered to the country."

"Don't be so damned stupid!" Joe retorted, slamming his fist on the table in irritation.

He was working through such a melee of emotions, from fury at the blatant audacity of Philemon Brown, along to hurt that he should voice such a personal attack. It was one thing to criticise him publicly. He'd ridden out such onslaughts before. But the inclusion of Irene was unforgivable.

"What have we done to deserve this shit?" he continued.

"Nothing. I wouldn't mind so much if I had had some fun with Shannon when she came down to the launch."

There was a long pause. The tension dissipated as they both relaxed into reverie.

"The same here with Irene, back home," Joe admitted finally.

Bruce laughed heartily.

"Are we pathetic or what? You're definitely losing your touch, Joe. Come to think of it, so am I. We must be getting old."

Joe considered.

"I must try and speak to Irene first thing in the morning GMT. It will be across the Atlantic by then."

"Yeah. I'll try and catch Shannon now. She's a very elusive lady at the moment, doing a whole bunch of publicity ahead of the publishing of her book."

Joe found Irene was unfazed by the whole business when he finally got through to her at midday in Britain.

"I know all about it Joe. The man's a nutter. It's as simple as that. If he has any sense, he'll plead insanity when all these legal processes you've told me about start happening. History is full of examples of people who overdosed on their own holiness. You have to feel sorry for him."

"*Sorry*? Irene, if I ever get hold of him, I'll tear him limb from limb! What he said about you . . ."

"Bless you, Joe, for wanting to spring to my defence." She giggled. "I'll tell you one thing. It has given me some street cred with the students already." Joe was nonplussed. "It's not everyday that a University professor is labelled as the concubine of a public figure. Concubine is such a splendid and old-fashioned word! Marmaduke, a friend and colleague of mine, has already picked up on it in New Zealand. He's on professorial exchange over there at the moment. He mailed me a message. It begins wonderfully. *My dear concubine, I always knew that you would make it if you tried!*"

Bruce was also left gaping. His astonishment began the moment his ex-wife appeared on screen.

"Shannon!" he managed in a strangled tone. "How—I mean . . . What have you been doing?"

"Do you like the new me?" She stood up and performed a couple of twirls. "My publisher has been urging me for some time to create a crisper, sharper image, with all the pre-launch stuff. I'm not twenty-five any more. So the long hair had to go!"

"You look great!" he admitted.

Shannon's hair sparkled with fresh silver tones and was cut into a simple shoulder-length style. She looked at least ten years younger.

"So what did you want to talk to me about, Bruce?"

"You know damned well what I've contacted you for!" he snapped.

His anger was in part a reaction to old feelings, old longings that were stirred within him as he beheld the refurbished Shannon.

"Oh, you mean that stupid man Philemon Brown? Ignore him, honey. That's what I'm doing. My publisher is convinced that it will put thousands on the initial sales of the book, perhaps tens of thousands. I ought to be grateful to the pastor in a way!"

Two baffled and frustrated wannabe knights in shining armour met up in the evening in the hotel bar to compare notes. They had expected sobbing ladies, who needed comforting, albeit via the screen, who needed acts of derring do done on their behalf. Instead, they were confronted by feisty females, who were brushing aside Philemon Brown as if he was an annoying flea. In fact, Irene and Shannon were both looking upon the incident of vicious and baseless slander as a career enhancing opportunity.

A couple of journalists passed through the bar. They spotted the two men huddled together and they grimaced. No doubt Mortimer and Dougall were plotting terrible revenge against the media who had publicised Philemon Brown. They gave the *BUSSTOP* chiefs a wide berth. A carapace of legalities that would keep the lawyers busy until Hell froze over surrounded these two now. It was dangerous even to ask them the time of day.

Joe and Bruce were not planning the downfall of the free press and television. They were not doing anything in particular. They sat in silence for a long time.

"Women!" sighed Joe.

Glasses clinked in the background. The occasional raised voices and a general hum of conversation filled the space. The sounds echoed dimly, as if they belonged to another world.

"I know!" said Bruce eventually.

* * *

Apart from Brian Hammond, the crew of *Ariadne One* was unaware of the furore that their minor problems had caused. Life flowed on as the spaceship powered its way towards Mars. Each person was glad of the disciplines imposed by the raft of experiments down in the payload bay. Although two weeks was nothing like the six months that the voyage would have taken prior to the development of the reactor that was currently blasting them through the heavens, it was long enough. It was easy to become impatient when landing on planet Mars was the goal at journey's end. In the meantime, everyone had to content themselves with revelling in the power and the technological know-how of the miracle that was *Ariadne One*.

Emily came into the bay to find Jackson frowning at a set of plants. Some were flourishing. Some were dead and others were wilting.

"I don't think you are a gardener somehow, Jackson!" she said. "It looks like you have a brown thumb, not a green one!"

"They're meant to be like this. Emily, can you understand this? I have to water this batch. I have to give these over here water *and* liquid feed. This lot are shut away in the dark for long stretches of time and I have to neglect that bunch totally. My four year-old niece could predict what will happen to them all! Why do they need to be on a spaceship headed for Mars?"

"They're out of Earth's atmosphere?" she suggested.

"Yes, but in a pressurised cabin with artificial gravity. And in air brought with us—albeit recycled—they're not in that different an environment. It's not even as if we're experiencing weightlessness, as astronauts and their experiments did on Apollo and the space shuttles. It makes no sense!"

"If someone wants to send plants on an expensive ride, that's up to them, isn't it, Jackson? It keeps us busy. Perhaps it's something to do with the total lack of insect life up here and the origin of the water, coming from our hydrogen power cells."

Emily was becoming uncomfortably aware of the way in which Jackson was studying her. Come to think of it, she had noticed him giving her sidelong smouldering glances for a while. She wondered if he was misinterpreting her actions when she helped him with the poker games. She was doing it out of kindness, to make the late replacement feel at home. He was a good-looking guy, rather like Brian in some ways, with those dark, dramatic looks and flashing blue eyes. Similar in build too. But . . .

Jackson grabbed her by the arm as she made to leave. He studied her, *very* slowly, from head to toe, his eyes lingering over every smoothly rounded part of her body.

"Has anyone ever told you that you are a very lovely lady?"

"Simeon tells me most days," she replied steadily, although her heart was pounding frantically.

"Ah, yes. Simeon. I hope Simeon realises how lucky he is."

"He does."

"If he ever stops appreciating his good fortune, I'm here waiting for you. I know how to take care of a lady. I know for sure I can do that a darned sight better than any damned ni—"

He stopped himself just in time.

Emily wrenched her arm from his grasp and fled. She wanted to slap him but the urge to be as far away from him as possible won out over everything else.

She ran headlong into Brian.

"Whoa!" he said. "Where's the fire?"

"Nowhere," she answered hurriedly, then thought quickly. "I was just getting in a little running. Keeping the fitness levels up. That's very important, isn't it?"

She didn't wish to become entangled in explanations just at that moment. Brian shook his head. This one was always so keen!

"I know our gym area is small, Emily, but it is effective. You don't need to pound round the ship."

He watched her go. This wasn't right. She was upset about something, almost ready to cry. What had brought this on? She could only have come from the payload bay area, which was where he was headed. He waited to see if anyone else would emerge from there. After a few seconds, Jackson sauntered along. He nodded affably to his Commander and carried on towards the flight deck.

Dear God, I do hope I'm wrong, Brian thought as he put two and two together.

He was beginning to dislike Jackson Metz anyway and this fuelled his unease. He would rather deal with technical difficulties any day.

He understood that the alarums and excursions with the AD249 had caused some kerfuffle downstairs. That was too bad. That was what all those folks were paid for, although he didn't like the thought of Joe Mortimer or Bruce Dougall being stressed out by what had happened. They were the voices of sanity, who knew what it was like to fly into the unknown, who appreciated what were the real problems.

Brian had picked Joe's brains at length about commanding a spaceship on a long-haul flight. Joe gave him the benefit of his experience but saved one piece of advice until last.

"I'm telling you what I found, with the people I worked with on the Zeus flights. You must develop your own style. You need a strong working relationship with your right hand man. Jethro Norman is the best one for the job. If he does it properly, he'll run the mission and allow you to amuse yourself with the space ship from time to time, just to humour you! That's how Bruce played it. I had the kudos of sitting in the big chair but he did the hard work! And he could pass the buck to me when it suited him—not that he ever really did that!"

Brian decided that he must speak to Jethro when he had a minute.

Yes, technical problems were one thing. Crew difficulties were quite another. The sooner they reached Mars, the better.

* * *

Justin was distraught.

"It will happen!" he whispered. "Can't we do anything to stop it?"

With a naturalness that had taken hours of practice, Sally put her arms around him.

"We can do nothing."

"We have to sit and watch again?" he cried.

"We have sat and watched for a long, long time."

"In our natural state, yes, when we didn't have the emotional and physical bonds and restrictions that we have now."

Sally hugged him a second time.

"Justin, not since the days before the destruction of Maldek have we had the chance to be so close to our brothers and sisters on Earth. Our previous visits back to the planet have been dismissed by all but a handful, who have been scorned for their honesty. And yes, they are our brothers and sisters, whatever we might say. We call them "cousins" in jest, to put some distance between them and us. The regrettable characteristics that we see amongst some Earth people—well, we possessed those traits once upon a time, before we learned a better way. We are embarrassed to be reminded that we could be like that—arrogant, scheming, power-hungry, and war-like. And even now, when we know so much better, we still make mistakes, as with the wrong that must be righted."

"Can't we appeal to a higher power to stop what is planned?" Justin wondered.

"No. We can't meddle."

"We're meddling with Bruce Dougall," he pointed out quite reasonably. "He's still alive. How can one intervention be meddling and another not?"

"That is quite different. We can't face up to our karma without him and we have quite a tangle of links with him and with Joe Mortimer."

"It's not fair!" Justin proclaimed.

"That sounds familiar! Justin, you embraced that bit of being human from the very beginning," said Tony, arriving to hear the complaining. "But now you are nearly the finished article! What's not fair?"

"What Ted—my link—has planned."

"It's hard, Justin. I know. I've been doing a bit of tuning into Earth. It's so difficult, whilst we're getting the balance with out human part. Ted must do what he has to do. We have to be ready for the fall-out."

*　　*　　*

Joe was enduring a restless night. Although he was worn out when he went to bed, he couldn't settle. His thoughts jumped from one topic to the next. He tried to concentrate on one thing—Irene. But tonight even she wouldn't stay in focus. He read for a while and began to feel sleepy. When he turned out the light, his mind was spinning again.

He got up and padded over to the balcony. He stood a while, looking up at the night sky. *Ariadne One* was out there somewhere, amidst those points of light. He envied the crew. They had only one thing to think about—the missions to Mars. And that was neatly divided into three parts, wasn't it? They flew to the planet, took the Lander down to the surface, and then returned in triumph. It was simple. In those terms, space missions always had been. Every time Joe and his crew pointed Zeus at the stars, the aim of each journey could have been summed up in a similar way.

He wasn't sure that he could explain what he was doing at the moment. With the present-day sophistication of communications systems, strictly speaking it was not necessary for him, or for Bruce, to be waiting fruitlessly near Mission Control, on the off-chance that they might be needed. They could be at home and still be able to make any decisions that needed making.

Joe almost persuaded himself. He wanted to go home, to be surrounded by familiar things and above all to be with Irene, even if it was for a very short time before he had to return. He got as far as working out when Vicky would be at her desk in London *BUSSTOP* and could organise flights home for him. Or perhaps Bruce's PA, Genevieve, could sort matters out for both of them. He was sure that Bruce didn't want to be sitting around here, any more than he did.

Joe stopped himself just in time. A whiff of danger, however slight, had come close to *Ariadne One*. Those in charge had to be *seen* to be in charge, even if in reality they were twiddling their thumbs. When the world watched and waited, feeling helpless, it was hardly appropriate for the authority figures to raise two fingers to the situation and push off home.

The world was very silent, almost as if it was watching and waiting for something to happen, holding its breath in anticipation. The sea was normally loud in the quietness of the night but the waves were whispering up on to the beach. The wind had dropped and all was still.

Admitting defeat, acknowledging that it was probably one of those nights, Joe went back into the room, put on the light and turned on the television. Automatically he searched through the listings for BBC World News. In his experience, this centuries old station was still the best broadcaster, with the fewest axes to grind. He might as well catch up with what was going on outside his present narrow experience here at Cape Canaveral, with his world view shrunk down to watching and waiting for the progress of *Ariadne One*.

The twenty-four hour rolling news programmes had been an integral part of the television landscape for so long that no one could imagine what it must have been like to have to wait for the next news bulletin, with scheduled programming interrupted only when something wonderful, terrible or important happened.

Joe blinked as he looked at the screen. The picture showed the flashing lights of the emergency services, huddled onto a small section of road, almost hypnotising the viewer. The complete roll call was there—police, ambulance, fire trucks and heavy rescue. The camera, obviously filming from a distance behind a cordon, panned over a road traffic accident. He could make out a large lorry with its front smashed in and the mangled remains of a limousine. There was no commentary.

For the moment, the pictures could speak for themselves and there was the running strap-line at the bottom of the screen.

Joe reached for his glasses. He couldn't quite make out the words. Or perhaps he was able to see and he couldn't bring himself to believe what he was reading.

When he took in the message, he removed his glasses in disbelief.

U.S. President Phoebe Harper badly injured in a car crash on the Beltway, Washington D.C. A lorry ploughed into the presidential car. Mrs Harper's driver and bodyguard declared dead at the scene of the accident, along with the driver of the lorry. The President has been rushed to hospital.

As Joe tried to digest what he was seeing, the scene switched to the news studio in London. The newsreader was wearing a black tie and a grim expression.

"It has just been announced from Washington D.C. that President Phoebe Harper has died as a result of injuries sustained in a car crash, which took place on the D.C. Beltway. After being freed from the wreckage of her official limousine, President Harper was rushed to the Clinton Memorial Hospital, which she formally opened only eighteen months ago. The President was declared dead at one ten a.m. local time. She never regained consciousness. Vice President Ted Rodriguez has already been sworn in as her successor.

"Over now to our Washington correspondents Tanya Fielding and Warren Buckley. First of all to you, Warren, outside the hospital where President Harper died . . ."

Joe shook his head. Death in a car crash always seemed such a senseless waste of life.

He met Phoebe Harper briefly in the hours leading up to the launch of *Ariadne One*. She was a smaller, more vibrant version of her screen persona, a fascinating woman to talk to. Widowed at a young age with two small children to raise, she had been appalled at the way in which the system tried to grind her down and keep her trapped by offering little assistance. She threw herself heart and soul into politics, burning with zeal to correct the many imbalances in society.

Above all, her conversation with Joe confirmed that she was committed to the Mars project long-term, come what may.

Was the new President equally keen?

Only time would tell.

Chapter Fifteen

"Dad! I'm not eight years old! I don't need to see my dog to know that she is all right. I trust you!"

Joe protested as his father insisted on luring Bonny to jump up and sit beside him so that the dog was visible on the screen.

"You may not be missing Bonny, but she's missing you," Neil remarked.

Bonny was in typical pose, head slightly on one side. When Joe spoke to his faithful companion, her ears pricked and she began a body shaking wagging of her tail.

"One satisfied customer!" Joe laughed. "So how are things back at the ranch?"

"Pretty much the same. Little Abby is growing more gorgeous by the day—and she isn't so little! Any more on the death of the President?"

"Not really. I guess you know as much about it as we do. I'm not exactly on the spot down here at the Cape. It's a bit difficult for any investigation into the accident to make much headway, when everyone who was involved is dead. Oh, Bruce Dougall and I have been invited to the state funeral in Washington D.C. Because I'm not royalty, I don't have a set of funeral clothes in my luggage at all times. I'll be off tomorrow on a hunt for the appropriate kit."

"First a royal wedding, then a state funeral. You're getting about a bit, Joe. You must be getting used to all this stuff. It's coming up with the rations!"

"Maybe. I think I was invited simply because I'm in the States. It would be a bit awkward otherwise because Bruce would have been asked, anyway. The Mars exploration programme was always close to Phoebe Harper's heart and I think Bruce had quite a good working relationship with her."

"Bruce Dougall! I take it you two haven't tried to murder each other yet, or you would be conducting this conversation from a prison cell."

"We're rubbing along very well, Dad."

Neil Mortimer shook his head in wonderment.

"Hmm. I still say he's going mad. It's all that dashing about at the incredible velocities that you generated with the new reactor. It must do things to some people, and it has done something to him."

"Maybe. But this must be the serene, all-seeing and thoughtful phase of madness, then."

"Are we talking about the same man, Joe?"

"Yes." Joe smiled at a long ago memory. "You know what Granny Mortimer would have said. The fairies have been and sprinkled the magic dust on him."

*   *   *

Preparations for the funeral of President Phoebe Caitlin Harper were in top gear. Away from the frenetic pace of organising the logistics of the event, her body lay in state in the Rotunda of the Capitol Building in D.C., for a nation to pay its respects. The cause of her death was reported as internal haemorrhaging from a crushed and torn liver after a truck smashed into her car. There was time for all of that later. For now, a nation simply needed to remember her and to give thanks for her life and her achievements.

The flag-draped coffin rested on the Lincoln catafalque, made and first used for President Abraham Lincoln after his assassination in 1865. There were pedestals of flowers and, equally immobile, stood representatives of the different branches of the United States Armed Forces, watching over their dead chief day and night. In the long-held tradition of the country, the guards faced the coffin, rifles held in the right hand, the weapon butts resting on the floor.

Outside the roped-off area, they came in their thousands and their tens of thousands. Despite the bitter winter weather, there was a never-ending tide of humanity waiting to spend those moments taking in every detail—the floral tributes, the ramrod straight backs of the military, the coffin that could have been overwhelmed by the surroundings but nonetheless managed to dominate the place.

Men, women and children were cold, hungry and thirsty by the time they reached their destination. But that was all part of the process of mourning, part of identifying with the grief. You could look into the eyes of a total stranger and know that he was thinking the same things, understand that she was experiencing the same emotions. The urge to draw near, to feel, to touch, to taste, to smell the experience was huge. The cordoned-off area in which Phoebe Harper lay at rest prevented some of that but all the senses were fully engaged. Fingers of the young and not so young touched the red ropes that separated them from the dead President and indicated a road of remembrance along which they were allowed to travel as they said their goodbyes. Hands slid up and down the brass supports punctuating the ropes. There was a murmur each time a petal fell from the carnations or roses—Phoebe's favourite flowers.

The perfume of the roses mingled with the dampness of the visitors, who were soaked by the fitful rain, sleet and snow that came sweeping across the city. The result was a smell that could almost be tasted in mouths dried out by biting winds.

Those who were in the Rotunda when the changing of the guard took place witnessed a little, quiet thing. The uniformed men and women who were leaving handed over the duty of care to those who were relieving them with no word said and with total ceremony. The President would never be alone and there was an odd comfort in knowing that, through the dark watches of the night, the silent vigil continued.

The Rotunda of the Capitol was a place of dignity, of tranquillity. Emotions were given fuller rein outside. The ever-present reporters for television and newspapers were penned into one area, a respectful distance from proceedings. They asked individuals and groups about to join the line why they had come, what they hoped to gain from this visit. They waited for weeping members of the public to reappear, to ask them how they were feeling.

One young woman, accompanied by a wide-eyed little boy aged about eighteen months, summed it up.

"It's like my mom has just died," she said, her lips quivering. "One day I'll be able to explain to my boy Mike that he was here for this. I'm pregnant now, so I'll tell my unborn child that he or she was here too, to say goodbye. We are all saying goodbye to the mom of our nation."

Carole Waterman, aged twenty-eight, from Alexandria, Virginia, beat the publicity experts to find the phrase of the moment. *The mom of the nation* was flashed round the world within minutes. A grand federal government-orchestrated event was cut down to its proper and human size by five words. Phoebe Harper won the hearts of the country during her time in office and, a little belatedly, that country remembered that she had family. A son, a daughter, a brother and a sister-in-law, nephews and nieces and grandchildren were enduring a loss too.

*   *   *

The weather mended itself for the funeral service of the late President Phoebe Harper. The temperature hovered around freezing point but the sun was bright in a winter-blue sky. Trees stood out against this backdrop, black skeletons holding up arms of grief and celebration. The forecast was for snow later in the day.

Washington D.C. was at a halt and had been for three days, as the proposed journey of the cortege was checked and double-checked, timed and security was put into position. A large chunk of the city's population, and groups and individuals from most of the states of America, were crammed along the route from the Capitol Building to the National Cathedral at the junction of Massachusetts and Wisconsin Avenues in northwest Washington, along with a fair sprinkling of international representation The crowd was probably at its most numerous along the mile-long stretch of Pennsylvania Avenue from the Capitol Building to the White House. There was barely a sound as the hearse and the accompanying motorcade glided by, pausing briefly near the White House.

About four thousand people were present at the Cathedral for the service. Black was the order of the day, relieved by the odd line of colour in a woman's jewellery and medal ribbons worn proudly. New President Ted Rodriguez and his wife Maureen were very obvious. There was the usual foreign representation. Joe nodded to Kevin Crane and his wife Janet. Her Royal Highness the Duchess of Cambridge was present to represent her father King Richard the Fourth.

The setting was tailor-made for a solemn national event going out on worldwide television. The Cathedral Church of Saint Peter and Saint Paul was a mere youngster in a line-up of such buildings. President George H.W. Bush had been present for the placing of the last finial in 1990. And yet its mix of mediaeval styles of architecture harked back to a much earlier age. The long, narrow building, standing on Mount Saint Alban, was a text-book collection of pointed arches, stained glass windows, intricate stone carving, flying buttresses and beautiful ceiling vaulting. Two towers stood over the west front and another crowned the crossing at the transept.

All this was the stage on which final honour could be given to the girl from Laurel, Mississippi, who attended a local United Methodist church as a child.

Joe was not surprised to find that he was seated next to Bruce inside the cathedral. His colleague was obviously distressed by the occasion before it even began, as he was by the sudden death of his President. He was not the only one to take off his glasses and sit like a statue, eyes bright with unshed tears. It was as if the very act of moving would have opened an uncontrollable floodgate.

Joe found his emotions stirred, although not for the same reasons. It was not always easy for a British person to appreciate the position of the President of the United States of America. In typical style, Britain had two leaders for the price of one—the Prime Minister and the monarch. The office of President rolled up and invested all that, and more, in one person. For Joe, it was the manner of Phoebe Harper's death that reached him. Anything that pertained to car accidents touched a wound within him that he would carry to his own grave.

The coffin was carried slowly up the nave by a detachment of Marines. In the end there was no contest as to who would have that grievous honour. Mrs Turner's grandfather and a great-uncle served in the U.S. Marine Corps. They paced in time with the tolling bell, shouldering the burden expertly, heads pressed against the sides of the coffin. It was as if they might be making one final check to make sure there was no heartbeat from their former commander in chief.

It was the singing of the Battle Hymn that was finally too much for many of the congregation.

> *Mine eyes have seen the glory of the coming of the Lord:*
> *He is trampling out the vintage where the grapes of wrath are*
> > *stored;*
> *He has loosed the fateful lightning of his terrible swift sword:*
> *His truth is marching on.*

Joe learned something during the service. His *BUSSTOP* colleague had a good voice. Suddenly that voice was silent. Like others around him, Bruce was unable to sing another note.

*   *   *

The astronauts on *Ariadne One* were sent the broadcast of the funeral service. They watched intently, just as they studied all film sent up since they had received the shocking news of the President's death. Gianfranco wound his rosary round his fingers and touched his crucifix repeatedly. Simeon held Emily's hand. In his other hand he held the bracelet given to him by Hagar.

Before the service began, the crew were involved in the usual spot-the-well-known people.

"She's a looker!" drooled Jackson, too busy leering at a screen image to be particularly moved by the death of his President.

Brian shot him an annoyed glance.

"That's the King's daughter, Princess Charlotte, Duchess of Cambridge," he said curtly. "She is Britain's next queen."

"You don't say!" marvelled Jackson, his thoughts written all over his face.

Masahide tapped Jackson on the shoulder.

"My friend, I'm sure that what you are thinking is treasonable under British law."

"And the King would chop your balls off—begging your pardon, Emily," Brian added hastily. "Speaking as the father of a daughter, however young, I'm sure he is Charlotte's father first and the monarch of Great Britain second. I'm surprised he let her marry her pilot hero."

"There's Joe Mortimer!" called out Emily. "And Bruce Dougall. Neither of them looks very good."

"I was right to think that we would give them a bit of a fright when the AD249 decided to have a paddy," Brian admitted. "I don't think they've quite recovered. We were too busy up here to consider that side of it too much. All that Mission Control saw were our different computers dropping off line. They didn't know what to think until my message got through to them. And now this on top of everything. Anyway, is anyone supposed to look good at a funeral?"

A funeral is a natural closing of a chapter. Everything is on hold until the ceremonies are completed. Now a stunned nation could wake up to the reality that Phoebe Harper was gone, buried in the family plot in Laurel, Mississippi and that there was a new President. Ted Rodriguez had been thrown into office under the most trying of circumstances—struggling to pick up the pieces after the death of a popularly elected President. He was the fallback guy, the default position in the Constitution, who now had to work hard to be seen as President in his own right and not just someone who was keeping the Oval Office warm until the next election.

Keeping one eye on the line of succession as laid out in Congressional legislation, he nominated Henry Sargent, the Speaker of the House of Representatives, to be his Vice President. With everyone desperate to recreate some kind of normality, confirmation of Sargent's new position was rubber-stamped within hours.

Ted Rodriguez made his mark rapidly. Two days after the funeral, he made a live broadcast to the nation. He spent some time eulogising and remembering his predecessor. Also, he was eager to display his credentials, as someone who would carry on President Harper's social reforms and policies, with one noticeable exception.

"I have to tell you, the people of America, that there was always one area in which President Harper and I differed. This is on the subject of space exploration—specifically about travelling to and exploring Mars. I will be scrutinising very carefully both this project and the long-term plans of *BUSSTOP*. Of course, I salute the huge achievements of the crews who flew the Zeus missions, especially our own Bruce Dougall, and as I speak *Ariadne One* is flying ever nearer to Mars. We have to be realistic about the huge amounts of money that such journeys consume. In the meantime, I look forward to great results and great benefits springing from this mission, not least the possibility put before us by Professor Hanson in Cambridge, England, that mankind will be making its first contact with other beings on planet Mars."

The unspoken *Or else* hung in the air for those who could sense it.

"Oh bugger!" Joe said when he watched the presidential speech.

The broadcast was sent on to *Ariadne One*. The crew looked at one another.

"Isn't it great to be loved and wanted?" asked Jethro, summing up the confusion of all.

*　　*　　*

There were so many news stories floating around in the United States of America. Those engaged in the business of packaging and putting out the information around the world were in the unenviable position of not knowing where to turn first. There was the ongoing churning and rechurning of the events leading up to President Harper's death, as well as a state funeral to chew on. *Ariadne One* continued journeying towards Mars and was very close now. At the same time the President was hinting that an ongoing space programme might not be a good thing.

On a vaguely related topic, Shannon Dougall's first novel, *The Last Millennium Party*, was launched with a razzmatazz that had not been seen in American publishing circles for a long time. It was a great read, worthy of the advance hype, and copies were flying out of the bookshops and out of the warehouses of online sellers the moment they were available. The demand for the electronic version was staggering.

Bruce found himself looking at a photograph of his revamped ex-wife in the newspaper, along with a glowing review of the book.

> "*Shannon Dougall has crafted a complex story, using meticulous research of the year 2000. Students of the era cannot fault her grasp of that odd time and yet the facts sit lightly and naturally within the narrative. The lives of one family are described and dissected in intricate detail but the reader's attention is grabbed and held because of taut plotting and the shifts of scene and pace. It is obvious that the author knows and cares about her characters passionately. So we care about them. I sense that she had great fun writing this story. So I was caught up in the fun too. This is an outstanding debut novel.*
>
> "*The writing style is spare at times but full of feeling and description when those things are needed. Her insights are so*

accurate that, as with any good writer, some passages must have been distilled from Ms Dougall's own life experiences. She has put herself firmly in the camp of authors who have turned their backs on the graphic sex scenes, which have marred story telling for so long. Her hints are far more provocative and exciting than the bald—and frequently bad—descriptions found in so many novels today."

Shannon had promised Bruce a copy of the book, which she would deliver personally. As she apologised on several occasions for not being able to make any kind of visit down to Cape Canaveral, he realised that, unwittingly, his ex-wife was turning the tables on him, using the script he used when the Zeus project kept him away from home.

"You can imagine how busy things are at the minute, Bruce. I'll be with you as soon as I can."

He knew that it was no more than he deserved.

"So when is the big day?" she asked finally one night.

"What?"

"You haven't been listening to a word! *Ariadne One* should almost be to Mars now, shouldn't she?"

"Yes. She will be establishing an orbit around Mars first thing tomorrow morning and then the Lander will go down to the surface."

"So January 14th 2110 is The Date, then? The one that will go down in the history books. I'll be waiting for all the news. Try and get *some* sleep. I know you too well, Bruce. You'll be awake most of the night."

*   *   *

Brian Hammond gave the crew the thumbs up at the end of the briefing.

"We're as ready as we ever will be, team. So far we have been following in the footsteps of the later Zeus missions. Establishing an orbit round Mars is as far as Zeus went. It's up to us to do the next bit and we will do it properly, and we will do it well. Good luck, everyone."

As the group dispersed, Brian murmured to Emily that he wanted a word with her. She waited until the others had gone from the flight deck. Brian had delayed this conversation with her many times, waiting in vain for the moment when she might say something to him. He hoped that he hadn't left it too late.

"Emily," he said, "am I right in understanding that you had a bit of trouble with Jackson?"

"It's okay!" she replied brightly. "He tried it on once. He's been quiet since."

"You and he have to maintain the Orbiter whilst we go down to the surface. I could leave Masahide here too, if you're concerned about being left alone with Jackson."

"Thanks, but no. I think even Jackson will be too busy and too on the watch to think about anything else. And I'd be ready for him now."

None of the *Ariadne One* astronauts could believe it was happening, that this was not another training morning. The manoeuvrings to establish an orbit above the planet went without a hitch. Masahide set up three cameras to film continuously as the spaceship swept around the planet.

"This is so beautiful!" whispered Simeon as the crew reviewed the footage before transmitting it back to Earth.

There was indeed a severe beauty about the planet. Its brownish-red emptiness beckoned and begged to be explored. The rugged cratered southern hemisphere was particularly appealing but this kind of landing was out of the question in such terrain. Developing craft to put down safely there was a problem to be solved by another generation.

Or was it?

Banishing the political machinations of Earth from their minds, each person got on with their appointed jobs.

"Synchronous orbit established above the landing site," Jackson reported to his colleagues and to Mission Control. "We can go at any time."

Inside Mission Control, breathing was almost an optional extra. A whole heap of people, with the latest computing technology could at their finger-tips, could only sit and wait for the time-delayed messages and signals to come through. It was up to the seven people on *Ariadne One* to get this right.

Joe Mortimer, Bruce Dougall and Hagar Turner were standing at the back of the room. Joe was berating himself. He should have stayed longer to help the crew after the falling-out with Steven Bradbury back in the summer! What was he thinking about, wanting to be part of some unimportant family holiday?

Bruce leaned up against the wall, head bowed. He had promised himself that he would still be alive for this event. So here it was, happening before his ears and eyes. What next? He couldn't fight the inevitable forever.

He was aware of someone moving closer to him. He looked up to see Hagar watching him. She squeezed his thumb.

"You should be pleased. It's going well."

The critical ship's telemetry readings started to come through. The pictures of the Martian surface silenced everyone. Jackson Metz's message raised a cheer.

"Ready for some history to be made?" Joe asked Bruce.

Bruce straightened up.

"I guess so."

*   *   *

Simeon and Emily stood quietly, foreheads touching.

"Take care," she said simply.

"I aim to."

"And just remember that this is for real, Simeon Turner. This isn't another practice, where Deanna can say *'That wasn't good. Let's do it again.'* You go and show 'em!"

"I will. And I've got these." He showed her the bracelet and the stone. "Even though she's millions of miles away, I'm not about to disobey my aunt."

Emily laughed. When she stopped, Simeon was gone to join the others, to be suited and booted prior to entering the Lander section of *Ariadne One*. She felt an empty ache within her momentarily and then she hurried to join Jackson. The quicker the Lander touched down on the surface, the quicker everyone would be returning.

She soon saw that her parting words to Simeon were wiser than she knew. The whole process was like the very best training session as she and Jackson listened in and played their part.

"This is Orbiter. Lander, you are free of the mother ship," Jackson stated.

"Thank you, Orbiter," echoed Jethro Norman's voice.

"Hypercone deployed," said Brian

"Confirmed. Inflated," replied Jethro.

Emily's eyes flickered across her screen.

"Lander, you are now in subsonic speed."

Brian and Jethro were into the tennis-rally dialogue that accompanied the final descent.

"Ready with the parachutes!" Brian ordered.

"Confirmed."

"Hit those chutes!"

"Deployed."

"Chutes away."

"Thrusters on."

"Masahide. Override! Correct thrusters for a one degree shift!" came Brian's voice unexpectedly.

Emily and Jackson exchanged glances.

"A slight wobble in Lander's descent," said Jackson, pointing to another screen. "Probably a gust of wind."

Everyone on board the Lander felt the craft crunch up against the surface of Mars. It was not one of those crater-drilling spectaculars of the early training days, but it was a harder impact than Brian would have wanted.

No computer was protesting. The Lander had survived the bump.

"Well done, everyone," Brian praised the team. "Orbiter and Mission Control, this is Lander. We have touched down on the *Amazonis Planitia*, the Amazonian Plain. We are sending out remote cameras to take a look around whilst we get ourselves ready to go out. I anticipate leaving the Lander in about two hours."

Back on Earth, Bruce picked up on the variation in the Lander's descent as everyone heard the delayed on-board dialogue.

"What was that?" he asked, his voice sharp as he indicated the read-out on the screen.

"Seeing as everything else is showing as normal, I would imagine the Lander has been caught in a slight gust of wind," surmised Joe. "Brian asked Masahide for a correction override, quite correctly."

When the words came through that confirmed the touch down, there was bedlam in the room. Chairs crashed over as they were kicked back. Bottles of champagne and glasses appeared miraculously from the most unlikely hiding places and there were a thousand toasts to everyone involved. Celebration was mingled with utter relief as kisses and hugs were exchanged.

Congratulations were soon winging on their way towards Mars and everyone had to keep reminding themselves that they were witnessing history. This moment had been so long in cooking that everyone was experiencing a prickle of uncertainty. But even if Brian Hammond decided that conditions were not right for leaving the Lander, this was the first manned vehicle to touch down on Mars.

"They did it!" Bruce was glassy-eyed. "They damned well did it!"

"Chop, chop Bruce!" said Joe. "You have a President to talk to, plus an Italian and a Japanese Prime Minister. I have my Prime Minister and the King to deal with."

As Bruce was moving away, Hagar put a hand on his shoulder.

"Did you ever doubt they would do it?"

Bruce was almost beyond words. He was impatient to analyse the film of the descent and landing. Waiting for this moment has been like the build-up to the perfect Thanksgiving or Christmas holiday. Could the reality match the anticipation? He remembered that he had noted the landing area as the last Zeus flight orbited Mars. He had wondered if people would be there in his lifetime. Now it was happening and he could hardly believe it. All that striving, all that hard work, the hoping, the planning, the arguments and the sleepless nights . . . It was all worth it now.

* * *

The Martian delegation waited patiently. It had taken humans such a long time to get here that another short delay was no problem. Justin was all for rushing over to the Lander craft the moment the dust had settled. Tony counselled caution.

"We don't want to scare them in any way. They will emerge when they are ready. Remember that this is a hostile environment for them, in terms of gravity and atmosphere. They will have to make certain preparations before they can leave the Lander."

"The craft came down very heavily," Sally observed. "It was taken off course momentarily by an air current. But I'm not sensing any damage."

On the Lander, everything was ready. This had been choreographed like a classical ballet. Brian Hammond and Jethro Norman would be the first people to step on to the surface of Mars. The other occupants of the Lander would have their turn later.

Brian entered the airlock and waited impatiently for the atmospheric pressures to even up. The outer hatch opened and the planet stretched out before him in the shape of the smooth Amazonian Plain. Dust danced across the surface, further evidence of what had knocked Lander out of stride momentarily. He reminded himself that he had a job to do and climbed down onto the ground.

He didn't know what to think, what to feel. The ground of Mars gave the same sensation under his boot as ground anywhere on Earth. But that was where the similarity ended. This was a harsh, alien landscape. For someone brought up in the hustle and bustle of modern towns, the total silence was the most unnerving part. The outline of *Mons Olympus* in the distance was the only point of reference in the featureless terrain. He was already aware of the sensation of apparently being one third of his body weight. He moved cautiously for a couple of steps.

"Brian Hammond, Lander Commander, to Orbiter, Mission Control and the inhabitants of Mars. We are landed on what we know as the Amazonian Plain. We come in peace to the planet we named after an ancient god of war."

He was aware of Jethro Norman standing beside him. He was a tall man and his space suit and helmet turned him into a looming figure. Brian could make out Jethro's usual slow and good-natured smile.

"Let's go explore," he suggested to the commander in matter-of-fact style.

When the film came through to Mission Control, it sparked off another round of merriment. Joe and Bruce knew they had drunk too much champagne and they didn't care. They needed peace and quiet later on to take in what the pictures and the data readouts were telling them.

Hagar disengaged herself from an over-passionate kiss with one of her computer staff.

"My office," she said softly to the *BUSSTOP* leaders. "Let them get on with it."

No one noticed the three of them slip away.

In her room, she steered each of the men wordlessly to a chair. She poured coffee for both of them and then opened a drawer and held up a bottle.

"Anyone for a strengthener in their coffee?" she wondered.

The bottle went away unopened when they both declined.

"I think I'm intoxicated enough," Joe said as he took the coffee mug. Hagar sniffed at his breath and nodded. "I'm drunk on events as well, Hagar."

"And how about you, Bruce?" she asked, turning to the silent American *BUSSTOP* boss.

Bruce put his coffee down very carefully, to give himself extra space to formulate his words.

"I'm not a parent," he began hesitantly, "but I guess this is how a mother or father feels when the child outstrips parental achievement. Up to establishing a synchronous orbit, *Ariadne One* was doing what we had already done. Now the crew is doing so much more. It's wonderful!"

"Yes, that's it!" continued Joe, moved to honesty himself. "I can remember Mum's exact words the first time she saw me flying solo. *'I'm married to one lunatic and now I'm the mother of another.'* I thought she was about to take off herself. She was floating with pride."

Bruce remembered a similar kind of conversation with his father. It was not long before he died.

"I could never do what you're doing in a million years, son. Joining the USAF and learning to fly. I'm only useful for looking after the family fortune. Up to this moment I would have said that I have achieved two good things in my life. I met and married your mother and I was jointly responsible with her for the producing of you. After today, I can add the fact that I have a boy who will get on with more than I could ever dream of."

It was not a memory for sharing in this company.

There was a knock on the door. The down time was over. A raucous deputation was demanding the return of the heroes of yesterday, so that everyone could continue crowing about the heroes of today.

"Tell me that one later," Hagar said to Bruce.

*   *   *

"I like this sensation of excitement!" declared Sally. "Here they come!"

Brian Hammond and Jethro Norman walked towards them purposefully, carrying large boxes. After a general walk around to get the feel of the planet, they had returned to the Lander to collect the first of many pieces of equipment to be set up on the planet's surface. They had the measure of the lack of gravity and there was confidence in their stride. The Martians waited, smiling.

Their smiles began to fade. There was not a flicker of acknowledgement or recognition on the faces of the humans, although it was difficult to get a clear view through the visors of their helmets. Their pace did not slacken.

The humans walked straight through them, as if they were mist.

Brian passed through Tony's left shoulder.

Jethro passed right through Sally's body.

"Did you feel that?" Brian asked Jethro. "I was really cold just for a moment. I thought the insulation of my suit was failing but I'm okay now. How strange!"

"Yeah. I was a bit shivery for a few seconds."

"Greetings!" Ichiro cried desperately. "We're here!"

"Ichiro, they can't hear us or sense us in any way," Tony told her. "Hush now."

A few minutes later the astronauts returned, leaving the monitoring equipment on the ground, awaiting set-up and activation. The Martians moved out of the way, having no wish to go through such a dispiriting experience once again.

"What went wrong?" Justin demanded as they watched the two returning to the Lander craft.

Tony frowned in concentration.

"We lowered the level of vibration at which we exist as far as we could, so that we could take human form. To drop any lower would have extinguished us. I can only surmise that the level at which we are operating is not low enough. Our brothers and sisters are not as evolved as we thought."

A long silence was broken by a very human sob from Sally.

Some hours later the Lander crew was ecstatic. Everyone had been out on to the planet's surface. More technical paraphernalia had been positioned over a wide area and was now up and running. Dust samples had been taken. Ground-penetrating radar readings were stored for the astro-geologists back on Earth. Slivers and slices of rock, cut to very specific sizes, were bagged and tagged. Conventional wisdom said that this plain where they had put down was a solidified lava flow or an old seabed from the time when there was water on Mars, or both. There was no telling what microscopic examination of the top strata might reveal.

"Your spelling hasn't improved much," Simeon murmured at one point as he looked over Jethro's shoulder and watched him label a sample.

Jethro gave him a sickly smile in return.

There was time for some fun, too. Masahide was a good gymnast and he took advantage of the thinner atmosphere to do some floor exercises that would have won him an Olympic medal. He was taking a big chance. If he had fallen undertaking a string of forward somersaults, he might have damaged his air supply backpack, which would have been catastrophic.

The crew were sending a continuous stream of reports to the Orbiter. These were relayed to Earth along with film of the events. Emily confirmed that all the monitors that had been placed on the plain were working perfectly, as were the time-lapse cameras that had been left in position.

"I can't believe that we have just done all that," said Gianfranco when they were gathered back in Lander. "And we have done it all *on Mars*! It doesn't seem possible, or real."

"It's the kind of thing you enjoy in retrospect," suggested Brian. "My mother is a school teacher, as I think you know. She has always said that she enjoys the trips out with her groups of young people when they are over and done with and everyone is safely back home. At the time, she's too taken up with what she's doing to appreciate what's going on. We'll be telling everybody about this for the rest of our lives. We've got plenty of time for it to become real."

"We have radio communication from Mission Control," broke in Jackson from the Orbiter. "Sit to attention, everyone. It's the boss men."

Joe Mortimer and Bruce Dougall sent their congratulations. Messages were played from President Rodriguez, His Majesty King Richard the Fourth and the Prime Ministers of Britain, Italy and Japan. Then Joe made the important statement.

"We'll be interested to hear from you ASAP what you have found on the planet, in terms of installations and beings."

"It looks kind of empty," added Bruce. "You are not so far from the source of the signals that were picked up last year by Professor Hanson. Is there some type of structure that you haven't shown us yet? Are you saving the best until last?"

Brian looked at his exhilarated crew soberly.

"This is when I really wish that the problem of instantaneous communication had been solved. I'm not looking forward to telling them and the whole world that there is nothing here. They will be sitting and waiting so eagerly for our reply. It's almost cruel."

Simeon looked out of the window, over the Amazonian Plain. It didn't make any sense but he had done what Hagar asked him. Under the cover of being busy taking samples, he had taken a moment to slide the stone from her back yard out of his pocket. He placed it near one of the cameras that Masahide was setting up.

"There you go, Auntie," he said quietly. "I can tell you exactly where your stone is, and with the cameras on-line, the world is seeing it without knowing. It'll be your secret. And mine."

Chapter Sixteen

"What do you mean—*it would be an almost impossible task?*" Ted Rodriguez almost snarled.

"Just that, Mr President," Bill Francioni, one of his senior aides replied smoothly.

Rodriguez glared at him but this man was not for staring down. Francioni was a long-serving White House staffer and a decorated former Marine, with a reputation for getting things done quietly but firmly. He wasn't likely to have a fit of the vapours because the President started throwing his toys about in annoyance.

"Sit down and explain yourself."

"Thank you, Mr President."

Francioni knew that he wasn't the first person to be seated within the Oval Office, facing a President and not knowing exactly what the tirade was all about. The newly promoted Rodriguez seemed angry out of all proportion to the facts that could be ascertained, so there was reason to hope that this could be sorted quickly by pouring some cold water on the situation.

"As I understand it," Francioni began calmly, "there is a possibility that a Good Samaritan medic may have helped Mrs Harper immediately after her car was hit by the truck and that person then disappeared when the emergency teams arrived." The President nodded. "You would like to find him. Why, may I ask?"

Rodriguez appeared temporarily floored by this question. He glared some more at Francioni. This man was a tricky one! He sat bolt upright habitually. The same height as the President, he made Rodriguez aware of his own slouched position. The bearded face and unreadable hazel eyes made him harder to figure out.

"Well," he blustered, "he needs to be thanked, doesn't he? He did his best to help the stricken President. That needs acknowledging."

"I wonder if it does. The very fact that he slipped away makes me think that he doesn't want the praise and acknowledgement. Some people are very modest."

"But he needs finding!" Rodriguez insisted.

"Very well, Mr President. What do we know about this unsung helper? Male, younger rather than older, white. There is an insistence from the emergency personnel who saw him briefly that he was not American or Hispanic. I don't know how they came to that conclusion. If we go with that, he could be from any European Union country, Australasia or South Africa. One person 'thinks' he might be British, for no particular reason."

"She heard him speak."

"He said the word 'Yes.'" Francioni smiled thinly. "Sir, do you have any idea how many doctors fitting those outlines work in D.C. alone, never mind in the surrounding states? Just because he was close to the Clinton Memorial doesn't mean he has anything to do with that hospital. Hell, he could have been on his way home from a dinner party!"

"He was dressed in scrubs."

"And so he could belong to any hospital in the tri-state area."

The President rose slowly. Bill Francioni stood as well. Because he had retained his military bearing, he seemed a good head taller than his superior.

"I want him found!" ground out Rodriguez.

"Then I will make sure that everyone does their very best, Mr President. May I remind you that you and Mrs Rodriguez need to be on your way in a few minutes? There are more important things going on than fussing about an unknown doctor who was simply trying to help."

Alone, Ted Rodriguez felt a real stab of fear. This was a loose end that he hadn't realised was still dangling. He thought that everything had been taken care of. He hadn't anticipated this kind of blunder.

His gaze drifted round the room, the scene of so many historic meetings, and the engine room of so many great Presidents. Already he was discontented because his staff was not creating a daily miracle for him. Not for the first time he had reached where he wanted to be, only to find that the place was not where he really wanted to be at all.

He shook his head. He had to go and be pleased at some reception now, to mark the safe landing of the astronauts on Mars. Thank God he had Mo to keep him sane through all this.

*   *   *

Brian looked around at the rest of the Lander crew.

"Are we all agreed then?"

One by one, the men nodded. Simeon hesitated before making the gesture. Brian picked up on this.

"What is it, Simeon? I want everyone's views."

"We have quartered the designated area," Simeon began hesitantly, and then he warmed to his task. "Each of us has walked as far as we dare at any one time, given our restrictions with exposure to the sun, radiation and cold. We have spent the night on the surface of Mars in this Lander craft. Now we send a message to Mission control saying the planet is empty. No sign of life anywhere."

"What's wrong with that?" wondered Jethro, a frown creasing his features. "We've checked for life signs with all our equipment. We can't do more than that."

"Our equipment measures what it is designed to measure!" Simeon hadn't finished with his doubts yet. "How about if there is life that our boxes of tricks can't measure?"

"We know that all such devices have their limitations. We have to accept that, Simeon." Brian smiled ruefully. "I think that you are being a romantic instead of a scientist. We would all have liked it if there had been a Martian delegation waiting to meet us when we arrived. But there wasn't. Finding life on Mars is a minor sideshow. Are we losing sight of what we've achieved already? Look out of the window! What you see isn't a computer simulation! It's Mars! We're sitting on *Mars* having this discussion! Deanna isn't about to open the door and look in to ask who wants coffee or tea! Yes, everyone got a bit carried away when Professor Hanson announced that she had picked up messages from Mars. *BUSSTOP* became rather tangled up in it because Joe Mortimer let her do a press conference through the organisation. Everybody soon stopped talking about it, didn't they, after a bit of silliness in Britain."

"Because they have been waiting for the Professor to be proved right!" argued Simeon.

"We can't fight Professor Hanson's battles for her," Brian concluded. "Nor Joe Mortimer's, for that matter. They will be waiting for our routine message at Mission Control. In addition, I'll pass on our conclusions about life here—or the apparent lack of it."

Whilst Brian was talking to the Orbiter to establish the relay link to Earth, Simeon looked out of the window that Brian had indicated. He found himself holding Hagar's bracelet.

His eyes widened and his mouth dropped open. There were seven distinctive figures on the near horizon!

The piece of jewellery dropped from his slack fingers and fell to the floor with a clatter. Busy with set routines, Jethro, Masahide and Gianfranco didn't notice. Brian was too engrossed in sending the news, both good and bad.

Simeon ducked down, retrieved the bracelet and put it safely in his pocket. He hardly dared to look out again. But he did.

The Amazonian Plain was empty. Dust devils whirled, twirled and sank. Other than that there was nothing apart from the barren brownness, which was already getting on his nerves.

Automatically, he moved to check the computer console that managed life support on the Lander. He was looking specifically to check on the carbon dioxide levels. It didn't take those levels to be raised too far before there were all kinds of strange effects on the human body. Unconsciousness, followed by death, was the best known one. But what about hallucinations, caused by breathing tainted air?

The carbon dioxide readings were perfectly normal.

Simeon sat for a while, staring out at the planet's surface, beseeching the forms to appear again. There was a tap on his shoulder.

"Prayer time is over," said Gianfranco in all seriousness. "I am tempted to join you but we must get on. We have work to do if we are to take off today and rejoin the Orbiter."

* * *

Mission Control had been in a state of uncontrolled delirium for some twenty-four hours as events rolled along in an inexorable tide. *Ariadne One* took up her orbiting position above Mars. The Lander bumped down onto the Amazonian Plain rather firmly but all was well. Brian Hammond went out on to the surface of Mars and didn't fluff his lines. He was followed by Jethro Norman and then by the rest of the Lander crew. Joe was tempted to take Bruce's pulse when they witnessed Masahide's gymnastics but no real harm was done.

The astronauts had spent the night in Lander Everything was going according to plan. It was as if everyone was watching one of those excellent practices in the simulator. Bruce berated himself for doubting the mission for even a moment. Nothing had been left to chance, after all. Joe looked and felt more relaxed than he had done since before the launch. The two heads of *BUSSTOP* were beginning to tell themselves the mission was a success. Bruce knew that it was worth having hung on this long, because he was starting to feel tired and weak.

Joe was passing the time of day with Hagar Turner in her office in an early morning visit.

"Another message due from the Lander soon?" she asked.

"That's right. Bruce will be joining us shortly then we can go and listen in."

"Excuse me, Joe," said Hagar as her messaging system came to life. "Terri!" she said, as she recognised the face on screen

Joe couldn't help but listen. Terri Boyle was the head of Mission Control's Medical Centre.

"Who is sick on my team that I should know about?" she continued. "Selena? I told her not to come in today."

"No. I think that Selena will have listened to me and will be at home until she feels better. Is Joe Mortimer with you? We've tried his personal communicator, with no luck."

Joe swore at himself. He was developing a habit of leaving the communicator in his hotel room, because when he was within Mission Control he reckoned he was easy enough to find. But he knew he ought to carry it anyway. Hagar spun the screen round for Joe.

"I'm here," said Joe, rather obviously. "What's up?"

"Sorry to bother you, sir. We didn't quite know who else to speak to. We've got Bruce Dougall here. He became ill just after entering the main building."

Joe sprinted from Hagar's office. After a shouted "Thanks!" in the general direction of the screen, Hagar ran after him. He was surprised that she wasn't far behind when he reached the Medical Centre door. They both took a moment to compose themselves and went in.

"Mr Dougall is suffering from general weakness and nausea," said Terri, with no preamble. "He's lying down and resting until he feels stronger and we can get the nausea under control. We've established that he threw up badly a couple of times before coming over to Mission Control. He's had medication for the nausea but it's taking a while to have any effect. It looks to me like overwork combined with a gastric upset. I am sorry, Mr Mortimer. I didn't know who else to contact."

Hagar noted the perfectly plausible medical lie, told in the best traditions of medical confidentiality. Bruce would have had to admit his illness to the people here. The routine questions to establish a case history covered the taking any medications or having any existing conditions. The game of bluff and double bluff had already begun, courtesy of the doctor.

Terri Boyle was a competent, I'll-get-straight-to-the-point medic with an oddly charming Texan drawl. She was small and slight, with the appearance of a fair-haired porcelain doll. But when she gave an order or made a diagnosis, everyone sat up and snapped to attention. Whatever was wrong with Bruce, Joe knew that he was in good hands.

"No need to apologise," he said. "There is no one else, really. One ex-wife up in D.C. and another one God knows where. Not a lot of choice. Can we see him?"

"Yes. Don't worry about this news getting out," Terri reassured them both. "There was no one around who would see and tell, and there wasn't much to see anyway. It's not as if Mr Dougall hit the floor. He stopped and leaned against a wall and one of my nurses happened to be right behind him as she was coming on duty."

Hagar paused in the doorway. It was a heart-stopping moment for Joe when he was ushered into the small room. The years fell away and he was back on *Zeus Three*. His right hand man was lying very still on the bed. His face was ashen and his lips were devoid of colour. His eyes were closed. His uneasy, snatched breathing was an indication of the nausea that was washing over him.

Joe sat down beside the bed. Aware of someone close by, Bruce opened his eyes. For a moment he looked confused.

"It's all right, Bruce!" Joe said. "We're in Mission Control Medical Centre, not on board *Zeus Three*. This is rather where I came in last time."

"Yeah." Bruce lifted his gaze beyond the end of the bed. "I must admit that I don't remember Hagar being on Zeus!"

"I would have loved to have been there!" replied Hagar in total sincerity, stepping into the room.

She was worried. Stretched out on a bed, with nothing to distract the eye, he looked very thin. Was Joe noticing this? Probably not. As a space flight commander, nothing escaped his eye, important or trivial. However, he was a man and this type of detail didn't register on the tracking screens of life. But Bruce couldn't keep up the pretence forever

"Some sort of stomach bug, then?" she went on, feeding him the lifeline of a story started by the doctor.

"Something like that," he said. "What's the time? There should be a message through from Ariadne soon."

"The message will arrive whether you're there or not." Joe pushed him back as he struggled to sit up. "Break the habit of a lifetime and do what you are told for once. There are a thousand and one reasons why you could be missing at the crucial moment. Hagar and I will pick the best one. Trust us. I'll come back and tell you all about it later on. You rest."

"I will," murmured Bruce.

He was in no fit state to argue. He had only felt like this once before, on *Zeus Three*. He was cold, deep down cold within, and his arms and legs were no longer properly under his control.

He was asleep by the time the door closed.

*   *   *

Vicky Tennant looked at the clock. She was surprised that it was not much later. She had been convinced that it must be nearly time to go home. But that landmark was still a long way off. She had plenty of work to keep her busy each day and the good news bulletins from Cape Canaveral were exciting. The Lander was down on the surface of Mars and there should be another contact with the crew very soon. Then *Ariadne One* would be heading back home. Vicky knew that she was playing a part, however minor, in history-making events. But without Joe Mortimer around, this little corner of the *BUSSTOP* building was dull and flat.

She could think warm thoughts about her boss again. Irene hadn't gone to the launch with him and the Personal Assistant was secretly delighted. She wouldn't have wished illness upon anyone, especially the nasty brand of influenza that was doing the rounds. But she was convinced that, because Irene had to stay at home, the end of *that* particular interlude had come about quite naturally. Mr Mortimer was rather used to getting his own way and he must have been properly miffed that Professor Hanson didn't accompany him to America.

Still thinking mildly vengeful thoughts about Irene and lovely fuzzy ones about the boss, she answered the messaging signal automatically. She was snapped into full attention when she registered the face on the screen.

"Jamie!" she exclaimed delightedly.

Then she really looked and saw her brother's pale, haunted face. His brown eyes were bruised with fatigue. His dark hair had grown a little longer than he usually wore it and it stood up like a row of exclamation marks.

"Hello, sis!" he said.

Even his voice sounded faint.

"Jamie, what's wrong?"

"Vicky, we need to talk. Really talk."

"Ah, you mean Talk. Right. Where are you? At your apartment?"

"Yup. I've got a day off."

"Give me a couple of minutes and I'll be back to you."

Vicky glanced around, even though she knew that no one would disturb her. She opened the door to Joe Mortimer's office and went in. She sat down at the communications console there and entered the access codes. Within a few seconds she was speaking to Jamie again.

"There. We're on a secure line now. I'm using Mr Mortimer's office. I can see you're bothered about something. What is it?"

"Vicky, it wasn't like they say it was! The President was stable and the lorry driver was okay after the tyre blow-out and—."

"Jamie—stop! I have no idea what you are talking about. Go back several spaces and start again."

Vicky had been saying variations on those words since Jamie said his first words as a tot. Once a big sister, always a big sister, even if the age gap was only a couple of years. He still had a tendency to launch into a topic headfirst, as he was doing now. But that didn't stop him being a good doctor by all accounts.

"Sorry, sis. The road accident that President Harper was in—it wasn't like that, with her seriously injured and everyone else dead."

"What do you mean?"

"The lorry driver had taken a bump to the head. He probably had mild concussion. The lorry had a tyre blowout and he lost control and smashed into the President's car. The limousine driver was dead, as was the bodyguard. I guess he may have saved the President's life. I had to move his corpse to get to Mrs Harper. It looks as though he threw himself over her at the moment of impact. She was in pretty good shape, considering the forces involved in the crash."

It took Vicky a few seconds to work out fully what he was saying.

"Jamie, you're telling me that you were there, at the scene of the U.S. President's accident?"

"I was first on the scene. I was on my way back home. I'd done an afternoon and early evening shift at the hospital. I had a meal at a small restaurant I like near the hospital and then I headed towards home. It was getting late. The Beltway was deserted, which was odd. The lorry driver called the emergency services whilst I went to see what I could do for the occupants of the car. Mrs Harper was the only one in there to be helped. I had my basic medical bag in the car so I was able to check her out. She was complaining of abdominal pain. My immediate concern was her spleen. I couldn't find any problem there and there was no obvious damage to her liver, which we've heard so much about. I think she was very badly bruised, that's all."

"She was complaining of abdominal pain," Vicky repeated, almost in a trance as she tried to assimilate the importance of what Jamie was saying. "She was conscious then?"

"Of course she was! And the lorry driver—he'd taken a knock on the nut but he was with it enough to place the Nine One One call whilst I attended to the President. He told me all about his new wife. He'd been married six weeks."

"There's been nothing in the news about anyone helping before the emergency services arrived. Absolutely nothing! We've been told that someone driving by on the other side must have seen the crash and called for help. Why has there been no mention of you?"

"When the emergency teams started to show up, I got out of the way—fast!" Jamie told her.

"Why?"

"Everyone was armed to the teeth."

"Jamie! How long have you been in the States?" Vicky could afford to be the patronising older sister for a moment. "You know that the average cop would rather go out minus his underpants than be without a gun."

"Police officers maybe, but paramedics and fire crews? I stepped back into the shadows and drove away. In all the hoo-ha no one noticed me—I hope. Sis, this is all wrong. Two people are dead who have no business being dead. The lorry driver and the President."

"Have you told anyone else about this?"

"No. It's taken me long enough to pluck up courage to call you. I knew that you could wangle a secure line somehow. Vicky, I'm scared. It doesn't make any sense."

It was one thing reassuring a little boy that there were no monsters in the wardrobe or under the bed. It was quite another to know what to say now. Vicky was frightened too. It was easy enough to see dastardly deeds in every corner these days but her brother was right. Something did not add up.

She could feel her insides straining tight with apprehension.

"If no one has approached you about this by now, then no one has a clue who you are. Just keep on keeping on. I don't know what other advice to give you. You could come home but lots of awkward questions would be asked, to say nothing of throwing away the opportunity of a lifetime. Do you think you can hang in there?"

"Yes. I feel so much better now I've spoken to you. But there's something else, which I haven't told you yet. President Harper was brought to my hospital. You would think that the place would still be buzzing. It should have been manic the day after."

"And it wasn't? And isn't?"

"That's right. I know the people who were on that back-side-of-the-clock shift. If Pete hadn't swapped duties with me, I would have been one of the team receiving the President in the Emergency Room. No one is saying a word about what went on."

"Medical confidentiality?"

"No one would be stupid enough to say anything outside the walls of the hospital but it's the way ER personnel cope—to share some of their difficult stuff with other people who understand what they're talking about. All I get from Pete, and all of the team, is that they must say nothing because of the inquiry that has been set up."

That seemed reasonable enough. Vicky knew that one of President Rodriguez's first announced actions was to call into being a full-scale investigation of the circumstances surrounding the accident and the subsequent death of Mrs Harper.

"And all records of the entire night have been removed from the hospital computer system—by an expert," he continued.

"Now how do you know that?" Vicky wondered.

"A couple of days back, I wanted to check some details of a patient I attended during that early evening. All ER records have disappeared from six pm to six am the next day. When I raised this with Systems, I was told that there had been a computer crash across the department and those files were all lost. Other staff have found the same thing. Yesterday I borrowed the seventeen year-old cousin of a colleague. Sandor is one of these scary computer prodigies. He's off to M.I.T. but I think they're already a bit nervous about exactly what they can teach him. Anyway, I said he was shadowing me for the day. I gave him my access codes and let him play on the hospital computer system. He said that he's never seen anything like it for removing every trace of those files. He's the one who said it had been done by an expert."

Vicky had thought that her insides were knotting up. Now she changed the analogy. They were turning to water.

"Look, Jamie, whilst the boss is away I can continue using this line. Call me here in office hours and I can get back to you. I'm beginning to wonder if you should come home. I'll talk to Mum and Dad. I'm sure we can come up with some kind of family emergency to get you out of there."

"No. Leave them out of it. Promise me that, sis. I'll tough this one out."

"If you are sure. It'll take *Ariadne One* two weeks to return from Mars. I don't think Mr Mortimer will come back home now until after the spaceship lands back on Earth, so we have secure communication. He's pleased with himself, as you can imagine."

"I'm sure. We're having a blow-by-blow account of what's happening on Mars."

"The same here. It's difficult to take it in—that it's all happening." Jamie agreed.

"Has Mr Mortimer said anything about his colleague, Bruce Dougall?" he asked

"Not really. It seems that they are being very civilised to each other, which is weird, because I understand that they have quite a history of not seeing eye-to-eye outside a spaceship. Why do you ask?"

"It's only my opinion, but I think he's one ill man."

*   *   *

There was total silence across the Mission Control room at the end of Brian Hammond's latest news. Whilst all that was being achieved delighted everyone, they were caught up on the hook of planet Mars being empty. A few individuals made themselves busy but most heads turned in the direction of

Joe, who was sitting with Hagar. After all, he had launched Professor Irene Hanson and her signals from another planet on an unsuspecting world.

"Let's go," said Hagar. "We can face the questions later. The media will love this!"

"Hagar, I'm not much of a betting man but I could have staked anything on there being rational, intelligent life on Mars!" Joe protested when they were seated in her office once more. "Professor Hanson tracked those signals. She wouldn't get that wrong."

"I'm sure she wouldn't. Of course, you are in love with her, aren't you?"

Joe's jaw went slack as he looked at her. She had no business knowing that. But this was Hagar, who seemed to be gifted with some kind of second sight when it came to other people's lives.

"What if I am?" he began aggressively and then calmed down and smiled ruefully in her direction. "Sorry, Hagar. Yes, I am. But I'd only just met her when she told me about the signals. I saw all her data, her readings, everything. My judgement wasn't clouded. Not then."

"And it isn't now," Hagar told him firmly. "You've just opened a new door on life, that's all. She's going to need you, Joe. I think you will need each other before this is all over."

"I'm sure we will. But in the meantime, I need to go over to the Medical Centre and speak to Bruce."

"D'you want some moral support?"

"No." Then, "Yes please."

Joe had expected any number of reactions from Bruce, who was awake and reading a book given to him by a nurse and generally looking a lot more human. What he hadn't anticipated was the complete calm with which this kicker was greeted.

"It was an interesting idea whilst it lasted," Bruce said in a very matter-of-fact manner. "But it doesn't detract from the success of the mission, does it? The Ariadne crew have done so much! Let's get them safely back to Earth and everyone will forget all about the possibility of meeting Martians. But it does raise the question of what the hell Professor Hanson was tracking. Do you know the poem *The Listeners*, by Walter de la Mare?"

"Poetry's not really my thing," Joe admitted.

"My mother loved poetry. This poem was her all-time favourite. She said that its opening was one of the best she knew.

"Is there anybody there?' said the Traveller,
Knocking on the moonlit door."

"Was there anybody there?" Joe asked, in spite of himself.

"Yes. It's just that they weren't there in the way the Traveller expected."

"That was Professor Dougall's poetry class!" observed Hagar. "So what are you doing, Mr Dougall? If I were you, I'd stay here for as long as you can. Terri is better than a personal bodyguard and the media will be everywhere when the news gets out."

"It's tempting but having to explain what I'm doing in a Medical Centre room just adds unnecessary complications. I'll check with Doctor Boyle and then Joe and I had better be ready to present a united front."

*　　*　　*

Blood trickled down from Jackson Metz's nose. He put his hand up to the injury gingerly.

"I think you've broken my nose, you bitch!"

Emily glared.

"It won't be your face I go for next time!" she promised, fire in her eyes. "Even better—why don't you make life easier for yourself and make sure that there isn't a next time? Go and clean yourself up. You're dripping blood everywhere and making a mess."

Metz stumbled away in a daze.

On her own, Emily shook with shock and reaction. Her colleague's conversation had become more and more suggestive through the previous evening as they shared the night watch. She had been unable to sleep during her off-duty times, worried about where he was. Tired and tense, when he made a move now she hit him with the first thing that came to hand—a small electronic notebook. Its rigid edges would have caused the injury he sustained.

Emily knew that this was partly her fault. Brian had offered to keep Masahide on board the Orbiter. She should have listened. But for now she needed to be organised, as would Jackson when he returned. There was one last delicate manoeuvre to be undertaken—Lander taking off from the surface of the planet and docking with the Orbiter—and then it was time to break free of orbit from Mars and head back to Earth.

Jackson sat down warily, as far away from Emily as was physically possible and yet still be working the same consoles. His nose was very swollen and badly misshapen. She opened her mouth to apologise and stopped. What was she thinking of? It was he who should be apologising to her. And that wasn't likely to happen.

"Orbiter to Lander!" she said cheerily. "We're looking good up here. Are you ready with a schedule for take-off and docking?"

*　　*　　*

The media reaction to the lack of life on Mars was surprisingly muted in America. Professor Hanson was British. Anyone could make a mistake. All eyes were fixed on the imminent Lander take-off and rejoining with Orbiter. This was the last dodgy bit and would be the crowning glory of the mission. The flight back to Earth was a mere detail. The Zeus missions had made that part appear to be routine.

Joe knew that the home press and television might not be quite as forgiving. He contacted Irene straight away.

When he saw the confusion and bewilderment on her face, he hurt for her. He wanted to be with her, to try to soothe those feelings away.

"Joe! You saw my data. You reverse-ran my tracking. People might not have wanted to admit that there was intelligent life on Mars. There was a great deal of fuss but, at the time, no one questioned the accuracy of what I found."

Joe remembered that afternoon in college with her, looking at the data, listening to the message, taking her to his parents' house so that his father could listen as well. That was where it had all started. He had to admit that now as he looked back. By the time he dropped her off at her house in the evening he was in love, something he had not allowed himself to be for many years.

He pulled himself back to the present.

"May I make a few suggestions, Irene? Next time I speak to you, I don't want to see you covered in footprints where the media have trampled over you. You remember Albert Wright?"

"The media man at *BUSSTOP*? Oh, he was a sweetie."

It was not a description that sprang readily to Joe's mind but it would do if Irene had to depend on him.

"Strictly speaking you are none of his business. You're not *BUSSTOP*. But I can be the boss when I have to be. His business is what I say it is from time to time, not that I think I'll have to be heavy-handed with him. He took quite a shine to you, Irene."

"Then he's *definitely* a sweetie."

"He has excellent judgement," Joe conceded. "I'll have a word with Albert and he'll be in touch with you. He can minimise the grief that you will have to go. He may be a sweetie but he can be a real bull-dog with the media people when he puts his mind to it, especially if he thinks someone has stepped out of line."

*   *   *

"It's almost superfluous to say that this is an historic moment." Brian Hammond looked round at the Lander crew. "A lot of moments have been historic since we took off from Cape Canaveral. But are you ready to make history one more time on this trip?"

"You bet!" replied Jethro.

"Good. Orbiter, Orbiter, this is Lander. We are ready to take off. Synchronise on my mark."

He looked over at Simeon and Masahide, who gave him the thumbs up.

"Lander to Orbiter." Emily sounded very close, not way up in the sky. Simeon wanted to be back with her. He would be soon. "We're ready when you are."

"Mark!" said Brian. "Fire those thrusters."

"Firing thrusters," confirmed Masahide, entering the sequence into the computer.

There was silence and stillness.

"A problem, Masahide?" Brian asked calmly.

"I don't understand," Masahide said. "Everything is working and on line."

"Orbiter from Lander!" Brian called. "We have a slight delay here. We're looking at a possible malfunction. Stand by."

The next five minutes crawled by as each crew member went about his designated tasks of checking different parts of the Lander's systems. This had all been practised on Earth, with Deanna throwing the most bizarre problems into the mix. They had never worked on the scenario when every system was not working whilst the computers said everything was functioning normally.

Brian had talked to Joe Mortimer about the outside possibility of not being able to leave the planet's surface, dooming the crew of the Lander and the Orbiter.

"It's something that you need to be aware of, as the commander. It's not something that you can do a simulation for," Joe had said. "The variables leading up to it are too scattered. And let's face it, doing a dummy run for your own death is not exactly good for team spirit and morale. It's very simple anyway. It will be down to you to hold the group together and you will have two choices. You can give up and sit there and wait for life support to fail. So you will all go to sleep and not wake up again. Or you keep trying to the very end to make things work, in the hope that something might have been overlooked. I know which I would go for."

"Let's keep checking, let's keep trying," said Brian to the other four. "We will have missed something, I'm sure." He contacted Orbiter. "We're still experiencing some difficulties here. Stand down the synchronising of our computer controls. When we get this ship off the ground, we'll have to do it the hard way—linking up under manual control. Send a message to Mission Control informing them that we have a total systems failure at the moment. We're a bit busy down here. Presuming that our telemetry readings are still reaching Earth, someone might have a bright idea. Ask for any suggestions."

On the Orbiter, Emily went deathly pale. Jackson sent the information back to Mission Control. Then he stood up to move closer to her.

"You stay where you are, Jackson!" she said, gripping the notebook tightly.

"Don't be so dumb, Emily! Your man is stuck down there and we're stuck up here. We can't return to Earth without the Orbiter, remember. It's an integral part of the ship. We're in this together, whether we like it or not."

"Contact Lander again and see how they're doing."

"Do it yourself!" Jackson said roughly. Then he relented. "Give them a few more minutes. They'll be working flat out down there."

Jackson Metz was correct. The five men were combing every inch of every system, in the hope that they might find some tiny flaw that was having a huge knock-on effect. Brian could see that his crew were becoming slightly panicky, making small mistakes.

"Let's stop for a minute or two. Then we can pool our ideas, start again."

Gianfranco brought out his rosary.

"*Ave Maria, gratia plena,*

Dominus tecum, benedicta tu in mulieribus, et benedicta fructus ventris tui Iesus.

Sancta Maria, mater Dei, ora pro nobis peccatoribus, nunc et in ora mortis nostrae. Amen."

"Latin now?" Brian wondered.

"Yes," said Gianfranco and crouched down.

Brian pulled him upright.

"What's that all about?" he asked.

"You said you would knock my bloody head off if I prayed to Our Lady again."

"That was then. This is now."

On the planet's surface, the Martians drew nearer. They knew things were badly wrong. Now that there was an emergency they could intervene and they were combining all their powers to help the astronauts, Orbiter and Lander, putting in place a temporary force field.

"Will their last message to Earth have got out before we put in the support?" asked Sally. "I hate being so . . . limited, not sensing things!" she concluded vehemently.

Tony assured her that even now a message from Jackson Metz was making its ponderous way back to Earth

"If only we could come right down to their level!" said Justin. "At least they would know we were helping them."

"We can!" laughed Tony. He pointed to the ground by one of the remote cameras. All the monitoring equipment had failed as they walked by it. "We can finally come down to their level. See what's here."

He bent down and picked up the stone that Hagar had given to Simeon.

"What good will that do?" Justin wondered.

"Touch it, all of you," Tony urged. They did, mystified. "We touch it and we are literally earthed. We are brought down to human vibration level with no harm to us. The stone was brought here from Earth. Hagar sent it."

Each saw in their minds an image of Hagar.

"Of course!" said Sally. "It had to be! I haven't come across that face for a long, long time!"

"Our brothers and sisters will be able to see us now," Tony continued. "Let's move. We haven't got much time. Or rather, they don't have much time before life support breaks down on the Lander, and the Orbiter can't get back to Earth on its own."

The wind was blowing fiercely, whipping up the dust. It made a wailing sound around the Lander, an unnerving ethereal choir mourning the loss of travellers who had strayed too far from home.

Brian gritted his teeth. He would have preferred something else to be the last sounds he heard. But in the meantime they must keep on trying to get the Orbiter moving.

"I knew I wasn't imagining things!" yelled Simeon suddenly. "Look out on the starboard side!"

Chapter Seventeen

Albert Wright was in his element. The boss had set him an interesting challenge—to stop the media pack tearing Irene Hanson limb from limb when the news was made public in Britain that there was no life on Mars. He relished the prospect of the tussle and looked forward to reacquainting himself with the delectable professor.

So, first he would—

Harry Chance, his assistant, burst through the door.

"Mr Wright!" he panted, out of breath. "Turn your screen on! The Mars Lander has problems. The crew can't get the thrusters to fire!"

Albert Wright knew straightaway that he would not have to worry about Irene's welfare. All attention would be on the Lander crew and the horrible possibility that the entire *Ariadne One* team might be stranded.

*　　*　　*

"Don't be frightened," said Tony gently to the five men. They were pressed back into their seats as far as they could go and he could feel their terror. "We are here to help."

"Who are you?" Brian managed to get out.

"My name is Tony. I'll introduce you to my brothers and sisters when we go outside. You will need to leave the Lander soon, least your protection becomes your tomb." He turned to Simeon, reading his thoughts. "Yes, Simeon, we are real." He held out his hand. "Touch. See? We know everything about you," he said in answer to the unasked question, "including your names. I am what you would call a Martian, in human form, as are my brothers and sisters. We have waited a long time to greet you. We have much to share and then we will take you home."

Everyone was in a half-faint of fear; they understood and followed very little of what was being said. Jethro picked up on the word *home*.

"How can we get home?" he queried.

"We will take you back to Earth," Tony promised. "We will repair the Lander, reunite it with the Orbiter and escort you home."

"What about the Orbiter?" asked Masahide "It can stay up there for as long as necessary on its own but the reactor . . ."

He surprised himself for a moment there. Usually he let other people do the talking. But he was convinced that this was some kind of bizarre dream, totally unreal. David would wake him soon. So whilst he was in this experience, he might as well say what needed saying.

"We will deal with everything," Tony said in reassurance. "We have created an area of environment on the planet's surface where we can all live comfortably. You will not need any of your cumbersome life support equipment." He opened the inner hatchway. "Please, you must leave this craft. Simeon, look at the panel you studied earlier when you saw us."

Simeon did as he was told. Life support readings were creeping towards there being a problem.

"I recommend that we go," he said firmly.

*　　*　　*

Bruce ignored the doctor's advice and left the Medical Centre, his head full of thoughts about how *BUSSTOP* would deal with grumpy media people, who could see their best headline evaporating. *Take Me To Your Leader* would have been such an unforgivable cliché but such a gift. He walked into the main Mission Control room and stopped as if he had come up against a brick wall. There was total silence. Each person was staring at his or her computer screens. Hagar was trawling through endless readouts. Joe was at the back of the room, leaning against the wall, arms folded, eyes down. Bruce went and stood next to him.

"Lander's stuck," Joe said briefly. "Her thrusters won't fire. The crew are working their way through the systems to try and isolate the problem."

"Life signs?"

"We're still registering five in the Lander and two on the Orbiter. That's something, I suppose."

"No!" someone cried. "No! No! No!"

In a few strides Joe and Bruce were over to that person and her console. She looked up at the *BUSSTOP* chiefs.

"I've lost all life signs on the Lander," she said.

"Computer failure again?" wondered Bruce.

"I don't think so," said the man next to her. "All systems are still registering and life support is—Jesus, Mary and Joseph!" he breathed suddenly. "All Lander telemetry has been lost."

"Life signs from Orbiter are gone!" declared another voice.

"Orbiter telemetry is lost!" a fourth person announced.

Joe and Bruce stood in the middle of the Mission Control floor. They didn't know which way to turn first as possible disaster echoed from every corner. In the silence, everyone became aware of a lone, desperate voice.

"Orbiter and Lander, Mission Control comm check . . . Orbiter and Lander, Mission Control comm check . . . Orbiter and Lander, Mission Control comm check . . ."

Joe was closer. He put his hand on the man's shoulder.

"It's okay, Keith. If there's anybody up there to reply, remember the time lag in both directions."

Bruce made his way over to Hagar's station.

"Well?"

"See for yourself," said Hagar. "Blank screen after blank screen. Nothing. Lander and Orbiter just aren't registering—and neither are the people."

"Ship-wide systems failure?"

"It's theoretically possible but I doubt it. And I can't think what could malfunction on Lander that would affect the Orbiter—or *vice versa*."

Joe and Bruce automatically looked in the direction of Dieter Goldberg, seated at the back of the room.

"Ladies, gentlemen," he said very softly, "make sure that all data on your computers is secure."

He gave the briefest of nods to Joe and Bruce, to remind them that, like him, they had matters to attend to.

Joe strode off in the direction of the office that was there for his use.

Hagar looked at Bruce.

"Shouldn't you be doing something?"

"Plenty. If you'll excuse me, Hagar. In the meantime, will you . . ."

"We'll keep on trying to re establish some sort of link with *Ariadne One*," she promised. "We all know what we have to do in such a situation."

It was only later that Bruce remembered something.

Hagar was a relative. Simeon was on board.

* * *

The crew of the Lander looked about them in astonishment. They weren't simply standing on the planet Mars without their protective suits and breathing gear. They were seeing a rainbow. Even that wasn't quite as it seemed. They were *in* the rainbow. They were part of it. The rainbow was the planet and the planet was the rainbow. The rainbow was generated by a massive crystalline structure. Wherever they turned, the crystal was in front of them, refracting light and making the colours dance around them. In turn they were touched by red, orange, yellow, green, blue, indigo and violet. Each colour generated different and complementary emotions within them. They were dizzy with joy.

"I could fly home without a ship!" Brian murmured.

Emily and Jackson were walking towards them through a waterfall of shades of colour. How they were here on the surface of Mars, the others had no idea. All that mattered was that they were out of the ship and they were safe. Tony beamed as Simeon and Emily embraced.

Tony introduced them to Justin, Sally and Ichiro. One figure stayed in the background.

"She is still transforming," Tony explained.

No one understood but it didn't matter. On some strange level they grasped exactly what he meant.

Emily wanted to cry out in fear as she looked at the other two beings and then she knew that nothing here would harm anyone. This was no place for the negative, the draining, and the frightening. Those things belonged in another place, which was already becoming a distant memory. She greeted them confidently.

"Hello. I'm Emily Alexander."

"We know. Greetings Emily."

Initially, their appearance was humanoid but as she tried to make them out they became light rather than substance. They towered over the crew, standing at least eight feet tall.

A strange sensation of peace came over the astronauts. It filled their bodies, filled their minds, filled up their senses to saturation point. It was like a drug removing pain, flowing through them like a tide, pushing the pain ahead of it until it finally washed over the distress and took it away.

All were wrapped in a continuous now of calm and contentment. All were drawn to these beings.

"Is it you, Jesus?" Brian murmured.

"Muhammad, peace be upon him!" gasped a stunned Simeon.

"The Buddha! The Enlightened One!" sighed Masahide.

"*Il Papa!*" wept Gianfranco, kneeling to receive the blessing of Pope John the Twenty-Third, a figure from the twentieth century for whom he had the greatest regard.

"Mother Theresa!" Jethro said. "I have always admired you so much."

"Artemis!" breathed Emily.

Jackson was astounded that he could name all of the *Ibo Loa*—the spirits, gods and goddesses of the Voodon way. Way back—wherever it was he had been—he had no knowledge of this. In rapid succession, like a film being run at high speed, he and the others could see and identify many such beings and people. There was Boudiga. Urania the muse of astronomy wore her star-spangled gown and held a globe. Dornoll the Amazonian warrior goddess stood near them, along with Hathor, the Egyptian goddess of the Moon, Venus, psychic work and healing. They lost count and lost track of those they saw but they touched, and were touched by, the wisdom and power of all.

"I don't understand," Brian found himself saying to Tony. "How are we all seeing such different people?"

"They are part of the essence of inspiration for the human race, a spark of the divine, great teachers, shining examples. If there had been a Sikh amongst you, he would have seen Guru Nanak. If there had been a Jew, she would have seen Abraham or Moses or Elijah. You are becoming one with the planet. As well as those you look to, you are seeing those of whom you have never heard but whose knowledge and grace will be needed by you and by your brothers and sisters on planet Earth."

Planet Earth.

The phrase was already gathering a distant quality, an echo from long ago and far away. It was a like a wisp of smoke left over from a fire, perhaps like the tendrils of mist that were creeping around and over them, making the colours that enveloped them pearlescent. Or perhaps it was a story they had been told about when they were very young and therefore they thought it was a memory. It had something of the nursery about it.

A riot of smells and tastes suffused them. For Brian there was home-baked bread and the fleeting aroma of freshly poured tea. Emily tasted cinnamon biscuits and bagels. Jethro was aware of eggs and bacon cooking. Simeon was enjoying the perfect roast chicken. Gianfranco was helping to make and eat *linguine* with pesto. Masahide was savouring green tea as he was surrounded by fragrant flowers. Jackson was overcome by the gorgeous smell of onions being fried to go with the hotdogs.

Everyone could see the parents, friends and partners who were preparing these things. They recognised them—and it caused no distress to know that they were elsewhere. Being here was all that was necessary.

Indescribable feelings of love surrounded them. Love was such an inadequate word—used, abused and overused in everyday language. But as each person looked at the others, they understood. The tears flowed and they could see.

A force beyond Jackson's control moved him until he stood in front of Emily.

"Emily! Please. Forgive me."

Emily held open her arms to hug him. In that moment Simeon knew what this man had done and had thought. He understood and forgave him too.

Sally stepped forward.

"Jackson Metz, this is a planet of peace, of love, of brotherhood and sisterhood. Your planet is meant to be the same. Your outmoded racist and sexist attitudes have no place in either world. This is your chance to start again. Will you take it?"

Jackson nodded dumbly.

"When you get home, love your wife as if your life depends on it," said Tony. "It may well do."

"I'm not married," he said, amazed that he could speak.

"Your girl friend watched *Ariadne One* take off. Do something about that relationship when you return to Earth."

Sally touched his battered and damaged nose, running her forefinger and thumb down the length of it.

"You don't need to be reminded of your past life. We none of us do. Be whole, Jackson, and stay whole." His nose was mended. She smiled at Emily. "Good girl! This may be the planet of peace and love but the human part of me remembers when I would have happily hit a man. Two, in fact."

Emily had a glimpse into Sally's mind. It was like walking round the outside of a never-ending house, looking in through windows. There were rooms full of people, sounds, emotions and events. Some rooms were flooded with light. Others were dark and Emily needed to turn away. She saw the images of the men to whom Sally referred. The one was wreathed in love, the other spiked with conflict. She knew who they were but she was not surprised. A small part of her had a lingering doubt as to whether she should have seen this.

"Don't be afraid, Emily," Sally reassured her. "We have opened windows into your minds and souls. A window is a two-way business. You can gaze in when you are ready, just as I can gaze in on you."

Emily looked around her.

"So this is where the rainbow ends. As a little girl, I always wondered."

"This is the beginning of the rainbow and the end of the rainbow. It is the middle of every rainbow seen in the sky. I'm glad you notice rainbows, Emily. I loved them as a human. I was so angry when people ignored them. I once made what can only be described as a speech to Joe, who didn't always take time to wonder and to appreciate such things. I told him: *A spaceship roars up into the sky and everyone cheers and claps. Colours are painted across the sky and no one bothers to even look.*"

"You loved him very much," Emily stated, seeing one image again.

"Yes, Sally loved him."

The astronauts were at home with the dual personalities of their Martian hosts. On one level each of them *was* their Earth figure, with all the feelings, hopes, joys and sorrows of that person when in the Earthly plane. And yet at a very deep level, the essential Martian was there, full and overflowing with the wisdom that they were yet to impart.

"Ichiro!" said Tony. "You have work to do. There are space ships to be attended to. And the rest of us have much sharing and caring to do. And learning."

Ichiro bowed to the astronauts. In another time and place the astronauts would have been awe-struck at being in the presence of the man who, along with Brent Dyer, had to be given most of the credit for the reality of the Zeus space ship, which led on to the Ariadne project. On Mars, they accepted that his reincarnation was someone they had to meet. Masahide was moved because he was in the presence of an honoured fellow countryman.

"I will take great care of *Ariadne One*," Ichiro promised. "Just as you have done."

The crew had only ever seen still and moving electronic images of Ichiro Matsushita, taken before the advent of the S-Creen film process, but there was no mistaking him. He was a little taller than Gianfranco, with an amazing shock of black hair and he really was as greyhound thin as the old pictures made him out to be. His face was lean, almost haggard it seemed, but Masahide knew he was reading Ichiro's Earth fate into what he was seeing. Until his sudden death, the designer was bursting with health and vigour.

Ichiro smiled and was gone.

Sally, Justin and Tony looked at one another. The full magnitude of their mission was clear to them. The learning process was also a two-way business. They needed so much detail. Like the humans touching down in Lander, the Martian delegation would only have one chance to get this right on Earth. What was already a complex mission had evolved further and the story was still being laid out before them.

Tony glanced over to their sister who was transforming. He had accepted, as had the others, that he did not need to know, until the moment arose, who this figure was. Now he knew the human name of the seventh being.

*　　*　　*

Mission Control and the *BUSSTOP* headquarters in Washington D.C. and London resembled disturbed ant heaps. But in much the same way as each ant would be carrying out an appointed task, everyone within the organisation was fitting in to the bigger picture.

All appropriate heads of state were informed of the problems on Mars. Assorted personal assistants and aides of national leaders were spoken to and the straightforward demand was made that their superiors be dug out of meetings, dinners, bed if necessary and pow-wows with their publishers where they were preparing the market ahead of time for their memoirs. This was far more important.

Family members were told of the situation. Specially trained staff made personal visits to the loved ones of each astronaut. There were tears, outbursts of shouting and abuse, which gave way to helpless sobbing. Then there was blank incomprehension. The golden touch of the Zeus team had made everything appear so simple, so routine, and so matter-of-fact. They had pushed the new design of spaceship to its limits and had orbited Mars. Landing on Mars and coming back was just the next step. Now there was the unthinkable being put before each group of people. Your son or daughter, your partner or significant other, might not be coming back.

Every tracking device of any appreciable power was glued to Mars, to see if any clues could be found by studying the planet. Early information, coming in from observatories that kept a routine eye on that part of the solar system, was not encouraging. It appeared that huge dust storms were raging across the planet. Joe and Bruce, who were doing their best to keep open minds about what might be happening, began to think darker and more desperate thoughts when they received that news.

The media were briefed via press releases. The reasons for this were simple. First, like the shocked families, television and the newspapers couldn't believe what was being announced and began an immediate shrill coverage of every fact, rumour and vague innuendo. Nobody would have wanted to be in the same room as any media representatives. Second, it was understood by the more thoughtful sections of press and television that those within *BUSSTOP* who might have something to say were too busy dealing with the problem. That's why there were such things as press offices.

And the media accepted it. Everyone was mindful of the legal picket fence that was in place around Joe Mortimer and Bruce Dougall over Philemon Brown. No one wanted any kind of extra accusations slapped down on the table.

Efforts were doubled and redoubled to re establish contact with *Ariadne One*. Orbiter's journey round the planet was tracked by the second to the moment it disappeared off screen. It was known down to the last gnat's whisker where Lander was settled on the surface of Mars and every walk each of the crew had made was plotted with total accuracy. Hagar Turner was hugely proud of her systems team. They could tell anyone where Orbiter, Lander and the crews were meant to be. It was just that nothing and no one appeared to be where they should be. There was nothing and no one to contact.

Hagar knew that counsellors from *BUSSTOP* had visited Simeon's parents. She would have known anyway because her brother contacted her. She sat in her office and watched Ishmael weeping and raging at her from the screen. She had worked all day to no avail and she was bitterly tired with that weariness which is unique to times when huge amounts of physical and mental energy are expended for no result. She was finding it hard to keep her own tears at bay.

At last Hagar put up her hands defensively.

"Enough, Ishmael! What do you think I have been doing for hours and hours? I've been trying to find Simeon and the rest of his crew. Don't you think I'm hurting? Did I do something deliberate to knock *Ariadne One* out of communication with us here?"

Ishmael blinked.

"I'm sorry," he mumbled. "Will you come over to see us tonight?"

"I shall be here all night, trying to solve this problem. You can see me any time. If we are to find the astronauts, it must be done soon." Ishmael swallowed hard. "I'm sorry. I don't mean to be harsh. I'm trying to say that I can best serve the situation by being here. I'll bet you're not alone."

"We have a few people here from church and Celia is rustling up a bite to eat. You know what she's like. Being busy helps her cope with things."

Hagar interpreted that as at least twenty visitors and a menu that would make an award-winning restaurant go pale.

That difficult conversation over, Hagar sat with elbows resting on her desk. Her chin was supported on her cupped hands. This was what she was here for. That was the only possible conclusion. She was waiting for some reassurance, some sign, because this was not what she had understood her mission to be. Or was it that her present limitations meant that she had a tendency to misinterpret what she thought she knew? Bruce was a good example. Whilst she had understood that there was something very wrong with him, she wasn't clear on the details until he confided in her.

Some of her words to him ran like a challenging audio loop in her mind.

"*When we've spoken about stuff before, have I been wrong?*" she had demanded.

Perhaps she was horribly wrong now.

Hagar didn't move her position when there was a knock on the door and she waited for the person to come in.

"Hello, Bruce," she said. "Are you seeking sanctuary? I'm hiding here for a while."

"I'm returning the compliment, coming to see how you are," he said. "You bustled over to the Medical Centre first thing to see me."

She sat up.

"Was that only this morning?" she marvelled. "I was reckoning on it being days ago. Should you be rushing about everywhere? You were pretty sick earlier on. I know you want to keep up the appearance of normality, but trying to do the Superman thing may not be a good idea."

"I can't sit around worrying about my health, Hagar. And to be truthful, everyone is beginning to wind down some. Everything that can be done has been done. Some things have been done for a second and third time, just to make sure. Your department has been outstanding. But—"

"—we have no idea what has happened to *Ariadne One* or her crew."

Hagar finished the sentence for him.

"Yeah. I know that Simeon's parents have been visited by one of our support teams. But what about you? Simeon is your nephew."

"I've got my support system here, with all you wonderful people," she stated in genuine gratitude. "I can't ask for more right now. So where's Joe Mortimer, if everything has been said and done?"

"Giving President Rodriguez a piece of his mind."

"I would buy a ticket to witness that! Why aren't you talking to our latest and brightest President? I would have thought that was your job. You chatted good and long to President Harper on occasions, if I remember correctly, and you didn't mince your words."

"I informed the White House this morning about our difficulties. Joe raced through his tasks very fast and I suggested that he might like to speak to the President in person. Anyway, he'll be better at it than me. Joe just plain dislikes the man. Rodriguez gives me the creeps. There's something about him."

"You've picked up on it too. Interesting." Hagar stretched her arms and flexed her fingers to ease the physical tension she felt. "Why is Joe rattling the doors and windows of the White House?"

"The President can't wait to get the crew dead and buried. He will have had to take Joe's call because he will be expecting *BUSSTOP* to have some memorial service plans. We will have to start thinking along those lines." Bruce stopped for a moment and bit his lower lip. "But not yet. Not yet."

Joe banging heads with the President of the United States of America was one of the last pieces of activity, which had covered a whole day. Yet for all this effort, two big problems remained. No one knew what had happened to *Ariadne One* and her crew and there was no sensible explanation as to why all readings had dropped off screen almost simultaneously. A catastrophe on Mars would not have affected Orbiter and Orbiter plunging to the planet's surface would not impact on Lander immediately.

One matter was still to be faced. If the crew was still alive and stranded, there was little that could be done. It might be 2110 but, as yet, nothing like the twentieth century children's stories of a future with International Rescue existed. Thunderbird Three could not power up and dash off to Mars to save the astronauts as they breathed their last gasp of air.

This was the stark reality. A long stretch of doing something—*anything*—that might help had, thus far, kept the prospect at arm's length. Now, as the To Do list was whittled away, the realisation was dawning. Perhaps it was better if there was no contact with the *Ariadne One* crew. A running commentary on increasingly futile efforts to get Lander off the ground would have been devastating, especially as the voices faded away one by one. Lander was not designed with self-sustaining life-support systems, as it was only meant to be away from the mother ship for a short period of time. A landing craft with a longer independent existence was what engineers were working on for the future.

In theory, Orbiter could stay up there forever but eventually the reactor would start emitting dangerous levels of radiation without a complete overhaul. And Orbiter could not come home without Lander reattached.

Hagar watched the minimal colour in Bruce's face drain away as he considered these possibilities.

"I don't think I can take this, Hagar," he said.

"You have to. We all have to. The whole world is looking this way."

She paused for a moment. It was as though someone unseen and unheard by anyone else was speaking to her. Bruce had witnessed this before, had not taken that much notice.

"Don't give up hope," she said. "You'll see."

"What hope is there, Hagar? I reckon I'm a fairly positive guy. I've had to be over these past months! What is there to be hopeful about?"

"Don't ever stop believing in angels, fairies and Santa Claus, Bruce. There is always room for the wonderful and the miraculous."

Bruce didn't know whether the sudden draining of strength from his body was physical or psychological in origin. He sat down heavily on a chair.

Hagar had just said, word for word, what his mother once told him. He was about to say something to that effect when there was another knock on the door and Joe entered the room. He appeared to be sleepwalking. Hagar jumped up and pulled a chair close to him. Bruce eyed him anxiously. Was Joe ill as well? Doctor Terri Boyle was spinning a convenient medical fiction in case anyone heard about his early morning faint. But perhaps there really was some virus floating about!

"Did the President give you a bad time?" Hagar enquired cautiously. Joe turned a vacant face to her. "Bruce told me that you volunteered to have words with him."

"He was okay." Joe shook his head at the recollection. "Well, he's a pillock," he qualified. He stared at Hagar for long seconds and then he turned his gaze to Bruce. "But I remembered something whilst President Rodriguez was ranting on about why Lander might have failed. I think I should be sacked on the spot for what I've done," he croaked. "Or, rather, what I didn't do."

Hagar went to her secret stash of bourbon. She slopped a generous measure into a glass and handed it to Joe. She and Bruce had joked about Dieter Goldberg and his tendency to exaggerate and fly off the handle. But Joe was no drama queen. If he thought he had messed up big time, there was every likelihood that he might have done.

"What didn't you do, Joe?" Bruce wanted to know, when he could stand the silence no longer.

"At the end of last winter, I took a call from one of our British engineers, Rob Masters. I couldn't be bothered to listen to him. It was a Friday and I'd had enough. That was the day you contacted me," he informed Bruce, "to tell me that Britain was being given overall control of the Ariadne project." Bruce studied the floor for a few moments. "I should have taken time to listen to him!" he berated himself out loud.

"What do you think he was going to tell you?"

Hagar's tone was quietly reassuring. She had never seen Joe like this.

"He started to tell me that he had been studying the wiring schematics of Ariadne's Lander—the originals drawn up by Ichiro Matsushita just before he died. I interrupted him and handed him back to my PA, who passed him on to someone else. He would only have tried to tell me about what he'd found if there were something wrong. What if the mistake he found has led to Lander being stranded on Mars?"

His chin sank onto his chest and his voice went down too. This was a Joe Mortimer that neither Bruce nor Hagar had ever seen before—uncertain, defeated, and scared. Bruce had seen his colleague devastated when he broke the news of Sally's accident, but that was insignificant compared to this.

Joe pulled himself upright and drank the bourbon.

Hagar took a few deep breaths. Bruce screwed up his eyes tightly for a moment, as if this simple physical act might summon every ounce of his concentration.

Their points were straightforward and designed to put Joe's mind at rest. Had Joe heard more as a result of Rob Masters' conversation with someone else? No. So it couldn't have been anything important.

Would *Ariadne One* have been completed without anyone else spotting a possible error? No.

Bruce saw the possible flaw in that one and crossed his fingers. No one had spotted the imbalance in the propulsion system of *Zeus One* prior to the first test firing.

Could Joe be sure that Rob Masters was about to reveal some glaring mistake? No, he couldn't.

And there was always the possibility that contact might yet be regained with *Ariadne One*. There had already been one panic, over her computers.

It was nearly midnight. Joe was surprised at how much time he had spent talking with Bruce and Hagar. He was far from easy about the failure of the Lander craft. If Ariadne was lost and no reasons were ever agreed upon for that loss, he would be in the worst possible position; he would never know for sure

There was one light on the horizon. Irene had left him a message, saying that he could call her at *any* time. She meant it. That was for sure. What time would it be in England? The simple maths was beyond the capability of his fuddled brain. For all he knew, the moon was probably green over Cambridgeshire and certainly Irene would be asleep.

"Here goes!" he said out loud, deciding that he would say nothing to her for the moment about his dark fears.

Irene appeared on the screen very quickly. She was wrapped decorously in a dressing gown but she looked deliciously rumpled.

"Good morning, Joe!" she said. "It is early morning here, as opposed to late night. I'm really sorry. I don't need to ask how things are going at your end. I can see it in your face."

"We've got nowhere," he told her anyway. "No contact, no indication of what happened when contact stopped. I think we've lost them, Irene. Seven crew and a fine ship that made Zeus look like some museum relic. I don't understand."

"Some things are beyond understanding at the time, Joe." Her heart ached as she heard the slightest catch in his voice. She wanted to make that go away. "Would you like me to come out to Cape Canaveral?"

"What—and walk out on the University?"

"You were prepared to give the launch a miss for me. I'm becoming positively bold in my old age. I've got a good teacher, you see."

"Bless you, Irene. I think I will be home in a few days. Now this is strictly for your ears only."

"Oh," she broke in, after she had listened for a couple of minutes. "That is rather final, isn't it?"

"It is. We need to draw a line under this, somehow. I had to smack the President about a bit because he was so cocky and certain about everything. But he's right. The *Challenger* space shuttle blew up before the television cameras of the world and Texas and Louisiana watched and felt the pieces of *Columbia* dropping down from the sky. No one was in any doubt as to what had happened in each case and everyone could accept that the crews were gone. We've got nothing. Nothing, that is, apart from dead air on the comm and blank screens. The longer this drags on, the worse it becomes for everybody involved. I'll talk to you soon and keep you up to date with what's happening."

*   *   *

Ted Rodriguez finished speaking and switched off the screen. After a few moments he became aware of his wife standing in the doorway.

"Mo! How long have you been standing there?"

"Long enough. You are a piece of work, Ted! I think you're enjoying this, aren't you?"

"How can you say that?" he protested. "We have lost six men and a woman out there on Mars."

"Save that for your television appearances."

"Mo! What's all this about?"

"I've been watching you since we first heard about Ariadne," Maureen said. "There's this secret little smile that you've got. I was watching the British Prime Minister on the television earlier. You know what a sombre guy he is. He doesn't give much away as a rule. He was destroyed. You could see that. And he's only got one citizen on board! Although numbers aren't important in a situation like this."

"You're weary, Maureen. It's been a long and difficult day. I won't be long. I've got a couple more jobs to do."

He was tired and he was furious with his wife for knowing his inmost feelings. He thought that he had the dignified grief thing nailed. She wasn't fooled, for some reason.

Rodriguez opened up a computer file. He gazed, as he often did these days, at the picture of Justin. But this time, he moved on to other photographs. Justin was dead but Jared and Lee and the others were very much alive.

There was something else to be done, which needed sorting out. He was still concerned about the unknown doctor who helped President Harper. That was scratching away in the back of his mind. He didn't need yet another item of unfinished business.

Philemon Brown had served his purpose well. He had put question marks over Mortimer and Dougall. But Rodriguez had no further use for him. Fate had played into the President's hands beautifully. The astronauts being stuck on Mars was more than he could have hoped for in his wildest dreams.

He shut down the file of pictures hurriedly, in his haste forgetting to add the encryption codes.

The President punched buttons to initiate another call.

"Operation Watchful. Terminate the subject!"

"You seem so keen on God, Philemon Brown," he said under his breath. "So you can move along and meet him a tad early."

*   *   *

Maureen Rodriguez was not the only person unimpressed by the President's statesmanlike sorrow at the possibility of the loss of the Ariadne crew. Philemon Brown was disturbed as he watched him in a White House news conference. The man seemed almost pleased.

The church pastor spent a restless night. The legal processes hanging over him were a worry. He had never dreamt that *BUSSTOP* would react in such a way. His fellow pastors and ministers took a relaxed view about it. Some saw the serving of papers as a badge of honour. You were not doing the Lord's work unless someone was so riled that they had to reach for the law. He had tried to speak to Rodriguez and instead he received vague messages of support via a White House aide.

About two o'clock, Philemon Brown started thinking back over what Rodriguez had said when he dropped by that second time.

> *"You have been so helpful with the cause, Philemon."* Cause? What cause? *"You have such a way with words, to make people think the unthinkable, to make them face up to unpalatable truths. I'll lend you one of my speech-writing staff. He can guide you in what you preach and he can hone your sermons for you. We want to say the right things to the people."* Guide? Say the right things? *"You have become such an ally in my stand against the Mars programme."* Ally? Against the Mars programme? *"I won't forget this."*

Philemon had favourite phrases in the Bible. One was *the scales fell from his eyes*, describing the healing of actual or spiritual blindness. The scales had certainly fallen from his eyes and he didn't like what he was seeing.

In the early morning he slid out of bed, making sure that he didn't disturb Darlene. He dressed quickly and tiptoed down to the front door. It creaked alarmingly as he opened it. He stood still, hardly daring to breathe.

No one had been woken. He closed the door softly and walked down the road. He needed to pray in church. He knew that he could pray anywhere but this morning he wanted to be in his own church, alone.

Brown entered the security codes at the side door of Braddock Road Full Gospel Church and slipped in silently. He turned on some lights near the front of the sanctuary and knelt down behind the communion table, looking along the length of the centre aisle, as if he was leading the congregation in celebration of the Last Supper.

"Father God, I've been holding hands with the devil!" he prayed out loud, desperation giving his voice strength and volume "Forgive me. Oh my Lord! I have blackened the names of good men and women. Forgive me!"

Tears ran down his cheeks. How could he have been such a fool? Yes, he had been used, but it was his own weakness, his own vanity that allowed the likes of Rodriguez to take advantage of him. He had allowed himself to become bigger than the message that he was trying to put over. Worse still, he knew he had lost track of the comfort and guidance that he should be proclaiming.

Philemon Brown's lips moved in silent petition to God as the laser dot of the rifle sight centred on his forehead.

*   *   *

Once Joe had digested the news from Washington D.C. that Pastor Philemon Brown had been shot dead in his own church, his first reaction was one of relief that Bruce couldn't possibly have done it. He was tucked up safely in bed in his hotel room. To be precise, it turned out that he was making an early morning room service call at about the time Brown was found by the church janitor, who was unlocking the building ready for members to come in to prepare for a prayer breakfast. The pastor was tumbled backwards by the impact of a single round to the head, sprawled down the steps surrounding the church communion table, with a massive pool of blood gathered underneath him.

Nonetheless, Joe still felt he had to speak to Bruce about it. He found his colleague in one of the restaurants, minding his own business and reading a newspaper over a final cup of coffee. He experienced a moment of revulsion towards hotels and everything to do with them. If he never went inside a hotel again, it would be too soon. At one time he would have said he liked being away from home in such places. He liked the anonymity, the attendance on every whim. After this stint, he really did want to go home and enjoy his surroundings for a very, very long time.

With Irene, of course.

"May I join you?" he asked Bruce.

"Sure. I can squeeze another cup out of this pot." He studied Joe for a few seconds. "Are you okay?" he wondered and received the slightest of nods in reply.

Two members of the restaurant staff were already anticipating the situation, swooping in with new cups and fresh coffee.

"Did you hear about Philemon Brown?" Joe asked casually as he poured himself coffee.

"I did. The lawyers won't like that. They were winding themselves up for a big and expensive action. And someone saved me the trouble and the ammunition, didn't they? Plus an embarrassing rap for murder."

"You didn't put out a contract on him, then?"

Bruce folded his newspaper.

"Shannon is the one with the exotic and exciting life these days!" he said ruefully. "Now how would I know people like that, who would organise a killing for me?"

"You wouldn't. I know," Joe conceded.

"He was a shit of a man, though. I can't pretend I'm sorry. Well, I'm sorry for his family. But not for him!"

"I imagine that Philemon Brown is busy sorting out God right now. Didn't anyone ever tell you not to speak ill of the dead, Bruce?"

"That piece of etiquette has come to my notice a few times." Bruce took a proper appraisal of Joe. He had to say something. "I thought I was the one who was supposed to be sick. You look like I feel. Do you want to take over the room I had in the Medical Centre? The nurses and the doctor there are very considerate." The look on Joe's face stopped him saying any more. Joe had shared his fears with Bruce and Hagar about the error he might have made, but that was as far as it went for the moment. "Okay. If you want to get on with the day, we'd better not take too long here. We have our own dead to worry about, haven't we? There will be plenty of people to mourn Brown. He's not our problem. We know that the world will turn out for our people lost on Mars. No praise will be too high for them, but where do we begin?"

Chapter Eighteen

"Thank you for coming here today," Joe said to the people dotted round the room. They were sitting in supportive little huddles. They knew. "I won't insult your intelligence. I'm sure that you have a good idea why Bruce Dougall and I have called this meeting."

The families of the *Ariadne One* crew had a more than an idea. As soon as they were told that it might be advisable to bring their counsellors, they knew. They sat in the Armstrong Suite, the plushest room that Mission Control could offer, waiting with dignity for the hammer blow to fall.

"We have been trying to re-establish contact with *Ariadne One* for many hours," Joe continued. "In all that time our computer screens have remained blank. There is no indication of either part of the ship being on Mars or in orbit and there are no life signs. Automated comm checks have been going out every fifteen minutes day and night, and they will continue to go out, but our radios are silent. We must conclude, with great sadness, that *Ariadne One* is lost and her seven crew have perished on Mars. On behalf of *BUSSTOP*, I want to offer my most sincere condolences. My thoughts are with you, as are the thoughts of my colleague here."

Bruce nodded. There was no point in adding any more.

Joe looked round the room. It only took a couple of seconds but it felt like forever. He took in their blanched faces and his heart ached for them. Ishmael and Celia Turner were accompanied by their *BUSSTOP* person. Hagar was there too and she studied the far wall intently. For some reason Georgina Hammond had come on her own. Her features were blank. Gianfranco Rosso's parents and fiancée sat with heads bowed. Jackson Metz's girlfriend clung onto her counsellor. Masahide's partner David hid his face in his hands. Jethro Norman's mother and girlfriend linked arms. Joe had to look away as the face of Emily Alexander's father crumpled and he gave way to his grief. Hagar reached out and held his hand.

There were two security men posted inside the room, and there were two more outside, to ensure total privacy and to keep out any enterprising journalists.

Joe flashed a sideways glance to Bruce, who carried on.

"Your counsellors will be with you for as long as you feel you need them. We are planning a memorial service for the crew of *Ariadne One* here at Cape Canaveral and *BUSSTOP* liaison personnel will be speaking to you about exactly how you would like your loved one remembered within the ceremony. In the meantime, if there is anything that you want to ask us, or if you think there is anything that we can help you with personally, please say now. Or you can speak to either of us privately and in total confidence at the end of this meeting."

Georgina Hammond stood up.

"Mrs Hammond," Joe said encouragingly, trying not to think about the two small children.

"There is something you can do for me," she stated in a flat, calm voice. "Give me back my husband!" she shrieked suddenly, leaping towards Joe. "You bastard! You picked Brian to go on this mission! You've killed my husband! You bastard! Give me back Brian!"

The security detail sprang into action but Georgina was quicker. She punched Joe in the face before they grabbed her. She struggled for a moment and then sank to the floor, sobbing hysterically.

Hagar was beside the wrestling group in a flash.

"Let her go," she ordered firmly and quietly. "She's in great distress. Do something useful, like getting some medical attention for this girl and for Joe Mortimer too."

In the furore, only she and Bruce had seen the long cut which ran from the left side of Joe's nose and down onto the cheekbone. Bruce was doing his best to stem the bleeding. As Hagar held the distraught woman with all her strength, she saw a beautiful diamond eternity ring on Georgina's right hand. That was what had caused the damage.

As the last of the families were ushered from the room by their counsellors, Terri Boyle and two nurses hurried in.

"A young woman in emotional shock here and over there the victim of a good right hook, with the addition of a diamond ring like a razor," Hagar reported succinctly.

"Are you okay, Bruce?" Terri asked as she took over tending Joe's wound. "I don't ask the injured a dumb question like that," she said to Joe. "Just hold yourself steady for a few more moments."

"Mrs Hammond was only after Joe, for some reason. I don't mind blood," Bruce said, looking at his reddened hands. "It's a good thing I'm not like my father. He was useless in that respect. I could audition for a slasher movie right now, couldn't I?"

The attempt at humour was his way of dealing with the trauma of the situation. He had anticipated many different reactions from families and loved ones, but not such naked anger and pain.

"We're okay here," said Hagar as a nurse dealt with the limp Georgina. "You go and get washed up, Bruce."

Joe had not moved or said a word. Georgina was not the only one in shock.

"Let's get back to the Centre," said Terri, taping a temporary pad over the gash on his face. "Then I can decide the best way of putting you back together, Mr Mortimer. This might be one for the medical superglue."

Only when they reached the Medical Centre did Joe speak.

"She meant it," he whispered. "She blames me for Brian's death."

"No," Terri was very definite about that. "She'll feel very foolish when she's herself again. She will be resting under light sedation for a while. And you—." She turned Joe's head to study his face from various angles. "—You are a very lucky man. If Georgina had landed that punch a bit higher, she could have damaged your eye. I'll do my best to make sure there is no scarring. You'll look a bit piratical for a while, but I'm sure that you can live with that."

The news of the assault travelled like wildfire. It simply added a human dimension to the sombre press release, which informed the world of the meeting between the *BUSSTOP* chiefs and the families of the astronauts.

* * *

The Cabinet Room within Ten Downing Street was an uproar of activity and a dazzle of television lighting. If Kevin Crane had been any more motionless, he would have been dead. He was going over his speech. It was on autocue anyway but, in his mind, he was trying to give the right words the correct weight and emphasis. And he was trying to keep himself under control. He had functioned in an emotional blur since Joe Mortimer had given him the kind of news that no national leader ever wants to hear. And it had stirred up memories of his own loss. When he paid an emergency visit to Buckingham Palace, all he could do was agree with what the King said he wanted to do. Joe had informed his former RAF pal of everything that was happening but Crane felt that he needed to go and speak face to face with the monarch.

"It's a bad business, Prime Minister, a bad business," said His Majesty. There were tears in his eyes for the astronauts, and for another. "I understand from Joe that Cape Canaveral will be organising some sort of memorial service for the astronauts."

"Yes, sir, and I will be going, to represent you and all the country."

"And I will go, Kevin!" The barriers of formality were breached by grief. "I will go too. Dammit, the Queen will go as well! One of our own commanded this enterprise and it has cost him his life. The least we can do is turn out for him."

"Yes, Your Majesty," the Prime Minister found himself saying, imagining the hissy fits that some officials would have, arranging all this in the time that appeared to be available.

He remembered the summer's day when Joe gave him the text of the speech that no one would ever acknowledge existed—unless the worst happened.

"This is the form of words that has been agreed between all the countries who might possibly have crew on Ariadne, Prime Minister. Each country fills in the blanks, so to speak. Put it away in some drawer or other. We won't need it. And I don't want you and Richard fighting over who would deliver it."

"That would be me, Joe, as I think you know. Buckingham Palace would issue its own statement and contact the families of any British citizens. But like you say, we won't need it."

How confident everybody was back then! It all seemed straightforward. This was the onward march of technology. The Ariadne flights were carrying on the great work started by the Zeus programme.

Further back in time, he and Joe had held that memorable press conference, announcing to the world that *Ariadne One* would take off soon, with Britain in overall charge. A comment that Joe made to him when they were chatting afterwards swam endlessly in his mind.

"In some ways the crew that is finally selected will be as good as it ever will be. There's nothing like experience. I can vouch for that! By the time we finished the Zeus series, we could have flown across the Universe! But there's also nothing like that first flight—not knowing what you can't do. You face up to any difficulties as a complete innocent. That's when the great strides of progress are made."

What difficulties had overwhelmed the astronauts? What couldn't they do? What couldn't they put right? Whatever had happened, Kevin Crane hoped that their end had been swift and merciful. Given the rapidity of contact failure with the ship, that seemed likely. It was the only crumb of comfort in an otherwise bleak outlook. As a Christian, he committed them to God in his prayers. But somehow that didn't seem enough anymore.

"Prime Minister," the television director was saying.

He became aware of the focused silence within the Cabinet Room.

"Yes, I'm ready."

"Just to remind you, Prime Minister, that this broadcast is live—going out ahead of the nine o'clock news headlines. Are you happy with that?"

It's a bit late to ask me now, he thought.

He waited as the countdown went to one and the inevitable call of *On Air!*

"I am speaking to you from the Cabinet Room of Ten Downing Street at this very difficult time."

Irene watched the Prime Ministerial broadcast at home. Debbie had come over to watch it with her. Alisdair was working late in the hospital to help cover staff shortages but he would have eyes on a screen, he promised.

"Everyone will have to stop bleeding all over the place," he said uncharitably, "and those who want to die will have to wait for a few minutes."

"Britain took the lead in this endeavour," Crane was saying. "I know that no crew could have been better prepared for what lay before them and we will honour them and remember them all, especially our own Brian Hammond."

"Those were his children at the launch, weren't they?" Debbie said, her eyes moistening.

Irene could only nod and reach for the tissues. Both women were unaware of several more minutes of the speech.

"Mars was their goal and it has become their final resting place. They went in peace as explorers and we pray that they will rest in peace. The crew of *Ariadne One* was international and today the world stands as one. I would like to conclude with a tribute first uttered in antiquity by Pericles. This was to remember the first Athenians who died in the Peloponnesian War. Somehow it chimes with this sad occasion.

"For heroes have the whole earth for their tomb; and in lands far from their own, where the column with its epitaph declares it, there is enshrined in every breast a record unwritten with no tablet to preserve it, except that of the heart."

*　　*　　*

"We want you to see something," said Tony. "We want you to see what is happening on Earth."

Some habits are very hard to break and all seven members of the *Ariadne One* crew looked about them for some sort of screen.

"No," chuckled Justin. "Look inside your minds. Concentrate."

Brian closed his eyes as he saw a harsh, bright light. It didn't make any difference. The light seemed to glow inside his brain. The others were having the same experience. A series of pictures raced before them—cities of the twenty second century. The images froze.

Jethro, Simeon, Emily and Jackson saw Washington D.C. Masahide saw Tokyo. Gianfranco saw Rome. Brian saw London. Lines of people were placing flowers in ever-growing piles. Each astronaut found that the focus of the picture could be sharpened if the mind was fixed totally on it. Brian recognised the London *BUSSTOP* building and the Americans realised that the crowds in their scene were at the Washington D.C. *BUSSTOP* headquarters. Masahide and Gianfranco knew that the flowers were being laid at their national Space Agency buildings.

This was unlike any conventional film record. They could feel the cold winds of winter, listen in on the conversations of those standing in line and those who had laid their flowers. They could smell the perfume of the flowers and hear the rustle of wrapping paper moving in the breeze.

"That is for each one of you," said Tony. "There is an outpouring of sorrow for you around the world. Each of you is seeing your own capital city but you are being remembered everywhere."

"Why?" asked Jackson.

"As far as Earth is concerned, you are dead. All contact with you and your ship was lost very abruptly when we took you and *Ariadne One* into our care. Neither people nor ship will register any longer on equipment on Earth because you are now on our plane of existence, at a level of vibration that is much higher than could be tracked by *BUSSTOP* or anyone else. Your superiors and your governments can conclude no other."

The crew watched dispassionately. Here, within the rainbow, they were safe and all was peaceful and calm. But even Paradise was pierced momentarily with the next set of images. Each saw saddened loved ones.

"Oh!" murmured Emily as she gazed upon her father.

National leaders appeared for each person. Brian straightened to attention when he saw the King. Then he looked wonderingly at Joe Mortimer and Bruce Dougall, who were careworn and tired.

"What happened to Mr Mortimer?" he demanded.

"Your wife punched him in the face," Tony told him. "In her moment of accepting your death, she blamed him and attacked him."

Brian opened his eyes wide, to see Tony smiling.

"She would," he said fondly, returning the smile. "She has two older brothers, who are still a pair of lunatics. She learned to stand up for herself at an early age."

"There has been a reconciliation. It was guarded on Mr Mortimer's part. He is still convinced that she will strike him again. She won't. She is deeply sorry."

Sally watched Brian as he frowned, deep in thought, something she had not seen any of the guests do since their elevation to the vibration level of Mars.

"What is it?" she inquired.

"There is something else I should remember," he said slowly. "Other people I should be concerned about. Yes! My children. How are they?"

As Brian enjoyed watching his children, Sally took Tony on one side.

"Is this wise?" she wondered. "They are dropping so deep into the experience here. They are becoming impervious to their life on Earth."

"It they were not, the pain would be unbearable," Tony reminded her. "They will have time to adjust on the return journey. Ichiro is working over *Ariadne One* from stem to stern. He has concluded that she will not stand up to our conventional travel mode. We will have to travel in human time. She is Earth's cutting edge technology, not ours," he continued, when Sally looked aghast. "She is powered with a primitive nuclear reactor. Earth is a long way off travelling across the stars by folding time and space, as we do. Her theorists have put the idea forward. That is all. Our visitors are not evolved enough to travel in one of our vehicles. The strain would be too much for them. We can't raise their level of vibration high enough. So it will have to be a human journey to Earth in the human craft. And besides, a long journey will give us a chance to adjust too. There will be the small matter of Earth chronology for us to deal with."

* * *

Bruce knew that nothing would be further from Shannon's thoughts but some kind of reversal of roles, even a revenge and a triumph, was accomplished. Once upon a time it had been his former wife appearing on a screen, resigned, emotional, alone, needing, whilst he was riding high, with the world at his feet. Today she was the latest hot property in publishing and he was . . .

Bruce was all too aware of the accusing glances that were coming his way, along with the wagging of admonishing fingers. In such a situation, everyone was desperate to apportion blame. No one had the slightest idea what had happened to Ariadne and, in the absence of wreckage or bodies to give some kind of a starting point, he and Joe made a good target to take pot shots at until a better one came along. Joe was saying nothing, but Bruce knew that he was still churning over how he had ignored Rob Masters.

"I wish there was something that I could really do for you!" Shannon's sigh was a mini tornado. "My agent and my publisher have tried, but the memorial service for your astronauts is a *very* exclusive gathering. Ex wives don't count. Have we got time to get married again? Never mind. Forget I said that. But you look like you could do with some support. I guess that you will be taking part? I won't ask what you're doing, because I know you won't tell me."

Bruce didn't have the energy to react or reply to any of what she was saying.

The conversation meandered on. Then Shannon's eyes lit up.

"I've got it! I may not be able to gatecrash your ceremonies but I can be in Cape Canaveral. I haven't given you the copy of my book yet, and I did promise. I'm on my way, Bruce!"

In the silence of his hotel room, Bruce went over what had been said and he felt so ashamed. Shannon had demonstrated a huge generosity of spirit and a consideration that he didn't deserve. As a child he had always been fascinated by the phrase *Heaping coals of fire upon someone's head.* He had never understood it. Today he did. Actions from the past, which he regretted bitterly, were burned away by Shannon's concern. Like any burning, it was painful and he hoped it was over, but he already felt better.

Bruce knew he had achieved something, even if he wasn't sure what it was.

*   *   *

In assorted locations across Cape Canaveral, the same words were being said.

"Time to go."

Three words. Short. Monosyllabic. The dull rhythm of a funeral bell. Counsellors, who had become friends, held their people for one last time and then it was on with the public faces and out into harsh reality.

Joe spoke to Irene before he left for the memorial service. She would be watching the event live on television at home. Beyond the bare bones of keeping the infrastructure of the country running, everything in Britain was shut down in a day of national mourning. This would be the first of many remembrances for Brian Hammond.

"That's beautiful, Joe," she said when he gave her a sneak preview of what he would be saying.

"I can't take any credit for it," he admitted. "Bruce is the expert in this department, I have discovered. He steered this one in my direction. I'll admit that I was stumped when I was asked if I had an appropriate favourite passage or poem that I wanted to read. It's amazing. I've spent most of a working lifetime with him and it's as though I've woken up suddenly and I don't know him at all."

"You'll be fine. Bruce has picked you a good 'un there. And you don't look too bad. That doctor in Mission Control deserves a pat on the back for the way she has put the cut back together. And most of the bruising has gone too!"

"Yes. I've had some new wonder treatment for reducing black eyes and other bumps and bangs. The doctor said I was a perfect guinea pig."

"You'd better go. You don't want to be late. Call me when you're done. I'll be watching every minute of it and following every word."

That was the only thing that would make this bearable.

"It's time for you to go," said Shannon Dougall, giving her ex-husband a hug. "You give it to 'em, Bruce! And you have chosen your words well. It is a true inspiration to use that! And what a hidden talent! I'll be watching every minute of it. And remember—I expect dinner tonight."

She kissed his forehead and pushed him towards the door of the hotel room.

That was the only thing that would make this bearable.

Cape Canaveral was at its sunny best for the time of year. The temperature was in the high sixties Fahrenheit and the breeze had died away completely. They gathered on the lawn outside the front of the *BUSSTOP* Mission Control building—the great, the good and the grieving. With no wind, the flags of the United States of America, Great Britain, Italy and Japan hung limply at half-mast. There could so easily have been a fifth flag, that of Russia. Illya Abelev, along with Arty Rowe, was like a man in a dream. He could have been on the Ariadne flight. The same went for Arty. They sat with the remainder of the reserve crew, who were counting their blessings.

The Mission Control building looked as though it had been scrubbed down for the occasion, glistening in the sunshine. If nothing ever happened here again, the huge expenditure on it had been worthwhile. In its short history it had been witness to and the hub of the tumultuous events of the Zeus flights. No one ever imagined that it would have to be host to something like this.

The memorial service for the crew of *Ariadne One* was a triumph of rapid planning and logistics. His Majesty King Richard the Fourth, accompanied by Queen Alice, headed the phalanx of foreign dignitaries. The Prime Ministers of Great Britain, Italy and Japan flanked the President of the United States.

But the clockwork precision, the thoughts, prayers and music of many faiths and belief systems and the cohesiveness of the occasion were lost on everyone. All present were submerged in their own bubbles of thought and preoccupation. Only afterwards would they be able to say, "Yes, that was just right."

Many surfaced when the two *BUSSTOP* chiefs made their contributions. Here were two people who had been out there and come back—several times. And over there was the remainder of the Zeus crew. Apart from anything else, they were a reminder that this day was the tragic exception.

Joe stepped up to the lectern.

"I am reading a poem written by John Gillespie Magee, a young American who volunteered for the Royal Canadian Air Force before the United States joined the conflict of the Second World War. He died in a mid-air collision in England in 1941. At that time, powered flight was still quite a novelty for most and the idea of travel into space was the preserve of the mad, the dreamers and science fiction writers. Yet his poem, *High Flight*, could easily describe some of the sensations of being in space. I share this with you now in remembrance of our astronauts. We hold them with love in our hearts.

> *"Oh, I have slipped the surly bonds of Earth*
> *And danced the skies on laughter-silvered wings;*
> *Sunward I've climbed and joined the tumbling mirth*
> *Of sun-split clouds—and done a hundred things*
> *You have not dreamed of, wheeled and soared and swung*
> *High in the sun-lit silence. Hovering there*
> *I've chased the shouting wind along, and flung*
> *My eager craft through footless halls of air;*
> *Up, up the long, delirious, burning blue*
> *I've topped the wind-swept heights with easy grace,*
> *Where never lark nor even eagle flew;*
> *And while, with silent lifting mind I've trod*
> *The high untrespassed sanctity of space,*
> *Put out my hand, and touched the face of God."*

Kevin Crane had always presumed, reasonably enough, that silence was silence. But he could sense the intensity of the stillness deepen, become something more, as the amplification system carried Joe's words to the assembled people. If pride was allowed on such a day, he felt it. The man was just right for the moment, just as he had been right for so many moments over the last five years. The Prime Minister knew that many had doubted his appointment quite openly. He was thought to be too young and totally lacking in administrative experience. The same charges had been levelled at Bruce Dougall.

It was Bruce's turn now.

"I have chosen a poem written by a friend and colleague. I was privileged to work with Gene Ward on the Zeus project. He was the engineer aboard all the flights that took us closer and closer to the reality of landing on Mars, which was the aim of *Ariadne One*. Like everyone who goes into space, Gene had to make sense of his experiences—from the totally thrilling to the totally terrifying. He chose the medium of poetry. He has given his permission for me to use his poem *They said*, which he wrote after the final Zeus flight. This is for you: Brian, Jethro, Masahide, Simeon, Gianfranco, Emily and Jackson. Rest in peace."

Gene Ward, in the midst of the Zeus team, tried to shrink a little lower in his seat and failed.

They said,
You are an explorer, you are a hero.
You are a shining example, they said.

I said,
Everyone is curious, everyone is a daily hero.
Lives shine from every corner, I said.

They said,
Have a medal son, tell us what it was like.
Write a book, be on the news, they said.

I said,
Leave me alone, I have walked in space.
I could hear my thoughts there, I said.

They said,
What will you do now that you've flown in space?
You're yesterday's man, they said.

I said,
I have been to the stars, where I will return in death.
It's all I ask, I said.

"Go, Bruce!" Shannon murmured from in front of a hotel screen.

Across America, there was the sound of literary agents and publishers trying to find Gene Ward's contact details.

After such powerful readings, delivered so well, there wasn't much left to say. No one was all that interested in President Rodriguez's speech. Out of respect for the memory of the dead, everyone listened politely. Rodriguez fumed inwardly as he went through the motions of his words.

He had spoken to groups and crowds for long enough to know that he had lost this audience.

Joe Mortimer would be going home now—and he could damn well stay there! The President eyed Bruce Dougall in a calculating manner. Enjoy your moment whilst it lasts, he thought.

A final tribute was paid by the United States Air Force.

Neil and Stella Mortimer were watching the broadcast at home. Philip and Daphne had joined them for the occasion.

"And now we wait for four aircraft of the USAF to fly the Missing Man Formation overhead," explained television commentator Luke Prentice. "This is an aerial salute undertaken at a funeral or at a memorial service. Generally the manoeuvre is used to honour a lost pilot. Today we have been witnessing the honouring of seven special pilots of the twenty second century—the crew who flew *Ariadne One*. The aircraft will approach the memorial location in a v-shape. The flight leader will be on the point and his wingman on his left. The second-element leader will be on the flight leader's right and his wingman will be on his right. The formation will fly low enough to be seen clearly and as it crosses over our location, the second-element leader will pull up and away from the group suddenly. The rest of the formation will hold position to maintain the gap until it is out of sight. This requires split second timing."

Stella looked over towards her husband.

"I hardly like to ask."

"Someone has given him the right information," Neil said. "Here they come."

Everyone at the memorial service rose instinctively as the approaching scream of fighter plane engines could be heard. At the precise moment of passing over Mission Control, the second-element leader executed a dramatic pull-up. Joe and Bruce stood to attention and were amongst the few who didn't duck instinctively as the sweeping explosion of noise ripped down through the sky. Bruce's eyes were fixed on the single plane flying away from the pack. A few old USAF hands shook their heads. As a one-time pilot in the Air Force, he should have known better. The pull-up plane represented the honoured dead and it was considered bad luck to stare at the departing aircraft. Looking at the "missing man" means that you might well be next.

"That was perfect!" rhapsodised Neil as he poured himself another glass of wine. "Of course, it has long been a UASF speciality. And it's not that complicated. I don't think they could manage the kind of stuff that we used to do."

Stella and Daphne exchanged glances.

Philip was so proud of his little brother. He had conducted himself admirably in the most trying circumstances. He recalled the evening when he had visited Joe and found him beset by uncharacteristic doubt about the Ariadne project. Bruce Dougall had put that doubt in his mind.

Philip had to wonder, if only for a moment, if he had taken the right course of action, encouraging his brother. Of course he was right. If everything had worked out according to plan, Joe would now be in the midst of being hailed as a national hero, along with the astronauts, and the celebrations and congratulations would be never-ending. As it was, all the Mortimer family could do was to be there for Joe when he came home.

That's what families do.

*   *   *

On Mars, safe inside the rainbow, the crew watched their own memorial service. It was the perfectly logical thing to do. Just as with the rest of the team, fragments of Earth memories plagued Jethro. Viewing what was effectively his own funeral brought to mind Tom Sawyer, the character created by Mark Twain. Tom crept into the church to attend the service being held for him. It was presumed he had drowned in the Mississippi River. In the end, unable to take the magnificent mourning any longer, he came out from his hiding place, was fallen upon by the congregation, and joined in the singing of *The Old Hundredth*.

Jethro toyed with the idea of what it would have been like, making such an appearance at this gathering in his honour. It might have been fun and he was sure that his hosts could have arranged it. But it wasn't that important. He watched impassively as his girlfriend Kate cried.

Brian looked at his wife and children. Susie was silenced by confusion. Tears trickled down Fred's face because so many adults around him were sobbing. He held his mother's hand.

"Will Daddy be coming home soon?" he asked.

There was not a flicker of reaction from Brian Hammond. Tony nodded. Sally was right. These people needed to be on their way home pretty quickly, before they became too deeply embedded in the ways of Mars. There was nothing wrong in that but their learning and their assimilation of new skills and arts were almost completed. They had a date with destiny in their own time and on their own planet.

And Tony had his own personal reasons for wanting to be on planet Earth sooner rather than later.

*   *   *

"I think that my one remaining brain cell is about to die, very slowly and very painfully," Joe decided.

"You've got a brain cell left?" Bruce wondered. "I'm on reserve battery. Some experts say that the larger species of dinosaurs had a second brain stashed away somewhere, probably in their butts. That's me right now."

They were silent for a while. The hotel mezzanine bar, which had been the spot from which they had been viewing the world forever, was uncharacteristically quiet. Michael, the bartender, watched them from a distance. He would be sorry to see them go. They spent very little but they brought a certain something to this corner of the building. Two wise old owls, perched on the same branch.

The media were still giving them a wide berth, even though that fool Philemon Brown was dead, killed by a person or persons unknown. It had been a fascinating time, Michael concluded, and definitely something to tell the grandchildren one day.

"The show's over. Everyone is going home," Bruce said eventually.

"And so must we." Joe hesitated for a moment. "We couldn't have done any more, could we?"

"Considering the crap hand that events have dealt everyone, I think miracles have been taking place here."

"I wonder if we'll ever find out what happened to our astronauts and the ship?"

Bruce thought for a few seconds.

"Do we really want to know?" he asked.

"We'll have to send the next flight to Mars in an act of faith. Then we will have a better picture. The crew will be able to check out any wreckage—or remains."

Bruce said nothing. He had been dogged by uncertainty all along about the *Ariadne One* mission and he was horrified to have been proved right. As Joe spoke confidently about more Mars flights, again he was filled with ideas he could not identify.

"The Missing Man formation was good," he said, changing the subject. "The USAF put on a good fly-by, didn't they?"

"They did. When I get back, my father will no doubt be ready with a full critique of it!"

As Joe said the word *back*, he was desperate to be there, to be home, to be back into some kind of normality—if anything could ever be totally normal again after the events of the past few days. The relentless sunshine of the Sunshine State was getting him down. It was winter. This eye-watering brightness wasn't right. There should be angry, heavy skies, threatening to dump yet more rain or snow on the countryside. He wanted to be out running with Bonny on a murky Sunday morning, the bells of Graffenby parish church muffled in the fog and gloom as they summoned the faithful.

He wanted the unique solid grey quality that London took on in wintertime. Generally too mild in the capital for snow or even any noticeable frost, the city marked out the season by draining itself of colour.

"I'm looking forward to going home too," said Bruce, although nothing had been said. "I'll travel back up to D.C. tomorrow. How about you?"

"My PA has promised me that she'll have me booked on the evening flight to London tomorrow. I'll leave you to it now, Bruce. I've got some calls to make."

"One of them to Professor Hanson, no doubt!"

The words were spoken with an impish grin, something that Joe hadn't seen on Bruce's face in years. It took him right back to the first time they met, before things came between them.

> *"Hi! I'm Bruce Dougall. It looks like we are to be partners in crime on this Zeus project."*

"No doubt I will be talking to the good professor," Joe said. "Enjoy your dinner with Shannon."

Chapter Nineteen

Bruce spent most of the flight back to Washington D.C. in silence. Shannon knew better than to break it. She contented herself dipping in to a chunky and mainly tedious magazine. She still found it slightly shocking to turn the page and read an article all about *The Real Shannon Dougall*. It was more than reading details of her life in cold print. It was a bit like being partly undressed in public. It was amusing to discover how many "friends" she had, who apparently knew so much about her. She averted her gaze from the inevitable photographs.

No piece that she had read so far mentioned one very important feature within the book. That would sort out the real friends from those who had spoken to her once at a writing seminar and those who were the figment of some editor's imagination. Only a small group of people, including Bruce, would pick up on it. It was strange that he hadn't said anything. She imagined that he might be embarrassed, or annoyed. Obviously he hadn't looked at the book yet. As keen a reader as he was, he wouldn't have been in the mood for fiction in these past days. Reality had shaped up into something far more urgent and attention grabbing.

Shannon turned to speak to him.

Bruce was fast asleep.

His air of dozy detachment persisted when they arrived at National Airport. Concerned, Shannon insisted on accompanying her ex husband in the taxi back to his apartment in Georgetown. He opened the front door, stepped inside, dropped his bags on the floor and just stood, looking around him.

"Everything okay?" she wondered.

"Sorry. Yeah. I had serious doubts at one point about ever seeing this place again."

"I can imagine. Look, you just do what you want to do and I'll sort a few things out. Coffee?"

Rain and thick cloud had reduced visibility and daylight to almost zero. As Shannon bustled round, she turned on lights wherever she went.

"I am grateful, but you don't have to do all this," Bruce said at one point, feeling outmanoeuvred.

"Someone has to!" she replied cheerfully. "I can see me coming back next week and finding you still standing there, looking out of the window, with your bags right where you dumped them. Here. Sit down and have some coffee."

Shannon left the room and went back to the kitchen to grab her own mug and a plate of cookies. She had excavated them from the depths of the pantry. When she came back, she put down what she was carrying and sat next to Bruce on the sofa.

She wasn't sure that she had ever seen the adult Bruce cry. When his parents died, of course. But even then, although he was in the USAF and seemed so grown up, the tight-knit gang who had worked their way through school together were all still just bits of kids. This was something different.

Shannon put an arm around him and was reminded again of how frail his body felt. She had been horrified when she gave him a hug before the memorial service for the astronauts. She waited for a while.

"You've needed to do that for days," she said.

"Probably since the moment I heard that Lander's thrusters wouldn't fire," he agreed shakily. "I guess we all knew then, deep down, that we'd lost the crew."

*　　*　　*

"Welcome back, Mr Mortimer," said Roland, taking over his baggage.

"Thanks. It's good to be back."

This short exchange of words took place in the airport VIP Arrivals area, away from prying eyes. At that point, Joe was sure. At last, he was really on the way home. On the plane, he could have been going anywhere. He was glad that Roland knew his job, and not just the driving bit. Sometimes nothing needed to be said. They walked to the car in silence.

It was only when Roland nosed the vehicle out into the open that Joe spoke again.

"That's better!" he observed with deep satisfaction.

"Sir?" queried the driver.

"The weather! It's wonderful!"

Roland raised his eyebrows. Cloud cover meant that he was driving with full lights on. The rain hammered down onto the road, creating plumes of water to go with the spray created by the traffic. The outer environs of the airport looked at their grimmest. And those black clouds appeared to be settled in for the day.

"You didn't like the weather in Florida then, Mr Mortimer?"

"I like wall-to-wall sunshine as much as the next person—in the summer. This is proper winter weather."

Roland decided that he wouldn't mind some winter sunshine. But Mr Mortimer's sun and sea visit had come with a terrible price tag. He glanced in the rear-view mirror.

The boss was fast asleep.

Joe stirred, as if some automatic homing device had been activated, as Roland drove into the village.

"Almost home, sir!" Roland announced.

Joe's face twisted as they went past the top of Pond Lane. He wondered if the staff and children at the school would be so keen to talk to him now.

He paused for a moment before getting out of the car at the house. Stable End, the object of his dreams for some days, looked just the same. The front garden was neat. There was little that needed doing at this time of year and Philip had promised to call round from time to time and to do any necessary tidying up. In sheltered corners, patches of snowdrops provided the first promise of spring. There would be further drifts in the back garden.

After Roland had departed, Joe wandered aimlessly from room to room. He picked up and put down objects in a random manner. There was the book he had been reading before he left for America. He opened it to remind himself of where he had got to in the narrative. The words stirred a memory of the excitement he was feeling at the time. *Ariadne One* was going to Mars and a dream was coming true.

The memory hurt and he dropped the book back on the chair.

There were vases of fresh flowers dotted around in ground floor rooms and he found a note from Daphne in the kitchen.

> *"Welcome back Joe! Women don't usually give men flowers, although I've never worked out why. An appreciation of beauty is universal. Anyway, enjoy them. Philip will bring Bonny back tonight, as arranged. Be warned. I'll be coming along for the ride, and your parents are hoping to tag along as well. There is plenty of food for anyone who feels peckish, so you don't need to panic!"*

Joe groaned out loud. As much as he loved his family, there were occasions when he really didn't want them around. But then he remembered the times when they were all he had and he knew that he couldn't pick and choose when they arrived. And deep down, he knew that he wanted to see Mum and Dad and Philip and Daphne, to be with people who would not judge and who could put so much into a hug or a slap on the shoulder and not have to say anything. He wanted some time with that group, to whom he was simply "Joe." He wondered if he could admit to them his possible mistake.

When he looked in a couple of kitchen cupboards and the fridge, he saw that the house was stocked like a siege camp. That was his mother's work.

He checked his messages. The best one was from Irene. He glanced at a clock. She would be in college but it was worth a try. He had not been able to discern any definite pattern in her schedule of commitments.

He was in luck.

"We're under the same sky at last," he said to her.

"It does seem a long time since Christmas," she replied. "Although it isn't. So much has happened, I suppose."

Joe told her about the promised family invasion.

"I can't complain," he admitted. "They've all been contributing to holding the fort whilst I've been away. And I can feed them all if necessary. I don't think the kitchen will hold another item of food. I left a few long-lasting basics in a cupboard."

"That will be your mother. That's what Mums do, Joe, given half a chance, for all kinds of reasons. My Mum did that for me a few times when I was a student. It's one way of kissing it better for an adult child."

Joe wanted Irene to kiss it better for real.

"Look," he said. "It is Thursday, isn't it? I'm totally confused by the days at the moment. The gang will be round tonight. Tomorrow I need to go to *BUSSTOP* and start picking up the pieces. I'll probably be growling at Bonny by the evening. I'll be no fit company for anyone. Let's meet up on Saturday."

They made happy plans. Joe agreed to something that he had never thought he would do.

As he worked his way through the rest of his messages, he wondered how Irene got on without family. She had none. He knew that her parents had died some years previously and she was an only child. But she had Debbie and Alisdair. He had seen first hand that they were her staunchest allies. That was good. Everyone needed someone to stand guard with a flaming sword.

*   *   *

Friday dawned in a smother of snow and a flurry of headlines. By the time Joe was ready to leave the house and set off for *BUSSTOP*, he was aware of two interlinked threads in the morning newspapers and television offerings. There were calls for an inquiry into the Ariadne disaster and a general review of the competency of *BUSSTOP*. In the meantime, all plans for further flights to Mars should be put on hold. Then there were the demands for his resignation. He should do the right thing and go.

If only they knew, Joe thought. They'd be demanding my head on a platter.

When he had driven the car into the underground car park at *BUSSTOP*, he sat for a while. He was no longer certain of the reception he would receive and he was sure, deep down, that he deserved only hostility. As he done so many times since that terrible moment of realisation whilst he was talking to President Rodriguez, he replayed the conversation with Rob Masters in his mind. This time, the same as all the other times, he was left with a question mark hanging over the matter.

Joe found much-needed strengthening. All the way up to his office, there were calls of "Good morning, Mr Mortimer!" and "Wotcha, Joe!"—depending on who was greeting him. These voices and the smiles that went with them carried the comforting impressions of the clanking of armour and the sharpening of weapons. This was an experienced army closing ranks round the leader in his time of need. Also, this was an example of the picture that Irene had put in his head—kissing it better for an adult.

One person who was sorely tempted to kiss Joe and fling her arms around him was Vicky Tennant. Instead she patted herself on the back for her admirable restraint and contented herself with a dazzling smile and "Welcome back, Mr Mortimer!"

She was about to launch into the list of people who wanted to speak to him, with the Prime Minister leading the field.

"Give me a moment or two to get my breath, Vicky. And this is by way of thanks for everything you've done whilst I've been away. I do appreciate your hard work. I would imagine that Kevin Crane is top of the list of people who want a word. We'll start with him. Some coffee would be great."

Vicky held the gift-wrapped box tightly as she watched him disappear into his office. From the shape of the package, she guessed the present was perfume. Even if it was the most disgusting concoction ever, she would wear every scrap of it. And what was going on here? Mr Mortimer *never* did anything like that.

"Take no notice of all the media chatter, Joe!" the Prime Minister was urging him a few minutes later. "It goes with the territory. When you are at the top of an organisation, you wear the biggest target on your backside. Someone wants me to resign on a regular basis. The pound is too high, the pound is too low, there's not enough investment in various sectors of the economy, schools are dropping to bits and so on and so forth. It's my fault entirely and therefore I should go."

"But have you ever been blamed publicly for the deaths of seven people?" Joe asked bluntly.

"No, I haven't." Crane gave him a shrewd look. He wondered what was eating at this man, beyond the loss of *Ariadne One*. "You're blaming yourself, aren't you? You haven't any intention of resigning, have you?"

"I have. I suppose I was considering it on the drive here."

"Don't even think about it! Not on my watch!" The Prime Minister's tone was unusually sharp. "I've never known anyone in a position of authority to be more conscientious than you. And that conscientiousness works its way down through an organisation. I would say the same about your American colleague, Bruce Dougall. You have both proved a lot of people wrong over the years. Now they are bound to try to exact a little petty revenge. Obviously we are setting up an inquiry and we will liaise with America. Otherwise there will be huge duplication of effort. This will be a proper technical investigation, of the sort that's done into any kind of major accident, be it road, rail, sea or air—or in this case, space. It will be to see if we can come up with some answers to what happened, not necessarily to apportion blame. As Transport Secretary, I was involved with parts of the investigation into the EuropeAir crash at Manchester Airport in 2100. It was an illuminating experience. It was incredible to see all the small problems and events that had to occur simultaneously to make a passenger jet apparently drop out of the sky like that. I can't even begin to imagine the complex chain of events that came together to down *Ariadne One*. I want to know what happened. That's all. I'm sure you do as well. And I have no intention of stopping the Ariadne programme. We go ahead, confident that we will learn from this tragedy. I won't let you be hung out to dry, Joe. You are a man of your world and I'm a product of mine. My skin is thick enough for the two of us. Now let's get down to some real business."

"Thank you, Prime Minister."

Nothing could completely take away Joe's lingering doubt but it was good to know that the Prime Minister was on his side.

"Think nothing of it. You are a winner and *BUSSTOP* will emerge from this all the stronger for it, I promise you." He bestowed a smile, something in short supply these days. "Successful politicians need a sixth sense for winners. It's the only way we get to look good."

*　　*　　*

Bruce stared at his office screen in disbelief.

"I don't understand, Mr President!" he said, totally stunned. "What have I done wrong? What has *BUSSTOP* America done wrong? I've just been speaking to Joe Mortimer in London. The Prime Minister is launching a full inquiry at his end and I'm sure that he—."

"I've already spoken to Prime Minister Crane. I told him we'd be doing things our way here. Quite honestly I don't give a damn what the Brits are doing, creeping about around the situation. I hold you and *BUSSTOP* totally responsible for the deaths of the Ariadne astronauts and I want you to act appropriately and straight away."

Bruce counted to ten, very slowly.

"Are you telling me to resign, Mr President? In *a screen conversation?*"

"Why not? I thought the idea of all this technology was to save time and effort. I can't see any reason why you should come over to the White House so that I can say exactly the same thing. Will you resign or do I have to dismiss you publicly?"

"Of course I'll resign, Mr President, if you have no confidence in me. With immediate effect." Bruce wrapped his dignity around him like a cloak. "Do you have someone in mind to take over from me?"

"You don't get it, do you? I won't need anyone to take over from you. I don't know what you've done during your time in office anyway. *BUSSTOP* is no longer a viable proposition. It will take months, even years, to find answers to what happened to *Ariadne One*. That is, if we ever find any answers at all. I'm not prepared to sanction further flights whilst there is no clear answer. And I certainly won't have an organisation like *BUSSTOP* sitting around on its ass doing nothing and swallowing endless amounts of money. I have plenty of people in Congress who think the same as me."

"You'll shut down *BUSSTOP?*"

"You are getting it—at last! I will suspend all *BUSSTOP* work prior to shutting it down. All your folks can go home and find themselves proper jobs."

"You can't do that!"

Bruce was immediately on guard for the hundreds of people whose livelihoods depended directly on *BUSSTOP* and the many more who would be affected indirectly. And what about Britain?

"Try me!" snapped Rodriguez.

"What does London say?"

"To hell with London! London doesn't know what my plans are yet and I'll thank you to keep your mouth shut, Dougall!"

This was definitely a case of nation not speaking unto nation.

"Do you want me to make a statement?" Bruce asked, already toying with a few diplomatic but choice phrases.

"No. Thanks for resigning. It makes things much tidier. My people will put out a statement on your behalf, along with my reply."

President Ted Rodriguez felt good when he had finished that conversation. He was exhilarated. It had been so easy! Dougall ought to grow himself a new set of balls.

He smiled sadistically as he recalled the look of complete devastation on Bruce Dougall's face. He'd get over it. He wouldn't starve. He had serious family money and he could cosy up to that ex wife of his now that she had hit the big time.

> *"We would like to thank you for your application, Mr Rodriguez, and for the impressive work that you have done over the three days of the selection board process. However, on balance, we feel that we must reject you. Obviously, we have very stringent criteria and, although you have many admirable skills and qualities, by those criteria we judge you to be unsuitable as a candidate for the next stage of the BUSSTOP space exploration programme."*

Those spoken words, like the letter saved on his computer system, were engraved upon the President's heart. Now, finally, after all these years, he was taking his revenge. Revenge, it was said, is a dish best served cold but there was an anger in him that had never cooled, that had kept him warm all these years, which had grown, twisted into new shapes and informed many of his actions. He looked about him in contentment. It was time to fool around a bit tonight. He hoped that Lee was in town.

In the meantime, he took a deep breath and savoured the moment of pushing the *BUSSTOP* chief into resignation. It was good. It was one to remember, seeing Dougall gazing stupidly at him

It was very good.

Ten minutes later it was Joe's turn to sit gazing stupidly as he looked at his screen. He wished he knew what to say that would help in any way. Perhaps, if Bruce had been in the same room, he might have been a bit more inspired. As it was, he had to deal with an electronic image, however realistic that image might be.

"Bruce, I can hardly believe this! Can the President do all that he says he will do?"

"I wouldn't bank on him making a mistake. He's a real street fighter of a politician and he's well advised. He wouldn't do something as high profile as this if he wasn't sure of his ground. Hell, this wouldn't have happened if Phoebe Harper was still alive!"

"She would have been as supportive as Kevin Crane," Joe agreed.

The two men looked at one another across the thousands of miles.

"Arty Rowe!" they said in unison.

They had come to the same conclusion when the replacement in the Ariadne team broke his leg. The only person who could have tipped off the media about Arty's freak accident was the then Vice President Rodriguez.

They thought it very odd but in the hustle and bustle leading up to the launch, the incident was pushed to one side. Now all those suspicions about Rodriguez came bubbling back to the surface.

"What is Rodriguez up to?" wondered Joe. "I think that your Mr President could do with a little scrutiny."

"And I know just the person to do it," said Bruce. "Bob Broomfield, my friend from school days."

*   *   *

"Bruce, I'm going to do you a big favour," Bob Broomfield said, frowning as he spoke. "It'll save your blushes and keep what's left of your reputation intact. I'll pretend this conversation didn't take place. I'm surprised at you! The President does something that doesn't suit you. Therefore the President's judgement must be in question. Don't even go there. And if you are fool enough to make anything of it, I can't and won't help you. I'll talk to you when you're in a better frame of mind. You've resigned from *BUSSTOP*, which is the most sensible course of action. If I were you, I'd get on with something useful, like clearing your desk and leaving the building."

Bruce blinked as the screen went blank abruptly. That had been a total waste of time. He had the vague impression of there being wheels moving within wheels. He had run up against something bigger than he had bargained for. Bob Broomfield, a person on whom he was sure he could stake his life, was far from just the right person to talk to. He didn't understand.

So there was nothing left to do, except to go. The hardest bit would be telling his loyal administrative staff, starting with Genevieve.

*   *   *

It was strange, being at home on a working day. Bruce had got used to it when his doctor ordered him to take that two-week break, so he would be able to develop new routines again. He wondered if he ought to contact Doctor Doherty now. He felt ill but it was his mind that was troubled, not his body, and there was nothing that anyone could do for that.

He had been buoyed by the reactions of everyone he met as he left the *BUSSTOP* building. His admin team stood in stunned silence as he bade them goodbye. In corridors that seemed endless today, he was stopped by individuals, who pleaded with him not to leave.

Bruce heard someone calling his name and the sound of running feet behind him. Angie Thompson from the legal department caught up with him.

"There you are!" she panted. "We called your office but Gen said that you had already left. We will fight this, Bruce. Don't worry. Let us fight this for you. Rodriguez is already doing a hatchet job on you. The White House statement announcing your resignation is actionable and that's just the beginning! Go home and have a good rest and leave it to the professionals. By the time you get home there will be a filter on your communications system. We have your list of people who contact you at home. Call us if you want to add any more names. No journalist will be able to get through to you. And legal papers should be in process right now. We're putting a restraining order area round your apartment block—again for the benefit of the journalists. If anyone steps off that far sidewalk, they're for it." Bruce started to thank her. "As far as we're concerned, you're still part of *BUSSTOP*. You always will be. It's only that jerk in the White House who thinks otherwise." She put a hand on his arm. "Are you okay?"

Fragments of sentences whirled around in his head now as he sat down. The glow of the supportive comments was gone and he was left with some stark and brutal statements.

> "... *keep what's left of your reputation intact ... Rodriguez is already doing a hatchet job on you .... I don't know what you've done during your time in office anyway ... I hold you and BUSSTOP totally responsible for the deaths of the Ariadne astronauts ...*"

That last bit echoed and re-echoed until his head ached. How could everything have gone so wrong? *BUSSTOP* should have been putting the final touches to the celebrations that would mark the triumphant return of the Ariadne crew, not fighting for its life.

Bruce knew he was discarded trash, something no longer wanted, crumpled up and thrown on the ground. It was a totally alien concept to him. He came from a loving, supportive family background, even if the key players were taken from him early. His time in the USAF put a polish on a healthy and sensible appreciation of his own abilities and potential. With *BUSSTOP* he reached for the stars literally and received the admiration and plaudits of the world. Up to the moment when he was told about his illness, the only real setbacks in his life had been his divorces, but they had been by mutual consent and, at the time, were seemingly the only way out of difficult situations.

And now this mess was his reward.

There was nothing to look forward to, nothing left. Nothing except accusations, pointing fingers and an increasingly wearying battle against the cancer, which he would lose sooner or later.

Shannon. He must talk to Shannon. She had asked him again if he was sick. When they met for that dinner back in the early fall, when she first told him about her book, her concern weakened his resolve. He so nearly told her then. Hagar knew. But she had her own problems to deal with and she was far away in Cape Canaveral.

Shannon did not answer when he called. Bruce left a message, wished he hadn't and stood suddenly, his mind made up. There was no point in struggling on any further.

* * *

"No! He mustn't do that!"

Simeon shouted so loudly that the others jumped. Their Martian hosts looked in his direction enquiringly.

"What's wrong?" asked Justin, knowing full well what was in Simeon's mind.

"Bruce Dougall!" Simeon wrung his hands. "Do you know what he's thinking?"

"Go easy on them, Tony!" urged Justin. "Remember that all our guests are still experiencing a lot of new things and they are still learning." He turned to look at the group. "I'll assure you all on this one. The end is not what you think."

"Simeon," said Tony, "if you can't take this, we can block your view of Earth until you feel stronger. You are all such promising pupils, but perhaps we are expecting too much from you too soon."

The crew of *Ariadne One* watched, wide-eyed and fearful. Yes, this was the first time they had felt anything approximating fear since their Martian-human friends rescued them. Deep within the rainbow, thoughts and concepts were being given to them that bestowed upon them breath-taking knowledge and abilities, all to be used in the future. But now it really was like being back in school, when a young person confronts that frustrating chasm between the theoretical knowledge, which can be wheeled out at the drop of a hat, and the practical experience, which has not yet been accrued. Their minds, their spirits, their psyches were being worked to a phenomenal level. With this incident they couldn't quite make the final connections with any clarity and they were bothered by what they saw.

Tony understood. This was the first sign of discomfort in the group and it was natural. They were still humans, however changed they might be by the time this process was over. Bits of the negative aspects of humanity were bound to peep through from time to time. Up to this point, attending class had been no hardship for them. It had been a total joy. This was where they got to try out their achievements. They were aiming for the perfect balance of emotional logic and logical emotion. This would be a marker of how far they had come.

*　　*　　*

Bruce Dougall went to a wall-safe and put in a number. He took out his handgun. From another location he fetched ammunition for the weapon and loaded it. The astronauts wanted to look away and they could not.

"Why are we still sitting about here?" demanded Emily. "We should be back on Earth, stopping this sort of thing. A good man is about to end his own life—for no reason at all!"

"Peace, Emily!" Sally soothed.

"How can you watch this? You cared for the man!"

"Yes, Sally cared for him. Remember, you are not *sitting about* here. You are learning so much in every Earth hour. There are still things that you need to know, including some more details about Bruce Dougall. So you are not quite ready to return home yet. You have a mission to fulfil that you can hardly comprehend yet. By the time *Ariadne One* takes us to the third planet, you will be ready. And I promise you that this is a scenario in which no intervention is needed from us."

*　　*　　*

Bruce sat down again. This would be so easy. It was the obvious answer. He had nothing to live for. It seemed that Joe Mortimer's life was about to start again. Good luck to him. Rodriguez was on course to scare up a real storm by the look of it. This would deflect some of it away from Joe. He checked the loading of the gun and released the safety catch.

It would be so easy. To find real rest at last, to move on from all the effort, was an idea that was beckoning seductively. He wasn't one hundred per cent clear on the mechanics of it, but he was sure that in some way he would meet up again with friends and family. The Zeus project had given him the spirit of an explorer and an adventurer. So now it was time to leave, with the minimum of fuss, and participate in the next great adventure. He hoped that some of the first people he would encounter would be the *Ariadne One* crew, if only to be reconciled with them.

Bruce lifted the gun.

As he shifted slightly in the chair, his left foot nudged against something. He thought he sensed someone nearby, even though he knew he was alone. Overcome by curiosity, he put down the gun and leaned towards the floor. It was Shannon's book, still untouched. He didn't remember putting it there. He picked it up and glanced at the front cover. He put the book on the table and opened it. He found himself looking at the dedication. His head came up and back momentarily, as if he had been hit very hard. Then he read it again, just to make sure that he wasn't imagining things.

To B.J. Remembering all the good times.

Within the rainbow of Mars, there was a collective sigh of realisation from the astronauts. They had been picking up parts of the *denouement* in advance and couldn't put it all together.

"Of course!"

Only Masahide was still confused.

"Bruce Dougall's full name is Bruce John Dougall," Simeon reminded him. "He went through a childhood phase of liking neither of his given names. For a while his close friends called him B.J."

"And Shannon was one of those childhood friends!" Masahide declared wonderingly.

"Yes. That's real class and style on the part of Shannon. She has dedicated her book to her ex husband under the noses of the world and no one knows!"

Tony beamed. These were really promising pupils. Of course, that was why they ended up on the crew.

Bruce didn't know how long he sat staring at the book, torn by a mixture of joy and disbelief. He came back to reality when he heard the door buzzer. In a dream, he went to see who was calling round and there was Shannon.

"I picked up your message," she said. "Bruce, what's wrong?"

"Nothing. I've been looking at your book."

Shannon followed him through into the main room. She took in the situation with one glance. Yes, her book was on the table. But so was Bruce's handgun with the safety catch off.

"I hope you found the book interesting," she said softly.

She picked up the gun and re-engaged the safety catch. Then she went one better and emptied out the bullets.

"Shannon, I—"

"Put the gun away, Bruce. You and I need to straighten some things out."

*　　*　　*

Joe had spent an increasingly frustrating late afternoon and early evening in his office, talking to various people who could offer him no way forward with the situation that President Rodriguez was creating. Finally, losing patience, he called the Prime Minister again. Kevin Crane was sympathetic but unsure what could be done.

"I wanted to give President Rodriguez a good slap when I spoke to him earlier, Joe. His treatment of Bruce Dougall is disgraceful, I agree. The trouble is, over this last century or more assorted American Presidents have declared a National Emergency for different problems and the declarations stand technically until somebody wakes up and does something about them. So the office of President has accrued a large array of powers that were never intended in the Constitution and any incumbent is quite within his or her rights to use them. I'll give you an example of what I mean. When the Watergate scandal surrounding President Nixon was investigated in the 1970s, the range of the presidential powers came under scrutiny by Congress. It was discovered that the United States of America had been in a state of emergency since 1950 because of the Cold War tensions with the USSR! Each President could do just about what he liked, with a strict reading of the law. Some pushed that date back further and said that the country had been on an emergency footing since the 1930s, when Franklin D. Roosevelt was trying to sort out the huge economic and social dislocations that America was undergoing. So a President hell-bent on doing something can do it, as long as he has an inventive team of constitutional lawyers behind him who can quote the appropriate chapter and verse."

Joe's expression became increasingly grim during the quick tour of American presidential history.

"Answer me this, Prime Minister. If Rodriguez carries out his threat and suspends and then shuts down *BUSSTOP* America, where does that leave the organisation in this country?"

"Up the famous creek without a paddle, Joe. Britain can't afford to carry on the space exploration programme alone. That was one of the key reasons for the founding of *BUSSTOP*. The pooling of talent and, most importantly—resources. *NASA* became a bottomless pit and both countries knew that they couldn't afford this kind of work on their own."

"So our *BUSSTOP* would have to go?"

"I shouldn't be saying all this to you without a ton of Civil Service advice, but the simple answer is yes."

"Fine." Joe felt as though a weight had been lifted from him. The guilt was still there, but he didn't have to carry on with a job that he no longer judged himself fit to do. "Prime Minister, I'm resigning as British head of *BUSSTOP.* I will have a letter couriered over to you in Downing Street and you will also receive the text electronically."

Joe then went on to outline his fears about the mistake he was convinced he had made, which surely contributed to the loss of Ariadne.

"Joe!" Kevin Crane exclaimed. "You can't blame yourself. You can't know for sure what this Rob Masters wanted to say. If it gives you some ease, you can resign, but I would much rather you didn't. You and your feelings of guilt will be better dealt with if you play a prominent part in the investigations into the loss of Ariadne, in your capacity as head of *BUSSTOP*. But whatever you do, please don't put any of this stuff about Masters in your resignation letter. I can guarantee that everyone will think that you have a guilty conscience about something anyway. But you don't have to go looking for trouble."

"Thanks for that, Kevin. There is another reason for leaving. Whilst I remain in office, my hands are tied. I can do nothing for Bruce beyond making a formal protest, which would be a total waste of time. As a private citizen, I can do what I like. So can Bruce. I think it's about time someone looked at Mr Ted Rodriguez. Bruce and I can focus the spotlights."

"That might be an interesting idea, Joe. Come over to Downing Street at the beginning of next week and we can talk about this properly. The very act of you turning up here will show the world that I support you. I'll put out the announcement through the Downing Street press office and give you a bit of legal protection to keep the news people off your back. We'll do the usual."

The usual. The media might as well give up and go home. They would be banned from the village, restrained from going anywhere near Joe or anyone he was with and could deal only with *BUSSTOP* and Downing Street. Events had moved too fast for this to be done after Irene's press conference about the messages from Mars.

"Thank you, Prime Minister, for being so understanding. But can you order all this protection when I'm no longer part of *BUSSTOP*?"

"Let me get the ball rolling, then you send over your letter of resignation. I have certain powers tucked away for a rainy day. Ted Rodriguez is not the only one who can stretch the letter of the law. Enjoy the headlines, Joe, and your weekend."

"I aim to."

Whistling tunelessly, Joe called Bruce at home and was confused when Shannon Dougall appeared on screen.

"Mr Mortimer!" she said, very impressed. "Bruce is not feeling so good at the moment. He's resting."

"Unless he's unconscious and can't be woken, I really need to speak to him. What I've got to say will be better for him than rest or any drugs."

Looking very mistrustful, Shannon disappeared to fetch Bruce. Joe noted that his colleague did look pretty rough when he came on screen. He hadn't been like that earlier in the day. Still, bad news took people in different ways.

Joe gave his colleague a quick resume of what he was doing.

"If Ted Rodriguez wants to crucify people, it will have to be a multiple event. You're not fighting him on your own, Bruce. Something tells me he's dangerous."

"You're doing this for me?"

"It looks like it. And anyway, in all conscience I can't stay in office after what I know I've probably done. Do you remember when we first met, to work on the Zeus project?" Bruce nodded. "What was the phrase you used about us working together?"

"I don't recall it."

"*Partners in crime.*" He lifted his tea mug in a toast. "To being partners in crime again. Only we're not the criminals. Well, we're not. Ted Rodriguez needs taking down a peg or two. I'm not sure what we can do or how the hell we can go about it but we ought to have a damned good try."

Joe saw an expression on Bruce's face that he had never seen before. It was an odd mix of vacant and curious. No. He had seen Hagar looking like that, when she was off into one of her profound statements.

"Thank you for what you're doing," Bruce said. "I get the feeling that Rodriguez will make his own downfall. But you're right. It doesn't mean that we have to sit around doing nothing."

Shannon had removed herself from the room discreetly whilst this conversation went on. When she returned, she was amazed by the transformation in Bruce. There was the hint of a smile on his face and he looked less like some wilted plant.

"Wow!" she said. "Mr Mortimer wasn't joking, was he? He has given you good news. What are you two up to?"

Following the ingrained habit of many years, an evasive reply was shaping behind his lips. Then he thought better of it.

Not telling people things had brought him toe-to-toe with death.

"If you really want to know, I'll get you up to speed."

*   *   *

The colours of the rainbow of Mars glowed brighter and stronger than ever. There was laughter, and further understanding.

"I saw those last scenes in advance," marvelled Simeon, "and I couldn't think how they could be when Mr Dougall took out his gun. Tony, there was someone else there, wasn't there? In spirit."

"You must learn to trust your vision, Simeon," said Tony. "If you truly see, it is so. You must all remember that. The talents were already within you. They have been woken, that's all. You must believe in yourselves. That's the lesson you have learned from this."

"I know that we must believe," put in Brian. "But I was convinced that the poor man would shoot himself."

"Perhaps in another reality, he did," Tony told him. "There are billions of parallel universes existing side by side, shaped by the decisions we made and the paths that we took. But with us, in our reality, he did not. That's all that matters. We have touched on alternative realities before. Let's save that for another occasion. For now, we need to shut ourselves down and leave these good people to live their lives unobserved for a while. We hold a watching brief. We don't spy on them out of prurient interest. Joe Mortimer and Bruce Dougall have sorting out to do which we can safely leave to them. There will be reckoning enough in which we will be involved."

"Class dismissed," Emily murmured to Simeon.

Chapter Twenty

The world of news reporting exploded.

Both heads of *BUSSTOP* had resigned. The word was out on the streets that the President pushed Bruce Dougall into his departure. The rationale behind Joe Mortimer's move was not so clear. His letter to the Prime Minister was scrupulously correct but spare to the point of being curt. There were no obvious clues, but his leaving must have something to do with the loss of *Ariadne One*. Was he acknowledging that he carried some guilt? And what was his burden of guilt? What would each of them do next? What would be the reaction of the British Prime Minister? Had the Prime Minister sacked him?

Hampered by the swiftly imposed legal restrictions on both sides of the Atlantic, television reporters were reduced to sending breathless dispatches from outside the *BUSSTOP* buildings. Newspapers set up headlines in the kind of typeface that was generally understood to be reserved for the Second Coming, the end of the world or—at a push—the death of a British monarch.

Given half a chance, the media swarms would have invaded Graffenby and sat outside Joe's house. Bruce would have been similarly besieged. But these days the news industry reaped a bitter harvest, the legacy of a hundred and fifty years of increasingly intrusive reporting. The trade-off was a tricky one. Some said, regretfully, that there would never be another investigative journalism *coup* like the *Washington Post* revelations about Richard Nixon and Watergate. But on the other hand, it was hoped that there would never again be the kind of disgraceful scenes witnessed in the late 1990s, when a princess was photographed to death and beyond.

The eye of the storm is said to be the calmest place. Joe was unruffled when he went for a run with Bonny on the Saturday morning. He guessed there would most likely be a sturdy band of reporters and photographers positioned outside the boundaries of the village at either end of the main road, sitting in these odd places to comply with the court orders. So he took a zigzag route that carefully avoided the locations. He knew how inventive caption writers could be. A perfectly innocent picture of him, running through the mist and the slush with the dog, would end up as *Joe Mortimer battles with his grief over the astronauts.*

Well, he did grieve for them. The seven people were active ghosts in his mind. But dealing with his thoughts was a private process, not something carried out round the roads of Graffenby with representatives of the media on hand to catch every sigh.

On his return, he contacted Irene, to reassure her yet again that he was on his way over to see her. Understandably, she had been worried about him the previous night when the story of his resignation broke. He hoped he had put her mind at rest when she called him.

Following Irene's instructions, he selected warm clothing. He had no intention of freezing, even in the noble cause of pursuing such a lovely lady.

As Joe drove out of the village, the little posse of reporters was there. A photographer took a few half-hearted pictures. There was a hankering within the group for the good old days, when some of them would have jumped into cars and kicked motorbikes into life and roared after the object of their interest. Joe was tempted to acknowledge their presence. Once, long ago, Richard had taught him the knack of the royal wave. But he thought better of it. That really would be a childish thumbing of the nose. The reporters were pegged down and he almost felt sorry for them. And also, breakfast television had shown the Friday night talk to the American people by President Rodriguez. Its contents were a dagger pointing at the heart of *BUSSTOP*, for those who were listening carefully. This might get tricky. *BUSSTOP* could well need the media before this sorted itself out

Joe could hardly believe that he was holding Irene tight and she was holding him. For a few moments, their reunion was beyond words, beyond kisses, beyond anything. Joe felt a deep-seated coil of tension unwinding within him. Irene decided that she had emerged from a struggle through the jungle, battered and dishevelled, the result of sharing Joe's troubles at a distance via a screen link after her own woes with the knee injury and influenza. Joe couldn't help smiling when they moved apart from a kiss. Irene wondered what was so funny.

"I was remembering what you said the other day, about kissing it better," he said. "I don't think I'm quite better yet."

*   *   *

Bruce stirred and wondered what had woken him. He reached out for his glasses to get a better view of the bedside clock. For a moment he recoiled in horror at the lateness of the hour and then remembered the previous burdened day. It had happened. It was not some feverish dream. And it was Saturday, anyway. Even if it wasn't, he was minus his job and plus a houseguest. But most importantly of all, he was still alive.

He lay very still for a few minutes, his thoughts in free fall. It was hard to let his mind even touch on what he had so nearly done.

He remembered Patrick, who sank slowly into the clutches of schizophrenia. There came a point when it appeared that Bruce was the only person who could get through to his friend. His family and his fiancée tried and failed.

Bruce had a long talk with him three days before he flew on *Zeus Two*.

"When I get back, we'll go down into Virginia for a break, Pat. We'll put a bit of colour back into your cheeks."

"That sounds good. I'll look forward to it."

The news was kept from Bruce until his return. On the third day of the space mission, Patrick committed suicide. The drug overdose he took was so massive that there was no way it could have been accidental or a cry for help.

As well as being deeply upset, Bruce was baffled. He trotted out all the usual platitudes to other friends, and to Shannon. *Unbelievable . . . surely survival is the first order of business with all living things . . . what drives someone to do that?*

And so on.

Now Bruce knew what drove someone to do that. His perceptions had shrunk momentarily to the point where the gun in his hand was the answer to everything. The lovingly maintained and polished weapon would deliver the final soothing caress to make everything better.

He could hear Shannon moving about and he wondered if she had carried out her threat of sleeping with his gun under her pillow.

"Then you'll have to disturb me," she reasoned. "But I don't think you want that gun again, do you?"

So this was what a nurturing goddess looked like. She was fifty, dressed in jeans and a sweater and crowned with that beautiful silver hair. And she had taken up temporary residence in the spare room.

Bruce got the impression that he was learning lessons again. Shannon was limbering up to move mountains for him. And Joe Mortimer—*Joe!*—had taken the radical decision to stand shoulder to shoulder with him very publicly and very dramatically. The unlikeliest of individuals were throwing him the necessary lifelines and making him reconsider who were the important people.

Yesterday he was being summoned by Death.

Today he was being called out by Life, to step into a landscape where some of the features were changed beyond recognition. It was a gift he was not about to waste. What was it that Hagar had said to him about still having things to do?

*   *   *

When he arrived with Irene, Joe had wondered what he was doing in such an unfamiliar environment. Now he was feeling quite at home as he inspected the runners for the next race in the parade ring.

"Aren't racehorses the most beautiful creatures?" Irene wanted to know.

A horse stopped right by Joe, to ensure that he had something to study. Obviously an old pro, this horse turned his head both ways to ensure that everyone photographed his best side. The lad leading him up managed to urge him forward into a trot. It was like watching a supple dancer striding out across a stage.

"They are," Joe had to admit.

"The Arabs have a wonderful saying about horses," she continued. "They say that Allah gathered together the south winds and formed them into the horse."

"That's positively poetic. I'll have to tell Bruce that one."

"Returning to the mundane, I like number six, Long Ever," said Irene.

Joe gave the horse a thoughtful look.

"No." He shook his head. "Jemima Swan is your man—or woman, rather. It's a mare, isn't it? Look at her feet. Hooves like soup plates. Perfect for this soft ground. Made from the south wind or not, your horse will get stuck in the mud with those dinky little feet."

Irene considered this in amused silence. A typical competitive man! He started out at Huntingdon racecourse not knowing one end of a Thoroughbred from the other. Three races in and he was the expert. The trouble was, he was making a very good point about the animals in question. Huntingdon had escaped the previous day's covering of snow. It had rained instead and the going was officially *Soft*. She placed her bet, knowing somehow that she was doomed.

The steeplechase was fast and furious. The Huntingdon track is wide, flat and invitingly open for a horse bred to race. Runners rarely hang about, even when the ground is heavy. Standing by the winning post, Joe was getting used to the moving earthquake that hurtled past them in each race but he decided that he'd still rather be on the launch slope at blast-off. And this time there was some drama that justified his preference.

At the feature open ditch jump by the stands, the leader clipped the top of the fence and tipped over in a perfect somersault. The rider was thrown out in front of the field and he was kicked by several of the horses as they powered by. There was a collective "Ooh!" from the crowd.

"And my father said I was going in for a risky way of life!" he observed to Irene as paramedics rushed to help the stricken jockey.

After another circuit of the track, Jemima Swan beat Long Ever in a driving finish, winning by a nostril.

"I won't gloat," Joe said with a smirk.

"No. You won't. You will collect your winnings and buy me something to eat. I'm starving. We can miss the next race. And it will be on screen in the restaurant. It's a conditional jockeys' event." He looked at her for clarification. Aha! He didn't know everything—yet. "Apprentice jockeys, learner jockeys."

Over a late lunch, Irene explained more about her love of racing.

"My mother's family were big fans. Way back, in the latter part of the twentieth century, one of my great grandfathers hobnobbed with royalty at the racecourse. Ask His Majesty to get out the family pictures from that era, with Queen Elizabeth the Queen Mother at the races. I'm sure that Ian Stirling will be in some of them. I don't attend race meetings very often because I can rarely persuade anyone to accompany me. This is a real treat, Joe. Thank you so much."

Racing Television had the news scoop of the day, and it wasn't anything to do with the miraculous escape of that third race jockey with no more than severe bruising. Racing journalists stared at two people, stared again to make sure, and then got busy contacting colleagues. They knew that they couldn't approach Joe. But this would give everyone the in they were looking for.

Race goers didn't give one particular couple a second glance. All were deeply involved in the business of the afternoon and well-known faces are often not noticed when put in a different context. Joe Mortimer and Irene Hanson were well out of their usual worlds.

By the time the last race was due, the temperature was dropping fast. A sinking sun hung red and weary in the sky. Joe understood that there was some problem with the glare of the setting sun combined with sudden blocks of shadow, which meant that horses and riders might not have a clear sight of some of the jumps. He wished that this contest would be cancelled. He wanted to return to warmth and civilisation. But Irene was having the time of her life and he had to be pleased for her when it was announced that the race would go ahead.

On the way back home, Irene's personal communicator signalled.

"Where are you?" asked her next-door neighbour Clara urgently.

"I'm with a dear friend, on my way back home after a perfectly lovely afternoon at Huntingdon races," said Irene, dreamily. "Why?"

"I thought you'd like to know that there is a very large group of reporters outside your house. They're blocking the lane. There are a couple of police officers here but they don't appear to be doing very much."

Irene relayed the information to Joe, who was annoyed with himself for not seeing that one coming.

"Damn! I never thought about that. Someone must have seen us at the racecourse! If you don't mind, you'd better come to my place until I can sort this out," he suggested.

Irene was not about to object.

"I know you said that you like dogs," Joe said when they arrived back in Graffenby. "Bonny is a very well-behaved animal as a rule. She's going mad at the moment when she sees me. She might jump about a bit and she is rather big for that. She won't notice that you're there when she's barging about."

"She must have thought you'd abandoned her when you were away for so long," was Irene's understanding comment. "She's doubly delighted every time you return home."

A four-legged fur ball missile launched itself at Joe when he opened the door. Realising she had a new audience, Bonny chased round in a tight circle several times and reared up to rest her front paws on Irene's shoulders.

"You are a lovely dog!" Irene told her, tousling her ears. "And you know it. Now get down, woofle pops, before I fall down."

Bonny sat at her feet, gazing up in adoration.

"I think I should be feeling jealous!" Joe said in mock-complaint. "Come on through, Irene, and I'll talk to Kevin Crane."

"Joe, it's late on Saturday afternoon. You're contacting the Prime Minister?"

"The PM won't mind. He's disturbed me enough over the years. I like to go straight to the top if I can. Police chiefs can be unhelpful, especially at weekends."

Irene was only vaguely aware of the discussion going on in the background. Her gaze drifted round the large room. She took in the stone fireplace and the paintings on the wall. Some pieces of furniture here had to be at least a hundred years old. She wandered over to the floor-to-ceiling book shelving in an alcove. She noticed that Joe had copies of all her books. Bonny joined her and leaned against her new-found friend, raising her head for the expected pat. She had obviously never known anything other than kindness and love. She was totally trusting.

Irene became aware of Joe calling her name. She walked the length of the room, Bonny shadowing her.

"Good afternoon, Professor Hanson," the Prime Minister began very formally. "I'm sorry that you've ended up in something of a mess. I can have the media people removed from round your property, but not before Monday morning I'm afraid. Strictly speaking, I should not be running this protection for Joe. I can't push my luck by making another fuss at the weekend. It could mean a rather uncomfortable time for you at home. But the police will get you in to your house and keep you safe. I shall have words with the appropriate people. You can be sure of that."

"Don't worry, Mr Crane. Thank you for everything you are doing."

"Are you hungry?" Joe asked Irene after the call. "I don't feel as though I had any lunch. It must be the cold. I'm a fairly good cook. D'you like vegetable curry?"

"Definitely. And all good chefs need an assistant."

"You're on!"

The kitchen became a hive of culinary industry. In between helping to prepare a mountain of assorted vegetables, Irene watched Joe. He certainly seemed at home on the cooking range and he worked with the casual ease that marks out the experienced practitioner from the hesitant beginner.

"How did you get into cooking?" she wondered.

"We were marched into it by Mum!" Joe reminisced, measuring out a mixture of wholemeal and plain white flour for chapattis. "No, that's not quite so. Philip and I fell into it when we were young, wanting to help Mum as children do. I think we were also supporting Dad. He was the one who was marched. He was the typical helpless male to begin with, apparently. When they married, Mum presented Dad with some cookery books. She had the right approach. She called them 'technical manuals.' As she ended up with two sons, she often says that she's glad she took the firm approach. Otherwise she would have found herself with a house full of men denying all knowledge of how to make a cup of tea."

"I knew there was a reason why I liked your mother the moment I met her."

"Which would have been at your book signing," said Joe, stealing a sneaky kiss.

"You've got a good memory!"

"I don't forget things about you, Irene."

Irene had never spent such a special evening. The meal was very good and the company was wonderful. She talked serious topics with Joe and they laughed and joked too. But as the time ticked by, she thought about going home. She would be cheek by jowl with a chunk of media people, who would be camped outside until Monday morning.

"Penny for them?" said Joe as they sat watching the flames devouring a log in the fireplace.

"I was thinking about my unexpected guests from the press and television." She snuggled closer to Joe, resting her head in the hollow of his shoulder. "I'm so gullible, I shall end up making them breakfast in the morning. What do they call it, when you end up bonding with your captors? Oh yes, the Stockholm Syndrome."

"You don't have to go home. How about making breakfast for us in the morning?" Joe stroked her hair. "Don't go. Stay here tonight. I can give you the contact details and you can tell the appropriate people that you're staying elsewhere. I'm sure the police outside your home will be relieved that they don't have to wrestle you through the front door."

*   *   *

Shannon sat on the floor, cross legged, something she had done since Bruce first knew her, when they were both about five years old. She sighed in fond exasperation.

"I won't even bother with *why?*" she said.

"Why did I come close to committing suicide?"

"No. With the place you found yourself by early yesterday afternoon, I can understand what you were thinking, totally. I'm talking about one of the factors that took you there. Why you felt you had to walk around all on your own with the knowledge of your illness."

"It seemed like a good idea at the time," he replied. "I didn't want people feeling sorry for me."

"I won't even pretend to understand that one, but never mind. I'm here to make sure you are in fighting condition for whatever comes next. There's an ass-hole in the White House who needs a wake-up call. Breakfast television this morning was full of people who are furious on your behalf. After that speech he made last night, Rodriguez needs to have a care—perhaps a truckload of care. Apparently the unions who represent workers at *BUSSTOP* and Mission Control are rolling up their sleeves ready for a fight if he goes ahead with suspending the organisation. Oh, and by the way, it looks like you have about six hundred and forty three written messages on the communications system. I'll bet every one of them is a message of support. What is it, Bruce?" she asked as a strange shadow, part smile, part sadness, part something else crossed his face.

"Regret, I suppose. Us. What should have been. I know it's no good going over old ground but—"

"It was Adam and Eve stuff, honey. Like most men, you are good when you're on a mission. You're better than good. When I talked, I didn't always want you to solve my problems. I'm not that dumb. I knew what my problems were. I simply wanted you to listen so that I could order my thoughts. And in the end, I couldn't compete against your ultimate missions, in a space ship. You were my protector in the schoolyard. I hoped that would continue. If we're talking about regrets, I'll tell you mine. I didn't revert to my birth name when we divorced and I could have published the book under any *nom-de-plume* that took my fancy but I used my name—*your* name. I've always been proud of wearing that badge so to speak, even at my lowest point. A lot of nonsense has been talked about my book. I know my limitations as a writer. It's comfort food for the masses." Bruce wanted to protest at the self-denigration but this was not the moment. "For all that, a lot of folks seem to like it and they've nailed it to the top of the best-seller list. There's no point in being modest about it. I am regarded as a success and I will do very well out of this financially. It's a pain in the butt always trying to look respectable for the fans when I run down to the store. That will calm down. But my greatest reward would have been knowing that you were saying to your friends '*Yes, she has done well. I'm so proud of her and she's all mine.*' I know I'm crazy but I still love you, Bruce. And I always will."

* * *

Vicky knew that this was the moment she had been anticipating for so long. Joe Mortimer looked at her as he had never looked at her before.

"I'm not your boss any more, Vicky," he said.

"Does that make any difference?" she asked archly.

"A lot of difference. Work place relationships are never a good idea and you must know that I have wanted to—"

Suddenly Vicky was aware of the communications system signal. She sat bolt upright in bed, the final threads of her dream dissolving as she saw that her bedside clock was telling her it was seven a.m. on Sunday. Einstein barked madly.

She raced through into the living room, dragging on her dressing gown, already rehearsing some sharp phrases for whoever was calling at this unearthly hour.

"Oh," was all she could say when she switched on the screen.

Vicky knew that it was her brother but she might have walked by him in the street. Jamie's face was pale and hollowed with obvious illness. He had a hacking cough.

"Hello, sis!" he croaked. "I'm coming home for some TLC from you and from Mum and Dad. The hospital has insisted that I take some time off. I'd probably make the patients worse, wouldn't I?"

"Will any airline let you fly?" she wondered. "They're none to keen on passengers who are obviously unwell before the journey even starts. They like to avoid in-flight illness dramas."

She was speaking with the voice of PA experience. Her previous employer had once been turned away from a flight on health grounds.

"My boss has had a word with someone he knows. I'll be on the morning flight from D.C."

A few facts slid into Vicky's sleepy brain.

"Jamie! By my calculations, it must be two a.m. with you!"

"I can't rest. It's a waste of time trying. And I'll have to be on my way early to the airport. Will you tell Mum and Dad?"

"You should tell them yourself. You'll be staying with them."

"No. Vicky, I want to stay with you. Please."

She saw his haunted, hunted look and noticed that his eyes were darting to the corners of the room where he sat. This was not a secure line and it dawned on her what some of this might be about.

"You make sure that you're on that plane!" she said briskly. "I'll sort out everything at this end. Give me your travel details."

She made notes in a flamboyant hand.

"Thanks, Vicky. I'll see you later."

Vicky sat by the blank screen for some time, thinking. In her wish-fulfilment dream, she had been reminded that Joe Mortimer was no longer her boss. When he announced his resignation on Friday evening she was broken-hearted. She felt devastated now. And those feelings had somehow led to her dream. She blushed hotly at the prospect of what would have happened next in her fantasy land and she was glad that Jamie's call had intruded. Otherwise she would never have been able to look Mr Mortimer in the face again. And now that he was no longer in *BUSSTOP*, he might be able to help. Her brother's knowledge was dynamite.

* * *

Irene was awake but she didn't want to open her eyes. She was wrapped in a blanket of warmth and remembrance of what she and Joe had shared the previous night. She had no wish to move out of it before she had to. Rain began to patter against the window.

She heard feet bounding up the stairs followed by the pad-click-pad of a dog's paws. There was a brief scuffle on the landing, during which she guessed that Bonny was being sent back down to the kitchen. The door opened as she sat up in bed and Joe walked in carrying a tray on which rested a teapot, mugs and a milk jug. He was dressed for running in a tracksuit.

"Good morning, sleepy head!" he said, smiling broadly.

He picked up something else from the tray that she hadn't noticed.

"Joe, they're lovely!"

Irene took the small bunch of snowdrops, still damp with the first sprinkling of the rain.

"And your tea, m'lady."

He presented her with a mug of tea and sat down on the bed beside her. She looked positively edible in that black sweatshirt of his. He put an arm round her.

"Or perhaps I should say Good morning, gorgeous."

Her glowing face was answer enough.

"I was beginning to wonder if we would ever get to this point," he said after a long pause. "It's been a lesson in patience, I suppose."

"The obstacles did become rather epic, didn't they? But the best things are always worth waiting for."

*   *   *

Vicky was glad to reach home with her brother. He was really poorly and the flight in a pressurised cabin would only have made things worse.

"Go to bed, Jamie," she said firmly. "Everything's ready for you in the spare room."

"No, I must tell you, I must show you," he replied in a desperate tone.

He was still insisting on this some time later as Vicky made sure that he had made it into bed. Einstein watched from his basket, not sure what to make of all this.

"You must see the film on my communicator. I recorded what I saw. You must see it."

"Later, Jamie. You need to rest."

"Justice! We must get justice for Phoebe Harper."

"We will," Vicky reassured him, feeling his hot forehead. "President Harper always struck me as a kind woman. I'm sure she wouldn't begrudge you a few hours sleep. Then we can look for justice."

"She was fine . . . watch the film . . . she wasn't badly hurt . . ."

Jamie's voice faded away as he relaxed into sleep. Vicky picked up his communicator and went to put it in a drawer in her bedroom. Then she knew it would be safe. There was important evidence on there, it seemed

She peeped back round the door to check on Jamie. He was deeply asleep. Einstein had sneaked in somehow and was snuggled up against him. Leaving aside his terrible pallor, in slumber her brother was still about sixteen years old. It really wasn't fair. He had pinched all the family looks. He had thick, dark, cow-like fringes of eyelashes. He hadn't got round to that haircut yet and he so he was sporting an impressive set of curls. He had the bone-structure that any male model would have killed for.

Vicky went in and rearranged the bedclothes over Jamie. Einstein's ears went back for a moment when he though that she was about to move him. But she gave him an absent minded pat and left the room.

Jamie had picked up some winter bug or other from his patients, no doubt, but there was something else going on here. She would have to talk to her cousin Briona again. The family thought she was totally mad but to Vicky she said things and did things that made sense. In the face of a raft of efficient pharmaceutical drugs for every possible ailment, she used herbal remedies. She talked about healing the whole person. Vicky knew that people were thinking along these lines a hundred years previously, rediscovering the skills that went back millennia. And then the knowledge was almost lost again, trampled underfoot by some key medical research breakthroughs. Briona was not to be swayed. And she often mentioned illness as *dis-ease*, the lack of ease in the body, mind or spirit. Vicky fancied that there was some dis-ease happening in Jamie. From their previous conversations, what Jamie knew was worrying. And now he was revealing that he had film evidence to back it up! No wonder he was ill.

Vicky couldn't put it off any longer. She had to talk to their parents on-screen. She wondered what she could say that would be truthful but which would not have them hammering on the door within the hour.

*   *   *

Bonny was stretched out on the floor, snoring gently. Irene sat close to Joe, her head on his chest. She looked endearingly waif-like, dressed in one of Joe's sweaters and a pair of his jogging bottoms. The clothes were very baggy on her. Although she was tall, there was a great contrast in their build. She had decided that her race-going outfit from the previous day was not appropriate for sitting around.

"What d'you reckon?" Joe asked as the recording of President Ted Rodriguez's television address ended.

"He certainly isn't enamoured of *BUSSTOP*, is he?" she observed. "Phoebe Harper was so keen on the space exploration. I'm surprised that she had him as her Vice President."

"No political partners will ever agree on all points. She must have thought it was a containable disagreement. It was. And I'm sure that she didn't know this man's real opinions on space travel. No one did! Mrs Harper didn't reckon on dying in office like that and at *BUSSTOP* we didn't reckon on there being such a catastrophe with *Ariadne One*."

Irene didn't know why a particular memory came to mind.

"We talked about Phoebe Harper's accident at work. There was a fascinating discussion one lunchtime. Dudley Merrick is a sweet soul. He is something else when it comes to his knowledge and application of it. He's a theoretical physicist who strays into areas like energy dynamics. He's the kind of chap who will prove to you beyond a shadow of a doubt that a bumblebee should be incapable of flying, because the wing area does not tally with the body mass. Anyway, we ended up with diagrams on pieces of paper all over the table because he looked at the physics of the accident, as we understood it to have happened. We were stumped. We could accept that the car driver might have been killed outright because that was where the lorry impacted. Possibly the bodyguard too, because he was on the same side of the car, seated behind the driver. But Mrs Harper should not have sustained life-threatening injuries like that. And the lorry driver should have been fine as well. It did seem odd that everyone ended up dead, with no witnesses." She shrugged her shoulders. "But I suppose there have always been questions raised when someone popular and loved dies suddenly. Look at the murder of President Kennedy. The conspiracy theories still rumble on nearly one hundred and fifty years later!"

Joe made no immediate comment. He wasn't a big one for conspiracy theories. Accidents and incidents happened. He had personal experience of that. But suddenly he was sure President Harper's death wasn't the random tragedy that had been portrayed in the media.

*   *   *

Tony nodded in satisfaction. His grand daughter was doing him proud!

"What are you up to?" Justin enquired, appearing through the rainbow mist.

"Encouraging my grand daughter," he said honestly. "And Joe. I know I shouldn't. But they both need some seeds of honest doubt sown in their minds about Ted Rodriguez."

"You're not doing any thing that I'm not doing. I keep trying to reach Ted. He has sunk to such a low vibration that I don't think he can be reached from here. I'm not sure what I will be able to do for him when we reach Earth."

"You'll know, when we get there. I think we will soon be on our way. Listen, Artemis of Mars is speaking to Gaia of Earth."

"Sister Gaia, greetings! I am returning your children and I lend you some of mine for a season."

"Sister Artemis, greetings! I have waited a long time for these events. Up to now humanity has not deserved this. My sons

*have treated their brothers and sisters with violence and contempt
and my daughters have wept. My children have contemplated the
destruction of the planet and claimed that it would be a victory.
Your children travel to me to right the wrong that was done with
no malice. My children are ready to move on. They are ready to see
that they caged and cramped and twisted the essential teachings
of the Cosmic Masters such as Lord Buddha, Shri Krishna and
the Master Jesus. It is time for them to see the truth."*

*"Sister Gaia, the rainbow cannot travel with my children.
Will you ready yourself for their arrival?"*

*"Sister Artemis, it is my honour to make the preparations.
Together, we must right the wrongs done in the destruction of
Maldek, Lemuria and Atlantis, and ensure that such calamity
never happens again. This will be a truly momentous time in both
of our histories."*

Tony saw Simeon approaching.

"Can you hear music?" Simeon asked him. "It's very faint and like no
other music that I have ever heard before, but it is so . . . special."

"You are hearing the music of the planets, Simeon. You have a rare gift.
Not many humans are blessed with the ability to hear it."

"It's like a conversation in music; first one side, then the other."

"Yes. Mars and Earth are conversing. It will soon be time to return to
Earth."

*   *   *

Vicky hoped that it wasn't Mum and Dad calling yet again to see if
Jamie was awake. It wasn't. It was Michaela, her *BUSSTOP* colleague from
along the corridor at work.

"Brothers and sisters of the world unite!" she said cryptically.

"I'm not following," admitted Vicky, even though she knew Michaela
was a trade union official.

"We're taking industrial action—both sides of the Atlantic! We're
protesting about the way Mr Mortimer and Mr Dougall have been bundled
out. But this is also a shot across the bows for President Rodriguez after
the not-so-subtle threat he made on Friday night. If *BUSSTOP* America
goes, that's us gone too. We're on strike from nine o'clock tomorrow morning
GMT and Washington will follow on at nine o'clock Eastern Standard Time.
We're hoping that Mission Control will join in too. They should do! We're
not demonstrating or anything like that yet. We're all staying in our tents,

so to speak. How anyone could be so stupid as to dump two fine people like Mr Mortimer and Mr Dougall is beyond me."

Vicky agreed. She was pleased that she didn't have to think about work. It gave her time to sort out Jamie—if that was possible.

* * *

The Vice President of the United States, Henry Sargent, sat reading a book, apparently unruffled by having to wait to see the President. Inwardly he was fuming. The last time he sat like this, he was a naughty school pupil waiting to be summoned to the Principal's office.

"The President will see you now, sir," said a child masquerading as a White House aide.

President Ted Rodriguez was a thunderous presence behind his desk in the Oval Office.

"What is so damned important that I must see you on a Sunday afternoon?" he asked, each word punctuated by obvious annoyance.

"I have been trying to speak to you since Friday night," replied Sargent quite reasonably. "As you know, I was still in Paris at the end of my visit to the French President. I got up in the middle of the night French time to speak to you when a conscientious member of my staff woke me to inform me about your speech. Your staff said you were busy."

"I was. I'm sorry your beauty sleep was disturbed!" sneered Rodriguez.

"You wouldn't take my call," he continued, ignoring the remark. "I spent most of yesterday on a plane or at home still trying to speak to you. No one would connect me."

"Have you got a thing about me?"

Ted Rodriguez sat back and pouted provocatively.

Henry Sargent sprang up from his chair. Rodriguez copied him instinctively. Both men leaned forward, resting their hands on the desk between them.

"And because you would not take any of my calls, when I might have been able to advise you, unions in Britain and in this country have called a strike in *BUSSTOP* and Cape Canaveral Mission Control. You are aware of these developments, Mr President?"

The President was shaken to the core as they both sat down and he thought frantically. He had never expected a reaction like this from Sargent! Apart from being the obvious person to appoint as his Vice President, Henry Sargent had an enviable reputation. When he was working the crowds on a whistle-stop tour of Alabama, a woman spoke to Rodriguez about Sargent.

"Thank you, Mr President, for picking such a gen'leman to be your helper at this difficult time."

Sargent was quietly spoken, polite and his speech had a very English cadence to it. There was a patrician air about him. He was much shorter than Rodriguez and a good ten years older. Blue eyes watched the world keenly and his fading brown hair tumbled across his forehead. But as they squared up to each other in those moments of anger, he was like some invincible god of retribution, twelve feet tall and filling the room with energy. He was a dangerous enemy.

Bruce Dougall was right when he described Rodriguez as a street fighter of a politician. He was used to thinking his way out of a problem very quickly.

"Henry," he said affably. "Let's not get too heated about this. I can't be blamed if two people decide to resign."

"You pushed Bruce Dougall and that gave Prime Minister Crane the green light to do the same with Joe Mortimer! And your speech on Friday night! Who wrote it?"

"I did."

A less well-mannered person would have clapped a hand to his head in despair.

"Congratulations, Mr President. You've now got a work force in two countries going on strike."

"They'll never see it through."

"Tell me why not? You made it pretty plain in your speech that *BUSSTOP* has no future. As far as these folks are concerned, they have nothing to lose. What will you do when both *BUSSTOP* buildings and Mission Control stand empty?"

"I'll be pleased, because everyone will then see that we don't need them!"

Henry Sargent stood up decisively. In that moment he knew that some outlandish whispers he had heard, and thus far dismissed, about the President must be true.

"Thank you for your time, Mr President. I'm so sorry to have disturbed you on a Sunday afternoon."

Rodriguez couldn't believe his luck. Another pushover! Dougall had gone down without a fight. Now his own Vice President. This was becoming too easy.

He went back to the private wing of the White House with a spring in his step. Where was Mo? He went into the study. Sometimes she used the computer. He stopped dead. His computer was on. There was a note on the console. When he saw what was on the screen, he knew what would be in the letter before he read it.

*"Do you think that I didn't know about these young men?
And all the others whose pictures are no longer on record because
they have served their purpose? I was prepared to ignore them,
even Justin. He was the first after we got married, wasn't he?
That was the situation that hurt me the most of all. After that
first betrayal, nothing ever causes quite the same pain. But that
doesn't mean that I haven't felt betrayed and humiliated every
time. I have been your faithful wife all these years. Now you
have gone too far with your attacks on BUSSTOP and Bruce
Dougall. I hear chatter about Phoebe Harper's death. I wonder
about that too.*

*"I hoped that we might have children, but it was not to be.
Up to now I would have said it was a cause of great sadness
to me. Now I only feel relief. I don't have to explain to young
people just what sort of person their father has shown himself
to be.*

"Goodbye, and may you rot in Hell!"

Ted Rodriguez knew he was a careless fool. The last time he accessed
the file containing all the pictures, he must have shut down the file without
the security codes. And Mo had found the pictures of the boys.

And what were these whispers about Phoebe Harper's death?

He calmed himself by deciding he would call Lee.

*   *   *

It had been a weekend full of interesting interruptions. Kevin Crane
knew that this particular Friday night, Saturday and Sunday would have
to be put in the memoirs. Talking with Joe Mortimer on screen a couple of
hours previously had been most revealing, with Professor Hanson *still* very
much in evidence in Mr Mortimer's home. Well done Joe! He didn't think
anything could top that.

A late call from Vice President Henry Sargent did. The American
looked troubled.

"Henry! What can I do for you at this time of night?"

"I do apologise for the lateness of the hour with you, Prime Minister.
You are aware of the impending troubles at *BUSSTOP*?"

"I am indeed."

"It is very disturbing and entirely of the President's making. I'm hearing
other things about him too, which I won't go into for the moment. But the
man is shaping up into a monster. An . . . emotional psychopath! Tell me
one thing honestly, Kevin. Did you sack Joe Mortimer?"

"No. He can see which way the wind is blowing and he's angry on Bruce Dougall's behalf. I promise you that he resigned. There are various things that made him decide he had to go. Everyone thinks that I sacked him and he's being polite about it, like Bruce Dougall."

"Okay. I need to have a little chat with you about that."

Chapter Twenty-One

Monday morning appeared with all the promise of the usual grey, drab winter's day. Towards the end of January, there were supposed to be the first signs of spring. And indeed, snowdrops like those presented to Irene dusted many woodland and domestic settings. Even in this sullen time, there was the stirring of new life, aided by a milder spell of weather. Apart from the brief visitation of snow on the Friday, this had been a much kinder winter so far in Britain.

Some individuals were far too preoccupied to notice what Nature was or wasn't doing. Vicky Tennant awoke to remember two things. She was on strike from today and Jamie was so much better. A long stretch of sleep and being physically removed from Washington D.C were combining to do the trick. She looked forward to having a long chat with him later in the day. But Mum and Dad would be calling round first.

*   *   *

Irene woke for a second morning with Joe. It was wonderful, and right.

"I'm glad you're here, for all sorts of reasons," said Joe.

He didn't need to say any more. Irene realised that it was just dawning on him what he had done. He had no job to go to this morning, or any morning for that matter. She spent a few minutes contacting college to explain why she would be late in. She was honest. She was at Joe's house and she was waiting for the media crowd to be moved on. Apart from anything else, there was no point in concocting some elaborate story when the simple truth could soon be discovered.

"I haven't got any teaching commitments first thing this morning," she said to Joe.

"Have you committed a sackable offence?" he wondered. "Admitting that you will be late into work, I mean. You can join me. Everyone seems convinced that I've been given the heave-ho, like Bruce. It's odd that Kevin Crane is not putting the record straight. He must have his reasons."

The Prime Minister was British villain Number One, in the newspapers and on the television.

Joe and Irene watched the breakfast programmes. There were scenes from outside London *BUSSTOP*. The front of the building was thronging with reporters and camera crews. There was no one else there. Even the early morning cleaning shift had not turned up. It made for an impressive show of solidarity.

The overnight news from America was even more encouraging. Everyone in Mission Control had decided to join the protest. They had nothing to lose either. They had sat through a miserable day when *Ariadne One* should have returned. There was little point in continuing the monitoring for the lost spaceship and the automated comm check was now discontinued.

This was when the world of space exploration really began to hurt. In the heat and panic of the tragedy, in the scanning of the heavens for any sign of *Ariadne One,* in the planning and execution of the memorial service, hands and minds were kept busy. Reality was creeping up on everyone and no one was in any mood for a President and a Prime Minister who treated their Zeus space stars in such a cavalier fashion. They couldn't do anything more for the Ariadne team, but they were damned if they would let Joe and Bruce be dumped so unceremoniously.

Irene received a message at about half past nine that the reporters had slunk away from her house reluctantly.

"I'll thank Kevin Crane for you," Joe promised. "I'd better drive you home and then you can whiz over to Cambridge and report for duty at college."

"Are you trying to get rid of me?" Irene wondered.

"No! I just don't want you joining the unemployed list along with me."

Joe calculated that Irene could not have been in college for more than half an hour when she contacted him.

"I'm flattered, Irene, that you can't go too long without talking to me!" he joked. "But isn't this a bit quick? Shouldn't you be tutoring Britain's finest young brains?"

"Half the college has woken up this morning coughing and sneezing at the other half," she replied. "I hope that I have cast iron immunity after my illness at Christmas and New Year. My students are languishing. Are you doing anything important?"

"I'm replying to some of the goodwill messages that are cluttering up my communications system here. The media can't get at me and I wouldn't say anything on principal anyway. I'm enjoying a bit of peace and quiet for a change. Why do you ask?"

"Could you come over to college and see me?"

"Wow!" His face lit up. "Every man's fantasy! Have I landed myself a beautiful woman who is also a sex maniac? Aren't I the lucky one!"

"Don't mock me, Joe!"

Her words took him back to that first meeting, when he drove over to Cambridge from *BUSSTOP*. The words were pretty much the same, except that then it was *Mr Mortimer*, not *Joe*. The steely glance and the sharp yet slightly worried tone were exactly the same.

"Sorry, Irene." He pulled himself together. "That was juvenile. What's happened?"

"There's something I want you to see. Well, hear mainly. Please."

"I'm on my way."

He remembered that first occasion. He had gone haring over to the college, not knowing exactly why he was going there. He had been struggling with a rare hangover, if memory served him right. Irene had said it was important to the Ariadne mission. She had then played him the transmissions that she had tracked from Mars, using Attila-running-Heinrich.

Joe felt his arms coming up in goose bumps and the hairs on the back of his neck were crawling. Surely not!

*   *   *

Kevin Crane was glad that this was a quiet morning within Ten Downing Street. Out in the real world he knew that he was being shredded by the media and gossiped about in every workplace in the land. But he judged that he could ride out this storm. It was best to say no more about Joe's departure because that would only lead to further speculative stories. The *BUSSTOP* boss—correction, ex-boss—had enough on his plate with the thoughts that were torturing him. The Prime Minister wrote himself a note as a reminder to get Joe over for a proper talk. When the world saw Joe Mortimer walk through the door of Number Ten Downing Street, to the accompaniment of an appropriate press release about his inclusion in the Ariadne inquiry team, it would settle down again.

Having given the authorisation that would sort out the media who were besieging Professor Hanson's property, he was supposed to be reading and annotating papers. Within a few minutes he had given up and put his pen down. The dream would not leave him alone.

Crane accepted that everyone dreamed every night. REM sleep was vital for health. He was one of these people who never remembered dreams. He knew a couple who recorded the events of their dream world in a journal, in luxurious detail. He had envied them, up until now. Be careful what you wish for . . .

He must have spoken out loud during the night-time experience because he heard his wife asking him if he was all right. The events that filled his mind were so powerful that he did not wake.

The air was filled with a misty rainbow. Figures approached him, people whom he didn't recognise. They introduced themselves as Tony, Justin, Sally and Ichiro.

"We are bringing them home," said the one named Tony.

Behind the four he saw the seven astronauts from *Ariadne One*. He started to walk towards them but Tony barred his way.

"They are not quite yours yet, Kevin. They will be. Only have patience."

"They're dead!"

"You think they are. How little you understand at present, and yet how great is your potential ability. We are bringing them home. Don't forget. We are bringing them home."

Alone in the Cabinet Room, the Prime Minister could hear those voices so clearly again and see the missing team in every detail. His glasses slid down his nose as he broke out in a cold sweat. It had been so real. It *was* so real. The crew of *Ariadne One* was there! But where?

There was a knock on the door. The Cabinet Secretary bustled in.

"Prime Minister! Why haven't you put out some kind of statement making it clear that you didn't dismiss—. Oh! You look as though you've seen a ghost!"

"I think I have. Seven ghosts to be precise."

"Prime Minister?"

"Never mind."

*　　*　　*

Within the privacy of the computer lab, Joe put his arms round Irene.

"You're shaking!" he exclaimed.

"It was a shock," she admitted. "I don't know what made me do it. I listened in on Mars, just like I did before. This is what I picked up."

The rhythmic pulses of a signal could be heard once again. More Random Error Code? How? Why? From where? But as Joe listened, he found he was hearing groups of letters that made sense.

"Replay once more, Irene."

He indicated that he needed something to write on. Automatically she handed him paper and a pencil and he began to write down the dots and dashes of Morse Code.

●●/●—●/●/●—●/● ●——/● ●—/●—●/● —●—●/——
—/— —/●●/—●/— —●●●●●/—— —/— —/●

"Not more Random Error Code?" she asked despairingly.

"No"

Joe was finding it difficult to believe what was on the paper in front of him.

"Then what is it?"

"It's conventional Morse Code, so I can make sense of it."

"What does it say?" she demanded.

"I don't think you want to know."

"Joe!"

"Okay, then. The message reads *Irene we are coming home.*"

Joe watched the colour drain from her face. He stepped in close and held her.

"Easy now," he soothed. "I thought you were about to faint,"

"Bless you, Joe. I'm not a fainting person. I wouldn't know how to go about it." Their eyes met. "And I don't know what to do about this."

*   *   *

Vicky and Jamie felt as though they had been through a wind tunnel. Their parents had blown in on a gale of concern and questions. Eventually Danny Tennant could see that they might be doing more harm than good.

"Mary, love, I think we should give it a rest for now. Jamie still looks very tired. Vicky, we'll do that shopping for you and bring it back this evening. How about that?"

"I thought they would never go!" Jamie sighed when his sister returned from escorting them as far as the lift to ensure that they were not just leaving her flat, but really were leaving the Gravely House complex in Barnet completely.

"They're just concerned. We wouldn't like it if they weren't. Now then, this film record you made of the accident."

Vicky set it up to play through the communications system.

"The quality isn't all that good," Jamie said anxiously.

"Jamie! I think you were more concerned with saving lives than making an Oscar-winner!"

The film began with the jerky motions of the person who was carrying the communicator running to the scene of the accident. Jamie's voice could be heard, using the outline script that had become known as the Good Samaritan Protocol, identifying himself and his qualifications, stating where he was, at what time, and his first impressions of what had happened. This convention for those helping at the scene of an incident had been in operation for some years. The record was often useful to local police and accident investigators, and medical people saw it as a legitimate way of protecting their backsides from later legal action that might be taken by relatives.

"There has been an impact between a lorry and a limousine. The lorry driver is climbing down from his cab. It looks like the lorry has had a tyre blow out, causing it to swerve." In the lights of the Beltway, a figure could be seen easing his way down to the ground slowly. "In the limousine the driver, male, is dead. A male in the back of the vehicle also appears to be dead. The female passenger pinned under his body is alive." The mini camera worked across the scene at a respectful distance. "I am ceasing recording to verify all this and to give what assistance I can."

The lorry driver could be heard in the background saying that he would call 911.

"Very professional, Jamie," Vicky murmured.

"Thanks," he said after a bout of coughing. "Training means that you go into an automatic mode. The remainder of the film shows us waiting for the emergency services."

Vicky watched intently. Two corpses were laid out on the side of the road, their upper torsos and heads covered with their own jackets. Obviously the driver and the bodyguard. The lorry driver was stretched out on the roadside next to his vehicle, his high-visibility vest folded to make a very flat pillow. He waved when he knew he was being filmed.

"I'm okay!" he called out. "The doc says that possible head injuries should lie down."

Phoebe Harper was also prone, her knees raised and supported in that position by some old cushions Jamie found in the back of his car.

"You had time to do all that?" Vicky wondered.

"I've learned to work at maximum speed at Clinton," said Jamie. "But the emergency services did take a very long time to show. I was thinking about giving them another call. The local cops and the first ambulance arrived when I was putting my stuff back in my car. When I saw the kind of guns the paramedics were toting, I knew that this was trouble. One of them asked me if I had helped. I said yes. I was elbowed out of the way and I took that as the hint to leave. I was expecting a knock on the door for days afterwards but obviously no one bothered to take down my car licence plate. They were more interested in the accident."

"It was the President, Jamie."

"But all the more reason to know who had been attending her, surely. I put Mrs Harper down on the ground because she was complaining of abdominal pain. It was a precaution. I couldn't find any obvious cause of the pain. I think she was badly bruised, thrown against the seatbelt. I've seen that many times both here and in D.C.—a car crash patient with a perfect bruise imprint of the seatbelt across the chest and abdomen."

"Did you realise it was the President?"

"Not to begin with. I did when she spoke. As you know, she had a very distinctive Southern accent. But the thing is, sis, those two people were alive and kicking when I left. What happened? And what do we do now?"

Vicky smiled wryly.

"As my former boss would say: oh bugger!"

"Very helpful."

"He might be our man, little brother."

* * *

"What?"

President Ted Rodriguez could hardly believe his ears. Bill Francioni spoke again with barely disguised irritability. Although Phoebe Harper could be a pain in the butt, she had always been on the ball.

"Representatives of the Seminole Tribe of Florida and the Miccosukee Tribe of Indians of Florida have appeared within the grounds of Mission Control at Cape Canaveral overnight. They are camped on either side of the runway that is used by our returning spacecraft. In case you are not familiar with the Native Americans of the area, these two groups make up the majority of the Seminole nation."

"Okay, skip the school lesson!" said the President grumpily. "What are they doing there, and how the hell did they get on site? What were the security people doing?"

"You must speak to head of security yourself, Mr President. He's as puzzled as we are as to how they went past all the checks. Part of the reason we have brought this to your attention is because of the statement that their leader has given about why they are there."

"And why are they there?" said Rodriguez, with inexplicable foreboding. Francioni braced himself.

"The leaders say that the Seminole are waiting for them to come home. They can't come home unnoticed. When the local police chief asked who *they* might be, the reply was 'The astronauts, of course.'"

The White House old-timer waited for the explosion, which never came.

"That's different," muttered Rodriguez, totally floored. "Is there any chance that the local LEOs can just run them out of town?"

"Not unless you want the eyes of the world watching, Mr President. Local and national television are already there. We reckon that the BBC will be there within ten minutes and after that—who knows? News Land is on track to give everybody a ringside seat. I'm sure that we can find them on television somewhere."

Bill Francioni struck gold straight away on the Oval Office screen. The man being interviewed was identified in the caption as *Martin, a spokesman for the Seminole nation.*

"Not very Indian-sounding," commented the President.

Bill Francioni cringed inwardly. This man was becoming a liability!

"The Seminole have English names as well as names reflecting their own culture. The Seminole are one of the most successful Native American groups when it comes to being part of today's world and yet retaining that culture. What did you expect, Mr President? Big Chief Sitting Bull decorated in beads and feathers? These are people of the modern age, as well as being representatives of an ancient way of life. The Miccosukee own a casino in addition to the 'Indian Village' where they educate people about their pre-Colombian way of life. As a group, the Seminole purchased the *Hard Rock Café* chain of restaurants early in the last century. They have fingers in plenty of commercial pies."

Martin was answering questions patiently.

"How long will we stay? We will stay as long as we are called to. I have brought members of my family and the family of a friend. We need nothing more. We do not have an obsession with time as so many do. We have no words in our language for such portions of time as *second, minute* and *hour.* Mission Control is empty. Its workers are on strike. We have heard the word. We answered the call that went out. We had no choice but to travel. They cannot return home and find no one here to welcome them."

"Martin," said the interviewer. "By *they* you mean . . . ?"

"The astronauts of *Ariadne One.* We have heard the messages. Some of us have come here to welcome them home."

The camera ranged over their tents. On all of them was fixed the sign *The Unconquered People.*

"They're mad!" exclaimed Rodriguez.

"I can't comment on that, Mr President," said Bill Francioni. "I'm giving you the facts as they are. About fifty Seminole are waiting for the astronauts to come home."

The President buried his head in his hands. On top of Mo leaving him, this was just too much. Nobody knew that she had left him, presumably for good. He was hiding behind a story, telling everyone about a friend needing her in some crisis. But how long could he keep that one going? Mo had turned herself into a pretty active First Lady and it wouldn't be long before questions were asked about where she was.

*　　*　　*

"Now how did you manage that?" Simeon demanded of Tony. "Putting us all in a dream for the Prime Minister of Great Britain and then those Seminole people waiting at Cape Canaveral?"

The astronauts' Martian teacher and friend smiled.

"Those who can hear the messages will hear them," he said serenely. "I should have spotted the latent ability within Kevin Crane sooner. He and his public face disguise have become virtually interchangeable. He has become very skilled at concealing the real person. He learned the basis of that very early, when his brother had to move on prematurely to the next stage of his life."

By way of an explanation of that last comment, Simeon was given the sight of the blazing wreckage of a plane, followed by a younger version of the Prime Minister saluting, reassuring and welcoming members of the armed forces who had died in service. He took a step back, as if trying to distance himself physically from the pictures.

"That was stupid!" he admitted. "I'm still getting used to seeing this stuff."

"I know you are," Tony replied proudly, "and you're doing very well. Anyway, some of our links are not very receptive at the moment. Bruce Dougall needs time to gather himself, in mind and body. Joe Mortimer has distractions, obvious and not so obvious. My grand daughter . . ."

He searched for a suitable phrase.

"She's all loved up?" Simeon suggested.

"That will do until I can think of something better. But put her with those computers and she is soon back on track. She couldn't resist listening in on us again so I sent her a message where, this time, there could be no mistake. I knew someone would do the honours and translate. I'm delighted that it was Joe. That was how it all began, with my first messages in Random Error Code."

"You sent those first messages, which Professor Hanson told everyone about?" asked Emily, appearing at Simeon's side.

"Of course," said Tony. "I had to make sure that somebody was listening. Somebody was." He considered how everything had meshed together so beautifully. "And it couldn't have been anyone else."

"So where do the Seminole come into this?" Simeon wanted to know, having lost track of the conversation.

"I can't control everything. As I said, those who can hear the messages will hear them. They were receptive. Our links will have to be told at another time. You will be flying *Ariadne One* back to the Mission Control runway. So that is where the Seminole have gathered."

* * *

Day One of the *BUSSTOP* and Mission Control protest ticked by on both sides of the Atlantic. Not much happened, apart from the mysterious appearance of the Seminole at Mission Control. That wasn't in the script. Not much was supposed to happen, seeing as all employees were staying out of sight. Kevin Crane spoke at length to waiting media people when he emerged from Number Ten to attend the House of Commons in the afternoon. He made it very plain that his sympathies were totally with the absent *BUSSTOP* people, which was a bit confusing seeing as he would make no comment on the departure of Joe Mortimer.

"You know the sequence of events that took place on Friday evening, when Mr Mortimer resigned" he said.

"But do we, Prime Minister?" someone called out.

"Don't you?" he parried as he got into his car.

Joe's visit to Downing Street couldn't come quickly enough.

Day Two and President Rodriguez made a mutinous but quiet situation worse. When asked in a routine press call about the one hundred per cent absence from *BUSSTOP* and Mission Control, he smiled with total insincerity.

"What about it? The country doesn't need these people. If you listen quietly, you can hear them digging their own graves."

Aides looked at one another and the press corps was a little taken aback. But the questions kept rolling

"Mr. President, what do you make of the Seminole presence at Cape Canaveral and the assertion that they are waiting for the Ariadne astronauts to come home? Do the Seminole people know something that we don't?"

"Some folks will do anything for publicity. The way I see it, the strike at Mission Control is just an excuse for them to develop *The Martin and Seminole People* show."

This was a car crash media meeting. For a few seconds Bill Francioni wondered how he could intervene and prevent this spiralling down from bad to worse. He thought briefly about wrestling the President to the ground. That was not a good idea with armed Secret Service personnel dotted around. You only had to look at the President in the wrong way for more than about ten seconds and you could hear those jokers taking aim. All he could do was pray that this session would soon be over. He was almost past caring about salvaging anything for Rodriguez. Apparently listening to every word, he was evaluating his retirement package.

Ted Rodriguez was touching on a newly rediscovered raw nerve of the United States of America. With Martin and his followers turning into an unexpected focus of this bizarre situation, many took it upon themselves to consult their computer files and find out about the history of the Seminole Nation. It did not make for pretty reading.

In the three Seminole Wars of the first half of the nineteenth century, the American government waged a long-running battle against the Seminole people in Florida, costing thousands of lives and millions of dollars. At the end of the third war, in 1842, many Native Americans were forcibly exiled to live west of the Mississippi. But in the end the government could not overcome the Seminole who had retreated into the Everglades. They were left in peace. Eventually the phrase *The Unconquered People* would become a kind of motto—because that's exactly what they were.

Those who were interested were reading about Seminole leader Osceola and getting to know Halleck Tustunuggee and Jumper. Then there were Black Seminoles like Abraham and John Horse. This was another bone of contention leading to the wars. The Seminole harboured and protected runaway slaves.

*   *   *

Bruce could only laugh at the man who had reduced him to total despair only days earlier. He was feeling positive after an unexpectedly good report from Doctor Doherty, who concluded that stress had caused most of his symptoms, not any real alteration in the state of the cancer. It was a case of laughing or being appalled that the supposedly educated leader of the foremost nation in the world could be so insensitive.

"Rodriguez could write a book!" he chuckled to Shannon. "How to Upset People. It might be a best seller like yours. In one silly sentence he has alienated all Native Americans and when the African American population realises how the Seminole helped fugitive slaves, no one there will be best pleased either."

Shannon agreed with him wholeheartedly. But for her, the best bit was hearing Bruce laugh like that. It was music to her ears.

"You pity him, don't you?" she asked.

"I think I do. I'll tell you for sure later. But I'll tell you this. American presidents have been assassinated for less."

Bruce had shared with her his thoughts on shooting Philemon Brown. Her reaction was predictable.

"Bruce! Stop it!" she began.

Then she saw him wink at her.

This was the Bruce she knew twenty-five years ago.

* * *

The trespassers on Mission Control land continued to fascinate the nation, and then the world. No one thought about trying to move them. When Ted Rodriguez testily demanded of the local chief of police why she wasn't doing something about the illegal occupation of government land, he was given short shrift.

"Mr President, if you are so concerned about them cluttering up the runway, you come down here and do something about it yourself!"

The Seminole group were not on the runway. They had created two camps, on the grass, either side of the runway. Police were in evidence, mainly to ensure that press and television people behaved themselves. The Native Americans greeted these observers of their actions with total courtesy and hospitality. They offered weary reporters food and drink. They were seemingly oblivious to the mechanical gaze of so many cameras. One young woman took everyone's eye. Tall, well made, her long black hair braided neatly, she moved amongst the media camp with refreshments. But all kept returning to Martin. He could have been any age. His face was beyond petty matters like time, with high cheekbones and an aquiline nose. Apart from fine lines around his eyes caused by too much squinting into the sun, his brown skin was unmarked and his expression untroubled. His straight dark hair was tied back with a strip of leather. Like the entire group, he wore modern clothes. But his dignity and bearing marked him out. He was the natural leader and head of his family. "It's as if," said one reporter, "we are occupying the place illegally, not them."

Which was probably true. Florida was originally Seminole land.

Watching the television coverage, Joe and Bruce noticed the same thing. The Seminole had set up their camp at the spot where the returning Zeus spacecraft generally came to a halt.

"Except *Zeus Two*," Bruce reminisced to Shannon. "For some reason Joe let me bring her in that time. It was entirely my fault. A perfect, sunny day and I let her drift a tad too far along the runway before putting her down on the tarmac. So I couldn't blame the weather. The craft looks like a plane and handles like one once you're down into the atmosphere but, unlike flying a plane, you can't go around and get your shi—sorry, your stuff together to do it again if you've screwed up the approach. Well, I didn't screw it up exactly. The people waiting for us had to walk a bit. I'm sure it didn't kill them."

Shannon remembered the incident clearly, but she wasn't about to spoil things by reminding him of that. She had mixed memories of waiting in the building at the end of that runway, put in place as part of the rationalisation that took place when *BUSSTOP* took over space exploration. The whole site had been cleared and levelled off, enabling take off, landing and Mission Control to be contained within the one complex.

*　　*　　*

Joe was remembering similar things with Irene.

"It's as if the Seminole know exactly where to be," Irene marvelled.

They watched live television pictures from the Cape Canaveral runway. Joe shook his head. He could almost see *Ariadne One* swooping down out of the sky, with representatives of the Seminole Nation providing an unusual guard of honour.

Joe's personal communicator sounded. He groaned.

"I shall start leaving this thing at home!"

Irene moved to clear away coffee cups but she couldn't help hearing part of the conversation Joe was having with a woman. She thought she recognised the voice.

"I see, Vicky," Joe was saying. "I'm at Professor Hanson's house. Hold on a moment. Irene!" She emerged from the kitchen. "D'you mind a couple of unexpected visitors? Can I be rude and invite my PA Vicky and her brother here? They have some important information that they think I can help them with. Would you like to speak to her?"

Irene held a brief conversation with Vicky and then moved over to the communications console to send instructions on how to reach her house.

"I'm forever doing this," she said to Joe. "You'd be amazed at how many people end up getting lost coming here."

"Your house is easy enough to find."

"I'd be worried if you couldn't find it! You found your way to Mars."

"I almost wish I was flying there now, with you as my right hand woman, naturally. I'm sure Bruce wouldn't mind being demoted for this flight. Then we could find out what's going on with the message. It doesn't make any sense. And yet . . ."

He glanced back at the television. The Seminole insisted that they were waiting for the astronauts to return home. The personal message for Irene was plain enough. *Irene we are coming home.*

Joe couldn't wait for Vicky and her brother to arrive. It would distract him from the crazy thoughts that were spilling out from the corners of his mind.

*　　*　　*

Hagar Turner looked out of the window. This was good. Plenty of people in the house. This was how it was meant to be. As well as Simeon's parents, Emily's father was here too. He seemed so *lost*. Hagar would have taken him in anyway, even without Emily's relationship with Simeon.

She felt a sudden glow of certainty within her. The scene outside the window was bathed in extra light.

"We're waiting," she said.

*   *   *

The sun had dipped behind the hills and mountains hours ago. Paola Scarlino stood looking up at the stars and the moon, which was riding on a fluffy cloud.

"*I wish I could take you there*," Gianfranco had often said when they stood here by the lake watching the moon. "*It's beautiful, if you can call anything so barren beautiful.*"

The waters of Lake Maggiore lapped sluggishly a few feet away. She turned and looked at the looming bulk of Pallanza immediately behind her. Inexplicably, the lakeside town looked bigger, blacker, and more important.

"I'm waiting," she said.

*   *   *

Georgina Hammond knew that the children should have been in bed long since. She still felt incapable of organising any recognisable domestic routine back in England and there was method in her madness. If she kept the children running around long enough, they slept solidly when they did reach bed and didn't wake in the night asking for Daddy. Also, more time filled with the noise of the youngsters meant less time in silence for her.

Fred and Susie came roaring in.

"Mummy!" Fred began indignantly. "Susie won't play properly!"

Georgina put an arm round both children and hugged them fiercely. She had these lovely little people, her children, Brian's children, *their* children. She felt sad for the partners of the other astronauts. They had a fistful of memories. Precious enough, but not a living legacy of love like these two.

"Mummy," said Fred, twirling a lock of her hair round his fingers. "When is Daddy coming home?"

Georgina had tried to explain. She had taken professional advice on what to say. She knew her children. She wasn't reaching them with what she was telling them.

She looked at them. The lamplight cast an aura about both of them, which startled her to begin with.

"We're waiting," she said with complete certainty.

*　　*　　*

David Templar put down his book. Tonight the words were blurring together, scampering across the pages like mischievous children. He couldn't concentrate.

"*You must keep up your studies!*" he could hear Masahide scolding him.

What was the point? What was the point of anything anymore? What was the point even of their cosy little house here in Lincoln?

Restless, he went to the back door and stepped out into the garden. It was late and in the frosty sky the stars were particularly bright. He picked out the various communications satellites that Masahide had named for him in the past. He was getting pretty good at identifying the major constellations now. Masahide would have been proud of him.

Correction. Masahide *was* proud of him. He knew that with a certainty that worked its way up through his body in a wave of warmth.

"I'm waiting," he said.

*　　*　　*

Leah Grant was talking to Kate Simmons on screen. They had become bonded through loss. Leah still cried when she thought for too long about Jackson, and Kate continued to find it difficult to come to terms with what had happened to Jethro. She replayed many times the film of the moments when he became the second person to step onto the surface of Mars. But the two women bolstered each other and spoke daily.

"I'm so much stronger today," observed Leah.

"I was about to say that!" exclaimed Kate.

They recognised something in each other's eyes, even if they didn't know what it was.

"I'm waiting," said Leah.

"I'm waiting too," said Kate.

Chapter Twenty-Two

There was confusion on both sides of the Atlantic. Everyone had had the chance to draw breath and take stock of what was happening. No one was quite sure what came next.

A whole work force was on strike. It had been done quietly and with no fuss. No one was being inconvenienced so far apart from the *BUSSTOP* and Mission Control employees themselves, who were now receiving no pay. There was no doubt that a hundred and one rules and regulations had been broken. There had been no ballot of union members. No official notice of intent to strike was given. But the total adherence to the call for industrial action was validation enough in the eyes of trades' union leaders. No one was locked out. Security personnel were ready to swallow hard and open up buildings for anyone who wanted to turn up for work. No one had any intention of doing that.

And there was popular support across both countries. The mood music said that President Rodriguez set the tone in his address to the nation by stating, however obliquely, that *BUSSTOP*'s days were done. The people within the organisation were registering their protest about this and about the abrupt departure of Joe Mortimer and Bruce Dougall in the only way open. So good luck to them!

Kevin Crane was inclined to take this view. He was furious with the President for dropping everyone into such a tricky hole but he wasn't about to waste time on a lost cause. He concentrated on what he might be able to do, which was to sort out the problems this was creating in Britain.

He was acutely aware of the possible knock-on effects that could arise if this action continued for long—especially the contracts for supplies and other external services that would suddenly be terminated. The recipients of information and knowledge gleaned from the space industry experience would find their own developments curtailed. Crane could sense the unrest rippling out into the wider arena. He would have to keep alert for the warning signs of further trouble.

"So what would be a good course of action?" he said to those within government who were insisting that 'something' must be done. "Tell me. My mind is a total blank. All suggestions gratefully received."

Cabinet members were equally blank.

The think tanks didn't seem able to think.

"Advise me," he demanded of the leading civil servants.

There had been a frantic checking of the legislation that brought *BUSSTOP* into being in Britain. It was agreed from the outset that *BUSSTOP* would have no overt military links. Whilst individuals might be poached from the Armed Services, especially the RAF because of the skills that they would bring with them, everyone from Joe Mortimer downwards was effectively a civil servant.

Kevin Crane was increasingly annoyed with the senior officials who trooped in and out to see him. All they were offering was waffle.

"There are thousands of you sitting in offices in Whitehall and across the country and not one of you can come up with a single sensible sentence," he concluded in an abrasive tone. "Do we just ignore it all and let these skilled people drift along, in the hope that everything will come right magically? Can you discipline a whole group of people? I suppose you can. But they know that they are losing their jobs in the long run, so what's the point? They are not being paid. I don't know what else can be done. I suppose its possible to drag them through the legal system but I'd love to see how even the most enterprising legal teams batting for H.M. Government could put hundreds of people in the dock. They have committed no criminal offence."

Similar conversations were taking place in Washington D.C. The major difference was that President Rodriguez had no sympathy whatsoever for the *BUSSTOP* people.

White House advisers who were desperate to stay in post made sure they found the answers that Rodriguez wanted to hear.

"Mr President, the Supreme Court ruling in the case of *Jedidiah Clawson Construction v. John Stringer* in 2101 is the most recent validation of the fact that a whole work force can be dismissed for breach of contract. We would suggest that employees at *BUSSTOP* and Mission Control fall under that category. We further suggest that Mission Control workers could be putting the country in danger because they are not carrying out their secondary task of monitoring space for the arrival of any extra terrestrials. Whilst they are not the only facility watching the skies, they are a part of the system. Remember the 1947 London agreement."

The President was not likely to forget it. He had been briefed on it and was surprised to find that it existed.

"Oh, and whilst we are on the subject, Mr President, if you'd like to sign these documents, we can start the inquiry into the *Ariadne One* disaster. There was overwhelming Congressional approval for the Board of Inquiry."

Ted Rodriguez would have been very surprised if there *wasn't* overwhelming approval. Bob Broomfield had spent enough time, money and effort massaging whole groups of people into seeing where their loyalties lay for the inquiry into the death of President Harper. They should be neat and dandy for the Ariadne showpiece without any extra trouble. Broomfield knew his job. When he said 'Jump', those under his watchful eye replied "How high, how far and in which direction?"

Rodriguez had to stop himself showing too much relish in front of an audience as he scrawled his signature in the appropriate places.

A Presidential Board of Inquiry was a relatively new weapon in the armoury of federal government. It was brought into being at the end of the previous century after other forms of fact-finding commission were falling into disrepute. He was looking forward to fetching this toy out of the box for some proper use. The Harper Board of Inquiry was being used simply to rubber stamp the accepted version of events surrounding the death of his predecessor. It was receiving minimal, routine media coverage. He anticipated the *Ariadne One* inquiry producing a lot more fun. It was an unexpected gift, a thorough try out of a Board.

He savoured the prospect of Bruce Dougall being put on the stand. He had never met the man face to face but he hated him. *He* should have been in space, not Dougall—a rich kid with too much money in his pockets. Joe Mortimer could be called to give evidence. He was told that those two didn't get on. This could be . . . interesting. With a bit of luck they would cut each other's throats and save the Board a lot of work.

Within hours it was announced that every *BUSSTOP* and Mission Control worker in the United States of America was now officially out of a job. A notice using the form of words validated by that 2101 court case would be sent to each person.

"So this is how it ends," Hagar Turner said to her brother.

"You don't seem all that bothered," replied Ishmael.

He wolfed down the remainder of the lunch that Hagar had prepared for him. Grief had affected him in many ways. He was permanently weary-looking. Like his sister, he was tall and well built. Since the disappearance of *Ariadne One* he seemed to have shrunk. His exuberant energy was dissipated and his movements were slower and more deliberate. The odd dab of grey in his hair was becoming an inexorable tide. But one thing that hadn't changed was his appetite.

"I'm not bothered, Ishmael. Because in every ending there is a beginning. And this will be a beginning that the world will remember forever."

Ishmael only half-listened. Since Hagar could first put a string of words together, she had said weird things that didn't make a lot of sense. He remembered an incident, which he hadn't thought about in a long while. Hagar would have been about five years old. The family were driving past the Children's Wing of the local hospital, which had stood proudly on the same site for many years, evolving gradually in ongoing modernisation.

"This is where I came when I died," stated Hagar.

The car had done a quick detour up onto the sidewalk and back down again whilst their father composed himself. Everyone was so shaken by what Hagar said that no one dared ask her what she meant. Ishmael knew that Dad often used to drive by the hospital after that, when the quickest route didn't take them that way. He must have been hoping that she would broach the subject once more. Hagar never said another word about it.

Yes, his sister Hagar had always been *different*. She lived alone and yet people were drawn to her like iron filings to a magnet. So many held her in the highest regard. He knew that since his promotion to being head of *BUSSTOP* America, Bruce Dougall looked upon her as a very special *confidante*. What could Mr Dougall do now to help? He was out of a job too.

"I have a mind to go over to Mission Control to speak to our visitors," she announced when the meal was finished. "Would you like to come along for the ride?"

"Hagar! They won't let you in. Whilst no one is forcing the Seminole to leave, the general public is not being allowed anywhere near them."

Hagar only smiled that smile.

"Are you coming with me or not?"

Cameras fixed on Hagar's car in a reflex action when she drove into the West Side car park, which was close to the perimeter gate leading to the runway and the Seminole encampment. The media people couldn't believe their luck.

"Miss Turner! Hagar! Why are you here? How are you feeling Mr Turner?"

Ishmael walked behind her, pretending that this was nothing to do with him.

"I've come to see my brothers and sisters, of course," she told them.

As Ishmael had predicted, the men and women of the security team weren't having any of it.

"I'm sorry ma'am. No one is allowed in. Not even you."

"Really? What a pity."

She was unruffled and looked at a figure walking towards the wire from the other side.

"Greetings!" called Martin from a distance. "Officer, why aren't you letting my friends in?"

"You know Hagar Turner?" a security guard asked incredulously.

"I have been awaiting my sister and my brother for a long time," replied Martin. "Welcome to you both!"

Under strict instructions to do nothing that would damage the goodwill surrounding this incident, the guards had no choice but to open the gate and let Hagar and Ishmael through.

*   *   *

Vicky Tennant was left with plenty of food for thought following her visit to her former boss. And it wasn't all to do with where to take Jamie's film evidence from President Harper's car crash.

As soon as Joe Mortimer answered her call and said he was at Professor Hanson's house, she knew. When she saw him with Irene, she knew she was right. Those two had the makings of a formidable couple and they were well on their way already. Vicky bowed to the inevitable and accepted that she would never be of any romantic interest to her boss. She could admit to herself now that she was only ever in that position in her own mind. To Mr Mortimer she was an efficient part of the office set up, nothing more. At last she understood the motivation for his gift of the perfume. Naturally, he was devastated by the loss of *Ariadne One*. Everyone was. What everyone did with those feelings was more individual. Vicky recognised the same quirky personality trait that also belonged to her uncle. When Geoffrey had been through some difficult time, he liked to buy treats for those around him and for himself. If he was able to react with pleasure to his own indulgences and enjoy the happiness that he gave others, it was an indication that he was still alive and he must be thankful for it.

Mr Mortimer's advice was simple, direct and very useful. It had taken Vicky all her courage to contact him and when he said where he was, that courage nearly failed her. She went through with it for her brother, for a little lady from Laurel, Mississippi and for an unknown lorry driver who made someone his wife and left her as a widow within weeks. She was so glad that she stuck to her guns.

All four of them watched the film intently, seated in Irene's living room. Vicky found herself noticing little details that had escaped her in the first viewing. Out of the corner of her eye, she saw Mr Mortimer making notes. He was taking this very seriously. Irene's eyes never left the screen. Vicky gave Jamie a secret thumbs up sign in the break in the film record.

"You had great presence of mind to do that filming, Jamie," Joe said at the end.

"It's one of those things that's drilled into students at medical school nowadays," Jamie replied modestly. "It's what you do if you come across some kind of incident. I'm sure that certain routines were hammered into you, sir, when you were in the RAF and then when you were an astronaut."

"That's for sure. And let's have less of the *sir*, Jamie. I never warranted it when I was in *BUSSTOP*. I'm a private citizen now and I'm Joe. Anyway, to business. To start with, you've got two people there who look in pretty good shape. According to official records, the lorry driver was dead at the scene and the President died in hospital after a battle to save her life. You are not mentioned in the report at all."

"And have you noticed that not a single vehicle passed by on either side of the road until the emergency services showed up?" Irene put in. "That's very odd!"

Vicky could appreciate the professor as a person now, not as some kind of rival. She was a sharp one!

They talked and swapped observations until everyone felt dizzy.

"This is all well and fine, s—Joe. What do I do now?" asked Jamie.

"You are the witness to something that is very wrong here," said Joe. "Are you prepared to go through with the inevitable shit—pardon me, ladies—that will come your way if this goes out to a public audience?"

"I am!"

Jamie looked firm and determined.

"Good lad. I'll speak to someone I know at the BBC. I've met some very interesting people over these last five years. I'll ask Stuart to contact you. Stuart has put together a few documentary programmes in his time that have rattled certain individuals. He's credited with some resignations, as well as the usual industry accolades and awards, although he has been quiet recently. He isn't the kind of person who rests on his laurels, so my guess would be that he is waiting for something to come along that really takes his fancy. He will *love* taking on the murky powers of America. How does that sound to you? And by the way, may I have a copy of your film?"

*　　*　　*

BUSSTOP personnel in Washington D.C. decided that they needed to step up a gear. They had lost their jobs. That was signed and sealed. They wanted to keep the indignation rolling. To that end, Bruce Dougall's PA Genevieve Stanforth was sent to visit her former boss, to invite him to join them.

She found it odd to be sitting in his home, drinking coffee and chatting casually. Mr Dougall had been a great guy to work for but there was always a sense of that proper distance between them. Now they were in the same place, as ex-employees of *BUSSTOP.*

Bruce saw Genevieve's eyes gleam with interest when Shannon brought in the coffee and said hello. He decided it was better to say nothing because, however he might protest, it would be all over Georgetown that he and his first wife were back together again.

"Thanks for thinking of me, Genevieve. But perhaps I ought to stay out of this one. Does anyone know what you will all be doing?"

"Only the police."

"And they won't be telling anyone. Would you like me to contact a few people? Make sure that you have some press and television coverage?"

"Thank you!" breathed Genevieve.

"I'm glad to be of assistance. There's stuff going on here that needs busting open. President Rodriguez is up to something. I wish I knew what!"

Bruce knew what was taking the President's attention right now. The legal papers, which requested the presence of Bruce John Dougall at the Presidential Board of Inquiry into the *Ariadne One* disappearance, were burning a hole on his desk. Apart from the fact that it was not appropriate for the former head of *BUSSTOP* to be waving a placard out on the streets of D.C., he would be otherwise engaged. He had a bad feeling about this Board of Inquiry. He wished he could march with everyone. A steady walk on a cold winter's day would be of more benefit to him than fending off danger in a snake pit

*　　*　　*

Joe had to stop and think for a moment. *BUSSTOP* expertise was scattered across the south and east of England instead of being gathered conveniently within one building. Finally he located the personal contact details of Nigel Slade, head of the legal department. It was good to chat. He hadn't actually spoken to Nigel since before Christmas, when the world was a different place.

The lawyer told him what he already suspected.

"Our international treaties of co operation mean that you have to comply, Joe. You have been served with a Notice of Warning. You need to be available to travel to the States if your presence is required at the Board of Inquiry. Of course, you could answer questions and give evidence via a screen link but I fancy that this President likes his pound of flesh. When an inquiry gets under way here, Bruce Dougall could be asked to come to Britain. The PM will be setting up a technical investigation, picking through the mountains of data." Tell me, thought Joe. He had visited the Prime Minister that morning.

"We would like to make some kind of sense of what went wrong. America is out to catch the eye and make a big show. If you are summoned, take your hard hat. It could be a bit lively. This is not the forum where you find out what happened. It's a set-up to find someone to blame."

*   *   *

Once he had recovered from the surprise of what he was watching, Stuart Bland knew that all his birthdays and Yuletide celebrations had arrived at once. He was a Father Christmas of a man, tall and chunky and white of hair and beard. Father Christmas might not have worn his beard in a plait or his hair in a ponytail, but these were minor quibbles. Jamie felt at home with him straight away.

Stuart gave him a concerned glance when he couldn't stop coughing.

"You're not well, my boy," he rumbled.

"Sorry. I came home from America because I needed to recover from this infection."

"You do realise that if we go ahead with this, it may get out at some point that you are behind it, however discreet we are. Then you may not be welcome back in America. I mean, have you got some special person waiting there for you?" Jamie said no. "That's all right, then. You can always find another job. People are a bit trickier to replace. Wait here a moment."

Stuart disappeared, leaving Jamie to marvel again about the splendidly unpredictable nature of the British character. He had been away from home, in America, long enough to appreciate his compatriots in a very different way. He wondered how many of the neighbours in this unassuming street in Barnet, north London, not far from where Vicky lived, were aware of the fact that the back of the house was set up as a film production suite?

Jamie was a little alarmed when Stuart returned with two glasses and a bottle of very expensive single malt whisky. It was half past nine in the morning.

"This is medicine for you, my boy. Me? I'm too old to care. Make sure you don't ever get that way. Keep it as medicine. As a doctor, you must be aware of the healing properties of the water of life, used in moderation."

Jamie felt the spirit burning a path down his throat. The fire in his chest settled into a comfortable and warming glow.

"It hits the spot, doesn't it?" said Stuart knowingly. "You do realise that this film is a ticking time bomb, don't you? Hmm." Jamie could almost see the ideas being tossed around in his mind. "Now this is far too precious to be handed over to News. To start with, I'm not sure that anyone in any broadcasting company would have the balls to show it. If they did, you might see a twenty second clip if you were lucky. Blink and it would be gone. This needs to be seen in its entirety, contrasted with the official version of events. Joe Mortimer is nobody's fool and he's a quick learner. He's as sure-footed as anyone round the world of media after his stint as head of *BUSSTOP*. That's why he suggested we meet, rather than you hand your footage to News. This needs a proper documentary-type approach. Don't look so crestfallen, my boy. I can have this ready to go in a very short time because I possess a whole batch of film that was never used for some long-defunct project, reconstructing a similar kind of incident, where someone stopped to help at the scene of an accident. So if I can make a copy of your film, I'll get cracking. I'll talk to you very soon, Jamie Tennant."

*   *   *

Bruce Dougall was a confident person. He had been from an early age. On his first day in school he thumped and then chased away another boy who was teasing a tearful girl. From that day on Shannon saw him as her champion. But the doughtiest of champions needed to stop and think about attending a Presidential Board of Inquiry, held within the hallowed precincts of the Senate building in Washington D.C. There was a fearsome array of Senators lined up to ask questions and Erik Dronfield was in the chair. Bruce knew that he had nothing to hide, nothing to be ashamed of but he harboured the sneaking suspicion that this was a process being undertaken to make some obscure point, not to shed light on the truth.

He was right. The questioning was relentless and he had to be nimble-minded to be able to answer questions fully.

"But Mr Dougall, if you had doubts about this project, which you obviously did, why did you not do more . . . ."

"Mr Dougall, that is a very unhelpful answer. We have here the report that you submitted to President Harper. Did Mr Mortimer accept your analysis . . ."

"That will not do, Mr Dougall! It is common knowledge that you had many disagreements with Mr Mortimer. Are you trying to tell me that you agreed . . ."

"Mr Dougall, prior to the landing of *Ariadne One* on Mars, there was a computer problem, with the system called AD249. I am led to believe that there were problems with an earlier form of that equipment when you flew on the Zeus programme. Would you call it carelessness, or downright negligence, that during the time between Zeus and Ariadne nothing was done to address this weakness?"

Who had let that one out? Bruce marshalled his thoughts and went through the work that had been done on the AD249 to improve its reliability.

He felt like Alice in Wonderland at the end of the book when the court hearing, to establish who stole the tarts, was racing out of control. Alice brought everything to an abrupt halt by declaring that all present were nothing more than a pack of silly cards. The author Lewis Carroll wimped out of the corner he had put his character into by making it all a dream. The people in this scenario were very real and there was no such literary device, however feeble, to rescue him. Bruce had to carry on.

It was compulsory television viewing for those who were free to watch.

"This is not seeking information!" declared Hagar hotly to an empty room as she watched.

The press took the same view. The front pages the next morning looked pretty much the same. All editors were doing some kind of compare-and-contrast exercise. Everyone had gone archive hunting for pictures from Bruce's space career. Leading the field by a big margin were the shots of his long space walk outside *Zeus Three*. Beside these were stills taken from the television record of the Board of Inquiry. Bruce was apparently calm and unruffled. But the strain on his face was there for those who looked. There was justifiable over-use of the *Grace under fire* tag but one publication went in for a more thought-provoking headline.

IS THIS HOW WE REWARD A HERO?

These events gave a new focus and a fresh impetus to the *BUSSTOP* personnel who were about to take to the streets in demonstration. They had something else to protest about now.

Shannon was thankful that Bruce wasn't required for a second day. He would be called back at a later date but today the Board would be listening to technical and engineering data from the company that built *Ariadne One*. Her anger flared briefly. Was this how a civilised country treated a very sick man? Then she remembered that she was part of a very exclusive group, containing herself, Hagar Turner and some doctors, who knew about that side of things.

Bruce said very little when he came home and he wasn't much more forthcoming the next morning, although his fury was obvious. And he wasn't concerned about his own well being.

"Whatever they are doing up on the Hill, it's not finding out what happened to our astronauts. Did you notice that, Shannon? I spent the whole day answering their damned questions but at no point were the people of the Ariadne crew mentioned! When Erik Dronfield was going on about the AD249 computer system, I was tempted to say *'Screw the AD249! What about Brian, Jethro, Masahide, Simeon, Gianfranco, Jackson and Emily?'*"

"I'm glad you overcame temptation. You might have been arrested for contempt of the process."

"True. It would have given them something to think about, though."

"After all that indignation, let's have some breakfast," Shannon suggested.

She glanced out of the window as she passed by and then she looked properly.

"Oh my!" she said, in such a tone that Bruce had to join her.

It was a sight to behold. Across the road at a safe distance, the media people were still shut within their invisible legal corral but the concourse at the front of the apartment building was full to overflowing with demonstrators who were waving banners and chanting. An eagle-eyed *BUSSTOP* employee spotted Bruce at the window. She pointed and shouted something and everyone was cheering and waving in his direction.

"They're doing this for you," said Shannon. "You ought to go out there and—"

She turned as she spoke and found that she was addressing thin air. Bruce was already on his way down to talk to the mob.

Bruce scanned the crowd as they chanted his name. Genevieve stepped forward.

"How about this, Mr Dougall?" she asked. "We're going right into D.C. We have our shadows." She indicated the police presence. "And some of your media shadows will be coming with us too. We thought we'd start here, just to let you know how much we care about you. You're as much a victim of whatever is going on as we are and yesterday's opening proceedings at the Inquiry were unforgivable. You get back indoors now. We're dressed for being outdoors in the Washington winter. You're not."

Bruce waved to everyone. The crowd erupted into cheers. Whistles were blown and there was a widespread clanking of cowbells. He knew who had supplied those! Some of the banners and placards were less than complimentary about the President. Someone had been busy on a computer system. Her banner contained a photograph of Adolf Hitler addressing one of the Nuremberg rallies. Ted Rodriguez was inserted into the picture so that he was standing next to the German Fuhrer on the podium. *Remember how he finished up* was the stark statement underneath.

Journalists were already talking to their editors and a working headline was born.

BRUCE'S ARMY.

As the impromptu army moved off, police officers were talking to their superiors. On every block passers-by shouted encouragement. Those who had nowhere in particular to go fell in to the ranks and were given placards to hold aloft. At this rate, the demonstration could be three or four times its original size by the time it reached the middle of Washington. The exchange of messages between cops on the street and bosses in offices grew in volume and urgency.

*   *   *

President Ted Rodriguez had spent some time in the early morning engaged in a fruitless search for his wife, contacting friends and relatives. If anyone knew where she was, they were very good liars. To all intents and purposes she had vanished.

His mood was deteriorating rapidly when he walked down corridors to begin the presidential day officially. He closed his eyes for a moment when he saw Bill Francioni, looking like a large storm cloud.

"Good morning, Mr President. We have an unscheduled visitor to see you. Leo Morrison from the Police Department. He says it is very, very important. A matter of law and order."

*   *   *

"We are ready to go. It is time," said Ichiro.

Tony, Sally and Justin stood beside him, looking pleased.

None of the Ariadne crew had considered how they would leave the planet's surface. Perhaps that was because they were so happy. This was where they lived now. Ichiro's words made them stop and think. The Lander was not designed for so many people and goodness knows where the Orbiter was. The other three Martian-humans, who had held themselves a little aloof since the bringing of the astronauts into the rainbow, joined them. The two, who had represented so much Earth wisdom, were settled into inoffensive human form. The seventh being, whom they were told at the time was still transforming, had completed the process. Everyone understood when they saw her. There was no need for comment. Simeon did wonder what reaction this presence would provoke on Earth.

"You still have doubts?" teased Tony, reading their confusion about the method of leaving Mars

"No!" replied Brian in the same spirit. "We're just being human."

"Then I'll forgive you. Brian and Jethro, you will take off and bring Lander back up to the ship as was planned in your original mission. I think you will find that everything is working properly. Ichiro will accompany you."

"In case anything goes wrong?" wondered Jethro.

Tony tutted. Ichiro beamed.

"I was the design engineer on the Zeus craft," he reminded them. "This is the offspring of my work. I must see her fly."

"Listen!" said Simeon.

He didn't have to ask if the others could hear what he could hear. He could see it on their faces.

"What beautiful music!" murmured Emily.

A basic melody, working up and down a scale, whispered in their ears. Harmonies that brought tears to their eyes slipped their way in and out of the melody. The music filled their bodies, filled their minds, gave them strength and hope. They had never heard the tune before and yet they knew it. The multi-coloured mist of the rainbow shimmered and vibrated to the sounds of . . . what? No one could name an instrument that was being played and yet there was a blending together of different kinds of music making that was more satisfying than the most perfect symphony, opera or popular song.

Just as the motifs of the tune wove a track through the melody, the beings of light appeared and wove a path between the shafts of colour within the rainbow.

"The rest of the planet has come to say goodbye," explained Tony.

Simeon and Emily saw varying expressions on the faces of their rescuers and teachers. Tony was thoughtful, as a traveller might be when setting out on a long journey, knowing he will return one day, but who will miss hearth and home whilst he is away. Ichiro looked much the same. Justin and Sally were excited children, off on the trip of a lifetime. But Simeon could sense more in them. On Mars he had learned his reading lessons well. Underneath the anticipation there was a very human feeling of apprehension. The journey for them was a bunch of roses—so much beauty, so much to enjoy but oh! the thorns that might pierce and tear during that enjoyment.

The beings of wisdom were content. This was a voyage that was part of their calling, as it had been many times before. It was their task to travel, to bring the light and the learning to those who needed it so desperately. Journey's end would see them return and their mission would be done.

In the seventh being, so recently transformed, Simeon felt a real pain; so much so that he found himself stepping back again. Emily's hand tightened round his.

"Artemis, give me the strength to do this," Simeon heard. *"It will be my crowning work and joy, and no one else can do it. One day I will return."*

The beings of light danced among them all. Jackson hadn't felt like this since he was a child; the tummy-fluttering excitement of Christmas morning or the bolt of pure joy when waking up before daylight and remembering that school was out and the long vacation had begun.

Each astronaut gave thanks to the planet and the inhabitants that gathered them in, cared for them and taught them beyond their wildest dreams. No words were said out loud. They knew that they only had to think their gratitude and it was received.

"Goodbye, my children," said Artemis of Mars. *"I know that I can call you my children now. We have enjoyed your company for a season. You must go home. Your loved ones await you. But you will tell them of us. You have been the pupils. Now you will be the teachers. You will return, the first children of Earth to be the children of Mars."*

The music of Mars commanded their senses. They had no sensation of anything else and they had no wish to experience anything else.

"And now we must go," said Tony.

Emily felt a brief lurching sensation in her stomach. A thousand lights twinkled before her eyes and she was standing with the others in the middle of the main space ship. Her senses reeled and she held on to Simeon.

"Of course, humans have never teleported," said Tony understandingly. "We brought you and Jackson down to the planet by other means, because there were only the two of you."

He touched Emily's forehead and her mind cleared.

"Thank you." She looked around. "The rest of you are all right!" she stated, almost accusingly.

Her colleagues were assortedly stupefied or immobilised by fear but not manifesting any physical symptoms.

Sally put a reassuring hand on her arm.

"On Earth you suffer from travel sickness, don't you? And the first time you went into space you were ill."

"I made a total fool of myself," Emily confirmed. "But I've been fine since then."

"You have travelled now. In a different way and through a different dimension, but travel is travel to the human body. Next time you teleport you will have no problem."

Emily hoped that she wouldn't be moving in a similar fashion for a long time—if ever.

They moved to the command area of Ariadne. Tony indicated the control panels.

"Emily, Jackson, you have a job to do. The Lander will be requesting permission to dock in a short while."

The strangeness persisted for some time. Everything in the *Ariadne One* mother ship was exactly as it had been when the crew left. Computers told Simeon and Masahide that the composition of the atmosphere on board was different but it defied analysis. No one was keeling over, so the air was breathable. They had to accept that it was so.

Gianfranco took a couple of minutes out from his duties to change the sign that had flown with them for most of the journey to Mars.

This time it read *EARTH OR BUST.*

On the surface of Mars, the Lander thrusters roared into life immediately when they were activated and the vehicle blasted away in a dust cloud. Brian watched the screen, as the smooth bleak terrain of the Amazonian Plain dwindled in size and then grew remote. In what felt like another life, when the Lander wouldn't move, he thought he would die there. He afforded the planet one final glance. He was sorry to be leaving and wished he could stay within the rainbow. The music faded from his ears and he knew he had to go home. The sensations of the farewell floated away like bubbles and burst. But the peace stayed with him. He couldn't forget the experience as he and Jethro walked through the music to the Lander, the strands of colour twisting and swaying around them in time to the rhythms.

He looked over to Ichiro. The Martians knew their every thought. He still found it a little disconcerting. He wondered if something might be said about his regret. But no.

"My dream come true!" sighed Ichiro. "A designer who is able to fly in his own spaceship!"

The docking was textbook perfect.

"I wish Mr Mortimer and Mr Dougall could see this!" said Jethro.

"Perhaps they will," replied their travelling companion.

The look of complete bewilderment was still evident on Brian's face when he and Jethro joined the rest of the crew and their guests. He realised that they were waiting for him to give some orders. He was the commander of this spaceship. He took a deep breath as his training reasserted it.

"Power up to Nominal and orbit Mars to check all propulsion systems. Then half power to break the orbit. Set the automatic systems for Earth, landing at Cape Canaveral. That's where we're meant to land. The computers are programmed for it." He looked across at Tony. "You've shown us that Mission Control is empty but someone will track us and pick up our transmissions. It will be one heck of a shock for everyone but we must tell the world we're on our way."

"No one can track us or hear us yet," said Tony. "We are existing on a level of vibration that cannot be picked up by Earth. We must all use this journey time to lower our levels."

"So no one will know about us until we pop out from behind the clouds?" asked Jackson. "That's asking for trouble."

"Not quite. I calculate that Earth will have about thirty-six of your hours in warning. By then we will be in harmonious vibration with Earth, so that this craft will register on all systems and radio messages will be heard. We don't want to frighten anyone. And some individuals will know in advance. Then we want to reunite you with your loved ones as soon as possible."

Real sadness about leaving the rainbow of Mars was still uppermost in the mind of each astronaut. But Tony's words made a gap for something else. For the first time they could think about families and friends in terms of memories that brought a smile to the face and a lift to the heart.

"The process has begun," he said in a low voice to Sally.

*   *   *

Bill Francioni had been witness to some things in his time. He wondered if he would ever be allowed to write his autobiography. He could almost see the legislation going before the two Houses banning it. But the meeting to which he had been summoned today would take some beating if he were allowed to publish the details of it.

President Ted Rodriguez was surrounded by assorted advisers, discussing the best way to deal with the tidal wave of humanity that was flowing slowly into the centre of Washington each day, gathering force and energy along the way.

Francioni couldn't see the problem. Like many tidal waves, the initial impetus came from an earthquake, a seismic shock. Everyone in *BUSSTOP* America had lost their jobs, from the top down. Now someone was on a twisted mission to make *BUSSTOP* take the blame for the Ariadne disaster, via the Inquiry. It wasn't enough that Bruce Dougall had been pushed into resigning. Hundreds, possibly thousands, were protesting, as was their democratic right. It seemed to be a very peaceful gathering. But here was the President talking about this demonstration as if it was a barbarian invasion battering at the gates of civilisation.

"Mr President" one adviser was saying, "if this group of people gets out of hand, you can use the Executive Order and proclaim a national emergency. We at *FEMA* will assist. Use Operation Cable Splicer. We talked about this stuff yesterday."

Francioni looked at the group of people with narrowed eyes. When had these discussions taken place? He had no idea who this comedian was, or who any of them were, but they were wearing all the correct clearance paraphernalia, so Rodriguez must have invited them, as he must have invited them *somewhere* the previous day.

"Yes!" The President's eyes sparkled. "You're sure about the state of emergency thing?" He glared at the silent television screen. "It's about time someone cracked a whip around here. Ah, hello Bill."

Rodriguez and his gang became aware of him waiting at the back of the room.

Long years in the White House had given Francioni an encyclopaedic knowledge of the Constitution, Federal law, the grey world of Executive Orders and the use of a state of emergency declaration. And he thought that nothing would surprise him any more. He was wrong.

FEMA—the Federal Emergency Management Agency—was set up ostensibly to ensure the safety and security of the homeland and to help people after a natural disaster. Its unspoken agenda made it potentially more powerful than the most dominant dictator could ever be, if the President called a national emergency.

It was a little known fact that, under Executive Order #11490, the President could declare a national emergency for pretty much any reason. *FEMA* could flex its muscles using Operation Cable Splicer and Operation Garden Plot, with the power to arrest and imprison citizens without due process of law, requisition property, transportation systems and food supplies, move large populations of people and suspend the Constitution.

Bill Francioni looked over at the television screen. Even with the sound muted, it was obvious that this was a totally peaceful group of men, women and children. There looked to be plenty of family dogs in evidence and some were joining the march on horseback. So who was this dangling the carrot of an unholy alliance with *FEMA* before the President?

We at FEMA. Who were these people from *FEMA*, here at the invitation of the President and talking emergency powers?

For one hectic moment, Francioni wondered if he was losing his grip. He reckoned on knowing everyone who needed knowing. But *FEMA* had become a shadowy organisation and those within it stayed out of view. He sat down, very concerned.

He was aware of someone saying his name. Ted Rodriguez was standing over him, looking genuinely concerned. There had been a general easing of positions within the room for a coffee break.

"Are you okay, Bill?" he was saying. "You went a real funny colour just now."

"I'm a tad tired, Mr President. My wife has been sick with this influenza. She is fine now."

"Why don't you go home and get some rest? We've got everything pretty much under control here. Because there may be some tough times ahead, I'm giving all key White House staff a week's vacation. Only the domestic help and Security will be around. This is why I sent for you. The word will be spread today. Messengers will go round. You can be the first to benefit. Have some coffee with us before you go."

The snippets of conversation Bill Francioni was hearing made his hair stand on end. These people were talking over coffee about compulsory registration of all US citizens and the use of concentration camps as if it were all some interesting academic exercise, a computer game, or a drill. And they didn't seem to care that he was listening. They were either supremely careless or supremely confident.

Looking round the room at the fat-assed, smug types that filled it, he sensed that these folks just knew they had the magic touch. Their attitude was contagious. The same self-satisfied smirk was settling on the President's face.

He *did* recognise one person here, because this one wasn't part of *FEMA*. Over in the far corner was Bob Broomfield, whose wealth would have made Croesus envious. He stood out, not least because he was a blonde, lean hunting cat amongst a herd of over-fed prey. He wondered why this person was at the beck and call of the President.

Francioni had lived his whole adult life by the expectations of duty instilled in him during his time in the Marines. It was his duty to warn the President, scream at him if necessary to get his attention. But it would be a waste of time. He would have to try and stop his boss by other means.

He had never left his work part way through a day. It was almost as though he was being dismissed. He didn't mind. He needed to think. Who could he approach? Henry Sargent was the one.

Francioni left the room thankfully. When he reached home, the first thing he would have to do was take a long soak in the tub. He felt physically soiled from having been witness to such a discussion.

Oh yes, he had done one or two questionable things in his long association with the White House. But nothing that couldn't be justified. Mostly he and his colleagues spent their time doing their best to prevent the leader of the day upsetting other national leaders, setting off World War Three, putting an iron-shod foot in it and generally looking terminally ridiculous.

Never had he heard a President talking so eagerly about undermining the very fabric of society to get a grip on a bunch of unhappy people, with *FEMA* in the driving seat.

Either Ted Rodriguez was very stupid or very dangerous.

Up to this point, Francioni knew which option he would have gone for. After today, he wasn't so sure

Chapter Twenty-Three

"Irene?"

Joe could see her moonlit outline standing by the window, staring up at the sky.

"Sorry, Joe. I didn't mean to wake you."

"How long have you been there?" he wanted to know when he joined her. "You're freezing cold! Come back to bed." She followed him obediently. "Heavens, woman! You're an icicle! What's this all about?"

Irene was grateful for the warmth of Joe's body.

"The garden looks beautiful in the moonlight," she said after a pause.

"Don't change the subject."

"That Morse Code message. I . . . well, I don't know what to think."

"Someone wanted to get your attention. He or she succeeded, don't you think?"

"Joe, have you ever had something happen to you that you can't explain?" Irene asked after a long silence.

Something stopped Joe trotting out the usual kind of answer he would have given. Suddenly this was a very important moment and it deserved a proper response.

"Yes," he said quietly. "Once or twice."

"And what did you do?"

"There wasn't anything I could *do*. I believe that everything is capable of an explanation. Sometimes we don't allow ourselves to accept the possibility of certain explanations because they're uncomfortable, or very different to what we would normally think. So the event becomes a mystery."

"*We are coming home*," Irene reminded him. "Who are *we*?"

"Irene! It's two in the morning!"

"Don't change the subject!"

Joe could hear the laughter in her voice, and the determination.

"Touché," he admitted. "You're the one who has to get up and go to work in a few hours. D'you really want to know what I think?"

*   *   *

Bruce was watching the main news channel evening programme, which was full of images of that day's *BUSSTOP* march. This was becoming a routine. The protesters started off each morning outside his apartment block and walked in orderly fashion into the centre of Washington D.C. He was proud to see that Genevieve had turned into some kind of spokesperson for the group.

"We will do this every day until people realise that we have grievances to be addressed—namely, the loss of our jobs, the proposed dismantling of *BUSSTOP* and the shabby treatment of our boss!"

Whistles and shouts of "Go, Gen!" rippled through the crowd behind her.

"You say that you want *people* to acknowledge your grievances," said the interviewer. "Do you include President Rodriguez in that?"

"You bet we do!"

There was more shouting and the clanking of cowbells.

Bruce was sorry that Shannon was not here to share this with him. She had decided that he would be okay and she could go home.

"The suicide watch is standing down?" he joked.

"Don't! Not even in jest!"

An angry Shannon made the bravest hearts fail with fear and Bruce apologised hastily for his bad taste in humour.

"But you don't get rid of me that easily!" she continued. "I'll be around from time to time."

"Shannon," he said hesitantly. "All that you've done. I don't know how to——."

"No thanks needed, honey." She took his hands in hers. "It's like it says in the book dedication."

He was missing her already.

Bruce couldn't be bothered to watch any more news. The world was still turning round. That would do for now. He reached out for Shannon's book and read for a long while. He hadn't got very far with it whilst she was staying. It was obvious that she found it difficult to know he was reading it. She was oddly shy about the fact that he was enjoying the story.

It was a good read, with a powerful narrative that swept everything before it. He had to be careful not to be distracted by playing "spot the location." He recognised various events from Shannon's life that were at the base of happenings in the book. By the special alchemy of telling the tale, mundane fact had been spun into fictional gold. But he knew what she was referencing in several instances. He couldn't recognise himself in any of the characters but, by the mysterious process of creativity, he was sure that unrelated bits of his life were in there somewhere.

He knew that it was time to turn in for the night but he was too comfortable to move for the moment and there was no Shannon to nag him.

Bruce slipped into the special world that exists between wakefulness and sleep. The everyday sounds seemed further away and yet each one was separate and identifiable. There was the background hum of traffic. The emergency siren of an ambulance wailed on into the night outside. Every natural click and creak of the building was audible, as it seemed to settle down for the night.

"Hello, Bruce."

He looked up. He took off his glasses, blinked several times, and put them back on again.

"I . . . you . . ."

He gave up.

"It's all right, Bruce," said Sally, with an encouraging smile. "There is nothing wrong with your eyes and you are still sane. This is not a dream." Bruce made to get up. "I'm not here. Not exactly. I am a projection of me. You need to know. We are coming home."

*　　*　　*

It was six a.m.

Irene wondered how she and Joe had ended up where they were. Not their physical location. They were sitting downstairs, with the fire rekindled, finishing the latest in a long line of mugs of tea. Bonny was prowling about looking confused.

It was the conversational minefield that they had crossed which Irene found mind-boggling. And looking at Joe's expression, he was equally rocked back on his heels.

During the long watches of the night she found herself recounting things which had either never been said out loud or which were secrets kept by Debbie and Alisdair and Marmaduke Dawson. She did something that she never thought she could do—give a fairly unemotional summary of her marriage to Ken Fielding.

"It took a while to work out what I had got myself into. Ken changed gradually. I should have known—the first time he hit me when we disagreed about something. He begged my forgiveness and said how much he loved me. That happened a few times. Then one Friday night I came home from work much later than planned. I hadn't let him know how late I would be. Ken flew into a rage and kicked and punched me, repeatedly. I managed to get away from him. Somehow I drove the car over to Debbie and Alisdair. I refused to go to hospital because I felt such a fool. It was my fault. I provoked him, didn't I? So Alisdair patched me up." For a moment, the superhuman control slipped. "I had done a pregnancy test just that morning. It was positive. Ridiculously early, but I was pregnant. The next day I began losing a huge amount of blood. Alisdair put his foot down and he took me to hospital. The pregnancy was lost before it was barely begun. I think that hurt more than my bruises and cracked ribs. Alisdair and Debbie were amazing. They helped me so much. The divorce was fast-tracked at arm's length. Most people never knew I was even married. I had worked hard to create some footholds in my world. I was thirty-two when I married and I was Irene Hanson. I didn't want to confuse matters by appearing with another name. So I continued working using my birth name."

Joe held Irene close; they clung to each other for a long time, survivors from the shipwrecks of their earlier lives, washed up on a new shore by a surge of honesty. There was nothing more to say. He had told her all about Sally and how at one stage she found herself very drawn to Bruce Dougall, as happy as she was with Joe. With an effort he recounted the tragedy of her death.

He was not completely surprised by Irene's story, although the details were harrowing. He suspected something that first day they met, when they visited his parents. He saw the fear in her when he came up behind her and spoke, taking her unawares.

The twin strands of what Joe told her flabbergasted Irene and she dealt with them in very different ways. The fact that he was accusing himself of being responsible for the loss of Ariadne, because he had not listened to an engineer, was a mere detail. She urged him not to be so hard on himself. The people who didn't think they'd done anything wrong were the real problem.

It was being told about Sally that grabbed hold of her. Apart from anything else, Irene knew that she was very privileged to hear about this. Although she and Joe were drawing closer by the day, he needn't have told her. Only his immediate family, and Bruce Dougall, knew anything about this very private chapter of his life.

She wanted to know so much about Sally. She wanted to see photographs. She wanted—.

Irene stopped that train of thought before it gathered speed. Now that she knew, the other things would probably follow in time. They had been engaged in a raw and total sharing which was as intimate as sex. Enough was enough for now.

"Irene, are you going in to college today?" Joe was asking.

Irene fought her way up through layers of darkness. Her eyes didn't want to open. Joe's face came into focus at close range. Her head was on his shoulder.

"Wha—at?" she mumbled groggily.

"You've been asleep for about half an hour. I think I have too. Are you going in to college today?" he repeated.

Bonny rolled over on the floor at Joe's feet, stretched her legs, and closed her eyes again, giving a shuddering sigh. This faithful hound stuff was exhausting at times.

"I'll have to," she said, struggling to sit up. "After the time off I had with my knee, the powers-that-be will go mad if I'm away any more."

"You could be ill just for today. No one can complain about that. Your students have been deserting you because they were poorly. I'm getting too old for this sitting up through the night business. I shall be going back to bed. You're welcome to join me. To sleep," he added firmly. "And if the Prime Minister calls again, which he is doing every day to ask me to reconsider my resignation, he'll just have to leave a message like everyone else."

"I'd better face the world," she said with genuine regret.

When Irene reappeared, dressed and approximately in her right mind, Joe had prepared breakfast. He served coffee with a real kick to it.

"If that doesn't keep you alert, nothing will," he said with satisfaction when Irene was on her third cup. "We were never big coffee drinkers in the family home. I learned the art of making coffee like that from Bruce Dougall. Flying long distance space missions is a bit like World War One trench warfare. You have bursts of mad activity, with long stretches of tedium in between. You need other things to do. Bruce taught the rest of the Zeus crew the tricks of how to play killer poker. He taught me how to make killer coffee."

Irene had never thought about the minutiae of life on board a space ship, even a ship that was designed to get to its destination as rapidly as Zeus. Joe's words conjured a picture of an odd domestic harmony amongst the stars—the poker school in one corner and the coffee school in another, with Bruce Dougall as the presiding genius of both.

"You didn't need poker lessons then?"

"No. Dad taught Philip and me from a young age."

"Who is the better player?" Irene wanted to know, her lips twitching as she struggled not to laugh. "You or Bruce?"

Honesty and pride jostled for position within Joe.

"I think we're quite evenly matched," he said in the end. "I'd love to see Dad play Bruce. I know he's eighty now but—"

"—the older they get, the wilier they get," Irene finished for him. "I'd better love you and leave you Joe."

"You look really tired." Joe was concerned. "Call me when you get to college. Please. I want to know that you got there safely."

*   *   *

Irene had given up looking at the clock. Time was apparently frozen. She grumbled sometimes about students who sat like puddings, saying nothing, making her work more like dentistry than teaching. Today everyone was revoltingly perky and on the ball.

"Professor, what do you say to . . ."

"But Professor, I think that . . ."

"I'd have to disagree with you there, Professor Hanson. This is . . ."

One young woman did show some thoughtfulness at the close of the tutorial.

"Are you all right, Professor?"

"A little tired, that's all, Coral. Thank you for asking."

Irene decided that she would sit down again for five minutes before even thinking about lunch. She leaned back in the armchair that was the pride and joy of her college study. Her eyelids were lined with layers of sandpaper and lead.

"Hello, Irene!"

Only the high arms of the chair stopped her falling to the floor as she jumped to wakefulness. Then she relaxed.

"I think it might be *hello again*. It is, isn't it?" she asked.

Tony's smile was wider than ever.

"You *did* understand. When I came to you before, that was a visit in the dream world. This time I am using astral projection. I wasn't sure that I had picked the right moment back then. You were heavily drugged, which is not good for any kind of communication like this, but your defences were down, as they are now."

"Defences?"

"The conditioning of your world, that says you can't possibly have a conversation with a man who is 'dead', whom you never met whilst he was alive. You worked out who I am and accepted it. I am so proud of you, Irene Hanson. But I am here to give you reassurance. Reassurance that many need. We are coming home."

"So *you* sent the message! What does it mean?"

Irene listened in amazement until her grandfather had finished.

"Joe! I must tell Joe!" she exclaimed.

"Wait until you are together again. He will know."

"Who appears to him? Who is telling him?" Irene wondered, putting pieces of a jigsaw together. "Sally?"

"Yes. Joe has never quite accepted what he has experienced whilst in the dream world. Be patient with him, Irene. He is not quite as far along this road of understanding as you are, mainly because he hurts too much, because he is too angry with Sally for leaving him. You love him very much, don't you?"

"Yes. It sort of crept up on me. There it was, done. Hopelessly in love."

"And quite right too!" Tony told her. "I know he loves you. So help him to acknowledge his grief, help him to be angry. He has never let either emotion have its moment properly. When he has wept, when he has raged, he will truly be yours, with a bond that can never be broken, on the earthly plane or beyond. Can you do that for him? You need to do this today because Sally is speaking to him even as I am speaking to you. He will be very vulnerable."

"Of course. I just wish I felt a bit more . . . energetic. We had a wakeful night."

"I know. It was a wakeful night of truthful sharing, which prepares the ground for this final sharing. Sleep for a while, my angel. You will have the strength and you will be given the words."

"Thank you, granddad," she murmured as she slid back into sleep.

The clock told Irene that she had been asleep for about fifteen minutes, if it was to be believed. She felt revitalised, as if she had enjoyed an uninterrupted night's rest. She sprang up and rushed down the corridor in search of her colleagues. Yes, she had things to do both here and at home tonight. But she had no intention of doing them without lunch.

* * *

"Your cough is much improved."

Stuart Bland twinkled at Jamie Tennant.

Jamie could only twinkle a smile back at him.

"I think you've been leading my brother along dubious paths," Vicky said. "But he is really getting better. Thank you for suggesting the whisky."

"Healers were prescribing it long before antibiotics, young lady. Anyway, what do you two fine people think of my little effort?"

The "little effort" was a thirty-minute demolition of the official version of Phoebe Harper's car crash and subsequent death, which was at present being nodded through a Presidential Board of Inquiry in Washington D.C. The narration was a masterpiece of hardboiled and sinewy prose, spoken by one of the leading voice over specialists, Paul O'Hara. Jamie's film was interspersed with a soft-focus reconstruction of what was said to have happened.

"It's great!" said Jamie. "And in such a short time!"

"I did tell you that I had all this "car crash" footage sitting around. Reconstructions are a pain in the backside if you have to start from scratch. It's uncanny how well my stock film fitted the alleged events. I want to run this past one or two people first, and then we shall get it out there. And hey ho for whatever happens next. Are you ready for whatever happens next, Jamie Tennant? Not weakening?"

"No, I'm not."

Vicky looked grimly sure as well.

*   *   *

"This is becoming damned silly!"

Ted Rodriguez thumped the table as television screens continued to show the *BUSSTOP* employees plus their many supporters trudging their usual march.

"All these other folks joining in," he continued, almost plaintively. "Don't they have anything better to do?"

"Apparently not, Mr President," one of his advisers replied.

Rodriguez felt at a disadvantage for a moment. What was his name? Murray? That was it. Murray Crellin. His floppy burnished brown hair and plump face belied his fifty-five years.

"Well, Murray, what do you suggest?"

"It's time to move, Mr President. Call the state of emergency and really get to work. It's what you want, isn't it?"

The President blinked. This was fantastic! He had never expected things to move as quickly as this.

"Of course it is."

His eyes raced across the group to Bob Broomfield. He owed a huge debt to this guy. His money and his influence had made so much happen already and he would still be very useful. On the principle that it is wise to keep your friends close by you and your enemies even closer, Bob was in on all this. Rodriguez was under no illusions about which label to stick on Bob. And this man would take the first opportunity to slip the leash. Would he turn to Bruce Dougall? The friendship of childhood and schooldays had remained tight. Rodriguez was banking on there being things that a man would not share even with such a close buddy.

The quiet man of business stood up to get himself more coffee. Those sharp blue eyes were disconcerting and his very short fair hair gave him a tough appearance. The President knew that he would always feel a prickle of danger when this one was around. He didn't have Richard Nixon's confidence in the total efficacy of having someone by the balls. Broomfield sat down again, nodded imperceptibly to the President and then spoke.

"You need some sort of reason for calling a state of emergency," he pointed out. "It needs to be something that is credible."

"Public disorder!" said Rodriguez promptly. "It guarantees that the majority will approve of any action taken. There's nothing like running battles in the street and a few buildings going up in flames to focus the mind. How can we do it?"

"Simple. Let's start with the demonstrators themselves," suggested Crellin.

"The *demonstrators?*" Rodriguez wanted to laugh. "They are so correct in what they're doing that it isn't true!"

"Leave it to us at *FEMA*. And Bob, I'll have a word with you later as to how we can move this on, once it has started."

*   *   *

Finally the anger, the pain and the distress were drifting away like the torn and ragged remnants of storm clouds. It had taken a while. Joe was physically and mentally exhausted.

"Irene, I'm sorry."

Irene brushed away her own tears.

"Don't start apologising! You've been saving that up for a long time. Sally was an important part of your life. Don't shut her out. Remember her gently, whenever you need to. I won't be offended."

"What's happening?" he asked. "You've been visited by your grandfather. Sally has visited me. And what they said . . ."

"Let's leave what they said for now. This is the second time Tony has visited me and Sally has appeared to you before, hasn't she?"

"Yes." He was shamefaced. "The first time, she spoke to me in a dream, two weeks after she died. I—er—told her to go away."

"I'm sure you didn't say that." Irene knew her grandfather was approving. "What did you say to her, exactly? Do you remember?"

"I said '*What are you doing here? You're dead!*'"

By the end of that short statement his voice was barely audible.

"A very natural reaction!" Irene said in understanding. "I'm sure that I would have said exactly the same in those circumstances. But she didn't go away, did she? So she understood."

"And to think that I came over to see you tonight to make sure that you were okay after a day's work with not much sleep!"

"That just about sums you up, Joseph Joshua Mortimer!" stated Irene very seriously. "You have received a bombshell—no, make that two bombshells with the actual appearance of Sally and then her message—and yet you still saddled up and came here, with no question, to see if I was all right. All your adult life you've been watching out for other people. You watched out for your crew and ship on Zeus. You watched out for your students when you trained astronauts. You've watched out for the whole kit and caboodle whilst you were head of *BUSSTOP*. Since Sally died, who has been on Joe watch? Who has been there to pick up the pieces at the end of the day? No one really, although I know your family do their best. I was talking about you to a colleague who is into astrology. I didn't mention your name, of course. You are a very interesting mix, born on the cusp of Leo and Virgo. All your adult life you have been the serving, dutiful, conscientious, perhaps even picky Virgo." She ruffled his hair. "It's time to shake that Leo mane and have a roar. Oh damn and blast!" she said as she heard the messaging signal. "I'll ignore it."

"It might be something important," Joe told her. "Or someone important. Or both."

It was the Prime Minister, looking decidedly uncomfortable.

"Good evening, Professor Hanson. Is Joe Mortimer with you? He's starting to behave like a truanting schoolboy. He seems to have taken to going out minus his personal communicator."

Joe appeared at Irene's shoulder. She looked at Kevin Crane and then at Joe. There was something about the Prime Minister—in his eyes perhaps? Whatever it was, he had the same look that Irene recognised in Joe and in herself.

"I know you want to talk about *BUSSTOP* with Joe, Prime Minister," she said. "May we leave that for the moment? Joe and I would like to discuss unusual experiences first of all. It's all right. We know."

*   *   *

"Now who is that?" Irene wanted to know some time later. "Everybody wants to chatter tonight!"

She flicked on the screen and was delighted to see Debbie's smiling face.

"Hello! I haven't spoken to you for ages and I've been hearing—" Debbie began. She looked at her friend more carefully. "Oh yes! What have you been up to, Irene Hanson?" Irene called to Joe, who came into the room, ducked down into view for a moment and waved. "Ah," she said, in perfect understanding, resisting the urge to jump up and down in celebration. "I'll call another time."

"No you won't!" ordered Irene. "Joe is busy in the kitchen, making us a meal." He took the hint and disappeared. "He is one of that endangered species—*vir domesticus*. Domesticated man."

When Joe reappeared to tell Irene that dinner was served, she was shutting down the screen.

"Should my ears be burning?" he wondered.

"No. You know that Debbie can be a bit . . . overwhelming. And she and Alisdair are very fond of you. We owe them an eternal debt of gratitude."

Joe could only agree, remembering all those occasions before Christmas when he visited the convalescing Irene at their house.

The food nodded towards Italy—*penne* drenched in a homemade tomato sauce and topped with Parmesan shavings, accompanied by a salad dressed with balsamic vinegar.

"You told me to use whatever I needed," said Joe. "So I did. As you know, I'm not a big one for meat."

"This is divine!"

There followed an eating silence of great seriousness. Then Irene waved her fork as a thought came to her in mid-mouthful.

"Bruce Dougall!" she pronounced eventually. "Do you think he has been visited?"

"By whom? You're thinking of Sally, aren't you?"

"I am. By your own admission, there was a spark between them." She looked at the clock on the wall. "Five hours behind, yes? Ask him! You won't need to, I'll bet. We saw it in the Prime Minister straightaway."

"I need some reason for contacting him, Irene. What do I say?"

"*Hello* is usually a good start." Joe frowned. "Seriously. I've always found that *I'm checking you're okay* works well with most people, and it doesn't arouse any suspicions. You could ask how fairly the authorities will be treating him. You're getting the full benefits and early retirement package from *BUSSTOP*. He might not, seeing as he really was sacked and President Rodriguez is stamping around like a bear with a sore head when it comes to the organisation."

Joe didn't need any of Irene's suggestions when he got through to Bruce later on. They both spotted it straightaway. The shock, the wonder, and the indescribable something else were all plain to see in Bruce's eyes the moment he came on screen.

"We know," said Joe.

*   *   *

The hardcore of the Washington D.C. *BUSSTOP* protesters did wonder if their support might start to dwindle. The bitterly cold weather continued and surely the novelty must wear off. But no. If anything, more people were joining them. There appeared to be a spontaneous rolling roster of non-*BUSSTOP* people. The same faces didn't appear every day but there was a gradual growth in the numbers on the march.

The demonstration took various routes and the organisers were scrupulous in their consultations with the local police, but each day they finished the walk near Constitution Gardens, which were completed way back in 1976 as part of the Bicentennial celebrations. The Washington Monument loomed over the immediate skyline and the historically minded might have wondered briefly what the first President of the United States of America would have made of all this.

Mostly they were more concerned with what the present incumbent of the post was thinking. There were increasingly hostile comments coming from his direction, attributed to *White House sources*. Those who knew how to read the auspices understood that these were angry squawks from the President himself.

Rightly or wrongly, Ted Rodriguez believed that inaction was making him look foolish. He cast bitterly envious eyes across the Atlantic at his brother in power, Kevin Crane. The British Prime Minister was also doing nothing about his rebellious *BUSSTOP* people but, then again, they weren't tramping round the streets of London every day.

Rodriguez couldn't figure it out. After a wobbly few days, Crane was back up there in his usual role as the unlikely darling of the masses, and all the huffing and puffing about the resignation of Joe Mortimer—surely the poster boy of his generation in Britain—had stopped abruptly.

The halt to hostility between the Prime Minister and the country could be linked to the moment when Mortimer had stepped through the front door in Downing Street and the information was leaked that the star of Britain's *BUSSTOP* would be given a prominent role in the Ariadne inquiry. It was an obvious ploy of support and everyone believed it! Rodriguez's team had done everything and more to persuade the opinion-makers that Dougall really had resigned of his own accord but no one accepted that for a moment.

The President's anger burned. Kevin Crane was doing nothing and he was praised in the international media. He, the mighty Ted Rodriguez, was doing nothing and was accused of weakness. He would give them weakness!

*   *   *

Genevieve looked back at the snake of people behind the front line of marchers. Perhaps fiery dragon would be a better description. The white breath of each person rose into the still air. Snow had fallen heavily overnight and the temperature was below freezing. Even though the sidewalks had been cleared, a new layer of frost was making them treacherous. A few little ones had tumbled over. Genevieve had helped one fallen child after he escaped from his family and started to hurry towards the front. Dogs either frolicked in the snow or picked up their paws in disgust. The horse riders decided to give it a miss today, not wanting to risk delicate legs and fetlocks in such treacherous conditions.

Everyone was very glad when Constitution Gardens came into sight. There was the usual large group of cops to funnel them into the agreed area. They knew it was total overkill that these officers were kitted out in full riot gear but if it kept everyone happy, so be it.

There was a squeal from the midst of the march.

"Mommy!" a child cried as she slipped and fell.

Everyone stopped instinctively. Those at the front hesitated, looking back. As they watched, the child was lifted onto someone's shoulders. Knowing that the problem was solved, those in the middle moved forward, bumping into those who were still stationary at the front. In that split second of disorder some people spilled onto the road, simply to avoid being crushed. Fortunately the weather meant that traffic was virtually non-existent.

Seb Healey, in charge of this police group, was already uneasy. He had been warned in no uncertain terms to expect trouble today. He had back-up waiting in side streets. The word was that the demonstrators were angry because they weren't receiving enough media attention.

"Go!" he yelled.

*   *   *

It was a disaster. There was nothing that could be done to tone it down or explain it away in any manner. Press and television reporters got their pictures and their information before they joined protesters who were fleeing. The deeply shocked and injured sat on the sidewalk or at the side of the road. Sobbing and screaming children had been rushed away by families. Some were bleeding from gashes to the head and face. This is what a mediaeval battlefield must have looked like. Slumped on the ground, leaning against a lamppost, Genevieve was in a daze. She clutched her arm as she spoke to her husband.

"Greg, what happened here?"

"I have no idea!" he said with barely-controlled anger. "But I have every intention of finding out. Hey, you! Over here!" Greg Stanforth's shout was uncompromising as he shouted to two paramedics. "I think my wife's arm is broken."

As they hurried to her side, Stanforth spotted Seb Healey. He didn't know who he was or where he came in the great scheme of police matters here in the city. But he did recognise him as the fool who gave the order to go in. Healey was tall but Genevieve's husband was taller and immensely strong—a testimony to his job as a visiting sports coach at the prestigious Madeira School located in MacLean, Virginia, not so far from D.C. Healey had shed his riot gear and Stanforth lifted the policeman up by the lapels of his thick uniform coat.

"My wife had better be okay," he said in a quiet snarl.

When he had said everything that he felt like saying, and had probably said some of those things several times over, he put the police officer down and strode back to Gen, who was being helped to an ambulance. Seb Healey straightened his coat and looked around nervously for cameras. The media boys could be hiding anywhere.

The media boys and girls were having a ball. There were still snappers hiding out in points of vantage. There would be some memorable photographs on the front pages the next day of Greg Stanforth having that nose-to-nose conversation with Seb Healey. The most dramatic shots, moving and still, were of the terrifying moments when the police waded into the peaceful demonstration, batons flying and heavily booted feet kicking individuals out of the way.

A tight-lipped and furious Bruce Dougall was seen going into the local hospital, to check that his former PA wasn't too badly hurt. He made an almost royal progress round the different floors to check on the injured, making no distinction between *BUSSTOP* people and those who were supporting them. Those who knew the man were impressed. He was no shrinking violet but power and confidence oozed from him.

He stopped to give an interview outside the front door of the hospital. It turned into an unofficial media call. His tone could have stripped the paint from the walls.

"In conclusion, I want to know what the hell has been going on here. I think questions need to be answered, all the way up to the White House if necessary."

With that parting shot Bruce walked away. The reporters and vision and sound crews melted obediently to his left and right, deferring to Moses as he parted the waves of the Red Sea.

A shaken Seb Healey spoke to the cameras.

"I was following orders," he said. "We were warned that there was likely to be trouble today in the demonstration."

"Trouble?" called one reporter above the disbelieving hubbub. "A kid slipped on the ice and snow! Who gave you this information about possible trouble?"

Healey looked over the pack of reporters and saw two very large men, built like wardrobes and dressed in three-piece suits and black topcoats, making their way quietly and purposefully towards him.

"I'm sorry, ladies and gentlemen, I'm afraid I can't say any more right now. My department will put out a full statement later on today."

By midday, the news had spread. The streets of Washington D.C. were crammed with angry workers, using their lunch break to register their protest at what had happened. Makeshift banners were waved. A large group stood near to the White House, shouting its displeasure in the general direction of the President's residence. Some looked as though they had no intention of returning to their places of work.

All over the city, rows of police watched from a cautious distance.

At just after four in the afternoon, truly shocking information was seeping out across Washington D.C. Seb Healey, the man at the centre of this controversy, had been found dead in the family home after he failed to turn up for a debriefing meeting about that morning's incident.

His gun was at his side. He had suffered a single shot to the head. It was presumed he had committed suicide.

A sad and angry President Rodriguez appeared on national television that night.

"Of course, there will be a thorough investigation into the tragic events surrounding today's demonstration," the President was saying as Bruce tuned in.

"Yeah, right!" Bruce said out loud.

He had the experience now to imagine Seb Healey's last moments. He knew all about that overwhelming loneliness, which had to be dealt with, and for which there was only one apparent solution. Bruce thought he had explored loneliness pretty thoroughly when he walked in space. But when he was out there, especially during the long, long inspection of *Zeus Three*, there was a majesty and a beauty to the backdrop of black velvet studded with a million jewels and more. But the isolation of deciding that nothing and no one could help any more was in a different league. It pushed the individual beyond the usual constraints of self-preservation, into the emptiest place in the Universe, where you talk to yourself and don't let yourself talk back to you.

Bruce paused the newscast, stood up and walked to the window. He looked out over the city. The memories of his moments of total despair were more vivid and fresh than he would have liked and he had to make a conscious effort to shake himself free of them.

He wasn't alone over *BUSSTOP* after all. And Sally had brought him the most incredible news about *Ariadne One*. However, in the end, he still stood on his own with his illness. Hagar knew and so did Shannon. They made an impressive support team but they could not take the cancer away from him. He wondered if Sally the Martian, or whoever she was, knew what was going on. What part of the real Sally was within this being and what did she make of it?

Bruce was straying into territory that made his senses reel. He would have to leave such thoughts for another time.

Watching the news again, he went back to suicide of Seb Healey. Surely there had to be something else preying on Healey's mind. He made an error of judgement, albeit a massive one, and he was probably badly advised. Many had done worse things and had done them wilfully. But Bruce was beginning to see that many people had an inbuilt flair for kicking their own butts for no good reason. He thought of Joe, beating himself up over a mistake that probably never existed.

"I am receiving disturbing reports of civil unrest in several states," the President was saying. Bruce was tempted to fast-forward Ted Rodriguez but he decided to stick with the man. "I have no idea how anyone thinks that taking to the streets and damaging property will help the cause of *BUSSTOP* employees, or shed light on the unfortunate events which took place this morning at Constitution Gardens. I give everyone fair warning and a chance to cool down. If this situation does not right itself very quickly, I will have no choice but to declare a state of emergency across the United States of America, using the powers conferred upon my office by Executive Order #11490."

Bruce sighed. He didn't like threats. This was a petulant bully stamping his foot. The only trouble was, he was sure that this schoolyard bully could do all manner of things under the terms of the aforementioned Executive Order.

And there had been no mention of Seb Healey at all. Bruce didn't like that either.

Something was scratching at the back of his mind. He reran the film of Healey starting to talk to the media and then stopping the conversation. The camera tracked round to show his departure.

Bruce had an eye for the small details, perhaps more so than Joe Mortimer. The moment-by-moment safety of a spaceship and its crew had rested as much with him as with the boss.

He noticed the two figures walking towards Seb Healey.

"Dear God, no!" he murmured.

Chapter Twenty-Four

"Gramps! What's the matter?"

Seven year-old Eryk tugged at his grandfather's arm urgently.

Brent Dyer turned and looked at the child as though he had never seen him before. Then he became aware of his surroundings in his son's house. He was seated by the fire in the family room. He smiled.

"Sorry, Tiger. I was thinking. Do you ever do that? You think so hard that you go to another place?"

"Yeah!" said Eryk with feeling. "In class. Then Miss Bucher gets mad at me!"

"Perhaps school isn't the best time to do it. I was thinking about an old friend and work colleague," he added, knowing that the child would give him no peace unless he gave some information about his reverie. "Ichiro Matsushita."

Eryk tried the name for size.

"Wow! Ichi—Ichir . . . That's too hard! Gramps, he should have another name!"

"He did. Those of us who worked with him called him Matt. It was simpler," Brent agreed.

Eryk was busy putting two and two together. He was old enough to understand something of what Gramps had done in his life. Brent could see the cogs going round. The boy had a very analytical mind for his age, leading grandfather to hope that grandson might follow in his footsteps. He was tall and chunky. Fair hair refused to be smoothed down and made him look rather like a punk rocker for the new century. He didn't appear to look like anyone in the family until he smiled. Then he became his grandfather.

"Matt helped build the space ships?" he asked after a pause, with that amazing smile.

"In the early days, yes."

The little boy took hold of his grandfather's hand.

"You look sad. Don't you see Matt any more?"

"Ichiro went back home one time to Japan to see some of his family. Whilst he was there, he died."

"Oh." Eryk was crushed momentarily by this information. "Gramps, it's stopped snowing. Will you come outside with me and make a snow rocket? You promised."

Eryk loved it when his grandparents called round in winter. Grandma disappeared into the kitchen and made all kinds of tasty meals. Mom was the greatest mom ever but she didn't cook too well. But the best bit was when it snowed. Everybody else made snowmen out the front and in the back yard. Gramps helped him make snow rockets, which flew all over the solar system, of course. He was able to lord it over his friends for most of the season.

His little sister Leanne assisted in the process by running up and down, shouting and throwing snowballs.

"You go get dressed for snow building," said Brent. "I'll be out in a minute."

On his own again, he returned to his preoccupation. Obviously, every time a spaceship took off, he remembered Ichiro. The design concept of Zeus was his and from that grew Ariadne but he hadn't *thought* about his friend for a long time. So why now?

Ichiro was so *real* in the dream. He was just as he was before he made that last trip back to Japan. Brent could remember every word that was said during the night.

"Nobody should blame themselves for the failure of the Lander thrusters, Brent. If anything, I should take the blame. I was doing too many things at once. I was overseeing the final stages of Zeus and already looking ahead and doing the preliminary work on what turned into Ariadne. When I died, no one thought that I might have made a mistake. My designs were taken over and completed. But we are bringing them home. It's the least we can do."

"Who are you bringing home?"

"The Ariadne crew. Seek out the others. Talk to Bruce Dougall."

Brent Dyer sat watching the fire until he heard a voice filled with the exasperation that only a seven year-old boy can muster.

"*Gramps!*"

*　　*　　*

The crew of *Ariadne One* drifted around in a waking haze. To begin with they did automatically what they needed to do to keep the spaceship heading safely for Earth. They drew on the ingrained long hours of previous space flight and the training and preparation for this expedition. But gradually they began to remember what they were doing and why they were doing it.

At first, everyone looked at pictures and keepsakes that they had brought with them on the ship and no one grasped what importance they had. Then the breakthroughs began. Simeon was looking at a bracelet that he had found in his pocket.

"Hagar!" he said suddenly.

The flood of chaotic images streaming into his mind steadied to a coherent narrative, which recounted the whole story from when his aunt gave him the bracelet to the moment when he saw the Martians for the first time.

Brian knew that the pictures on his personal computer system were special but he struggled to remember why. When he was undertaking a routine check of the ship, memories raced through him. They jolted his body as well as his thoughts. He knew everything in an instant—meeting and falling in love with Georgina, their marriage, the birth of Fred and then Susie. It left him breathless. He wanted to run and look at the images at that very moment. Somehow he managed to complete his task before rushing back, locking himself in his quarters and feasting on the memories. He couldn't wait to be with them.

Simeon was alarmed to see tears in Emily's eyes.

"My Dad!" she said. "How long have we been gone? He will have been so alone and lost."

"No," Simeon told her. "You'll find that Hagar has been busy there."

The Martians watched, fascinated, as the thoughts and concerns of home returned to the human consciousness and nestled easily alongside the huge amounts of knowledge that had been assimilated on Mars.

"Once they start asking me why Lander's thrusters wouldn't fire, I think we're almost there," Ichiro said to Tony. "I have spoken to Brent Dyer."

Tony sensed human worry about what Dyer would do next.

"Give him time. We must remember the limitations of humans, however sensitive they are and whatever their potential. You have opened the door for him, as Sally and I have done for the others. They need to come to terms with what they have seen and what they have been told. They have to walk through the door themselves. It could take some of them a while. We can't kick them through it, as tempting as that might be."

*   *   *

Through the medium of television, the whole world looked on in appalled fascination as the United States of America apparently ran out of control. In Richmond, Virginia a bystander was shot and seriously wounded by local police as they struggled to gain control of a large mob. The country erupted as this and other stories of violent law enforcement were publicised. Everyone forgot about *BUSSTOP* and its peaceful marching in Washington D.C. It was as if the cause it was trying to bring to everyone's attention—the disbanding of the space organisation—had never existed. A collective madness was descending as old scores, real and imaginary, were settled on the streets of towns and cities across the country.

Local police and the National Guard were fighting a losing battle.

Television and press correspondents tended to lead a peaceful existence, dotted across the face of the country, and they liked it that way. Domestic reporters were happy filing reports about cats stuck up trees and hostility between cheerleader groups. Foreign reporters scanned local and regional news for items that might be of interest to the folks back home. With a snap of the fingers, everyone was a war reporter and the front line was everywhere.

President Rodriguez sat with his inner core of new advisers—Murray Crellin and Bob Broomfield very much to the fore.

"Mr President," said Crellin. "All the White House staff that you put on vacation are clamouring to come back and help you. This could be a bit tricky."

"Not at all." Rodriguez grinned wolfishly. "They can try to come back." He turned to another member of the team. "Dan, have the clearances all been cancelled?"

"Yes, Mr President. And the notices are good to go."

"Excellent!" Rodriguez turned back to Crellin. "It's a matter of thinking ahead, Murray, as you have said several times to me. When all these folks turn up for work, they will find that their security clearances have been voided. Not only will they not be allowed within the White House, they will each be given a letter terminating their employment here with immediate effect. They have all breached their contracts by taking unauthorised vacation."

"But you told them that they could all take a—"

"I told them what, Murray? I said no such thing. Dan, is there any trace of anything on the White House system saying that these members of staff could take time away from work?"

"No, Mr President. I don't know what you are talking about."

Murray Crellin's grin was widening to match that of his boss.

"Mr President, it's a pleasure doing business with you."

*   *   *

Bruce came to the latest four-way screen conversation with Kevin Crane, Joe and Irene with important news, although everyone's immediate concern was his safety. Was there rioting anywhere near him?

"I'm okay," he said to them. "There hasn't been any trouble round here, yet. As you can imagine, Genevieve is devastated. She's as confused as everyone else. No one can quite work out how there is a peaceful demo one moment and the country going up in flames the next. But long story short, I've had an interesting talk with Brent Dyer. He called me last night."

"That's the man who designed the propulsion system for Zeus and Ariadne?" asked the Prime Minister, dredging through his memory.

"Yeah. And he's been visited too. He had a dream. Ichiro Matsushita."

"That's going back into the past!" put in Joe from home when Irene looked blank. He didn't really want to talk about this person but someone had to keep the conversation going. "Ichiro Matsushita was the overall design engineer of Zeus. He worked very closely with Brent Dyer. He returned to Japan for a family holiday and died. It seems he had a cerebral aneurysm, which had been there from birth, most likely. This was a bomb primed to detonate within him and his time ran out whilst he was staying with his parents. He died in his sleep. The work on Zeus was completed without him and, when his computer was checked, the designs for what would later be named Ariadne were at an advanced stage."

"Is Mr Dyer all right?" Irene enquired from her computer lab.

"He will be," Bruce said. "Like the rest of us, he's having some difficulty getting to grips with it all. Ichiro told him the same as we have been told—the astronauts are being brought home. And Ichiro is taking responsibility for the non-functioning of the Lander thrusters." Joe closed his eyes for a moment. Every time he thought he had locked away his lurking fear, something let it loose again. "I invited Brent to join this link-up. I guess that was a bit too much, too soon. He'll talk with us next time."

Four people, brought together into an unlikely family grouping by shared experience and knowledge, were eager to make the tally five—or more.

"Do you think anyone else will have some kind of—er—visitation?" Kevin Crane wondered.

"Who knows?" said Joe. "I've been keeping some contact going with Brian Hammond's wife and the partners of Gianfranco and Masahide. I'm beginning to wonder. They seem different, suddenly."

"I've found that with the folks connected to Jethro, Emily, Jackson and Simeon," Bruce added. "And, of course, Hagar is just . . . Hagar. You haven't lived, Prime Minister, until you've met Hagar Turner," he said by way of explanation. "Simeon Turner's aunt."

"Perhaps," suggested Irene, "they've got some sort of reassurance that makes even less sense than a visit."

"Georgina Hammond would come straight out with it if she'd had a visit!" Joe observed dryly.

"Yes," said the Prime Minister with a broad smile, remembering her physical attack on Joe. "She does seem to have the confidence to say and do anything where you are concerned!" His face straightened. "Bruce, I'm concerned about the way things are going on your side of the Atlantic. It seems that the President is very likely to carry out his threat and declare a federal state of emergency. Anything might happen then and it probably will. I'd like you to consider very seriously travelling over to Britain. We don't want you stuck in D.C. when the astronauts return."

Kevin Crane was not about to admit to anyone, least of all a U.S. citizen, that his working relationship with Ted Rodriguez had deteriorated to the point where he was dependent on the chatter that British Intelligence could pick up, to have any idea of what was happening in America. Other European leaders were experiencing the same problem. His Majesty was properly miffed that his Prime Minister was being treated in such an off-hand manner and he was all for turning the clock back three centuries and ordering the Royal Navy to sail up the Potomac and burn down the White House.

"The astronauts and their rescuers are returning to Cape Canaveral," said Bruce. "And Bob Broomfield wouldn't see me stranded." He began to wonder even as he said the words. "He's an old school friend. He'll get me there, if there are any difficulties."

Kevin Crane could hear alarm bells ringing in his head. *Bob Broomfield.* That name kept cropping up in several of the reports that were on his desk. He made a mental note to have a separate talk with Bruce when this meeting was done.

*   *   *

"Isn't it strange?" asked Irene that night as they finished dinner. "Here we are, all accepting that the Ariadne astronauts are being brought home by a group of people who are dead!"

"Are you beginning to doubt what's happened?" said Joe, casting the tail of an angry eye in the direction of Bonny, as if daring her to go anywhere near a guest and beg for food, even if it was Irene.

"Of course not! I've been thinking about it all afternoon. I think that the friends and loved ones we're seeing are the Martians, using a bodily form we can understand." Millions of miles away there was rejoicing on a spaceship. "I don't know why we didn't make the link before. After all, my grandfather said he sent the messages from Mars."

"I think we've been too busy taking it all in to think straight. And I think you and I might have had other distractions, as well. So planet Earth is finally to be invaded by Martians."

"I'd hardly call it an invasion, Joe!" Irene protested. "Invaders don't drop by for a cosy chat before they storm the barricades!"

"Visited, then. Visited. It was never like this in the old time films and books. I suppose death and destruction and women being carried off make for better action in stories than a peaceful arrival."

Joe was still for a moment, making a decision. However peaceful the Martians might be, and whatever their motivation, the world would never be the same again. It was time to stop messing about. He had delayed once before and look where that got him! He reached across the table and took Irene's hand in his.

"I love you, Irene. And I'm happy to see that you have a bit of time for an old fossil like me."

Irene thumped his shoulder with her free hand. Joe stood up, moved round the table and went down on one knee beside Irene. She turned to face him, hardly able to believe what she guessed was coming next.

"Joe. I—"

He put a finger on her lips.

"Shh. I know I'm a bit of an old has-been now but, Professor Irene Elizabeth Hanson, will you marry me?"

* * *

"So how long has this information been swilling round the system?" Kevin Crane wanted to know.

This may have been a screen conversation but Stuart Bland could feel the Prime Minister's irritation buffeting him.

"Not long," he replied airily. "And it has not been swilling anywhere. Only—" He did a quick calculation "—six other people know about this, and that includes my voice over person, who wouldn't breathe a word. I know too much about him," he concluded comfortably. "And my broadcaster. You are the first person who has seen the film other than those people. There's nothing like starting at the top."

"Six!" Crane was aghast. "How do you hope to keep control of so many?"

"Prime Minister! This is not Downing Street, or Whitehall. They are a dream team to work with"

"In my experience, lurking behind every dream team is a nightmare waiting to happen. I'm more likely to believe you, Mr Bland, if you tell me who is your informant and give me the identity of his or her associates. That knowledge will rest with me."

"I know it will. When the next edition of the Oxford English Dictionary is produced, you ought to be there within the definitions of *discretion*. Very well, then. Doctor Jamie Tennant shot the film. I deliberately removed that information from the soundtrack and did a few things with his voice to disguise it. In the end I decided it was better he was unidentifiable. His sister Vicky knows."

"Vicky Tennant? Joe Mortimer's PA?"

"The same. She asked her boss for help when young Jamie came back from the States with his film. He suggested me. Oh, and Professor Irene Hanson has seen the footage as well."

"I see. And who is your broadcaster?"

"The BBC is showing it. For the sake of speed and shock, which is of the essence, I've probably got less for the film than I could have done. But then, I didn't have to work too hard. It's still a pity I couldn't have trailed it on the open market. There might have been a lively bidding war. But a lot of the impact will come from total surprise so I've had to forgo that. One of the senior programming people at the BBC is an old friend. Michael Zindoff. I think you've heard of him. As you know, the BBC has a weekly current affairs slot. The topic and the film can change right up to the time of airing." The Prime Minister knew this very well. He had stolen a march on his political rivals by doing an interview for this programme when he was positioning himself to become leader of the party. "When I told Michael I was running it past you first of all, he perked up no end. I think he's looking forward to hearing from the Honours Committee and Buckingham Palace."

*   *   *

When the British Prime Minister scolded his country for the way it behaved towards Joe Mortimer and Irene Hanson after the original announcement about messages from Mars, everyone felt suitably chastised and humbled and made a silent promise not to do such a daft thing again. When America listened to a Presidential broadcast, in which it was treated to a roll call of the states where there was serious trouble, Ted Rodriguez was obviously boiling with rage. A nation felt as though it was being thrashed within an inch of its life, and the worst was still to come. A state of emergency was declared, with *FEMA* at the helm alongside the President.

"There is a list of Executive Orders. These are published in the Federal Registry and they are therefore law. I will use these in consultation with *FEMA*. We can, and we will, suspend laws, suspend the Constitution and take what powers are necessary."

Rodriguez listed some of the Executive Orders that might be called upon first, including the compulsory registration of the whole nation, arrest and detention of any individual without due process of law, the seizure and control of highways and seaports and control of communication media and all airports and aircraft.

"I *will* have law and order in this country!" he stated very firmly. "Foreign nationals might think about leaving, if they have no essential reason for being here."

Bruce began to wish that he had taken more notice of Prime Minister Crane's suggestion that he travel to Britain. He was one well-informed man. But what he had hinted at regarding Bob was horrifying.

Bruce knew he had to stay. Apart from anything else, he must have a moment of reckoning with his old friend.

There was a sharp intake of breath around the world as governments and officials digested the full impact of what had been announced in America. Several countries recommended that its citizens left as soon as possible. Kevin Crane was advised that it was best to hold a watching brief on this one, although anyone who contacted the Foreign Office was told it was not a good idea to travel to the United States unless it was absolutely necessary.

The Prime Minister bided his time, because he knew something that no one else knew.

The broadcasting of Jamie Tennant's film was not announced until the day it was due to go out. Then there was a full-on publicity campaign that whetted everybody's appetite without showing a frame of the action or giving away anything but the barest hint of what was to come. By midday, Greenwich Mean Time, most major television companies around the world were clamouring to be able to show the documentary, including the American networks. Zindoff knew what he was doing, Crane had to admit. This was worth a knighthood for services to broadcasting, at the very least.

The sharp intake of breath grew to be a cyclone of disbelief, which followed the time zones round the world as television schedules were altered and the half-hour demolition job went out at prime time. No accusations were made in the narrative. Stuart Bland was way too experienced to score cheap points that could see him in the hottest of hot water, and in court. The details of the two versions of the President's accident spoke for themselves. Viewers with more than two brain cells to rub together were left asking all kinds of questions.

The *FEMA* people were unimpressed the next day when President Rodriguez summoned them to the Oval Office so that he could launch a tirade and wave newspapers at them, which carried screaming headlines about the documentary and wondered on inside pages what the hell had been going on.

"Mr President!" said Murray Crellin. "The death of your predecessor was nothing to do with us. I take it, then, that it was something to do with you."

Crellin was making no judgement. He was simply disappointed that the President had apparently breached the Eleventh Commandment: *Thou shalt not be found out.*

Rodriguez spun on his heel and prepared to yell at Bob Broomfield.

"Don't start on me, Ted!" warned Broomfield. "I was the . . . master of ceremonies, you might say. I picked and introduced everyone that you needed. It was up to them to perform."

"Then you picked the wrong people!"

Rodriguez's fury was tinged with fear. Already thousands of people were clamouring to speak to him on screen and in person, including representatives from most of the world's embassies, asking for his opinion and comments on the BBC programme. Additionally, no one could believe that the sittings of the House of Representatives and the Senate had been suspended. It would only be a matter of time before shocked White House personnel went to the media to tell how they had lost their jobs.

He looked round the room. Instead of the familiar, friendly faces he had dismissed using low cunning, he saw only a ring of hard features, hatchet-sharp with malice and self-interest. Most of all, he longed to see that major pain in the butt, Bill Francioni.

"May I remind you, Ted," Broomfield said smoothly, "that you spoke to all the people concerned as well. You were pleased enough with them then. They did a perfectly good job in our practice run with that jerk from breakfast television. You must speak to each of them again and find out who was so dumb that he didn't even take down the licence plate of the doctor who stopped to help."

"That's your job!" Rodriguez flared.

Bob Broomfield had nearly had enough. In the normal run of things, there wasn't much he wasn't prepared to do to back a winner. He had got where he had got by spotting the perfect investment opportunities and knowing when the most unlikely individual or the most unpromising situation was the way to go. But he didn't need his business acumen to tell him that Ted Rodriguez wasn't a real winner. He wanted to *have* won, without putting in all the hard work first.

As the President marched up and down the Oval Office and the *FEMA* boys made their suggestions, Bob Broomfield finally faced up to a rare sensation. This wasn't just a case of having his money on the wrong horse. Everybody made mistakes. It was more than that. He had done what he thought was right to protect his family, and it was the wrong thing. If that wasn't bad enough, with this knowledge came a thought that impacted him like a bullet as he remembered his school days and a sparky, generous friend who did his math assignments for him on a regular basis.

"Bob, I never have worked out how you did so well in business when you're practically allergic to numbers!"

Bruce Dougall had teased him about that again only last summer, when he came to stay with the family.

"You go with what you're good at and you find others to fill in the gaps," he replied nonchalantly. "I cultivated a few people shamelessly in the early days when I saw that they had real ability with figures. Then it got to the point where I was able to afford to employ proper bean counters."

Broomfield had to think on how badly he had mistreated Bruce. Phoebe Harper was the staunchest ally of *BUSSTOP* and had a lot of time for the former astronaut. And he had been part of the plan for her removal. He shivered in the overheated room as he recalled his friend calling him, appealing for help when this jackass Rodriguez sacked him.

His personal communicator saved him. He excused himself and stepped out of the room to take what turned out to be a routine business call. When he came back in and Crellin was asking if the President had any names that he wanted to put on the list of those to be detained without charge, his mind was made up.

"Ted, that was my wife," the businessman lied. "There's a bit of a domestic emergency at home and I'm needed. I'll see you tomorrow."

He was half way to Bruce Dougall's place before he stopped to think. Bruce might not be in. He had always been a very outdoors kind of guy. But there was a dank mist settling over everything, creeping and writhing its way between buildings. It was like nothing he had ever seen before. Anyone with any sense would be warm and toasty indoors.

It was turning into a day of unpleasant surprises. Bruce looked grim when he opened the door to Bob. There were none of the usual cheery greetings.

"You'd better come in," he said curtly.

Broomfield wasn't sure now whether he was visiting a friend or being given the role of Daniel stepping into the lion's den. Bruce was watching him with narrowing eyes. He didn't invite him to sit down.

"Bruce, I've got a few things I want to talk to you about."

"So have I," Bruce replied in a flat tone.

Bob Broomfield never saw the punch coming. Apart from anything else, he had forgotten momentarily that Bruce was left-handed. He had the weird sensation of being airborne for a second and then he was sprawled on his back on the floor, his head spinning and his face on fire where the blow had landed.

"That's for Phoebe Harper!" he heard Bruce say.

He gave up trying to focus until he could see just two Bruces.

"Give me a hand to get up!" he begged. "The room is still going round."

Bruce stood over him. Broomfield was genuinely frightened. This man had always been easy to read. He was toying with the idea of doing the decent thing, but part of him wanted to complete a thorough job and dole out a good kicking. Slowly, reluctantly, Bruce reached down and pulled Bob to his feet.

"Sit there," he said, indicating an easy chair.

Bob half-fell into it.

"How do you know?" he asked, prodding his jaw tentatively.

"I have my sources."

"You don't know the half of it. Let me tell you, please. For a moment there, I thought you were going to carry on, Bruce. But I know you wouldn't kick a man when he's down, literally."

"It's the best time to kick him."

"Who said that?" Bob wanted to know, sensing a quotation in there somewhere.

"A twentieth century Archbishop of Canterbury apparently, according to Joe Mortimer." There was precious little humour in his smile. "So it seems I've got God on my side. What's going on, Bob? You might as well fill in the gaps for me. I'm guessing that there are some gaps, which might begin to explain why you have been doing what you're doing." He studied his left hand. "I'll have bruised knuckles anyway. I can always hit you some more."

Bruce could see that Bob was scared. He had never felt so liberated. He had nothing left to lose and it was a heady sensation.

*　　*　　*

Whilst Ted Rodriguez was chasing a situation that was taking on a life of its own, he received what was probably the most humiliating blow of all. He kept trying to contact Lee, with no success. It dawned on him, rather late in the day, that Lee was an Australian citizen who had obviously taken the President at his word about foreign nationals going home. He was upset that his friend didn't contact him before leaving.

Now the whole world was hearing from Lee Reckett with a vengeance.

It was a classic kiss-and-tell exclusive, the likes of which newspaper journalism hadn't seen in years. The Australian tabloid running the serialised story was printing round the clock, sensing a goldmine as copies of the newspaper were changing hands for silly prices. The gist of the story was round the world within minutes but everyone wanted to savour the words and talk about it with friends, family and colleagues.

Lee gave his reasons for dishing the dirt: "I have been driven from my adopted home by Ted because of the unrest and the state of emergency. And the film about the death of Phoebe Harper shows that something is going seriously wrong with his country."

The dollars that were changing hands for his exclusive weren't mentioned.

And he made it plain that he wasn't the only man who had taken the President's eye. The stampede was on. Every sensationalist journalist was on the hunt for other boyfriends. And where was the President's wife in all of this? She was conspicuous by her absence and her silence.

The same photograph and film footage headed every news report in every country. A global audience studied the image of a bronzed and muscular fair-haired young man with pale blue eyes, which seemed to be permanently on the verge of weeping.

The American internal security forces knew that a very clever and devious politician had played them. Rodriguez had covered his tracks in an expert fashion and there was a reluctant acknowledgement for how he had done it. There was not the slightest hint of homosexuality when routine checks were run. Otherwise his political career would have been ended long ago. That is, if it would have ever been allowed to get started in the first place.

*   *   *

"It's a different way of being proved right, Joe," Irene mused as they sat in Saturday languor at her house. "When you told me about Sally, you said that it is possible to keep your private life private, if you really want to. I get the impression that these revelations about President Rodriguez are a real surprise to everyone."

Joe looked at the *Shock! Horror!* front page of the newspaper

"You have to feel sorry for the poor sod. This will be the end of him. National leaders can bluff their way through most things, but this is making him look ludicrous and no one can survive that for long."

"It's a terrible thought, but perhaps someone will kill him," said Irene. "The Americans have a very chequered history with their Presidents, don't they? They have bumped off popular leaders, as well as the unpopular."

Joe knew that he must have another warning word with Bruce on the subject of shooting people. His attitude to homosexuality had been made very clear in his antipathy towards Masahide; and the astronaut, living quietly but openly with his partner David, was light years removed from Ted Rodriguez.

"Never mind everybody else's secrets, Irene. We have some news to deliver ourselves. You go and glam yourself up for the family dinner. I need to call Bruce."

*   *   *

The body language and the tone of voice gave away true feelings. These were men and women who put on neutral faces with their working clothes but their anger, their disgust and their unease were expressed in other ways.

Vice President Henry Sargent handed out generous libations of bourbon.

"Drink it up, my dear," he said to one dubious White House staff member. "It will do you nothing but good."

Chelsea Brannigan sipped tentatively at her glass and then knocked back the contents.

"What the hell! I'll go and kill him myself!" she said vehemently.

"That's better!" the Vice President observed. "So, ladies and gentlemen. I'm flattered that you have turned to me. I've had on-screen conversations with most of you, but I'm not sure where we go from here. The way you were all dismissed from your posts would be laughable, if it were not so serious. As you are well aware, a President can do his job with almost no reference to the Vice President. I was only appointed because the Constitution said that there must be a VP. And now that the constitution has been suspended . . . A state of emergency is the most elastic of commodities in this country and *FEMA* coming in on the act and using all those Executive Orders makes it a very dangerous situation. I'm sure we shouldn't be meeting like this."

Bill Francioni put down his glass with a clatter

"Henry! You're the Vice President. We are your guests in your formal place of residence at the Admiral's House. What law or Executive Order could we possibly be breaking?"

"Probably a law that Ted Rodriguez made up whilst he was eating breakfast this morning. I don't mean to be flippant but this is what we are reduced to—rule at the whim of one man."

"That's true. And it's one man backed by one very scary organisation," Francioni had to admit.

There was a knock on the door and Meryl Sargent, Henry's wife, came in.

"Henry, there are some gentlemen who insist on seeing you. I said you were busy."

Four police officers shouldered their way into the room. Bill Francioni noticed that they wore the badges and insignia of *FEMA*.

"We received a report that there was some trouble here, Mr Vice President," said one of them. "Everything all right?"

"Trouble, officer? There has been no trouble here. My friends and I were just having a quiet drink together."

The police ruse was childish and transparent. The Admiral's House had its own security teams.

The senior officer took in the identity of each person in a glance.

"Okay. You need to know that *FEMA* police are taking over the safety of this residence. The existing teams are being stood down. Things are very tense at the moment, Mr Vice President. I think it might be an idea if your *friends* all went home. It's dangerous out on the streets."

"They will be on their way in a few minutes," Sargent promised.

He could do no other. And as he said goodbye at the door to his visitors, parked police cars were in evidence.

"Where will this end?" he whispered to himself.

Alone, he poured another reflective drink. He was raising the glass when Meryl bustled in again.

"Doesn't anyone know it's the weekend?" she complained. "There's Bob Broomfield here to see you."

"Have you become lost?" Sargent asked when Broomfield was seated. "Ted Rodriguez is running the White House these days."

"Cut the funnies!" The Vice President noticed a massive bruise and swelling on Broomfield's jaw. "Listen. Please. I need your help."

Vice President Henry Sargent did listen. He had heard a lot of worrying rumours. What Broomfield had to say confirmed and underlined them, giving substance to his worst nightmares. Equally shocking was the bit that came next—the family burden that Bob carried, a burden that enabled the President to blackmail him in such a cavalier manner. Bob managed to tell the story with only a slight tremor in his voice. The least that Sargent could do was to take it all in with an outwardly calm exterior.

"You don't need me to tell you that you're playing a dangerous game, Bob," he said at length. "You've decided to become a double agent, so to speak. You've seen sense, even if it is a little late in the day. All credit to you. But if Rodriguez has the slightest suspicion that you are playing this game, you know that he won't hesitate to make public what he knows about Belle. And he'll take you apart for light amusement afterwards."

"I know. I've managed to tell Bruce and I've managed to tell you." Bob's eyes were haunted. "I'm big enough and ugly enough to look after myself. So I think I can move on and tell the kids." He stopped and smiled wryly. "Kids! They're adults."

"But they are still your children and Belle is still their mother," Henry pointed out.

"I know. But in the end I can't carry the can for Belle's behaviour, and neither can the girls. I couldn't have done more for her. Her sexual preferences have become more and more bizarre and have overwhelmed her. A man who loves her is no longer enough. Someone has to stop Rodriguez, and it will have to be an inside job. The President of the United States is running amuck! If the price is Belle and an uncomfortable time for the family, that's the way it has to be."

"What *is* eating Rodriguez?" Henry wanted to know some time later. "Do you know? Apart from being a closet gay all these years, that is. What is this all about?"

Broomfield accepted another drink thankfully.

"I usually leave the parlour psychology to others, but I dug around and found out something about him that is very relevant. As a young man he candidated for the *BUSSTOP* space programme. He was turned down. So I guess all these years he has felt rejected and angry."

"How on earth has he kept that one off his resume and out of the public domain?" the Vice President wondered. "You can be sure that Phoebe Harper didn't know anything about it. Well, the information must be there. You found out. You don't need to tell me how."

"I won't. But I had to call in almost every favour and debt on the list to get at this one, once I had an idea of what was there. He had covered his tracks very thoroughly, Henry, mainly by threats. He is one mega-devious guy. Look how he has fooled everyone with all these . . . boyfriends."

"Uhu. And from being angry and rejected over *BUSSTOP*, he has ended up plain angry," Sargent marvelled, understanding "He has felt it for so long that he's forgotten what he is angry about, apart from being well on the way to wrecking our space programme. Does Bruce Dougall know?"

"He does now. He knows that when Rodriguez was gunning for him, it was the unsuccessful envying the successful."

"You'd call Ted Rodriguez unsuccessful?" the Vice President exclaimed.

"Henry! You know what's going on. Is that a success? The Founding Fathers must be spinning in their graves. I had to put a stop to Bruce being arrested when I saw his name on a list!"

"What was the charge?"

"Come on, Mr Vice President! You don't need charges in this state of emergency."

"I do apologise," Sargent said with a gracious incline of the head. "It's taking some adjusting to, that we are not living in an approximation of a democracy. So. What happens next?"

"I think there could be some help coming from a very unexpected quarter. It was a very long talk that I had with Bruce Dougall. We covered some pretty amazing ground. I'm still not sure about some of it. Bruce has a better grasp of what will happen but I think there are some areas where he's still a tad hazy."

"Was he the one who hit you?" Sargent asked.

"Yes. That's not important right now. I want you to listen very, very carefully. I don't think I've gone mad. Well, not yet. And I've never seen Bruce as calm and rational about anything and we go back a long way, as I think you realise. Hold on all comments until I have told you the whole story. I hope you don't mind me taking up your Saturday afternoon, Henry. Perhaps I ought to apologise to your wife in advance. This is going to take us a while to trot from Go to Whoa."

Chapter Twenty-Five

Hagar Turner woke very early, two insistent strands of thought marching through her head. She couldn't remember having any kind of dream but she knew that the ideas had been placed in her mind whilst she slept. That had happened to her on other occasions, most notably when she knew she had to give Simeon the bracelet and the stone from the back yard.

The first was information, plain and simple. She smiled. The knowledge was like a big hug and it made her feel good. Well done, Joe!

For once, she hesitated over the second thought, which was forming into a set of instructions. Normally she went with her instincts. But today she wanted to be really sure and she railed silently at her present limitations. This could be tricky, what with the state of emergency and a President who seemed to be losing it. For herself, Hagar wasn't worried about walking into danger. But she did pause to consider the consequences of leading others into that peril, especially if they didn't fully comprehend what it was all about.

When Hagar went to stay with her grandmother as a child, she was sent to church and Sunday school. Most of what she was told washed over her head. But she remembered some of the roistering stories about characters from the Old Testament. She loved Gideon, the original wimp who didn't want to be God's warrior. He challenged God to give him a sign to prove that he was the one for the job. This time, *she* would demand more from those who watched over her and guided her.

"Here's the thing," she said out loud. "Show me. I'm open to persuasion."

Hagar turned on the television news whilst she ate her breakfast. She watched for a while and then she knew.

For once the headlines weren't completely full of President Rodriguez, what he had done, what he was saying, or how many countries had shut their embassies and withdrawn their staff in protest at his thousand and one transgressions. Instead, there was a lead story that had all the experts scratching their heads. No one could offer any kind of rationale for this weather phenomenon. A grey line of mist and fog was following the Atlantic coast of America round its contours from Washington D.C. down to Cape Canaveral and it was beyond explanation.

Hagar knew. She had seen those fingers of fog in her visions. In her dream world, they were tinted with the rainbow colours, beckoning, encouraging. And, as ever, she knew why she was drawn to them.

"Hello!" she whispered.

It was time. They were coming home. And then, could it be, might it be time for her to travel home?

First things first, though. The astronauts were coming home, Simeon included. She felt sorry that his mind was being shielded from her for now. Never mind. All would be revealed when the time came.

Hagar sat down and thought for a moment. She didn't need that many people. Powerful computers saw to that. What she did require was a handful of key individuals, who could watch over the electronics with understanding. And they must be characters who were used to the way she thought and reacted and would do as she asked without question, however bizarre the things might be that she said. Also, they had to be people who had the ability to be able to take on board what was about to happen.

She made a list of names and began contacting this special group.

*　　*　　*

President Ted Rodriguez knew he was in a waking nightmare. This was not at all what he intended. He had imagined what it would be like, so many times. After trouble had been whipped up on the streets deliberately, the state of emergency was declared. He was hailed universally as the strong leader, doing the tough but right thing for his country in a time of difficulty. Presidents, Prime Ministers and monarchs from all round the world fell over themselves to congratulate him on setting an example of firm government.

It wasn't playing out like that.

The documentary about the death of Phoebe Harper apportioned no blame directly. It couldn't do, but the implications were plain enough. The consensus of opinion was that if the doctor's communicator film was genuine, the interference to alter the course of events must have come very high up. Who *was* that doctor, anyway?

Rodriguez's inner circle found some very clever individuals to explain away the footage of the accident. They focused on the doctor. If his evidence was real, why was he remaining anonymous? And what about this filmmaker guy who helped him? His stock-in-trade was causing trouble, much of it unfounded. This official rumour-mill turned itself inside out to try and sow some seeds of doubt.

From the safety of Australia, Lee was making him a laughing stock in daily serial form. None of Ted's other friends could be contacted. He had to presume they had gone into hiding. He had no idea where Maureen was but, thank God, she was lying low and staying quiet. As a result of finding his unencrypted computer file, she knew the identity of other young men. Lee didn't have that information. He only knew that they existed.

The country was becoming a nervous, jumpy and sullen place. Curfews were imposed and travel restrictions put in place. Prisons and detention centres were bulging at the seams because it was becoming a crime to say or even think the wrong thing. And still there was dissent. Rodriguez was furious when Bob Broomfield removed one name from an arrest list.

"Have you taken leave of your senses, Ted?" Broomfield wanted to know. "It may be a while since Bruce Dougall was out in space, but elementary school kids still know who he is and what he did. A public figure like that would have to be charged with something. What's his crime? Standing up to the battering that the Board of Inquiry handed out to him?"

The President had to concede the point.

Canada and Mexico had not closed their borders formally but because they were urging their citizens in the strongest possible terms not to travel to the United States, the end result was the same.

No one could give the President advice on how to make any of this better. The best that Murray Crellin and his team could dream up, to try and turn round the Phoebe Harper situation, was to attempt to smear her.

"The bodyguard was travelling in the back of the car with the President," said Crellin with a leer. "That's not usual protection protocol. I'm sure there must have been something going on between those two. Shall I set up an investigation?"

Even Ted Rodriguez knew there were some things that just weren't done. In life, Mrs Harper was the ministering mother who doled out the hugs and kisses and the occasional smack to an adoring nation and, in death, she was becoming a secular saint. Despite the fact that Laurel, Mississippi was a long journey and an obscure destination for many, total strangers from all over the country were appearing on a regular basis with flowers for her grave.

He looked at his advisers in despair. Well, he wanted people who thought like he did. Now he had got them. He was learning the wisdom of the old adage *Be careful what you wish for; you might just get it.*

This morning he wanted to cry when he was given the news that Hagar Turner, *BUSSTOP*'s leading computer expert, and a small group of space flight managers had entered the Mission Control building at Cape Canaveral.

"Why were they allowed in? Where was Security?" he almost shrieked as he sat in the Oval Office for the daily meeting.

Everyone shuffled their feet and their papers.

"Security had no choice but to let them in, Mr President," said Murray Crellin after a long pause. "It turns out that they all had valid ID and their electronic passes still work. We will get the clearance stuff cancelled. Then, once they leave through the perimeter gate, they won't be able to get back in."

"Why weren't the passes and ID cancelled? Well?"

Another long pause.

"The authorisation to do that never received the final signing off, Mr President," Crellin stuttered. "The person who should have done it forgot to do it."

"Who should have signed that authorisation?" Rodriguez demanded, relishing the thought of humiliating someone.

"Because Mission Control has such a high security grading, it was you, Mr President. And you sacked them, didn't you?"

Crellin's voice was almost a whisper.

Rodriguez stared at the table.

"Get out!" he said sharply.

"Mr President?"

"Get out! Get out—all of you!" he yelled.

Everyone pushed back chairs hastily, gathered up documents and fled.

The President sat with his face in his hands for a long time.

"Oh, Ted!" said a much loved and recognisable voice.

He sat up and looked round the room wildly. There was no one there.

"We'll soon be with you. Don't worry."

"No!" he begged hysterically. "No! No! No!"

The tears ran down his face.

*　　*　　*

"Good morning! No, of course, it's a late good afternoon with you, Joe Mortimer."

Seeing Hagar Turner's smiling face was always a tonic but, on this occasion, Joe was more taken with where *BUSSTOP* America's mother confessor was located. He put on his glasses to make sure.

"Hagar, are you sitting where I think you are sitting?" he asked.

"I'm in my office at Mission Control," she confirmed. "I'm just off to see my group down in the Control Room. We have all systems powered up. Fortunately, everything was left as it was. No dismantling has taken place."

Joe didn't waste time or breath asking how Hagar had managed all of this. She was an amazing woman, to say nothing of being completely mysterious.

"So what now, Hagar?"

"They are coming home and they will soon be with us. I suggest you get yourself over here to the States. I have been talking to Bruce. Go and stay with him first. Then you will be able to travel to Cape Canaveral. He is expecting the two of you."

"The two of us?" queried Joe, with a totally straight face.

"No one is thinking that you will leave Irene behind. She is part of all this."

The gleam in Hagar's dark eyes suggested that she knew more about Irene than the facts that Bruce would have given about the visits that they had all experienced.

"How do you—? Never mind," he concluded, realising that there were many things about this whole business that defied explanation—for the moment. "Will we be able to get to D.C? And will we be able to move on down to you? I understand that there are all kinds of restrictions on travel to and from the States, as well as internal embargoes."

"Bob Broomfield, Bruce's old friend, is sorting it all out. He was advising the President for some reason but now he trying to do the right thing and redress the balance. He has set himself up as a sort of Trojan horse inside the White House and he will make stuff happen that way."

"From what Bruce has told me, with the sort of money Bob Broomfield has got, he could afford to raise a private army, trundle his tanks along Pennsylvania Avenue and park them on the President's front lawn," commented Joe. "I'd be tempted if I had that kind of clout! But I understand. If he did that, he's no better than Rodriguez, is he?"

"I think that's the idea. Get yourselves organised and give Bruce your travel details. Bob will smooth the way. And don't worry about the families and loved ones of the astronauts," she reassured him, apparently reading his thoughts. "It's all under control. Just for once, let other people do what needs doing."

"I like the sound of that. Don't forget that the Prime Minister and Brent Dyer are in our loop."

"You can contact your Prime Minister. I'll allow you that, Joe. You know him better, anyway. We'll deal with Mr Dyer. Now get your butts moving!"

*   *   *

Irene smiled at Joe and she put her hand over his as the plane climbed steeply into the sky.

"I remember you saying once that you wanted someone to hold your hand on a flight to America. Well, here I am. Better late than never."

"What have we done, Irene? What are we doing? What will we do?"

"We're going to America," she said, not catching the drift of his questioning. "The astronauts are on the last leg of their journey home. Goodness knows what will happen after that, but it should be interesting!"

"No. You, your post at the University . . . everything!"

"Oh. That! I'm not bothered, Joe. I think my time there is done. The research has been wonderful, and I have been privileged to work with some young people who will make us all sit up in years to come. But some of the nonsense that surrounds academia gets me down and I can live without it."

Irene thought briefly about the stormy session that had developed with the college hierarchy when she asked for unpaid leave with immediate effect because she needed to travel to America on urgent business. She was told in no uncertain terms that, if she insisted on travelling, she need not return. It was monstrously unfair but not surprising. Sir Arthur Downey, the Master of the college, was a rabid misogynist, who was always concerned that there might be even one woman, somewhere, daring to have a good time. He had been scowling at her ever since Joe had returned from America after the disappearance of *Ariadne One* and she was obviously so happy.

"Are you sure?"

"I am." She held up her left hand, where a ring now sparkled. "I presume that you haven't changed your mind about this? So. When our adventure is over in America, I could be vindictive and take Downey to an employment tribunal for constructive dismissal. But I'd rather that we just got on with life, crashing about as everyone does from time to time, loving each other, enjoying ourselves. I'll write some more books. You can do . . . whatever you want to do. It sounds all right to me. How about you?"

"It sounds perfect."

"What do you think you will do?" Irene wondered after a couple of minutes.

"I'll sit back for a while. I've spent my whole working life as a human doing, not a human being. You said quite a bit about my star sign. I'm partly a Leo. Leos are supposed to have a lazy streak in them, aren't they? Perhaps it's about time I indulged that for a while. You write and I'll laze. I like the idea of being a kept man, for a few weeks at least!"

* * *

Brian Hammond knew that his eyes must be crossing as he continued listening to Ichiro's explanation of what had gone wrong with the thrusters on the Lander. Basically, the radiation from the sun and the temperature variations on the planet's surface had overwhelmed a small but crucial part of the Lander's electrical system. But the engineer was enjoying having an audience and he was sharing every last detail, as well as blaming himself for mistakes he made in the wiring schematics ideas that eventually turned up in *Ariadne One*.

"This was not your fault!" said Masahide. "You were only thinking out loud, so to speak, when you put those design ideas onto your computer. It was like doodling. I wouldn't want people to see my doodles!"

"I was not thinking clearly," Ichiro confessed cheerfully. "I know now that the increasing pressure of the aneurysm was pressing on my brain before it finally burst. Very late in the day, someone did spot that I had not built sufficient tolerances into the electrical system. Nothing was done about it. But we would never have met you all if the Lander had functioned properly."

"And we had to meet you," said another voice.

Tony had arrived unobserved to join the huddle round the large screen. Brian was really glad to see him, if only to be let off Ichiro's technical hook.

"You've said that before," put in Jethro. "Why?"

"We have made you aware of some of what is happening on Earth in America. That situation must be resolved."

"It must," agreed the second in command. "But there's something else, isn't there? Much bigger too. When all that knowledge was being given to us, on Mars, there was something missing. Am I right?"

"You are a perceptive man," Tony praised him. "You all ended up on this mission because of your levels of intuition. We are nearing Earth. We will soon be able to communicate with the planet and then its tracking stations will begin to find us in the heavens. So I must explain to you some final things. You must know of the situation with Bruce Dougall, and you need to hear more about the planet Maldek."

Brian's eyes had uncrossed and he closed them for a moment. As important as all this was, he wanted some quiet time to think about his family for a while. But for now, it appeared that school was never quite done.

The end was in sight, though.

* * *

Only a year previously Joe would have said that he would rather sleep out in the street than be under the same roof as Bruce in any kind of social context. As he relaxed in Bruce's home with Irene at the end of an easy and hassle-free journey, with only minor delays for the fog, a moment of introspection made him see just how far he had travelled in his attitude. And, as he had been noticing for some time, his colleague was a different person these days.

Talking to someone on screen was not the same as talking face to face, whatever claims might be made for the new technology, and Irene appreciated the force of Bruce's charm and personality as he welcomed her and Joe and congratulated them both on their engagement. She could quite understand how Sally's head was turned, however briefly, all those years ago.

In pride of place on the wall in the main room there was a photograph of the Ariadne crew. They were all so *young* and dramatic and good-looking and gave the appearance of having just stepped off a film set. It was very similar to the picture Joe had on display, and Neil and Stella owned one too, but she hadn't given it much thought up to now. She met and fell in love with Joe the man but she would have been lying if she said that there wasn't an element of fascination with the public figure. She was meeting Bruce as the famous astronaut and former head of *BUSSTOP* America, just as Sally met him when he was a headline maker of the day.

Irene noticed that Bruce had well-thumbed copies of her books on one shelf, sitting oddly with a major collection of poetry. She was flattered. Her literary agent and publisher despaired of the American market. Oh well, it was wholly appropriate that this man should be an exception to the rule.

It was easy to talk and both transatlantic voyagers stayed alert, despite the time difference. In the early evening Bruce opened bottles of wine and unexpectedly brought out beautiful old dishes containing olives, large shards of Parmesan cheese and fresh figs wrapped in ham. He shook his head when Irene complimented him on his good taste.

"There's a great deli down on the next block. Stefano is my guide to all things Italian."

It was easy to forget why they were gathered together.

"There's something I need to tell you both," Bruce said finally during a natural pause in the conversation. "This is important."

By the time he had finished, the colour was gone from Joe's face and Irene knew that she was holding the arm of the sofa with one hand and grasping Joe's hand with the other.

"Why didn't you tell me sooner?" Joe demanded.

The speaking of those words broke the dream he had on that family holiday last summer, when he could only remember that Bruce told him something vital and terrible. Here was the rest of it. It was like watching a film or a television programme again and taking in all the details missed in the previous viewing.

"Cancer!" exclaimed Irene. "Does your doctor have any suggestions as to a possible cause?"

"He thinks so." Bruce looked directly at Joe. "The long space walk I did on *Ariadne Three* must have exposed me to some unknown form of radiation."

"That's impossible!" Joe protested. "The airlock sensors picked up nothing when you came back in and you sat in that hospital for days being checked over for every known culprit that might have caused you to be unwell on the return journey. I know how long you were there. I gave those doctors hell to try and get some answers from them," he admitted ruefully to Irene. "It was hard work, being angry for so long." He paused. "That makes it sound insincere. I *was* angry, for real. Furious, that top-notch doctors couldn't help one of my team."

"Every *known* culprit," Bruce went on. "The doctors are talking some *unknown* form of radiation. Tests and machinery only find what they are designed to find." He looked tense, as if ready for a big effort. "I'll admit now that I blamed you for a long time after the diagnosis, Joe." Pieces of jigsaw fell into place for Joe. "I blamed you for sending me out there, even though I had the time of my life doing the walk. And it was my job."

"It was," Joe agreed. "But I'm sure that I would have thought just the same if I was in your position."

Irene left the room discreetly, saying that she had to make a call on her personal communicator because it would already be pushing midnight in England.

She spoke to Debbie for some time. She longed to tell her friend that Alisdair was now proved right in the diagnosis he made last summer when he watched Bruce on television. That would have to wait for another time. She still had plenty to relay to England.

But, more importantly, Irene could give these two proud men the opportunity and the privacy they needed to make any apologies and effect the reconciliation that they were edging towards. She knew that there was another unacknowledged elephant sitting in the corner of the room but matters had to be dealt with in proper order.

*   *   *

The media were very happy with the unexpected turn of events at Mission Control. Interest in the Seminole encampment was beginning to wane but the arrival of key personnel in the Control Room sparked everything into life again. It didn't take specialist correspondents long to work out that these were some of the people who would have talked down *Ariadne One* in the normal run of affairs. What was it that the Native Americans had said when they appeared at the end of the runway? They were waiting for the astronauts to come home. Surely it was more than coincidence that these folks had turned up. It looked as though they were staying in the Mission Control building and accepting hospitality from the Seminole. Reporters spoke to the *BUSSTOP* specialists when they were out in the encampment and everybody said the same.

"We are waiting for them to come home."

Under the terms of the state of emergency, Ted Rodriguez could do just about anything he wanted, if he was brave enough. His courage was beginning to fail him. He could have sent in specialist teams to drag out the *BUSSTOP* people from Mission Control but he didn't fancy the spectacle of unarmed civilians manhandled by the military being flashed round the world. He could have forced the media to leave but there again, ugly images would have been put out before press and television were completely gone from the site. And when he put these suggestions to his advisers, they shook their heads.

"Of course, it's up to you, Mr President, but . . ."

As events became more complex, they lacked the breadth of vision to see what to do next. And like their boss, they didn't have much of an appetite for a fight.

It had been so easy to begin with. It made Rodriguez think it would all be easy. Getting rid of Philemon Brown was like disposing of the trash. Dispatching Monty Silverton was a good practice and therefore the removal of Phoebe Harper was assessed as simple. It was. But a small mistake—the failure of someone to confirm the identity of the doctor who helped—had busted that wide open. The President had made another small but crucial mistake himself. He had been having such fun barring his staff from the White House that he forgot about something that turned out to be much more important—the fact that some of the dismissed workers at Mission Control still had live ID and entrance passes. And it never crossed his mind that, some day, his relationships with a string of gorgeous young men would come to light.

And he had another problem to deal with. Justin was plaguing him from beyond the grave. The young man was there, in Ted's waking thoughts and in his dreams. The nights were the worst because, as the President awoke after each dream, for a few moments he was convinced that Justin was still alive.

*   *   *

"Justin! Behave!" said Sally when she saw him sitting in a corner of the spaceship's command area in a meditative position. "He is beyond understanding any of your messages now."

Justin opened his eyes.

"I suppose he is," he said with genuine regret.

Tony returned from a complete tour of the ship.

"She feels right, Brian," he told the commander. "We should soon appear on screens on Earth. Send out your first message. There will be no time delay on your transmissions. Ariadne could not withstand the strains of time and space being folded to make the journey but we can speed along your radio messages. Try now."

The entire crew crossed their fingers out of sight as Brian opened up the comm system.

"Mission Control, this is *Ariadne One*. Do you read us? Please respond, Mission Control. We are on instantaneous communications."

"We read you, *Ariadne One*." The voice at the other end was not in the least bit surprised. "It's good to hear from you. We are picking up your telemetry and your position. We estimate that you are about thirty-six hours out, give or take. Do you concur?"

In the Control Room, Hagar nodded as screens came to life and Brian Hammond's voice was heard. There were a few moments of wild cheering and individuals rushed up to each other before haring back to their consoles. Hagar went over to the comm board.

"*Ariadne One*, this is Mission Control," Brian, his crew and his guests heard. "Stand by. Someone wants to speak to you."

"*Ariadne One*, we are receiving you loud and clear," said Hagar. "It has been a while. You are registering on all systems. You're all okay? We confirm that we are picking up seven life signs plus . . ." She pondered for a moment, wondering how to phrase the description of this hitherto unseen reading. ". . . plus seven echoes."

"That's correct, Mission Control. We have seven guests on board, from Mars."

"That's fine by us, *Ariadne One*. How are you doing, Brian?"

"Really well, Hagar. Really well."

"Enjoy the journey, *Ariadne One*. We'll have a party for you here when you get back. And we look forward to welcoming your guests."

Hagar looked up at her saucer-eyed accomplices.

"Okay, ladies and gentlemen," she said. "We won't need to do much for ship or crew until they are finally through the atmosphere. They have a compliment of Martians on board. Hence the instantaneous transmissions, I guess. They will be looking after things there. I did say that we would be making history. I suppose we'd better go and share the moment with our media friends. The whole world needs to know about this."

There were a lot of missed heartbeats whilst many, many people checked the date to make sure that it was not April Fool's Day. The media had received a recording of the conversation with Brian Hammond on *Ariadne One*, released by Hagar.

The television news channels were in uproar. Special editions of daily newspapers were hitting the streets at all hours of the day because editors assessed this to be such a fast-moving story that conventional deadlines would make the front pages out of date before they appeared.

The world was scared and angry.

It was scared because this crew of astronauts who were coming home were supposed to be dead. They had been mourned across the world. So what was going on here? And most picked up on the fact that there were Martians on board *Ariadne One*. When Bruce Dougall said that America had never really recovered from Orson Welles' radio dramatisation of *War of the Worlds* in the 1930s, he wasn't entirely joking. Films and television stories about alien invasions continued to mine a rich vein of fear in the 1950s and 1960s, fuelled by the tensions of the Cold War. Although there was a much more reasoned attitude to the possibility of life on other planets these days, that time had left its mark in the collective consciousness. The majority of people were still little children who were afraid of the dark and who expected monsters to turn up in flying saucers.

It was angry because there was a school of thought reckoning that, for whatever inexplicable reason, Miss Turner and her colleagues had gone out of their minds and were perpetrating some kind of sick joke. It was a particularly cruel hoax to play on the loved ones of the astronauts.

The pay-per-teardrop journalists and the publicity specialists went looking for these stricken groups, so that everybody could Share In Their Pain. The men and women associated with Brian Hammond, Jethro Norman, Masahide Shimamoto, Gianfranco Rosso, Simeon Turner, Jackson Metz and Emily Alexander were nowhere to be found.

Casting the net wider, comment was sought from Joe Mortimer and Bruce Dougall. They wouldn't be too keen on opening up old wounds. Anyone with a grain of sense and empathy could imagine how hard those two must have been hit by the loss of *Ariadne One*, to say nothing of losing their jobs in the subsequent fall-out. And Irene Hanson had to be worth a few paragraphs because she lit a blue touch paper when she announced that messages were being received from Mars. None of them could be located.

Brent Dyer's relations were suspiciously vague about where he was. His was a tight family, who appeared to be born with built-in radar when it came to sons, daughters, spouses and grandchildren. When Amelia Dyer said that her husband was on some kind of business trip, the woolliness of her language caused eyebrows to be raised.

The British Prime Minister was another obvious candidate to speak about events down at Cape Canaveral. The Downing Street press office issued a brief statement informing everyone that Kevin Crane had been called away unexpectedly to attend to personal matters and that everything was left in the capable hands of his Deputy, Tomas Kaminski, who had nothing helpful to say regarding the return of *Ariadne One.*

If anyone was knew where Kevin Crane might be, no one was saying.

The opinions of the Italian and Japanese Prime Ministers were sought, as the memories of their citizens were being sullied. These leaders were out of the country and no one would say where they were for the moment. Second-in-command figures were holding the fort.

No one seemed capable of putting together the obvious two and two by seeing that all these elusive people couldn't just have disappeared without some prior warning. So it was as though some giant hand had come down from the sky and snatched them up into another dimension.

The instrument of removal was Bob Broomfield. His hands were of normal size but the length of his reach and the power he commanded impressed even Bruce. On his say-so, within hours the astronauts' families and the politicians were flitting through airports and checkpoints like shadowy ghosts, apparently unnoticed and with no questions asked. What amazed Bob was that only the Italian and Japanese premiers were at all surprised by their summons. Everyone else welcomed it, expected it, and obviously knew more about what was going on than he did. And he felt Bruce had told him some pretty incredible stuff.

When everyone was safely gathered in, staying in different anonymous houses within the City of Cape Canaveral, Bob met up with Bruce and Joe for a quick consultation. *Ariadne One* was a day away. It should have been twelve hours, but for some reason the spaceship had slowed right down.

"We're doing a bit of sight-seeing," was Brian's explanation over the radio.

Tony had asked him to put the brakes on, to make sure that all the players were in position.

Bob Broomfield looked ill. He was almost asleep on his feet. He hadn't rested in twenty-four hours and he wouldn't rest until everything was sorted out. Joe could sense a kind of manic energy seeping out from him. He noticed a fading bruise on Broomfield's jaw as this fixer enumerated what he had fixed.

"I'm glad you're on our side," he said.

Broomfield rolled his eyes.

"I need to go back to Washington now and persuade that w—pardon me, the President of the United States—that he should be here for the landing of *Ariadne One*. Are you happy with everything, Bruce? Because if you are, my private jet is waiting for me."

With that, he was gone.

"You're the dark one, Bruce," Joe admitted. "I know he's your friend but I take it that you must know where the bodies are buried. No one is *that* accommodating, or wears himself to a frazzle, without a very good reason."

"We both know things," said Bruce cryptically.

*　　*　　*

The President and the businessman were alone for this talk in the White House.

"You will travel to Cape Canaveral, Ted." Bob Broomfield's voice was quiet but firm. "Do you want to look even more of a fool than you are already? You aren't about to be the only person missing from the muster. You've ringed Cape Canaveral with tanks and infantry. It will look a bit dumb if you're not there as Commander in Chief. Your Vice President is on his way down there as we speak."

"He doesn't have permission to leave D.C!" The President's laugh was manic. "No one has!"

"But they've already gone. Henry Sargent. Bruce Dougall. Joe Mortimer and Irene Hanson are there. The list is endless."

"Who said they could go? Who let Mortimer and that woman enter the country?"

"I did, Ted. You appointed me as one of your advisers, sharing in your emergency powers. You did well to call an emergency. It means that I have been able to get the right folks to Cape Canaveral and the crazy sightseers are safe at home. It couldn't be better."

"You traitor!" Rodriguez hissed. "You've turned against me, haven't you? You're going to tell everyone what we've done. I will do some telling too, remember!"

"No Ted. I'm not saying anything. You will tell the world yourself what you have been up to. Bruce Dougall knows most of what has happened one way or another and he can guess the rest. You will accompany me to Cape Canaveral tomorrow morning. We will be there in nice time for *Ariadne One* landing. And no, you don't need to take a planeload of staff with you. You can take your bodyguards, if you're that bothered. But everyone will be more interested in witnessing a miracle than in taking a shot at you."

*   *   *

The damp blanket of fog was still wrapped around Cape Canaveral. Ordinarily, an incoming plane or spaceship would have been diverted to another location. Hagar appeared to have taken over the role of Flight Director and she said that everything was fine. As trained pilots, Joe and Bruce wanted to question this. Even with modern day instrumentation, such weather was still to be taken very seriously and Ariadne did not have all the kit that a commercial airliner or military plane possessed to minimise the dangers. Like Zeus, she flew for such a short time in conventional airspace that it wasn't worth installing yet more equipment. It was Mission Control's job to help land her safely. But then they remembered that there were Martians aboard, who probably knew what they were doing.

Both men wanted to be inside the Control Room but Hagar was definite on this matter.

"You do what you've got to do and we'll do our bit. You need to be out there to welcome everyone home."

"You've got Simeon aboard," Bruce pointed out. "You should be on the runway too."

"Simeon's parents are here to welcome him. I've all the time in the world to catch up with my nephew."

Most of the world was still terrified. Places of worship used by every religion and every denomination in every country were crammed, as some kind of reassurance was sought. In buildings that didn't already possess them, viewing screens were installed hastily. The members and adherents of Philemon Brown's church wondered what their pastor would have made of all this. They still missed him and they wondered again that so little progress had been made in finding those responsible for his murder.

The tension on one matter was eased when the missing Prime Ministers appeared for the landing at Cape Canaveral, each accompanied by a small staff. The prospect of three national leaders being mislaid somehow was worrying. They seemed fine and there was time for recriminations later. They were mingling with all the other people whom one would expect to be present to welcome home a triumphant space flight. It was easy to pretend that none of the dramas surrounding *Ariadne One* had happened. The presence of the Seminole was a reminder that this was a bit different. All stood waiting, oblivious of the dreary weather.

"The President doesn't look too happy," Irene commented. "If I didn't know any better, I'd say he had a gun pointing at him."

Bruce glanced over at Bob, who stood a couple of paces behind Ted Rodriguez. His right hand never left his coat pocket.

"Perhaps he has."

Georgina Hammond was waiting with her children next to Brent Dyer. Fred had recognised a familiar face and made a beeline for him.

"I think you should be able to see this time, soldier," Brent reassured him.

In the Control Room everyone was rigid, willing *Ariadne One* through the communications blackout caused by re entering Earth's atmosphere. Jethro Norman's voice was heard again right on schedule.

"Okay, *Ariadne One*. Basically you've got dead calm here," the meteorologist concluded at the end of her approach weather report. "Just the fog to contend with."

"The runway lights are on," confirmed Hagar. "Do you need a steer? Computer landing systems are ready and waiting. Your only problem is a runway full of people hanging around for you and getting a bit chilly,"

"Thank you, Mission Control. We understand," Brian Hammond confirmed. "We're on a direct line, straight in. I'll try and pedal a bit harder. We don't want anyone catching cold. Forget your computer controls. We're coming in on manual."

Outside, eyes strained to see that black dot on the horizon and binoculars raked the sky.

"Here she is!" someone said.

A murmur ran through the watching crowd.

Irene was standing between Joe and Bruce.

"Don't forget to breathe, you two!" she murmured.

Just as they had never seen this type of spaceship take off—because they were part of the crew in Zeus—the same thing applied to landing.

Ariadne One glided down towards the runway, landing gear extending as if she was stretching her legs after a long rest. There was the slightest flurry of dust when her wheels touched the ground, the graceful swan settling onto the water with barely a ripple. Landing chutes were deployed and the final braking systems went into action as her weight settled fully on the wheels. She whispered to a halt within two inches of the markers.

"Brian Hammond is bloody good!"

Joe was pride personified. He was sure that Brian had brought *Ariadne One* in under manual control. The little wiggle that the ship had executed as she came over the end of the runway, to centre her, did not have its origins in any computer command.

No one moved. No one knew what to do.

At last the main door opened and the steps unfolded.

Chapter Twenty-Six

The procedures, the lists of dignitaries and the endless details about who would do what, when and where for the scheduled landing of *Ariadne One* had grown ever bigger in a massive computer file. When contact was lost with the spaceship, and all hope of anyone still being alive faded, those plans were quietly deleted and each person involved tried to forget about everything that was supposed to happen. This arrival was apparently unorganised and spontaneous and all the better for it.

Brian Hammond appeared in the doorway of *Ariadne One*.

"Daddy!" yelled Fred, breaking the awe-struck silence.

He ran forward, followed by his sister and their mother. At the bottom of the steps that led down from the spaceship, the family merged into a four-way hug. Georgina's face underwent a series of transformations as the sadness, the tension and the worry slipped away, to be replaced with the radiance of pure joy. Brian held on to his wife and children with an iron grasp.

One by one the astronauts emerged and figures detached themselves from the waiting groups, hurtling over to the middle of the runway. By the time Emily was swung off her feet by her father, there was hardly a dry eye in the crowd. The Seminole, led by Martin, began to sing and dance in celebration. Everyone else started cheering and clapping. Cameras fixed on Joe Mortimer and Bruce Dougall. No one would ever be able to describe accurately the expressions on their faces, any more than either man would be able to put into words exactly the emotions they were experiencing as the crew of *Ariadne One* truly came home.

One person unaffected by the moment was the President.

"So where are the Martians?" he demanded petulantly.

Bob Broomfield sighed. If Ted Rodriguez had been present when the angels sang for the shepherds in Bethlehem, he would have criticised the lead tenor for being slightly behind the beat.

416

But in one way, Rodriguez was right. An expectant hush settled over the runway. The astronauts were safe and well, if a little bemused by the warmth and enthusiasm of their welcome. So where were these guests from Mars that Brian Hammond had mentioned so casually his first radio message back to Earth? A buzz of anticipation worked its way around the crowd.

Brian untangled himself from his wife and children and went back inside the spaceship to where the Martians were waiting.

"At the moment, no one will be able to see us," Tony reminded him. "We need to earth ourselves, just as we did on Mars. If you take each of us by the hand, at the bottom of the steps, we will become visible. Our vibration levels will travel through you into the ground and undergo the final necessary lowering."

Brian went back outside. This could be interesting. The crew had become used to the different things that the Martians did. He wondered what Earth would make of it all.

There was a choked sound of confusion from the spectators as the two figures of wisdom materialised, seemingly from nowhere, on the tarmac. The man and the woman were unrecognisable to anyone as a friend or family member but the surprise came from the way they appeared and the fact that they were in human form. Only five people were expecting that.

Bob Broomfield shoved President Rodriguez forward and he recovered his manners enough to step out and welcome the visitors to Earth, and specifically to the United States of America. The Martians introduced themselves as Sophia and Adam.

Four individuals were obviously apprehensive, for those who cared to look. Brent Dyer shifted his weight from one foot to the other. Irene's face was very pale and she recognised the blank mask that was settling across Joe's features—his defence against the world when he unsure or nervous. Bruce was studying the ground intently.

"Ichiro! Matt! My old friend!" shouted Brent, running to meet his colleague as eagerly as Fred had bolted to his father.

The cheering and singing began again as the two men flung their arms around each other, laughing and thumping each other on the back.

Kevin Crane nodded in particular recognition as Tony materialised at the foot of the steps. Irene's legs didn't want to work.

"Go on," Joe whispered. "You know that they're here only for our good. That's your grandfather, remember!"

Despite the dream and the visit, Irene was still overawed by what was happening. Tony walked towards her, smiling broadly, the crinkling round his eyes imparting that special warmth to his expression.

"Granddad!" she managed finally and rushed into his embrace.

For all that Joe encouraged Irene, he was equally dumbfounded when Sally appeared. He stood and stared, such a muddle of emotions flooding through him and overwhelming him. This was every dream and every wish rolled into one, with a generous dash of nightmare thrown in for good measure. He had yearned for Sally down the long years. Now he couldn't move as she came nearer and nearer. She was just as he remembered her when he left to fly on *Ariadne Four*. That curl of hair still grew in a complete corkscrew over her forehead. It was an antidote to his last memories of her in a hospital bed as her failing brain was slowly entombed in a failing body.

"Hello, Joe," she said, kissing his cheek.

Joe could only pull her close and hold her tight for a moment.

"And hello, you!" Sally continued, turning to Bruce, who was equally overcome by a conflicting mixture of feelings.

Most people missed their moment of reunion because general attention was grabbed by a muffled cry from President Ted Rodriguez who had spotted someone strolling so casually towards him. A look from Bob Broomfield stood down the protection officers who were taking aim. From the President's reaction, Broomfield was sure that this was someone Ted knew—even if he was startled to see the young man. Droplets of moisture from the foggy air beaded on Justin's eyebrows. The overhead runway lights glinted on his diamond earring.

"Hello again, Ted," he said quietly. "I've come to help you. I've come to take you home."

He moved in closer, grasped Ted's hands and kissed him. There was a united intake of breath from the crowd.

"Oh God! No!"

The scream from Rodriguez was unmistakable this time as a seventh figure appeared at the foot of the steps of *Ariadne One*. Even Kevin Crane found himself gaping in disbelief as those around him called out in confusion and tried to understand what they were seeing. A woman in the Italian Prime Minister's party was led away. She was heard murmuring incoherent prayers.

Rodriguez continued holding Justin's hands, in terror.

Phoebe Harper looked up at him.

"We've had to break just about every rule in the book to do this!" she said in a ringing voice. "But then, you've broken a few rules yourself just lately, Ted Rodriguez! There's a bit of sorting out to be done here."

President Ted Rodriguez fell against Justin and slid to the floor in a dead faint.

*   *   *

"How is the President?" Irene asked her grandfather.

"Resting. A doctor wanted to put him under sedation. He needs to sleep, not to be filled full of pharmaceutical chemicals. We have given him sleep."

"You must remember that we don't possess your skills yet. We don't have any other way. If we want to ensure someone is quiet and sleeps, we do use—er—pharmaceutical chemicals, Granddad."

Granddad.

The word tripped off the tongue so naturally. Everything seemed so right, so natural. Irene did give herself a little pinch to make sure that this was not another of those complex dreams. She really was sitting in a house in the City of Cape Canaveral talking with her grandfather, Tony Johnson, who had died before she was born.

"Correction!" said Tony. "You—the people of Earth—did possess those skills once. You lost the knowledge, along with so much else."

The pangs of nervousness, unease and uncertainty began again within Irene, like a physical pain. Such comments reminded her that this was *not* her grandfather. He suffered a heart attack and died following routine surgery, many years ago. Tony knew what she was thinking.

"It's all right, my angel. It's only natural that you should be frightened on one level, as glad as you are to see me. Think of the families of the astronauts! As far as they are concerned, their loved ones really have come back from the dead. Of course, they weren't dead. We were caring for them on Mars, but that's how it will appear to them. And they *are* Brian, Jethro, Masahide, Gianfranco, Jackson, Emily and Simeon. Nothing added—apart from great wisdom—and nothing taken away." He saw Irene glance at the clock. "Joe is out doing good things," he soothed. "He'll be back as soon as possible. He and Bruce are bringing some order to today. Two fine men." He indicated Irene's ring. "And you think one of them is particularly fine."

"I haven't said anything to you," Irene stammered, blushing. "No one knows really, apart from Joe's family. And Bruce. And it's the last thing anyone is about to notice at the moment. I presumed you knew."

"I did. I do. I know what goes on in your life, Irene, and I'm so glad. This is Tony Johnson saying this, not the Martian *alter ego*. I've watched over you all your life. I never had a moment's doubt that you would say yes when Joe proposed to you."

Joe Mortimer and Bruce Dougall were indeed trying to bring some order to proceedings. Everyone was in a daze—and the President was in a state of collapse and shock—so they did what came naturally to them. They put their feelings and their needs on one side and took charge. Their first obvious concern was the astronauts and their families. They were confident that they could leave the sorting out of the dignitaries left standing at the side of the runway to Henry Sargent and Bob Broomfield.

It was not within the remit of Joe or Bruce to do most of what they did—even if they still had been the heads of *BUSSTOP*. But someone had to make the first moves, so they made them. They paid rapid visits to where each of the groups was based, made sure that everyone was coping, and then went on to the next thing. They were invited to stay at all the parties that would undoubtedly go on for days, but these were celebrations for family only.

Bruce paused to announce that there would be no debriefing, no press meetings, nothing with the astronauts for forty-eight hours. Seeing as *BUSSTOP* America was in limbo thanks to the President, he decided that he would call the shots. The crew of *Ariadne One* needed that time—and probably more. These people had been given up for dead, with no one having any idea what had happened. The world could hold itself in patience for a few days longer before hearing their story.

In a spirit of total hypocrisy, Bruce ended his comments by hoping that Ted Rodriguez would be feeling better soon. Rodriguez was last seen being helped to his feet by Justin and being taken to a car, incapable of doing anything other than putting one foot in front of the other

Whilst the Ariadne crew was not about to face the world, Joe decided the media needed something and he held an impromptu and rumbustious conference inside Mission Control. At one point he wondered if he might need to send out for a whip and a chair in the style of an old-time lion tamer, but eventually he began to get the message across. Of course there would be no interviews with the astronauts for a day or so. They needed time alone with their loved ones. And the Martians were not here as some kind of amusing freak show. They had travelled to Earth to do a job, probably several jobs. Exactly what their tasks were would become clear later. They would speak when they were ready.

"But Joe!" one reporter carried on protesting. "We must insist . . ."

"Insist?" Joe didn't know whether to laugh or cry. "You're in no position to *insist* on anything. In the future, people will look back on this as one of the most significant days in the human history of planet Earth. No one will be interested in what you are fussing about. Thank you, ladies and gentlemen."

"But Joe, what is the nature of your relationship with the woman called Sally? And obviously she knows Bruce—"

Joe stood up and everyone was silent. He seemed to be glowing with energy. He walked out of the room and no one followed.

Bruce was in the Control Room, talking to the *ad hoc* team that Hagar had assembled to bring *Ariadne One* home safely. At last he turned to Hagar.

"How about that then?" he said.

"Yes," she agreed.

No more was needed on the subject.

"You must go and see Simeon," Bruce suggested to her. "He was asking for you a while back when I dropped by. There's a party to end all parties happening. He won't rest until he sees you."

"I know. I'll be on my way shortly. You have someone to see too, Bruce. Don't put it off. It's important. It's part of your future."

That word. *Future.* Even now, when he was on a total high and felt he could go out and take on the world single-handed, Bruce hesitated over it. Hagar seemed to know what he was thinking.

"*Oh ye of little faith,*" she quoted, digging around in her Sunday School and church memories. "You'll see. I know you have other matters to attend to, but get yourself to meet Sally properly as soon as you can!"

The whole situation was moved along ably by Bob Broomfield. Bob's first task was to remind Henry Sargent that he was the Vice President and that he must take charge, due to the incapacity of the President. On the spot, Sargent announced the lifting of the state of emergency imposed by Ted Rodriguez and then set about being the gracious host for the foreign visitors. He invited them to fly back to Washington D.C. with him. The city offered more in the way of hospitality than Cape Canaveral and he needed to meet with the Speakers of both Houses of Congress and various groups to get some normality flowing. He would need to speak to the nation, and indeed to the world, through a television broadcast to spread a little reassurance.

Kevin Crane would much rather have stayed in the area. Apart from anything else, he wanted to see the people with whom he now felt he had a special bond—Joe, Bruce, Irene and Brent. But he showed a pleasantly neutral face to everyone and knew that he would be able to catch up with the important folks at another time.

For the moment Phoebe Harper said that she would stay in Cape Canaveral with the other visitors from Mars, within the Mission Control building.

Her reappearance was raising some unique problems, not least of which was the fact that, technically, America had two Presidents, something that had not been seen since the United States became disunited through civil war. What was she here for? Would she tell everyone about what really happened in the car crash? Would she expect to be President again? What was going on with Ted Rodriguez?

The questions were endless. And everyone would have to wait.

*   *   *

Irene did wish that this part of the experience were a dream—a dream from which she would wake very soon. It was something that she knew she had to do, but the certainty didn't make it any better. Sally gave her a glance of total understanding as they sat on a sofa together. Irene hated her and was ashamed about it.

"This is very difficult for you, Irene," she said. "You and Joe have just found each other and you think I have come to take him away."

Irene looked round the room. She was glad that this was all taking place in the anonymity of a borrowed house thousands of miles away from rural England. Whatever the outcome, she didn't want her home, or Joe's, filled with the memory of these events. Joe had not got round to showing her a picture of Sally and the woman was stunning, with her mane of black curls, the dark eyes and the high cheek bones. To say nothing of the fabulous figure, with legs that stopped somewhere round her ears. Irene was jealous too and she didn't like that sensation either.

"Something like that," she said faintly.

Whatever else Sally might be, she was honest.

"Please don't worry," Sally told her, putting a hand on her arm to emphasise what she was saying. "Mars has lent me to Earth only for a season, using the form of Sally. It's confusing, I know. I'm not here to take Joe away from you. You are making him so happy and the Sally part of me thanks you for that."

"Then why are you here?"

"I've come for Bruce. He is dying."

"I know he's ill with cancer. He told Joe and me the other night. He seemed quite upbeat about it all."

"From what he knows and feels at the moment, he will be. I shouldn't be telling you this yet, Irene, but I will. Someone needs to be prepared. He truly is living on borrowed time. If things stay as they are, he will die very soon. Ah," she said, noting the tears that came to Irene's eyes. "Bruce is an easily acquired habit, isn't he?"

"He's a sweetheart," Irene agreed, sniffing. "And I've only just met him."

"That's about right. Most men have to turn on the charm deliberately. He doesn't even have to try. So women love him and most men envy him for it. Don't cry." Sally enveloped her in a hug. "What happened to Bruce in space was a terrible accident. We are here to help him. We can't cure him here."

"How?" sniffed Irene, not picking up on Sally's comment about an accident. "Other than curing him, I don't see how you can help him."

"Patience, Irene. Patience."

*　　*　　*

Across the City of Cape Canaveral, there was some massive readjusting to be done. In the midst of each manic celebration, complete with popping champagne corks and flying streamers, there was an island of quiet and reflection as two people had to come to terms with what had happened. Georgina sat close to Brian, with the children in dancing attendance. Kate sat close to Jethro. Paola and Gianfranco smiled at their guests but didn't really see them, and it was the same for Leah and Jackson. David looked at Masahide as though he never wanted to stop looking. Simeon and Emily were involved in a joint merriment and Ishmael and Celia Turner and Doug Alexander could still hardly believe it was happening. The arrival of Hagar at that house gave everybody chance to take stock whilst she spoke privately with her nephew and his girlfriend.

The astronauts of *Ariadne One* had journeyed further than anyone could comprehend. But, in many ways their most difficult expedition was about to begin as they walked once more in the land of the living, when everyone had started to accept that they were dead.

*   *   *

Joe was drained, physically, mentally and emotionally. He and Bruce had spent what felt like a lifetime dealing with a thousand and one practicalities. They could fight their own battles but there were moments when impenetrable bureaucracy stood in the way. Then a situation was sorted by summoning Bob Broomfield in person or asking him to glare or bark via a screen or personal communicator. They were very glad that Bob was batting for them.

In many ways the day had become exactly what Joe had hoped for in his craziest fantasies. No one would ever forget those precious moments of meeting on the runway. But in other respects it was a million miles away from what he was expecting. He understood that Martians were bringing the astronauts back to Earth, using human form to make matters as straight forward as possible. What he hadn't anticipated was one of those Martians in the guise of the President's dead gay lover and another turning up as a reincarnation of Phoebe Harper.

And then there was Sally. Even though Joe knew that Sally would step off that spaceship, he was not ready for the hurricane force feelings that were rattling through him and shaking his very being.

He sat back in his chair now, eyes closed. Irene was quiet. This was not the time for idle talk

"We're not here!" he moaned when the door buzzer sounded. "We've stolen Ariadne and we're on our way to Mars!"

"It must be important," said Irene, getting up. "Otherwise our guard dogs wouldn't let them through."

One of Bob's thoughtful rabbits-from-a-hat was a formidable security detail for each place where *BUSSTOP* and Ariadne personnel and Martians were staying, to keep away the media and the multitudes of the simply curious.

"Oh. Come in," Joe heard Irene say. "We're through here."

With an effort, Joe sat up straight, just in time to see Bruce and Sally enter the room. He flinched. Meeting Sally on the runway that morning had been . . . whatever it had been. He knew that he must see her again but he was hoping to do that with a decent night's rest under his belt. That was not to be granted to him, obviously. And Sally arriving with Bruce just rubbed salt into the wound.

"Irene and I had a chat earlier on," Sally said. "We fitted that in whilst you two were still busy sorting out the world. We need to talk now."

Irene knew full well that *we* did not include her.

"I'll make us all some supper!" she said brightly. "A vanload of provisions arrived earlier on. Another of Bob Broomfield's master strokes, I suppose. Or Mr Sargent perhaps. He seems to be working miracles from D.C." She stopped, unsure, aware that she was prattling nonsense. "This is going to sound like a very silly question, Sally. Do you eat? I mean, you are a Martian and—"

"A very thoughtful question! Now that I am in fully acclimatised human form, yes. It has taken us today to adapt. If you look outside now, you will see that the fog has lifted. That was for our benefit, until we could adjust to the very different atmosphere."

"Supper for four it is, then!"

Irene took herself off to the kitchen, knowing that this would be a difficult one for all concerned.

"I should never have become a bone of contention between you two," Sally said when neither Joe nor Bruce knew what to say. They were sitting in an agony of silence and embarrassment. "What could have become a great friendship, that went beyond the confines of the teamwork in the spaceship, was marred. I think that you've had a taste of what that friendship could have been recently."

"This is honesty time, isn't it? It's what this is all about, I suppose?" Joe asked after a few moments. "Saying what hasn't been said before. Bruce, you said that you blamed me for your cancer—sending you out on that space walk. Well, for a long time I blamed you for Sally's death."

Bruce took that one very calmly and waited for more. Joe drew in a light, shaky breath.

"It sounds bloody stupid now, but I reckoned that Fate—or whatever you want to call it—decided that if there was going to be any sort of conflict over you, Sally, no one should have you at all. And so you were taken away from us."

"Some events are terrible, random accidents," Sally said. "My death was one of them. It's what you do with the aftermath that's important, the real lesson to be learned."

"I didn't do very well, did I?" Joe murmured.

"I shouldn't have taken any notice of you, Bruce," Sally said with genuine regret. "I had the love of a wonderful man. But it was always my weakness, that I was susceptible to flattery. And you know how to flatter, Bruce Dougall. You always did."

"And I was old enough to know better," he admitted. "Fortunately, I did—in the nick of time. This is not the place for lies. I promise you, Joe, that though she was sorely tempted, Sally was true to you."

In the kitchen, Irene was trying to make as much noise as possible. But in the end she had to stop chopping and stirring and generally clattering about. She crept to the door of the family room, listened for a moment and then opened it. She feigned not to notice the trace of tears on all three faces. The atmosphere was emotional but positive.

"The Hotel Hanson is open!" she announced. "Chicken and vegetable curry and rice. Joe has got me into the ways of curry."

"Curry!" said Sally with real enthusiasm. "What was that restaurant that we used to go to, Joe?"

"The *Taj Mahal*," Joe reminded her. "Irene, I hope that you've made plenty. When it comes to curry, Sally can eat anyone under the table."

*   *   *

There was no blueprint, no guide, and no precedent for what was occurring. A fiction industry in book, film and television had grown up around what would happen when humans encountered beings from other planets, either in the course of exploring those other worlds or when the aliens arrived on Earth and wanted to be taken to The Leader. But nothing could have prepared the world for the exact style in which this event took place. The visitors from another planet hitched a ride on a spaceship that was presumed lost, along with the crew who were thought to be dead. Four of the Martians were in human forms that notable people obviously knew and the fifth was a total shocker to everyone.

Reaction divided the planet into two groups. There were the watchful sensitives, who were attuned to powers and concepts beyond the rigid constructs of thought that had dominated the human inner life for so many centuries. They rejoiced and welcomed these events as a natural development in the progress of the Earth and its inhabitants.

The majority were overcome with degrees of fear. No one who saw the beaming faces of the Ariadne astronauts as they stepped off the spaceship or the gentle expressions of the Martian-humans could have spotted the slightest evidence of violence, hostility or any idea of an "invasion." Even when Phoebe Harper spoke to Ted Rodriguez before he collapsed, her admonition was given in the manner of a beloved aunt delivering a lecture to her nephew for his own good. But the whole package was completely different, scary, rushing in from left field.

Fear led to suspicion. Although the people who stood on the runway at Cape Canaveral had been assembled very hastily, the whole thing had been underwritten with a certain smoothness, as though a handful of folks must have known in advance that something along these lines would be happening. Some things never change and, rekindling the style of the excesses in late twentieth and early twenty-first century reporting, certain tabloid newspapers came up with front pages that scaled new heights—or plumbed new depths, depending on the reader's viewpoint.

"Now *that's* one for the scrapbook!" exclaimed Irene, looking over Joe's shoulder as he studied the British newspaper front pages on screen.

This one was particularly eye-catching. There were photographs a-plenty—a montage of Brent Dyer meeting Ichiro Matsushita, Irene laughing with her grandfather, Joe and Bruce speaking to Sally.

ARE THESE LEADING FIGURES REALLY ALIENS? demanded the banner headline without a blush.

"I always wondered why I was different!" Joe began grimly, and then he couldn't help smiling. "I shall make sure I have some serious words with my mother! It's a good job that your grandfather didn't openly acknowledge Kevin Crane on the runway. He could have done, because he had a long chat with the Prime Minister in that dream. Can you imagine what the rags would have made of that?"

Irene was imagining.

"I think our Martian friends are well up to speed on the eccentricities of planet Earth," she said. "Joe, are you all right?"

It was a sudden question, her first allusion to the meeting between Joe, Bruce and Sally the previous evening. Joe followed her line of thought, which was surprising. She wondered if it was prolonged exposure to the Martians that was making everyone more tuned in to others.

"Yes," he replied eventually. "We were all bloody fools and now we can let it rest. And I hope that Sally can be your friend whilst she's with us. She's not your rival."

*   *   *

Only a handful of people knew that Ted Rodriguez was detained within the Medical Centre at Mission Control. Henry Sargent spoke in a masterful broadcast to America, in which he announced that he was in charge now and that President Rodriguez had been ordered to rest, having worked so hard through a difficult time of transition following the death of Phoebe Harper. He was so calm, so matter-of-fact that he made people forget what they had seen happening before their eyes at Cape Canaveral. The nation, and the eavesdropping world, simmered down.

The Medical Centre was a logical place for the President to stay. It was equipped to undertake the initial handling of the carnage that would be caused by a major mishap at take-off or landing, involving a whole crew and many people on the ground, so a single helpless patient in a state of mental collapse was a mere detail. The staff had been summoned to care for him and it was easier to guard the stricken President in this confined area. Security was tight anyway for the Martians. Apart from the medical teams, only Tony was allowed to see him to begin with, to deal with his confusion.

This time, Tony brought Justin with him. It was obvious that Justin should take over the higher-level care and he was quite capable of delivering it. Rodriguez was sitting on the bed. When he saw Justin, he scrambled down and began backing across the room.

"No!" he whimpered. "Please, no!"

"Ted, did I ever hurt you?" Justin demanded. "Do you think I'm about to hurt you now?"

Ted had retreated so far into himself that his dark eyes were dulled and almost lifeless. For a moment there was a spark of true comprehension and remembering, shining through the haze of realisation and guilt and horror that clouded his mind.

"You never hurt me," he said slowly. "Except when you died."

He was standing in the corner of the room and he crouched down, covering his face with his hands.

"I'll take you home, Ted," Justin told him. "To Mars. You can recover there and, bit by bit, you can become the person you were always meant to be."

Justin led him, limp and unresisting, back to the bed.

"Lie down and rest, Ted," he soothed. "Sleep."

Justin's hand rested lightly on Rodriguez's forehead.

"You never hurt me," the President muttered as he drifted into sleep.

"No one said this would be easy, Justin," Tony said, seeing his anguish. "The human feelings we experience are part of the price we must pay."

"And the hardest bit is now to come!"

"Facing an innocent victim is difficult, always. The personal tasks are nearly completed. Irene and Sally have spoken together, as have Joe, Bruce and Sally. The two men did some reconciling before we arrived."

"So now it's Bruce," Justin sighed.

"Bruce," confirmed Tony. "And after that, addressing an international forum and facing the media of the world will be no problem at all."

*   *   *

Bruce was confused by the request from the Martians.

"You all want to see me," he repeated. "Just me. You don't want Joe? How about Brent, or Irene?" He was clutching at straws. "Or Prime Minister Crane? No. Just me."

"Just you," confirmed Ichiro. "You may want to speak to those people after we have met. You may tell who you wish but our business is with you."

Everyone was assembled in the house that Joe and Irene were using.

"You might need some friends to talk to afterwards, Bruce," said Irene, thinking on what Sally told her and having an idea what this might be about "They've obviously got some important matters to discuss with you. We won't be listening but we'll be around when they've gone."

This was like facing some very tough interview board, with seven people ranged round the room. But these faces radiated kindness and love. Tony, Justin, Sally, Ichiro, Sophia, Adam and Phoebe all looked at Bruce. He managed to look back without quaking. He felt nervous, for some strange reason.

"This meeting with you has always been a vital part of our mission," Tony began. "In fact, it's the central plank. Everything else has been gathered around it. We have to speak to you and make our peace with you. It's part of our karma, which we must face up to and deal with before we as a race, as a planet, can move on. This can't be dressed up to make it any more palatable. Bruce, we are responsible for your illness."

Bruce sat back in his chair and then leaned forward again, the movements enabling him to get his mind into gear.

"How?" he asked, quite reasonably.

"The doctor who cares for you is right. He is a talented man. He will go far. You were exposed to radiation on your space walk—a form of radiation that, at present, is unknown to this planet. In our normal Martian forms, the seven of us were conducting an experiment. We made a mistake. Mistakes are not the exclusive property of planet Earth! The resulting cloud of radiation drifted much further than we anticipated and calculated and so we had not made any effort to neutralise or disperse it. You were caught in one edge of it as you checked the exterior of *Zeus Three*. All these years later your cancer developed. We need your forgiveness."

"Of course I—"

Sally held up her hand, cutting him off.

"You must hear it all, Bruce, before you're so generous with your forgiveness. Your doctor prescribed you a particular medication and that has helped you."

"Yes. ZFF. It has given me my life back."

"It has, partly," Sally observed, making Bruce frown. "ZFF is the breakthrough oncologists have been looking for. Doctor Doherty is a real pioneer. But you were actually too ill for it to do you a lot of good when he prescribed it for you."

"We have been holding you up and keeping you strong for some time," Tony admitted. "You could not die—as the process is labelled here on Earth—and move on in the natural order of things until we had the chance to speak to you like this, whilst you are still a corporeal being. It has been part of our ongoing retribution to keep you in a reasonable state of health. The amount of energy needed from us to do this for you is draining and exhausting for each one of us. That is our burden. We apologise for the time when you were weakened during the flight of *Ariadne One* to Mars. You were driving yourself so hard that it was difficult for us to keep up with you. But the point is, Bruce, that on Earth you don't have much time left. You will die soon."

Once more Bruce experienced that hollow, empty sensation as the bottom of his world fell out from underneath him. It was a reliving of the original diagnosis from Doctor Doherty.

"*On Earth*," Tony reiterated. "We can't help you here. We can't bend the laws of this planet that far with the alteration of the vibration levels necessary. Your scientist Nikola Tesla had the right idea. His teeming mind developed a system to cure cancer based on harmonics. Any living thing can be killed with sound at the right frequency, including cancer cells. At the time, three million dollars, thirty scientists and three years would have seen his theory perfected. But the opportunity was wasted, as has happened so often on Earth, and the knowledge continues to be wasted because drug companies can see their profits being eroded by such a simple concept. Come back to Mars with us. There we can cure you of your cancer—and additionally, you can evolve with us into the next stage of our existence, as pure energy and thought. We know that you have always wanted to make a difference. You have, on Earth. That goes without saying. But this world and the countless other worlds out there stand on the brink of a huge jump in knowledge and in their way of life and understanding. We need teachers and guides like you."

"What if I chose to stay on Earth?" Bruce wondered, his mind spinning.

"You will die a human death, which you should not fear," Tony encouraged him. "One of the greatest disservices done to the people of Earth has been the development of fear about death. You will still become spirit and light but it will be the difference between . . ." Tony stopped, searching for inspiration ". . . being part of the ground crew and flying in Zeus. It may be that you wish to die on Earth. That's understandable. It is the planet that bore you and nurtured you. And maybe you will want Shannon with you in your last days."

"No!" said Bruce very abruptly. "I wouldn't do that to her. She knows I'm ill but I want her to remember me as I am, in a reasonable state of health, to quote you."

Tony smiled an understanding smile.

"You still care for her, very much. Don't you?"

"Yes. I do," Bruce admitted.

"Make sure you tell her your thoughts and feelings then, whatever you decide to do. And we will respect your choice, Bruce. I know you are a man of courage. You were ready to face death at your own hand, although in karmic terms that is never the answer. You saw it as the next great adventure. Wisely you turned away from that idea. Travel with us and the adventure of the whole universe is yours."

"I will be returning to Mars soon," said Sally.

"I will be taking Ted Rodriguez with me at the same time," added Justin. "Ted is the alien on this planet. The evil he has done is beyond repair here. And he is a gay man playing at being heterosexual so that he can be "respectable". It's the deceit that is reprehensible, not the sexual orientation, and it adds to his list of wrongs. Your astronaut Masahide, by contrast, is an honest and noble person."

Bruce was reaching information overload, to say nothing of trying to cope with the information that his life would end far sooner than he anticipated.

"Will you all return to Mars?" he wondered.

"I have some family duties to perform," said Tony. "Then I will return."

"I have some design work to do with Brent," Ichiro continued. "I have no idea what that man is doing sitting around in retirement! But then I will go home."

"We will stay for a season." Adam and Sophia spoke in unison. "We will guide those who need guiding then we will return home."

"I will travel home too, Bruce, when my duty is done," Phoebe confirmed.

"But whatever you decide about your future, we need resolution to your past—and our past." Tony looked genuinely troubled. "Bruce, we seek your forgiveness. We are trapped in the now by the consequences of our actions. We cannot move on. We cannot evolve as we are meant to evolve."

"It was an accident, wasn't it?" Bruce said. "I was in the wrong place at the wrong time. The classic cliché. Joe could have done that walk. Any member of the crew could have done it. We were all trained to be outside the ship in space. There was no malice intended. I understand that and I forgive you."

As he spoke those words, Bruce felt a curious lightness of body, mind and spirit that he had not experienced in a long time. It was though a huge weight had dropped away from his shoulders. It gave him the faintest idea of what the Martians must be experiencing.

One by one, the Martians thanked him as they left the room. Tony was the last to go.

"Thank you," he said. "We are freed and we can free your world now from many of its constraints. Take time in your final decision. Think about whether you want to stay or travel to Mars. No one is rushing back yet. The seven of us all have a teaching role to fulfil first. You will have time to be a teaching figure too. Apart from anything else, Ted Rodriguez is not well enough to travel yet—even in the way we travel."

Joe and Irene bade the group of visitors farewell. Then they stood, frozen by uncertainty.

"This is silly," said Joe and opened the door into the family room.

Bruce was sitting quietly.

"Hi!" he said.

"Everything okay?" Joe wondered.

"Yes. I've just been told I shall die soon."

Joe put his arm round Irene.

"Come and sit down," Bruce invited them. "I've got some things to tell you."

Chapter Twenty-Seven

Henry Sargent decided that he would remain in the Vice President's residence whilst he was stand-in President, for a while anyway.

"Ted Rodriguez could just as easily be resting in the White House as anywhere else," he said. "I wouldn't go barging in there under those circumstances. So I'm quite happy here. And so is Meryl."

No one would have minded if Sargent was working out of a busted down henhouse in the far end of West Virginia. What delighted a battered nation was the way in which he put the right people around himself so quickly in an attempt to return affairs of state to a more even keel. The *FEMA* team slunk away. The Vice President had enough to think about without conducting a witch-hunt for those who had helped Rodriguez. That could come later. Right now, every ounce of strength that the country could muster was needed in repairing the damage that the President had done. And one of the Rodriguez's main assistants in his madness had been Bob Broomfield, until he decided to stand up and be counted. Bob was Essential Man Number One for the moment. Sargent knew why Bob had acted as he did. Discretion was the thing for now. At some point there would have to be a reckoning regarding who did what, including an airing of the problems faced by the Broomfield family. But such considerations were for another time.

Everyone's combined determination meant that those involved in the landing of *Ariadne One* ended up with five days of comparative peace. Sargent told a breathless world that the astronauts and the Martians needed time to adjust. And he wasn't far wrong as far as the space crew were concerned. Not only had they been away from the planet but also they had been in another dimension. It gave them time to start to describe some of their experiences to their families, in preparation for the inevitable press and television conference that was being organised, to be held within the media centre at *BUSSTOP* in Washington D.C. And after that would come the endless sharing of thoughts with space experts of every kind.

The promise contained in the line-up of those facing the media meant that there was virtual war over obtaining accreditation for this gathering. The astronauts would tell their story, another group of people including Joe Mortimer and Bruce Dougall would say their piece and then, finally, it would be time for the visitors to address planet Earth for the first time.

"*Including* Joe and Bruce?" reporters said to each other, momentarily losing sight of the fact that this media call included Martians, even if they were in human guise. "Who else will be sitting with them?"

No one knew.

"Do I have to plead?" Henry Sargent wondered when he invited Bruce over to ask him if he would take his old job back. "I will, if you want me to. Everyone else is about to be given a notice of reinstatement at *BUSSTOP*, including your Genevieve! I'll literally grovel too, if that will do the trick. But you may have to help me up off the floor afterwards. My doctor tells me I have the beginnings of arthritis in my knees."

"I'll take the post, on a temporary basis," Bruce replied without hesitation. "I'll do this to help you out and to restore some kind of normality. I might be doing . . . other things as time goes by."

"I can't say that I blame you, Bruce. You have been rewarded in a strange way for all your work down the years. Yes, I know Rodriguez needs to be in a funny farm, but even so! You deserve to go off hunting and fishing or whatever for as long as you wish. But thank you for stepping into the breach for a while. Apart from anything else, you can keep that media pack in order. You have officials to take care of press and television but all these crazies know you and you know them. I would rather that they didn't start killing each other before the conference even begins. Could you bang some heads together and pour the oil on troubled waters so that we at least start in a calm and orderly fashion? Everyone's going stupid this time, not just the usual suspects. You can hardly blame them. Will you do it? It's a cheek, asking a man of your talents to be in charge of a big kids' conker fight. Sorry, I had a misspent youth in England," he said hastily when he saw Bruce's baffled expression. "I'll explain some other time." As much as he was tempted, he would regretfully have to leave the stories of his one hundred and forty niner for later. "But the end result of this press call will be something much more important, won't it?"

"It will," Bruce promised. "I'll do my best. Joe and I just hope that the Ariadne crew will have things to say that will make some kind of sense to the outside world. The media people will only stay fascinated by the *Back from the dead* bit for so long before they start in with the tough questions. Brian and the team are travelling up from Cape Canaveral with their families and our visitors today. Bob has commandeered the hotel for them all. Joe and I are hoping to do a debriefing session with the astronauts later on. We all need to get an idea of what happened. Oh, and the President is being transferred to that clinic here in D.C. and then the Martians can go on helping him."

"I don't know what we would have done without Bob these past days," Sargent reflected. "Well, I don't know what we would have done without you and Joe, period. But Bob is a subtle steamroller. He makes things happen! I can quite understand why Ted wanted him as one of his backers, however he recruited him"

"Yes," Bruce agreed, recalling the astonishing admissions that Bob stuttered out to him bit by bit. "He's an underrated man of action."

"True. Tell me again what our guests intend to do with Ted Rodriguez. I feel rather bad about him just languishing and nothing happening apparently. I understand that the Martians have already started the healing process, but it's nothing that I can comprehend."

"They are doing plenty, Henry. It's just that what they do doesn't bear much resemblance to what we would do. They represent a highly advanced civilisation."

"You could be a spokesman for them!" said Sargent shrewdly. "I'll bet you're wishing you could be on the next Mars shot."

*   *   *

Joe and Bruce said little. They made the odd comment and asked occasional questions when no one could think of the next thing to say. They sat in a hotel suite and listened to, and pieced together, a wonderful narrative from the returned astronauts. Joe continued the habit of a lifetime and made notes but at one point he put down his pen and simply watched these people. He knew them well and he had monitored their progress over the years, as they grew from novice space travellers into the accomplished individuals who had been picked for the greatest challenge yet. He looked on them with something like paternal pride. He knew them very well and yet there was something *different* about them. As they spoke of their experiences, they . . . well, different was the only useless word he could come up with. He had noticed this with Sally. She was unmistakably the young woman he had loved and yet she wasn't. Did that mean that the Ariadne crew were part way to being Martians?

Joe understood completely what these people were trying to say. But he had an advantage, as would Irene, Kevin Crane and Brent Dyer when they listened. They had all shared in this amazing experience of the Martians coming to Earth, albeit from the sidelines. And Bruce? Joe stole a glance over at his colleague. He was not sure what this extraordinary man would do next, but part of him seemed to be half way to Mars already.

Afterwards Joe had a private word with Brian Hammond.

"You explain it like that and the whole world will have a good idea what went on out there," he reassured the commander of *Ariadne One*.

"Do you think so, Mr Mortimer?" Brian wondered. "I know what I want to say. I can still see, hear and feel what I experienced. It's as if it's all imprinted on my mind and has become part of me. I'll never forget a single detail. But putting it into a form that means something to others? That's another matter. I've lost Georgie a couple of times when I've been trying to explain."

Joe gave him an encouraging slap on the back.

"That has been the burden of the creative artist and the scientist alike down the centuries—knowing how something is and trying to show everyone else so that they understand too. You'll be fine. Bruce and I are performing as well. No one's escaping that easily. We'll have a good talk about it all when we're done!"

"I just can't wait for it to be over!" said Brian with great feeling. "Then we can all start getting back to normal."

Joe knew that *normal* would never be quite the same again.

* * *

Sean Moynihan, a reporter with one of the big Dublin-based daily newspapers, crossed himself.

"Holy Mary, Mother of God!" he whispered to his neighbour. "You couldn't be making this up, could you?"

Between them, the astronauts were painting a broad and vivid canvas of what had happened on the surface of Mars after Ariadne's thrusters failed to fire and contact with the spaceship and the crew was lost. They invoked all the senses to describe their experiences. Amongst the audience, mouths stayed open for a very long time as they shared in the story. The seven were elevated to a Hall of Fame that contained those who had silenced a media conference for more than five seconds.

Bruce grabbed the advantage when they had finished speaking and jumped in to thank the group for their efforts. Then he asked the reporters if they had any questions.

"*Sensible* questions," he said firmly, impaling a few sensationalist journalists on his glance. "None of this *How did you feel when the thrusters didn't fire?* nonsense."

The conference was almost as much in awe of Bruce as it was of the astronauts. The questions were sober and restrained as everyone reached out for their professional instincts and carried on.

Michael Charolambous, one of *BUSSTOP*'s media liaison officers, took over for the next part, as Bruce was in the spotlight. A room full of people simply goggled as the others joined him. They expected Joe. But Professor Irene Hanson? And Brent Dyer? And what was the British Prime Minister Kevin Crane doing with this lot?

There was a profound silence as each of the participants explained their unwitting part in the events that had put the world into a holding pattern whilst it waited to see what happened next. They detailed their exact links and experiences with the Martian visitors prior to the arrival of *Ariadne One*. What an amazing story, with Irene Hanson and the grandfather that she never knew! And Ichiro and Brent Dyer! And as for Kevin Crane . . . Some journalists had never been quite sure that he was human. He gave the appearance of always being so controlled, almost remote. Androids were the stuff of science fiction and a few political correspondents were convinced that a maverick genius inventor had slipped one into British politics. They couldn't imagine him being capable of having such an incredible contact dream.

As the revelations went on, the tabloids realised that a secret drama had been played out in amongst the Zeus space programme, with Joe, Bruce and Sally caught in the eternal triangle. The ambitious were already dreaming about what their front pages and major articles might look like the next day, when Bruce dropped yet another news bombshell—his terminal illness, and the space walk that was the cause of it. He spoke quietly, unemotionally, as did the others. This was too much, after hearing about Sally's death and the particularly tragic circumstances underpinning it. There was a wave of muted activity as walls and the ceiling were studied carefully and the odd tear blinked away from moist eyes. Only a few stopped to consider the torment it was causing very private people to tell it all.

As Irene said something to support a comment that Bruce made, she gestured expansively with her left hand. The lights winked and flashed on the diamond ring she wore.

"Oh yes!" she said, following the line of the animal-caught-in-the-headlights gaze of those who had noticed. "You probably won't know about this. Seeing as we are all being very honest and very detailed, Joe Mortimer and I are engaged. There hasn't been an appropriate moment to announce the news so far."

After a definite pause, there were many calls of "Congratulations!" which were almost drowned out by the sound of the majority slumping in their seats.

"*We surrender!*" their body language sighed. "*We're defenceless! We can't take any more!*"

There had been no element of calculation in this. Astronauts, Martian links and Martians had met the previous evening and decided that complete openness was the only way to go.

"Good news is there to be shared. That is obvious. And when you have made a mess of something, talking about it is part of the healing and the reconciling process," Tony told them. "However difficult it might be. Everything means everything. Are you three all right with that?" he asked Joe, Bruce and Sally.

They nodded.

"We have just as tough an admission when it's our turn," Tony admitted. "We have to tell planet Earth that we are responsible for the premature death of one of the icons of the age."

There had been no element of calculation in this. The Martians had journeyed to Earth with a remit for the truth, but everyone was attending a master class in the use of total honesty as a pre-emptive strike.

Bruce caught the eye of Michael Charolambous as he wrapped up what this group had to say with some well-considered remarks. Charolambous moved over to stand by him.

"I don't think they can take much more for the moment, Michael," he said softly. "We'll be sending for the paramedics soon. Give them all a fifteen-minute break. Then everyone will be a bit fresher for the Martians. They have some heavy duty stuff to deliver."

The move to the exits was not the usual stampede. Thoughtful knots of journalists drifted out together, trying to make some kind of sense of what they had been hearing.

Joe walked over to where Sol Freeman was sitting. He had made no attempt to leave his seat.

"Lost the use of your legs, Mr Freeman?" Joe wondered.

He had never had a lot of time for this writer, who used his newspaper column to criticise the space programme on a regular basis.

"Please tell me that this is some kind of elaborate hoax, Joe!"

Freeman's tone and face were beseeching. He seemed faintly desperate.

"Now why should a huge number of people go to all this trouble to pitch such a yarn to the world if it's not true?"

"Well, I have been less than enthusiastic about the *BUSSTOP* programme over the years," Freeman admitted.

Joe was angry.

"You are mesmerised by your own self-importance!" he growled. "Each person who has spoken has turned his or her guts inside out to give you lot the full picture—and all you can think about is your damned column and how you can save face because you can't accept that you might actually be wrong!"

"Joe," a voice spoke quietly behind him.

Bruce was waiting for him a few paces away.

"Please don't tell me I'm not allowed to kill him!" Joe muttered at him.

"The line to do that would start with me, Joe. Let him stew. And don't allow him to spoil this day. I know it's hard work but today is special."

The reporters filed back in obediently after their much-needed break. The seven Martians were already in place and they smiled serenely as they were stared at intently.

"Have we got something wrong with our human appearance?" Sally murmured to Tony.

"No," he whispered back. "Remember that in many ways these are a primitive people, with a backward and ignorant culture. They are checking to see that we haven't got two heads or six arms or some such thing."

Bruce called proceedings to order and welcomed the Martians.

"The floor is yours," he said graciously and sat down.

Previous expressions of incredulity were nothing compared to the facial gymnastics of the audience now as the visitors admitted to the errors that had caused Bruce Dougall's illness and his impending death.

"We have spoken at length to Bruce about this and we have made our peace with him," Tony said, with an air of finality which none but the foolhardy anyone would ignore. "This has long been a part of our mission. It was the very beginning of it, in fact. We had to do this, or we could not move on and evolve as the inhabitants of planet Mars."

"Why?" someone asked instinctively, hardly realising she was speaking.

"The deeds we all do become the wings that lift us higher or they turn into the chains that imprison us," Tony answered. "We were imprisoned by the knowledge of what we had done, even if it was an accident. Through your Earth years, we hoped that Bruce might be lucky—that he would suffer no ill effects other than the frailties he suffered during the flight home on *Zeus Three*. But deep down we knew that it was a false hope, and false hope is also a chain. We had to watch as Bruce became ill. Our real hope lay in the fact that plans were well advanced for the first visit from Earth to Mars."

"You said it was *part* of your mission," said Joelle Moulinat, the same reporter, wondering at her own cheek. "What else have you to do?"

"We have to teach." Tony indicated Sophia and Adam. "These beings represent all wisdom that has come to Earth. You have so much to learn. And a turn of circumstances means that we have yet another role to play."

Phoebe Harper smiled and nodded. "A fine country has had a leader who lost his way. The damage that was done must be undone."

Many of the people in the room still found it difficult to face Phoebe Harper squarely. They tended to glance away in the hope that, when they looked back, she wouldn't be there. After all, most of them had covered her state funeral. And no one felt brave enough to ask about Ted Rodriguez. That was way too scary. They had tittered immoderately over the newspaper exclusives regarding his secret gay life but what was being dealt with here was obviously about more than deceit and indiscretions. It didn't take a huge leap of the imagination to guess that he had a hand in Mrs Harper's death, along the lines of the machinations that were hinted at in that amazing British television documentary. No wonder he had collapsed when she appeared and spoke to him at Cape Canaveral.

"So when can we hear some of this teaching?" asked Joelle, obviously elected spokesperson by dint of everyone else's silence and her thirst to know.

"Soon," said Sophia, charming everybody straight away with the musicality of her voice. "But not here. We will be moving to Britain to teach. From time immemorial Britain has been a natural hub of this planet and a focus of energy and wisdom. Adam and I need to be settled and centred, that we may show you, the people of Earth, what you have missed and what you need to know. Our brother, whom you know as Tony, will be travelling with us. Apart from anything else, he has family business to attend to."

Tony beamed at Irene and Joe, who smiled back at him.

There was so much more that everyone could have asked but Sophia's statement brought this time of sharing to a natural close.

There were all kinds of immediate repercussions from the media conference. Within the hour, British citizens started to walk with a swagger and secret lift of the heart that had not been known since the heady days of Empire. Americans resigned themselves to being the poor cousins yet again, although they were wildly proud to own Bruce Dougall—now cast firmly in the role of the tragic hero.

There was personal fall-out too. Bruce had been home for about ten minutes when Shannon appeared on the doorstep. He wondered if she was tracking him via satellite.

"I came here with every intention of being mad at you!" she declared, brushing aside all social niceties and parking herself on the sofa. "But now I'm here, I can't do it! I couldn't believe what I was hearing on television!"

"I'm sorry that you had to find out some of the details via a press conference," Bruce said in genuine apology. "Since we knew for definite that Ariadne was returning, everything has been so crazy that no one has had a moment to stop and think."

"I know, honey. All that stuff about your state of health. That you will die soon. It really is true?"

"The Martians aren't here to deal in lies, Shannon. It's true."

"Oh, shit!" she exclaimed vehemently.

"I'm sure a best-selling author isn't supposed to say that. Although I remember that one of the characters in your book goes in for far worse language." He shook his head. "I thought you were here to yell about Sally."

"Bruce! That's the least of my worries. That's long ago and far away. And if we were to be held to account for what we *thought*, as well as what we did, we might as well all give up now! I'm concerned about you."

"The Martians will take care of me." He saw her incomprehension and her fear. He realised how improbable that must sound to her. "Stay to dinner. Joe and Irene will be back soon. You've met Joe before and Irene is a wonderful lady. And they might have Tony with them, so you'll get to meet a Martian. And I hope we can all help you to understand what will be happening."

Bruce still wasn't sure the next day whether Shannon had understood fully what had been said. He managed to track down Bob Broomfield, who took time out from performing miracles for the acting President and arrived promptly to visit his old school friend. He sat down and looked about him warily. Bruce gave him a querying glance.

"Last time I called round it all got a bit violent," Bob reminded him. "I don't do well as punch bag, Bruce. But I guess I deserved it on that occasion."

"You did. But that's all sorted and I've almost regretted hitting you since I knew what that asshole Rodriguez was about. I need your help, Bob. A big favour."

"Name it and it's yours."

Bruce outlined what the Martians had told him when they were all still in Cape Canaveral and the options that were open to him. His friend took it all remarkably calmly. It seemed that complete honesty was becoming the routine order of the day.

"Knowing you, I can't imagine that you'll sit around waiting to die," Bob judged correctly. "You'll go to Mars. Great! So, where do I fit into this?"

"Shannon. I've tried to explain it to her. I think she's too upset to take it all in."

"I'd heard that you two were getting quite cosy again."

"That's not the point. Bob, when I leave, will you look out for Shannon?"

"With the greatest of pleasure!" he replied, with a smile that widened by the second.

"Bob," Bruce said in a warning tone. "You're still a married man, technically. You aren't the one who should be splashed across the front pages."

"No," Bob told him. "I've had a long talk with the girls and Belle. We all talked together. Not just about what Belle has done, but how it meant that Ted could coerce me." Bruce tried to imagine a family conversation of such savage frankness. "Belle and I are divorcing. My lawyer will use all the right phrases on the paperwork." His smile was as wintry as the weather. "I've envied you being with Shannon since we were all about ten years old. But I promise you that I will help Shannon in whatever way she needs."

*   *   *

Professor Marmaduke Dawson gazed at Irene adoringly from the screen.

"Good God, Irene, you certainly know how to put the world in a tizzy with your own piece of news. Joe Mortimer! Congratulations, my dear. I can't say I'm surprised."

"Really?"

"Really. Do you remember the last time we met up and we had dinner in Cambridge?"

"I can hardly forget it, Marmaduke. You flattered me with your after dinner offer."

"Not flattery, Irene. It was meant, sincerely. Anyway, I recall that when I mentioned Joe Mortimer's name, you were all over alike in patches."

"And women are supposed to be the ones who fantasise!" Irene laughed. "I hadn't even met Joe at that point—apart from a fleeting official hello sometime previously when I gave a lecture at *BUSSTOP*."

"But you liked the idea of him!" Marmaduke persisted. "Now, are you two planning some kind of celebration bash?"

"It's one of our first things to do as soon as we return to England. And, of course, we'll be delighted to see you. If you can hang around long enough, come to the wedding. We've set ourselves a bit of a tight schedule, for various reasons," she said, thinking of Bruce. "Can you wangle the time?"

"I'm finishing here in New Zealand any day soon. A bit early, I know. I think I've earned remission for good behaviour. Seriously, the New Zealand prof has got to come back home for personal reasons, so we've all decided to draw stumps before tea. Now what's all this about you leaving the University?"

*   *   *

442 | Gillian Coleby

Home.

It was a very special place. Having seen so little of it recently, Joe appreciated just how special it was. As a child, he listened to his mother reading him *Wind in the Willows*. He never understood the part when Mole rediscovered his house after months of adventuring with his friend Ratty. Being away in space or undertaking long training sessions had not provoked this kind of reaction in him. But now he understood. He walked from room to room, touching different objects, standing at various windows and taking in the view and feeling only contentment. And all this was underpinned by the heart-warming knowledge that home also equalled Irene.

Joe was sure that he would sleep for a week but it was his turn to be staring out of the window in the small hours of the morning, with Irene wondering what he was doing and then joining him.

Stars were glowing and pulsating with incredible energy in a clear, frosty night sky. Joe knew quite a bit about them. Not as much as Irene, but enough. And he was still concerned about what Bruce had decided to do.

"Bruce?" she asked simply.

"Yes. Has he made the right choice, Irene? And is it that obvious what I'm thinking?"

"No. It's not." She glanced in the direction of the room where Tony was sleeping. "I'm sure that some of the Martian abilities are rubbing off on us. Bruce has picked the right way forward, Joe. We only struggle with it because it's beyond our immediate experience and every day understanding. Of course part of you wants him to stay here. I'd like him to stay, and I've only met the man recently! But for what purpose? If he remains on Earth, he will grow weaker and die. Then we can nod wisely and talk about *a painful illness, bravely borne*. In other words, he died in agony and was probably afraid and didn't say anything because he didn't want to upset anyone. We could all be thoroughly miserable at his funeral because that's what we're conditioned to do and it's satisfying. It's all rather selfish, isn't it, in a macabre sort of way? You know I have exaggerated a bit. But you get my meaning, don't you?"

Joe kissed her hair.

"Has anyone ever told you that you are a very wise woman?"

"Don't let the Master of the college hear you say that!"

"He is a—"

Irene put a hand over Joe's mouth.

"Be rude about him some other time. Let's watch the stars for a while. Sally is right. You could have had a great friendship with Bruce. You're realising that and you're trying to make up for lost time. Remember, we should always want the best for a friend. Look at that sky! What more could you wish to give someone?"

*   *   *

For a celebratory gathering organised at short notice, the turnout was impressive. Stable End had not seen such an influx of revellers in years as people rolled up to celebrate the engagement and impending marriage of Joe and Irene, who wanted to share their happiness with everyone. Never quite off duty, even though he didn't have a job any more, Joe commented to Irene that this party would take the public eye away from Sophia and Adam, who were not yet ready to speak.

Friends and family were simply delighted that two people had found each other and were making each other very happy. The popular press had been plunged into brief mourning. One of the longest speculative stories in the history of newspapers, with Joe Mortimer at its centre, was drawing to a close. And it turned out he had been making fools of them all the time. On the basis that most people love a happy ending and are delighted by the prospect of a wedding, the tabloids were remarkably forgiving and set out to ensure that readers were given every titbit of information.

Debbie and Alisdair MacIver were very proud guests at the party.

"It's only right," Debbie found herself saying to people in the course of the evening. "Irene was responsible for Alisdair and me meeting. I'm glad that we did a bit to help these two on their way."

Alisdair watched in friendly amusement. Wherever Joe was in the room, his eyes rarely left Irene. The doctor had to admit that she did look wonderful tonight, wearing a cerise dress, with pearl earrings and necklace.

"Joe," he said at one point. "I've just heard that a delegation has landed from the planet of Mercury."

"Yes," Joe replied vacantly. "She is, isn't she?"

Even Joe had to wake up when Marmaduke Dawson arrived. He made an entrance into the main gathering to cries of welcome from most of the group. He was the kind of person who would have bumped into someone he knew in the middle of the Gobi Desert. And no one could miss him. He was a lion but showed himself to be a pussycat as he kissed Irene soundly on both cheeks and then took hold of Joe by the arm.

"It's good to meet the fellow who has finally swept Irene off her feet! Make sure you take good care of her. I—. Good God! Who is that?"

Joe looked where Marmaduke was looking. The professor was transfixed.

"That's Vicky Tennant, my PA at *BUSSTOP*. She's a very efficient young woman."

"You worked alongside that . . . that vision?" Marmaduke gasped. "And all you can say about her is *a very efficient young woman*? You're obviously not made of stone but I am shocked by you, Joe Mortimer! Excuse me!"

Marmaduke made his way over to Vicky purposefully. Part of her was always in PA mode and she was aware of the importance of this man. Well used to chatting with total strangers, she shook his hand.

"Hello, Professor Dawson. I'm Vicky Tennant."

Marmaduke kissed her hand.

"Victoria! A vision like you should always use her full name. You are Victoria, the goddess of victory."

"Are you joking?" she asked uneasily.

She glanced around her. Was there someone here who might have got the professor to do this for a bet?

"Let me get you another drink, my dear, and we must talk. I'm Marmaduke, by the way. And you are most definitely Victoria."

The very sound of her full name being spoken by him was like a caress and it sent shivers of expectation coursing through her.

Joe stood for a while with Tony, watching the group.

"You've never really said anything about Irene and me," Joe said.

"Sorry, I forget that you can't read thoughts. Well, not with total ease yet. Joe, if you need approval or want a blessing, it's yours, with my every good wish. Don't fret about Bruce, either."

"I'm sorry he couldn't be here tonight." Joe tried to change the subject. "He'll come to England for the wedding."

"And then he will travel to Mars. That's the bit you don't feel so easy with."

"It's because I don't understand, I suppose," Joe admitted. "Irene told me off good and proper about that! I want to understand."

"You understand far more than you realise," said Tony with great fondness. "And you have travelled further than you ever travelled in space. Think back a year of your time. Irene was someone whose books you read. You could barely be civil to Bruce and the unspoken hostilities between you were a cancer in themselves. You were three disconnected people, who have established and re-established connections. And doesn't it feel better? And could you have imagined, a year ago, that you would be hosting such a party as this and one of the guests would be a Martian?"

"*The deeds we all do become the wings that lift us higher or they turn into the chains that imprison us,*" Joe remembered.

"If you understand that, Joe, the rest will come naturally."

Vicky had never guessed that simply talking with someone could be so enjoyable. Marmaduke was a fount of knowledge and his learning was leavened with a great sense of fun. She laughed more in an hour with this man than she had done in a long time. She felt the stress of the past weeks ebbing away. It had been a difficult time. There had been the loss of Ariadne, supporting her brother, putting up with the wrath of their parents when they discovered that they had been shut out of very important knowledge, as he admitted to them what had happened in America, and then being strong for Jamie after the documentary was broadcast. That was before she moved on the incredible return of the astronauts and the Martians and everything that had emerged from that.

It was as if all that baggage belonged to another person.

Irene came over and asked, very apologetically, if Marmaduke could go and speak to someone about his forthcoming publication on the twelfth century civil wars between King Stephen and Matilda. She had noticed that he and Vicky had barely moved from the corner.

She returned from pointing Marmaduke in the right direction to find Vicky looking a little lost.

"Marmaduke will soon be back. Agnes just wanted to ask him a few questions. He's a great person, isn't he?" she said, unable to resist the temptation to nudge the process along. "I've known him a long time. Joe broke your heart, didn't he?" she asked apropos of nothing, knowing that she had to go for it. "I know that at no point did he say or do anything out of order. You carried a torch for him and he was always the perfect gentleman to you—a little too perfect, I'm sure. And then I came along." She remembered the surge of anger she felt when Sally materialised from *Ariadne One*. "You must have hated me. I'm sorry for any distress I caused you, however inadvertently."

The two women looked at one another in perfect understanding.

"Ah! Two beautiful ladies!" exclaimed Marmaduke as he strode back with arms wide open. "How about a great big hug?"

"I've got my own teddy bear," said Irene, sliding out of the way. "I'm sure Vicky could do with a hug though."

Marmaduke crushed Vicky in his arms.

"How many months have I been gone?" he wondered.

"About five minutes."

"And every second was a fraction of pain, because I was away from you. I have never felt such pain!"

Marmaduke kissed Vicky's hands and her cheeks.

"Victoria, you are the woman of my dreams. Where have I been all your life? I will court you the old fashioned way until you say yes. You are my vision and my goddess, put here to be my partner, my friend and the mother of my children. I am here, in the humble hope of being your partner, your friend and the father of your children. And I will be your rock. Good God, Victoria! If I were having this conversation with you on the eve of battle, I would ride out there tomorrow and kill a thousand men. Fortunately, these are more enlightened times and war is generally considered abhorrent. But I will slay your dragons for you." He raised an appreciative eyebrow. "And I'm sure that you do a good line in dragon slaying yourself!"

Vicky wanted to say so many different things at once. What *was* this man rambling on about? It was all a bit scary. They had only just met, for heaven's sake! She doubted he was drunk. He had savoured two glasses of Chateau Neuf du Pape, accompanying the first glass with a comprehensive wine-tasting commentary and some complimentary remarks about Joe's taste in vintages.

At the same time, she liked what he was saying and wanted to hear more. In a weird way it was *right*. She looked at Marmaduke Dawson and had the sensation of arriving home after a long journey.

The contradictions within her meant that she ended up saying nothing and she glanced round from time to time, hoping that no one was overhearing.

At the end of a long and enjoyable evening, there was the inevitable and protracted process of everyone leaving. Tony made himself useful by running between the front door and the milling guests, announcing that taxis had arrived for different people. This left Joe and Irene free to say good-bye to everyone.

"Thank you for coming, Marmaduke and Vicky," Joe said. "Excuse me if I talk shop for a moment with Vicky, Professor. I haven't really had a chance to speak to her tonight! Vicky, I'm sure you've been told that the Prime Minister really wants to get *BUSSTOP* up and functioning again. He'll have to find himself a new person to be in charge. My time is done there and my resignation stands. Thanks for being such a great PA. I'll recommend you to my successor."

"Mr Mortimer, I was only ever your most efficient piece of office equipment. You never saw me as a person."

"As a goddess," Marmaduke murmured in correction.

"Yes, it seems that I am a goddess incarnate to Marmaduke, not just your answering machine."

Joe saw Vicky as he had never seen her before. Her light brown hair was long and smooth, reflecting the light. Her blue eyes sparkled behind the lenses of her glasses. She was of medium height and slim but she still had curves in all the right places. There was love and kindness in that face, an inner beauty shining out that was enough to make any man put his hand in his pockets, shuffle his feet and wish he were a better person.

Joe was so taken aback by the woman he was looking at that he didn't notice Irene wink in approval at her.

"Thanks again to both of you for coming. And thank you for all your hard work at *BUSSTOP*, Vicky. I'll be in touch."

"You're welcome, Mr Mortimer." Her gaze met Marmaduke's for a moment before she turned back to her former boss. "Thank you for inviting me tonight, and congratulations. I'm sure that you and Professor Hanson will be very happy together. And just one little thing. My name is Victoria."

Chapter Twenty-Eight

Vicky Tennant was glad on this particular morning that she was on her own in the flat once more. Their parents had swept up Jamie in a scorching firestorm of reproaches following the broadcast of the documentary and his confession to them that he was the doctor who helped Phoebe Harper. They railed at Vicky for respecting her brother's wishes on secrecy until he chose to say anything to them and they made Jamie feel like a naughty boy for throwing away a good job in America. Mum and Dad forgot sometimes that their children were adults and, when they were on this track, nothing and no one could shake their belief that the two of them were still vulnerable school pupils.

Actually, Vicky did feel slightly vulnerable when she awoke. Hence she was glad of the space. She went hot and cold in turn when she remembered how rude she was to Joe Mortimer at the end of the party. He was on Cloud Nine and probably didn't even notice. But Irene Hanson seemed to approve.

This brought Vicky to the crux of last night.

Marmaduke Dawson.

He might have been dismissed as a very vivid dream. Everyone appeared to be having them within the context of the Martians coming to Earth. But Marmaduke's contact details, on an ornate business card, were real enough in the bottom of her evening bag. She knew she was smiling as she recalled their conversation, which ranged effortlessly across a multitude of topics. Then there was his heartfelt protestation of devotion to her and his declaration of intent to make her his very own.

Well, his honesty was like an ocean breeze. He was a breath of fresh air after some of the men she had met; and following on from Mr Mortimer, who didn't know she existed as a person, it was completely exhilarating. Oddly enough, at the time that exhilaration struck her almost dumb and made her a passive bystander in what was happening. It was only now that she was thinking about it all and enjoying the evening in retrospect.

Marmaduke kept dodging in and out of her thoughts whilst she went through the mundane routines of getting ready to face the day. It would be good to get back to work at *BUSSTOP* soon, with a new boss thank goodness. That's what she was: an efficient PA. It was what she did best.

At the other extreme, the professor saw her as being cut out to fulfil some kind of Mother Earth role, combined with being an intellectual muse. Twice during the evening Marmaduke had said to her, "You are superb to talk to, Victoria. You are challenging me to think in different ways."

Suddenly, Vicky rather liked the idea. The thought of protecting the backside of another thoughtless boss and covering for him—it was bound to be *him*, wasn't it?—in the time-honoured tradition of good old-fashioned flannel, was exhausting. She had been taken to another world as Marmaduke talked about his stay in New Zealand and how he would be a University spare part for a while.

"I wasn't due back until the end of this academic year," he explained. "I don't think anyone knows what to do with me. I shall be a bit like Paddington Bear: *at a lewse end.*"

That recollection made Vicky grin. She went and looked at her Paddington Bear, complete with his hat, duffel coat and wellies. He stood on a chair in a corner of the main room. He was a family antique from the 1970s, loved, handled with care and passed down the generations. Marmaduke's eyes lit up when she told him about her treasured bear.

"Now *that* I will have to see, Victoria!"

Vicky believed in first impressions. As a PA she had to put over the right unspoken and spoken messages to others and she had become very deft at judging people herself. Mr Mortimer didn't count, so the only person who foxed her completely during her time at *BUSSTOP* was Bruce Dougall. She watched that gut-wrenching press conference, along with most of the world. It now transpired that he had been busy playing out a very private drama in his own life and another one with his colleague. So it wasn't surprising that she read him wrongly, especially as she was taking in Mr Mortimer's prejudices at the same time.

Oh yes, she believed in first impressions. And her first impressions of Marmaduke were good. He was a kind man, she judged, and sincere. His heart was in the right place. The fact that he walked and talked in capital letters just added to the fun and he had the bold appearance to go with it.

By the time Vicky had finished breakfast, it was a respectable hour to start contacting anyone. She went to her bedroom and took Marmaduke's card out of her bag.

*　　*　　*

Up to now, Sophia and Adam had been something of an enigma. The human forms of the other Martian visitors all meant something to someone. The personal links of Tony, Sally and Justin had been laid bare for everyone to understand. Ichiro Matsushita was a figure who resonated with most people of Brent Dyer's generation. Although no one wanted to think about it too much, everyone knew who Phoebe Harper was, even if her mission was still unclear.

Now it was time for these two characters to take centre stage.

Those who were expecting them to be sat cross-legged in some remote rural fastness were in for a disappointment. They were quite at home in a television studio in West London with a select audience, which gave them people with whom they could talk and interact and hold a discussion instead of having to address the soulless stare of a camera.

In the minutes leading up to the live broadcast, Adam and Sophia laughed and chatted with their audience.

"That's an interesting question!" Sophia told a man at one point. "Don't forget it. Ask it during the broadcast. Adam and I will be able to use it to make some important points."

They were sitting there like a couple of old hands, as if they were veterans of a thousand television events. The director Tara Wilson was surprised and then she wasn't. If these people were supposed to personify all wisdom come to Earth, it was to be expected. Modern wisdom needed to be media savvy. Tara had seen enough people pass through the studios to know that these two would come across well to the millions of viewers.

Adam and Sophia had that radiance about them which was so noticeable in the other Martians and in the Ariadne astronauts. And yet they weren't a bit scary. Both were of medium height and average build. Sophia's long fair hair glistened under the studio lights. Tara had known several prominent individuals over the years who had been described as "serene." Up against Sophia, they were pale copies of the real thing. Her wide smile, her lustrous skin, the welcoming face, the shining and welcoming blue eyes all came together to create a warmth that drew people in to a place where they could truly relax and be themselves.

Tara studied Adam on a monitor screen. This was another openhearted person. Power and tenderness mingled in his appearance in the most extraordinary way. The short brown hair, the dark eyes and the gentle face were guaranteed to put anyone at ease. As she crossed the studio floor close by him, Adam smiled at her reassuringly.

"Excuse me being so personal," he said to her, "but I have to tell you that your daughter and your son will be fine. You have been anxious about both of them. I am giving you this knowledge so that you can lose your worry about them and be the mother that they need."

Thank you seemed such an inadequate phrase but Tara could think of nothing else. Sophia watched Tara straighten and brace herself as she walked back, a jet-haired, black-clothed figure who had suddenly lost a crushing burden from her mind.

"There were many specific locations that we could have gone to within the British Isles," explained Adam in answer to the opening question about why they had chosen to begin their teaching in a television studio "There are places of huge energy and great importance but the fact that we are in Britain is enough. We might well set one part of the kingdom against another if we favoured one place over another. We are content to be on neutral territory, so to speak. Being in the right country is enough for us. Why do you think that these lands have been a source of fascination and the desire of many other nations throughout recorded time, and prior to that? Why is it that this tiny group of islands has spent a large part of its history punching well above its weight in world affairs? The English language is the language of world communication in a way that speakers of the ancient Greek and Latin could only dream about. The British Isles are a natural hub of your world."

Joe, Irene and Bruce were part of the invited audience. Joe leaned over to speak to Bruce.

"I'm imagining that every US Navy ship in an Atlantic port is heading out even as we're listening, sent by a green-eyed top brass," he murmured. "Their mission will be to seed the ocean with explosive devices. *If you're so damned wonderful, stay in your own country.*"

"With the rest of the Navy getting there as quickly as possible," Bruce agreed. "But perhaps Henry will have more sense."

"Oh, surely part of the fleet will stand off the Thames estuary and lob in some long-distance weaponry towards London!" Irene contributed with a totally straight face.

Another question from the audience really set the ball rolling.

"In the past, when there was all that stuff about UFOs and people saying that they had seen beings from other planets, did that really happen?"

Sophia nodded.

"In times of great danger, when it looked as though mankind was close to destroying itself and the planet Earth, there were visits, especially early on in the atomic and nuclear ages. Your scientists ripped from the heart of the Universe one of the secrets of power, without the knowledge and the wisdom to go with it. Humanity made such huge strides technologically in your twentieth century without corresponding advances in spirituality." Sophia was aware of some raised eyebrows in her audience. "I am talking about spirituality, not religiosity. Those who walk in love are the true spiritual warriors. You spent your twenty first century coming to terms with that. We did not want Earth to suffer the fate of the planet Maldek. We have longed to be with you for many seasons but mankind did not deserve it and we could not get through. There was too much war, too much brutality and life was cheap. The Lord Buddha said *Action and reaction are opposite and equal.* The Master Jesus taught *As you sow, so shall you reap.* The karma of this planet kept us away in all but the times of gravest danger. Now it is time for the people of Earth to move on. Lessons have been learned, sometimes at a terrible cost and we on planet Mars had our own karma to face."

A camera swung in the direction of Bruce Dougall, who was watching and listening, oblivious to the processes of a studio.

The obvious query about Maldek was raised.

"As a race, humanity prides itself on knowing its history through fact, myth and legend," said Adam with a sad smile. "You don't realise that these headings are false divisions of the one and only body of knowledge, which teaches all things. But as you learned, became sophisticated in many ways, you have lost much and know less of your history now than a small child. The violence of your past means that you have destroyed your civilisation twice—in what was known as Lemuria or Mu and in the days of Atlantis. And before that we destroyed a planet—Maldek."

"*We?*" queried a sharp listener.

"We once were as you are," Sophia continued. "We truly are brothers and sisters. We were one. We inhabited the planet Maldek, positioned between Mars and Jupiter. The planet Earth was a place of rest and refreshment. We journeyed here to wonder and learn as an ecosystem was born in a young world. We witnessed the first cells in the water, which then grouped together. We watched the waters give birth to life. We enjoyed the spectacle of life emerging from the water to live on land. We walked with the very first creatures, which eventually would one day develop to be called dinosaurs. We studied and rejoiced in a plan of God Itself unfolding. But we grew complacent and perhaps too comfortable at home on Maldek. In the course of foolishness, fear and greed, we experimented with atomic and nuclear power and caused devastation and uncontrollable explosions. The Sun was dimmed as it lost a third of its mass and the Universe still echoes with the death cry of so many pure souls. A chain reaction destroyed all life on Maldek and the planet was reduced to a mass of fragmented rock. As well as the deaths, the loss of knowledge was incalculable. Only those away from the home planet visiting Earth or Mars were left. The asteroid belt is all that survives of Maldek. We all learned the most terrible lesson. We can still hear the cries. Be glad that your hearing is dulled. But here on Earth your learning was dulled too. You almost forgot the lesson. Your attitudes and your history became a chasm that we could not bridge. You discovered once again the terrible power of the nuclear reaction. You began to repeat the history of Maldek. Chernobyl so nearly copied our mistake. When you had developed atomic and nuclear weapons, you contemplated assured mutual destruction and said that such a thing would be called victory. We so desperately wanted to join hands with you, our stranded brothers and sisters, as we learned from our mistakes and evolved. But we had to watch as you struggled, stumbled and fell and picked yourselves up again whilst you moved along the slow path. Only now have we been able to meet up with you once more. And it is ironic that one of the major factors in enabling us to reach out was an error on our part, in harming our brother Bruce.

"You are now at the dawn of a time of great change and transition. So we are here. We can make the journey together because we have already been there and we know. There is an old Earth phrase *Been there, done that and got the T-shirt.* We can say that in all honesty."

The unexpected colloquialism provided a safety valve of laughter within what was becoming the claustrophobic atmosphere of Studio Nine.

"Since the dawn of true sentience," Adam continued, "we have looked around us and asked *Why am I here? What is my purpose?* Everyone on planet Earth at this moment can answer that question in a way that no other generation of mankind has been able to answer it. You are all here to be part of the process of moving on to the next stage of evolution and the reconnecting of the family, which was stranded on Mars and Earth. Some will play a bigger part than others, but the whole of the Earth is involved, just as the whole of Mars is involved. Those of us who travelled back with your astronauts are merely representatives of Mars, chosen because of our part in the terrible wrong." Adam studied his audience—and hence the world—with something approaching a stern expression. "Remember not to travel along the road of error, as you have done many times before with many different teachers. We are teachers, nothing more, nothing less. We are not here to be adored, worshipped and then crucified! Beware of the barbaric sport of building up individuals and then tearing them to shreds in public! You've been doing that since Roman times at least. It was messier then, with such things as lions and arenas and public executions, but your forefathers did not have the benefit of television."

"Don't forget," continued Sophia in a lighter tone. "Our journeys are inextricably linked yet we are just another pebble on the beach."

"This is powerful stuff, Victoria!" exclaimed Marmaduke as he sat watching the broadcast with her in her flat.

Victoria agreed, clutching Paddington Bear as if her life depended on it. Marmaduke patted the space on the sofa next to him as Einstein stalked around on stiff legs, his eyes never leaving the visitor.

"As you may have gathered, I'm a big Paddington fan. But in the end his appeal is limited. Please put down that bear and come and sit here with me. I might do lots of other things but, as a general rule, I don't bite. And I'm old enough to know how to behave."

Vicky put the bear back in his accustomed place and sat next to Marmaduke. They continued watching and listening for a few minutes and then she sighed.

"I don't think I can take in any more," she admitted. "We can always catch up with the rest of this later on."

"A good idea! It's rather a philistine attitude but I can only take being the witness to so much history at one time—and yes, I know I'm a historian! I could murder a cup of tea."

Over tea, Marmaduke felt that he had to say a few things.

"I do apologise if I embarrassed you at all last night, my dear. I do tend to bang on a bit. It's just that I say what I think. I meant every word of what I said at Joe Mortimer's place. I still do mean every word. I have never said it to any woman before. That's why I've got to forty-seven without making any kind of serious commitment. I've never met anyone I wanted to say that lot to—until I met you. But I am so sorry if I upset you in any way."

"I wasn't upset," Vicky assured him. "A bit stunned, I suppose. But when I thought about it all this morning, I liked it. I felt . . . cherished."

"*Cherished*! What a wonderful word. May I cherish you some more by taking you out to dinner? I imagine that we might have any restaurant to ourselves. It could be quite cosy. Everyone will be glued to their screens."

"Unless they're like us and they decide to view again later."

*   *   *

It was late when Joe, Irene and Bruce arrived back at Stable End but they were too full of what they had heard to contemplate sleep straight away. Tony was eager to listen to their thoughts. He already knew every word of what had been said by Sophia and Adam.

"I've never heard of Maldek," said Bruce.

"Neither have I," chimed in Joe. "First job on your list, Bruce, when you get to Mars is to go and check out the asteroid belt. You're a lucky sod." He turned to Irene. "Do you know about Maldek?"

"Yes. The observations that led to the idea of a missing planet have been around for a long time and it is a golden oldie of astronomical debate. It looks as if Sophia and Adam have given us the definitive answer."

Tony could have given them every possible fact and figure about the planet but he preferred that it came from his grand daughter. Joe and Bruce were key *dramatis personae* on a worldwide stage and they were suffering from a touch of what could only be described as Martian Fatigue. There is such a state of affairs as too much of a good thing and he was happy to see the three of them clustered round Joe's computer instead of having to hear yet more information from one of the visiting group. Irene called up an animated diagram of the solar system and gave them the benefit of her considerable knowledge.

"Titius of Wittenberg was the first person in the modern era to describe the spacing of the first seven planets in our system. This, confusingly, is known as Bode's Law, published in 1772 by the director of the Berlin Observatory, one Johann Bode. An anomaly within that spacing pointed to a missing planet. Ready for the mathematics?"

"I am!" said Bruce eagerly. "You might need to speak more slowly for Joe!"

Joe managed a slight smile. It was an old running joke.

"No squabbling, children!" she admonished. "Take the basic sequence 0, 3, 6, 12, 24, 48, 96 and 192. After zero, you have each number being doubled to give the next. Add four to each of those numbers and divide by ten. What do you get now?"

"0.4, 0.7, 1.0, 1.6, 2.8, 5.2, 10.0 and 19.6," supplied Bruce with impressive speed.

"That progression of figures sounds familiar," said Joe, wishing it wasn't quite so late at night.

"It should be!" laughed Irene. "Give or take the odd per cent, these numbers give us the number of AU—astronomical units—that each planet is from the sun. Of course, this is done from the point of view of Earth. One AU is the distance of Earth from the Sun, which is about 93,000,000 miles. We have to take Neptune and Pluto out of the picture because they don't fit the Law but there is a gap at 2.8. Bode's Law predicts a planet should be there and instead we have the asteroid belt."

"Most astronomers have long held that the asteroids were builders' junk left over from the formation of the Solar System billions of years ago," Joe pointed out.

"Not quite all of them," Irene told him. "Professor Michael Ovenden, based at the University of British Columbia in Vancouver, Canada, spent a large part of a working life time building a case for the asteroid belt being what was left of the missing planet. He put forward the theory of The Principle of Least Interaction Action. Without getting too technical, his premise predicts the orbits of the major moons of Uranus and Jupiter." She tapped on the console keyboard to bring those bodies in. "And, with an error of less than one per cent, it predicts the orbits of all the planets from Mercury to Neptune. But he maintained that the whole thing only held together properly if there was once a large planet where the asteroid belt now sits. It was there until about 16 million years ago."

Tony watched, awash with pride. He wanted to cry. He was so happy to see his grand daughter doing this. Her position in the University was in question, although now Sir Arthur Downey was desperate to keep her on board because she was winning popular global acclaim. Tony hoped that she would have the strength of character to tell the old fart what to do with his job. But anyway, once a teacher, always a teacher. She did not need to sit within hallowed precincts to guide people to an understanding. She needed to be out in the world, explaining in a way that ordinary people could understand.

He lowered his head and smiled a secret smile as he saw and he knew her future.

In the night Tony was concerned about another potential teacher. As a Martian he did not need sleep, as the people of Earth would understand, but the human part of him was tired by the end of a day. And living within the lower frequencies of Earth, the amount of energy needed to keep Bruce on his feet was a continuous drain on the whole Martian party. So some rest was a good idea.

It was an absolute necessity for Bruce and Tony was not pleased to find him downstairs trawling through reams of information on Joe's computer.

"Do you want to make it to Joe and Irene's wedding in one piece and travel back with us to Mars?" he asked when Bruce became aware of the fact that he was watching.

"Of course!" Bruce said indignantly. "It's just that I wanted to read some more about Maldek."

"Bruce, in a while you will have access to the sum total of knowledge out there! And you won't need a primitive box of electronics to access it."

"I'm sorry. It's what we do here."

"So tell me what you have learned."

Tony listened approvingly to Bruce's clear and concise summary of his reading on further "proof" of the existence of Maldek. Many meteorites from the asteroid belt are magnetised as if they had cooled in the magnetic field of a large rotating planet and they have a crystalline structure consistent with *slow* cooling over millions of years. Such cooling of a small meteorite can only happen if it was once part of a much larger object, probably thousands of miles across. Some scientists believe that tektites, which have landed in a few areas of Earth, come from the asteroid belt and their spherical and glassy molten rock and metal composition could only have been created by a thermonuclear explosion. And iron meteorites show more than ten times the exposure to cosmic ray particles—again consistent with being parts of a planet destroyed by a thermonuclear explosion.

"How am I doing?" Bruce wondered.

"Very well," replied Tony. "But what you should be *doing* now is sleeping. Promise me you will go and rest?"

Tony listened to Bruce's feet going up the stairs. A door opened and closed.

He sat for a while enjoying the night silence of the countryside. In his Earth life he had managed to make his home in such surroundings after an urban upbringing in the East End of London.

Another door opened and there was a lighter tread coming down the stairs. This was becoming ridiculous.

"Hello! What can I do for you?" Tony asked when Irene appeared in the doorway. She looked confused. "Never mind, my angel. Sit down here with me. It's obviously not the night for peaceful sleeping. Joe seems to be the lucky one so far. What's on your mind?"

"Nothing in particular. I didn't want to disturb Joe. It's all so *exciting*, isn't it? I'm like a child. I can't settle."

"And you have an exciting time ahead of you, Irene, as someone who can make sense of things for those who are uncertain and perhaps afraid. You and Joe will make a great team. Your astronomical knowledge and his practical experience of being out there in the solar system will be formidable when they are put together."

"I'm glad that we will be of service." She looked at him and then looked away, unsure. "Granddad, I wish I could have met Joe ten years ago."

"You meet people when you are meant to meet them. Ten years ago neither of you would have been really interested in the other. Well, perhaps you might have enjoyed some casual sexual encounters before you moved on. You are both attractive people. The two of you were far too wrapped up in what you were doing. And you both still hurt too much to have dared to engage your emotions. Aren't you happy with all that's happening now you've met Joe?"

"Yes. But some children would have been nice. I'm too long in the tooth to consider such a thing."

"I understand. But you are both parents." Irene gulped. "You know that Sally was pregnant when she died. And I can tell you that your daughter is a beautiful soul."

"My *daughter*?"

"Your child, who was not born, is a girl. She is a soul of comfort, guiding those like herself who never had the opportunity to come to this side of life. She brings them to their loved ones who have already crossed over. Perhaps she should have a name, Irene," he finished quietly as the tears began running down her face.

Tony put his arm around his granddaughter.

"I don't mean to upset you. But it is a message that you are meant to have tonight. Learn the lesson taught by John Edward, one of the great teaching souls of the first part of the twenty first century. *Those who are meant to get the messages will receive them.* The messages can bring us great joy, although they may pierce our hearts to start with." Irene managed a very wobbly smile. "Good girl. But the messages are always there for our education and progress."

"Do you know the details about Joe's child?"

"I do. But that's for Sally to tell Joe, when she judges he is ready. And you will be the first person he tells."

"Fiona," said Irene with great firmness. "Her name is Fiona. It's a name that has been in our family for a long time." She giggled self-consciously. "Hark at me! Telling you something which you already know."

"Fiona," said Tony thoughtfully. "Fiona Hanson. It has a good sound to it. That would have been her registered name, Irene. As you said to Joe, only a handful of people even knew you were married and if your pregnancy had progressed, you would have left your husband, for your own safety and for the safety of your unborn child. I'd like to share something with you. What you would call doubt here on Earth is not something that has any currency in the spirit plane of life beyond death. In spirit, I was present when you were born. I blessed you when you were minutes old. But your pain and the loss of your child were my pain and loss as well, and agony for your parents too. For a moment of your time we lost the vision of your future. Only for a moment, though."

A thousand questions surged through Irene's mind, prompted by Tony's remarks.

"Go back to bed, my angel," Tony said firmly. "We can talk some more at another time." He put his hand on her brow. "You will sleep. I promise."

* * *

"Whilst you still look back to yesterday and all that it entailed, you cannot be promoted to tomorrow," pronounced Adam. "Let go of the past and all its resentments! If certain people and situations haven't travelled with you to your future, then they are not meant to be there."

Another teaching session from Sophia and Adam was in full swing, broadcast live to a waiting world from Studio Nine. The topic had settled on the arrogant waste of wisdom. This waste came about because of what humanity had done with the teachings of the Masters who came to Earth at different times to give guidance on living.

"Religion was never meant to pit nation against nation, or to divide countries, or split communities and make the son stand against his father and the daughter harden her heart against her mother!" Sophia said, with tears in her eyes. "Confucius, Buddha, Jesus, Mohammed, Aristotle, Moses, Mani, Lao Tzu, Mahavira, Abraham, Sabellius, Christian Rosenkreuz, Dalai Lama, Mother Ann Lee, Abul Baha and so many others came to bring interpretations on the wisdom at the centre of the universe—not to provide a harsh measuring rod for who is "right" and who is "wrong." The secret at the heart of the Universe, within the heart of God Itself, if you will, is both simple and complex. It is the challenge to give and to receive. These tasks require very different but, at the same time, complimentary graces. If all can give freely and receive equally freely then life can open up to be all that it is meant to be. A person never stands so tall as when he or she bends down to lift someone up and the one who has fallen is equally blessed."

It was time to lighten the mood. Adam nodded.

"We are all children at heart, and we all love a story. I shall tell you one. Once upon a time, in a peaceful place of worship, a grey cat came in to join the group, attracted by the serenity of the people and the location. It sat in the corner, watched everything that went on, appeared to understand what was happening and left when the group left. Each time the people gathered together, the cat was there, sitting in the same place. Individuals began to talk about the importance of the cat, why it was there, how it helped with their worship and contemplation.

"Over the years, everyone expected the cat to be present. Books and other scholarly works were written on the exact significance of the cat sitting in the corner. Of course, there was the heretic publication stating that the cat sat there because there was a piece of carpet on the floor and the sun shone in that spot during the time of gathering. Then one day the cat no longer appeared. The animal had been turning up regularly for at least fifteen years so it was presumed that it had died of old age. Everyone was sad but said that life must go on.

"But the worshippers became fragmented. Some said that a replacement cat must be found. Some claimed that the cat had been the representative of God and must not be replaced. Others said that it was merely symbolic and should not be replaced. A heretic wing said that the cat was never there—it was a mass delusion. Those who said that there must be a replacement cat fell out over what colour the cat should be. There was the Grey Wing and the Ginger Wing, plus the unspeakable White Wing. The peace and tranquillity that had attracted the cat in the first place was destroyed, perhaps never to be regained. No cat ever came to sit in that place of worship again."

The studio audience laughed in all the right places and fell silent after the last line of the story.

"Sects and schisms, followers of this way and that, muddling doctrine and dogma with the vision of how to lead a meaningful life have been the downfall of all religion," observed Sophia. "You have broken the simple laws of the Masters who brought them—and you have broken their hearts. Who cares what anyone wears, or what language is spoken in times of thinking and contemplation? We are all spiritual beings. And our only weapons should be love and a fierce and certain hope that the best is yet to be!"

Some in the studio and many round the world remembered the dramatic accounts given by the astronauts of when they first met their rescuers on the surface of Mars. Each astronaut saw the figures of wisdom in the guise of their spiritual founders or inspirational people. Would something like that happen now?

"No," said Sophia, reading thoughts. "That was a special moment of sharing with the crew of *Ariadne One*, who needed it. Here it would be a cheap conjuring trick. We would ask you to think carefully about what we have told you tonight. We are all children of the light. The people of Mars and the people of Earth must be ready to move forward together."

* * *

"That was giving it with both barrels, wasn't it?" Marmaduke asked Vicky. "The world was ticked off good and proper the other night but this is real tough talking."

"The Martians have made all this effort to get here, so I suppose they will say it like it is," she ventured. "If I understand correctly, they will all go home to Mars eventually. They want us to get things right."

"Well said, my dear! Well said!"

Marmaduke couldn't remember the last time he had felt so content. Outside a rising wind threw the occasional handful of sleet against the windows and made sparks from the fire dance up the chimney. Everything about the front room of his cottage was suffused in a glow, which had nothing to do with the soft lighting. He knew that it had everything to do with Victoria being there. They had shared a meal, they had shared their thoughts as they watched the Martians together and they had shared some first gentle kisses and embraces.

Joe Mortimer wasn't blind and he wasn't a fool but he had let this wonderful woman escape. Still, he had found himself another wonderful woman. Marmaduke could only conclude that it was all meant to be and he wasn't about to argue with such an arrangement. Victoria had brought Einstein with her and he was curled up and snoring. Even this hostile little tyke was coming round to seeing him as top dog.

* * *

Justin had run the gamut of just about every human emotion, with a dash of exhaustion thrown in for good measure. He was caring for Ted, which was a kind of purgatory, and he was searching for Maureen Rodriguez. It was very important that husband and wife met again before he took Ted back to Mars, however briefly. And it was vital that he spoke to Mrs Rodriguez himself. He had to make his peace with her.

Justin reasoned that Maureen was probably not far away. She had a lot of friends, mainly located in the D.C and northern Virginia area. Family members were too obvious a hiding place and he knew they were telling the truth when he contacted them and they told him that they were as worried as he was. Because he had no direct link with the woman, he could not sense her with his limited powers.

He was feeling defeated on this particular afternoon and not enjoying the sensation of frustration in his search for Mrs Rodriguez. Obviously she had some very loyal friends. And Ted seemed to be making so little progress. It was difficult to reach his tormented mind and Justin found himself buffeted by impenetrable waves of pain when he tried.

He looked out of the window. Snow was falling in a silent freezing blanket, transforming the world. Ted turned restlessly on the bed, uneasy even in sleep.

There was a knock on the door. When Justin opened the door, he knew straight away the identity of the woman standing next to the nurse.

"Hello," said the stranger. "I understand you've been looking for me. I'm Maureen Rodriguez."

*   *   *

Over in Georgetown, Shannon Dougall stood at the front window, watching the snow working its magic on the street. First the ground was dusted. Then the windward side of the trees, the fences and the road signs began to acquire an undercoat of snow. The breeze danced, as if taking a lead from wild music, and the growing curtain of snowflakes spun round accordingly.

Unbidden images slipped into Shannon's mind as she remembered a particularly manic late afternoon snowball fight that she and Bruce enjoyed. By the end of it they were both black and blue and soaked to the skin. Darkness was falling. Shannon was triumphant because Bruce surrendered after she subjected him to a final twenty second bombardment. They might have been only eleven years old but they knew that if Shannon went back to her house in that state, her mother would perform a vertical take-off from Runway Two Left and they would both be caught in the blast. Bruce took the only course of action open as he saw it and marched Shannon home with him.

Mr and Mrs Dougall understood and rose to the occasion magnificently. Whilst Bruce's mother bundled Shannon away for a hot bath, his father contacted Mrs Pierce to explain that Shannon had fallen over in the snow and was a bit wet and bruised and so would it be okay if she stayed with them for the night? Shannon appeared on screen, scrubbed and glowing and wrapped in a dressing gown and looking very cheerful. Mom couldn't really say anything other than express her gratitude.

"I still owe you one for that, Bruce," Shannon whispered.

The front door buzzer broke her reverie. Bob Broomfield was standing on the porch, a blonde snowman.

"I was just passing," he said. "I thought I'd look in and see how you are. I know Bruce is away in England."

Over coffee, Shannon shared with Bob the memories of the snowball fight.

"I've not heard that one," he admitted. "I guess that if no one knew, no one could accidentally tell your mom what really happened."

"That's exactly what Bruce said! To this day my mother doesn't know what happened that afternoon."

"What price that I don't tell her?" Bob teased.

He was alarmed when Shannon's face creased up as the tears began to flow. He didn't rate himself very highly with crying women and this wasn't Shannon's way at all. But it was symptomatic of the depth of feeling that she still had for Bruce. To his dying day, Bob knew that he would never understand why they divorced. He sat next to her and patted her arm awkwardly until the storm was apparently past.

"What's wrong?" he asked.

"Bruce! He's going away. To Mars. He might as well be dying!"

This time her body was racked with sobs. Bob appreciated that this was something she had needed to do for a while. And there was only one thing he could do. He gathered her close to him and cradled her head against his shoulder.

*   *   *

Maureen Rodriguez didn't know what to do or say and couldn't put a name to what she was feeling as she looked at her husband. Always a big man, he seemed smaller, shrunken. When he stirred and woke, she grabbed Justin's hand instinctively. Ted stared up at her. His eyes cleared momentarily in recognition.

"Mo!"

"I'm here, Ted. I'm here."

She sat on the edge of the bed and kissed his forehead. He smiled at her, closed his eyes and slept again.

Maureen turned to Justin.

"Is it necessary to keep him drugged like this?"

"He is not drugged. Martians do not need drugs. We are keeping him calm and rested using our own methods."

Maureen remembered belatedly that this was not really Justin. Justin had died more than twenty-five years previously. A Martian was using his form.

"Why were you so insistent that I see him . . . like this? I'd much prefer to remember Ted as he was, however flawed he might have been. I loved him."

"You need to see how ill he is, so that you will understand why it is necessary for us to take him back to Mars to restore him. And the Justin part of me needs your understanding and forgiveness."

"Forgiveness?"

"Ted was already married to you when I met him. It was a detail he conveniently forgot to mention for a long time. I would never have become involved with him if I had known. To me he was a very sweet and caring man and I couldn't believe my luck."

"Justin, it sounds to me as though we were both fooled."

Chapter Twenty-Nine

"You really have gone native!" Sally laughed.

Tony almost looked annoyed.

"It's not every day that we get the chance to be part of a living museum. Why shouldn't I contact you by screen? And anyway, I'm finding telepathy over long distance really hard work here on Earth. In these low vibratory levels, Britain to America counts as very long distance. I feel so *limited*."

"So do I if, I'm honest," Sally admitted. "I caught myself speaking to Justin on screen yesterday. How lazy is that?"

"It's perfectly normal in the circumstances. So how are you doing with finding all the people who were directly harmed by Ted Rodriguez and his plans?"

"I think I have visited and spoken with everyone. Justin hasn't been able to identify anyone else through the mind link he managed to create with Ted. The list was long enough as it was. What was that fool trying to do? I have been through everything with these people in my travels. The family of Monty Silverton, the breakfast television man, is a good example. They were so angry and unforgiving at first, of course, but also so confused."

"I think that's a fairly usual reaction when you find that your husband or father was used as the practice run for another murder," Tony observed wryly. "Were they all right in the end?"

"Yes. The oldest son did say that, if he ever had the chance, he would kill Rodriguez. But seeing as he won't have the opportunity, I think we can let that one ride."

By the end of the conversation, Tony was doubly glad that he had chosen the human way of communication. He and Sally had a lot of ground to cover and it would have been a huge effort to do this via the Martian method.

The Martian party were all feeling the strain of working within Earth conditions. Once Justin had met up with Maureen Rodriguez and could concentrate fully on Ted, he found a way into the former President's mind. The effort cost him dear. Ichiro seemed to be having the best of it, luring Brent Dyer back into activity with the plans for the necessary building project that had to be carried out quite quickly. But he was frustrated by the slowness of the intellect of a man considered to be a genius by human standards. Ichiro had to help the thinking process along a little for his friend and colleague.

As Sally indicated, she was the sounding board for every emotion in the book during her hunt for the families of victims of Ted Rodriguez. That was a tough call. Seeing as Rodriguez was in no fit state to face these people, she had been sent on this task. It was difficult and she faced several awkward first minutes. Because Phoebe Harper was now with her family, Sally's call to that group was thankfully brief.

Adam and Sophia were about to set off on a worldwide teaching tour. Simple enough, humans were thinking, but the two had a few surprises in store that would be a labour and a half to carry out within Earth conditions. Phoebe was spending that precious time with her family, which was an emotional drain on her human part.

Tony felt stretched, pulled in too many directions at once. And *his* human emotions were in full play where Irene and Joe were concerned.

He sat by a window and watched the peaceful countryside. Irene, Joe and Bruce were out and he was glad of the solitude at Stable End. An occasional car passed the house and that was it. Bonny trotted in and joined him. The dog raised a hopeful paw to him. Tony stroked her glossy fur. Every home should have a Bonny. It was amusing watching the dynamics between the animal and Bruce. Tony knew that the American had called Bonny a "flea-ridden mutt" on more than one occasion prior to meeting her. But her one-ear-up-one-ear-down I Think You're A Wonderful Human appeal hadn't taken long to work. One charmer was clean bowled by another.

Bonny understood that a walk wasn't happening right now. She sat at Tony's feet and rested her chin on his knee. Tony went back to his thoughts. He shared Sally's bewilderment at what Ted Rodriguez was prepared to do. In the quietness, he had a chance for his Martian sensibilities to come to terms fully with a man who had displayed the very human and very male quality of indifference as he murdered his way into the White House. Monty Silverton and Philemon Brown were cast aside when their usefulness was over. Phoebe Harper didn't die alone, not that she perished in the accident anyway. Dexter Melton, the driver, and Frank Travis, the bodyguard, died in the impact. Manny Cartier, the truck driver, paid the penalty later for doing what he had been signed up to do. He was newly married and short of money and lured by the promise of more than he could imagine. And no one must forget Seb Healey, the police officer who died after the Constitution

Gardens debacle. The official line was that he committed suicide, distraught by the mistake he had made. This gave his family an extra cause of pain, as they were all devout Roman Catholics and they viewed suicide as a terrible sin. At least Sally was able to put their minds at rest on that, even if swapping the words *suicide* and *murder* didn't take away the grief at the loss of a loved one.

Those who carried out twisted orders of Ted Rodriguez would have to be dealt with through the due process of law, as the authorities saw fit. This was not within the remit of the Martians. Tony was sorry for Henry Sargent, who would have to display the fabled Wisdom of Solomon when this lot was picked over, not least with Bob Broomfield.

It was time for Phoebe to step up to the plate, as Bruce would put it. Tony had to speak with Joe when he came home, because it was time for a Martian to visit a King in his palace.

*   *   *

Justin appeared to be reading the document. It was an ordinary enough action on the surface yet it was anything but ordinary. Henry Sargent was out of his depth here as he tried to grasp the idea that this young man was reading the contents of the paper directly into the mind of Ted Rodriguez. His eyes flitted between the Martian and Ted, who sat passively in the chair by the bed, head down, eyes fixed to the floor and arms folded. Bob Broomfield was motionless, as was Bill Francioni.

At one point, Justin stopped reading.

"Peace, Henry," he said quietly. "Just let the process happen."

He returned to reading for another minute before putting the document down.

"All done?" the acting President wondered.

"That part is," said Justin. "I could ask Ted telepathically if he agrees with what I have written down on his behalf but, obviously, the three of you wouldn't know what either of us said. It is very difficult to talk to him. Something deep within him broke when he saw me and then Phoebe Harper at Cape Canaveral." He took Ted's hands. "Ted!" he said in a voice that compelled the man to leave his confusion and attend. "Look at me." Ted managed that. "I've read back to you your confession of your misdemeanours. Are you willing to sign this statement?"

"Yes," he croaked.

Justin put a pen in Ted's hand and placed the paper on the bedside table. Laboriously Ted scrawled out his name: *Edward J. Rodriguez.*

"If you gentlemen would like to sign as witnesses to this now?"

Justin proffered the pen to Henry Sargent, who signed and then passed the pen to Bob Broomfield. Then Bill Francioni added his name.

"Thank you," said the acting President to Justin.

He didn't know what else to say.

"It is part of what we came to do," Justin replied.

"But at what price?"

Sargent was a compassionate man. Justin's distress was as obvious as the sweat on his brow.

"The pain to my human side is payback for harming our brother Bruce."

Our brother Bruce. That phrase again. Suddenly Bob Broomfield felt a flash of anger and a momentary possessiveness of Bruce Dougall. He and Bruce had been like brothers all their lives, putting aside the shameful moments when Rodriguez got in the way. What made it worse was that he was used to throwing dollars at a situation and this was something that money couldn't solve. Like Shannon, Bob had to let Bruce go.

The Presidential bodyguards were waiting by the door when Justin ushered out the visitors. Mistrust was written all over their faces, mingled with relief that Henry Sargent, Bob Broomfield and Bill Francioni looked pretty much as they did when they went in. Sargent held his document case tightly and his eyes were damp. Broomfield looked more pensive than usual. This President was turning himself into a security nightmare.

Justin was glad to shut the door on them. Ted stared up at him beseechingly. There was no real need for communication, verbal or telepathic, but Ted deserved some comfort.

> *"You will come to understanding, one day Ted,"* Justin promised him silently. *"We all have to grow and we grow through understanding. Sometimes the understanding hurts, doesn't it? I'm here to help."*

Bill Francioni allowed Henry and Bob to chatter on the journey back to the White House. He couldn't get Ted Rodriguez out of his mind. Yes, the right thing had been done, reinstating all the advisory staff that Rodriguez had dumped in such a childish but effective manner. He had jumped at the chance to stand as a witness to sign the statement. It would be a chance to enjoy the final triumph over a man who had riled him beyond belief and pushed the country to the edge of a precipice. But instead, he felt pity. He expected to experience anger. But instead, he saw the unshed tears in Rodriguez's eyes and wanted to cry them for him. He remembered the smart and cutting things that he planned to say if he ever came face to face with the chief again. But instead, his heart ached for a man destroyed by his own shortcomings. And he wondered at his new and tender thoughts.

* * *

"This is not a frivolous request, Joe," said Tony.

"I know it isn't," replied Joe. "I'm guessing that Richard has a part to play in everything that's going on because of his links with me."

"You are becoming more perceptive by the moment!" Tony told him happily. "We need someone to travel to different countries as an ambassador with Phoebe Harper. Not everyone is interested or engaged in what we have come to do and there are pockets of outright hostility to overcome in some parts of the world. A respected crowned monarch will certainly help the cause, because some do not understand the physical manifestation of Mrs Harper."

Joe and Tony were talking in the kitchen. Joe nodded in the direction of the main room, where he knew Irene and Bruce were poring over data on the computer.

"That sounds reasonable enough. But talking of perception, you don't need much of it to see that Bruce is not so well. He's doing a good job on Irene but he's not conning me. Aren't you helping him any more?"

"We are doing our best. Ironically, it was easier supporting him when we were millions of your miles away on Mars. The vibration levels are so low on planet Earth and many tasks are very difficult, especially when we are trying to do so many things at once. This is part of what we have to do. We have to raise everyone's awareness and lift up their vibratory levels so that we can move on together. I—"

"Joe! Granddad!"

Irene's panicky voice cut across whatever Tony was about to say next.

They rushed into the living room to find Irene sitting next to Bruce on the sofa, looking very anxious. Bruce was leaned back, his eyes closed, his face paper white and drawn. He looked up at the new arrivals with a fixed stare. Bonny was in the process of stretching out across his feet, showing her concern.

"I thought he was going to pass out!" Irene exclaimed.

"I can help him but I shall have to be totally anti-social until tomorrow," Tony said as he sat on the other side of Bruce and placed a hand on his forehead. "On Mars, we can be in different places doing different things simultaneously. Here on Earth we are severely limited. That is having a knock-on effect on Bruce. He is weak and in pain. If I can concentrate solely on him for a while, he will be restored to us. Help me to get him upstairs, Joe. He needs to be in bed."

Bruce had said nothing but he groaned as he stood up and he looked shamefaced at this admission of frailty.

"Don't even think about it!" Joe told him firmly, knowing that his colleague was about to apologise. "We've all had enough sometimes. Don't try to speak. Tony will make you feel better."

A sombre-faced Irene shut down the computer when they had left the room. She wandered into the kitchen and switched on the kettle to make some tea. After a seeming age Joe came back downstairs.

"We must trust Tony on this one like we've never trusted him before," he said heavily. "Conventional medicine would have Bruce in a hospital side room heavily sedated, with a round-up call for friends and family to come and watch him die. In the meantime, I have a job to do for Tony. You seemed to get on well with Richard when you spoke to him on screen that time. D'you fancy another little screen chat with His Majesty the King? I'll bet he will jump at the chance to meet a Martian in the guise of your grandfather. I spoke to him the other day and I think he was feeling a bit left out."

* * *

"It certainly is a wonderful idea," said Richard thoughtfully to his guests. "I reckon I've been a bit of a spare part in the recent events, Joe. You have been hogging all the limelight, along with the Prime Minister. You want me to go on a goodwill, ambassadorial visit round the world with Phoebe Harper! Well, your sister in Phoebe's form," he added, inclining his head to Tony. "This would be to back up Sophia and Adam's teaching? I suppose it would be a charm offensive as well, to win over the sceptical. Nothing would give me greater pleasure. I am presuming that the PM will bestow the government's blessing upon this."

Joe was delighted. This was vintage Richard. He had picked up the knack of learning fast at an early age and this was a good example of it. As Prince Richard in the RAF, he made sure he was kept up to date with what was happening. As His Majesty he had the whole Palace system and Kevin Crane to brief him. He couldn't go wrong. And as the one-time astronaut hopeful, he couldn't wait to be involved in the plans of the Martians.

The King, Joe and Tony were meeting in one of the smaller, less imposing Palace rooms. It was presided over by a rather severe portrait of Queen Victoria.

"Don't be put off by the old girl!" Richard chuckled to Tony, noticing him glancing at it from time to time. "My wife has suggested that this particular picture ought to be put in the cellars to frighten the rats and mice away. I had to chide her for being disrespectful but, between you and me, I couldn't agree more."

"The human part of me could be intimidated, Your Majesty," said Tony. "I wonder what she thinks about a Martian sitting in her palace. I'll ask her sometime. But seriously, Sir, you would be willing to do this? It will be a demanding schedule."

Richard waved a hand.

"Of course I am! I'm sure that Mrs Harper will lend me strength and inspiration. And cut out the Sir bit. Protocol wearies me at the best of times and I'm sure the rule book doesn't cover visitors from other planets!" He sighed in contentment as he poured tea for his guests. "I'm sure you know, Tony, that I wanted to go gallivanting across the stars like Joe here. I had the backing of the RAF, the same as Joe, but the family weren't having any of it. It has always been a regret and I don't like regrets. Now that regret can be taken away. The stars have come to me, in a way, with your group visiting Earth. Thank you. Joe, I'm disappointed that you did not bring the delightful Irene with you. No colleague Bruce Dougall either. I would like to meet him."

"You will," Joe said. "At the wedding. He's come over a bit early. Henry Sargent reappointed him as head of *BUSSTOP* America but obviously there isn't a lot to do at the moment that can't be dealt with through routine administration. Bruce must be taking the most public sick leave ever."

* * *

Bruce Dougall was not a very patient patient.

"I've never had to convalesce in my life!" he grumbled to Irene.

"I don't think that word was actually used," said Irene with a brittle smile. "The suggestion was made by Granddad that you go quietly for a while. Nothing more."

She was still utterly enchanted by Bruce but he was being a typical man now that he was recovering from being laid aside, however temporarily. He was totally outraged.

"But—."

"No buts, Bruce. You ought to be grateful that you're still alive. Tony sat with you all that night. It was hard on him and even more of strain on your metabolism as he dragged you back from the brink. That's why you need to take it easy for a day or two. He must have performed the Martian equivalent of heroic medicine. Probably took you apart piece-by-piece and put you back together again. I don't know what he did, Joe doesn't know and you have no memory of it but it must have been fairly spectacular. So settle down."

Bruce subsided, seeing the steely side of Irene that he had not come across so far.

She was in fighting mood, although she would have put her conversation with Bruce under the heading of *tough love*. It was Sir Arthur Downey, the Master of the college, who was driving her nuts. He had worked out that Irene was in almost permanent residence at Stable End and had spoken to her again on screen to try and lure her back into the fold. Irene wasn't remotely interested anymore. When she made a simple request to be able to go to America, she was being disloyal to the college and scuppering the entire University system. And it was highly probable that once Downey knew she was with Joe, she was the painted whore of Babylon for good measure. But the Master changed his tune after Irene was bounced into the world's consciousness as one of the primary Martian links. He could see something in it for himself and for the college. Suddenly she was a valued member of the academic community and she must have misunderstood what had been said in their final heated exchange.

"Which do you reckon is your sharpest cook's knife, Joe?" Irene asked him when he returned from London with Tony. "Fool that I am, I would still like to be merciful when I slit Downey's throat. And Bruce is just like a naughty little boy. He's a flea in a bottle! No, I suppose he's bored."

"I think I've got just the remedy!" Joe turned to Tony. "You're only concerned about physical exertion, aren't you? Would a poker tournament be okay?" Intrigued, Tony nodded. "Yes! I'll get Dad and Philip over. I can finally get to see Dad and Bruce go head to head over a poker table! I know that Sophia and Adam are doing their first international broadcast tonight but we can watch it tomorrow. And I'm sure you know what they will say, Tony."

"Did somebody say poker?" Bruce wondered as he drifted into the kitchen to join them.

"I did! Bruce!" Joe announced. "You will get your backside kicked tonight. I'm inviting Dad over to play you. And my brother Philip too, if he can make it."

Bruce lifted his head, a warhorse scenting battle.

"We shall see," he said, smiling the smile that hadn't been seen for a day or two. "If memory serves me right, your Dad taught you and your brother to play, didn't he? So you'll go about things in the same way. Once I see where you're coming from, I should be able to thrash all three of you."

Joe looked quite put out. Irene could see that the cure was working already on Bruce. It would be worth Joe's pride being a little dented. And a mini-healing was happening with Joe. Once upon a time, the fate of the world would have hung on a card game with Bruce, but now he was taking a far chirpier view of it. Everyone was moving and growing in the most unlikely ways.

*   *   *

"But we can't—"

Brent Dyer stopped in mid-sentence when Ichiro sighed like a hurricane. They were working on Brent's computer and the engineer was struggling to keep up with the Martian's thought processes. It was like being back in class. No, class had always been a joy. Brent lapped up information from an early age, the more challenging the better. As a teenager, when he began to have a proper understanding of his own abilities, he developed the itch to solve the unsolvable. He won the plaudits of an astonished world when he turned the theory of a propulsion system into reality so that the journey to Mars became a feasible proposition.

Not being able to get his head round something was a new sensation for Brent and he didn't like it.

He looked up at Ichiro from under his brows.

"I guess we can," he concluded humbly.

"Of course we can!" encouraged Ichiro. "Brent, I really do need your help. I'm not humouring you by involving you in this project. I need the Earth perspective but you are letting some Earth ideas get in the way. Why did you say that we couldn't do this?"

He indicated the schematic on the screen.

"It goes against the laws of physics," Brent replied promptly.

"The laws of *Earth* physics! And how many times has that book been rewritten since the time of Isaac Newton? Remember that we are building the first portal to link Earth and Mars. Mars laws come into play as well. Brent, why did we make such a good team?"

"Because we trusted one another, I guess. We trusted one another's judgement."

"Exactly. Will you trust me now? Good. Close your eyes. Pick a really happy day when you were about . . . ten years old." Brent opened his eyes for a moment, saw that Ichiro was in deadly earnest, and closed them again. "Got it? Stay with it, stay with how you felt then, with what you were doing. Who are you with?"

"My Dad."

"Excellent. Your Dad has just brought you this problem to solve." Ichiro restated his idea. "How will you deal with it?"

Brent was silent for a while and then his eyes snapped open and he turned back to the computer. He worked on the console in total concentration for a few minutes. Ichiro watched the years falling away from his friend. His mind had cut loose and there wasn't anything that couldn't be done.

Brent punched a final button with a flourish. Ichiro looked at the screen and felt the quiet satisfaction of the teacher knowing that the student has grasped the concept.

"That will do very well. Exactly right. Mars and Earth are places within everyone's basic and narrow understanding but we also belong in another dimension. We belong everywhere and we are everything. The theories of Earth have served you well, Brent. But go and be ten years old with your Dad whenever you need to fly beyond the bonds of Earth to find your answers. Before too long you won't need your father any more. Not in that respect, anyway. There is so much knowledge out there. Don't be afraid to grab it with both hands."

*　　*　　*

The dinner table was loud and full of laughter. Irene noted that Bruce didn't have as much to say for himself as she would have anticipated, but one look at his face was enough for anyone to know that he was very happy. Neil Mortimer was in his element with a fresh audience. Joe and Philip exchanged understanding glances and heard the stories one more time. Tony, Bruce and Irene were lapping it up.

"You were quiet," said Joe to Bruce as the dinner came to an end. "Saving yourself for the big match?"

"I was appreciating a class act, Joe. I never realised that your Dad did all that stuff. I knew his background in the RAF but not the detail. I was remembering as well. You never really talked about your family when we were out there in space."

"It didn't seem right, what with both your parents being dead at an early age," replied Joe, almost embarrassed at having been found out in this small act of consideration.

The card game was set up on the dining table. Irene admitted that she hadn't got the first idea about poker, so it was no use her trying to play and getting in the way. Tony excused himself for obvious reasons.

"I can read your minds," he reminded them. "I would know what cards you are holding. Hardly fair."

Neil looked uncomfortable with this statement and took Tony on one side.

"You know what I'm thinking?" he wanted to know.

"Not the exact detail. I would have to concentrate for that and it would be an invasion of your privacy if I did it without your consent, or unless there was an urgent need because you were unable to communicate in a conventional human manner. But I know that you look at your two sons with huge pride and love and you are wishing that you could have persuaded Stella to come with you tonight. She is not feeling very well and she knows that she will meet me at the wedding. And you still cannot quite believe that

Joe has got himself sorted out with a good woman in his life. I read those broad generalities unless I am invited further in." He patted the elderly man on the shoulder. "Because you spent your working lifetime doing amazing things, Neil, I don't think you realise what an important part you have played in the Martians coming to Earth."

"Me? What have I done? Apart from being Joe's father, of course."

"That's very important in itself. I sent the messages from Mars that Irene picked up. Those who are meant to get the messages receive them. She turned to Joe for help, which sowed the seeds of their relationship, but you helped Joe identify that it was Random Error Code being transmitted. And because you and your wife were so matter-of-fact about it all, Joe and Irene could be too, which set them on their path in these matters. Now go and give them hell in that poker game!"

"I shall indeed. Bruce Dougall seems a very personable chap but walloping an American is always a good thing!"

* * *

A nation can be the same as a person. The macrocosm and the microcosm are one. Just as an individual can find that all emotions are spent, cauterised by event piled on event, a country can be in a similar position. The United States of America had been chained to a runaway train of sensation and emotion since the death of President Phoebe Harper. The publication of the confession from Ted Rodriguez was no more than the national express hurtling round the sharpest bend yet, a defining catharsis.

A lot of things made sense now. Fortunately the usually astute and vocal groups within the country were as battered and tired as the rest. Henry Sargent jumped in with another understated but effective broadcast, where he promised that those who had carried out Rodriguez's orders would be brought to justice.

"This process will be undertaken quietly and without a lot of fuss," he said, in a tone that brooked no argument. "That is something that we have not always been very good at in this country. We have received the deserved mockery of the world for it. There will be no show trials, with television and press capturing every moment. But every investigation will be reported fully, I promise. Right now, confidence has been shattered. I hope that through this search for justice, and through many other efforts, I will be able to rebuild that fragile and precious thing—your belief and trust in the federal government."

I hope I am right, he would later confide to his diary. *The last thing this country needs is a witch-hunt. Too many good people will get swept up with the trash. I'm thinking primarily of Bob Broomfield. I WILL have to say something about Bob to the nation and the world. But what? He was important to the President whilst he was under duress. Without access to the influence and the money that Bob provided, Rodriguez would have needed another whole team working together, which I doubt he could have organised. Fortunately Bob made a very brave decision and began trying to redress the balance. The Martians arrived at just at the right moment. I wonder if those two events are linked in any way?*

*   *   *

"Father Christmas!"

Irene and Tony were talking quietly about family as they sat in the kitchen. Joe's loud exclamation was from the heart.

"I think that might be the half-time whistle," said Irene. "Time for refreshments."

"Perhaps a sponge and towel as well!" added Tony.

"It's poker, not rugby."

A glance at the piles of tokens indicated that Bruce and Neil were level pegging in the poker war. Joe and Philip were not doing so well.

"I don't understand, Dad," Philip was saying disconsolately. "You taught us everything you know about the game and you're taking us to the cleaners."

"Ah," grinned Neil with a waggle of his eyebrows. "It's every man for himself tonight. I taught you most everything *you* know. That doesn't mean that I taught you everything *I* know."

Bruce's smile was a little fixed. This was tougher than he had anticipated. Neil was a ferocious opponent. Philip was good and Joe . . . well, he didn't think Joe was concentrating fully. When he woke up, he was still as good as he ever was on the Zeus missions.

Joe wasn't giving the game one hundred per cent of his attention. He was marvelling still that his father and Bruce were battling this out. A shaft of mental sunshine fell on a memory from last summer. He had walked Bonny along the seafront at Minehead and found Natasha enjoying the air outside the holiday house, a refugee from the poker game indoors. She reported that Neil was winning. For some reason Joe could remember his reply word for word.

> *"He will. Continuously. I've only met one person who I think could really take him on at the game and that's Bruce Dougall, my Zeus flights colleague. Those two playing would be a true clash of the heavyweights. It's a pity it will never happen."*

No one had a clue then, he least of all, about the chain of events that would unfold. Dad and Bruce locking horns over a hand of cards just about summed up the futility of predicting the future with any degree of accuracy. Along with Irene and a Martian in the form of her dead grandfather offering snacks round the table.

Instead of leaving the room when play recommenced, Irene and Tony made a fascinated audience of two. Irene watched without much understanding. Tony knew only too well what was happening.

The action swirled on. Having Irene in the room made Joe put his entire mind to the job in hand. Philip was determined to show his father that he had learned a trick or two along the way. Neil was having the time of his life and Bruce . . . well, Bruce was just Bruce, the same as he was all those years ago.

"Who will take me on?" he had announced to the wide-eyed crew of *Zeus One*, producing a pack of cards.

It had been a slaughter of the innocents, with only Joe still upright at the end of it.

At about eleven o'clock, the general consensus was that Bruce and Neil had ground out a honourable draw, with Joe and Philip only a fag paper behind them. Bruce extended his hand to Neil.

"Wing Commander, it has been a real pleasure. I can see now why Joe was always so damned tricky to play. And thank you, Philip."

"Did you ever do any work up there in space?" Philip wondered.

"Occasionally," Bruce replied.

*   *   *

Sophia and Adam were in France, on the first stage of their teaching mission across the world. They were in the old university town of Laon. They did not need their Martian skills to sense the underlying hostility in the audience, springing from their previous statements about the importance of the British Isles and the pre-eminence of the English language.

"Good evening, ladies and gentlemen," Adam began. "Thank you for coming here. And we welcome a world-wide audience via television."

The murmur of astonishment that started in the town hall was repeated round the world as television viewers watched in assorted time zones. When the figures of wisdom had taught in London, they spoke in English and the broadcast was overdubbed with simultaneous translations into other languages. Sophia and Adam had overcome the restrictions of Earth now and everyone was hearing Adam speaking in his or her own language.

They didn't understand it at Pentecost in Jerusalem, more than two thousand Earth years ago, Sophia reminisced telepathically to Adam. *I wonder if they will get it now?*

The audience in Laon and the worldwide audience of billions soon settled down because they were caught up in what was being said.

"I have chosen to speak about Death in tonight's gathering," Sophia announced. "We sense that so many of you people are preoccupied with it, whether you realise it or not. You talk about it with fear and in whispers. What you mourn wholeheartedly is simply the next state of being. You accept that you are conceived, grow in the womb and are born. You go through different stages of physical and mental development and growth. Then you age. All these stages you accept. But you rail against Death. Think of a crystal with its many faces and its millions of reflections of colour and light. Each spark, each flash, each colour is part of the whole. The fragments of the whole are uncountable and yet they all belong together. Thus it is with what you call Life and Death here on Earth. They are only two faces of the millions of strands of being and existence. Moving from one to another is as natural as the light dancing from one surface of the crystal to the next. Each one of you danced into this Life. Each one of you will dance into this Death. Each one of us is dancing through time and space, progressing with each step. Every one of you was called into being in this plane of reality, bringing your gifts and your personality to a particular time and situation. This was the result of an immense labour in the heavens, as well as the labour of birth. Surely you don't think that such a work of art will be thrown away? That is how some of you view Death, as an end, a final discarding of everything. It is a very arrogant view, but understandable. When a race of beings thinks that it is the only one, such strange thoughts can creep in. Each one of us is a true work of art—a work of art in progress. You learned lessons before you came here; you learn lessons and grow whilst you are on this earthly plane. You will learn lessons as you move on. We are all learning continuously. My brother Adam and I are learning. All seven of us from Mars are learning. Our mission to Earth has grown to be far more complex, but as most of you are now aware, our initial impetus came from the knowledge that we had to right a wrong done to an innocent man who was aboard *Zeus Three* and who was part of the peaceful reaching out towards us. That has been a lesson for us."

*   *   *

Joe's mind was maddeningly alert after his father and brother had left. He decided to check the computer for any new messages. He smiled when he read one. Then he put on his glasses to enjoy the text all over again.

I felt that I must write and offer my congratulations on your engagement and forthcoming marriage. We met, if you can call it that, on the seafront at Minehead last summer. My son Nat asked you if he could pat your dog and you kindly said yes. I recognised you and I told Nat afterwards who you were. He was furious that I didn't say anything, but we are all entitled to our time off duty and you certainly deserve yours!

Thank you for taking the time to bother with a little boy. I think he will dine out on the story for the rest of his life. I hope that you and Professor Hanson will enjoy a long and happy partnership.

Best wishes
George Miller

"Joe! Whatever are you doing reading messages at this time of night?"

Irene's voice could be heard a long way away. He looked round and smiled.

"This one is a bit special."

He explained the background and Irene read over his shoulder.

"So many loose ends being tied up," he mused. "So many circles being completed. It's funny, I was thinking about the holiday earlier on. I told Natasha then that I would love to see Dad and Bruce play cards but it would never happen. Look at everything that *has* happened since I was by the seaside and you were in Scotland. It hardly seems possible."

"And everyone is well on the way to being a totally different person," Irene added.

*   *   *

Sally was watching the television broadcast of Sophia and Adam's teaching. She turned to her hostess.

"What do you think?" she wondered.

"They are saying it like it is," said Hagar. "Just as we knew they would. The world will understand and rejoice. Brent Dyer and Ichiro will soon have the portal built, won't they? They really are working on that first portal to Mars, aren't they?"

"Not long to go," Sally confirmed, hearing the longing in Hagar's voice. "We could hardly borrow the spaceship again to return to Mars and flying in it makes for such a long journey! I don't think that I could stand it. The Martian part of me salutes Joe and Bruce and their crew as total heroes for putting up with those desperately slow speeds! And Brian and his crew as well."

"The Martian part of you is forgetting something," said Hagar. "Before Brent Dyer worked his magic, journeys from Earth to Mars would have lasted six months, so they didn't happen. The practicalities of that time span restricted the human race to sending only automated probes to the planet's surface until the problem was solved."

"That's right!" sighed Sally, her human memories stirred.

She recalled Joe talking to her about *Ariadne One* when he had been given command of the ship.

"If this works, anything is possible, Sally! Mars could be two weeks away."

"If there are to be the links between the two planets that we have longed for," she continued, "this portal must be completed soon. Ichiro has had to pick up Brent and carry him at various points, so to speak, but the design is done. They will be joining you here tomorrow. Nobody knows why they are coming to Cape Canaveral."

"Then may I come home now?" Hagar looked wistful for a moment. "Of course I've got ties here but I can always come back and visit. I've done all I needed to do here. Surely it must be time for me to come home."

Chapter Thirty

"Sister Gaia, greetings!"
"Sister Artemis, greetings!"

Artemis of Mars and Gaia of Earth spoke joyfully to one another.

"Sister Gaia, I can hardly comprehend it. We are to be reunited after so long. The first portal is almost complete."

"Sister Artemis, it is a time of great happiness!"

"And, Sister Gaia, it is the culmination of a lesson for us all. When my children first decided that they must right the wrong, they had little idea of how much more they would be achieving. When beings of good conscience are stirred by that conscience, only good can come of it."

"Sister Artemis, I celebrate the achievements of your children. I am breathing easier as they criss-cross my surface on their missions. The levels of vibration are being raised for myself and for my children. We are ready to step into our future."

"Sister Gaia, we will be able to join hands again and dance to the music of the spheres, in such a way as we have not done since the destruction of Maldek. I know that as we speak, Sophia and Adam are teaching all your children about Maldek, and the lessons we must learn from its tragedy."

"Sister Artemis, there have been times when I have feared so much for my children. On many occasions I have stood as witness to a dress rehearsal for their deaths—and mine. It is wonderful that their eyes are being opened."

"Sister Gaia, I am ready to receive your wounded children, namely Bruce Dougall and Ted Rodriguez. We will heal Bruce. He

has so much to do. We will minister to Ted, so that he can move on. Many of your children and my children—our children—will be able to use all the portals that will be built. Healing and learning and enlightenment will be for everyone. And we are about to see a time of celebrations on Earth."

*   *   *

Joe and Bruce were fighting a quiet, continuous behind-the-scenes battle to keep the crew of *Ariadne One* out of the public eye. In their estimation, the astronauts had given testimony enough to the whole world. Joe was no longer head of *BUSSTOP* in Britain but seeing as his successor, Jeremy Tremayne, was only just getting his feet under the table, the media crowd continued to listen to him. He had always tried to play fair with press and television during his time sitting in the big chair at *BUSSTOP* and that brought its own rewards now. Also journalists were mesmerised by him because he could so easily have taken his job back and he had decided that he did not want to do this. They guessed he had resigned to show his support for Bruce Dougall. Bruce was head of *BUSSTOP* America once more, although no one knew how long that would last.

Bruce helped himself to an attitude that was there for the taking. He might as well use it when it came to protecting his people. It may have appeared slightly calculating but the feeling was a fact. Many were treating him like an unexploded bomb and he knew it was because they understood that he was dying. So when he asked for something—in this case, privacy for the astronauts—everyone tumbled over themselves to respect his wishes, to begin with. As he observed to Joe at one point, Sophia and Adam had a heck of a lot more teaching to do on the subject of death. And to be fair, no one knew what he and the Martians had planned.

Naturally, there was a never-ending line of assorted experts who wanted to talk to the seven members of the flight crew. The crowd control was organised by *BUSSTOP* on both sides of the Atlantic but it was Jeremy Tremayne, a member of the reserve crew for the Zeus flights who, frustratingly, never made it onto one of the missions, who orchestrated all this from his end and won his spurs in the process.

Meetings between the *Ariadne One* team and specialists of every stripe were private and well spaced. Joe advised a grateful Jeremy on this but they knew that the real problem for the crew members would not be with eager experts who wanted to hear about Mars. Brian, Jethro and the others couldn't wait to spill the beans, as long as they weren't overwhelmed with such gatherings. Joe in particular could appreciate that, once the initial euphoria of the back-from-the-dead scenario was over and done with and the champagne corks were tidied away, there might be some difficult readjustments to be carried out between individual astronauts and their loved ones. They needed time and privacy. He only had to remember his own reaction when Sally appeared to him in that first dream, so long ago: *What are you doing here? You're dead!* Families were just beginning the long journey towards some kind of acceptance of the loss of children, husbands and boyfriends—even though nobody knew what had happened to them—when the lost ones reappeared in the perfectly framed shot worthy of old-time Hollywood. They had obviously undergone the most wonderful and life changing experiences whilst their nearest and dearest were being fed through the wringer of bereavement.

And the Ariadne crew were altered. Joe knew that from talking to them and the difference was there for all to see. There was calmness, a radiance, an impression of quiet wisdom, in the faces and the eyes of all seven. He noticed it most in Jackson Metz. He had agreed to this man joining the team with a heavy heart, as the replacement for the replacement member of the crew. When the time was right, these seven individuals would start teaching. But not yet. They still had to make sense of everything they had experienced and get back to living life here on Earth.

The crew of *Ariadne One* were particularly grateful for the protection that *BUSSTOP* on both sides of the Atlantic could provide when it came to the media. But as the days and weeks slid by, representatives of television companies and newspaper groups forgot the promises they had made to Bruce and prowled round in decreasing circles of frustration, pestering the astronauts with offers of more and more fantastic sums of money for an exclusive inside story. At one point Jeremy Tremayne, with Joe at his elbow, was struggling to keep control. Bruce came to the rescue with a very simple tactic. He was fed up with being Mr Nice Guy. In a screen conversation with a group of American newspaper editors, he lost his temper

It was only the fact that, in popular opinion, he already had an advance on sainthood that prevented every American newspaper front page consisting of two words on the morning after his outburst. The media people retreated in contrition, realising for once that they had pushed too hard.

Whatever difficulties the astronauts might be facing up to behind closed doors, a stream of people contacted Joe and Irene and Bruce about forthcoming events in the summer. Jackson was the one who started the ball rolling.

"Mr Mortimer, Leah and I are getting married. On August twenty third," he informed Joe. "I would consider it a great honour if you and Professor Hanson could come over to the States to be at our wedding. I guess by then the prof will be Mrs Mortimer, won't she?"

"She will," said Joe proudly. "Congratulations, Jackson!"

"I can hardly believe that Leah accepted my proposal."

"I think everyone has had a bit of a wake-up call as a result of your mission, haven't they?"

Jackson nodded, recalling the events on *Ariadne One* and on Mars that he had shared with no one. The Martians knew and his colleagues knew but that was different. Perhaps one day he would tell Leah all about what happened.

This on-screen conversation seemed to open a floodgate. In quick succession, Joe heard from Gianfranco, Jethro and Simeon and Emily with similar invitations.

"That's surely it!" Joe declared to Irene, who was already planning a series of shopping expeditions with Debbie. "Brian and Georgina are married and Masahide and David are as hitched as they can be."

For some reason it had escaped Joe's notice that same-sex civil partnerships had been alive and well in Britain for over a century. It was only a matter of time before Masahide spoke to Joe, who found himself putting yet another date in the diary. The final surprise came from Brian Hammond.

"Georgina and I are holding a ceremony to renew our vows in July, Mr Mortimer. We would be thrilled if you and your wife could be present."

Your wife. It was the first time someone had used that phrase to Joe and it was a bit of a shock. It would take some getting used to but he liked the sound of it already.

The same invitations were offered to Bruce, who was graciously cautious.

"My plans are a little vague by summer," he explained. "Thank you for asking me. I can't make any promises."

As yet, what he was doing—to say nothing of his destination—was not for public consumption.

It did indeed seem to be a time for the tying up of loose ends. One thing puzzled Joe. Tremayne had invited Vicky to meet with him to talk about continuing her job as PA to the head of *BUSSTOP*. She declined the offer, saying that she was doing other things now. She might not have travelled to Mars but Vicky Tennant had seemingly passed through some kind of transformation as well. Joe couldn't forget her parting comment as she left the engagement party.

"*My name is Victoria.*"

It was not only what she said, which was strange enough. It was the way she said it, with a special kind of confidence and conviction. Like the crew who had journeyed to Mars, she was changed.

Irene had never said anything about the incident at the end of the party. Joe decided to raise the topic of Vicky as they sat in a central London restaurant enjoying lunch, after a private visit to see Kevin Crane in Downing Street. Guiseppe, the owner of *La Casa*, had a tender regard for his regular well-known customers. Joe was on that list and he and Irene were treated like royalty.

"I am so excited, Mr Mortimer, that you have come here today with your beautiful lady. Enjoy your meal."

By the time the beautiful lady Irene had gone through a brisk summary of what was what, Joe was sagging, looking as though he had been hit by a thunderbolt. Victoria carried a forlorn torch for Joe all the time she worked for him. At the engagement party she met Professor Marmaduke Dawson and the two were now very much an item. The University hadn't had such fun in years. The staff hadn't thought it could get any better than Irene telling Sir Arthur Downey what he could do with his job. But that delicious situation had been overtaken by the simple fact of Marmaduke and Victoria falling for one another big time.

Not for the first time, however briefly, Irene envied the male of the species his tunnel vision. There had been a three-ring circus of life and emotions going on around Joe and he was oblivious to it—apart from her resignation, of course. A woman became involved with the process as a matter of course and sometimes it could be damned hard work.

Joe stirred his coffee unnecessarily. For a moment he wondered if Irene would take the spoon away from him, as Bruce had done once.

"So you mean to say that all the time . . . Vicky, I mean Victoria . . . she was hoping . . . she wanted to . . . oh bugger!"

He ground to a halt and studied the froth he had created on the surface of his coffee.

"Something like that," Irene agreed. "Every day must have been a torment for the poor girl in a way, because I'm sure you always managed to behave correctly, even if you were being brusque or were annoyed about something. And as she said herself, to you she was never more than the most efficient piece of office equipment. And then she met Marmaduke at our do. It's the talk of the University. Every man is jealous of Marmaduke and every woman who is single and looking is cursing because another of the good guys has been claimed. And Marmaduke is a good man, I promise you. Always larger than life, but a good man."

"Marmaduke won't do anything silly like resigning, will he?"

Joe continued to be uneasy about Irene's departure from the college, even though his wife-to-be looked as though she had been let out of prison. He couldn't bear the thought of being connected, however remotely, with another professor biting the dust.

"Why should he? Marmaduke has given everybody a titbit of gossip. It's not at all the same as the feathers that I ruffled! I had a difference of opinion with Sir Arthur Downey, and I'm glad I did. It had been building up for some time. I really enjoyed telling him to go forth and multiply! But the important thing is that Marmaduke is a total sweetie pops underneath it all. I was interested and tempted myself, in my younger days."

Joe rubbed his eyes in bewilderment.

"Take me home and mop my fevered brow, Irene. Then try and explain the mysteries of women to me."

"Certainly. And I will now admit to you that I added Victoria and Marmaduke to the invitation list for our wedding. They have accepted, by the way."

*　　*　　*

The grip of winter relented. On a perfect spring day, with the promise of so much more weather like this to come, friends and family gathered together to witness the wedding of Joseph Joshua Mortimer and Irene Elizabeth Hanson, in Graffenby's ancient parish church of St Margaret of Antioch. Tony Johnson gave away his granddaughter and Bruce Dougall was the best man. The bride's attendants—Debbie MacIver and Sally Tillman—took all eyes. They were tall figures, dressed in the palest lilac and grey.

Alisdair MacIver watched his wife adoringly. In another time and another place he would have given away the bride but he ceded that honour to Tony very happily, just as Joe's brother Philip was delighted to see Bruce be the best man. Once upon a time Philip would have anticipated filling the role for Joe—although over the long years following Sally's death, he never imagined in his wildest dreams that his little brother would ever actually go through any kind of ritual that required a best man. Seeing Bruce standing there, in formal attire, was the final acknowledgement of the mending of a rift that should never have happened in the first place.

Irene was radiant, lit from within. Her height and build were complimented by an ivory suit, cut along the same lines as the outfit she had worn for the wedding of Princess Charlotte. The tailored jacket and the flowing skirt were becoming the hallmark of her public appearances. Alisdair couldn't help remembering her previous wedding. Whatever might happen in the future, he knew that there would not be a similar disastrous outcome. And he was not the only one who acknowledged Irene's true generosity of spirit when she insisted that Sally took part in the day.

Joe had been in a daze prior to the wedding. After he had had one or two incoherent conversations with family members during the morning before the ceremony, Bruce kept everyone away.

"Joe's in shock," he said. "Happy shock. Leave him be."

He sent Joe out on a run with Bonny and threatened the gathering media people with murder and destruction if they tried to follow.

Joe seemed okay now, saying words that made sense when it was his turn.

Family aside, the congregation was an eclectic mix, a testimony to the many people that the bride and groom had come to know over the years. Marmaduke and Victoria smiled continuously. The remaining Zeus flight crew and most of the reserves were there. Gene Ward may have flown over from America but probably he felt capable of making the journey without the assistance of a plane. Thanks to the unexpected publicity that Bruce gave one piece of his work at the memorial service for the crew of *Ariadne One*, he had just agreed terms with a major publishing house for issuing a book of his poetry. Hagar Turner watched the proceedings fondly. Stella Mortimer wept buckets of happy tears. As she said quite reasonably afterwards, "Irene's mother isn't with us physically, so I cried as the mother of the groom *and* the bride."

Neil blinked a lot during the service and supplied his wife with the tissues.

After the first couple of minutes everyone forgot that His Majesty King Richard the Fourth and Queen Alice were present. They were two more guests, that was all. But Neil couldn't help being mischievous and whispered at one point to Stella: "We'll all have to be on our best behaviour. There's Ricky boy and his missus come along from the big house."

When the bride and groom emerged from the church, they had more than the official photographs to deal with. There was a sizeable line-up of press and television, bombarding the newly-weds with their inevitable chummy requests.

"Joe! Over here! That's the boy!"

"Lovely, Irene! Just hold that position for us darling! Super!"

This isn't as bad as I always thought it would be, Joe said to himself as Sally moved into his line of vision whilst the photographer rearranged the group.

"That's because you're older and wiser. We wouldn't have wanted all this, nor could we have coped with it then."

Sally's voice spoke into his mind. Joe looked away hastily, almost scared.

After the ceremony, everyone went back to Stable End to drink a toast to the happy couple and to reminisce whilst caterers put the finishing touches to a buffet meal.

Marmaduke was his usual blunt self when he spoke to Joe and Irene.

"I was a bit surprised when I saw that you were getting married in the local God house," he admitted.

"As ever, the Anglican church remains the organisation which exists for the benefit of those who don't belong to it," Irene reminded him.

"But having been in the place for a while, I understand why you picked St Margaret's," Marmaduke said knowingly. "A wonderful old building. Early twelfth century in origin, I would say. And the dedication is a giveaway. My guess is that someone who had been on the First Crusade dug deep into the moneybags to build the place when he, or she, returned. Some noble women accompanied their husbands on that venture." Marmaduke's historical faculties had been working overtime. "I think the grey cat could sit in there down the years and watch the world go by. It must be one of the few places where he could be quiet."

"What?" Joe began and then remembered the powerful story told by Sophia and Adam. "Oh yes."

"It was so peaceful in the church," added Victoria. "Timeless. Made that way by all the thoughts and joys and sorrows that have been brought there over the centuries to be shared. Thank you for inviting us."

Joe was startled. He had never known Vicky to be so eloquent. Correction. He had never got round to knowing Victoria Tennant at all.

In the hugs and kisses and handshakes, Irene spotted the ring on Victoria's left hand.

"Congratulations, Victoria! Well done, Marmaduke!" she said. "You should have said."

"Oh no!" Victoria looked uncomfortable. "This is your day. Please don't say anything to anyone here. Not now, anyway. Marmaduke only proposed first thing this morning and said that I must wear the ring that he'd bought me, straight away." Yes, thought Irene. That's Marmaduke! "Mr and Mrs Mortimer, I do hope that you will be able to come to our wedding, when we get around to planning it."

Joe was on the verge of saying *God help us! Not another one!* Irene knew this. She trod on his foot and smiled encouragingly.

"I've always had a fancy for a wedding around Christmas time," put in Marmaduke unexpectedly. "In the college chapel, of course. A dark afternoon, with all the candles and the lights of the Christmas tree shining away."

"That sounds beautiful!" said Irene, picturing the scene already, as she was very familiar with the chapel. "We'll be there, wherever and whenever."

Tony had overheard most of the conversation and he moved closer to talk when Marmaduke and Victoria drifted away to speak to other guests.

"Well, Mr and Mrs Mortimer. How does that sound then?"

"It sounds . . ." Joe considered, looking at his wife. "It sounds just right."

Joe was feeling things that he had never felt before, not even with Sally.

"It *is* just right," Tony agreed, looking across the room to where the King held Bruce in animated conversation. "Who would have thought?" he continued. "All these wonderful things have come out of the terrible fact that we accidentally harmed one man."

"Did you know?" Irene asked. "Did you know from the beginning how much you would be doing?"

"No," Tony admitted. "The burden of what we had done weighed us down. The whole of our planet was suffering. We could not think clearly or work as we wanted to work. We were like Jacob Marley in *A Christmas Carol* by your Charles Dickens, dragging our chains behind us. All we could do was wait for Earth to come to us. The complexity of what we were faced with only became clear gradually. And Joe, will you finally stop beating yourself over the head about not listening to Rob Masters? I don't know, no one knows, if what he would have said was of any significance when it came to the Lander failing to leave Mars. If it wasn't important, it wasn't. If it was, there's no such thing as coincidence. It made matters much simpler for the seven of us to get on the same vibration level as the Ariadne crew when those thrusters didn't fire. We would have had to go about things in a much more complicated way if Lander had taken off as planned. And I'm sure Mr Masters has never given the business another thought. He has never got back to you on the subject, has he?" Joe shook his head, relief replacing an underlying tension. "And he hasn't sold a story to a newspaper or television programme." His face crinkled into its usual warm smile. "This is far too solemn a topic for a wedding day! And I mustn't monopolise you. I'll still be here when everyone has gone home."

I'm glad you will be, thought Joe.

There was something else that he wanted to talk to Tony about.

* * *

Ichiro stepped back to admire their handiwork.

"That is superb!" he enthused.

"But will it work?" Brent wanted to know.

"My friend, when did you turn into the voice of doom?" Ichiro asked.

"I think I've been out of action too long," Brent confessed.

"I think you have! Maybe we should take you back to Mars along with Ted Rodriguez. Not to keep you there, but to shake you up, dust you down and send you back refreshed and renewed."

They were standing in the corridor near to the door into the space flight room in Mission Control at Cape Canaveral. It looked as though the two of them were staring at a blank wall.

"I think we should keep the portal like this, cloaked, when it's not being used," Brent said.

Ichiro was leaning against the opposite wall, head down, eyes closed.

"Sorry," he acknowledged after a pause. "I was speaking with our brothers and sisters on Mars. Yes. The portal is ready at that end. I will test it out. I'm sorry that you can't come with me this time. We will deal with humans coming back to Earth once the first journeys have been made to Mars."

Ichiro walked towards the wall, which opened into a tumbling riot of rainbow colours, lights struck from the facets of a crystal. The engineer was absorbed into the kaleidoscope and the wall was itself once more. Whilst Brent was still trying to assimilate what he had witnessed, the wall dissolved into particles of light again and Ichiro stepped back into the corridor. The wall solidified again.

"Perfect!" he stated with a brilliant smile. "Brent, I could not have achieved this without you. We can now start building portals to Mars all over the world, in every major town and city."

"What? Today?" Brent wanted to know with some alarm.

"No! Today we have achieved enough. Your wife has travelled down here, hasn't she? Good. Then we celebrate."

*   *   *

Everybody had gone. Joe made no claim to be the tidiest person in the world, although Irene was improving him by the minute. But even he had winced as he looked at the littered appearance of Stable End's main room before the catering staff got to work on it. Everything was back in order now.

One ivory shoe hurtled through the open door and crashed down onto the floor, followed by the other, as Irene kicked her feet free ahead of entering the room.

"That's better!" she murmured as she sat down and gazed around. "We did make a bit of a mess, didn't we? That was one amazing clean up. I'm glad that I didn't have to do any of it."

Joe wasn't about to say that the carpet hadn't looked so good in years.

Bruce returned, his inevitable shadow Bonny following him.

"I hope your dog doesn't have a hangover in the morning," he said. "She became frantic when she realised that all the glasses were being taken away. She was rushing round, lapping up all the dregs she could find."

Tony joined them, carrying a tray of glasses.

"I'll put these in the kitchen," he informed them. "The catering team manager said that he would come back tomorrow for anything that was missed. I rescued these from the garden and from one of the cupboards in the second floor bathroom,"

"That's nothing," said Bruce, seeing Irene's puzzled look. "Some years ago I went to a function at Bob and Belle's place. A few days later, builders doing routine maintenance found perfectly intact plates and glasses on the roof. And the stuff had been used. Work that one out if you can!"

Irene decided that she wanted a long soak in the bath.

"I'll be up to scrub your back in a minute," Joe promised.

She kissed Bruce's cheek.

"Thank you for being an absolute star today!" she told him.

Bruce was obviously tired. He made his goodnights, offered a further round of congratulations and went upstairs.

"In the meantime, Joe, you need to speak to me," Tony continued, entering the room from the kitchen as Irene left by the other door. "That's all I know, without prying. Something frightened you. What is it?"

Joe recounted the incident during the photographs when he had made an observation to himself about the presence of so many reporters and Sally replied straight back into his thoughts. Tony sat back in his chair and stretched out his legs. He steepled his fingers against his upper lip—something that Joe had seen him do several times when he was thinking deeply in a human way. Obviously it was a characteristic of the original Tony.

"What was wrong with that?" he asked of Joe. "The raising of the vibration levels of Earth, and of those who live within her care, means that you will become more aware of each other. You are becoming more aware."

"I know! I know! I welcome this. But the first thought-sharing shouldn't have been with Sally."

"Ah," said Tony, understanding the problem now. "The *first* thought-sharing? I don't think so. Sally may have spoken directly into your mind because she is a Martian with the ability to do so as the vibration levels increase. And you had a bond with Earth Sally, a powerful bond that you cannot ignore. Also, you were thinking about something that touched upon both of you. When you were together, you were both horrified at the thought of the media turnout if you married and thus put your relationship into the public domain. But Joe, you have been increasingly aware of certain other people and their thought processes for quite some time, haven't you?"

"Irene," Joe said slowly. "We do seem to know what the other is about to say."

"And I would venture to suggest Bruce too."

Joe's smile was forced.

"You have to let him go, Joe. He must go back home and put his affairs in order before moving on, in this life and in the voyage of many lifetimes to come." Tony stood up. "This will never do. Your bride can't sit growing cold in her bath. Move yourself!"

*   *   *

It was as though certain things had always been so, even though in reality they were temporary and extraordinary arrangements. Any changes were uncomfortable. Joe drove Bruce to the airport with a heavy heart.

"We'll see you at Mission Control," he said. "Take care until then, Bruce."

Tony had explained to everyone at Stable End what Ichiro and Brent Dyer had been up to at Cape Canaveral. Irene said to Joe afterwards that she knew she would never be surprised again.

Joe stood at the viewing window to watch Bruce's plane lumber down the runway. Like his friend, he knew the litany of the cockpit at take off—a routine that had not changed since the early days of flight: *V1—Rotate—Gear up.* But unlike Joe, Bruce would have managed to get himself invited onto the flight deck by the time the plane was levelled out.

Joe watched the aircraft become a distant dot in the sky and then disappear completely through the low cloud cover. He continued to stare for a while, willing the plane to return Bruce safely to D.C.

"It's hard to say goodbye, isn't it love?" said the woman standing next to him, casting a sympathetic glance in his direction yet not recognising him. "I guess you were seeing off family?"

All kinds of complicated replies jumped into Joe's mind but in the end his answer was simplicity itself.

"Yes."

*   *   *

"You're what?"

Simeon and Emily made a stunned row of two on one side of the dinner table at Hagar's house and Simeon looked at his aunt almost fearfully.

"I am your aunt, Simeon," Hagar explained. "But I am also from Mars. I was sent here to complete a task. It will soon be fully accomplished. It is nearly time for me to go home."

"So you knew all along what would happen!" exclaimed Simeon. "You knew that there would be problems but that we were all right on Mars and—"

"Not at all," Hagar corrected gently. "I knew scattered facts, which initially made no sense. But I had to follow my instincts and I had to trust. There were plenty of moments when I was as scared and unsure as everyone else. I was terrified when Mission Control lost contact with you all on Mars. I had to struggle long and hard to find the answers there. Before you left, I knew I had to give you that bracelet and the stone from the back yard. I didn't know why at the time. They were both useful, weren't they?"

"You're telling me!" said Simeon fervently. "The stone is on Mars, just as you said it had to be. Would you like the bracelet back?"

"No. That will be something to remember me by when I leave. Its design is from the Voodon tradition, by the way."

"I knew there was something special about it!"

Emily had been silent up to now. Hagar smiled.

"You were a sensitive young woman before all this. There will be no stopping you now. I look forward to a visit from you when I am back on Mars. But I'm not going just yet. I will be here for your wedding, as I will be for all the other weddings associated with *Ariadne One*. Tony and I will attend them all on behalf of Bruce Dougall, who will be leaving Earth soon."

Emily picked up on the way Hagar said *Tony and I*.

"Yes, Emily," Hagar confirmed. "The Martian being known as Tony here on Earth is my soul mate from many lifetimes ago. We will travel back home together at summer's end when our Earth duties are done. Ichiro will be here for a season, as will Phoebe, Sophia and Adam. Each will return home when they have done all they can. Each has a huge task. Ichiro will build many more portals with the help of Brent Dyer. Phoebe will travel the world with the King of England and Sophia and Adam will continue to teach."

*   *   *

Bonny sprang up and followed Joe to the front door. Joe was surprised to see Sally waiting on the step.

Joe continued to astonish himself, that he could be so calm and rational in the presence of Sally. It was part of the relentless learning process.

"Come on in!" he said. "Tony's out, if you wanted to see him. Irene is doing the sights of Cambridge with him. I could have gone too but this is time that the two of them need together. I know he's not leaving yet, but Irene is aware that his days here are numbered. I can do the conducted tour bit any time."

"It's you I came to see," Sally admitted, "and I chose today because I knew that you would be alone, apart from your wonderful dog."

Bonny walked to heel with Sally. The dog rolled over onto her feet when she sat down. Joe didn't know whether to be pleased or nervous about this arrival. He had a moment of clarity as to why Sally was here but he didn't quite trust his new instincts yet.

He was amazed to find that he was right.

"I have come to tell you of your child, our child. Tony has told Irene about her child and I know she told you. Our son is also a beautiful soul."

"Our *son*?"

"He was destined to care, and so he does. He watches over those in distress and those who are ill and injured."

"Our son the doctor?"

"In a way, yes. He has always been close to you, Joe. As close as I have been. And he is on watch for those around you. He was with Bruce in his darkest hour, along with Bruce's parents, of course."

Joe had the sensation of a film running in his mind. The scene was vivid in every unforgiving detail.

"No!" he said involuntarily, flabbergasted at the terrible revelation given to him. "So Bruce . . . when he was sacked . . ." He wanted to rid his mind of the images, especially the torment showing on Bruce's face as he lifted the gun. "He really was going to kill himself, wasn't he?"

Sally nodded.

"Look again. Look deeper into what you have seen. Step into it, be there, if you feel that you can. Close your eyes."

Joe saw again the moment when Bruce picked up the gun and he wanted to shut down the picture immediately. But he couldn't. He found himself being drawn into the image, as if he was being physically moved against his will. He was standing in one corner of the room, watching as a bystander. Then he saw. Behind Bruce was a nebulous outline. Was it a person? Hands appeared to reach out towards the man who was about to take his own life.

"Come back, Joe." Joe felt Sally's hand, cool and reassuring, on his brow. "I hope that wasn't too frightening for you. You needed to see it."

Joe wasn't sure how long the silence lasted. At last he looked up.

"That was . . . our son?"

"Yes. He made a difference, however small."

"He should have a name!" said Joe.

"Of course, although it's not vital. Remember that the Good Samaritan has lived for centuries without a name. It was his act of kindness and compassion, cutting across the barriers of the day, which was crucial. But I know that, to humans, names are important."

"Andrew," Joe announced after a pause. "Andrew Bruce."

"That's perfect. When you see small lights twinkling in the darkness at night, it isn't that you've flown one space mission too many. It will be Andrew, watching over you and Irene. You two have so much to do. People here on

Earth will listen to what you have to say in a quite different way. And you will have things to say, even though you don't know it yet! That is why you decided against returning to *BUSSTOP*. You know, in a manner yet unformed, that there is other work to do. Those of Earth will read Irene's books with a different mindset. When Mars is only a step away through a portal, that is inevitable. You could both do with an extra guardian angel and Andrew will be there. At the moment, the portal is one-way traffic only for humans. Ichiro and Brent Dyer needed to have one established for those who need to travel to Mars now. But before too long they will have a return system up and running for the people of Earth. So, Joe Mortimer, you will reach Mars one day. You won't have to trek in a flying bomb like Zeus or Ariadne. And maybe, just maybe, as you travel about you will meet a soul called Andrew. He may not be in any recognisable corporeal form, although I can't be sure of that. He is as resourceful as his father! But you will know him and he will know you, as he will know Irene and she will know him. In the same way you will both know Fiona. Soul recognition transcends all limitations."

Joe couldn't wait for Irene to return. He had so much to tell her, and so many things to ask Tony.

*　*　*

Irene was well able to stand up for herself. She could have gone back to college for the last time on her own to say a few goodbyes and collect her books and some personal possessions. She had been doing things on her own for a long time. But now there was Joe and he wouldn't countenance her going anywhere near Sir Arthur Downey unless he was at her side.

Downey was a broken man. He began to ask Irene one last time to reconsider. Joe took a step closer and the Master fell silent.

"May I wish you both all the best for the future," was what he did say.

As Irene and Joe walked down the corridor towards her study, they heard uneven footsteps and laboured breathing behind them.

"Professor! Professor Hanson!" a voice called out.

Irene turned to see Sid bustling along to catch up, as fast as his elderly legs would carry him.

"Sid!" she said warmly. "It's good to see you again. Sid, this is my husband Joe Mortimer. Joe, this is Sid Brotherton, one of the security staff and everyone's Dad, I guess. Sid has been associated with the college for as long as I have."

"Longer," replied Sid, shaking Joe's hand and almost bowing as he did so. "It's good to meet you, sir. Really good. I'd already been working here some time when I first met the Prof. She was a student then. I've tried to keep an eye on her over the years. You've got that job now, Mr Mortimer. I couldn't think of a better person to do it."

Joe nodded in a vague, self-conscious way.

"I've kept your study locked, Professor," Sid went on.

They had reached Irene's room. He produced the pass tag with a flourish and opened the door.

"Bloody hell, Irene!" said Joe when he saw the amount of books and files, neatly arranged on antique shelving. "I can't see this lot going in the car."

Sid coughed importantly.

"If I'm not interfering, Mr Mortimer, Professor Hanson, I can get some lads to crate up this lot and send it over to you in a van. You just take your personal bits and pieces, Prof."

"Can you do that, Sid?" Joe marvelled.

"When you've been in the place as long as I have, sir, there isn't much you can't do. It would be a pleasure to do this for you both."

It was a deal.

Irene hesitated as she looked at the armchair. Like any object, it was the storehouse of many memories, the most recent of which was her grandfather's visit to her before *Ariadne One* returned to Earth. It could be found a corner somewhere in Stable End. There were enough rooms, after all! But what was it that Sophia and Adam had said about hanging on to yesterday and not being promoted to tomorrow?

"Sid, would you like this chair?" she asked.

Sid was still thanking her as they moved on to the computer lab so that she could download her research data. She could have done that remotely, from Joe's house, from her house, from any computer. But she wanted to make sure that there were no mistakes. At the lab door, the security man shook Joe's hand again.

"Goodbye, sir. Now, if you don't mind, I'm going to do something I've always wanted to do."

He hugged Irene and kissed her on both cheeks.

"Goodbye, Professor Hanson. I expect to see you in the headlines, for all the right reasons, of course!"

*　　*　　*

The group of people in the corridor outside the door into the Mission Control nerve centre looked like a crowd in the limited space. There was a murmur of sympathy as Justin stepped forward with Ted Rodriguez. Justin nodded to Tony and Hagar as he escorted a sleepwalking Ted towards the portal.

"Thank you for making me so welcome here on Earth," he said to everyone. "I will see all of you again, sooner or later."

He guided a shuffling, oblivious ex-President towards the wall. The explosion of colour opened up like welcoming arms and they were gone.

Joe watched everyone's reaction. Marmaduke held Victoria's hand very firmly, as if he couldn't believe the circumstances that meant she was his. Joe didn't know why he was compelled to invite these two over to America to witness this, but somehow they seemed to have been part of the whole story, a thread woven in and out of the narrative. Bruce didn't mind. Apart from anything else, Marmaduke fascinated him in the classic role of an English eccentric.

Irene leaned against Joe and he became aware that his wife was crying.

"Hey, what's the matter?"

"I hate goodbyes," she sniffed.

She noticed that Joe swallowed hard when Bruce appeared with Sally. They had all said their farewells previously, in private, but this was still going to be difficult.

Irene cleared her throat.

> "At last they were beginning Chapter One of the Great Story which no one on Earth has read: which goes on forever: in which every chapter is better than the one before. That's C.S. Lewis by the way. The Last Battle."

Sally stood quietly near the portal. She held out her hands to Bruce, who turned for one last time to look at Shannon. Shannon was in tears but she smiled through those tears as Bob Broomfield put an arm around her.

"I feel like I'm sneaking away," Bruce said. "Especially when I've had the best wishes and thoughts of so many landing on my desk."

"Think of the wedding and think of the media presence cubed," Joe told him by way of reassurance. "Ichiro and Brent will show the portal to the world, when you have all gone through it. That wasn't right for this occasion. It's world—altering and yet so very personal. You wouldn't have wanted a media pack crashing about. And I don't think they would have fitted into this corridor! Henry Sargent and Bob here will do all the explaining that's needed." Bob nodded. He was finding this tough and wished that he could cry as openly and freely as Shannon. "So will I. And if I understand it aright, you'll be able to return one day. *Bon voyage*. I almost envy you. To live in another world, another dimension. Don't forget us." He held Bruce tight for a moment. "A smooth journey, bro, wherever you go and however you travel. You deserve all this and so much more. And I know we'll all meet up again in one way or another."

Today Bruce looked really unwell. The burden of illness was showing because he didn't have to pretend any more. A few paces forward and his life would be starting over again, in ways that he didn't yet fully comprehend. With Sally, he stepped into the vortex. But they did something different before they vanished. They stopped, turned and waved.

Joe was about to say to Irene, "Well, look at that!" but he didn't. Intuitively he knew that Irene wouldn't be seeing what he was seeing.

Bruce was just as he had been when Joe first met him, the youthful Puck of the stars.

Then they were gone.

"Yes, that was just for you," said Tony to an open-mouthed Joe. "To help you understand."

"It had to be, didn't it?" Joe asked Irene. "This couldn't have ended in any other way. In the best stories, the hero always gets the girl."

THE END

Breinigsville, PA USA
28 January 2011
254377BV00001B/19/P

9 781456 825683